Hexes and Ohs

A WITCHES PARANORMAL ROMANCE COLLECTION FROM THE NEW ROMANCE CAFÉ

T L Hamilton

Serafina

JaX

Kendall

Tasha Blythe

Kassandra Cross x.

Lily Kendall

Emmy Lee

Kit Blackwood

Wynter Ryan

Sabrina Bosque

Jenna D. Morrison

Amber Nicole

Kate Prior

Taya Rune

Anita Harlan

Rebecca Conrad

Angel W. Smith

Salem Cross

Jeana Louise Skinner

Rubi Jade

Contents

WARNING DISCLAIMER: This collection is suited for Adults 18+ only. Stories contain sexual situations and adult language. All characters depicted are of legal age.

Introduction

This anthology is brought to you by The New Romance Café and Romance Café Publishing, a community of romance novel fans and writers, born out of the desire for a safe space to discuss our shared passion for romance, as well as empower and support authors of the genre. Join us every day for your dose of romance in the Café:

https://www.facebook.com/groups/thenewromancecafe.

Our novelettes are paranormal witches themed romance, with varying degrees of heat. They are penned by both emerging and established bestselling authors, under a common goal of raising funds for Breast Cancer Research.

This project would not have got off the ground without the help and support of some very important people. Firstly I would like to thank the coordinators: Anna, Jenny, Sofia and Shanti. A huge thank you to all the authors for contributing their stories. Here's to many more books published!

Most of all, we'd like to thank you, our readers, for buying this book and supporting our fabulous community. Happy reading!

Andie Wood

The Witch Next Door

BY TASHA BLYTHE

Twenty-two year old Stella Weiland might be a hereditary witch living in a sleepy seaside village populated mostly by her kind, but she couldn't be further from a stereotypical evil hag if she tried. Shy, sweet, and a complete innocent not only when it comes to any sort of wrongdoing, but also in the relationship department, she's shocked to the core when her interfering cousin magicks a surprise birthday gift straight onto her living room carpet. Especially when the present in question isn't just any old boring present—but a man!

One

"I *didn't see him coming, Rowena."*

The soft, melodic tones stroked Dax's senses. And even though the voice trembled, the inherent power in it socked him straight in the gut like an immense fist.

"You didn't see him coming, Stella, because you wouldn't let yourself. You've guarded your heart for so long, you managed to set up a roadblock in your mind."

Interestingly enough, the second voice, though holding a sort of smoky appeal, didn't have the same effect on Dax as the first.

" We have to send him back!"

Again the plaintive, shaky voice. Maybe its strange power was the reason for Dax's floating, out-of-body sensation? True, the speaker's presence seemed to have a direct correlation with the tingles that sparkled throughout his entire being.

Either that, or Dax was dead.

I could be a human firefly? he thought, on a deep, inner sigh. Then he tried to shake his head, but it wouldn't move. *No, that's ridiculous.*

A million fireflies in the shape of a person?

But no, that couldn't be right either. Even though on the whole, it didn't seem to be too bad a description.

"Of course, we're sending him back." The second voice drifted closer, close enough for Dax to make out an outline in the roseate glow that filled his vision. A feminine outline with cascading dark hair.

"I don't mean next door. I mean back, *back. To wherever he came from before he arrived here in Aitken."*

A sweet longing filled Dax. *Please let me see you,* he pleaded with the owner of the first voice. *Or come nearer, at least. Because I want to be near you. Because I feel like everything will be wonderful, perfect, glorious, if only you are near.*

"Stella. You know we can't mess with people's lives like that. He's here where he's meant to be, at the time *he's meant to be. Not on your living room floor, granted. But here in Aitken, at least."*

"But I'm not ready for anyone in my life, Ro. And Kilarney magicking him here, throwing him at me like this? Well, it only highlights it. Besides, he can't be the one, Rowena, he truly can't, because he's not of the blood."

"'Of the blood,'" the firmer voice declared. "What does that matter when it comes to love? Nothing. Love transcends those kinds of boundaries."

"Ro, please. You need to support me in this."

Can I support you? Dax wanted to ask. *If you'll only let me nearer, I'll support you. I'll stay by your side all of our days.*

"Besides. You see how he reacts to you? And that's when he's half out of his senses. If you'd only stop hovering by that door and come further into the room —and let yourself feel—you won't want to fight. You'll accept it's a done deal, and be able to savor love in all its splendid and breathtaking magic. In fact, love is the true magic."

"If I come over there, will you help me send him back?"

"Back next door? Yes, sure I will. So stop stalling, come over here, and let's get it done."

Dax arched his back on a moan. "Please." The intense longing came out as a ragged thread of sound.

And then she was there. Filling his sight while a wild carousel of multicolored fairy lights whirled around her head.

A vision. An angel. A goddess.

His heart rose, fifty fireflies beating their wings as one, and all determined to burst through his chest wall. Straight out—to her.

She bent closer, and he almost cried with joy.

Then darkness began to close in, as though reality was nothing but dissolving friable fragments, or that he was being buried alive.

No. NO.

Two

Stella stood under the archway that divided the kitchen from the living room of her charming little whitewashed cottage, the back of her hand pressed against her lips.

Hovering, she didn't dare set foot in the space her new neighbor had occupied the day before. Though it was Stella's space—turned into her own over time, and with loving care—she couldn't bring herself to trek across the large, round, hooked-rag rug where the stranger had appeared out of thin air without the tiniest prickle of warning.

Standing confused for a moment, disoriented, shaking his head, he'd reached out one pointing hand in the stereotypical, 'I have a question' pose. Seconds later, he'd collapsed, longish legs folding underneath him as if they, too, were made of nothing but rags. Of course, just in the nick of time, as though tossed through the ether, a tasseled silken pillow had slipped lightning quick under his head to prevent its striking the floor.

"Ta da!" Kilarney had trilled, her delighted voice echoing and bouncing around the room. *"I might currently be in Marrakech, but it doesn't mean I forget your birthday, cousin!"*

A man. Kilarney had sent Stella—a man. Shy, awkward, now twenty-two-year-old, never-had-a-boyfriend Stella Weiland.

An equally young-looking, beautiful man, it must be admitted. With curling hair the color of fragrant cinnamon sticks, and long lashed, clear hazel eyes.

But a man! On her living room floor! And not just any pretty, well-formed man, but—

Her soulmate.

Supposedly. But then, Rowena—who'd been here with Stella on a birthday visit—had confirmed it with a single glance. And terrifyingly, her longtime friend and mentor was never wrong.

Not batting an eyelid, Rowena strode over to where he lay, calmly looking the out-of-his-senses man over. "Yes. Kilarney, your Aunty Vella, Rainey, and Leonora are all entirely correct in their assessment. He is your fated mate. Besides which, I've seen him before."

"What? You haven't said anything to me about that."

"Yes, a few times when I've been thinking of you, he's cropped up in a vision. And no, I never said anything, because whenever I tried to introduce the topic of men in general, or *a* man specifically, you shut it down."

And Stella couldn't explain to herself even why she'd always done that. Relationships, especially of the romantic sort, had somehow seemed like a new, foreign, and scary land to a very private and introverted witch.

It was bad enough when the guys in question were of the blood. They came off as darkly arrogant and cocksure, and seemed to want to bring magic into everything. Infuse it with innuendo, or make their witchcraft a competition. Maisie though, for instance, thrived on such things with her Luca. Winking, she said it added extra spice and flavor to 'certain shared activities.' But such things only freaked Stella out, sending her scuttling ever deeper into her protective shell, drawing her magic over her head like a shawl.

And then, if they weren't of the blood? How was one to explain, well —anything?

After working with Rowena to send the young man packing back to where he belonged next door, Stella had sat at the table, barefoot, her flowing cotton dress floating around her ankles. Forehead aching, and her hands still unsteady, Stella sipped the soothing chamomile tea Rowena had kindly brewed for her.

"So he's moved in next door." Stella gripped the fragile, delicately patterned porcelain. "How does he come to be doing that when it's Lacey's parents' cottage?"

Rowena gestured to Stella's teacup. "You don't want to do the honors of reading the accompanying explanation?"

Stella shook her head. Her stomach was too unsettled and jumping around for that.

"All right." Rowena set down her own cup. Bracing her hands against the edge of the round, wooden, country-style kitchen table, she stared into the dregs of the tea. Her dark, almost violet eyes swirled with mists and portents, shimmering to a pale lavender before subsiding again to their original color.

Her voice settled into placid, matter of fact tones. "His name is Dax

Brandon, and he's twenty-three. He's a friend of Lacey's. He was looking for a place to stay that was quiet and atmospheric. Somewhere to stir up his creative juices."

"Creative juices?"

"He's a creative." Rowena shrugged. "And he doesn't mind peace and quiet. And picturesque. In fact, that's what he was specifically looking for."

Stella nodded. "Okay. But why here in Aitken of all places?"

"He'd heard of it from Lacey, and he's always wanted to come here. Coincidentally, at the same time, Lacey's parents were quite keen to rent the house out while they're traveling around Europe."

"Okay," Stella said again, lifting both her knees and hugging them. "None of it matters, anyway." She dropped her chin onto her knees. "Because I wouldn't know what to do with him if I tried." Hearing her own words, her face suffused with heat.

Trying to avoid what she imagined to be Rowena's patient yet pitying look, Stella stared at her bare toes. "And I don't just mean *that*. I mean, at all."

Rowena swept back her masses of raven black hair, her golden bangles clicking. "Stella love," she sighed. "You're overthinking this *way* too much. Sometimes these things are easy. Easier than what you might expect. There doesn't always have to be struggle and high drama. For instance." She leaned over the table, cupping her palms under Stella's nose. A rich, pinky-red lotus bud twinkled into being. "Some loves unfold as naturally as these petals."

As Stella watched, they slowly unfurled, tender yet strong, filling the air with a fragrance so sweet Stella's throat ached.

Rowena placed the flower in the center of the table, then stretched with the feline grace of a cat as she stood. "So let it be, sweet girl." Bending, Rowena kissed Stella on the top of her head before making her way to the door.

As the chimes tinkled over the lintel, Stella's cherished mentor paused with one hand on the decorative bronze doorknob. "By the way, can I tell you that Dax Brandon is an absolute sweetie? He's a songwriter and musician. He loves animals, is kind to his mother, and has a *very* open mind."

Three

The attractive male voice carried from the patio next door and in through Stella's kitchen window. She paused with her hand to the tap, her eyes focused on the billowing lace curtain and the bee buzzing around the pot of meadowsweet on the windowsill.

"You weren't wrong about me coming to Aitken, Lacey. It feels right here. Everything. I can't explain it, exactly. Except that I can breathe here. The air's different somehow."

He paused as though he was listening to Lacey's response.

"And this cottage...But I'm telling you, the cottage next door, *that's* something else. Magical. Yeah, I can't take my eyes off it."

Stella shrunk back as if he could see her, blood rushing in her ears, and her heart pounding.

He continued merrily on, obviously unconcerned at the possibility of anyone listening in. "The music is writing itself here. Literally. When I wake up in the mornings, the words are just there. Like all I have to do is pluck them fully formed from my mind."

Then he laughed. And the happy, carefree sound had Stella spinning and slumping back against the edge of the sink, a protective hand laid over her heart.

Oh, God.

"I know. I swear if this place wasn't on the map, I'd think I'd accidentally strayed into a faerie realm.

Silence stretched for a good few minutes, during which Dax must have been listening to Lacey rattle on about Aitken.

What could she be saying? 'We're all witches here?' Stella cringed inwardly, waiting for the laughter. The exclamations of patent disbelief. Or the judgment.

None came. Instead he talked music, an appealing thread of boyish excitement in his voice.

"You want to hear one of them? Oh, all right, all right. Just for you. Hold up. I'll go get my guitar and prop my phone up. No. What? Acapella? Really? You sure? I'm warning you, it'll be a bit rough."

He made a self-deprecating sound. And then cleared his throat. "Okay, you asked for it. Here goes..."

It took two seconds of the pure notes filling the air with exquisite sound for Stella to throw her hands up in a warding off gesture, and to back away from the window.

Oh, no. No!

She couldn't bear this. *She couldn't.*

Her heart jerking, she ran, soft bare soles on polished floorboards, until she reached her bedroom. Pelting into it, she made a hasty gesture and the door slammed shut behind her.

She stood wringing her hands for a minute, before, snap decision made, she turned and climbed into the romantic tester bed and pulled the patchwork covers almost to her chin.

"Stella," a voice chided her from the ether, her favorite well-meaning cousin, butting in once again. *"You're being a bit ridiculous, you know that?"*

Stella clutched at the covers. "Stop using your glass to spy on me, Kilarney. *And* treating it like some kind of magical phone."

"I mean anyone would think the guy's a psychopath," Killie continued, unchastised, disembodied yet resoundingly present. *"Intent on digging your heart out with a blunt teaspoon, garnishing it with sage, popping it in a baking dish, and sliding it into the oven. Instead of a proper sweetheart."*

Stella's cheeks heated as she stared at the patterned quilt. God, she had to admit she did feel ridiculous, huddled in her bed like a child. Her heart thudded in her ears, and clutching the covers, her eyes swept around the room. "Is anyone else with you? Can anyone else see me?"

"You'd know that already if you opened yourself. But you're in too much of a tizz, aren't you, even to use your own magic to push back? You've shut yourself right down. So I'll tell you. It's only me with the audacity to poke into your business. To be so cruel as to prod you and to make you face your fears. But I'm not cruel enough to set up a circle of spectators so we can all watch and laugh at you."

Stella's heart squeezed in relief. Well, that was something. Bad enough that she'd embarrassed herself in front of her cousin, without putting on a show for the whole extended family peering into their glasses, or a stray party of friends.

"You know I'd never make game of you or your fears, Stella. But I do want to ask you this. What are you actually so afraid of?"

Stella plunged her hands into her pale blonde, tumbled curls, tugging at them. "I don't know. I don't *know.*"

"Something must have happened to make you so over-the-top afraid of relationships," Kilarney reasoned

"I—um." Biting her lip, Stella traced the patterns on the quilt with a fingertip.

"Think about it. Really think. What is it you're most *afraid of out of the whole deal?"*

Unbidden, a scene trickled into Stella's mind, of the shy, hopeful ten-year old version of herself waiting for a boy beside a pond. Her friend Blair, or she'd secretly hoped, maybe more than a friend?

A few minutes of nervous waiting, and he came, pushing aside feathery fern fronds that clung to his slightly older, stronger frame. He grinned under an appealing mop of dark hair, and moved to sit close beside her, bumping her hip with his.

Stella's heart fluttered wildly, stealing her voice. Skillfully though, over a matter of minutes, Blair drew her out, as he always did. Until finally, with a bold wink, delighting her, from behind his back Blair whisked a bouquet of daisies tied with a yellow checked ribbon. The gesture gave Stella courage to present her own gift—a small piece of polished lapis lazuli to aid him with his schoolwork.

He turned the brilliant deep blue over in his hand, stroking it with his thumb. "May I thank you for it?" he asked.

"Of course," Stella returned, taken aback by his formal phrasing.

Leaning forward he dropped a hasty, smacking kiss on her startled lips. Then just as suddenly he dropped to the ground in a crouch, hopping around like a frog. *"Ribbit! Ribbit!"* he croaked.

Uproarious laughter filled the glen, as two other boys crashed through the ferns. "Look! Look!" declared one, pointing. "I told you the witch would turn him into a frog!"

Blair collapsed into laughter on all fours as the second boy boldly stepped forward. "Here, I wanna try.

Dropping the daisies, Stella ran.

Coming back to the present, she covered her mouth with her hand. "I guess it's the intimacy I fear," she murmured, more to herself than to Kilarney. "Letting myself be seen, and known. Not—not just in a physical sense. But my whole self. Trusting that knowledge of—and access to the deepest part of me—to someone else. I'd feel too exposed, Killarney."

"You've always been shy and intensely private, this is true."

"And I guess it's fear of the unknown, too. These feelings and sensations crowding me are kind of thrilling and nice. But also strange. It makes me wonder if I'll be overwhelmed. If they'll take me over. *He'll* take me over until I don't have control over myself anymore."

"Stella, I'm sure he doesn't want to take you over. He wants a companion. A partner. Not a lapdog or a slave."

"It sounds silly when I say it out aloud." Stella bowed her head, pleating the quilt between her fingers.

"Fears usually do. Because they're largely irrational. And saying them aloud challenges them. It steals some of their power. But it's lucky we have an antidote to them, as well."

"We do?"

"Courage."

Stella shook her head. "But I'm not courageous, Killarney. I'm the very furthest thing from it. That's the whole point we're making. That I'm lacking in any kind of courage."

"Stella. We all need to grasp our courage in both fists at times. Having courage doesn't mean you're not afraid. If you weren't, you wouldn't need courage then, would you? No, courage means choosing to face your fear when you are afraid. It's a deliberate choice you make. And you can do it. You, Stella Weiland. I've seen you do it many times."

"You have?"

"Of course I have. In situations where you were uncomfortable, but pushed through anyway. Usually though, it's been for someone else. This time, you need to do it for yourself. And for Dax too. I mean, how sad for him, if you deprive him of the love of his life."

"Kilarney."

"No. I'm serious. There's another person involved here. And you have to consider him too when you're busily running away."

"You really expect me to feel sorry for him?"

"Not necessarily sorry for him. But you do have to consider him as well. That's all I'm saying."

Stella folded her arms. "Okay, fine. What am I supposed to do then? Go marching over there, and say 'here I am?'"

Kilarney laughed. "*Um, not that precisely. But then, from what I know of him, he probably wouldn't even object to it, he's that easy going and good natured.*"

Stella scowled. "Perfect in fact."

"Now, now. No need to get snarky, Stell. In fact, come to think of it, he's probably more good natured than you are."

"He probably is."

"But back to the point. All you have to do is to go about your normal daily life. And incidentally, that means no locking yourself up in a fortress. No hiding trembling in your bed. No latching every window, or creating a sound shield to stop you overhearing his truly first class voice. And definitely no *upping the ante on your protective wards to include Dax Brandon."*

Stella blinked, lifting a finger. "That's a—"

"No. I mean it, Stella. Courage, remember? Life as normal. And if you happen to cross paths during that ordinary daily life? Well, good. Try and be a tiny bit open to new experiences."

Stella's chest heaved as she released a monumental sigh. She hugged her knees and rested her chin on top. "All right. All right, Killie, I'll try."

Four

And Stella did try, she really did. Okay, so she didn't go outside when she heard Dax out on the patio. Or pretty much at all, to be honest. But she didn't hide in her bed again either when she heard him singing, and she didn't even close the windows.

And she didn't get in a panic—much—and close off when she heard the miracle that was his voice. That wondrous instrument that trickled inside her like molten honey, warming her from the inside out.

Wooing her with the beauty of his words, so that Stella began to understand that while he didn't have magic as she did, he possessed his own version, no less powerful in its way.

She found herself deliberately stopping to listen, becoming spellbound for long minutes at a time, pulling up a kitchen chair and tilting her head to catch the quieter passages. Humming under her breath. Shaken rudely out of her blissful reverie, and feeling strangely lost and bereft—an unaccountable sense of loss—whenever he packed up and went back inside.

Then came the day when he brought out the little pipe.

Oh. What glory! Such magical refrains. Stella's heart lifted, thrilling to the sounds. But they were too soft. She must have the fullness of them. So, hands clasped at her middle, her feet drew her closer, little by little, until they brought her through the house, down the front steps, along the path, through the side gate in the overarching shrubbery.

In fact, her spellbound feet brought Stella right to the player sitting on the patio steps, with barely even the consciousness of having moved.

Halting, he looked up, a hank of caramel hair tumbled onto his brow. "I think I must have summoned you. Did I? From next door?"

Stella came back to earth in a dizzying rush, the tantalizing, irresistible music having stopped. She sucked in a breath, panic seizing her. Palm to her chest, she took a step back, preparing to flee.

Jumping to his feet, Dax held up both hands. "No. No. Please don't go."

He tucked the pipe in his back pocket, and they stood facing each other in Mirabel and Varian's garden. Bursts of verdant life surrounded them, greenery and splashes of color, a fairytale setting for two fated lovers to meet properly for the first time.

His hazel gaze tracked over her face, leaving heat in its wake. "Hang on. I know you." His voice infused with wonder, he lifted an involuntary finger to the stray lock of hair by her cheek. "I've met you before. In what feels like a dream," he mused. "Or another life."

Stella cast her eyes down, nerves insisting she deflect. "That's only the cheesiest pick up line ever."

He gave a self-deprecating laugh, unoffended. "It would be," he admitted. "Only it isn't."

She couldn't deny the truth of the statement, yet what could she say? My interfering but well-meaning cousin Kilarney magicked you into my living room the day you arrived in Aitken, which also happened to be my birthday?

No, hardly.

Instead, remembering Killie's insistence on courage, Stella lifted her chin and tried something simpler, and more to the point. "Do you believe in witches?" she asked.

His eyes met hers, knowledge passing into them in the space of a heartbeat. "Of course I do, because you're one, aren't you? You must be. Lacey is a witch, and if I'm right, you're her good friend Stella.

Stella nodded. "Does that bother you?"

"No, why should it?" He lifted his shoulders. "There is magic in everything. This whole world is built upon it. I tap into this universal magic as you do, only in a different way."

Stella's heart sighed, an unknown weight slipping from her shoulders. *Oh, he understands.* Her lips curved, and she felt the welling happiness shine out of her eyes, turning them she knew into sparkling silver.

His eyes widened, and he released a breath. But he didn't back away, horrified at the change. Instead he reached for her hand, enfolding it in his own warm clever one, his expression earnest and his heart in his eyes.

"Will you walk with me?"

Stella nodded.

Together they meandered around rose bushes, through flowering arches, across a humpbacked bridge over a little fish pond. They talked of everything, and of nothing. Of witchcraft and of music. Of dreams.

Blushing, Stella explained what Killarney had done. "I'm sorry. She really shouldn't have done that. It wasn't right to take such liberties with you."

Dax smiled, his hazel eyes glinting. "I can't deny that from what I remember, it was a rush like no other. I can easily believe it was a heady kind of magic. In a way I think I've been trying to express that same sensation through my music ever since."

"And I think you must have succeeded," Stella admitted. "Especially today."

Dax nodded, thoughtful. "Perhaps you're right. It did bring you to me, after all." He turned to face Stella more fully, grasping her other hand as well. "And yet, I still feel like I can't take all the credit. It's as though being in your presence that other time fundamentally changed me. And changing me, changed what comes from me." His brow creased. "Do you know what I mean?"

The wondrous thing was that Stella did. In the same way their first magical meeting had changed Dax, hearing his sublime voice and his heartbreakingly pure refrains had changed Stella over the last week. Seeping down into her soul and communing with it. Warming it, and setting it to a steady flame.

A flame now fed by his presence, the touch of his hands, warm and strong. The contact sending delicious tingles throughout her body. His steady, clear, enraptured gaze revving her heart like an engine.

He lifted her hands, thumbs tracing light circles on the backs of them. "I hope you don't mind me saying this. Because in a strange way, it doesn't feel too soon. You see, I knew I loved you the first time I saw you. I'm in love with you again now. And I feel like if it were possible, I'd fall in love with you anew each and every time I see you for the remainder of my life."

"Oh, Dax." She lay her palms either side of his cheeks, allowing him to share the vision of possibility that burst into life in her mind. The sum of their days in a curling, closely entwined ribbon of light. The present, and the promise and the future. The small valleys of heartache, and the towering mountains of sunlit joy.

He gasped. But it was a warm, happy, hopeful sound.

Then, enraptured together, they fell down in a sheltered, grassy corner amongst the sage and the milk thistle, the nodding bluebells, the happy-faced marigolds and the snapdragons.

He cradled her head in his hands, the silken curls, waterfalls of gold through his fingers. "I swear I've dreamt of you and of this moment, like a thousand times, and I'm only just realizing it."

Leaning down, he brushed his lips over her forehead like a benediction.

Then over both eyelids, as gentle as the brush of butterfly wings. By the time he got to her lips, sinking into them velvet soft, all her fears had dropped away, as naturally as the trees shedding their flame-colored leaves in the autumn.

Ready for Dax's sunlight in her life? His lips on hers?

She hadn't known it before—but she'd been born ready.

About the Author

Tasha Blythe is the Romance pen-name of the Children's and Young Adult's author, Joanne Creed from Queensland, Australia. She has published a gloriously illustrated Christmas picture book, entitled The Shop on the Corner. Her work appears in various anthologies, notably the best selling, and Book Excellence Award winning finalist, Spooktacular Stories: Thrilling tales for Brave kids.

Joanne considers herself an incurable romantic. She is addicted to Pinterest, and all things cute and furry, such as bunnies with floppy ears, and hamster Gifs

You may find her on Facebook as Joanne Creed Author, and on her Writer's Group, Jo's Dreamer's. She is on Twitter as Joanne Creed, and Instagram as jodreamers73. Her website is www.joannecreedauthor,com,au.

It Was Only a Curse

BY SABRINA BOSQUE

Emma is convinced that finding true love is just a wild goose chase... until Adam comes soaring into her life, a curse on his tail. She's the only one who can break the enchantment. But can she do it before it's too late? Or will her secrets make this situation even worse?

One

Clink

A SILVER CHARM BRACELET TUMBLED INTO THE GLASS, SINKING swiftly. Withered, crushed leaves were sprinkled on top.

"Reveal to me the pure essence of my love," the soft female voice chanted. A golden aura enveloped the bracelet, lifting it effortlessly to the surface. Delicate fingers scooped it up, concealing it within a clenched fist.

RHYTHMIC MOANS SOUNDED FROM DERRICK'S ROOM. THE creaking of the bed and occasional grunts completed the picture.

"Yes, baby!" The throaty voice was followed by a resounding slap.

And that slap might as well have been across Emma's face. She closed her eyes, collected her wits, and marched into the room.

She expected it. She was prepared for it. And yet, seeing her boyfriend Derrick naked in bed with an equally undressed woman bouncing on his cock, head thrown back, moans leaving her lips with every motion, was like having a spear thrust through Emma's chest.

She froze in the dimly lit corner, while the fervent couple continued, blissfully unaware of her presence.

Happy memories flashed before Emma's eyes: the dates, the laughter, the 'I love you's'.

Her gaze dropped to the charm bracelet adorning her wrist, a token gifted by Derrick from a magic shop for their six-month anniversary, as he knew she loved dabbling in magic.

"Let this be the symbol of our love," he'd said when he put the bracelet on her wrist.

She'd been so happy then, staring into Derrick's eyes as if he was the only man in the entire world for her—the one who not only loved her, but understood her too.

Emma removed the bracelet, clenching it in her fist while she contemplated hurling it toward the entwined couple. Instead, she calmly dropped it to the floor and walked away.

Two

Emma awoke the following morning feeling crushed.

The breakup had been brutal. Derrick refused to take no for an answer, and after hours of crying and begging for forgiveness, he resorted to threats and recriminations.

She stretched her tired limbs and rubbed her swollen eyes, resolved to forget the entire ordeal. The charm bracelet she'd left behind jingled on her wrist, making her freeze.

How did it get back on her wrist?

Had Derrick come into her room and put it on her? A surge of horror coursed through her and shivers wracked her body. She sprang from the bed and meticulously inspected every point of entry.

The door to the balcony was unlocked! She lived on the third floor, and although difficult, it was plausible for an intruder to scale that height.

Emma locked the door and drew the blinds on all her windows.

If Derrick had done this, there was no telling what else he could do. She removed the bracelet and discarded it into the trash as she went to take a long, hot shower.

A WEEK LATER...

Emma strolled along the Arcane Bridge, her gaze fixed upon the serene expanse of the lake before her.

What a hellish week.

Derrick continued hounding and stalking her, pushing her to the brink of sanity. And the bracelet—the one she was holding between her fingers—refused to disappear! No matter what she tried—concealing it in locked drawers or discarding it—it stubbornly reappeared on her wrist every morning.

The last rays of sunshine vanished behind the trees, and darkness enveloped the park.

"Let this be the symbol of our love." Emma scoffed, releasing the bracelet, watching it plunge into the lake.

Turning away, she sauntered down the bridge.

Splashing noises in the water made her turn to see a majestic goose with silky gray feathers, black head and neck, and green eyes shining in the moonlight. Did her bracelet disturb this goose so much it abandoned the lake?

"Sorry, goose," she murmured before walking away.

Three

This isn't happening. This isn't happening!

Adam screamed inside his head. Perhaps he did scream out loud, except a loud, terrifying honk came out instead!

He flapped his wings in agitation, then paused and tried again. Yes, he had wings! Because Adam wasn't Adam anymore. He was a goose!

This must be a dream!

Adam squeezed his eyes shut, trying to wake up, but when he opened them, nothing had changed. He was still a fucking goose.

He wanted to cry, but he couldn't. Because, apparently, geese don't cry. *Do they?* Adam tried again, and his wings started flapping instead.

Damn those wings!

Panic created a knot in his stomach urging him to find his way home.

Where was his home exactly?

Everything looked disorientingly different from his new height. The landscape loomed vast and unrecognizable, lacking any distinctive landmarks. "Honk!" he cursed.

Damn. He couldn't even curse properly anymore. Something weighed heavily around his neck, though he couldn't discern its nature. What in the world?

Confusion mounted as he waddled toward a path, any path, driven by the urgency to escape. Agitated flapping of his wings propelled him forward, each attempt revealing a fleeting moment of flight. Astonishment accompanied this newfound ability.

I can fly!

Soaring through the park, he eventually recognized the path that would lead him back home. *Woohoo!*

However, a persistent calling tugged him elsewhere. Should he listen? It felt like some primal instinct, perhaps a migratory pull.

He didn't need to leave for Florida or wherever geese migrated. Wouldn't that be something...

Landing on the balcony, Adam surveyed his surroundings. Now what?

With a determined push of his beak, he managed to nudge the balcony door open, creating a crack sufficient enough for his entry. Weary, confused, and lost, he stepped into the apartment with the sole purpose of sleeping it off. Surely, this was a dream.

He navigated his way into the bedroom, employing his wings to leap onto the bed.

Everything will be better tomorrow.

He simply needed to get some sleep.

Four

"Aaaaah!" Emma scrambled off the bed and landed on her ass. There was a strange man in her bed. There was a strange man *in* her bed! And oddly enough... feathers?

"What's going on?" the man asked, his eyes wide with confusion, his voice groggy from sleep, as he scanned the room.

"I'm calling the police!" Emma cried, her initial shock giving way to determination as she frantically searched for her phone.

"Wait, don't!" The man leaped out of the bed, then dashed back in, realizing he was completely naked. "What the hell happened last night?"

Emma tore her eyes away from the unsettlingly captivating, yet unnerving, sight of the naked man in her bed. He had broad shoulders and muscled arms... strong enough to strangle her if he wanted to. She caught a glimpse of powerful thighs as he stood, before he hid them beneath *her* sheet...

"You tell me!" Emma cried. "How did you get into my house?"

He looked around, wide-eyed, his breathing labored. "I have no fucking idea."

"How drunk were you to climb into a stranger's home! A stranger's bed?"

"I wasn't drunk," the man croaked, his voice troubled. "I don't drink at all. I'm a triathlete."

He certainly had the body of an athlete. "How did you get here then?"

"I—" he absently patted his body, then froze, his gaze locked on his hand. He brought the hand closer to his face, dropping the sheet in the process.

"Oh my God! Cover yourself!" Emma shrieked, squeezing her eyes shut.

"I'm sorry, I don't know what's happening. I need to leave."

"Please." Emma waved a hand. She peeked through her fingers, but the man still remained by the bed, clutching a sheet to his chest.

"I can't leave like this," he hesitated. "I'll get arrested. You wouldn't happen to have any clothes?"

Emma surveyed the room. "Where are your clothes?"

The stranger scratched his jaw. "I don't... remember."

Emma sighed in frustration and went to her closet, keeping a cautious eye on the bewildered, naked stranger in her room. A twinge of sympathy tugged at her heart. "What's the last thing you remember?"

"I was swimming last night in the park when..." He shook his head, as if trying to clear a fog. "I must have blacked out."

Emma handed him a pair of gray sweatpants Derrick had left at her house, along with an oversized t-shirt. "I'm sorry, that's all I got."

He examined the clothes with a slight tilt of his head. "Better than nothing." As he reached for the clothes, Emma's eyes widened.

Dangling from his wrist was the bracelet she had thrown into the lake the previous night.

"WHERE DID YOU GET THIS BRACELET?"

Adam snatched the clothing and glanced between his wrist and the woman in front of him. "I don't know. Why?"

Her eyes widened, and a blank expression settled on her face. "Because it's mine."

"I'll happily give it back," Adam snapped, tugging at the bracelet that refused to come off. He blew at the errant lock of jet-black hair that fell onto his eye, his body tense and perspiration covering his skin. "Let me get dressed first."

He dropped the sheet and sat on the bed to put on the pants. The woman stared at him—or rather, through him—not even caring or acknowledging his nudity anymore.

"I threw it into the lake yesterday," she said, her voice trembling.

An unsettling chill ran down Adam's spine. "Why?"

She shook off the unease. "Because my cheating ex gave it to me."

That wasn't strange at all. "What does this bracelet have to do with me?"

She swallowed and then grimaced, shaking her head.

"What?" Adam turned toward her, the tight clothing cutting off his circulation in the most uncomfortable places.

"It's... nothing."

"Humor me."

She spoke hesitantly, "This isn't the first time I threw it away. And it isn't the first time it returned."

Adam looked around the room. Was he being pranked? "It returned?"

She shrugged. "This time, it made *you* bring it back to me."

"This is absurd!" he exclaimed, frantically fiddling with the clasp of the bracelet. "What's his name? Your ex probably drugged me and put me in your bed as some sick form of revenge for you breaking up with him."

"Revenge for cheating on me?" She scoffed before pausing in thought.

This was the only logical explanation. It would also explain his drug-induced dream of turning into a goose. "Why the hell can't I take this off?"

"Here, let me." The woman approached him slowly and took his hand in hers. A jolt of awareness surged through him, and Adam gasped. So did she.

They both froze, their hands intertwined, their breathing heavy. For the first time Adam truly noticed the petite woman whose bed he found himself in. She possessed soulful brown eyes and lovely curves to her body—which he should not be looking at!

After a charged moment, she wrapped her hands around his wrist and began working on unclasping the bracelet.

It wouldn't budge.

She persisted, warm fingers grazing his skin and sending shivers down his spine. Adam gazed at the top of her head and had an inexplicable urge to bury his nose in her silky black hair. He cleared his throat. "What's your name?"

She glanced up at him, surprise and confusion evident in her dark eyes. Her soft, rosy lips parted on a sigh, and neither of them seemed able to break eye contact. "Emma," she finally said.

"I'm Adam." They stood like that for a long moment until he pulled his hand back. "The bracelet is clearly broken. Probably on purpose." He sat on the bed and patted the empty space beside him. "Now, tell me all about your ex."

Five

Next morning, Emma awoke to a pleasant, languid sensation. She stretched, only to find a strong arm encircling her midsection, pulling her closer to a firm, muscled chest.

"Aaaaah!" Emma wriggled out of the tight hold, covered herself with the sheet, and sat up, her back pressed against the headboard.

Adam sat up as well, his hair ruffled, sleepy lines on his cheek, morning stubble shadowing his handsome face.

The damn psychopath was in her bed again!

This must be a joke. Or he was deliberately trying to drive her insane.

If so, he was a damn fine actor because he started and glanced around with eyes filled with shock. "What the hell am I doing here again?"

"Yes," Emma snapped. "What are you doing here?"

He pressed a hand to his forehead, looking miserable. "This must be a joke."

"My thoughts exactly."

Emma scrambled from the bed and stalked out of the room, determined to find out how he got into her house. She had locked all the doors and windows before going to bed, except for her bedroom window, which couldn't open fully.

Emma checked every possible point of entry, but they were all locked. She returned to her bedroom and scrutinized the half-open window. She leaned closer, sticking her head out. She could squeeze through it, but there was no way Adam's broad shoulders would fit.

"Tell me everything that happened last night," she demanded.

He scratched his jaw, and a ray of light caught one of the charms on the bracelet—her bracelet.

He was still wearing it.

The suspicion that had originated yesterday now firmly took hold of her mind. She almost didn't hear Adam recounting his usual activities from the night before. His day seemed completely ordinary. He went to work, had dinner, then went to confront Derrick, but the scoundrel wasn't home. And his new girlfriend insisted he'd been out of town for a few days.

Derrick moved on fast, not that Emma cared. *Bleh*. She was just surprised he continued messaging her while living with another woman.

"And then..." Adam paused, his brows furrowing. "I don't remember what happened next."

It seemed like as soon as the sun set, his memory was wiped, and he wasn't in control of his actions. Two nights in a row!

"I don't believe you." Emma observed his reaction closely.

He let out a defeated sigh. "I don't know what to tell you."

"How about the truth?"

Adam scrubbed his face. "There's something else, something even stranger than anything I've told you before."

Emma scooted closer on the bed. "Yes?"

"These past couple of nights, I've had the strangest dream." He paused, a grimace twisting his features. "I dreamt that I was... a goose."

Emma blinked. Whatever she expected him to say, this was nowhere on her list. "A goose?"

"Yes, a goose. I fly around the city, enjoying the wind on my face... And then I feel a pull that tugs me away."

"A pull?"

"Yes, I can't explain it, but it feels like it's leading me home. And then I wake up, finding myself in your bed."

Emma's mouth opened. She didn't know how to react to something this... bizarre! "Maybe you're sleepwalking?" *Sleep-flying*?

He shrugged. "Maybe. But why am I sleepwalking into your bed?"

Emma stared at the bracelet, her initial suspicion strengthening with every passing moment. She couldn't confide in Adam, not yet. She needed to be certain. "Here's the plan. You'll go about your day as if nothing happened. Go to work, do your usual activities, and I'll do the same. Then, we'll meet for dinner, and see what happens after the sun sets."

"Sounds reasonable," Adam conceded and stood.

Emma blinked, her cheeks burning, and her heart pounding loudly. "We need to get you some clothes first.

Six

Emma laughed so hard her ice cream fell onto the ground. "Look what you did!"

"What did I do?" Adam playfully took a bite of his ice cream.

"Ew! How do your teeth not hurt doing that?" Emma covered her eyes and peeked through her fingers. "Now give me your ice cream."

He chuckled and resumed their walk. Emma caught up to him and patted him on the shoulder. "You made me laugh. Therefore, it's your fault my ice cream fell. Therefore—"

"Therefore, therefore," he mocked but extended his ice cream toward her. "Here. We'll share."

She accepted and took a long, hard lick.

He paused, his gaze penetrating and his eyes hooded. "On second thought, I'd rather you eat it all."

Emma blinked innocently and continued walking.

"I'm surprised by how much I'm enjoying myself," he said suddenly.

"Really?" Emma raised her eyebrow.

"Considering why we're even here."

"Oh."

"I almost never just hang out anymore. I need to do a lot of work for my little startup. I need to work out more and harder to reach my athletic goals. Life has become a race. And whenever I idle, I feel guilty."

"But not now?" She threw him a side-eyed glance.

"No," he huffed. "Perhaps because we're trying to reach a goal, it doesn't seem meaningless."

"And there I hoped you thought I was worth it."

She wanted to fluster him because *she* was flustered. Instead, he looked at her under those hooded eyelids, emerald green eyes shining with the setting sun. Then, slowly and deliberately, he took the ice cream from her, his fingers grazing her skin.

Emma swallowed as a frisson of awareness coursed through her entire body. She sucked in a deep breath, inhaling the scent of fresh grass, summer, and Adam's spicy cologne. "What now?" Her voice came out breathy, so she cleared her throat while her cheeks burned in embarrassment. What was wrong with her?

Her phone buzzed, but she ignored it.

Adam raised a brow. "Who's that?"

She grimaced. "Probably Derrick. He's been messaging me non-stop for days. Even though he lives with his new girlfriend."

Adam winced. "What a pig."

Emma huffed a laugh. "Except, that's an insult to pigs. I don't know how I didn't see the real him. We were together for eight months."

"Love is blind." Adam shrugged. "And people can hide their true selves until they achieve their goal."

Emma turned toward him. Was he speaking about himself? "And what is your goal?" she asked, staring at him in complete darkness now that the sun hid over the horizon.

"My goal is... Honk!"

Startled, Emma jumped back with a screech, covering her face. When she peeked at the spot where Adam had been standing, all she could see was a gray goose with a black head and green eyes, wearing her bracelet around its neck.

Emma ran through the streets clutching a goose under one arm, holding a heap of clothes in the other. *This isn't happening, this isn't happening!*

Luckily, she was close to her apartment, and the goose was surprisingly docile, not even attempting to fly away. In her haste, Emma didn't notice a dark figure lurking near her apartment building and almost ran into it, stopping abruptly and dropping the goose in the process.

"There you are," a familiar voice emerged from the shadows.

"Derrick?" Emma stepped back. "What are you doing here?"

"I came here to win you back."

Emma's nose twitched. "That's not going to happen."

Derrick stepped toward her and grabbed her arm, squeezing it painfully, pulling her closer to him. "I love you. You're mine."

Emma twisted her arm away. "Leave me alone!"

Derrick lunged at her, and Emma screamed, shielding her head with her arms, expecting a blow. But none came. She cautiously lowered her arms to see Derrick running away, an angry goose chasing him, pecking at his shins.

Seven

"I turned into a goose?" Adam asked, his voice muffled as he pulled a shirt over his head. "In front of you?"

"Yes," Emma insisted. "But you also chased away my no-good ex. So I can't complain."

Adam was utterly confused. He remembered bits and pieces, but not the whole story. "I can't even begin to wrap my head around this."

"I know exactly how you feel. But I found various sources on the internet, and a few spell books we can go through to figure out what happened and how to undo it."

"You don't waste time, do you?"

"One of us has to keep a human head," she joked.

Adam chuckled and picked one of the books. "Okay, let's see what they say."

❧

THEY COMBED THROUGH EVERY RESOURCE BUT FOUND NOTHING helpful. Most sources indicated that curses only broke through actions contradictory to the curse, which with Emma's limited knowledge of magic, meant nothing to her.

"I say we call it a night," Adam said and stretched on the sofa. "Eat some ice cream, watch a movie."

Emma let out a chuckle. "Ice cream?"

"Yes, ice cream solves all problems."

"Even curses?"

"Especially curses," he responded, his voice lowering as he drew her closer.

Butterflies fluttered in her stomach. "I don't think it's a good idea for us to..."

"To?" he prompted, his finger gently tucking a stray lock of hair behind her ear.

"To be more than... friendly. We don't know what's going on."

He let out a sigh tinged with sadness. "What if I need a distraction?"

Emma bit her lip, her eyes now focused on Adam's mouth. "Something brought us together. You might regret..."

Before she could finish her sentence, Adam's lips were on hers. He started with a gentle kiss, tugging on her lower lip, freeing it from between her teeth. As her lips parted, his kiss grew deeper.

Hungry. Hot. Demanding.

Emma let out a deep sigh and welcomed his tongue inside her heat. Her hands cradled his head and neck, her fingers sifting through his silky hair.

Snaking his arm around her waist Adam tugged her to straddle his hips. Their kiss deepened, their tongues dancing, swirling, tasting each other. Emma moved her hips, rubbing against the hard erection pressing against her thigh, and a guttural moan left her lips.

Panting, Adam broke away an inch, their breaths and gazes locked in a thrall-like state. “What were you saying?”

Emma shook her head. “I don’t remember.”

And then she kissed him.

Adam grabbed her ass and pressed her closer to his entire body as he kissed her hungrily. He took off his shirt and Emma greedily roamed his chest, arms, and shoulders with her hands.

In a matter of moments, their clothes disappeared and their mouths traced each other’s skin, learning the taste, the topography of their bodies. Emma felt like a ravenous animal who wanted—needed—one thing. *Him.*

He pressed his cock against her center, the hot rod lighting her veins on fire. She moved her hips and they both groaned, his features strained as if he was holding on by a thread. “Are you sure that’s what you want?” he asked, his voice thick with passion.

“Yes, Adam, yes!” Emma moaned and was rewarded with a hungry kiss.

He held her by the waist, his fingers biting into her flesh and entered her in one swift thrust. Emma whimpered against his lips and heard an answering growl.

She moved her hips, taking him in deeper, her head thrown back, her back arched.

He moved, and all thoughts disappeared, save one.

More.

As if he heard her thoughts, his eyes lit up and an animalistic grin touched his lips. And he gave her more. Oh, so much more. With every move, he fed her passion, driving her wild. It was raw, primal, exciting. They couldn't stop. Every time one of them would move away an inch, the other would pull them back. Their bodies melted into each other, their moans a persistent sound in the room. Until their passion exploded in a moment of pure bliss.

Emma didn't know when she'd fallen asleep, but she awakened with the widest grin on her face.

She turned, patting the pillow next to hers only for her smile to fade. Adam wasn't there.

Frowning, she sat up and looked around.

That's when she noticed a lump moving under the sheets. And it was moving toward her!

Emma let out a guttural scream and jumped out of the bed.

The sheet fell back, revealing a big gray goose.

Eight

Days passed as Adam and Emma continued to meet every day in their pursuit of breaking the curse. They delved into magic books, sought guidance from fortune tellers, and Emma even reached out to her witch friends behind Adam's back, revealing the full truth. However, every source echoed the same message: the curse was unbreakable by any magical means.

In the meantime, Adam's periods in goose form lengthened while his human form aged rapidly, as if the two were merging. Given that geese rarely lived beyond thirty years, it seemed that his human form wouldn't either.

Emma's desperation reached its peak when Adam arrived at her apartment, looking like he had aged decades overnight.

"I think it's getting worse," he croaked. "I'm going to turn into a goose soon. I can feel it. Since I don't know which transformation will be my final, I wanted you to know..." He smiled wistfully. "This curse has ruined my life, and it'll probably kill me. But oddly I don't regret it."

"What are you talking about?"

"We met through this curse. And I can't imagine never knowing you." He traced her cheek with his knuckles, his wrinkled hand shaking. "I lo—"

"No!" Emma covered her ears. "Don't say it."

"Why not?" Adam took her hands, staring at her with a lovelorn gaze.

She couldn't bear it anymore. "Because I'm the reason for your curse."

He immediately dropped her hands. "What?"

"I blessed my bracelet to show me a way to true love. Derrick was becoming distant and I... I-it's complicated."

Adam recoiled. "You cursed me into loving you?"

"No! I blessed myself! But it didn't work. Or maybe it did... It revealed Derrick's cheating. Then I threw the bracelet into the lake and it must have latched on to you."

"You knew the reason behind my curse the whole time and you kept lying to me?"

"I wasn't sure. I didn't want you to hate me."

He huffed, his dear features twisting into a grimace. "Too late now."

"I never wanted this, Adam. You have to believe me!"

"Do I love you only because of the curse?" he growled.

"What?" Emma stopped short, horrified that he would ever think that.

"Well?"

"No!" She cried, although the terrible thought was now stuck in her mind. *Did he?* She felt numb. "I don't have that kind of power."

He scoffed. "Apparently, you have enough to make me believe I loved you!"

Emma closed her eyes, her heart breaking into a million pieces.

"I can't believe you lied to me!" He turned away and reached for the door handle.

"Where are you going?"

He shook his head and turned the handle. "Away from you."

Nine

Adam awoke the next morning, brimming with renewed energy and a sense of vitality he hadn't felt in... weeks. He burst out of bed and hurried into the bathroom, his gaze fixed on the mirror. To his astonishment, his youthfulness had been restored, and he was no longer trapped in the form of a goose. He glanced at his wrist, only to find the bracelet gone.

The curse had been broken! His heart leaped with joy. *I should tell Emma!*

Oh my God, Emma!

Regret washed over him as he remembered his hurtful words and doubts from the previous day. The curse had broken and he loved her still! Which meant the curse had nothing to do with his feelings toward her. He needed to go to her. *Now.*

Rushing to her apartment, he pounded on the door, his excitement mingled with trepidation. When the door swung open, his breath caught in his throat.

"Adam," an elderly woman greeted him with a warm smile.

"Emma?" His voice quivered with disbelief.

She nodded. "You look so beautiful, so young."

"What the hell did you do?" Adam barked, barging into her apartment.

"What I had to," she replied softly. "You were fading away, and I couldn't find a way to reverse the spell. So I transferred it to myself."

Adam rummaged through her kitchen, as if it would help him break the curse, then finally stopped and banged his fists on the table. "It didn't work, damn it. I still love you!"

Emma recoiled, tears rolling down her cheeks. “I’m sorry.”

"I'm not going to lose you." Adam stepped closer, taking her trembling hands in his. "Curse me back."

She shook her head, her voice filled with anguish. “It’s my curse, my burden... My love.”

“I don’t accept it.” Adam grabbed her wrist and tugged at the bracelet with all his might, until it snapped, radiating a brilliant glow.

Both of them watched as it soared through the air, landing on the floor a few feet away. Their eyes met, and Emma's astonishment transformed into pure shock before she collapsed.

Adam caught her in his arms, holding her tightly against his chest. As she stirred and lifted her head, he found himself gazing into Emma's youthful visage once more.

He glanced between her and the bracelet, bewildered. “What the hell just happened?”

“Reveal to me the pure essence of my love,” Emma whispered. “The curse has played out.”

“How?”

“It led me to my true love.” She cradled his cheek, her eyes filled with awe. “It gave you the form of a goose, a symbol of loyalty and eternal love. Geese mate for life, you know. And in our readiness to sacrifice ourselves for each other, the true nature of our love was revealed.”

"You love me," he whispered with a hint of wonder.

"I know you're angry with me because of my reckless spell.” Emma took a step away from him. “There's no forgiveness for me."

"Too bad," Adam replied, his hands tenderly cradling her face. "Because I forgive you."

“You can’t,” her voice was teary. “I stole your life and I can’t live with myself knowing this.”

He chuckled softly, his lips caressing hers in a gentle kiss. "Then you'll have to learn to accept it, because I love you. And apparently, geese mate for life."

About the Author

Sabrina Bosque is a steamy paranormal and fantasy romance author. Can she promise an endless flock of poultry-related shifter heroes? Not exactly. But you can join her in exploring a world of shifters, monsters, witches, dark and enigmatic, flawed anti-heroes in books filled with both quirky and heartbreaking moments.

Want more? Sign-up for Sabrina's newsletter and unlock a steamy epilogue and deleted scenes from her story *It Was Only a Curse,* along with exclusive updates on her upcoming releases.

www.sabrinabosque.com

Goody Halfmoon's Magical Hoodie & Her Hollywood Hottie Mishap

BY JEANNA LOUISE SKINNER

Goody Halfmoon — a disabled, plus-size Witch In STEM — is volunteering at a charity mud run when Hollywood heartthrob and uber-geek, Harris Colville, borrows her hoodie to wipe his face—WHILE SHE'S STILL WEARING IT!!! Their unexpected encounter leads to a bizarre twist of fate: her magic and his DNA combining, accidentally creating his perfect genetic twin. As Harris desperately searches for his mystery "Hoodie Girl", he discovers more than he bargained for: his dying clone—hardly an ideal set-up for romance. But caring for him together sparks a magic neither he nor Goody can resist.

(Note: This is a work of fiction, inspired by the time the author met her favourite actor at a charity mud run and he did indeed use her hoodie as a towel while she was still wearing it! All other events have been dreamed up in their entirety by the author's imagination.)

*

"Oh, my days, Goody! The streets are saying Harris Colville *is* here!" Kiel's voice climbs several octaves as he jogs up to me.

My best friend's aura is vibrating; his colours skipping through the spectrum like a rainbow on steroids. I can't blame him. Just the thought of my favourite Hollywood actor taking part in today's run has my stomach doing that flip-floppy, just-missed-a-step-going-downstairs thing. This is my third time volunteering at the Mud and Mayhem Charity Run, but Kiel is here as my Emotional Fangirl Support System. He only signed up because Harris Colville— an ambassador for this year's chosen charity—*might* show.

"A little help?" I grit my teeth, wrestling with an uncooperative folding table like a Deep South alligator wrangler.

As well as being the bestest bestie ever, Kiel is also a talented lab assistant —no one can generate a DNA expression protein faster. He's also distractible as fuck, wickedly funny, and when it comes to keeping a secret, locked down tighter than a bank vault on a public holiday.

He's the only person who knows my secret:

I'm a *real* witch!

Kiel takes the table from me before I can hurt myself. "I don't know why you don't just use magic instead of struggling."

"It's not an infinite resource, I've told you. I'm not allowed to just frack for it like an irresponsible local witchy authority."

"Witchy-Frackery sounds like fun though."

Once we've put up the table and unrolled the big 'WATER STATION' banner, I get busy filling cups. And I try not to think about how much of the universe's magic I'd have to illegally extract to ensure Harris Colville shows up today...

BY MIDDAY, MOST OF THE COMPETITORS HAVE COME THROUGH but zero sign of Harris. An early autumn sun shines down on the moorland, toasting my marshmallow face and neck, and I'm about to remove my charity-emblazoned hoodie when a new group appears over one gorsy ridge. My heart stops. They're at least thirty yards from the water station but I know it's him; I'd recognise that man mountain anywhere. Six feet of heaven in a megawatt smile.

Harris and his group jog up to the table and most of them gladly accept the water, but Harris declines. Instead, he says:

"You wouldn't happen to have a towel I can borrow?"

I steel myself to look at him. I've dreamed about this moment for over a decade. It doesn't disappoint, even with his gorgeous, carved-by-Michelangelo face completely covered in mud. Those eyes. They twinkle at me with the brilliance of stars in a midnight sky.

I recover quickly. Proud of myself, I pick up a cup.

"I'm sorry, Harris." (*I said his name-I said his name-I said his name!*) "I don't, I'm afraid... Would you like some water? Maintaining body fluids is the single most important thing for ensuring healthy intracellular and extracellular function pivotal to human survival."

"Oh..." he blinks. "No, thank you." His voice is chocolate brownie rich and it's all I can do to not ask if he'd like some extra sauce on top – *me*!

But he's still gazing at me with those impossibly bright eyes.

A pause. And then:

"May I?" He's gestures to my arm.

"*You may!*" Kiel yells back, but I can't look at him because Harris Colville is still staring at my right arm and tilting his head in the most adorable 'puppy dog begging for a treat' fashion. *He wants to use my hoodie!?* Anyone else and I'd tell them where to go, but when it comes to *HIM*, I'm mush. I am not proud of it.

"Sure, hold on," I splutter, grabbing the hem and making to lift it over my torso, but Harris stops me. He takes hold of my sleeve but not my arm, so that he's gripping the fabric and not me. It's like he knows how breakable I am.

"There's no need to take it off, if... this is okay with you...?"

And then, he raises his own arm, still holding the hoodie with my arm inside it, to his glorious face and begins wiping at the mud in his eyes.

I'm dead.

Harris Colville is using me as his towel.

I glance at Kiel, who's staring at us with an expression worthy of a million reaction memes. The moment seems to last forever but just as I think it, Harris gently lets go of my sleeve—leaving my arm hanging by my side; a weird extra appendage which doesn't belong to me.

He's talking again, but it's like it's coming from an alternate universe.

"You're a lifesaver, thank you." Harris Colville smiles *that* smile, but I'm choosing to believe it's a smile he's reserved just for me and not the same one loved by a billion other hopeless fangirls, fanboys and fan-persons the world over. That the wondrous lambency in his eyes isn't mere gratitude. That the way he's looking at me now—like he's the thirstiest man in the history of forever and I'm tallest, thickest, juiciest drink of water he's ever seen—means something beyond my wildest fantasies.

"You too!" I reply on autopilot.

Could I be any more of a moron? Pull yourself together, Witch.

Would it be so bad to use a little magic? A teeny-tiny spell couldn't hurt. Before I can talk myself out of it, I waggle my fingers in Kiel's direction. Once he's under the Forgetfulness Charm, I square my shoulders and beam at Harris.

"The second most important thing for human survival is support, so I've — err — been giving out motivational hugs... Would you like one?"

Thankfully Kiel doesn't react to my obvious fib; the spell is working.

My cheeks burn brimstone hot. I want the ground to swallow me whole again.

But Harris chuckles. "Well, I'd better top up my supply of both, then."

He drains a cup of water and then, smiling shyly, saunters around the table in that self-possessed way that only very famous people embody, like he's tuxedo-up and about to present an Academy Award, rather than standing in mud-drenched shorts and t-shirt in the Middle of Nowhere, Devon. The next moment, I'm engulfed in the biggest bear hug this side of Goldilocks, breathing his expelled air and uncaring that he's still covered in seven shades of mud and sweat. His body is tough and solid, like one of the obstacles on the course come to life, and I'd like nothing more than to climb all over and under him, have my own event for a good cause. The Goody Halfmoon Benevolent Bedroom Fund is gladly accepting donations, and I'm sure Harris Colville has charitable goodwill to spare.

I giggle into the concave space at this throat, forgetting the colour of everything. For a moment, there's only me and Harris, and the way he's gripping me to him. I've never felt this safe.

"What's your—

A voice hollering his name skewers his question, cutting through our intimacy. He stiffens, head swivelling to find his friends waving from the edge of a dip in the terrain. I pull away gently. Reluctantly. Only then does he let go. Then, thanking me again, he runs off into the distance.

Kiel is still staring at me like I've grown an extra head and I don't know whether to laugh or scream or dance with delight.

But what I do know is, I'm more in love with Harris Colville than ever.

❧

"I ONLY NEED SOME FILES, WAIT IN THE CAR IF YOU LIKE," I SAY to Kiel as we pull up at work hours later. We both took the day off for the run but there's always a billion things to do and deadlines to meet, especially when you're on the cusp of a breakthrough in genetic cloning.

"Don't be ridiculous." Kiel is already out of his driver's door and halfway round to open my side before I can argue. "You'll try to carry too much and end up hurting yourself."

He's not wrong. My hypermobile joints bend and break at the slightest touch. It's like I'm made from glass. I'm grateful to my bestie for looking out for me but it's times like these when the keen sting of being a plus-size, disabled Witch in Stem pierces me deepest. I have to work four times as hard as any man to be taken seriously. I've lost track of how often people automatically address Kiel and ignore me, even though I'm the lead scientist and he's *my* assistant.

We head into the glare of the lab, Kiel side-eyeing me.

"You've been in a right mood since we left. I thought you'd be floating on air.

I fish in my bag for my keys and sigh. "I was. I *am*. Sorry for being such a witch."

He smiles at our standard joke.

"But?"

Gathering up files and vials, we head for the secure frozen embryo store.

"Oh, you know how much I hate having to prove myself. How I'm always banging on about Women in Stem and equality and everything?" I turn the key in the lock and place my palm on the sensor. Kiel does the same on a matching pad on the other side. It's a dance we've practised many times and now we're as synchronised as an Olympic Artistic Swimming team. "Well, Harris Colville appears, and I turn to mashed potato. It's embarrassing how rapidly the feminism left my body."

"*And?*"

"And I used a Forgetfulness Charm on you so that I could lie to Harris about giving out motivational hugs in the hope that he would think I'm more outgoing than I really am and want a hug too, please don't hate me." I blurt it all out fast, like a penance.

"Goody Halfmoon, I'm proud of you." Kiel's smile is that of a graduation day parent. "I always knew you had a little Elphaba Thropp in you."

"You're not mad?"

"Nah, but I'd rather be your flying monkey than your guinea pig next time."

"There won't *be* a next time because as you know, there'll be a price to pay for the magic I used today. The pollution caused by my Witchy-Frackery."

I'm too hot, which is ridiculous considering we're in the 'fridge'. I'm still wearing my now mud-stained hoodie. There's a large patch of the stuff on the right sleeve where Harris used it, and two thoughts collide in my brain like atoms.

1. Harris Colville's sweat is in that patch, which means Harris Colville's DNA is in that patch.

2. I'm the world's leading genetic scientist on research into gene expression and human cloning.

No!

I push the idea away from me as quickly as it spawned. It's immoral, illegal and downright dangerous. Not to mention it wouldn't work anyway because impending breakthrough aside, we're nowhere near achieving full human replication. But Harris' bear-like arms and the way he'd looked at me with those intensely bright blue eyes brand themselves upon my heart and sear into my soul, and I shiver.

Very hot now.

Shoving all my paperwork and paraphernalia at Kiel, I rip off the hoodie as if it's burning my skin, but I move too fast, and my right ankle gives way sending me stumbling into him. He lurches backwards and we watch – almost in slow motion – as the jumble of reports, research and vials goes flying into the air along with the hoodie. Their arc carries them towards the fragile frozen embryo station.

"No!" I cry, throwing out my hands on instinct; they glow and tingle with a burning unconnected to my earlier warmth. Magic explodes from my fingertips, a golden beam which illuminates the 'fridge' and Kiel's shocked face, before landing squarely on the embryo station and my hoodie, fusing them into a glowing, magical disco ball. The ball spins and grows, humming with electricity. I drop my hands but it's too late.

Kiel and I back out of the chiller, as the glowing orb continues to pulse, growing and changing shape, until it fills the room. Eventually it begins to recede and dim, finally morphing into the form of a human man. And not just any man.

Harris Colville.

❧

"I *HAVE* TO FIND HER."

I stare at my assistant and closest friend, Lesley, willing her to remember her own wild goose chase in the name of love. To understand the urgency bubbling inside my chest. I haven't been able to stop thinking about *her*: the woman with the magical eyes, knockout curves and kindly donated hoodie at the mud run. God, she'd felt so right in my arms. We were a perfect fit; two lost puzzle pieces from life's broken jigsaw, found each other at last. I *have* to know if she feels the same.

"The charity says it'd breach GDPR to give out her details. They've agreed to pass a message on." Lesley smiles and shakes her dark head. "I get it, Harris."

Her phone rings as I crumple onto the sofa. There's a script for my next movie on the coffee table but I can't concentrate. I can't eat, I've barely slept. It's maddening that a stranger could have this effect on me but just the thought of Hoodie's violet hair and eyes—dye and contacts, of course, but who cares when they make her look that fucking desirable—does strange things to my insides. I've lost count of the times I've imagined us together, the ways I've fantasized about running into her, seducing her, claiming that wickedly plump body and those deliciously pink lips for my own. It's like someone peeked inside my head and cloned my ideal woman: big, beautiful and brainy.

"Did you say *cloned*?" Lesley loads the last word with incredulity.

Shit. I must have spoken aloud, but no, Lesley is still talking into her phone. Her face morphs through shocked disbelief to something akin to dawning realisation. Eventually she hangs up and for the first time since I've known her, she looks lost for words.

"Spit it out then."

But she shakes her head, moves to the bar, and fixes two large glasses of whisky, before handing me one.

"Sit," she says in the oddest tone. "You're not going to believe this, but... we've found her. Or rather, she found you."

❧

THE LAST TIME I'D BEEN THIS NERVOUS, I WAS NINETEEN, auditioning for a major Hollywood player. I'd stayed up all night drinking coffee and promptly threw up in the director's face the moment I opened my mouth to read my lines.

I didn't get the part.

My stomach churns as I raise my hand to the buzzer. I can't believe I'm going to see her again. Goody. The gorgeous woman with the hoodie. The scientist who—if what Lesley described is to be believed—has successfully created the world's first human clone. A clone of me. It's enough to make anyone anxious.

I shift my weight from foot to foot, but then a scream and the sound of glass breaking crash through the silence. Goody! It's like I've developed a kind of sixth sense. I just know in the pit of my chest that she's in danger. I pound on the door, throwing my shoulder at it, but no use. It's a secure building for a reason. But then the door swings open anyway and I almost fall clean through it.

"Oh great, two of you. That's all I need."

Goody greets me with a resigned sigh and the balloon of hope I've been carrying around this past week goes pop. She turns on one Converse-clad foot, purple hair flying, and leads me into the hi-tech building. Several loud bangs disrupt the silence, amplifying the fact that the place is empty when it should be teeming with activity. I follow, mesmerised by the graceful, almost careful way she walks; those generous hips and thighs swaying like the sea. Then she stops, eyes wary and says:

"He's in here."

We enter what was once a laboratory, now split into two clear sections by a wall of glass which reaches from floor to ceiling. Could this day get any more surreal? It's like something out of a bad science fiction movie—and I should know. But then, a rapid movement beyond the glass wipes almost everything from my brain—everything except Goody—as I come face to face with my clone for the very first time.

"I'M SORRY I WAS RUDE BEFORE."

I hand Harris a mug of tea with a shy grin. I hadn't meant to take my frustration out on him but it was such a shock seeing him standing there banging on the GenETech door immediately after yet another fight with his clone, that something inside me had snapped.

Why is he here? Oh my god, he's probably got a massive legal team preparing to sue. Save my poor, broken bod. But... he doesn't look *angry, so what's going on?* I blow on my tea. Might as well give him the truth. In for a penny and all that.

"When I was sixteen, I found out I was a witch. I thought that would be the craziest thing to ever happen to me." I pause, letting this intelligence sink in, but Harris' godlike face doesn't change. He just watches me, those brilliant eyes occasionally darting to his clone, now sleeping off the sedative I'd given him; long legs dangling over the edge of a makeshift cot.

Gulping, I continue, "Then there was being diagnosed with one of the rarest hypermobility diseases in my twenties, realising I'm not just a clumsy hot mess always bumping into things and breaking bones like breadsticks. And of course, I never imagined I'd become one of the leading names in my field. But all of that pales into insignificance compared to this past week. The mud run, meeting you, you borrowing my hoodie—"

I take a large swig of tea to avoid his gaze. Too hot! Shit! Spitting it back into my mug, I press on, hoping he didn't notice.

"And then everything that happened after. It was a complete accident; you *have* to believe me. I was doing too much as usual and I lost my balance and fell into my lab assistant, Kiel. All my research went flying into the embryonic chiller, along with my hoodie"—I nod my head in the direction of the fridge—"and I tried to stop them from damaging it, but... I accidentally summoned my powers and created you.

Well, a clone of you..."

My face burns with the intensity of a NASA space shuttle during re-entry. *'Five-hundred-degrees Kelvin,'* my science brain whispers unhelpfully. I fidget in my seat, worrying at a loose thread on my skirt, still unable to face him. But then a cool, strong finger tucks under my chin, pressing my head up with a firmness I can't resist. Harris Colville is staring at me again, but this time it's with something akin to wondrous confusion.

"Only," I whisper, scared by the intensity of him and how it seems hardwired to my sudden lack of self-control, "he's not like you, because he doesn't have your memories or character or soul, or whatever it is. He's basically a baby, an overgrown baby who doesn't know his own strength."

"Empty-Headed Harris Colville," Harris says at last, referencing an infamous and less than complimentary review he once received.

The brevity cuts through the tension and we both laugh. He sweeps his dark curls from his forehead, puppy dog eyes round and bright.

"I don't want to be rude – *again* – but why are you here?" I ask.

He laughs again. "You have your lab assistant to thank for that. He may have, err, accidentally called my management to let them know about your discovery... Now, when you say you're a witch..." The famous smile is back but it's tinged with doubt.

I nod, and repeat the words slowly, like I'm talking to a child, making a mental note to unalive Kiel in the most painful way I can imagine.

"I mean, I'm a real 'honest-to-Hecate-Long Lost Owens Sister-Sabrina the Teenage-I-can-do-magic' witch. It's fine if you don't believe me." Now it's my turn to smile but inside, I'm a tangle of hot nerves.

Harris stands and strides across the shiny tiled floor. He shakes his head, chest puffing in that way peculiar to men whenever their version of the world is challenged. My final thread of self-control snaps and I wiggle my fingers at his tea on the desk where he left it. Cost of Magic be damned. I'm tired, low on spoons, and my grasp on reality is slipping out from under me. This'll show him.

The mug rises into the air, tea inside sloshing up the sides; a tiny, stormy, tan-coloured ocean in a teacup. It takes all my concentration, but I guide the cup through the air, feeling the ebb and flow of the universe pushing back against it. What I'm doing goes against all the natural laws of science, a fact which is never lost on me. Harris halts in his pacing, eyes widening to impossible size. His mouth drops open and he smacks one large hand upside his forehead. The sound echoes throughout the empty lab.

I bring the mug to a stop at precisely the right spot for him to grab the handle and lift it to his lips, which he does as if in a trance. Draining the tea, he swallows, then drops the mug which crashes to tiles, splintering into pieces.

"You-you *are* a witch!"

"I DID TRY TO TELL YOU," GOODY SAYS, SMILING IN THAT mysterious and oh-so sexy way.

We've cleared up the broken bits of mug and we're sitting at the desk again. Her violet eyes shimmer with bemusement, while my clone's loud snores cut through the silence. And I thought this week couldn't get any weirder. She's a witch. An actual witch. And she created my clone. Perhaps I've stumbled into one of my fever dreams; I get them a lot when I'm cutting carbs for filming, but I've been eating well lately, so this must be real.

Goody sighs. She's obviously exhausted and no wonder given everything she's just told, and showed, me. She yanks the cuffs of her cardigan down over her wrists, causing it to fall from her shoulders. Snatching at the knitted material, she wraps it around herself, hugging her stomach and chest, but too late – I saw the bruising at her throat.

I'm out if my seat and at her side in an instant.

"Those aren't normal bruises, Goody, hypermobility or not." I tug the fabric from her hands and my heart sinks as the enormity of the damage is revealed. Her pretty pale skin is a patchwork quilt of black, blue, purple and green mottling which extends from her collarbone and snakes up and around her throat. I want to be her comforter. Her protector.

"Who did this to you?... Not *HIM*?"

My brain thunders, lightning splits my heart in two. How can he have hurt her when he's supposed to be me and I—

I'm suddenly banging on the glass, fists aching with the effort. Yelling and cursing, I hear myself threaten to kill my own clone. I'm way out of control, character, and my mind, but I can't help it. I'd do anything to keep her safe. But then Goody is back in my arms and the world makes sense again.

❧

"HARRIS, STOP! IT'S NOT HIS FAULT. HE'S A CHILD—NOT EVEN that—a living, breathing lifeform with the body of a human being but without its intelligence. He didn't mean to hurt me. And besides, I can take care of myself. I'm just fragile, that's all."

I wedge myself in between the glass and Harris's chest and flailing fists, circling my arms around his waist, finding my safe space in that spot where his throat perfectly fits my head. It's crazy but it feels like home. Breathing him in, I wait for him to calm, for his heartbeat to steady before I speak again.

"He's dying."

Maybe it's professional disappointment, or perhaps it's just a culmination of everything that has happened lately, but I'm struck at how emotional I am. Tears spike my eyes and I dash them away with the back of one hand, laughing at my foolishness.

"My accidental scientific breakthrough probably won't last another night. I've been trying to keep him comfortable, to medicate him through the pain, but he doesn't understand. Hence the bruises. And like I told you, I break more easily than most people, so please don't be mad at him." I shake my head, the tears unstoppable now. "If you should be mad at anyone, it's me."

But Harris only gazes at me. Eyes burning.

"How could I ever be mad at you? My brilliant, brainy, beautiful witch."

I gasp.

Did he really just say that? But I don't have time to ponder it further because he's looking at my sleeve with a familiar expression.

"You wouldn't happen to have a towel I can borrow?"

He smiles and this one is a dialled up to the max, full wattage, eat-your-heart-out-Hollywood, knee-trembling, spine-tingling, panty-dropping smile-to-end-all-smiles, and I'm in no doubt that he's been saving it just for me. So, laughing, I say:

"I'm sorry, Harris." How perfectly his name coats my tongue this time round. "I don't have anything like that, I'm afraid. Would you like some water?"

We turn in unison to look at the perfectly acceptable row of tea towels hanging by the big laboratory sink.

"Hmm, I am thirsty for something."

Chocolate brownie voice, extra sauce. I melt in the middle. Into him.

He looks down at my sleeve again.

"May I?"

"You'd better!" I reply, meeting his gaze.

If it's possible, he grips the fabric of my sleeve with even more care than before.

"There's *every* need to take it off, if... that's okay with you...?"

But then to my utter shock, he releases the material and instead grips the hem of his own t-shirt, lifting it up and over his head in one smooth movement. Do they teach men how to do that? Is it something they pull them out of class for at school, while we're learning about periods, boys get lessons on t-shirt removal during acts of seduction? But a moment later, all coherent thought has flown my brain because a now bare-chested Harris is bringing the t-shirt to my face where he begins wiping at the tears in my eyes. I try to remember how to breathe, to take in every sensation, but it's overwhelming. The shirt smells so good—but he smells even better. My hands take on a life of their own, exploring his hard hairy chest, abs and back, as if I'm trying to divine water from his skin. Thirsty indeed.

"Hold on," he whispers, discarding the shirt.

Then he cups my face in both hands, gazing at me with undisguised adoration, and traces the path he made with the t-shirt with the sweetness and softness of his lips.

I'm dead.

Harris Colville is being my towel.

He pulls back, searches my face.

"Where do we go?" His voice is gruff with desire. "No offence but I can't love you here—not in front of him."

HARRIS' CLONE DRIFTS AWAY. I HOLD HIM UNTIL I'M SURE, trying to wrap my head around the juxtaposition of how, only moments earlier, the real Harris had been similarly in my arms. He's currently sitting on the other end of the bed, holding his genetic twin's hand. This must be so surreal for him.

"He's gone," I say. "He looks peaceful."

Harris moves to sit next to me.

"To say I'm still weirded out is an understatement, but it's for the best. At least he's not suffering anymore." He pull me close and we're silent for a while.

Leaving the glass room, I turn off the light with sense of finality. What on earth am I going to do about his body? But that's a problem for tomorrow. Days like today don't happen to people like me, witch or not. Mere mortals don't get to kiss movie stars, let alone do all the things to and with them that I've done with Harris Colville during the past few hours. The man has stamina. Yawning, I stretch my arms up over my head, examining my bones and muscles for any tell-tale signs of damage, but I'm surprised to discover that apart from the odd ache here and there, I appear to be intact. Harris is an exceptionally gentle lover, as well as an exceptionally gifted one. But I'm realistic enough to know the score. At least I can make this easy for us both.

I take a deep breath.

"It's okay. I understand."

"You understand what?"

"You'll go too. I get it."

"You do *not* get it." He sweeps both hands through his hair. Blue-sky eyes filling with thunderous clouds . "I am in love with you, Goody—I don't even know your full name."

"Halfmoon," I reply, my voice small.

"Halfmoon..." he chuckles, long strides making short work of the reduced lab space. "You really *are* a witch, aren't you?" Then he turns to face me, shaking his head.

"I know it's crazy. I know it makes no sense. I'm scared you'll complete your cloning research soon and then you'll create your perfect guy, with or without magic, and I'll be discarded, failed experiment, or a spell gone bad. And to that end, I admit to being slightly terrified but also completely and utterly enchanted by you, both as a scientist and a witch."

He places his palm over his chest, near his throat.

"But I love you, Goody Halfmoon, and I need you here, where you fit so right, like a perfect clone of my heart."

I collapse onto him.

My safe space.

About the Author

RONE nominated Jeanna Louise Skinner pens plus-size romances with a sprinkling of magic!

Jeanna has CRPS and ADHD and she loves writing fat positive fantasy characters with disabilities and neurodiversity. She lives in Devon with her husband, their two teenage children, and a cat who sounds like a goat. Jeanna is currently working on a romcom series of spicy fairy-tale retellings called *The Bluebloodsuckers* about a fictional, modern-day, European royal family—who just happen to be a coven of vampires! Book One in *The Bluebloodsuckers Series, Pumpkin Spiced, a Cinderella*-inspired romcom about a fat and stabby swordsmith witch—wielding a glass dagger in place of a glass slipper —and her Prince Charming who turns into a vampire on the stroke of midnight, is coming soon!

Her cosy, witchy, "*Practical Magic* meets *Inkheart*" fantasy romance *The Book Boyfriend* is available in paperback, e-book and *audiobook*. https://mybook.to/TheBookBoyfriend.

Instagram @jeannalstars

https://jeannalouiseskinner.com/

Dear Soldier

BY ANITA HARLAN

In the enchanting setting of 1918 New Mexico, immerse yourself in a heartfelt tale of love. Meet Larkspur Point, a nurse dedicated to her patients' well-being and the healing power of her own witchy heart.

As WWI ends, a soldier's letters find their way to Larkspur, forging an unexpected bond across the miles. Through his eloquent words, she glimpses a soul yearning for solace amidst the chaos of war.

Amidst the frost-kissed air and the anticipation of Yule, Larkspur and the soldier find themselves intertwined in a delicate dance of affection. Will their shared letters blossom into an enduring love?

One

August 1, 1918

Dear Soldier,

It is the hope that this first letter of mine finds you safe and well wherever in Europe they have you stationed. It's my prayer that you are far from the trenches and that this dreadful war will be over soon.

I suppose I should tell you a little about myself so you aren't left wondering who this wordy nurse is rambling on in her writings! I work as a nurse in Blue Point Convalescence. It's a new hospital that was set up to help our brave returning witches. At the moment, we are one of the most advanced hospitals in the state thanks to Mayor Mays giving us such a large donation to equipment and proper care in the forms of herbs among other things. My aunt is one of the head nurses there while I'm still starting out in my nursing career.

If you've never heard of Blue Point, I promise you I won't laugh. We're a smaller town in New Mexico. I'm not from this area but moved here about eleven years ago with my family. If it helps, we're a few hours train ride Southwest of Albuquerque.

New Mexico has some of the most beautiful landscapes I've seen in a long time. If I can ever get my hands on some photographs or post cards, I'll have them sent your way. I recently saw some colorized postcards and even they don't really do the scenery justice. They can't even capture the colors of lovely sunsets that we have. Sometimes if it's quiet, I like to stand outside and watch the sun set over the horizon. It gives me a very peaceful feeling. I hope that you can also find comfort in watching the sun, moon, and stars.

While it's truly a lovely area, the only thing I don't like is that it gets hot and dry in the summer. I'm <u>not</u> like my Aunt Hope, where it can <u>never</u> be too hot! She would be right at home in Death Valley. There are times I don't know how she can do it. In some ways, I imagine I'm the black sheep of the family as I'm the only one who can't stand the heat. Ha-ha!

What about you? Do you have any exciting information about where you're from? Any sort of fascinating legends you can share? I find stories and mythology to be fascinating.

I suppose I've bothered you enough with my letters. Be safe out there, brave soldier, and I hope to hear from you soon.

Sincerely,
Your nurse

❧

August 28, 1918

My Dear Nurse,

Never in my life would I have believed I would start off a letter in this manner! There's a joke in here somewhere, but I'm not sure where.

It's very kind of you to write to me. Thank you. We soldiers always enjoy receiving letters from people, be it family, friends, or even nurses who won't yet tell me her name. Maybe one day I'll be able to convince you to reveal your name to me. I'll bet it's a lovely one.

Don't worry about writing too long letters to me. I enjoy receiving any sort of correspondence, be it short or long.

As for me, where do I begin? When asked to tell someone about myself, my mind always goes blank and I don't know where to begin. I enlisted when they were first asked for volunteers, which would be around December 1917. I forget the exact date but it was shortly after Yule.

I come from a smaller family. It's just my parents, my younger sister, and I. I'm afraid there's no real exciting story for me. Before the war, I was a bricklayer, apprenticing under one of my father's friends. It's good work, but I'm not sure that's what I want to do with the rest of my life. I wonder if any of us will go back to our old lives when we return.

My sister is going to be married when her sweetheart returns from the war. I still have vague memories of when she was a tiny baby and now she's old enough to be a bride. I'm <u>not</u> ready to feel this old yet! I can still remember using my skills to make little light shows for her to entertain her at night. I *suppose in some ways this gives me the opportunities to do the same for her children when she has them.*

I'm not from New Mexico, but they briefly stationed there me during my basic training. I remember that summer heat all too well. A great many of us would end the day as red as lobsters! There were times that I thought I would look like a ripe tomato for the rest of my days.

I can assure you that I'm safe and sound and intend to stay that way. I'm currently stationed in Europe but I can't say well because of the censors. Oddly enough, this area has helped me improve some of my foreign language skills. Languages have never been my forte, so my being able to carry on a very basic conversation is a genuine triumph for me.

I'm afraid that's all I have time to write for today as I need to fall into line for roll call.

Thank you for the kind letter. I'll write to you if you keep on writing to me.

Your soldier

❧

September 9, 1918

Dear Soldier,

Can you believe it's almost October already? Where has the month gone? My mother always said the older you get, the faster time goes. Does this mean we're getting older yet?

Do you think you'll reveal our names to one another? I always think of you as my dear soldier, but sometimes wish I had a name to attach to how I envision you. I won't tell you how I picture you, but I can assure you it's a lovely image. I always imagine a greatly talented witch with magical hands. Do you do the same for me? There are times I like to imagine that there are other couples out there, just like us exchanging letters.

I'm sorry for the shortness of this letter but it will be a busy day for me and I need to get ready for it.

Sincerely,

Your nurse

❧

September 1918

My Dear Nurse,

I forget what day it is, but I never have forgotten you. You and my family are the only ones who have continuously written to me. I do genuinely appreciate that.

You may hear frightening news coming from Europe, but you mustn't believe all of it. Most of it is gossip meant to get people agitated. We do get a great laugh in the trenches seeing what the enemy has written about us. My personal favorite is how we allegedly are dressing up in discarded women's dresses and putting on plays to entertain ourselves. I haven't been able to witness that...yet. Some papers even have hysterical cartoons depicting us. We will point at the illustrations and go "Lookie here, boys, here's..." and list whatever soldier's name the drawing looks like. We do find ways to entertain ourselves with various magic and put herbs that were sent to us by our families in our foods to keep us healthy.

The war can't last forever and it looks like it may be coming to an end. We've beaten the Germans back again and again. They say the war will be over by Yule and with a little luck it will be!

What do you think will become of us after the war? Will we still write to one another? Might you be so kind as to tell me your given name and where I can send you my letters?

Always,
Your soldier

❧

October 31, 1918

Dear soldier,

I hope this letter reaches you safely. I want to reassure you I haven't forgotten about you or our promise to write to one another. We don't know how true it is, but we've heard rumors about the Germans sinking some of our ships that may have been carrying the mail on it. Either way, I'll continue to send you letters until you tell me to stop. Between you and me it's privately my hope that you never tell me to cease my writing.

I received your last letter, but it was damaged somewhere along the lines. I wasn't able to make out all of it, but I saw your request to see a photo of me to keep with you. I won't send you a picture...just yet. I like it we're anonymous. I think it would be more enjoyable if we were to meet one another face to face after the war.

Happy Samhain. May your ancestors be with you this night and all others.
Your (always writing) nurse

My Dear Nurse,

I know you'll soon be hearing some frightening news about some battles in France, but I want to reassure you I'm alright.

I'll write more when I can.

Your soldier

Two

Jackie

December 1, 1918
Blue Point, New Mexico

The ambulance I'm stuck in with six other soldiers jostles us every which way on the dirt roads. We're bounced around in there as if we're nothing more than mere rag dolls. Some knucklehead got it in their brain that us traveling via the unpaved dirt roads was a faster route to the hospital. What they failed to mention was how much rougher the terrain would be. Why couldn't they just send us to the hospital or have the doctors perform a summoning ritual? Was there something we didn't know? There were people who are against our kind but could they be here?

Another bump and I strike my shoulder, sending pain radiating through it. I hiss in pain through tightly pursed lips. The medicine the doctor had given me was starting to wear off. A broken clavicle was a not so nice parting gift from the Germans in the last few days of the war.

I didn't even feel it, let alone realize what had happened to me at first. I hardly remember any part of that day. Perhaps it is for the best. What I remember was how my heart was beating so fast and it left me half deaf because of the rifle fire. Out of nowhere, something dark gray came barreling towards me. I barely had any time to react, or even create some sort of shielding, when it collided with me and bowled me over onto my back. Whatever it was, it knocked the wind out of me. At first, I was too frightened to even notice the pain. Scrambling onto my feet, I raced back to the safety of the trenches as if my very life depended on it. I fell into the safety of the trench in an uneven heap. It's only when that once dull ache became a stinging pain that refused to go away did I give in and pay a visit to our doctor.

Even our doctor grimaced at the ugly-looking bump that had formed near my neck. Between my howling and cursing in pain, he pushed my clavicle back into place, giving me strict instructions not to agitate it. The rest of the recovery was on me, however long that took.

When peace was declared, that meant I'd be taking a one-way ticket straight to a convalesce hospital. To be honest, I didn't think that meant I'd be returning home. Not that I'm complaining about *that*.

My only issue was I didn't want to go to a hospital of any kind. I would take a bed from someone who needed it much more than I did. That made me feel terribly guilty. Someone out there was in far worse shape than me and needed care more urgently. I gave it all I had, but my protests fell on deaf ears. They would send me to Blue Point hospital until the doctor deemed me well enough to go. Once I was discharged, I could leave the hospital, hop on a train for half a day, and make the rest of the journey home on foot. If my memories were still correct, home wasn't that far from the train station. Maybe only a few miles and I could walk that in my sleep.

The need to distract myself during the rest of this ride rises within me. I'll be bouncing off the walls if I'm forced to endure this last leg of the trip with no sort of entertainment. It's then I remember the letters my nurse was kind enough to send me. I read over the last of her writings again and again, noting her neat script. I could read those letters of hers all day.

The ambulance gradually comes to a stop. The echo of the door slamming shut once, and then three times, followed by an exasperated sigh.

"Only three slams this time. Last time it took four," a badly burned soldier next to me says.

"I believe that the lowest common bidder made many of the things us have to work with," I comment.

There's no time for more sarcastic comments as they throw the back doors open, bathing us in the harsh sunlight of the day. The most severely wounded are pulled out first and taken inside to their respective wards.

"You're next, but you're on the bottom ward," a doctor in an all too large white coat tells me.

"I'm fine. It's just a broken bone that's already healing. Keeping me here will only take up a bed for someone who needs it more than me. Someone can finish the healing job and then they can send me to the nearest office—" I argue as I'm ushered out.

"You haven't been discharged yet, so in you go. Your pajamas are on your bed, so go in there and get changed. Leave your belongings on the nightstand next to you. No more arguing."

Rather hesitantly, I trudge my way inside, shoving my letters back into my coat pocket. My uniform suddenly feels so dreadfully heavy. I feel like I can fall, crushed by the weight of it at any moment. Has it always been this way, or am I only noticing it now? Sighing, I undo the buttons on my uniform and replace it with a scratchy set of pajamas. Folding up my clothing as neatly as I can and set them on the nightstand. This brought me to the question of where was my uniform going? I don't want anyone being able to go through my meager belongings. Thrusting my hand inside my coat, I pull out my letters and shove them under my pillow followed by the few coins I have in my pocket. I take one last glance at the bedside table next to me. It has a sheet of paper and a pencil on it. Funny how I hadn't noticed that before.

John Jacob Hall, there are times you couldn't pour water out of a boot even with the instructions written on the heel. Of all the places they could have sent you, they sent you to the hospital where your dear nurse works, my mind reminds me.

The butterflies inside me intensify. What ward does she work on? How will I go about meeting her?

I run a hand through my dark hair, trying to calm my mind that was filled to the brim with ideas.

I could write her a letter or even make her a Yule card. What I lack in any sort of art skills hopefully I'll make up for in my writing out what's in my heart. I won't sign my name to save us both the humiliation in case she doesn't reciprocate my feelings.

My luck may very well be turning around thanks to that sheet of paper and pencil beside me. Though it's not in my neatest writing, I scribble out a quick letter to her.

My dear nurse,

Would you believe it I'm here? I'm in Blue Point Convalescence! Before you worry, I promise you I'm not seriously hurt. The doctor who treated me said I should make a full recovery.

I'll make every effort to continue to write to you and hopefully even meet you during my stay here.

Your soldier

Taking in a deep breath and letting it out, I look over the letter. My heart flutters wildly in my chest at the thought of being close to her. May the Gods hold I hold dear help me. I think I'm in love!

Larkspur

HURRYING DOWN THE HALLWAY FOR A FEW MOMENTS OF QUIET, I open up the door to my quarters and step inside. Immediately I'm greeted by the sight of my little rag doll Tabetha, or Tabby for short, lying on my pillow. She is one of the very few things I brought with me to the hospital. Though I'm far too old for dolls, I could never part with her as Ma had made her out of one of my old dresses that I had outgrown. Tabetha looks up at me with her blue bead eyes and the faded embroidered smile on her face. Her yellow yarn hair is tied back into two braids, just like the ones I used to have to keep mine in. The hem of her dress is decorated with little pentacles that are starting to fade and come apart. I need to repair them sometime soon. She was my favorite Yule present I had received that year when I was still a little girl.

"You know, Tabby, sometimes it doesn't feel like the war is over," I say, lowering myself onto the bed. Taking her into my hands, I smile down at the little doll. She has been with me through the best of times and has helped me through the worst. "What do you think happened to my dear witchy soldier? With the war being over, I imagine he'll be sent home soon wherever that is."

I set Tabetha in my lap. She stands out so much in her finery against my drab uniform. The person who designed our clothing wanted us to look as frumpy as possible. If we looked nice or wore flattering clothing, they feared it would distract our patients from their recovery process. Today is a day where it feels like a lifetime since I've last worn nice clothing. It would be a pleasure to wear a pretty dress again.

I kept the letters I received from my soldier hidden underneath. Each night I prayed to the Gods he would return home safely to us. Too many had been sent back to us in flag-draped coffins.

At the start of the war I imagined our country's brave soldiers in the trenches, fighting to keep us safe. At first it was a romantic idea until it wasn't anymore. I saw the wounded that returned to us and those who came back in a casket. No longer was it the romanticized idea of our men fighting, but a prayer that they would survive this terrible conflict.

Every letter I received from my dear soldier was a relief. It meant that for at least one more day, he was alive. The Gods would shine down upon him for one more day. In my correspondence, I would try to keep it as light and as cheerful as I could. For my December letter I'm already planning out in great detail what I'll write to my soldier. In some way, we're in the same boat as we're both spending our first holiday away from our families. It doesn't escape my notice that I do have some slight advantage as I'll have my Aunt Hope with me while he won't have any family overseas. I hope his friends will help ease the pain of being alone for the holidays. This letter will be extremely important for me to write. To help bolster his spirits, I plan on telling him all about this Yule in such great detail that he'll be able to imagine himself there.

My poor brave soldier.

Hugging Tabby to me with one hand, I stretch out the other out to my pillow. My fingers brush against the envelopes and I pull them out. Flipping through the envelopes, I settle on a random one to read. I always smile to myself when I see his handwriting. Quite often, I feel as if I'm talking to an old friend rather than a stranger who was fighting overseas.

Dear Nurse,

You must promise me you won't laugh too hard at what I'm about to tell you. You simply won't believe what happened to me today! A whole bushel of us mud crunchers (our slang for infantry) were getting transported back to a large base. Well, they parked us on a not so gentle slope and instead of jumping out like we were supposed to, the first fellow fell out! So what do I do? Trying to be the hero, I grab onto him but he was far heavier than I expected. Before I know it, we're both tumbling out of our transportation and are flat on the ground! Neither of us were hurt, but our egos were more than a little damaged from the incident. Now to make matters even worse, our sergeant witnessed the whole thing! He made the two of us do push-ups until everyone else got out of that jeep. They certainly took their time sliding out of there as they feared sharing our fate. After lugging all my gear around all morning and then doing so many push-ups, I was more than a little sore that afternoon. But I will always have enough strength left in my arms to write you a letter.

What's it like being a nurse for fellow witches? Do you have any funny stories to share? Is it true that they make you practice your stitching on oranges? Speaking of oranges, Adelia would be more than happy to savagely impale any of them before her with a needle. She's never cared for them, but I've always loved them and she would give me hers. When I was a young boy, I decided I was going to show off and shoved a whole orange in my mouth. I was successful in getting it ***into*** *my mouth, but getting it back* ***out*** *was an entirely different story. Let's just say it took my father prying my jaws open, some careful maneuvering, and then a large sneeze on my part to get it out of my mouth. I lost three baby teeth in the process. One day, I may be bold enough to tell you* ***all*** *the details. You might even write a book about medical misadventures and mine can be the first essay!*

Your soldier who vows never to shove a whole orange into his mouth ever again!

Even now I'm wondering if my dear soldier exaggerated the story to make me laugh. No matter, it made me smile then and chuckle now.

A low knocking on my dorm door catches my attention. I turn just in time to see my Aunt Hope entering the room. She stops next to me, smoothing down her apron with her hands. "Larkspur dear, I know it's not the best time as your shift is almost over, but we have some new patients and I need you to help me take their information."

"Yes, Aunt Hope," I dutifully answer. Woe to anyone who dared defy a head nurse, especially Hope Madden! Aunt Hope had more than her fair share of determination, and certainly wasn't afraid of putting her foot down when she felt the need.

Shoving the letters back under my pillow, I place Tabby near it. Hopping out of bed, I stand up straight in front of Aunt Hope. They expected me to behave just like any other nurse in front of her. Our relations meant nothing while we were under this hospital roof.

"Where would you like me to start?" I ask, looking at her.

"You'll be on the bottom ward with me. I may need you to help me feed the patients, so don't stray too far. Let's go."

Four

Jackie

Somewhere along the lines between my arrival here and now, I had fallen asleep. I wake up with my arm draped over my eyes and a dull ache in my clavicle. Far better than the stinging pain I had been in. Pulling my arm away from my face, I stare up at the ceiling, blinking rapidly until my eyes can adjust to the light.

Using my good arm, I push myself up into a sitting position. What time is it? I look for the sign of a clock in the room, only to find one above the door. Four o'clock. What time did I arrive? I hadn't bothered to look at any sort of time piece when I was getting changed.

It's still early enough that I'll probably get some sort of dinner. I didn't think to realize how hungry I was until my stomach rumbled. What hospital food tastes like is anybody's guess, as I've been fortunate enough to avoid it. It can't be any worse on the hardtack that we loosened our teeth on each time we tried biting into it. I should have lined my uniform with my rations. It was practically strong enough to stop bullets! Whoever it says that an army marches on its stomach clearly has never sampled the canned food we had.

The door opening catches my attention. I lean over to get a better look at our newest visitor. It's a nurse who looks about my age. It feels like a lifetime since I've last been able to see a girl. I feel like a voyeur for looking her over, and I hate myself for doing it, but I don't stop. She looks just like how I imagine my nurse of the letters to look like. She's a pretty lady with blonde hair that's gently tied back in a bun. There's a few loose strands of hair that frame her face, but that makes her feel even more real to me. She has gentle blue eyes that I rather like.

Another person soon enters after her. Just like the blonde nurse, I watch this motherly figure that follows. Her black hair is fashioned in a style like my mother would've worn. She has large brown eyes that look at us patients kindly. She appears to be a woman that we would retreat to if we needed a mother's love and understanding.

The older nurse stops in front of my bed. Taking some paperwork off the bed frame, she looks it over. "You're a new one, I see. Mr. John Jacob Hall. Well, Mr. Hall, you're a little thin too, but we'll have you fattened up soon enough. You'll need something with saffron for strength. My niece Larkspur is a fine cook and will be able to make something for you. She tells me I am to do the same for her soldier from that pen pal writing program when we get the chance to meet him. The last letter she received from him was that he was wounded but alright. Poor fellow. I hope he heals up quickly."

"Yes, ma'am," I quietly answer, looking down at my hands. My mouth speaks before my brain has the opportunity to catch up as I ramble away. "I hope to be released from your fine establishment before you have the opportunity to fatten me up *too much*. We should leave some of that for my mother."

"We'll see about that, young man. Larkspur dear, would you be kind enough to fill out the paperwork from Mr. Hall?"

"Yes, ma'am," Nurse Larkspur answers.

I look from Nurse Larkspur to her aunt. Is it common here for family members to work at the same hospital? Blue Point isn't a large area, so bodies may be scarce. I want to ask more questions but know it would be rude to do so.

Nurse Larkspur walks around to me, where she stops by my side and her aunt leaves. Offering me a small smile, she asks, "So, Mr. Hall, would you mind if I ask you a few questions?"

"Not at all, but no one ever calls me Mr. Hall or John. My family calls me Jackie."

"That wouldn't be proper in our hospital, Mr. Hall." Squaring her shoulders, she asks me my basic information such as name, birthplace, and my army information. Terribly boring stuff that I had to fill out multiple times before. They never ask you the exciting questions about what type of dinosaur are you the most interested in or if you believe magic is real. When she's done, she places the paper into a folder. "Are you in any pain?"

"I'm comfortable at the moment," I answer truthfully.

"Good. Dinner will be ready shortly. We have a kitchen staff but my aunt and her friends temporarily took the kitchen over and made soup and biscuits for everyone. Be sure to bring your appetite or she'll be rather put out with you."

I smile broadly at the idea of a hearty dinner. This doesn't even feel real. I haven't eaten anything home cooked since I was sent to basic training. I feel like I'm in a dream. For a second blessing, I get to spend a few moments in the presence of my nurse. I can't decide which I like more. Grinning a little, I tell her, "It's been a long time since I've had a good meal. Before I forget, your aunt mentioned a pen pal program. I was in one too, with a nurse from this state."

"I'm not surprised, as the letter writing program was started in New Mexico." She gently rests her hand on my shoulder. I enjoy the feeling of warmth it has to offer. "Now that the war is over and you're back in this country, I hope you get to meet her soon. I'm sure you have a lot of catching up to do."

The letter, you fool! Give her the letter! My mind suddenly screams at me.

This was going to be a bit more difficult, as how was I going to give it to her? Was I just to hand it to her and say, "read this"? That wouldn't be proper. Would it be better to hide it and let her find it herself? I could magically send the letter to her but I don't even know where she lives! I'm running out of options and precious time. I need to decide and fast!

Somehow fortune smiles upon me as she's distracted for a moment by a patient asking, "When do we eat?"

Turning from me, Nurse Larkspur answers, "Dinner is served at six. I'll be right with you, Mr. Claflin."

The diversion gives me a few precious seconds to slip the letter into her apron pocket. I don't think I've ever slipped someone a note so quickly in my life and I've always been good at slight of hand. Once the deed is done, I fold my hands in my lap trying to look as innocent as I possibly can.

"That's all I'm going to be thinking about now," I confess to Nurse Larkspur. "Making us wait those two hours will be torture."

She gives me a patient but knowing smile. Slipping past me, she moves to the next patient, some fellow called Claflin. My eyes follow her movement. Who is he? He wasn't in the ambulance with us. After she asks him the same series of questions, it's onto the next man. Out of the corner of my eye, I see Claflin rise from his bed and walk to me. Leaning in close, he hisses in my ear, "I saw what you did there. You put that note in her apron. You think you're so sneaky, don't you? Why did you do it, eh?"

"I don't know what you're talking about," I lie, looking as innocent as possible.

"Mr. Claflin, please stay in your bed for now. You can stand up and stretch your legs after we have an official head count," Nurse Larkspur gently says.

He frowns at me. Turning his attention away from me, he retreats to his bed, which unfortunately, is next to mine. I'll have to be more careful when writing, let alone slipping my dear nurse my letters.

One wouldn't think trying to appear pathetic and uninteresting would be a chore, but it certainly is. I scoot myself around just enough so that I can lie down in bed with one arm thrown behind my head. My body remains in such a position with a dull ache in my shoulder until a person pushing a large food cart enters. In an instant, my pain completely disappears and I'm sitting bolt upright in bed.

Pins and needles prick me all over my body. For the first time in what feels like an eternity, I get proper food! Praise the Gods! We're each dished out a healthy amount of soup and two biscuits each. My plate just barely touches my table when I seize upon it as if my very survival depended on it. Forgetting any sort of table manners, I greedily drink the soup and shove the biscuits into my mouth in such big chunks I may easily choke if I'm not careful. The warmth of the broth, the taste of the herbs. Such decadence! I imagine even the king of England doesn't eat as well as this. Cleaning my plate, I push my table away from me. Having a full stomach certainly feels good.

Rolling over onto my side, I close my eyes and slowly drift off into a semi-peaceful slumber with the thoughts of Nurse Larkspur on my mind.

Five

Larkspur

Having taken all of our new patient's information, I make my way to the common area. Earlier in the day, I had heard the orderlies have a chat about setting up and decorating a Yule tree. Stopping by the door, I take a peek inside to be greeted by the sight of shiny baubles that cover the tree so heavily I'm forced to wonder if there even *is* a tree under all those decorations? Beaded trim in shades of gold, red, and green have been pulled tightly around the tree from top to bottom. Ornaments hang from every available branch. Some are in the shape of spheres, a few boats, and some mercury glass. If I didn't know the tree had been carefully placed there, I would fear it would fall over and land on some unfortunate. Still, I have to admire their determination to get everything on that tree. Such a fancy tree may very well do our patients some good. They deserve happiness and something cheerful to write about to their loved ones who may be too far to visit.

My mind travels to thoughts of Mr. Hall and his mentioning of the pen pal program. I wonder who his nurse is? Do we know one another or are he and my soldier friends? I hope he can meet her soon. That would be a lovely Yule gift for the both of them.

Taking a step back, I stick my hand into my apron pocket to notice something that wasn't there before. My hand reaches in to pull out a folded up piece of paper. How did that get in there? Opening up the sheet of paper, I read it over.

My Dear Nurse,

Please forgive my writing, but I can't contain my feelings. Can you believe fortune may have smiled on me as I'm in this hospital with you? I could hardly believe it myself until I saw you there! Never in my life would I have thought I'd be grateful for a war injury. I'll heal up in no time under your tender and loving care.

I wish to talk to you and reveal my name. I'll try to find more ways to write to you until we can talk.

Always,

Your soldier

For a split second, I don't *want* to believe it's a letter from him. My heart flutters at the very idea. The man, my dear soldier, whom I've grown to care for is here, but where? The last place I visited was the bottom ward for the patients with the broken bones and other minor treatable injuries. Is he in that room or was the note slipped into my pocket earlier and I just hadn't noticed until now? The bottom ward is where I spent the most time, so it seems most likely it came from someone in there. The temptation to find Edith, the most gossipy girl I know, and ask for her help to figure out who wrote this rises within me. Alas, she's busy somewhere so my questioning her will have to wait.

Drat.

Folding up the letter and tapping it against my fingertips, I mull over my options on learning his identity if no one has any information on him. I wonder if I can tempt him into confessing by telling someone that I found their letter? Pushing the letter back into my pocket, I start walking again in search of Aunt Hope. She's superb at coming up with clever ideas to get the truth out of someone. With a warm face and a trusting personality, she could even get the most hardened criminal to admit to his deeds. She would say if her charm failed she could always use a truth spell on them.

Going from room to room, I find my aunt and Edith in the dining area that us nurses had claimed as our own. Edith, for some reason, was never very social with us newer nurses but preferred to talk to the more established ones. That is, unless it came to the local gossip around Blue Point. In that case, she'd talk to anyone. What little information I had of Edith was her grandparents were Greek immigrants and they settled in New Jersey. Why she came all the way out here is anybody's guess.

Edith looks up from her mug and at me. "What brings you down here? I thought you were busy with all that new patient paperwork."

I shake my head. "I just finished and came to speak to my Aunt Hope. I can come back later if this is bad timing..."

Pushing her chair back, Edith climbs out of her seat. Grunting lightly, she says, "No, it's getting late and I have an early day tomorrow morning. Goodnight."

"You've got something on your mind. What is it?" Aunt Hope asks me after Edith has left the room.

Rummaging through my pocket, I produce the letter and hand it to her. "The soldier I had been writing to put this letter into my pocket. It must've happened on the bottom ward when I was taking new patient's names. I recognize his writing so I know it's him but I don't know his name. He didn't sign it."

Looking over the letter, Aunt Hope folds it up and hands it back to me. "Whoever this boy is, he sounds rather smitten with you. Until we know who he is and to be safe, you shouldn't allow yourself to be alone with any patients here. Not everyone has the best of intentions. It's not just your job or a letter of recommendation at stake if you're caught fraternizing with a patient. It's also your reputation not only here but among our community. Let's not forget that some of the older higher ups don't approve of the idea of a young, attractive nurse out on the floor. They worry it'll distract the patients."

Solemnly, I nod, clasping my hands in front of me. "I'll always make sure I have a nurse or one of the orderlies with me at all times when I'm on the floor."

Aunt Hope's head bobs. "I'll be with you tomorrow morning. Soon it'll be time for bed. You have a busy day ahead of you tomorrow."

Kissing Aunt Hope goodnight, I hurry to my bedroom with thoughts of my soldier on my mind. As much as I don't want to admit it, there is a part of me that finds this exciting. It reminds me of the board inside the classroom that some of my classmates would write the names of whom they liked. My name got listed once, but no one had signed their name. There are times I still wonder who that was. Wouldn't it be a laugh if my soldier was the one who wrote my name on the board all those years ago.

Opening the door to my bedroom and stepping inside, I remind myself to pay close attention to the patients tomorrow and see how they react to my presence. Odds are very strong that my soldier will pay closer attention to me to see if I read his note.

Plopping down on my bed, I take Tabby into my hands. "Who do *you* think it is that gave me that letter? I can't say I'm in love with him as a person, as I don't know who he is. I hope he's as sweet in person as he is in his letters." Setting Tabby to the side, I change into my nightgown and climb into bed. Tabby rests on the small nightstand by my bed as I shut my eyes with thoughts of my dear soldier in my mind.

Six

Jackie

I COULD HAVE SWORN THE HALLWAY LEADING TO THE COMMON area was this way. I slowly turn around studying the pristine white walls and old looking doors that line the area with no exit to be seen. So just where *am* I?

You're in a hallway, you dolt, my mind tells me.

Forcing my mind back, I retrace my steps. We are allowed some time to leave our ward and go into other patient friendly parts of the hospital. Some wanted to go outside while I wanted to explore the common area. I wanted to see what they had done with it, as I had overheard a rumor of a Yule tree being set up there. I took another left somewhere along the lines and ended up here. Perhaps I should've taken a right back there, but what if there were other twists and turns there? Somehow I feel like Theseus in the labyrinth but, unlike the mythological hero, I lacked a length of string to help me find my way back.

Someone will find you eventually. Now if they'll find you alive or just your skeletal remains to be seen. Jackie Hall, you're not some Gothic writer, and that was dramatic even for you, I think.

That someone comes in the most unexpected but a much desired form. A nearby door opens and Nurse Larkspur steps out. We make brief eye contact and she looks just as surprised to see me as I am pleased to see her.

"I'm sorry, Mr. Hall, but patients aren't allowed back here. This area is only for the medical staff," she says, clasping her hands in front of her.

I feel the heat rise in my cheeks. "Forgive me, Nurse Larkspur, but I got lost. I was looking for the entrance to the common area and I must've taken a wrong turn somewhere. I'm sorry if I'm overstepping my bounds by using you first name but I don't know your surname."

She smiles patiently at me, which makes my heart flutter lightly. "No, it's alright. My name is Larkspur Point, Mr. Hall. I would dare say you took a wrong turn somewhere. You're in the entirely wrong end for the common area. If you started on the bottom ward, I'll walk you back and over to it."

Nodding, I anxiously wait for Nurse Larkspur to show me the way. I intentionally keep my pace a bit slower than usual so we can spend a few more precious seconds together.

"How's your clavicle feeling, Mr. Hall? Do you need our doctor to perform a healing to help it along?" Nurse Larkspur asks to make conversation.

"Better, thank you, but again, I must insist that call me Jackie. Everyone else does. My sister is the one who came up with the name for me as she couldn't pronounce John Jacob and my father would call me 'Jack'. It really struck when I was in the Army, as we had three men, myself included, all named John. There was me, John Alexander Bell, and John Daniel Hall. What are the odds of there being *another* John Hall in the army? But then, it's not a terribly uncommon name, either." I find my cheeks reddening as I realize that I've been rambling. Poor Nurse Larkspur, I'm probably boring her with all my talk. I glance up at her to see that she's been listening to me the whole time.

"Take a right here," Nurse Larkspur instructs me. "I can't say I've met any Larkspurs here, but there were some other women with flower names. For a while, out west, it was common for parents to name their daughters after flowers. It's very similar to how gemstone names are becoming popular for girls now." She laughs a little. "I'm sorry. I was just thinking of something. When I was a little girl, my parents gave me a doll that I named Tabetha. I think it's funny. I didn't give her a flower name. Forgive me, I sometimes talk too much and can reveal too many details."

"I don't mind. When I was a boy, my mother gave me a toy lion for my birthday. I immediately came up with a backstory for my stuffed animal. I said that my lion was a boy and his name was King Victor. I named him after the Queen, but I insisted that he have a *boy's* name and I didn't want to call him Albert."

Nurse Larkspur giggles lightly, giving me hope. Smiling at me, she says. "In some way, with your silly stories, you remind me of that soldier that I've been exchanging letters with. In a good way, of course."

Her small admission makes my heart flutter in excitement. If she's referring to her dear soldier, then there's a chance that she may like me too. Grinning, a little to myself, I ask, "Might I enquire to the identity of this person?"

Nurse Larkspur's cheeks turn a pretty shade of pink. "I'm afraid I can't say as he hasn't revealed his name, but I think of him fondly." She stretches out her arm to point to the door. "That'll lead you to the common area, but you'll have to be back inside for a head count by lunch. We'll have someone come and collect all of you shortly before it's time."

Giving a quick promise to be inside by then, I watch Nurse Larkspur turn and leave. My mind floods, threatening to overflow even with thoughts and ideas. It *couldn't* have been a mistake. I ended up in the medical wing rather than my planned destination. Everything happens for a reason, right?

Is it too early to tell her I'm her dear soldier? If I don't, would another opportunist may try to steal my credit if she were to tell anyone else? What man wouldn't want a pretty lady like her to be his sweetheart? There may only be one chance of confessing everything to her.

If you want to get the tiger, you have to go into the cave, I tell myself.

Hurrying to a nurse's station, I pilfer a piece of paper and a pen. Once again, I scribble out the first words I can think of.

My Dear nurse,

I have enjoyed the brief moments we have spent together chatting.

I must tell you I'm from the bottom ward. It's my wish that we can continue our talks and spending our time together. I'm going to do my best to continue to find ways to reach out to you.

Your always loving soldier

For once I don't bother re-reading my letter as I'm too busy folding it up. How do I get the letter to her? I most likely won't get the opportunity to hide it in her pocket again. For a moment I think of reciting a spell to send it to the room she came out of, but I don't know if that's her quarters. One of those pesky rules my magic obeyed was I could only send something somewhere if I knew where it was supposed to go. I certainly wouldn't want to give the wrong idea to the wrong person. The only option available to me may look as pathetic as possible and hope that they take pity on me. If I can find a sympathetic medical staff member, I can ask them to give it to her. Of course, that runs its own risks of my looking like a deviant if someone were to get the wrong idea. However, it's a risk I may very well have to take.

Looking around the room, I spot a young nurse placing some files on a table. Hurrying over to her I speak, "I'm sorry for troubling you, ma'am, but I need to get a letter to someone."

She looks me over. "It's Nurse Edith Burton, and I'm not some mail delivery service for the hospital. If you want a letter sent, you'll have to do it like everybody else."

"It's not like that! It's for Nurse Larkspur Point. It's from someone that she knows and is important to her. I was entrusted to get it to her, but I don't know where she is. I'll gladly pay you for your deed once it's done."

My heart is in my throat, waiting for her answer. In a flash, her hand stretches out and snatches the letter from my hand. "I expect payment as soon as I slip this under her door."

"And you'll have it."

She waves the letter in my face. "But if I find out you're lying to me..."

My hands raise up in a gesture of surrender. "I promise you I'm not. Thank you for your help. If you'll meet me in the bottom ward when you're done delivering the letter, I'll have your money for you. You'll find me under John Jacob Hall." My plans for spending some time outside have quickly changed. Now I need to stay inside the bottom ward until this nurse returns. Turning, I stroll on back to my bed where I pull out a few coins to give to the nurse.

This quiet time also gives me an opportunity to think. Maybe I should make something for Nurse Larkspur for Yule? If she isn't interested in me, I can save it for Adelia to pass onto her children when she has them. This leaves me with the question of what do I make? Nurse Larkspur had mentioned her little doll. Maybe her doll would like a friend? I could probably scrape together some fabric to make one. My sewing skills aren't exactly up to par, but it's the thought that counts, right?

I remain seated, playing with the coins in my hands while my mind mulls over potential ideas. Occasionally, I glance up towards the door to see it empty. Could the nurse have gotten distracted with something or someone? The sound of footsteps captures my attention. Looking up, I see Nurse Edith approach me with her hand outstretched like that of a beggar. I place the coins into her open palm. Her fingers tighten around the coins so quickly it's as if she's afraid I'll change my mind and snatch them away from her. Frowning at me she tells me, "Next time you should deliver the letter to her yourself at room number three."

Seven

Larkspur

RETURNING TO MY BEDROOM, I OPEN THE DOOR TO FIND AN unexpected letter that's somewhat crumpled up on the floor. It looks like someone had roughly shoved it through that narrow slot between the door and floor. Bending over, I pick up the sheet of paper to examine it. Who could it be from? Turning the paper over in my hand, I feel my heart skip a beat.

The letter is from my soldier! I would recognize his writing anywhere.

I must tell you I'm from the bottom ward...

Deep down I know it's still infatuation that I'm feeling for my dear soldier, but what if it could be more? If he's as charming in life as he is in his letters, I feel I could be happy. His sensitive writing reveals such a loving soul. Maybe there's still a chance that I can find him before the day is over.

"I see you got his letter," Edith says from the doorway, making me jump.

"Yes, yes, I did. How did you know about it?" I ask, and suddenly feel foolish. How could she not know when I'm holding it in my hands?

Edith smirks. "There was some loon in the bottom ward who had me give it to you."

This certainly piques my curiosity! I'm unable to resist the temptation and ask, "Do you remember what he looked like? Anything distinguishing about him?"

To my annoyance, Edith shakes her head. "There's nothing remarkable about him. I will tell you I think that if this writer fellow has any courage in him, he'll tell you his identity to your face. This letter writing nonsense is pure foolishness. We aren't children passing notes to one another in class anymore." She pauses long enough to change the subject. "Doctor Smith wants the patients to have some time outside today. It's supposed to get cold enough to snow this evening. Let's get to it and get them outside so they can get some fresh air. I'll start with the bottom ward while you work on the spinal one."

I don't say it out loud, but of course Edith would want the easier ward. Forcing a smile on my face, I cheerfully say, "I'll see you outside."

❧

SOMETIMES I FEEL MORE LIKE A PACK MULE THAN A NURSE. NOW is one of those times. Bracing my feet against the uneven dirt, I push hard on Clements' wheelchair. The poor man had lost the use of his legs when a bullet severed his spinal cord. I know it embarrassed him that I, am woman half his size, was struggling to push him to a pleasant area out of the sun.

"Right here is fine. I don't mind, really," Clements meekly says.

"No, a fellow patient not paying attention to where they're going may very well run you over. They can get a little rough when playing their sports. Besides, we're not going too far." I argue. Taking in a deep breath and holding it, I briefly close my eyes to prepare myself to push this bear of a man again.

Did Clements just get easier to move? The sudden and unexpected movement causes me to stumble. I may have very well fallen against the wheelchair had someone's powerful arm not wrapped around me. I'm pressed hard against a warm body.

The actions surprise even Clements. He tries hard to twist around in his seat to see who this new person is, but is forced to tilt his chin back to get a look at us.

My rescuers grip on me loosens, allowing me to stand up straight. I'm surprised to see Mr. Hall is the one who has been helping us.

"I thought you could use a little help." Mr. Hall glances down in my direction seconds before his cheeks flush bright red. Helping stand me upright, he rambles, "I'm sorry if I hurt you. I was only trying to keep you from falling over."

"I'm alright, thank you," I say, getting a better look at him. He's rather adorable in an innocent way with his shy but warm smile and innocent baby face. His dark hair needs to be brushed as it falls over his forehead. His light blue eyes are studying me. I open my mouth to ask him how his clavicle is healing, but I'm interrupted.

"Larkspur! Could you come inside, please?" Aunt Hope calls out for me from the doorway.

"Coming!" I call back. Turning to the two of them I say, "Excuse me. I'll return when I can." I practically run back to the building. It won't be long before it gets too chilly for the patients, or us to be out in the elements. I hop up onto the steps and hug myself. "It's going to be getting cold soon."

"It is, and maybe it'll even snow for Yule. I need you to help change the bedding in the bottom ward while they're all outside." She grabs my arm and whispers, "You must be careful. That young fellow was standing too close to you. You don't want him to try to put a spell on you."

Nodding, I hurry past her to take the clean sheets out of the closets. I don't know how much time I'll have before the patients' exercise time is over, so I have to be quick about it. The last thing I need is Aunt Hope to catch me alone out there with them.

Grabbing the oversized laundry basket, I pull it along behind me to throw the used sheets into to be laundered. I enter the bottom ward to thankfully find it empty. I can use the excuse that I won't have to worry about wasting time chatting with someone or startling a patient. Starting at one end of the room, I work as quickly as I can, pulling off one sheet, throwing it into the basket, and then putting a new one on in its place.

I pause by Mr. Hall's bed and I can't help but smirk to myself. I believe he's one of the few patients we have who actively tries to make his bed look as neat as possible each morning. There's hardly a crease to be seen in the blanket and even the pillows themselves look like they were carefully placed there. There is a part of me that feels guilty over the fact I'm going to have to undo all his work. Stepping to the side, I feel something crunch beneath my feet. Pulling my foot back, I look down to see a set of carefully bundled letters. Bending down, I pick them up and turn them over in my hands. My knees grow weak when I look over the writing on the front of the envelopes. That's my writing! But who do these letters belong to? My head swivels between two beds. It's either Mr. Hall or Mr. Claflin who was the recipient of my letters, but which one? I don't even know who to return them to.

"Do you need help with anything?" someone says from the doorway.

Looking up with my heart beating rapidly, I look into a somewhat familiar face. "Thank you, but no. I'm almost done with changing the sheets. If you don't mind coming back in a few minutes, I'll be out of your way. It's Mr. Claflin, isn't it?"

"It is, and you mustn't fret. I don't mind waiting here." He nods towards the letters. "I see you found my letters. Did you enjoy the most recent one I sent to you?"

Eight

Jackie

Instead of escaping to the common area to admire the Yule tree, I decided today I would go outside for some fresh air. Keeping my hands inside my pockets, I slowly walk in a loose circle around the perimeter of our exercise area.

I meander past the others debating how their baseball game will be played and to the apple tree. Sports never held much of an appeal to me. Now, climbing trees, *that* was something I could get behind. As a boy, there wasn't a tree that I couldn't top...or come tumbling out of. Stretching out my hand, I rest my palm against the bark.

I am calm, I am present, I am grounded, I think to myself, imagining roots growing out of my feet and securing me to the earth.

What should I do for Larkspur if she meets me under here? Should I try making a grand gesture of trying to impress her with my skills? Would it be better to wait patiently for her? Choices, choices, and not a single solution in sight.

"Hey, Hall! Have you seen Claflin around anywhere? We want him to be the pitcher!" Grengo yells out to me.

I can only shrug. "I didn't see him come out with us. He must be still inside somewhere."

"Can you get him, will you? Try the bottom ward first."

Nodding, I walk back inside the hospital. Walking as quickly as I can, I make my way to the bottom ward where I hear Larkspur speak. "I'm terribly sorry, Mr. Claflin, but we will have to discuss this matter later. Perhaps tonight in the common area after dinner is served."

Peering around the door frame, I see Claflin with his back to me. I don't trust him not to say something that could taint Nurse Larkspur's view of me. Stepping out from the doorway, I say, "Claflin, the men want you to be the pitcher in their baseball game."

Turning to me I see a look of annoyance crosses Claflin's face. He frowns at me but says nothing.

"It was nothing serious, only some letters that he wrote. Mr. Claflin now knows better." Nurse Larkspur shoots a quick glance at him. "Now if you two will kindly wait outside until I'm done with my task of putting clean linens on the beds."

I coldly eye Claflin. "Yes, let's go outside. It would be rude for you to keep the men waiting." I walk side by side with him until I'm certain we're out of earshot. Grabbing his arm, I give it a quick squeeze. "I know you're up to something."

Claflin rolls his eyes. "I don't know what you're talking about." He shoots me a chilly glance. Sneering, he tells me. "I know you're sweet on Nurse Point. I've seen the way you look at her, but you're nothing and she can do so much better. She probably doesn't know that you exist outside of the hospital. You're just another name to be discharged and forgotten about. I'll bet you haven't got any magical abilities."

"And I suppose some uncouth brute such as yourself is any better? Don't you think it's time to go back to that dank cave water that you regretfully spawned from?"

In the blink of an eye, Claflin seizes me by the front of my pajamas. His other hand is clenched in a tight fist and I'm pressed against the wall by an unseen force. My hands and ankles are pinned rendering me helpless. I've never encountered such power before. It doesn't help me that he's taking aim at my face. My heart beats fast in fear that he'll actually punch me. The rest of me is gearing up for a pummeling.

Trying to sound tough I hiss "Let go of me! Try that stunt again and I'll make sure you regret it."

"What's going on here?" Larkspur asks.

Her sudden appearance makes both Claflin and I jump. We look to see her walking towards us with Nurse Edith trailing behind. Nurse Edith moves in between our bodies. She places one hand on his arm and another on his chest. It's a far too familiar and even intimate gesture that makes me suspicious. Are they up to something?

Claflin is the first to recover. Stepping away from me, I find myself free from his grasp. "Nothing, just a soldier's spat. I look forward to discussing things with you in the common area tonight. Hall, why don't you come with me outside? We have much to talk about."

"I have nothing to say to you. I gave you my message that your presence is requested outside," I grumble.

Nurse Edith frowns at me. "Mr. Hall, you shouldn't be so rude. It's improper of you to be alone with a nurse, and the fresh air will do you some good. Now you two behave yourselves and go outside."

I frown though reluctantly agree. Claflin and I both stare straight ahead, not saying a word to the other. I take a quick glance in his direction to see his jaw is tightly clenched. Mine is too.

Stopping by the door leading to the outdoor area, I say, "I hope whatever team you're on loses." As I have no intention of giving Claflin the last word, I spin on my heel to head off in the bottom ward's direction. The Gods only knows what lies he's been filling Nurse Larkspur's head with. My heart beats fast in my chest. I may have to speed up my plans to tell her the truth and that I'm her soldier.

Nine

Larkspur

"What is it, Mr. Hall?" I ask when I see him again. "Did you forget something?"

"Yes! I think I forgot something in here. Um, this may sound silly, but I don't suppose there are any playing cards around here? I was thinking of playing some card games. My sister knows how to play Zodiac and I thought I'd learn how to play."

Ignoring my question Nurse Larkspur motions for me to come close. In a low voice she says "I saw him use a spell on you. Are you hurt?"

I shake my head. "I'm fine. I've just never encountered magic like that before. He was so strong." In a louder voice in case anyone was hearing I ask, "I'm also looking for some fabric scraps to make a gift for someone. I don't suppose you have any that I may have?"

"I'm afraid I don't have any fabrics, but I'll see if I can find anything for you. As for cards, check the common area. Before I forget, I found my letters between your bed and Mr. Claflin's." Reaching out, I take the papers off Mr. Hall's nightstand and hold them out as if they were an offering. "I know they belong to someone in this ward and I want to return them to the rightful owner. I know he's here somewhere, and I would like to meet him."

Mr. Hall steps around the bed and to me. He takes the letters from my hands and I feel a tingle of excitement when our hands touch. I notice how close our bodies are, yet I don't take a step back. Smiling gently, he says, "I know the man who was receiving them. I'll make sure he keeps them in a safe place." He smiles sweetly at me, causing my heart to beat fast in my chest.

Is it wrong that I want you to be my soldier? I ask myself.

"Thank you," I answer. Thinking quickly, I decide to test the waters to see if Mr. Hall knows more than he's letting on about my letters. "Speaking of the letters you've received, have you had the chance to meet your pen pal yet?"

"Not yet. I'm still working up the courage to tell her. We men can be as bold as brass, but the moment we're in front of a pretty lady we revert to shy schoolboys. I don't suppose you have any advice to give me?"

Reaching up, I gently rest my hand on Mr. Hall's arm. It's an action that makes him smile again. It does me too. "We ladies can become just as timid as you men around the opposite sex. The best thing you can do is to be yourself. Don't act like something you're not because you never know who will like what you hide. Be honest with her about who you are and things will work out. My shift ends early two days from now. We can meet up in the common room at five and you can practice on me to help build your confidence so you can tell her. However, you must promise to tell me how it went when you meet her. I'll see what fabrics I can scrape together for you today."

By the end of the day, I'm able to scrounge together a small pile of fabrics for Mr. Hall. I had gathered them from old clothing items that were too old to be fixed. I wonder what he'll come up with? Is it a gift for someone? He mentioned having a younger sister.

Maybe he's making something for you, I think. A girlish feeling rushes through me. How romantic that would be if he were to craft me a homemade present. Yet, I know I shouldn't get my hopes up. It may not be for me, after all.

No matter whom it's for, it'll be a sweet gesture. He'll also need scissors and thread, too, I tell myself. At least those are easy to get.

Going through our old junk drawer, I find a pair of scissors and some mismatched thread. It's far from perfect, but hopefully it'll work for him.

Carrying the items I make my way back to the bottom ward to find it empty. I carefully set the items on Mr. Hall's bed before leaving the area.

Tomorrow I'll get to see him again. How I wish it were already five in the afternoon and we were in the common area! I want to look into those lovely eyes from him and learn the identity of his nurse. I want that nurse to be me.

"You certainly have a look about you," Edith remarks from behind. In a few bounding steps, she's caught up to me. "Thinking about a certain someone?"

"No one in particular," I lie.

"Well, I'd stay away from that Hall fellow. Mr. Claflin said that he's the one who's been writing you the letters and Hall looks at you funny. He said I shouldn't tell you, but I thought it would be better if I did. I just want you to be careful."

Aunt Hope's promise for me to always have someone with me when alone with a patient rings in my ears. While I can't see Mr. Hall being anything but the perfect gentleman, I know better than to tempt fate. "I'll be careful."

❧

THE COMMON AREA IS FAIRLY BARREN SAVE FOR JACKIE, MYSELF, and Aunt Hope. Fortunately for us, Aunt Hope is an intentionally terrible chaperone and busies herself with her needlepoint. Jackie and I sit across from one another on the floor by the Yule tree. He looks almost bashful in his hospital issued pajamas and me still in my nurse's uniform. He has such a sweet innocence about him that reminds me of my dear soldier. I enjoy thinking of him as Jackie instead of Mr. Hall, which now sounds far too formal.

He has a nurse he needs to confess his feelings to and she may not be you. My mind scolds me. Clapping my hands once in front of me to clear my mind and the air, I say, "Right, how is your project coming along?"

"It's coming along. I'm a little tired from being up so late last night working on it. My sewing skills aren't the best, but I hope she enjoys it. I know you say she will, but I truly hope it."

"I'm sure she will. Now tell me about your nurse. What does she like?"

Jackie jumps lightly at my sudden action. "Well, mostly wrote and talked about things back home. She said the area that she lived in was beautiful and that she wished I could see it. She sent me her photo after I requested it, but I suppose most people did. I sent one back, but I think it might've gotten lost somewhere." He shrugs. "I mostly told her about my misadventures of being a soldier in the Army. The censors were incredibly strict on what we could write." To my surprise, he turns the question around on me. "But what about you? What do you like?"

I like my dear soldier, I think.

"I enjoy helping people," I say. Glancing away from him, I rub the back of my neck. Why am I suddenly so shy around him? I'm normally not one to become so timid around men. I want to say more, but my mind goes completely blank. What do I tell him? Maybe tell him about the holidays and my family's traditions?

Somehow I'm saved from my thoughts by a shout of "Look at that! Can you believe it? It snowed. It actually snowed out in this neck of the woods."

"Snow?" I repeat, as if I didn't hear the word correctly. "It wasn't supposed to snow until Yule, and that's only a week away."

Jackie's face turns from the door to me and then back to the door. Aunt Hope and I can see the gears turning in his head. I don't need to be a mind reader to know he's weighing his options between going outside and joining the antics or staying in here with us. If he goes out he'll need a coat and shoes on so he doesn't freeze.

And there you go, thinking like a nurse again. Then again, you are his nurse; I tell myself.

Jackie turns his face back to me and the Yule tree behind us. I glance over his shoulder to see a young blond fellow with glasses, Mr. Lee, from the limbs injury ward. Mr. Lee creeps so silently towards Jackie that even I can't hear his footfalls. How can a man with a thigh injury be so stealthy? I open my mouth to say something but I'm stopped by Mr. Lee putting his finger to his lips. As quickly as he pleases, he pulls back the collar on Jackie's pajamas and dumps a handful of snow down it. Jackie's blue eyes grow wide and his chest jerks. He lets out a squeal that's so high pitched it could break glass.

"I got you good!" Mr. Lee cackles. He's bent over at the waist, laughing so hard that his face is turning red.

"I'm going to get you for that!" Jackie declares. Forgetting that Aunt Hope or I am in the room with him, he jumps to his feet, chasing after Mr. Lee.

Aunt Hope bursts out into loud laughter at the entire exchange.

"Put on your jackets!" I call out after both of them. Springing to my own feet, I give chase after them. I use Jackie's playful threats of vengeance as a guide. The sound of a door slamming shut signals to me they've both made it outside. There's no way they could've stopped long enough to put their coats on. If they freeze out there, then it'll be a tough lesson learned. I take a nurse's cape from the hanging hooks by the door, wrap it around me, and follow them outside.

Throwing a quick glance over my shoulder, I see Aunt Hope hurrying towards me with a grin on her face. "I'm only here to watch all the excitement. You don't suppose they still put rocks in snow balls, do they?"

Her question causes my eyes to bug out. Someone could get seriously hurt! Taking in a deep breath and holding it, I throw open the door to reveal the chaos outside.

If one didn't know better, they would assume we had a small blizzard outside. Grown men don't bother making snowballs but hurl handfuls of snow at one another. Just about every one of them is laughing.

One throws out his hand and a shield of swirling light appears in front of him.

"Hey, no magic shields allowed!" Mr. Lee announces, seizing a handful of snow.

Another ducks down, covering his head with his arms, as he runs past Aunt Hope and I. It's good to see them so carefree, even if it's just for a little while.

I barely have the time to blink when I get hit by something cold and wet. My entire world goes white. I reach up to pull away at the snowball that struck me right in the eye socket.

"You hit the nurse!" Mr. Lee calls out.

"I would've hit *you* if you hadn't of ducked!" Another person says.

My vision begins to clear, revealing Mr. Lee and another man that I don't recognize. I should feel annoyed but I feel mischievousness. Bending down, I scoop up some snow and pack it. "Did I ever tell the two of you that when I was growing up, I played baseball with the neighborhood boys? Guess who was the best pitcher was." Taking careful aim, I hurl the snowball towards the two men. I'm rusty when it comes to pitching, but the ball hits its target. It's not long before I'm forced to retreat, shrieking, and covering my face. I didn't expect half the patients to gang together and try to playfully pelt me with loosely packed snowballs.

"Mind where you're throwing those things, young men!" Aunt Hope chides them.

"Some help *you* are!" I call out to her.

Someone strong gently takes me by my hand and pulls me away. I open up my eyes to see that it's Jackie who is shielding me from the barrage. "Come with me and I'll rescue you!" He laughs. Turning back to the crowd, he jokes, "You brutes! Shame on all of you for attacking a defenseless lady!" Jackie guides me away from the building and out into the snow. What is he thinking? I don't ask when his foot catches on something causing him to fall over, taking me with him. Jackie lands flat on his back with me falling onto him. He makes his best effort to catch me, which he just manages to do.

"Larkspur!" Aunt Hope cries out.

"Are you alright?" I whisper to Jackie, not yet climbing off of him.

Jackie's head bobs. He tilts his chin up slightly and take a few precious seconds to look into his warm eyes. There's such a kindness in them. Gods help me, I desire I could remain in his gentle embrace and that I could feel his lips pressed against mine. The very idea makes my cheeks flush. I lean into Jackie. Our lips are so close I can feel his warm breath against mine.

Suddenly our moment is broken by someone pulling me off of Jackie. When I'm able to regain my footing, I see that it's Mr. Claflin who ruined our moment. He stands over me with a frown on his face.

"You must be more careful. He could have hurt you," Mr. Claflin coldly says. "At this rate, I'll have to watch over you myself to protect you from... men like him."

"I'd be more worried about *you* hurting our nurse. You seem to be the type of rake who would do such a thing and not think twice about it," Jackie retorts. "You had no qualms about using your magic against me."

Aunt Hope runs to Mr. Claflin's side. She pulls me away from him and dusts the snow off of me. "Larkspur, let's go inside. Now. We'll let the men discuss this."

I don't want to leave Jackie but am pulled inside by my very determined aunt, who is busy clucking over me and checking me for any sign of injury. While I'm not hurt, I could cry. I wanted that kiss from Jackie!

Ten

Jackie

CLAFLIN FROWNS DOWN AT ME. NOT GIVING HIM THE opportunity to continue to glower at me, I climb to my feet and brush the snow off my pajamas. I shiver but say nothing.

Out of the corner of my eye I see Edith come marching towards us, looking like a thundercloud. She plants herself by Claflin's side. Sneering at me she says, "I saw what you did with Larkspur. I suppose you think that was terribly smart of you? Grabbing a nurse and pulling her out into the snow like that? What were you planning on doing with her? Nothing good, I imagine. Men like *you* never have good intentions."

"That is none of your business. Keep out of it." I answer coldly.

Claflin rolls his eyes. Folding his arms across his chest, he asks me, "And you think you could get Miss Larkspur's attention? You don't even have the courage to speak to her and tell her the truth!" He nods towards Edith. "Fortunately, my dear Edith has been kind enough to tell me everything. We both agree that you are a pathetic little man. Hardly a witch at all. I've hardly seen you perform any magic. I don't know why anyone worries about you worming your way into their lives. Look at you; you're so *ordinary*. Were you *really* injured by shrapnel, or did you intentionally hurt yourself to be medically discharged? I suppose *some* alleged medical tragedy is the only way you'd be able to get some girl, even an empty-headed one like Larkspur. At least she's a pretty face."

"You're just some school bully who feels entitled to a girl. Well, you're not. Your delusional sense of self-importance likes to write checks that your character cannot cash. Why do you hate me so much? I did nothing to you."

"You're a sneaky little coward and I don't like fearful men." Scowling, Claflin pushes me. I soon retort the same, shoving him harder. Claflin stumbles back, which gives me a small feeling of satisfaction. It doesn't last long. Claflin charges me, grabbing me around the waist, sending us both pitching backwards. I land first back first into the snow. The cold is already sucking the strength out of me, but I can't let him win. We punch holes in the air and snow more than we do each other's bodies. Somehow he's able to land a blow to my clavicle. The same one that I broke during the war. My eyes grow wide and someone lets out a terrible scream. It takes me a moment to realize that the person who's hollering is me!

"That's enough!" Doctor Smith yells.

Yelling and cursing, Claflin is pulled off of me. Where did my fellow patients come from, and why did they wait so long to end the fight?

The cold numbs my aching bones, but not as much as I would like. My chest heaves with heavy breaths. I prop myself up in the icy snow that leaves my hands and feet numb. My chest heaves as I pull myself up into a standing position.

"What in the God's name is going on here? I'm going to hang each one of you up by your toes!" Doctor Smith shouts.

I look to see him racing towards as if the hounds of hell were chasing after him. Larkspur follows him, looking as if she's running as fast as she can. "I heard shouting. What happened?" She gasps. She holds her skirt up so high that we can all see her knees with each step she takes. It's then something terrible happens. Something that we can't see in the snow trips my beloved nurse sending her face first into the ground. She barely has enough time to stop herself as her face comes inches from colliding with the snow. My legs react before my mind has an opportunity to catch up. As if acting on instinct, I make a move to hurry towards her but I'm stopped by Doctor Smith pressing his hand into my chest.

Larkspur scrambles to her feet. She gives her apron a quick shake to rid herself of any remaining snow. "I'm not hurt. Will someone *now* tell me what happened?"

"Ask him," Edith says, and jerks her head in my direction. "Larkspur, I warned you he was up to no good, but you didn't listen."

Doctor Smith ignores the two of them. "My dear nurses, would you two kindly escort Mr. Claflin inside. I need to take Jackie inside and examine him. I could hear his shrieking all the way from my office."

I can't help but feel my heart sink at the idea of Claflin talking to

Larkspur. What lies is he going to fill her head with? I need to tell her the truth.

Claflin shoots me a freezing glare, stomping past me.

Larkspur waits until he's past her before she turns around and follows him. She turns her head to give me one last look. She mouths "talk later" before climbing up the steps and entering the building.

"Inside with you before you turn into an icicle," Doctor Smith says. He nudges my arm, which makes me move.

My numb feet feel as if they're made from stone. They're so painfully heavy to lift trudging through the snow. I ignore the looks from the other patients. They part away from Doctor Smith, and I like the sea. Eyes look away from me and faces tilt downwards. A few patients murmur amongst themselves, but I can't make out their words. Forcing my attention forward, I walk up the steps to the hospital doors. Opening the door, I'm blasted by the warm air. The sudden heat causes an immediate and unpleasant reaction in my body. My hands and feet feel like they're on fire while there's a pounding pain in my clavicle.

I'm guided to the bottom ward where Doctor Smith pokes and prods my bones with one hand. He keeps the other hand clasping my shoulder. He presses his thumb hard into my clavicle. I hiss in pain through clenched teeth. If he didn't have such a firm grip on me, I would've pulled away.

"You certainly didn't help the healing process," Doctor Smith says. "However, you need to watch your temper. What started all of this?"

I glance away from him, not wanting to admit that Claflin and I were squabbling over Nurse Larkspur. I open my mouth and say, "Just some soldier's argument."

"That's not what I heard it was about," a woman says from the doorway.

I peer over Doctor Smith's shoulder to see Nurse Edith leaning against the doorframe. She nods her head in my direction. "That one is sweet on Larkspur. He even had me deliver a letter to her. If you ask me, he's up to no good. She might not be either."

"I swear my intentions are nothing but noble!" I protest. "I only wished to speak to Nurse Point in private."

Doctor Smith looks me over. "Speak to her about what, young man?"

Eleven

Larkspur

Words want to come out, but none will. I stare at Claflin with disbelieving eyes. The moment I think I have something to say, they instantly disappear. After what feels like days standing in my spot I choke out, "You took a swing at Jackie? How could you? What were you thinking?"

"Larkspur, come with me," Aunt Hope gently says to cut an argument short. She reaches for my arm, but I shrug her off.

Mr. Claflin snorts. "The idiot had it coming. He's the one who started it after all. Why are you so bent on defending him?" He pauses and even squints at me. "Wait, you don't *like* him, do you?"

I look away from him; I don't like the way he's behaving. Jackie has been nothing but kind to me. He reaches out for my shoulder, but I brush his hand away. The words come out before I stop them. "I don't like the way you're behaving. You know what? I don't believe you are my soldier from the letters. You aren't behaving like him."

Mr. Claflin dramatically rolls his eyes. "Your precious little imaginary soldier who wrote to you? Do you truly believe in that? You're in love with an image. This soldier doesn't exist, and he may never have. It's easy to pretend to be anything you want to be in writing. You need to get your head out of the clouds and see what's in front of you. You're so blind you can't even see *me*."

What was spoken in anger shouldn't hurt, but they do. Mr. Claflin is right that anyone can pretend to be anybody in writing, but my dear soldier seemed so genuine and loving. Not at all like how Mr. Claflin is behaving. I snap, "I'd rather be alone with my letters and an image than to be with someone like you! You and Edith seem to be rather chummy, so maybe you two should discuss your mutual dislike of Jackie and I."

Edging her way in, Aunt Hope separates the two of us. She carefully pushes me back. "I think you two have argued enough today. We should all step back until cooler heads can prevail. Larkspur, go report to Doctor Smith that Mr. Claflin is fine. He should be in the bottom ward or in his office by now. Mr. Claflin, please return to your ward."

Keeping my chin up, I turn and leave the room in search of Doctor Smith. My feet stop just outside the common area. I run my hand through my hair. There's no reason Doctor Smith would be in the common area. It's unlikely he'd be in his office, especially after Jackie was hurt.

"That was quite the scene you two made," Aunt Hope tells me.

I jump a little, surprised that she's so close to me. She must've been following me this entire time, and I hadn't of noticed. I run a hand through my hair. "I know I shouldn't have flown off the handle like that, but Mr. Claflin made me so angry with what he said. It's not becoming of a nurse or your niece, and I'll make more of an effort to do better next time. I should make sure Jackie is alright."

"He's most likely fine, but I agree that speaking to him is a good idea."

Nodding quickly, I walk out the door and to the bottom ward in hopes Jackie is there. To what I believe is my good fortune, Mr. Claflin isn't there yet but Jackie is. They don't yet notice me, but poor Jackie is almost cornered by Doctor Smith and Edith. He seems to shrink under their looks. Doctor Smith slaps some papers against Jackie's chest.

"Don't you know fraternization is highly frowned upon in this hospital?" Doctor Smith admonishes Jackie.

"I only wished to speak to Nurse Larkspur," Jackie chokes out.

"Speak to me about what?" I ask, startling them.

Doctor Smith turns to look at me with surprise etched on his face. Edith frowns at me. Jackie's face turns as white as a sheet. Doctor Smith is the first to recover. He marches over to me, papers clenched tightly in his hands. "I don't suppose you recognize these?"

Taking the envelopes into my hands, I turn it over to recognize my own handwriting. "I wrote these..."

"He also paid me to slip that one letter under your door," Edith adds. "Mr. Claflin has also noticed some suspicious behavior from him."

Jackie's eyes frantically dart from Edith to Doctor Smith and then to me.

He sputters, “I was going to tell you under the tree! I was just too afraid to say anything at first.”

Doctor Smith frowns at me. “Nurse Point, you were allowing a patient to fraternize with you and you didn’t report it? That certainly doesn’t look good on your record or place in this hospital. It is inappropriate, as patients and staff are required to be separate. It’s in your nurse’s code.” He looks to Jackie. “I will have further words with you later, young man. In the meantime, I need to speak to Nurse Point about the choices she made.”

My cheeks burn hot under his reprimanding. As much as I hate to admit it, Doctor Smith *is* correct. I should’ve reported the letter as soon as I got it and been moved to a different ward. I only have myself to blame for that, but Jackie shouldn’t be punished for my lack of action.

“As one of the head nurses, I believe it’s my duty to scold my charge,” Aunt Hope says, entering the room. “I’ve heard enough of what’s been happening in our hospital. I agree that they both need to be spoken to, but I should dole punishment out. As it should be between Edith and Mr. Claflin if they have also been fraternizing. Come, Larkspur. We have much to discuss.” Taking me by the hand, Aunt Hope leads me out of the room. We walk down the hall leading me to wonder what she has in mind for me. To my surprise, she brings me back to my quarters and opens the door. I step inside first, with her closing the door behind us.

I go to Tabetha and pick her up in my hands. Fiddling with her, I say, “I, I know what you’re going to say. I shouldn’t be in love with a letter writer.”

To my surprise, Aunt Hope answers differently than expected. “I was your age once and I don’t entirely blame you for not reporting your and Jackie’s actions and talks. I can see where it would flatter you to have a young man interested in you. However, I *am* disappointed in you for not telling me. I could’ve at least helped you in hiding the fraternization! That young man, your soldier, is a shy but sweet sort. You should give him a chance. If you don’t, there will be a day you’ll be sorry that you missed your opportunity.”

“But what do we do? What about Edith and Mr. Claflin?” I ask.

“You stay put and leave that to me.”

Twelve

Jackie

"I'LL BE FILLING OUT THE PAPERWORK TO HAVE YOU transferred to another hospital. Perhaps one closer to your home will be more fitting for you," Doctor Smith tells me before sending Nurse Edith out of the room.

Nurse Edith turns to go, but not before giving me a smug, satisfied smile. I suspect she'll go to Claflin and gossip to him about what had just happened.

Forcing my gaze straight ahead, I straighten my back like I did back when I was a soldier. "With all due respect, Doctor, I'd rather be discharged so I can spend Yule with my family. Don't worry about how I'll get home, I'll find a way. Nurse Point doesn't need to be dragged into this anymore than she already has. You also mustn't punish her. It's all *my* fault. I'm the one behind it all, the letter writing, the fraternization, and the fight I got into with Claflin. It's all on me. Nurse Point was an innocent bystander."

"I see. Either way, you'll be leaving tomorrow morning after you have your breakfast. What will happen to Nurse Point's career will be discussed at great length between the powers that be. But I will see what I can to grant your request to be discharged. Your uniform has been cleaned and will be returned to you soon so you can at least leave looking the part of a proper soldier. I suggest you begin to pack your belongings. It shouldn't take too long to get the answer to your request."

I watch as Doctor Smith leaves the room and me to my thoughts and the growing dread in my stomach. My actions may have cost a person their job and I'm not alright with that. As much as it aches my heart to admit it it may be best that I leave and finish my healing process at home. I can only hope that Nurse Larkspur won't receive a severe punishment and be dismissed.

Moving over to my bed, I sit down on it and run my hand through my hair. A wide range of emotions I didn't even know I had boiled up in me until they overflow. My lower lip trembles. I purse my lips tightly, only to have tears well up in my eyes, threatening to spill down my cheeks.

"Get ahold of yourself!" I hiss to myself.

Get ahold of yourself, I mentally repeat over and over again. I won't do anyone any good if I'm a near hysterical mess. What was it they told us in the service? We are one; we are calm; we are collected; we are brave soldiers. Somehow I didn't feel like one.

"Well, well, young man, you certainly know how to keep things interesting around here," Larkspur's aunt tells me, making me jump slightly.

My eyes snap open to see her walking towards me. As hard as I try to push it back, I can feel the heat rising in my cheeks. I didn't want anyone to see me in such a state. "Nurse Madden," I mumble. "I sincerely wish to apologize for any trouble I may have caused. Doctor Smith says I am to be released from this hospital tomorrow. Please extend my best wishes and apologies to your niece." Reaching into my pocket, I pull out the doll I had been making. Holding it out to Nurse Madden, I continue. "I've been keeping it here for safekeeping until I found the right time to give it to Larkspur. I don't wish to cause any more trouble, but if you'd be kind enough to give this to her, I would be greatly in your debt. I meant to give it to her for Yule, but fate had other plans in mind. It's a little companion for her doll, Tabetha. Even little rag dolls need friends."

I'm cut off from my ramble by Nurse Madden, holding up her hand. "I will not give it to her, young man."

My heart sinks into my gut. The little doll I had made feels like it's heavier than a boulder. If it were possible, my arm would've fallen off under the weight of it. Rather reluctantly, I draw the toy back to my chest.

She smiles at me. "That's because you are. Tomorrow, you are going to meet her in the common area and under the Yule tree, you're going to tell her everything. She deserves to know the man behind the letters."

"Me?" I squawk, my eyes growing wide. "I know I wanted to speak to her in private about it, but what do I say? I haven't even had the chance to prepare the speech I was going to give her!"

"You have all of tonight and tomorrow morning to do so. I'll make sure Doctor Smith and others are distracted, so you're not interrupted. In the meantime, I suggest you get cracking." Giving me a brief but patient smile, Nurse Madden turns on her heel and walks out the door.

This is something I can't write out in a letter and that's not because I'm lacking a pen and paper. I'll have to prepare my speech in my head and memorize it for her. ...Or I'll have to speak off the cuff and from the depths of my heart.

Glancing down at the little doll, I sigh. "And what would you say?"

The little drawn on eyes stare back up at me.

Somehow, I sense this toy I made with love in my heart will help give me the answers.

Thirteen

Larkspur

"You need to speak to Jackie in the common area this morning. He has something important to tell you," Aunt Hope says to me.

"Did he say what about?" I ask, walking alongside her. "What about Mr. Claflin and Edith? What's going to happen to them?"

"I don't know, but Doctor Smith also wishes to discuss their behavior with them. A transfer for Edith may very well be in order. Right now you need to focus on yourself, and you should spend your time focusing on Jackie and yourself."

Aunt Hope guides me into the room, where I see Jackie shifting his weight from one foot to the other. He looks so different in his uniform. He doesn't resemble that shy, awkward young man I first encountered but a dashing soldier.

My heart flutters in my chest. I don't run to him but I quicken my step into the room, only to stop by him. "Jackie! I mean, good morning," I say shyly. "My aunt told me to meet you here under the Yule tree this morning."

"Yes, and I'm in her debt for that. Larkspur, I want to start by apologizing for any trouble I may have gotten you into because of my actions." He raises his arms up only to lower them again. "I spent half the night trying to think of some big speech to give you, but I couldn't think of anything. It all sounded so...wrong. I, I don't know what to say, but your kind letters kept me going through the war. I'd read them repeatedly each night and I'd think of you. I wanted to believe that a special girl was waiting for me and wanting me to return. Larkspur, I fell in love with you through those letters. I love those letters, and I love you." Reaching into my pocket, I pull out the little rag doll. I take Nurse Larkspur's hand into mine and gently press my gift into her palm. "I also made this for you. I wanted to give it to you over Yule, but fate had other things in mind for me. Tabetha might like a little friend.

I gaze down at the little doll. A smile forms on the corners of my mouth. "This has to be one of the sweetest gestures a man has ever done for me. Thank you." Still smiling, I touch his face. He leans into my touch. "Jackie, while I don't know what will happen to my position here, there is something that I do desire. I know my dear soldier from the letters he sent, but now I want to learn about my Jackie Hall in person. And I want two things from you."

"And what's that?"

"I want you to kiss me like you almost did when we were out in the snow. You have given me the most wonderful Yule gift this year." I smile as Jackie slides his arms around me, gently pulling me to him.

"But we don't have any mistletoe to kiss under," Jackie tells me with a teasing grin spreading across his face. "And the second?"

Two can play at this game.

"You need to teach me how to play that Zodiac card game." Taking Jackie by the collar of his uniform and pulling him in close, I whisper against his lips, "Who needs mistletoe?" Leaning in, I press my lips against Jackie's. It's not long before he's returning my kiss.

Jackie smiles at me after our kiss ends. "I want us to spend Yule together and for us to be happy."

"We will," I promise. "We'll be so happy every Yule we share together. I know this year's will be wonderful because I'll have you by my side."

A WESTHAVEN MAGIC SERIES NOVELLA

BY MIKAYLA RAND

Normally a senior at Westhaven College of Magic shouldn't have problem passing Curses 301. My dismal spellwork proves otherwise.

Luckily, the best Curse Breaker at Westhaven College is my childhood BFF. Too bad to him I'm just Cal, the nerdy potions girl who uses him as guinea pig.

I do my best to learn the magic during our nighttime practice sessions but when his next breath depends on me getting the antidote right, I risk losing more than a degree.

Can I channel the magic I need to save him or will I doom the only man I've ever loved?

Disclaimer: This Flash Fiction is suited for adults 18+ only. The work contains sexual situations and adult language. All characters are of legal age.

One

Calla

"I'M NEVER GONNA GET THIS!" I GROANED, FALLING BACK ON THE lawn in the courtyard outside Westhaven College's cafeteria. The afternoon sun shone through the red and orange sugar maple leaves like stained glass in an old church window, a poetic distraction from the turmoil that was my life.

"You'll get this, Calla, all you need is... help," Kenzie said, her tone sly.

I turned my head towards my beautiful new friend, her long hair obscuring her face from view.

"Help, huh? Got some mysterious curse-based knowledge you've been hiding from your friends? Cause I am all ears, kiddo," I teased the Freshman. With a swish of my fingers, I used my magic to flick drops of water at her.

Elemental magic was a part of every Magic User's essence, and each of us had at least one underlying elemental skill that they could control. Mine was the ability to manipulate water in any form.

She shrieked, holding out a pale arm, her gray eyes alight with laughter, the port wine stain around her right eye visible for a few seconds. "*Kiddo*? Please, oh ancient one, just because you are a Senior doesn't mean––"

"I am a Senior and that means I am entitled to every leg up I can get, so I can graduate on time! That includes torturing underclassmen for their secrets!" I rolled over, my fingers curved into mock claws. Kenzie's elemental magic hit me in the chest, her gust of wind so strong I barrel rolled in the opposite direction. Her rare giggles of pleasure rang out, filling the courtyard, and I felt an answering grin splitting my face.

I loved making people happy and, based on what little I knew about Kenzie, she needed a lot more laughter in her life.

I stopped rolling, covered in leaves, and suppressed a shiver. I sat up and surveyed the damage; my clothes were now damp from my tumble across the lawn. With a concentrating frown, I drew the excess water from my clothes and directed it back into the ground, away from me.

"That was impressive Kenzie! You're really getting the hang of things," I complimented her.

"And you are practiced at ignoring the truth. You need help and you *need* to ask your brooding bestie," she teased.

She was right of course. Maddock was a gifted Mage of the Dark Arts and most likely my savior. Unfortunately, he was also my Kryptonite.

I'd met Maddock when he had moved to our small Magic User community of Locksley, outside Asheville. I remembered his first day of school. He was tall for a nine-year-old, his hair golden with wavy locks haloing his head. In the standard school-issued navy polo and khakis, he'd looked like the boy next door, friendly and approachable, until the class had swarmed him at recess.

Maddock's green eyes had stared down at us imperiously. His arms crossed, he had declared he would hex anyone who dared to touch him. Tendrils of grass had twisted up from the ground and wrapped around our ankles in warning, the blades easily broken when my spooked peers turned and ran, falling over one another in their haste to get away. I stood there and giggled, the grass tickling my skin. He'd turned his scowl on me next but he couldn't fool me, I'd seen his lips twitch.

I think that's when I decided it would be my mission to make Maddock Cane smile. The universe seemed to be on my side too, we continued to be placed in the same classes, lived on the same block, we studied together, and ended up being accepted into the same college. We even shared the same magical focus: Body Magic.

I felt a prickle of awareness along my spine, the sensation drawing me out of my memories. Kenzie was trying, and failing, not to look too gleeful after her announcement which could only mean––

"What exactly do you need help with, Cal?" Maddock queried, his resonant voice doing things to my system that shouldn't be legal.

I leaned back, the crown of my head resting on his shins. Dressed in black slacks, a crisp white button-down shirt, and black tie, Maddock observed me as imperiously as he did in our youth.

Shooting him a sunny smile, I gave in. If I didn't tell him, he had ways of finding out and they were *not* fun or delicious as I wished.

"I'm failing Curses 301..." I confessed.

Maddock growled low in his throat.

My lady bits perked up.

Kenzie squeaked.

"That's a Junior course, Cal." Disappointment laced his voice.

"I know." I beamed, knowing full well the sunnier I was, the more it would piss him off. An incensed Maddock was a sight to behold.

Too bad he 'beholds' me as one of the guys.

I internally sighed, knowing that his repeated use of the boyish nickname my older brothers had given me planted me firmly in the friendzone.

Maddock stepped back and I sat up.

"Meet me in practice room six at nine tonight, I already have it reserved," he exhaled, before walking away without warning.

"Sure thing, Mad, thank youuuuu," I brightly called, his answering grunt all the acknowledgment I needed.

"Name one of y'all's babies after me," Kenzie deadpanned.

"Shut up." I groaned, flipping her off.

Two

Calla

Westhaven College was a massive campus in the Appalachian Mountains, built slightly out of phase with the rest of the world to keep out the rest of the non-magical folks, including the population of critters indigenous to the mountains. You had to portal there, or you'd get lost in the forest.

The main mansion had four wings and was surrounded by five student dorms and various cabins for families of staff.

Body Magic, Mind Magic and Soul Magic occupied the North, East and West wings respectively, the South wing being reserved to the administrative side of the school as well as the cafeteria and staff lodgings.

Leaving Kenzie at the Freshman dorms following dinner, I dashed to my room in the Senior dorms, across campus. Maddock may think of me as 'Cal' but I didn't want to smell like one of the guys. A quick shower and a wardrobe change later, I slipped my three-inch yellow tourmaline wand in the pocket of my cropped cardigan and put on a magic-amplifying silver ring with a small citrine stone on my thumb. I grabbed my black boiled-wool witch's hat—a gift from Maddox I loved to wear. A quick twirl and a swipe of clear gloss later, I dashed out of my room into the common room I shared with Aubry.

Their head snapped up from their Kindle when I entered, the colorful crystals strung on gold wire jingling in between and around their elegant black antlers. Their dappled brown fur was mostly hidden by the comfortable gray sweats they lounged in. Aubry was a lesser demon from the city of Dis, in the realm of Hell, and someone I knew better than anyone other than Maddock.

They let out a low whistle, their large amber colored eyes sweeping my form. "Dang, chick! Look at you! You are wearing those jeans! Tell me this outfit isn't being wasted on a study group!"

I laughed at my otherworldly friend. "I am going to go study..."

Aubry groaned.

I snickered. "If it makes you happier, I'm meeting Mad at a practice room to study for my Curses midterm."

Letting out a squeal, they abandoned their Kindle and leapt up, running at me faster than humanly possible. I braced for impact, Aubry may have lived on this plane for the last three years but they often forgot how strong they were. I was enveloped in a gripping bear hug that left me wheezing. I weakly patted their back, once again struck with the thought that demons were cuddlier than history mentioned.

"Oh shoot, sorry!" With a sudden release, Aubry set me down.

I teetered back on my heels, giving myself a moment to breathe deeply. "Nah it's okay, hopefully tonight will be a positive step toward us becoming an 'us'."

Aubry grinned hopefully at me and, with a forceful smack to my bicep, they said, "I have faith in those jeans, Maddock will be unable to keep his eyes off of you."

❧

"CAL, YOU'RE NOT CONCENTRATING." MADDOCK'S infuriatingly even yet disappointed voice reached me from his spot leaning against the far cobblestone wall.

Frankly, I didn't know how he could stand it, we were in the basement of the North Wing and it was frigid. Dressed in a dark blue Henley and black jeans with black boots, he couldn't possibly be any warmer than I was, yet he was attached to that wall like it was heated.

Not that there was anywhere else to rest, since someone had taken the chair that matched the desk. He probably was in the most relaxing place in the room... far away from me.

I sighed, putting my arms down at my side, my yellow tourmaline wand warm in my right hand. "Listen Mad, I am trying––"

He made a noise of disbelief in the back of his throat.

"I. am. I concentrated on the damn apple," I gestured to the apple he had brought, resting innocuously on the desk two feet in front of me. "I used my intent to poison the skin, and then said '*venenum ab intus,*' like the damn book says--"

Maddock crossed the room picking up the juicy red apple, peering at the skin. It did have a slightly deeper read gloss that before I cast the spell, I was sure of it...

"If you would just--"

Maddock took a bite out of the apple; my stomach dropped to my knees.

"What the *fuck*, Mad!" I grabbed the arm holding the apple trying to pull it away from his lips. "That's fucking enchanted, you dumbass!"

He chewed thoughtfully. "It is, though not enough to please Mage Makutu."

Panicking more than was necessary, I ran over to the cabinets on the nearby wall, pulling out the standard tabletop caldron. I grabbed a box labeled 'bezoar stones', a loose ginger root, powdered peppermint, and a satchel of milk thistle. Drawing water from the air, I directed it into the pot and tapped it with my wand. A cheerful flame erupted beneath the vessel, and I hastily mixed an antidote.

All the while I frantically concocted a cure, Maddock strolled leisurely, finally joining me at the counter. I glanced over, noting his suntanned skin was wan, and sweat had broken out across his brow. My pounding heart rate kept time with my boiling elixir, my intent laser focused while I ran my wand along the rim of the caldron. A golden shine all but blinded me from its intensity and the potion turned from a dull yellow to a vibrant chartreuse. I grabbed a cup and directed a portion inside, not bothering with a ladle. I reached up, grabbing the side of his face and forcing the cup to his lips.

"Drink."

Three

Maddock

CALLA LOOKED LIKE SHE WANTED TO EVISCERATE ME; THE internal fire she lacked when she cast the curse showed up with a vengeance when she mixed her counter curse. She was the only Mage I knew who could imbue potions without vocalizing the focusing words necessary to lock in her intent. She could speed up the cooking time, faster than any of the literature hinted was possible. I'd never seen one of her potions fail, once she perfected the recipe, and her tinctures once applied left me feeling... loved.

She force-fed me her antidote and my resolve to stay distant crumbled a bit more when I felt her hand on my neck.

She was brilliant, beautiful, and so damn bright... I was certain any entanglement with me would snuff out her light. Calla needed people, thrived on the chatter and the interactions. I was logical, restrictive, unable to articulate my emotions well. The darker magical arts were where I excelled and somewhere I could be left in peace.

But I wasn't sure I wanted peace anymore.

I craved her.

I finished the potion, her alchemy rushing through my system, swiftly curing me of my self-inflicted ills, and warmth settled in my chest.

"What the *fuck* were you thinking?" she hissed.

"Nothing better than practical experience. The midterm involves casting curses and breaking them." I refrained from leaning into her hand; it still rested on my jawline.

"You can't do risky shit without a failsafe! What if you'd died?" Calla sighed. "I think they are expecting counter curses, not potions, Mad," she added, turning away from me, her hand sliding from my neck as the other put the cup down on the counter.

I caught Calla's hand before it made it to her side and brought it to my chest. "You brewed that potion in under ten minutes. I counted. I am cured. You're allowed to bring reagents to the midterm as long as you can blend and administer your solution before the end of the test."

"Sure, and if the curse isn't poisoning? How am I supposed to make a cursed locket drink?" Calla scowled, her hazel eyes telegraphing her displeasure.

My thumb swiped the back of her hand and she shivered.

I smirked, the obvious answer right in front of her but she was too furious with me to put it together.

"Why must it drink when it can absorb? Metals are porous. If you can make it imbibe, like your tinctures into a person's skin, it's possible."

Calla's eyes went unfocused. I watched her clever mind work the problem. Her dream was to create a line of beauty products that healed and drew out a person's natural beauty. I didn't fully understand what she meant by that, but I had been her test subject for the last decade. She'd mastered potion absorbency, anything she mixed sunk into skin faster than most of the products available for sale.

Knowing what would come next, I drew her over to the desk. I walked to my messenger bag and brought out a blank notebook and the purple ink pen she liked.

I handed her the items, and she came out of herself long enough to take them from me then she began writing out formulas and ingredients, her pen flying across the page. I watched her genius, uncaring of the passage of time. Once or twice, someone came up to the door to use the room for the time they'd signed up for. I stared them down through the small pane of glass in the door until they left.

Around midnight, Calla put the pen down, having filled out pages upon pages of possible recipes to try. Try she would, and if I had anything to say about it, I'd be with her. Already, I thought about how I could rearrange my study schedule to accommodate any testing she might need.

"Oh Mad, I am sorry, what time is it?" She stretched, her midriff on display drawing my focus.

Calla made me feel things I didn't usually encounter with others. I'd seen plenty of midriffs around campus but hers was different. I wanted to caress the softness of her waist and draw her close. The thought made my cock twitch.

I left the countertop behind and joined her at the desk, skimming at the last page of her formulas. "It's after midnight," I said, flipping back a page to scan the contents.

"Oh Goddess, you are usually in bed by now, I'm sorry." She placed a cold hand on my arm, the chill noticeable through my sleeve.

I frowned, taking her hands in mine. "You're cold."

"It is fall, nights are getting colder," she said with a shrug. "I'm sorry I zoned out. You had reserved this room to work on your Curse Breaker certification, right?"

I let go of her hands to retrieve my sodalite wand from the wand pocket in my jeans. "Initially yes, but you needed the space more." I took her hand and pulled the citrine ring off her thumb.

"You're always watching out for me," she sighed, watching me scrutinize her ring.

I tapped the ring with my wand, '*æstus sustinens*'. My enchantment wrapped around the ring with the intent to keep her hands warm. I waited to feel the spell sink into the ring, then I slipped it back on her thumb. "This should help."

She let out a contented noise and the urge to pull her against my body resurfaced.

I turned away to pack up my bag as a distraction.

"Now that we've made this breakthrough, I can surely figure out the rest alon--"

I interrupted her. "No. We should continue in this fashion. I believe it's the most efficient way to prepare you for your midterm."

"But your studies..." Calla put her hat on and swept her hair behind her shoulders.

"I can bring cursed items for us both to practice on," I reasoned. "If I fail, you can rub it in my face when your potions succeed."

Calla snorted. "Uh huh, sure, like that'd happen."

Four

Calla

MADDOCK AND I MET NIGHTLY OVER THE NEXT TWO WEEKS, testing my potions. I brought them to class and, surprisingly, Mage Makutu was impressed with my results. I wasn't foolish enough to think this meant that my midterm was in the bag, but it was a confidence boost.

Things were different with Maddox too. It felt like something had shifted in him, and it gave me hope.

"He's wearing down," Aubry voiced from my four poster bed while I got ready for a Friday night study session.

I stood in front of my mirror in a pink strapless bra and matching pink panty set, shimmying on a black sweater dress over my head. It was off the shoulder, and I hoped it would draw his attention.

"I agree," Kenzie said, cuddled up to my mountain of pillows. "He can barely contain himself. Did you see how he almost put his arm around her at dinner?"

"He was reaching for my cell phone, and I dropped it." I rolled my eyes while I situated the neckline. "Honestly, y'all are reaching."

"No, he's different, Calla. He's..." Kenzie trailed off looking towards the ceiling for help.

"Horny," Aubry supplied, making me drop my hairbrush in shock.

"I don't think--" I began.

"Don't you want him to be though?" Aubry asked, mischief in their eyes.

"No, she wants a relationship. If Calla wanted to get laid, she could, have you seen her ass?" Kenzie reasoned. "She wants––"

"For the speculation to stop. What do y'all think?" I twirled slowly for my friends.

Aubry wolf-whistled and Kenzie did a loud tongue trill.

And yeah if he's not horny, maybe this dress can change that...

My phone rang, Lady Gaga's Bloody Mary chimed from my dresser, knocking me out of my thoughts.

I put the phone to my ear with one hand while fluffing my hair with the other. "Hey Mad, what's up?"

"Someone replaced the reservation list for this evening. We no longer have a room. Practice rooms two, four, and six are in use and I can't even"—he paused—"use the odd number ones."

My lips tugged at the corners in spite of the news; Maddox hated odd numbers and the fact that he considered them for me made my heart melt a little. "Oh, that's okay. Maybe tomorrow night—"

"HE CAN COME HERE," Aubry cried from my bed, Kenzie tackling them trying to cover their mouth, "YOU CAN BOTH STUDY HERE, MADDOCK."

The other side of the phone went deathly quiet.

"I'll be there in ten minutes, depending on the foot traffic," he replied before ending the call.

"What the fuck Aubry?!" I whisper-hissed like Maddock was still on the phone.

"No, it's perfect! In ten minutes, we can do a quick chuck and run, and then you two will be alone!" Aubry pleaded, pushing Kenzie off of them.

"They have a point, Aubry can stay with me tonight," Kenzie flopped down on the bed pushing her hair behind her ears, "Then it's just you and him. Alone."

"Fine, for all the stars in the sky, let's do it," I kicked off my chunky heels scooping up the discarded clothing choices from the blue armchair.

A KNOCK SOUNDED AT MY FRONT DOOR. *OH BOY.*

Taking a deep breath, I opened the door.

"Hey, Mad."

"Your roommate was in the hall with a duffle bag," he stated.

I gestured for him to come inside, "Yeah, some people don't have the constitution for cursing."

Maddock smirked as he entered the living space. "Should we practice in your room? To hide our fearsome task from your roommate?"

I snorted. "Maybe that's a good idea."

We walked to my room; the door still open from my frantic cleaning session. Maddock set his bag down in my armchair, rummaging around for something, his back to me. I let my eyes appreciatively roam his body, his cream button down shirt tight enough to show off his muscular form, his leather belt holding his jeans snugly on his hips, and I admit I was an ass girl and those jeans did him *all* the favors.

I looked away when he turned around, my hand going to my neck, and I cleared my throat. "So what's the plan for this evening?"

Maddock sat on my bed, holding a small brown box. "It's time to move to blind tests. We've done well with testing specific curses and you've known what they are and you have been able to act accordingly." He opened the box and showed me a simple gold chain with a large jade pendant in the shape of a phoenix.

I joined him on the bed, sitting close enough that our thighs touched. "I know you won't tell me what the curse is but can I, I mean, will I..." my stomach dropped at the imagined outcomes.

"You are more than capable of breaking this curse." His tone was so confident that I felt reassured.

"Alright." I leaned into him, our shoulders bumping briefly. "I guess there's no time like the present."

Maddock unbuttoned the first three buttons on his shirt. My eyes unashamedly took in the tawny skin he revealed. He took the necklace out of the box, slipping it over his wavy blond hair down to his neck, tucking the medallion inside his shirt. His eyes locked with mine and, with the most tender smile I've ever received from him, his eyes unfocused, the life behind them dimming. A heavy breath expelled from his body and he fell back into the bed. My heart thumped loudly, the ominous tempo amplified in my mind. The world around me slowed. I rotated, my eyes widened in shock. He didn't move. He wasn't breathing. His pallor was that of death, his eyes unseeing, and suddenly this wasn't a practice.

Maddox was dead.

I lunged at the pendant, the need to be wrong so powerful I forgot to breathe. I ripped open his shirt, the white pearlescent buttons ricocheting around me. I tried in vain to lift the phoenix pendant off his skin.

The phoenix. Revival. The thought scraped across my panicked mind and I leaped to my potions chest in the corner of the room. He couldn't swallow but the pendant could be removed. At its core, the curse was the same problem we'd been tackling for weeks.

I rummaged through the compartments, bottles clinking together. Faster than I'd ever mixed before, I grabbed dried ground lavender, cayenne pepper, and St. John's Wort, throwing them into my personal mini cauldron. Flicking the flame on, I poured in purified rainwater collected during the waning moon, then I stirred the mixture counterclockwise with my wand while sprinkling in Jiaogulan and setting my intent towards removal of evil and the promotion of life. The potion bubbled furiously while I whisked, lighting up my room with an eerie gray light. Finally, on the eighth rotation, the potion glimmered, the concoction turning a deep emerald color.

I collected the mixture with my magic, spreading it out in the air for it to cool. An agonizing minute passed before I formed the tincture into a sphere and brought it over to the bed. Carefully I climbed onto the bed and straddled Maddock's waist. I took a deep breath, willing myself to be focused on banishing evil, removing the medallion, and encouraging life. With this firmly affixed in my mind, I directed the potion onto the jade phoenix, the verdant mixture absorbing into the medallion and his chest.

Five

Calla

THE PHOENIX ABSORBED THE POTION, AS DID HIS SKIN. I WAITED on a breath until there was a clink followed by the medallion breaking into fourths. Maddock took a great gasping breath, blinking slowly until his eyes focused on me.

As I stared into those infuriatingly calm pale green eyes, my emotions overwhelmed me and ran in rivulets down my cheeks. I gave into the strongest underlying feeling, relief, and kissed him. Warm and firm, his lips ghosted along mine tentatively, almost searching, like we knew the directions to where our hearts really beat, but somehow, we had forgotten where that was.

Tingles raced down my spine when his hands skimmed up my back. He pulled me tighter into his frame, deepening our kiss. Our noses brushed and he flipped us around, his body now covering mine. Teeth nipped across uncharted territory, curving down the side of my neck, sending signals of pleasure to my clit. I moaned, my hands sliding into his golden locks, keeping his attention on a particularly sensitive spot. I felt my panties dampen, the need to squeeze my thighs together becoming unbearable.

His hand cupped my breast, his thumb finding my nipple through the dense cloth, rolling the aching bud. My back arched off the bed at the indulgence. Not to be outdone, my fingers left the satin strands of his hair and curved into his chest, my fingernails scraping the skin of his pecs.

Maddock let out a hiss, his hips bucking into mine, his hard length ground into my needy pussy.

"Calla, by the Goddess, you deserve better than me." His voice roughened with more emotion than I'd ever heard from him before. "I wanted you to find someone just as incandescent as you are."

I made a noise of protest deep in my throat and grabbed the back of his neck before pulling him down in a punishing kiss, anger coursing through me. With a nip, I broke away and growled, "You're it for me, Maddock Cane. Next time you think you can make a decision that involves both of us, don't." Thumping his nose, I scolded, "Also, what the fuck? I told you, you can't do shit like that–"

Bracing one arm over my head, Maddock kissed me deeply, his tongue caressing mine, trying to soothe my temper, his hand trailing down to my hip. He pulled away, his forehead resting on mine. "You said I had to have a failsafe. The jade was cursed to mimic death. In a few hours I would have naturally risen from the dead if you couldn't dispel the enchantment."

His hand slipped under my skirt pushing up the fabric. I huffed, his hand sliding over the waistband of my panties, "So what, I would have thought you were dead for *hours* until you just rolled over and said 'Hi'?"

"No," Maddock smirked, his hand sliding inside the lace, my legs eagerly falling open, the hussies. "I knew you were more than capable of breaking the curse, I doubt I was even ensorcelled for more than twenty minutes."

His hand possessively cupped my mound while I considered his words.

I sighed both in pleasure and defeat. He would stubbornly argue that he had followed my directions, and we could get into a rip-roaring argument, but I'd be damned if I was going to let a disagreement keep us from finally being together now.

"This is not over," I admonished, my breath hitching, his fingers traced my slit.

"I never assumed otherwise," he chuckled, his thick fingers swirling at my entrance to collect my wetness and spreading it along my folds. Finding my clit with ease, his finger made deliciously wide circles that made my eyes roll back in my head. His clever fingers drove me wild, the need for him to enter me growing with each pass.

"Please, Maddock," I moaned.

I almost sobbed with relief when one of his thick digits slid into my vagina. He peppered kisses down my chest as his finger moved inside me, curling to rub a spot that had me gushing in response.

"Let me taste you," he rasped.

I nodded my consent but groaned when he stopped.

"I need your words, Calla."

"I want you between my legs showing me how sorry you are for *ever* thinking of depriving me of this. Make me come so hard that I can't remember why I was angry with you to begin with," I commanded, Maddock's eyes going molten at my directive.

"Take off your clothes," he said, before shrugging off his shirt.

I pulled my dress over my head, shucking my underwear while watching him divest my bed of pillows.

"Come back to bed, I want you to sit on my face," he told me matter-of-factly.

I faltered, but he raised a brow in challenge. "I'm trying to follow your directions, will you let me?" He laid down on the bed waiting for me to decide.

Hell. I scrambled onto the bed.

"Straddle my face and grab the headboard."

I did as I was told, my stomach giving a slow flip when I felt the hot air of his breath against my nether lips.

Maddock groaned. His hands stroked the outside of my thighs before he gripped them tightly, bringing me in closer. Like a starving man at a feast, he devoured my pussy, licking and sucking on my swollen bud. I tried to be considerate of his air supply, but I could barely concentrate, gripping the headboard for everything I was worth. His tongue speared my opening, and I lost my head, grinding down on his face. If anything, the lack of oxygen seemed to spur him on and I was lost in the sensations of decadence until I was achingly close.

"Mad, "I need--" I begged, unsure of what exactly I needed to push me over the edge. But he knew. With a light nip on my clit, just enough pleasure pain to shock my system, he brought me over, my orgasm shaking me to the core, my cries of ecstasy decidedly pornographic.

I sagged against the headboard, and he gave my hips a squeeze and I let him up. I shivered at the picture he made, his silky blond hair disheveled, fluorite green eyes heavily lidded with lust, and my juices glistening on his lips and chin. *Fuck.*

He smirked, scooping me up, wiping his face on his ruined shirt before he kissed me gently. His fingertips ghosted down my neck, his kisses leaving my lips and traveling to my ear.

"I'm a stubborn ass but I'll be damned if I go another day without tasting you on my lips one way or another," he whispered against my heated skin. "You're it for me, Calla Storm, and now there is no escape."

I sighed contentedly, happy with my fate, "It's about damn time."

THE END.

About the Author

Mikayla Rand's childhood was filled with stories of magic. When she wasn't jumping purposefully into fairy rings, leaving out tasty treats for unicorns, or trying to find the second star to the right, she was making up fantastic stories for her friends.

Though she resisted growing up for as long as possible she did what southern girls are taught to do and stayed on the path: she finished college, married her sweetheart, worked her full-time job, and had a kid... and quietly went stir crazy.

Now a little older and wiser, like most of her heroines, she sees the merit of straying from the path, and if there is a sexy werewolf in the bushes, well, that's a legitimate excuse to be late to dinner.

Learn more https://mikaylarand.com/

Also By Mikayla Rand: The Vanity of Devils https://books2read.com/TheVanityofDevils

Donkey Business

BY D A NELSON

When Verity Ash meets the handsome new vet, sparks do not fly. He's mad her donkey, Harry, is sitting on his car and she thinks he's rude. But Harry can see the two have potential and goes out of his way to bring them together.

*

Verity Ash switched on the electric kettle and unhooked her mug from the mug tree. She fetched her tea bags from the cupboard and popped one into the mug. Then she stood in front of the kettle willing it to boil. She could have used magic to make it boil faster, but her mother had drummed it into her never to waste her gift. It was only to be used in her witchcraft and for the good of others.

The witch stared at the kettle and wondered if her mother, God Rest Her Soul, would know if she just...

She was about to raise her finger and cast a spell when her cell phone rang. Giving the kettle one last hurry-up-and-boil look, she lifted the phone from the kitchen counter to see who was calling. It was a number she did not recognise. She answered.

'Hello?'

'Is that Miss Ash?' said a deep male voice.

'Yes.'

'Do you have a donkey?' The man sounded tense.

'I have many donkeys,' she replied. Verity ran the Three Oaks Donkey Sanctuary in the outskirts of the tiny village of Rowanberry. Housed in an old farm, the sanctuary not only looked after unwanted and ill-treated donkeys, but dogs, cats, goats, chickens and any other animal that needed a home. She wasn't fussy who or what she took in.

'This is a large grey one with a crooked ear and wearing a red harness with your sanctuary name embossed in it,' the man replied.

'Ah! That would be Harry you're talking about,' she said. 'What's he done now?'

'What's he done?' The man's voice went from tense to furious in a second. 'He's only gone and sat on the hood of my sports car!'

Shit! Verity bit her lip to stop herself from chuckling and composed herself. 'How do you know he sat on your car?'

'I can see him out of the window doing it now!' the man barked. 'Come and remove it!'

Before she could respond, the man told her where he was and demanded that she respond immediately. Then he hung up.

❧

'Well!' she said to no one in particular. 'What a rude man.' She looked down and saw her white terrier cross, Lulu, at her feet.

The address the man had given was the local veterinarian's practise on the other the village. It was only a ten-minute walk and the day was nice, so Verity walked, Lulu at her heels. She arrived at the vet's practise to find an irate looking young man with dark hair standing beside an expensive sports car trying to cajole a stubborn ass off the hood.

'Move you monster!' he demanded as he pulled the animal by the harness, but the donkey was staying put. He waved a carrot under Harry's nose. The stubborn animal took a sniff of it, but didn't bite. He wasn't that stupid. The man looked up when Verity and Lulu approached. He had startling blue eyes. Verity withheld a gasp. He was one of the most handsome men she had ever seen.

'Hi, I'm Verity Ash,' she said suddenly feeling nervous. She held out a hand.

The man snorted but did not take it. 'Get this filthy animal off my car, will you?' he said. 'There had better be no damage. If there is, you're paying for it!'

'And it's nice to meet you too,' she said, failing to keep the sarcasm out of her voice. She turned to her errant beast and, hands on hips, addressed him: 'Harry Ash, get off that car, right now, or there will be no oats for you tonight.' The donkey looked at her, sighed and then slid off the bonnet. 'Go home and I'll speak to you later about this,' Verity instructed him. 'Lulu, you go with Harry and make sure he goes right home.'

The little white dog gave her a bark and then followed the donkey as he plodded through Rowanberry towards the farm. Verity turned back to the man who was inspecting the paintwork of his vehicle.

'He's scratched it,' he said. 'Look!'

Verity looked down to where he was pointing. There was indeed a scratch and a slight indent where the beast had put most of his weight. She went over and pretended to inspect it. With a quick flick of her finger, the scratch was erased and the dent removed.

'Where? I can't see anything,' she said innocently.

'What? It's there!' The man pointed to the spot again and was astonished to see the damage was not there anymore. 'What happened? I was sure there was a scratch.'

'You need to get your eyes checked,' Verity replied. 'Good day.'

She turned about and followed her animals back home. It had already been a tiring day. The goats had gotten out again, she had received a large bill from the outgoing vet for a prescription for arthritis pills for an elderly cat and now Harry had been misbehaving. Forget the tea, she thought to herself, when I get home, I'm opening a bottle of wine.

Harry was standing at the farm's front door when she arrived, Lulu at his feet. He looked at her defiantly.

'What were you thinking of, you daft creature,' Verity snapped. 'What did you do that for?'

'He nearly ran me over,' Harry replied. 'He came haring around that corner and nearly took me out. I saw my entire life flash before my eyes. It serves him right, speeding through the village like that. I was just minding my own business and...'

'You still shouldn't have done that,' Verity scolded.

Harry gave her a hard look and tutted. 'You have no idea how hard my life is since...'

'I know... since you were turned into a donkey by an evil witch and doomed to live for eternity as an equine,' she said. 'I know the story, Harry, you don't have to tell me it. I've heard it millions of times already.'

'Well, you don't know what it's been like,' he replied. 'It's been three hundred years and your family have never once bothered to try and undo the curse.'

'Now, that's not true. You know various ancestors have tried and failed to do it,' Verity answered. 'The curse is just too strong. You shouldn't have tried to defraud the witch in the first place.'

'I did not defraud her!' he replied, his voice snippy and about an octave higher, 'I was trying to do business with her.'

'By stealing her money, her wand and her Grimoire and trying to sell it at market?' Verity replied.

'Well, it wasn't quite like that, but...'

'Look, I know you're bored around here and that you don't have many people to talk to...'

'I only have you to talk to since your parents passed away.'

'Yes, well, if humans heard you talking, they would freak out,' she said. 'Anyway, that's why I don't shut you into the paddock with the other animals. That's why I allow you to wander. But, honestly, Harry, could you just try for once and behave yourself?'

She opened the farmhouse door and went inside, followed by the donkey.

'You know I was born under a mischievous moon,' Harry said.

'Doesn't mean you have to be mischievous,' she reminded him.

She walked down into the hall and to her kitchen where her mug with the teabag was still abandoned on the worktop. She went to the fridge, pulled out a bottle of white wine and a can of heavy ale and placed them on the kitchen table. She fetched a wine glass from the cupboard and an animal feed bowl from under the sink. The glass she filled with wine, the bowl with the ale. Then she carried them both into the living room, sat down on the sofa and placed the wine glass on the coffee table. The bowl she placed on the floor near her feet. With a flick of her finger, she switched the television on and then took up her glass. Harry sat down on his haunches and drank ale from the bowl.

'Is that new cop series starting tonight?' he asked.

'Yeah.'

'Can we watch it?'

'Only if you promise not to sit on that man's car again.'

'You know I can't make promises,' he reminded her.

'Well, try not to do it again,' she said. 'Who was that man, anyway?'

'The new vet. Finn Somebody.'

'Huh.' She tried to feign indifference, but inside her thoughts were whirling through her head. A gorgeous man had moved into the village and he was the vet. But he's nasty, a voice in her head reminded her. Yes, but maybe he'll change, she reasoned. A leopard doesn't change its spots, the voice replied.

❧

THREE DAYS LATER, HARRY WENT MISSING FROM THE FARM. At first, Verity was not unduly worried, he had gone AWOL before and always came home. However, when the donkey failed to return for dinner, she knew something was up. Harry never missed a feed. She left the farmhouse with Lulu intending to get into her 4X4 and drive around the area looking for her equine friend, but stopped short of her vehicle when a sports car drew up. A dark-haired man in sunglasses got out. It was the new vet.

'Miss Ash,' he said, 'I'm glad I've caught you, I've just been told that there's a donkey stuck in the Mousel Marsh. I'm going there to see if I can help the Fire Service get it out and thought I'd stop by to see if it was one of yours.'

Verity looked down at Lulu and then up at Finn. Harry! 'I think it might be,' she replied, 'one of my donkeys is missing.'

'Which one? Oh, wait a minute. Don't tell me. It's the one that sat on my car, isn't it?' he replied.

She nodded. 'How did you guess?'

He replied with an eye roll, then said: 'I had a feeling about it.'

'His name is Harry.'

'I remember,' he said. 'Look, can I give you a lift to the marsh? I'm heading up there now.'

She thought about it for a second. It would make sense to get a lift, she thought. If Harry is okay, I can walk him home. If he's hurt himself...no, I don't want to think of that. 'Yeah, that would be great. Can I bring Lulu? She's Harry's best friend.'

'Yes, of course.'

MOUSEL MARSH WAS ONLY A FIVE-MINUTE CAR JOURNEY FROM the farm and there were two fire appliances complete with flashing blue lights parked at the entrance when they arrived. Firefighters were walking to and from the marshland, carrying ropes and other pieces of equipment. Verity jumped out of the car and, leaving Lulu in the car, rushed over to the nearest fire engine. The team leader was busy giving out instructions to a firefighter and didn't see her at first. Then he looked up and a broad smile broke over his face.

'Verity! How are you?' He walked over to see her and gave her a hug.

'I'm fine, Bill, but I think one of my donkeys is stuck in the marsh,' she said.

'It's Harry, isn't it?'

'Yeah, sorry.'

'Well, we're just going in to take a look. Want to come with us?' He looked down at the training shoes on feet. 'Have you got boots or something? It's pretty wet and muddy in there.'

'I'll be fine, I just need to check he's okay.'

'And what about you?' Bill looked at Finn. The vet stepped forward, hand out to shake.

'Hi, Finn Everly, I'm the new vet,' he said shaking Bill's hand. 'I was called out to give whatever help I can and check that the donkey is okay.'

'Good, good,' the firefighter said, 'now follow me. I was told he was about quarter of a mile in.'

As Verity and Finn followed Bill into the marshland, the witch cursed her donkey under her breath. She could see Harry sitting some way away surrounded by fire fighters attempting to drag the stuck beast on to its feet.

'That bloody nuisance of a former warlock,' she muttered under her breath.

'Did you say something?' Finn asked.

'What? No.'

The way was rough underfoot and once they left the path, the ground became uneven and pitted with holes and muddy areas. Verity stumbled a few times, but was so irritated by the situation the donkey had got himself into, she barely registered them.

'Are you alright, Miss Ash?' Finn asked as he hurried after her.

'Yes, fine. Why do you ask?'

'Are you still angry with me because of the incident with the car?' he asked. 'You know, I should apologise for my behaviour. I was angry, but not at you.' She glanced back at him. 'Actually, I was probably just nervous. It was my first day at work and the car was new and well...Harry was sitting on it...'

She stopped in her tracks and turned around to look at him. She folded her arms.

'Well,' he continued, 'what I'm trying to say is I'm sorry for snapping at you.'

'Apology accepted,' she replied, 'and I'm sorry for Harry sitting on your car. He's a nuisance, that donkey.'

'Well, no harm done and, well, it got us to meet, I suppose.'

Verity frowned. What the hell is he going on about? She thought. 'Yeah, I suppose so,' she replied. 'Now, can we just get on with getting Harry out of here.'

The donkey had chosen the wettest, most difficult part of the marsh to get stuck in. As they approached, they could see several of the firefighters were thigh high in water. They had a rope tied around Harry's neck and one around his belly, and were pulling with all their might, but the beast remained stuck. He brayed angrily as they tugged.

'Evening, boys,' Verity said as she approached. The firefighters looked up and greeted her. 'I'm sorry about this. I don't know how he got out this time.'

'No worries, Verity, girl,' the nearest firefighter said. He was a man in his late 30s. 'Just another day in the life of Red Watch. Though I think this is probably the most stuck Harry's ever been. I don't know how he does it.'

Verity threw Harry a look. 'Just lucky, I suppose. Hold on, I'm coming in.' She stepped off a drier area into the deep wet marshland. The ice-cold water made her gasp as she waded towards her animal. 'Let's have a look then,' she said. The firefighters back away from the animal allowing Verity to inspect Harry. 'What the hell do you think you were doing?' she hissed at the donkey as she inspected his forelegs.

'I don't know what you mean,' Harry whispered back. 'I just happened to wander in, all donkey-like, and got stuck.'

She looked up at him. 'I know you, Harry Ash, you've done this on purpose to annoy me.'

'As if!'

'Can I help at all?' Finn was now in the water wading out towards them.

'No, it's okay, I don't think he's hurt,' Verity replied, 'just a bit stuck.' She moved behind the donkey and with a flick of her fingers used magic to loosen his hind legs. Harry moved his legs.

'Oh, look at that!' said the firefighter. 'He just needed his mum to come and get him. Right, lads, let's get in there and pull him out.'

With Verity pushing his rear, and the firefighters and Finn pulling on the ropes, they soon dragged the muddy beast to the dry land. Harry gave himself a shake, hee-hawed and began to nose about the marsh grass looking for something green and tasty to eat. Finn gave the donkey a quick health check whilst Verity turned to his rescuers.

'Thank you all, so much,' she said somewhat breathless from all the exertion. 'And I'm so sorry he got out again.'

'Well,' the firefighter said, 'he is called Harry.'

Verity looked at him blankly.

'You know? Like Harry Houdini, the escape artist?' He chuckled. 'That's what he is...Harry Houdini the donkey.'

As the firefighters tidied up and returned to their appliances, Verity grabbed Harry's bridle and began to haul him back to the road.

'Can I help at all?' Finn asked. 'Can I drive you home or something?'

'No, that's okay. We'll just walk home, it's not far,' she said.

'Are you sure?'

She faced him. 'Yes,' she replied. Then seeing the disappointment on his face. 'But thank you so much for coming out and making sure he was okay. I appreciate it.'

'Any time.'

The three of them walked amiably to the road. Verity let Lulu out of the car and, once Finn had driven off, Verity rounded on the mischievous donkey.

'What the hell do you think you were playing at?' she demanded. 'You could have been killed.'

'Verity, darling, you know very well that I cannot be killed, not since... well, you know!'

'Yes, but you know better than to walk into that marsh. You were putting others at risk.' She could not keep the irritation out of her voice. She looked around for Lulu and found the little dog running alongside the donkey.

'Well, nobody was hurt, were they?' Harry replied. 'Now, let's get home. I'm starving. I hope you've done me a good dinner.'

'Is that all you can think about?'

'What else is there?'

They walked on for a few minutes in silence, then Harry said: 'That vet is a bit of a dish, isn't he? Very handsome. Why don't you ask him out?'

'What?' She looked at Harry and wondered if he could mindread for she had just been thinking about Finn and how nice it was he had showed up. And how gorgeous and thick his hair was. And how dreamy his eyes were. 'I suppose so.' She could feel the blush travel up her neck to the roots of her hair.

'Well, you could do worse,' Harry said. 'He's a professional man with a good job and gorgeous hair.'

'I don't think so. I'm not looking for a man, thank you very much. I'm quite happy on my own.' That wasn't actually true, but she was not going to admit it.

'What do you mean? You've been on your own for far too long now. Time you got back in the saddle and found yourself a new stallion.'

She gave him a withering look. 'Did you think that up all by yourself?'

'It was good, no?'

'It was corny.'

'So, how about it, Ver? I'm just worried you're going to end up an old maid.'

'I'm only 26.'

'Exactly. An old maid by the standards of my day.'

'Let's stop talking about it,' she said.

'But...'

'No, I'm not talking about it. I'm fine. I'm not lonely. I have you and all my animals to keep me company and I'm happy,' she said firmly.

'But Ver...'

'Do you want me to use a muzzling spell on you?'

Harry looked at her and then huffed. 'No. Okay, I'll be quiet, but just think about it, okay?'

❧

THE FOLLOWING DAY, WHEN VERITY WENT AS USUAL TO OPEN the barn to let the horses, goats and chickens out she found that the door was already opened. She went inside to see that all the animals were accounted for with the exception of one.

'Harry!'

She quickly let all the animals out, fed and watered them and then stomped back to the house in the worst temper she had ever been in. 'I'm going to kill that bloody donkey warlock' she muttered as she entered. She grabbed her car keys and rushed back out again. 'If I find him stuck anywhere, he can just stay there. I'm going to leave him and he can starve to death for all I care,' she said as she slipped the key into the ignition of her 4X4 and turned the engine on. 'That bloody, bloody beast!'

There were two places Harry was fond of disappearing to and they were both on the other side of the village. However, as she drove past the vet, she happened to look into the business' garden to see the familiar grey shape of her missing friend. Stomping on the brakes, she brought the car to a standstill then put it in reverse and reversed back to the surgery. Parking outside, she leapt out of the car and clumped over to the garden gate which was lying open.

'Harry Ash, you come back here right now!' she growled as she entered the garden and stamped towards her animal. 'How could you do this to me again? Don't you think about what you're doing? Don't you know I have other things to do, better things, than chasing you around all over the village?'

Harry looked up and grinned.

'Come here, you stubborn, horrible animal,' she yelled. She ran over to him and attempted to grab him, but the equine was too quick. He trotted out of the way and ran down the other end of the garden. 'Come here you awful beast!' She ran after him.

'What's going on?' a sleepy face appeared at an open window in the flat above the surgery. It was Finn looking all mussy haired and handsome. 'Miss Ash!'

'Verity, call me Verity!' she puffed as she chased after Harry.

'Verity! What's going on?'

'Well, you can see what's going on!' she snapped. 'Harry's gotten out again!'

'Hold on, I'll come down and give you a hand.'

Moments later, Finn appeared in the garden in a white bath robe and desert boots.

'Morning,' he said with a grin. 'So, he's out again, is he?' Verity gave him a look that showed she was not amused by him stating the obvious. 'Nice pyjamas,' he added.

Verity looked down and gasped. She had forgotten all about her attire. It was normal for her to go out to the barn first thing in the morning in her pyjamas and a pair of gardening shoes to let the animals out. Then she would return to the house to get showered and dressed. But her routine had been broken by the escape of Harry and now she was out in public looking like a scarecrow with no makeup and hair that stood on its ends.

'Oh my God!' she said, embarrassment washing over her. 'I forgot I wasn't dressed.'

'You still look good,' Finn said. Then seeing her discomfort, he added: 'Don't worry about it. It's early. No-one's going to see you. Come on, let's catch this beast and then maybe I could make you breakfast.'

It was a full five minutes before Harry allowed himself to be caught. Now tethered against the garden gate munching on some lovely sweet grass, Harry was content to be by himself whilst Finn invited Verity inside.

'Look, I don't want to put you to any trouble,' she said still embarrassed by the way she looked. 'I'll just take Harry home and...'

'You're not,' Finn assured her. 'I was hoping to see you today anyway.'

'You were?'

'Yes,' he replied. 'Look come inside and have some coffee. I'll make us an omlette and I can tell you all about it.'

Verity looked at Harry and the donkey winked at her. Bloody mule, she thought.

'Alright,' she said at last. 'But make it tea, I don't like coffee.'

'What? Who doesn't like coffee?' said Finn feigning shock.

❧

An hour later, Verity found Harry sitting down on the grass enjoying the early morning sunshine. He had easily untied his tether from the gate, but had evidently decided to wait on his mistress rather than disappearing again.

'Oh, you're still here then?' she said as she waited for him to get to his feet and follow her to the gate.

'Of course!' he replied. 'So, how did the breakfast date go with Finn?'

'It wasn't a date...' she began then something occurred to her. 'Did you...? Were you...?'

'Spit it out, girl, I don't have all day.' Harry trotted out of the gate and walked at her side up the road towards the farm. The car would have to be retrieved later.

'Did you escape on purpose so that I would come down here this morning?'

'Why would I do that?' he replied innocently. Before she could answer, he continued: 'Oh yes, I'll tell you why...because you couldn't snare a man if he leapt into your arms and demanded you kiss him, that's why!'

'What are you talking about?' she asked.

'You know what I mean,' he said. 'You're useless at finding a man. So, I thought I'd help out.'

'By running down to his garden.'

'Yes...and...'

Her eyes narrowed. Then she looked aghast. 'Oh, you didn't!'

'Yes. I. Did.'

'So, you deliberately got stuck in the marsh and sat on his car?'

'That just about sums it up.'

'But why?'

'Why?' The donkey rolled his eyes. 'The girl asks me why!' he said to no-one in particular. 'I'll tell you why, Miss Ash...you needed a kick up the arse to get going on your love-life. I had to do something before your ovaries shrivelled up and your beauty faded. Life is too short, my love, and I had to do something to speed things along. If I hadn't introduced you to Finn, you would still be moping around the house wondering why you didn't have a man.'

'I don't mope,' she protested.

'Oh, oh, what's wrong with me, Harry? Why does no one fancy me, Harry?' he said mimicking her voice.

'I was very drunk when I said that and you weren't supposed to remember it,' she snapped.

'Yes, well, I did remember it and I decided to do something about it and I've done something about it. So, you are welcome!' he shouted.

She was silent.

'So, did he ask you out?' the donkey wanted to know. She huffed and said nothing. 'Well? Tell me.'

'He might have.'

'So, my plan worked then?'

'It might have.'

'You. Are. Welcome,' he said triumphantly. 'So, where's he taking you then? That French restaurant in town? Oh no! The Italian on the river? Or maybe that old pub that's about three miles down the road? Come on, spill the beans.'

'Well,' Verity began. 'I will tell you, but you have to promise me one thing.'

'I promise whatever it is.'

'Say I promise.'

'I promise.'

'Okay, so he's asked me for a drink in the pub...'

'A drink in the pub!' Harry sounded outraged. 'Is that all? Why in my day we treated a young lady correctly... there was no drink in the pub for us... I would have wined and dined you and...'

'Harry! Harry!'

'What?'

'Shut up! I knew you would be like this.'

'Be like what?'

'All uppity and annoyed.'

'I'm not annoyed. I was just saying.'

'Well, just don't. I need you to be quiet while I tell you what I want you to promise.'

'Okay, then, my lips are sealed.' He closed his mouth and looked at her.

She breathed in. 'I need you to promise...'

'Uh-huh?'

'...that you will leave me and Finn to have our date in peace.'

'I don't know what you mean? I would never gatecrash a date.'

'You did before.'

'Did I? I don't recall.'

'You appeared when I was dating the farmer.'

'Yes, well, I never thought he was good enough for you,' he admitted.

'Well, I'm telling you now that if you gatecrash my date with Finn, I'll have him castrate you,' she said.

Harry looked outraged. The whites of his eyes were showing as he stared at her in disbelief. 'You wouldn't.'

'Wouldn't I?' she said. 'Promise me!'

The donkey looked away and pursed his lips.

'Harry? I said promise me.'

'Alright, alright, I promise not to gatecrash your date,' he said. Then he added: 'But you'll tell me all about it?'

'I'll tell you about most of it.'

'Even the kissing part?'

'We'll see.'

About the Author

Dawn Nelson is a Scottish award-winning author and journalist, living on the banks of the River Clyde in the west coast of Scotland with two kids, two small dogs and one chicken. She writes both fantasy and romantic suspense. Find out more:

https://danelsonauthor.com/

https://medium.com/@dawnnelson-46858

Facebook: https://www.facebook.com/authordanelson

Twitter: https://twitter.com/danelsonauthor

Threads: https://www.threads.net/@dawnnelsonauthor

LinkedIn: https://www.linkedin.com/in/dawn-nelson-95210221/

Tik Tok: https://www.tiktok.com/@danelson70

Pinterest: https://www.pinterest.co.uk/danelsonauthor/

Goodreads: https://www.goodreads.com/author/show/1351494.
D_A_Nelson

Instagram: https://www.instagram.com/dawnnelsonauthor/

A Witch's Bounty

BY WYNTER RYAN

The life of a supernatural bounty hunter is one of danger and loneliness. But six months ago, a ray of sunshine broke through my bleak existence in the form of Kat, my little virgin witch. She showed me a life I never knew existed. A life of love and laughter, and how did I repay her? By almost getting her killed by a dangerous monster. A monster I'm still hunting today.

To save her life, I broke her heart. She'll never know of my sacrifice. But I'd rather have her hatred on my conscious than her blood on my hands.

One

Kat

"You know I look ridiculous, right?" I tug at the zipper of my skintight black leather bodysuit, willing it to pull up to my chin instead of ending at the middle of my chest. I stop tugging when the zipper doesn't budge. I guess everyone in the bar will have a front-row seat to my wardrobe malfunction by the way my breasts are straining at the seams of my Halloween costume.

"Come on, Kat, you look hot. You'll have every guy in the bar crawling all over you. Just look at the sexy vampire at the end of the bar." Rhea, my soon-to-be ex-best friend, points to the far side of the room.

Rhea convinced me to attend the Halloween Party at the new bar in town, "The Demons Den," her idea was that I dress as my namesake while she's dressed as a sexy witch.

I brush my chin across my shoulder in what I hope looks like a casual movement to get a better look behind me at the guy Rhea has deemed sexy.

She's not wrong. He's gorgeous with his dark hair, piercing blue eyes that smolder into mine. He smirks, knowing his sexual appeal. But he's not my type. My type has dirty blonde hair, forest green eyes, and a soft beard that tickles my inner thighs. I sigh, thinking about my ex-boyfriend, Rafe.

I snap my gaze back to Rhea when the sexy vampire starts walking toward us. Hopefully, he didn't mistake the longing in my eyes for him instead of Rafe.

"Oh my gosh, he's coming over here." Rhea gushes, "How do I look? Is my hat on straight? How about my boobs?"

"You look gorgeous as always. Your hat is on straight. And your boobs are perky as ever." I roll my eyes as she squishes her breasts together.

Caught up in reassuring Rhea about her appearance, I don't hear the vampire approach our table. "Ladies." I jump at his hypnotic voice whispering in my ear. "Can I buy you a drink?"

Most women would be melting at his attention but not me. It's been five months since Rafe broke my heart, and I'm still not over him. He was the one, my soulmate. Or so I thought.

"I, um, actually have to go to the bathroom." I push away from the table, weaving through the large crowd. As always, Halloween night brings out everyone in our supernatural community. Some human, most not.

I reach for the bathroom door handle, but before I open it, something in the hallway catches the corner of my eye. "Rafe," I whisper into the hallway.

His head turns toward my voice. His eyes widen and roam up and down my body taking in my body-hugging Halloween cat costume, including the cat ears headband and the cat's tail.

His jaw clenches, and his hands tighten into fists at his sides, but he doesn't stop walking down the hall. If anything, he speeds up. Taking a left turn out of my sight.

He's not getting away from me before I give him the piece of my mind I never got to give him when he broke up with me. Five months ago, I was too shocked by his hateful words to do anything. I stood motionless while he told me we were through. But not today. Today I'm going to settle the score once and for all.

I straighten my shoulders and stomp after him. I turn the corner just in time to see him slip into one of the backrooms of the bar. The door silently clicked behind him.

Taking a deep breath, I throw open the door, ready to give Rafe hell, when he rushes to my side and glances into the hallway before pulling me into the room, closing the door behind us.

"Kat, what are you doing here? They can't find us back here." He spins me around to look at him.

"What are you talking about? Who can't find us?"

He runs his hand through his hair, messing it up, giving him that rakish look I love. I mean, I loved, not love, I remind myself.

His phone vibrates, and he pulls it out of his pocket, his eyes scanning the screen, "Shit, we're too late. They're on their way back here."

Two

Rafe

It's not how I imagined my reunion with Kat, but I never expected to see her at a place like this.

I can't believe she is here. I've done everything in my power to keep her safe. And on the one night, I need total concentration, she shows up looking sexy as Hell.

"I don't have time to explain what's going on right now, just that some evil guys are on their way into this room, and if they find us in here where we don't belong, they're going to kill us."

All the blood drains from her beautiful face, and my heart squeezes at the thought of losing her permanently. For even in the afterlife, I doubt she would forgive me for all the pain I've caused her.

The door handle rattles, and she thrusts her right hand in the air toward the door, using her witch powers to hold off their entry into the room.

"I can't hold them off forever. Do you trust me?" She asks, the shouts on the other side of the door getting louder.

"You know I do, Kat."

"Then unzip your pants."

"What?" My cock, which was half hard already from seeing her in that tight, form-fitting outfit that shows off her delectable curves, is now hard as steel, ready to burst out of my pants.

"We need to pretend that we are back here for a sexual encounter, and since the zipper on my stupid outfit is stuck, you're going to have to take your pants off, and I will suck on your cock."

Her words are so matter-of-fact about the plan, but the lust flaring in her eyes tells me she is just as affected as I am by her suggestion.

"I don't know if that's such a good idea." The thought of her sweet little lips wrapped around my cock again has it leaking pre-cum, making a mess in my underwear.

"It's not like I've never had your cock in my mouth before." She rolls her eyes and sinks onto her knees before me, "So, unless you want to die, I suggest you hurry up and take off your pants."

I unbuckle my belt and slip my pants and underwear down my thighs. My hard cock springs forward, bouncing on my abs, pre-cum glistening on the tip.

Kat looks at me through her long eyelashes and licks her lips, "Are you ready?"

At my nod, she opens her mouth and takes my cock deep into her throat. The sensation is better than I remember. I gather her hair in my hand and begin pumping into her mouth as she moans around my cock.

Sadness replaces the desire in her eyes as she drops her hand, releasing the invisible force holding the door shut.

The sound of wood splintering and hinges ripped from the frame echoes through the room.

"What the fuck?" The first guy says, bursting through the door. By the smell of him, he's a werewolf.

"Looks like we are interrupting a couple of lovebirds." The second guy, also a werewolf, snickers, stepping over the broken door that's now no better than a pile of firewood.

Kat pulls her mouth off my cock with a pop and stands up, spinning around to look at the two intruders, giving me a chance to pull up my pants. "Jimmy, you said we would have privacy back here." She turns around and sticks her lower lip out at me in a pout.

"Sorry, Carla, the bartender told me we could use one of the backrooms," I say, going along with her use of fake names.

"Of course, Ray would tell you to use one of the backrooms. They all have cameras except this one. He's an incubus. He likes to watch." The first werewolf explains with a shrug. "You got lucky and picked the one room without a camera."

"Why I never!" Kat spins on her heels and marches toward the door. I follow her lead and scramble after her.

Freedom is inches away until a dark figure blocks our escape. "I wondered where you ran off to, little kitty." The voice of my nightmares comes from the shadows. "I thought I recognized you as Rafe's girlfriend, but I wasn't sure until now." He grabs her wrists and pulls her to him. She shrieks when she sees his face, no longer hidden in the shadows.

"Let her go, you dirty blood-sucker." I lunge for him only to be held back by his two lackeys.

"Such a temper from a cold-blooded bounty hunter." His blood-red eyes glare at me. "I'm going to enjoy killing you slowly, human." He spats, a look of disgust crossing his unholy face. "Take them to the warehouse and lock them up. I'll return for them later. And make sure to tie her wrists together so she can't use her powers."

"What about him, boss?"

"What about him? He's human. He doesn't have any powers." The wolves blanch at my six-seven size solid frame. "Just tie him up." Wallace stomps out of the room, taking his vampire stench with him.

I give Kat a reassuring look, knowing there is no way I will lose her again. I didn't break her heart to save her life, only to still lose her.

Three

Kat

THE WOLVES LEAD US OUT THE BACKDOOR TO THE ALLEY. I LOOK around, searching for an escape. I notice a car waiting close by, but nothing else. This alley is secluded from the main road. This might be our only chance to escape. We are goners if we let the wolves take us to the warehouse.

I fake a trip and fall to the ground taking one of the wolves with me. Rafe plants his massive shoulder in our other captor's stomach, causing him to crash into the garbage cans lining the alley.

I roll to Rafe's legs reaching for the switchblade knife he always carries in his left boot. Stupid wolves should never have bound our hands in front of our bodies. My hands find the knife, and I pull it from his boot.

Rafe bends down next to me, holding his wrist out to me. I release the switchblade with a pop and cut through the rope around his wrists. Once free from his restraints, Rafe takes the switchblade from me and cuts through the rope binding my wrists together.

The wolves are almost on top of us by the time Rafe finishes freeing me. I don't have time to think. I throw my unbound hands in the air, one aimed at each wolf, hoping to slow them down, but instead, my magic blows them to pieces. Leaving nothing but ash.

I stare at my hands, too shocked to move. I can't blow things up. I can only slow things down or hold things back and sometimes freeze things for a short time. But this is new.

"Come on. We have to get out of here." His rough command pulls me out of my trance.

"Where are we going?" I manage to say, following him through the dark alley.

"It's a safe house. We can regroup, and I'll tell you everything."

❧

Rafe

I UNLOCK THE DOOR TO THE SAFE HOUSE. I KNOW I PROMISED TO tell Kat everything once we arrived here, but I need to make sure she is ok first.

"There's a bathroom on the right. You can shower and get the grime from the day off your body." At the mention of her body, my cock pulses against my zipper, wanting to get closer to her.

"I'm going to need help with the zipper."

My cock swells even bigger mistaking her request for help with her zipper instead of mine.

"Um, sure." My hands shake as I reach for her zipper.

"It's stuck. You're going to have to use your knife."

My head snaps, gazing into her eyes, "Hold still." I place my hand between the top of her zipper and her chest. My fingers slipped between her luscious breasts, causing her breath to hitch. I pull the zipper towards me and gently slice through the fabric until she can slide her arms out and push the body suit the rest of the way down her curvy body. Leaving her naked to my roaming eyes.

"Take a shower with me." Her eyes plead with mine. "Make me forget."

My control snaps, and I crash my mouth onto hers needing to taste her after so many nights without her.

I pick her up and carry her to the bathroom, sitting her down only long enough to start the shower and take my clothes off and for her to kick off her boots and finish taking off her body suit.

It's a tight fit in the shower, but we make it work. I want to take care of her, so I lather her hair with shampoo, working my fingers over her scalp.

"Mmm, that feels so good." She moans, causing my cock to bob between us, searching for her heat.

The water runs down our bodies, and I pull her back against my chest, my cock slipping between her ass cheeks to her clit. I continue soaping her body, rolling her nipples into my palms as she rocks her hips back and forth, my cock hitting her clit with every thrust.

She arches her back and comes on my cock. I hold her close as she rides out her climax.

I turn off the shower, wrap her in a towel, and carry her to the bed, gently laying her down in the center.

“I need to taste you,” I say, wedging my shoulders between her thighs, dislodging the towel from her body.

My first lick across her clit has her hips thrusting into my mouth and calling out my name. “You taste even better than I remember.” I groan against her pussy.

“Rafe, I’m going to come.” Her body begins to buck wildly, searching for her release.

I thrust two fingers into her pussy, and her body convulses around my fingers as she comes.

I kiss my way up her body licking and sucking each nipple into my mouth, wringing another moan out of her. “Rafe, stop teasing and get up here and fuck me.”

Her nipple slips out of my mouth with a pop, “Is my little witch greedy for my cock?”

She nods and thrusts her hips into mine, “Now, Rafe.”

“Your wish is my command.” My cock pushes into her heat, the walls of her pussy squeezing it tight. “Fuck, Kat, you feel so good.”

I bend down and capture her mouth with mine as I plunge the rest of the way inside her. Her walls flutter faster around me, and I will my body to slow down, or I’m going to come too quickly. But I can tell she needs it hard and fast, so I pick up my speed, slamming into her repeatedly until she cries out her release.

A tingling sensation flares at the base of my spine, alerting me that I’m seconds away from coming in her hot little pussy. We’ve never used protection before, but now it is different. Our relationship is different than it was five months ago. I should pull out, but before I can, she wraps her legs around my hips and pulls me tight against her letting me know she wants to feel my cum inside her.

My body surges forward, and my come spurts inside her welcoming womb. I rest my forehead on hers and stare into her eyes, praying this means she forgives me.

She leans forward and kisses my cheek, “It’s time to talk.”

Four

Kat

Luckily this is a shared safe house, so there are clothes my size I can change into. Once we have both cleaned up and changed into fresh clothes, Rafe begins his story.

"I'm not an accountant like I told you. I'm a bounty hunter."

"I figured you weren't an accountant the first time I saw the switchblade in your boot." I scoff. Men, do they really think we're not that observant?

He blinks several times before continuing, "I didn't think about that." He shrugs. "I've been tracking Wallace for the last six months. He's one of the most wanted demons in the Underworld. He escaped me once, vowing to hurt everyone I loved." He takes a deep breath, "I couldn't let anything happen to you, Kat. I love you.

"Oh, Rafe, I love you too." I run my hand across his cheek. "I know you would never let anyone hurt me."

He grabs my hand, pulling me against his chest, "That's just it. I thought I was saving your life by letting you go, but he still got to you. I couldn't live with myself if anything happened to you."

His speech warms my heart, "Then let's do this together." I scramble onto his lap, caressing his face with my hand.

He grabs my hand, stilling it against his face, "No, you are going to stay here where it's safe, and I will take care of Wallace once and for all."

"With my new power, he's no match for us," I argue.

He kisses my palm, still held against his face, "Sweetheart, your power is too new. You're not even sure how it worked when you blew up those two werewolves."

"But..."

"No buts. You are going to stay here, and that's final."

❧

Rafe

SHE REALLY ISN'T VERY GOOD AT BEING INCONSPICUOUS. I'VE sensed her following me since I left her at the safe house twenty minutes ago. I knew that as soon as her mind was made up, there would be no stopping her. I've made peace with the possibility of dying at the hands of Wallace, but I'll make sure he burns in Hell before I let him harm one hair on her beautiful head.

I retrace my steps leading us back to the alley where we escaped Wallace's men the first time. Now all I have to do is keep Kat in the shadows and wait for Wallace to show his blood-sucking face.

The sound of a gun being cocked is the only thing that alerts me to his presence. The feel of cold steel on my temple reminds me how dangerous he really is.

"You're not very smart, are you? But most humans aren't." His gun dips a little on my face. "Returning to the scene of the crime. You killed my men, and that's not something I can easily forget."

He pushes me forward, and I use the distraction to grab my gun in my left boot.

"Over here, you big meanie!" Kat steps out of the shadows waving her arms.

Wallace whips his head in my direction, causing me to still my movements, "Are you going to let your girlfriend fight your battles?"

"Kat, get out of here!" I yell into the alley.

"No, I'm not leaving here without you."

"Enough! I'm done listening to the two of you drone on." Wallace levels his gun at me, but he explodes into a fiery ball before he can pull the trigger.

"I did it!" A smiling Kat stands behind the now extinguished ball of fire, with her hands raised.

That was too easy. I wait for Wallace to regenerate, but he never does. I dump my flask of Holy water. I carry on his ashes, ensuring he won't rise again.

"We did it!" Kat jumps into my arms, wrapping her arms around my neck and legs around my waist.

I squeeze her tight, "Yes, you did, Sweetheart."

Epilogue

Rafe

It's been two years since we vanquished Wallace, and the Underworld still hasn't recovered from losing one of its most powerful leaders. The Underworld is in utter chaos, demons fighting demons trying to take the throne Wallace left behind.

Kat and I opened our own supernatural private investigator service, specializing in protecting the innocent and punishing the guilty.

"Hey, husband." Kat comes barreling into the office, plopping down on the corner of my desk. "I'm going to need some time off."

A smile breaks out on my face, and I pull Kat into my arms because only one thing would take her away from her love of fighting demons, "Are you..." I can't even get the words out before tears stream down her face.

"Yes! We're pregnant." She squeals and jumps into my arms.

About the Author

Wynter Ryan is a nurse by day and a romance author by night. Her love for romance novels started when she picked up her first Johanna Lindsey book with Fabio's flowing blonde hair on the cover. From that moment on, she was hooked. After twenty years of being a romance reader, she finally crossed over to becoming a romance author. If you enjoy a quick, short read with no cheating and always a happily ever after, please sign up for her newsletter for new releases and old favorites. https://author-wynter-ryan.com/newsletter-sign-up

And They Were Broommates

BY KATE PRIOR

Astrid is breaking her lease. The tower isn't big enough for her and Jason, and the town only needs one resident witch. She's tired of competing with him over every little thing.

Except, the lease-breaking ritual goes wrong, and they end up with a strange bond letting them hear everything the other is thinking. They didn't need a psychic link to know they hated each other, but now they can't hide everything else they think about each other.

MOONLIGHT MEETUP

With the last of the candles lit, the spell laid out before her started to glow. A low hum rippled through the night, prickling at her skin, the air stinging with magic. Astrid pulled back her hood and squinted into the darkness.

"What did we say about turning up to the ritual fifteen minutes late with a latte?"

Across the clearing, a figure stepped out of the shadows, indeed holding a paper to-go cup.

And he was fully dressed.

Astrid bristled. *Some* people knew to show up to a ritual sky-clad like the invite said to, and some people were Jason.

Under her long black cloak she was freezing her tits off, because in the middle of October it was a shivery 40 degrees. Of course Jason would show up in his jeans and a band t-shirt and the sleeves of a flannel rolled up, looking far cozier than he had any right to. This was the guy she had to share a lease with.

Jason rolled his eyes.

"Guess it's for me, then," he muttered, bringing the paper cup to his mouth.

Astrid narrowed her eyes. "What?"

He just hummed through a long sip of whatever was in the cup, probably just drawing it out to annoy her further.

When he didn't answer, she sighed and started unfastening her cloak. "Let's just get this over with."

“This could have been an email, y’know,” Jason grumbled, pulling the invite from his pocket. It was turning into an urgent reminder– the paper folding itself into a bird to peck at him. He snapped his fingers and it burst into a cloud of cinders.

"It really couldn't, the ritual calls for two people. And you still have my email marked as spam."

He didn't deny that, just began shucking his outer layers.

Jason had long, *long* black hair, smooth as a curtain falling over his shoulders as he shuffled off his pants. Like he was either hoping to be an extra in a Lord of the Rings remake, or an L’Oréal commercial.

It was a good thing he was on the other side of the summoning circle. The full moon was certainly a revealing time.

Revealing the tower’s lease, that was, Astrid reminded herself. The ritual to remove her sigil from the tower’s foundation could only be performed under the full moon, and she needed the other tenant’s magic to break the contract.

A few months ago, the local council posted a notice to appoint a witch for all residential magical problems. The realty office, however, had made it a little too clear that neither of them had the funds to lease the traditional witch’s tower on their own.

It had been remodeled late last century, but not in any conducive way to cohabitating. The hot water in his shower would go out if she turned on the dishwasher, and he would hear through the too-thin walls when she had a date over, and she could always complain about the whole place smelling when he had a spell in the slow cooker.

A year and a day until Jason goes the fuck away, she'd promised herself the hour she met him. She'd made it this far, but another week with him would be too much.

This town had really only needed one witch, after all. She was just going to have to concede it to Jason, as much as she hated it. She was just going to have to move on and look for a place in need of a singular witch that didn’t require a dual income to get by. Hopefully she would find something a step up from living in a gingerbread house.

She tossed her hair out of anxious habit, and cast her cloak aside, Astrid straightened her back and locked her shoulders. She couldn't let him distract her.

The pair of witches laid their hands at the edges of the spell, and after a few moments, the ground began to fall away within the circle, rumbling as things shifted beneath the surface. When the dusty earth cleared, the tower’s foundation layer was visible from the center, both their sigils carved into it.

Astrid gritted her teeth and spread her hands further apart to get a better grip on the spell. Magic was hard to guide the flow of even in the best of circumstances.

"Don't do it like that," Jason called from the other side of the circle, like he knew any better. He'd been in this residency exactly as long as she had, thank you.

"I know what I'm doing–" Astrid snapped back, when the vein of glimmering magic twisting through the root writhed, and snapped.

The burst of energy knocked her back into the grass, light flickering bright for a second and then out.

For several moments, Astrid could only contemplate the full moon overhead, slowly coming back to her senses.

"You ok?"

"Ugh. Peachy," she called back, brushing her hair out of her face as the clearing came back into focus.

It is insane how great her tits look tonight.

Astrid's brow furrowed. That was a weird thought, definitely not on her list of priorities. She glanced down, and did appreciate that despite the cold puckering her nipples, they did look pretty good for not being in her push up bra.

No, because of the cold, that weird thought came again. Then after a pause, *she wears a push up bra?*

Astrid frowned, before separating her back from the grass. Jason was also starting to get up from where the spell had thrown him. He was staring back at her, a look of puzzlement reflecting her own.

The ritual ground beneath them was scorched, but her signature remained on the lease.

Ah, shit. Now she's gonna blame me for fucking up her spell.

Astrid blinked. He hadn't said that out loud.

His eyes met hers, the realization dawning in them. Then they dipped for a fraction of a second. *Titties.*

Two

TAKE IT LEASEY

Jason didn't need a telepathic bond to know that Astrid hated him.

"For the love of Hecate, stop staring at my tits," Astrid muttered from the other side of Jason's desk, tossing her hair out of her face in an anxious tick. She had a heavy tome propped open on her knees, but neither the book nor the thin t-shirt she'd donned obstructed his view.

He was just as tired as she was, but neither of them was willing to sleep until they found a fix. Of course his mind wandered every few paragraphs, he couldn't exactly pay attention when she was right there, her thoughts as noisy as if she was reading out loud.

He was just starting to wonder if he could maybe convince her one of his thoughts was her own idea. And the idea would then be to leave him alone.

"It won't work, idiot," she snapped. *Shit. I wish I'd thought of that first. I would have done a much better job of convincing him.*

She glanced back at him, glowering with her arms crossed over her chest, looking for something to snap back about when she realized he must have already heard her.

"Hearing you planning to insult me is really something else."

"Just fix this. We wouldn't be in this mess if you hadn't broken my concentration."

It couldn't have been that. The ritual she had laid out had seemed a little strange, but she'd been in such a rush he hadn't really paid attention.

"Was that even the right spell to use to break our contract? It shouldn't have reacted like putting a fork in the microwave."

There was a sting of indignation that he'd assumed she'd used the wrong spell, and he felt it as keenly as if it was his own.

You don't need to think something AND say it out loud. It's like there's an echo in here, she shot back, and he could feel the force of her eye roll through the bond.

Jason turned away from her in the desk chair, searching for a moment's peace. His eyes fell on a slip of paper mostly tucked in the desk drawer. Half a thought, barely formed in his mind before he seized on it– thinking hard. *Shit, I can't show her this.*

He slipped both his hands into the drawer for barely a second before closing it, then standing up and walking two steps away.

Astrid, predictably, was in his chair the second he left it, yanking open the drawer. Her attention scanned the contents, and she didn't see him grab the back of the chair until he was rolling her out the door.

Jason bolted the lock the moment the office was empty, pausing only to hear her indignant yelp. The sound nearly brought a smirk to his face.

"Let me back in! We don't have time for you to dick around, I can't spend another day living like this!"

"We're not getting anything done like this. Do your research in your own room."

Jason sighed and sunk into his chair, the wood creaking with equal resignation, and began flipping through the index of his grimoire, searching for any mention of conjoined minds.

Hearing Astrid's thoughts was too much like hearing her voice in the room, though clearer and smaller all at the same time. It was easy to ignore what she was saying if he focused on his own thoughts.

And she thought *constantly*. Her mind went from one topic to the next incessantly, like a figure skater gliding from one trick into another. It was like she was narrating her life to herself, and then as if she was a talk show host, and then running through every possible permutation of an argument with no one in particular. It never ended.

Excuse me, I wasn't judging you for all the long-ass pauses between all of your thoughts, came from nowhere, startling him back from his desk.

The door was still closed, and she was still physically gone, just not psychically.

Jason crossed the empty room to his backpack over by the door. He dug out some earbuds, and plugged them into his phone. Next, music.

Ew, is that dad rock? Her voice came again barely a few seconds into the song, but this time the music helped obscure her words, though her derision was still palpable through the link.

Complain more and I'll change it to talk radio, he thought back quickly, and felt a wave of her disgust.

He had never heard so much from Astrid before. He wasn't surprised that she seemed to have an opinion on everything she'd ever laid eyes on, but she had never been so detailed and expansive, like you could dive into a pool of her, a universe made up of her.

Still, there was no working with Astrid. She could be as annoying as she was clever. Being in the same room and being able to read each other's thoughts would be unbearable.

Since they had become roommates, it seemed Astrid was determined to get underfoot. He had quickly learned that whenever he heard her stomping around upstairs, to slip away to one of the other floors, to circumnavigate the whole tower if he must. Every time he saw her she locked eyes with him like a fox chasing down a rabbit, and he did not enjoy being made to feel like a rabbit, his heart rate picking up to match.

She probably noticed that by now. If not after the ritual, how every time he closed his eyes he couldn't shake the image of her shedding that cloak in the misty midnight air...

Jason almost rolled his eyes at himself. Now, of all times to linger over that.

Three

THINKING OF YOU

Astrid settled into the bathtub, the warm, shallow water lapping at her legs.

This was a hundred times worse than simply living with him. He might have just taken up residence in her skull. Even if they managed to actually break the lease now, was she fated to be stuck with him in her head forever? Could she leave the country and still hear him? Or would he always be talking somewhere in the corner of her mind?

At least it was the weekend. She didn't know how she was going to get anything done with Jason in her head, judging the very way she thought.

Then again, she barely accomplished anything with his interference before this. It had been one time – she'd nearly knocked him into the local wishing well when he was trying to replenish it, and now he couldn't let her finish a potion without undermining each ingredient choice.

The echo of Jason's music had lessened, his thoughts in the back of her head had dulled. She could feel the comfort of his bed, the clear satisfaction of melting into the mattress as he fell asleep.

Finally.

She should have gone to bed too, but she didn't know when she would next have the privacy she needed. With one of them unconscious, there might be some semblance of alone time.

She liked baths, especially with a bit of herbs and salts sprinkled in. Rosemary for beauty and youth and lilac to soothe, a bit of Epsom for fun. It was like a potion where she was an ingredient.

Astrid sighed and laid back in the bath, letting the water warm her. She toyed absently with one of her nipples, teasing it into a point, the minimal pleasure of it starting the familiar ache of arousal low in her belly.

That was another thing besides hygiene that was going to be harder now. Who knew when she would get another chance to pleasure herself without Jason listening? It was bad enough when she worried he could hear her vibrator through the paper-thin walls.

Astrid took the soap into the bath with her, dunking it in the water and rubbing it down her body.

Then– a flicker of a thought that wasn't hers.

Astrid stilled, clutching her chest, trying not to think of anything at all. Did Jason wake up?

The next thing she got wasn't a clear, coherent thought. It was hazy, more sensations and images than words, sensual touches and feeling of soft flesh in his hands.

Of course, horny dreams from Jason.

She knew she shouldn't be seeing this, but there wasn't any way she could look away. Maybe she should go wake him up.

For a moment Astrid thought she had glanced in the mirror, seeing herself naked, but the mirror was too fogged up to properly reflect.

She frowned when she realized she was looking at herself from a different angle. Outside herself. Astrid glanced at the door, but the lock was still turned.

Jason was dreaming about *her*.

Four

TUMBLE AND DRY

I *need to get to the laundry too. I'm out of socks*, came Astrid's thoughts as Jason was tossing his freshly-stripped sheets into the washer, for reasons he would not mentally revisit if he could avoid it. She must have heard him wondering if they needed more laundry soap.

Toss them in, I'll run it in a minute, he sent back. That morning had been strange. They'd never had so many civil interactions– her letting him know the milk in the fridge had expired and him responding that there was a new carton hidden behind the pizza box. When he had felt her delight from smelling the bacon he was cooking, he added a few more strips to the pan, and not ten minutes later she asked if she should make enough coffee for the both of them.

They had made some mindful efforts to avoid each other for as much of the morning as they could after breakfast, her going through her many checklists, searching through her mess of a room for the tome she had gotten their lease-breaking spell from.

He had opted for another day in the study, flipping through as many books on the subject as he could find.

Solitude never lasted all that long, however.

"Morning, Astrid," he nodded as she came into the study. He tried to ignore the way she blinked with surprise, and even a little warmth at being greeted. She looked away quickly.

Her thoughts zipping by filled his head as she busied her attention with a display cabinet. There were clusters of crystals glowing with an inner light, bottles with murky contents moving in their shadows, a number of tools in cases, some more tightly bound than others.

For a moment, Jason wondered if there was any harm in just letting her work in there with him, if he was going to have to hear her nonstop anyway.

"Of course not," she grumbled, and thankfully left it at that.

The problem was, clearly she was still in the middle of a laundry day. Her only clean shirt left was a little too small, highlighting the soft fat of her belly and baring every detail of her chest. She'd dug out a long breezy skirt that may have covered her legs, but moved with her. It hinted at their soft shape, making his mouth go dry. He swallowed and tried his damnedest not to wonder if she'd run out of clean underwear too.

Book, book, book. Reading now. Right now, he thought, hoping she wasn't paying attention.

Shielded by the desk, trying to put his mind on anything else.

He watched Astrid out of the corner of his eye, as she swept from one bookcase to another, peering into cabinets, poking carefully at anything not shielded by glass. Her thoughts glanced by quickly enough he couldn't get them all.

While her back was turned, Jason tried to adjust the way his arousal was starting to tent his sweatpants, straining uncomfortably against the fabric. He ached to be able to stroke himself.

"Eep!" Astrid let out a sudden little noise, startling back a step.

Jason caught himself against the desk halfway to standing up. He could feel the slightest flutter of sensation low in his stomach, coaxing his cock to stiffen. "Is there– er, something wrong?"

"No." A touch of red in her cheeks.

He looked around for what could have startled her, but nothing on the shelves had fallen or jumped out at her.

He waited with baited breath to hear her thoughts, but she just stared at his bookcases, reading the titles to herself. And author names. And serial numbers.

Either she was getting better at hiding her thoughts, or she was just that weird.

Jason watched her a moment longer, but she didn't react to him thinking she was weird, too absorbed in the book titles.

He slowly lowered himself back down, but he wasn't fully able to return his attention to his work. Now that his arousal had been piqued, he could smell that lilac scent she wore, his cock could not go down again quick enough.

He couldn't bring his eyes down to the page for more than a second. He kept finding his gaze on her, the little way she tossed her hair out of her face to peer closer to the glass of a cabinet.

As he watched in the reflection of a glass cabinet. There was that look she had again, the fox hunting a rabbit. His heart pounded in his chest. He cleared his throat, snagging her attention away from some centuries old urn. "Anything look like it'll help?"

She crossed her arms over her chest, turning to face him, and he couldn't help but notice the way it pushed her breasts together.

The mere sight made his cock twitch in an enthusiasm his nerves did not share.

She sort of winced then, her shoulders stiffening. She gave herself a little shake and sat on the edge of his desk. "Not that I can tell. I think the best bet is to find the book with the ritual we used and work backwards."

"It probably wouldn't be in here."

He watched the way she twisted in her seat, crossing one leg over the other daintily, giving her hips a little rock, and nearly gasped as he felt a matching squeeze of sensation, the little flare of pleasure it gave her to squeeze her thighs together. The only way it could have felt better was if it was around his cock.

"What are you doing?" He gritted his teeth to hold back a groan. She was up to something, that much he could see now. All her little mannerisms, her little noises, were going to be his undoing.

She played the part of innocence. "What do you mean?"

Experimentally, his hand went to his cock beneath the desk, and gave it a small tug.

Astrid went rigid, a whimper escaping her tightly pressed lips.

"You know I can feel you doing that, right?"

"Which begs the question," she said, but with the pointed look she gave him, she didn't even have to ask or think it. She knew he was rock hard over her.

Astrid's eyes widened.

Ok, maybe she hadn't realized that.

"I heard you dreaming about me naked," she whispered, eyes alight with curiosity and her hunt. "But I want to know *why*."

Five

COCKED AND CORNERED

In so many of the months they had lived together, Astrid hadn't felt like she truly had the upper hand once.

Now she had him.

"I can feel you thinking, 'don't think about it' on a nonstop loop. You could have just thought it and then I probably wouldn't have cared that much," she shrugged, enjoying the feeling. "But now I'm extra curious."

Astrid held Jason's stare, pausing a moment to fully take him in— the lean stature he had even sitting down, the length of his fingers, the way he held himself. The gaunt, unimpressed look he always had turned heated.

She felt his hesitation intensify momentarily, before he mentally cast it aside.

He pushed his chair back, revealing his cock jutting from above the band in his sweatpants, hard and flushed with want, his hand curled around the base.

Her eyes widened. Even though it didn't answer anything new, somehow the sight of just how aroused he was from her walking around the room made all the little echoes of thoughts and sensations she'd been getting through their bond all the more real.

Her brow furrowed. "But you hate me."

But even as she said it, she thought of all the tense little moment's they'd shared the last few months, and wondered how many of them had similar explanations.

Her inquisitive eyes darted across him, from his face to his arousal. She hadn't realized her heavy breathing until she noticed how his chest rose and fell, that the same flush in his cheeks warmed hers.

"You get under my skin," Jason ground out, the frustration in his tone becoming dark with need. "You're always one step ahead of me, you're even in my dreams."

"I wasn't trying to–" she started to say, and cut herself off with a gasp, her back arching a little. He palmed his cock openly, and as she rolled her hips back against the desk in response.

Then his all too keen gaze went to her hips.

She could feel his surprise, how the last thing he expected was for her to lay further back on his desk, lifting her skirt and spreading her knees for him to see her dripping cunt.

She was always willing to up the ante with him.

Jason slowed his strokes, neither of them able to hide the clear pleasure they were experiencing in reaction to each other's personal palming.

"Again," she whimpered, voice needy, her eyes on his cock as she drew her fingers between her folds, wetting them to stroke her clit.

He stroked faster, feeling the sensations of her delicious wet cunt around her fingers as surely as he felt his own hand, her breasts heaving with every thrust, reacting as if he was fucking her open. She lived for how her every movement affected him, one hand dipping into her shirt to play with a nipple, feeling his hungry eyes.

A new wave of arousal struck her, heating up her skin as she felt the echoes of his need for her, how powerful she felt draped across his desk, taking his fantasies into the palm of her hand and reinventing them into her own.

Then her knees twitched involuntarily together, eliciting a strangled gasp. Her release was already budding, tight and fluttery.

"No, I'm not going to come before you," she gritted her teeth, thrusting her slickened fingers into herself hard. Her pleasure streaked through him like a lightning bolt, echoing in a feedback loop.

Within moments he was spilling across his lap, groaning, her voice joining in, the sound of her pleasure intertwined with his as her climax unfurled, squeezing tighter, hotter, wetter, her pleasure riding his, ushering them to completion.

The pair of them were left gasping in the aftermath, their releases twisted together through their bond.

It was oddly quiet.

Six

Astrid held Jason's stare for an agonizingly long moment. She only broke it to toss her hair over her shoulder in that way of hers. It seemed to have the power to silence all of his thoughts.

If only she'd known that yesterday.

She glanced back at him, her brow furrowed. "You... can't hear my thoughts anymore?"

Jason blinked.

He watched as she removed her fingers from within herself, drying off the sticky sheen left on it with a corner of her skirt. Low in his stomach, his body, an ache to arouse, crying out against his spent weariness, to be alive with want again at the sight of her rosy, wet cunt, open and inviting.

Then she paused, apparently realizing she needed to air her thoughts for conversation now.

"I didn't expect that to be what resolved it, but I'm not complaining," she shrugged. She hopped off his desk, letting her skirt fall back over her legs like nothing at all had happened.

Jason nodded, and slid the band from his sweatpants over his cock again, the skin still over sensitive from his climax. More to add to the laundry.

It was a lot quieter now. Eerily.

"Oh, this was the book that had the ritual," she started to say, spotting one on his desk, when his hands came down on top of her own before she could open it.

Astrid held his gaze, clenching her teeth. "Hey, give it. I need to look up what went wrong."

"It's not your book, this is one of mine," Jason's face was an unimpressed mask. It had to be, because not once in the last few months had he ever conceded to her. Every bickering, every utterance, had to be responded to.

Except maybe everything that had just happened.

Astrid deflated a little. Even without hearing her thoughts, he knew she wanted to stare him down. He held her gaze until she let out a long suffering sigh, dropping her shoulders.

"Fine," she huffed.

His grip loosened imperceptibly at her perceived defeat, and that was all she needed to snatch the book under his hand away.

"HA," she cackled, her eyes alight with triumph. She turned away with a little twirl, and immediately began parsing through the pages.

Jason couldn't help but let out a little impressed laugh. Yeah, ok, she got him that time.

But things were settling back to normal a little too quickly. "Hey, can we stop and talk about this for a second?"

"No, we can't. Now that I've got some privacy in my head, I want to leave everything in that particular baggage until I've forgotten what we put away. And we only have tonight before the full moon is gone, if we're going to do the ritual again."

"Astrid, you can't still want to break the lease."

Jason stood, taking a step towards her– she stepped back. She started to turn away but encountered the bookcase, and he seized upon the chance.

He put his hand over hers again, not to trap a book this time, but to hold her.

"Look, you knew what I was thinking at any given moment before you ever started hearing my thoughts. No one's ever known me like that before," he said, hoping she could hear the honesty in his voice, now that she didn't have the benefit of his thoughts to confirm it.

Even without the bond, he felt her attention under his hand, her fingers flexing underneath his, the heat of his hand against her cold fingers. Now that he knew what it was like to be in her head, he could only imagine what she was thinking, chasing down any possible conclusions with her usual ferocity.

"I know you feel it too. Don't go."

He reached up to her face, brushing her hair out of her eyes. He could feel her fighting against her anxious tick.

He watched the little movements of her eyes, the tension in her mouth as she steadily flipped through one page after another. The renewed pink in her cheeks as her shoulders tightened, and then relaxed.

"Seeing as our ritual turns out to be a couple's therapy spell..." she started to say, her face becoming a much deeper red. "I don't actually have a lease breaking ritual for us to do."

His attention darted to the book, as she tried to peel stuck-together pages apart.

Then she placed her hand on his chest, a cautious foray into the sort of tender feelings they'd been too busy sniping at each other to have before. "Maybe this tower's big enough for the both of us."

He couldn't stop himself from grinning.

"Bookmark this page," Jason said, folding one of the corners down, then setting it carefully aside. Her hands were finding fistfuls of his shirt as he leaned her back against his desk.

"We'll need it again for tonight."

About the Author

Kate Prior is an illustrator by day, podcaster by night, and romance author in all the little between moments. She writes fluffy, steamy office romances featuring necromancers, orcs, and other creatures that go bump in the night.

You can find her most places as @bykateprior, or sign up for her newsletter at kate-prior.com.

Spell Mates

BY SERAFINA JAX

Always Lilith... Never Eve!

I've always known I wasn't enough in the eyes of my mother—the most powerful witch in all the southern states. My magic never behaved the way it's supposed to, like I'm missing that special ingredient to complete any spell. But what really takes the cauldron? My own blood torturing me.

Trying to force me to marry a mage twice my age, I never thought in a million years saying no would land me in Scorchwood Penitentiary, fighting for my life. Or that three complete strangers would be my salvation.

Of all the hexed-up things!

One

Eris

"Witch please!"

That's the last thing I remember saying to my mother before I woke up here, shackled to a cold, metal rack... and it smells like someone's over-cooked their dead man's fingers.

Pain grips my throat as I try to swallow. My mouth feels like the bottom of a dried-up cauldron. Squeezing my eyes shut, I replay the meeting my mother called before our coven and attempt to recall what she said for me to react the way I did. Testing the shackles, they too bite into my skin and I catch something out of the corner of my eye.

"What the hex!"

"I warned you when you were little, I wasn't someone you could trifle with, Eris." The astral form of my mother hovers in front of me.

Her ability to project her ghostly form across distances has always pissed me off, popping up in places I never expect to see her. Like the time I eluded her clutches and found my way to a Shamanic tattoo artist—yeah, I can't help but smirk, thinking about the magical ink he infused into my skin. Even better, she wasn't able to remove it.

Always Lilith—Never Eve... words to live by, but it cost me and more than the lock of hair the Sharman demanded in payment. It was pretty much the beginning of the end.

"Who..." The words get stuck in my throat as the collar around it tightens, nails digging into my flesh.

"Don't test me, child. Things can be worse than this, trust me." Her shimmering, transparent form hovers closer and I catch the twitch in her left eye; the one she gets when things are out of her control. "Comply with my decree and this can all end."

The shackles banding me to the rack constrict even further, the cold steel biting into my skin. Reaching deep inside, calling to my magic, it recoils, burrow into the depths of my soul. My mother's cackling laughter only confirms my suspicions about my location and everything that happened today comes flooding back.

"I'll give you kudos for trying," she nods at me, the corners of her mouth pulling up in twisted delight. "Even if you were a witch of significant power, which you're not, no one ever escapes."

Barbs and curses sit in my mouth like some spoiled brew, and her enjoyment of this situation only grows. She even has the nerve to swipe a tear from her cheek. Asteria McGregor is one of the most powerful witches in all of Scorchwood—probably in all the southern witch states, if I'm being honest. Doesn't mean I'm afraid of her... well, not usually. The fact she has me chained up in Scorchwood Penitentiary like some common miscreant gives me pause. I know my mother loves control... over everything. I never imagined defying her decree would land me here, though.

"So, the gravity of your precarious situation has finally sunk in; good. Perhaps now you understand your place in the coven."

If my mother were physically here right now, her right foot would be tapping up a storm and that twitch, well let's just say its presence mars her beauty and she knows it. Apparently, I'm the only witch who sets it off though and, in the past, it'd always been a warning to cool my hex. Right now, it's like a red broom to a familiar.

Straining at the collar, she watches on and I know she's wondering how far I'll push it. Scorchwood Pen is known for its torture devices and my mother had a hand in creating many of them, including the one around my neck. If I struggle much more, the nails tearing at my skin will sink in too deep to repair, even with magic, and my mother knows it.

"Eris! Cede to me. Marry Jareth and this can all end." Her astral form floats around the rack and the image of her pacing the length of our rather ostentatious covenstead fills me with a small measure of satisfaction.

Opening my mouth to speak, the collar tightens a fraction more and all that escapes is a whimpered squeak.

"No, Eris! Not this time. I refuse to listen to any more of your nonsensical, patriarchal bashing. Your father should have never indulged your behaviour, especially after I warned him that your magic wouldn't even come close to what we expected."

My father is the only one who ever understood me. Understood the way I feel inside. Indulging my behaviour, as my mother calls it, was his way of letting me explore what was missing from deep within me. He would sit with me in his great library for days as we researched why there was such a disconnect with my magic. His death broke me even further and whatever protections he placed over me died with him.

Nothing happened the way it should after his death and the doubts I had, still have to this day, eat away at me. My mother's adamance that finding me a suitable husband was the only way to save the McGregor Coven didn't truly hit home until this morning.

"He..." the pain is too much, and I clamp my mouth shut, holding the scream in like an unspoken curse.

"Enough, Eris. There is little time left to salvage this agreement. Jareth is the best match you could hope for." Pausing her floating in front of me, the collar around my throat loosens unexpectedly, cool air brushing over my skin. "You do not deserve a Mage of Jareth's level. In my opinion, you'll only bring down his standing, but the offer was made. Securing your seat at the table of Merlin will catapult Coven McGregor out of the darkness which has befallen it. And so you will do your duty as a daughter of Lilith, because Hecate knows you're good for nothing else."

And there it is, the last strand of Deadman's rope curling around my neck, squeezing the life from me more so than my mother's stupid torture collar. This has nothing to do with me and everything to do with my mother's machinations and desires. Well, this witch isn't having a bar of it, not now—not ever.

"Hex you, witch!"

Two

Eris

From the vague conversations I've been able to listen in on from the guards at my door, I've been out cold for almost two days. Not sure exactly what my mother did to me, but it packed a wallop. My head feels like I've been on a cauldron hop or taken some bad eye of newt. Snickers alert me to a guard lingering at my cell door, my skin crawling at his presence.

"What the hex do you want, Jocus." Pain flares through my already suffering mind as the guard curses me for all I'm worth, not that his words have any effect on me.

Jocus is an unflattering term used to describe people born with no magic, many of who work in the penitentiary. I can see why they work here though, it's an easy way for them to satiate their rage against the people they once called family. The witches of Scorchwood are some of the cruellest in all of witch kind—my mother is their head bitch… I mean witch.

"You think yourself so mighty," the guard mocks at my door as I swing my legs off the bed, the shackles having apparently been removed. "Look how far you have fallen, little witch."

"Let's get one thing straight from the start." I wave a hand nonchalantly in the air. "I am not and have never claimed to be mighty. In fact, you might say I am the very antitheses of that idea. My motto is—Hex the Patriarchy, either that or Save a broom, ride a warlock." The giggle I feel brewing dies quickly, my body thrashing in agony.

"You are our prisoner," the guard's sick voice cuts through the pain. "There is no escape from The Scorch, even *if* you were a powerful witch. What little magic you have recoils from my power."

To prove his point, the pain returns and the metallic tang of blood fills my mouth, my teeth clamping down on my tongue. Every muscle and even ones I didn't know I had, clench and spasm and my cheek slaps hard onto something cold. Desperation begins to take hold as my nails drag across the stone and I realise I'm on the floor.

"Had enough?" Malicious laughter is quickly followed by another belt of pain. "Oops, my finger slipped."

Breathing hard, the scent of wet earth and... ew, crap, fills my nose and I push up on shaky hands. I knew the Council of Elders gave the guards the ability to punish their prisoners at the touch of a proverbial button. I didn't realise how severe the punishment would be. Kneeling on the cobbled floor, the eyes of the guard watching my every move, makes my skin crawl.

"Creeper," I mutter, pushing to my feet, but only manage to stumble and smack my head on the wall, which brings another round of demented laughter. "I hope you get warts on your dick and it falls off!"

Resting my back against the wall, I scan my cell, which takes all of two seconds. Four walls, a door with three bars up high, too high for me to see out, even if I stood on my tippy toes. Rubbing at my head, I squint at the bars in my door. There's barely any light coming through them and the thought of going over to them to look out fills me with a dread I've never known. I know my mother needs control, like a wart loves a toad, but this is insane.

I'm not the most powerful witch in the world and for whatever reason, the disappointment it gives my mother has led to this. Staring up at the roof, my mouth pulls down in a grimace at the things growing there and I turn away.

"Why, for Hecate's sake, would you leave me, father?" His death was... unexpected and unexplained, and my life went to hell in a cauldron soon after.

"Looks like you've been permitted yard time, little bitch... I mean witch," comes the sickly voice of who I presume is a guard, but with my mother neck deep in this, I wouldn't be surprised if it was that snake of a familiar of hers transformed.

Cruel laughter echoes through the walls as the door swings open and a dappled ray of weak sunshine stretches across the cell towards me. Leftover magical flotsam dances across its length and I sweep my fingers through it, a small sense of peace settling over me.

"I'm surprised you didn't burst into flames," the voice sneers, and I swear I hear a twitch in his voice.

"Unless there's a stake out in this yard you speak of that you intend to tie me to and set alight, it's not gonna happen, jerkwad... I'm not a fucking vampire." I don't often use human curses, but I think in this instance it's warranted. Taking a chance, I shuffle towards the door, half expecting it to slam in my face. When it doesn't, I jump out of the cell like a banshee's on my ass.

Another door across from me creaks open, pale light streaming through, and I wonder what time it is. Blinking to adjust, the surrounding space illuminates and the realisation I am in the tower cells slams into me. The Tower juts into the sky and can be seen for miles. It's meant to hold the worst of the worst, those witches who have gone against the laws set down eons ago and yet I'm here—by myself, it would seem. I don't hear another soul and there are twelve other cells besides mine here.

Doubt creeps across my skin like a ghost in search of a host to inhabit and the thoughts I've had about my mother searching for power are blown out of the cauldron. She *is* the power and everything I thought I knew comes crumbling down around me like dried up mandrake.

"Oh, did the poor little witch work out just how... hexed she is?" There's way too much enjoyment in his tone and I spin around, trying to find exactly where his voice is coming from, but I'm alone. There isn't another soul here and what started out as me defying my mother, well let's face it, because it's fun, is turning into a witch's worst nightmare.

Making a beeline for the open door, I step out into a dingy courtyard, a tree... more like a pale dead thing sticking out of the ground in the centre. I'm surrounded on all sides by grey stone walls rising into the sky and the pale sunlight that manages to creep over its edges barely illuminates the space.

The door slams behind me, the sound echoing off the walls in what can only be described as a death knell, and my heart lodges in my throat. Spinning back, it takes two quick steps to get back to it. The small viewing window, with three thick bars, doesn't afford me much of a view.

"Hey! Is anyone there?" Twisting from side to side, shadows move in the darkness and I squint to catch them. "Hellooo."

I may as well be a lump on a log for all the attention my yelling and banging is getting me. Pacing in the small courtyard, the distinct grunts of people... no, men, being forcibly moved on the other side of the walls have my nerves on edge. Bubbles pop and grow in my stomach and the magic I've tried to reach before surges through my veins uncontrolled.

"For Hecate's sake!" I cry to the sky, clouds of darkest pitch rolling in to cover the weak sunlight. "Mother, if this is your doing..."

The words die in my mouth as the scent of rose, apple and cardamom wrap around me. My magic swells and burns like a phoenix in flames, and I swear my skin is melting from my bones. Screams rip from my throat as I tear at my clothes, the world around me turning to inky ash. Hysterical laughter begins to build within me at the thought this is my mother's doing and my body thumps against the door of its own volition, as if desperate to get to something on the other side.

Red haze blurs my vision and I swear the sky above me mirrors my pain, bolts of fiery red, scorching across it.

"Lilith, embrace me," I manage to hiss out as a line from one of the many books I scoured with my father floats to the surface of my thoughts.

Sky above me. Earth below me. Fire within me.

Repeating the mantra over and over, hooded faces appear over me and the sensation of being dragged, my skin tearing and my mind ready to snap it's last wand, but when a male face comes into view and then two more, my heart soars. It sings. It clamours for their touch.

"Shh," the one closest to me kneels down, eyes like the malachite crystal I keep under my pillow for protection, stare down at me. "The pain will pass."

"Who..."

"Rowen," he answers my unformed question, the tenderness and relief on his face shattered as tortuous pain rips through all of us and I am left with nothing but an ache I cannot soothe.

Sky above me. Earth below me. Fire within me. Love surrounding me.

Three

Rowan

Cold seeps into my skin as I breathe for a moment, exhaling the bitter pain still traversing my body. I'd heard that Scorchwood Penitentiary had spells and devices to torture its inmates, but this is something else. It doesn't matter though because all the years of searching have finally come to an end. She's here, the one I've been longing for over more lifetimes than I care to remember.

"Rowan? Rowan!"

"Yes, Bastian, I'm fine." Bastian is the newest member of our trio, and when I say new, I mean we met almost ten years prior. Like me, though, he'd been searching for something missing in his life. Something he never quite understood.

"It's her, isn't it? It's really her." I envy Bas's enthusiasm, the joy he still finds in the simplest of things.

After waiting for so long to find her, I should mirror his happiness and find comfort in the fact that the one woman in all of time and space made for me and the men who have become like brothers is but one cell away. Bitterness and cynicism steal those parts of me away. The obstacles thrown at me have put me in a position not unlike this before. No, I cannot let those emotions swamp me... yet.

"Cullen?" Bastian calls across to the man whose rage rivals my bitterness. "Cul..."

"Yes, Bas! I'm fine, just fucking swell," Cullen growls, his footsteps echoing as he paces the tiny cell.

We've only known Bas for a decade, and for Cullen, it's been hard going. Most days, he can't cope with the sunshine he brings into our little trio. I can guarantee today is one of those days, especially in a place like this. Of the three of us, Cullen has suffered the most at both the hands of men and witches alike. The scars he carries both inside and out are a testament to their brutality, and this place is just another reminder of their cruelty.

"Rowan, what happened to her? Will she be okay?" Sitting up on the pathetic excuse for a bed, I'd honestly prefer a bed of nails. I rest my back against the wall, drawing one knee up.

"It's the bond, Bas." He still has trouble accepting the fact that I have lived more lifetimes than his mere seventy years on this rock, but when witches can live to be thousands of years old and even rise again after death, he shouldn't be shocked.

In the grand scheme of things, Bas is still a babe—probably explains his enthusiasm. He hasn't had eons to have his hopes driven into the dirt.

"Why didn't we react like her? I mean, she was beautiful and scary all at once and my heart swelled like the waves of the sea, but..."

"It's this place," Cullen grunts, his anger giving way to anguish. "It dampens our magic. She was outside, connected to the elements."

As if to emphasise his point, Mother Gaia releases a mighty roar, the walls of this prison shaking. The moment I stepped across the threshold of The Scorch, my magic reacted; clawing at the invisible restraints holding it back. The closer we got to her, though, the less control the restraints had. Even now, my magic howls within to be released, and a sudden cry from a cell across from me makes it thrash at my insides wildly.

Launching off the bed, I press my face to the small hole in the door, my fingers desperately clinging to the bars as her wails increase.

"What the fuck are they doing to her?" Cullen bellows, his face pressed into the bars of his cell across from me. "Fucking Jocus! Get away from her."

Wraith-like shadows flit to and fro and even though I can't see Bastian, I can sense his distress. We've only ever seen Bastian lose control once in the last decade and there wasn't much left of the tavern we were lying low in. If things weren't on a wand's edge, I'd let him explode, but he needs to keep his magic contained if we're to get out of here alive with the woman crying out across from us.

"Bas! Listen to my voice. Do you hear me?" Nothing. "Damn it, Bas, don't you go and jinx us all now!"

"If you fuck this up, Bas, not even the Goddess Divine will be able to protect you," Cullen yells across the space between our cells.

"I... I can't," he cries, pain evident in his tone.

"You can, Bas. I know it hurts, but it'll hurt a lot more if you lose control. Breathe, just like we practiced after Candlewick." Inhaling, I've never been much for prays or incantations, they've never served me well in the past. But now when we're so close, I'll take any help I can get.

Wrapping my fingers around the amulet they missed when searching me, I close my eyes and coax a small wisp of magic to my fingers.

"Elements of night. Elements of fire. I summon thee. Goddess Devine, protect the one of our heart."

Repeating the mantra, Cullen's bass tone joins in, our summoning prayer vibrating across the space. When a third voice joins ours, the triangle is complete and I release a heavy sigh. The very young are full of joy, but they're quick to anger and lose control. Bas's voice completes and seals the protection chant and her cries turn to whimpers and slowly fall silent as her tormentors flee from our power.

"Rowan..." Cullen calls across to me, his cell next to hers and I feel it the instant something changes. "Something's coming, Rowan."

"Not something," I frown, the power in the air unmistakable. "Someone."

"Who is it?" Bas's tone is tight, his magic still pushing the limits of his control.

"My mother," says a voice like the sweep of angelic wings and I have to push down the urges she invokes in me. The need to feel her body beneath me writhing in devotion.

"We're not afraid of her," Cullen barks, the bond between us strengthening the longer we're near her.

"You should be." I can't see her face, but I don't need to. In my heart I feel everything she does and even through all my doubt I push as much calm as I can through the bond to her.

"I'm Bastian but you can call me Bas," he introduces himself, his magic's wild storm ebbing. "And Cullen is next to you."

"That's awesome," she deadpans and a lick of sarcasm dances across my mind, the corner of my mouth kicking up in approval.

"And you are?" Bas persists, a sighed laugh escaping.

"Eris," comes her reply, and the surrounding air explodes with a darkness that claws at my soul.

"I told you things would not go easy if you refused my order." There, standing in the middle of our cells, is someone I hoped never to see again, and all the pain of my past clamps around my heart as I slink back into the shadows of my cell.

"Hard to accept anything when you've been out cold for days, *mother*," Eris quips, but I sense the edge of fear and it mirrors my own.

Reaching deep inside, I skirt around the suppression magic they've placed over The Scorch and reach for Cullen and Bas.

"*Listen and don't interrupt*," I instruct, knowing the longer I speak to them, the higher the risk of them discovering their suppression spells has a weakness. "*Cullen, you need to cause a distraction. I don't care what, just something huge. Bas... when I tell you, release your magic, let it free.*"

"*But...*" Bas's doubt is a burden I must bear and I can't be too angry at his inability to obey my command.

"*She is the one who will pay the biggest price, Bas. I can't explain it all now, but I will, I promise. Trust me, brother, please. We need to get her out of here. If we don't, none of us will see the sun rise again.*" I take his silence as acceptance and reach across the void to the woman across from us, Eris. To be so close to our fated mate and yet it feels like an entire world still separates us... *Goddess, if I ever meant anything to you, heed my call, I beseech thee.*

Four

Cullen

Fucking Rowan and his secrets! I don't know how the hell I trust him, but this bond, it's like an invisible string that's pulled us together since before I was born. In fact, I wouldn't be surprised if he knew Goddess Devine herself, he's that old.

Straining to see the woman standing outside Eris's cell, everything about her screams necromancy. Her aura pulses with darkness, a darkness I know only too well. But I'll be fucked if I let her mess with a woman who's haunted my dreams for centuries. A woman whose body I know like the back of my hand though I've never touched her. Goddess, the things I've done to her in my dreams and now, there's nothing but a wall between us. Well, a wall and a woman hell bent on who knows what.

"If it's a distraction you want, Rowan, then that's what you'll get." Pooling magic in my hand, whispering to it, snakes slither through the cracks of my cell as Eris's mother taunts her daughter.

"You leave me no choice," she shakes her head and her woeful attempt a lamentation makes my blood boil, but as the air fills with a magic, dark and malevolent, the ecstasy I felt at finding my one is wiped away in an instant.

"Over my dead body." Closing my eyes, I enter the mind of one of my wraith snakes, slithering into Eris's cell.

Her body contorts at unnatural angles, her eyes rolling into the back of her skull as the woman she warned was her mother chants malign words, the scent of rot and death filling the air.

"Who the fuck is this witch?" I call across to Rowan, who's suspiciously quiet. Eris's screams curdle my blood and watching her mother's words torture her into some form of submission raises the stakes. "Rowan! What the fuck is going on? Answer me, you son of a cyclops!"

"She's binding her powers." He reaches across the link, the strain in his tone making my own magic falter.

"Is that you, Rowan?" Eris's mother turns to his cell, continuing to chant her spell, and I know it's now or never.

"It's been some time, Asteria," Rowan answers, another one of his bloody secrets coming to life.

Forcing myself to ignore Eris's pain, a heart I declared as black, revolts; hammering in my chest. Calling to my creations, I layer them one over the other around Eris, cocooning her in my darkness. Every thrash of her body and tormented cry tests my resolve as the wall between us begins to crumble.

However they're suppressing our magic gains strength and a stabbing pain in the back of my head makes me see stars, but I can't stop—not now. Not this close. Caution went out of the cauldron the moment we allowed ourselves to be captured and dragged here, and I push my magic further. The door to my cell rattles and I force it to splinter, aiming the shards of wood in Asteria's direction.

"Do you think I don't see what you're doing?" she mocks, the shards bouncing off her as if they were merely wisps. "You are no match for me, Rowan. You and your band of outcasts. I cursed you once..."

"Clearly that didn't stick," Rowan taunts in return as I step out of my cell, shattering my brother's doors as well.

"I am not that young, naïve witch anymore." Whatever secrets Rowan hasn't told us pisses me off and judging by the look on Asteria's face as he steps into the light, murder isn't far from her thoughts.

Using Rowan as the distraction, I turn my wraith snakes into silken ribbons and wrap them tenderly around Eris, lifting her still thrashing body from the bed. "*Whatever you're going to get Bas to do, it needs to be now. Whoever this Asteria is, she's a few ingredients short of a spell.*"

Asteria's chanting ratchets up several decibels and the walls begin to fall down around us, the guards long gone, and Eris strains against me.

"Rowan!"

"Now, Bas!" he cries, Asteria's attention locked onto him.

The air pushes from my lungs as I'm tossed across the room, a wave of magic ripping the tower roof off. Icy spears of rain puncture my skin. Somehow I've managed to curl my body around Eris's, stormy eyes filled with terror staring up at me.

"Hey," is all I can manage, as her hand lands on my chest, her touch awakening every sordid fantasy I've had.

"For Hecate's sake," Rowan skids to a stop beside me, Bas limping in next to him. "Put that damn thing away before she goes running for the hills!"

Glancing down between us, my clothes are nothing but tatters and my cock, hard and ready, pokes into the side of her leg. "Sorry 'bout that."

"I don't know who you all are, but my body feels like I got run over by a rogue broom and my little witch is ready to dance naked under the full moon. Could someone please tell me what the hex is going on?"

"Isn't it obvious?" Bas tilts his head to the side, but Eris shakes her head. "We're bound. Fated to be each other's from this day to our last. We are a circle, no beginning and no end."

Rowan offers out his hand to her, and we all watch her reaction. There's not an ounce of hesitation to be seen and the satisfied lilt to Rowan's mouth as her palm slides across his is worth all of this.

"Lilith told me you'd come one day, but I never believed her. I always thought I was destined to be alone."

"You'll never be alone again." I get to my feet and the three of us close in around her protectively. Within the blink of an eye, we're standing in a field, snow melting on Eris's cheeks.

"So, we're outcasts now, huh?" she sighs, the warmth of her breath heating my chilled body.

"We've always been outcasts," I smirk, unable to stop myself from running my nose along the column of her neck, inhaling her scent.

"Well, at least I won't be an outcast alone."

About the Author

Serafina Jax lives in Australia, home to the mysteriously dangerous drop bears, and the secretive Yowie. And where the term '*yeah, nah*' is a perfectly acceptable answer to most questions. Summers are her least favourite time of the year, as temperatures get hotter than Satan's ass.

Writing has always been her secret passion, and she has found inspiration in the *classics;* Star Wars—or anything star related in the title. Harry Potter—no, she's not Gryffindor. Hunger Games—team Gale all the way. And her favourite Christmas movie—Die Hard.

To find out what shenanigans Serafina is up to next and all the gossip on her upcoming works, you can stalk her in all these places.

https://linktr.ee/SerafinaJax

As You Witch

BY LILY KINDALL

Yes. A pleasing word. An agreement, a promise, a blessing… and a curse.

Full time witch and beauty waxer, Durga, discovers this when she meets Luan. A professional model, he's tall, gorgeous, and totally into her. He's also cursed to agree to whatever anyone asks of him. Sparks erupt, but "yes" isn't music to Durga's ears when she knows Luan can't say no.

Luan knows magic is the stuff of con artists. But he can't deny he's in over his head where Durga is concerned. Is he really powerless to say no? Or does he just not want to?

One

"I am *not* overreacting!"

In direct contradiction to Durga's claim, glass shattered on the counter as a jar of incense caught fire under pressure from her powers. Sandalwood smoke billowed outward, choking her, and making her eyes water.

Great. In addition to "not overreacting" about my sisters' stupidity, I'm talking to myself and breaking things.

Durga yanked a broom out of her closet and glared at her iPad, where she'd talked to them only moments before. *I'm not the only one who cares Alma had the guts to kick us out of our pack. Why couldn't they be here to confront her with me?* Tiny red-gold sparks ignited above her head like a firecracker halo and she struggled to rein in her anger and energies that threatened to set off her smoke alarm.

Again.

She waved her hand impatiently, causing the smoke to circle and gather, mentally directing it out a window to linger under her illuminated *Waxing Moon of Austin* sign that advertised her dual witch and hard wax services.

Seeking calm, Durga focused on the sweeping motion of the broom. But that attempt quickly faded as the clinking of her bamboo chimes preceded a customer and a frisson of awareness on the back of her neck. A whisper of power clung to the newcomer like a thin veil as he moved around her showroom.

She tightened her grip on the broom as the feeling passed. *I'm getting jumpy.*

She closed her eyes and focused on her breathing. His footsteps stopped and she thought she felt the stirring again, but like the incense dissipating from her jar, it evaporated the instant she reached for it.

Durga watched her customer browse with his back to her. A tall man with broad shoulders, wearing a black leather jacket and blue jeans wandered among her rose quartz and calcite, running his fingers over the smooth crystals. Carefully, Durga reached out to the stones with her senses, seeking their reaction to him.

Nothing. He was one hundred percent human.

Stop being paranoid.

Plastering on a smile, she approached him. “Can I help you?”

He turned around, and Durga’s breath caught.

No one should be that sexy without some sort of warning label. Clean-shaven with russet brown skin, closely-cropped thick black hair, a strong jaw, and deep umber eyes, he exuded sexual prowess. Full lips drew into a smile, and when he arched his brows, a silver ring in one of them caught the light.

“Do you run this place?” He spoke with rolled r’s and a hint of nasal vowels.

Gods, an accent too? Krishna help me.

“Full-time witch and esthetician, at your service.” She brandished the broom as proof of her occupation, noticing how he bit his lip, almost as if he were holding back laughter. *Why come in if you don’t believe in witches?* “I’m Durga.”

“Luan. Pleasure to meet you.” Durga swallowed hard at the way he pronounced *pleasure*. “Do you take walk-ins?”

“Not usually, but I can make an exception.”

His smile grew, releasing butterflies through her entire body.

Get a grip! she chided, leading him to her back room. Behind her, Luan rustled fabric as he removed his jacket. Just thinking about the opportunity to use her magic on him had her breath speeding up.

“So, tell me, Luan, what do you...” Her words faded away, and her jaw dropped when she turned around.

Luan stood shirtless, full set of six-pack abs and broad chest on display.

Durga reached out a hand to his chest, then caught herself, snatching it back. “What... just what kind of magic did you say you need?”

He laughed, shoulders shaking with the hearty sound. “I’m not here for hocus pocus. I need a wax.” He took the hand she’d pulled away and put it on his chest, letting the tiny hairs there tickle her fingertips. He winked. “But you can cast a spell on me any time.”

Durga bit back a moan at the firm muscles under her fingers. “Is that so?”

A shadow flitted over his eyes, but he smiled broadly.

There!

As he nodded, she caught the sensation that had eluded her when he'd first walked in.

Shit.

Two

"Absolutely." Luan's entire body sizzled in Durga's presence. Anything she wanted, he would make happen.

And she wanted *him*.

He turned up the charm, stepping closer so she could feel more of his toned physique. He bit his lip again, holding her gaze. Thick ebony hair, smooth skin, and toned legs that extended for miles out of her short black skirt. *Hell yes.*

"Show me what you got, *gata*."

Her smile faltered for a fraction of a second, but she recovered quickly. "Gata?"

"Mm," he acknowledged. "It means 'beautiful' in my language. Did I offend you?"

"Just surprised. Is that what you use on all the girls?"

"Of course."

She actually snorted. "I'll try not to be too insulted. Next time, don't admit to recycling lines."

Luan frowned. *I didn't.* Despite how sexy most women found his Brazilian accent, he never used Portuguese to compliment them. That felt too close to home.

I just need a wax, not to flirt outside of work. He licked his lips. *Even with a woman as sexy as her.*

Durga furrowed her brows and shifted her hand to sit over his heart, which was pounding. He took a deep breath, trying to get himself back under control.

"Luan? Are you okay?"

"Fine." No, that wasn't right. He felt like someone had stuffed cotton so deep into one ear he could reach it from the other.

"Can I get you something? Tea?"

"Yes, please."

He swallowed thickly as the cottony feeling built into a jackhammer behind his eyes. *I hate tea*.

The edges of his vision dimmed until he could only see Durga's eyes. Like two pools of melted tiger's eye, deep brown swirled with gold. He was falling forward into their depths, and he could swear her pupils slitted like a cat's.

"Luan." Durga's voice sounded muffled and distant. "Don't close your eyes. Come on, look at me."

Luan complied reluctantly. Her words came out in slow motion.

"Are... you... o... kay...?"

He opened his mouth to tell her *no*, but couldn't make his mouth form the word. All that came out was a moan.

Durga removed her hand, and Luan slumped forward. The world spun, and when he opened his eyes again, he was laying on her waxing table, gazing up at the ceiling.

She tossed something onto the counter and it rolled to the center, spinning on its uneven axis before stopping. A dull tiger's eye stone, roughly the size of a 50 centavos coin. Luan gulped. The patterns of swirls in the pebble were *identical* to what he'd seen in Durga's eyes.

"What–" Luan tried to swallow through the cotton that had moved to his mouth and throat. "What did you do to me?"

She stiffened but didn't turn around. "It's what I *couldn't* do that you should be worried about. Do you have any... Crap. I *really* don't need this."

"You don't need *what*? What the hell is going on?" Adrenaline flared with his anger, and he shot upright before his body was ready. Durga's cool hands on his shoulders kept him from pitching forward.

"Someone cursed you." Her voice was deadly calm as she held him and Luan shuddered. "And the fact that I couldn't pull it off you just now means they aren't fucking around."

❧

Luan blinked several times. How long had he been out? And why was he clutching Durga's broom like a hockey stick?

"I hate the cold," he said, repeating the last thing he remembered telling her. "You couldn't have asked me to do something besides try out for an ice hockey team? Strip naked or something?"

"You're joking." Durga gaped at him. "Did you not get what I said about the Yes Curse? Damnit, don't answer that. You'll agree no matter what."

She touched his bare chest, and warmth spread from the contact. Despite the heat, he shivered. An image of her sliding her hand down the muscles of his abs and lower still slipped into his mind.

"What are you doing?"

"Clearing your head."

Oh no, you're not. He glanced pointedly down at her hand, now *glowing* red-orange. "It feels like you're trying to set me on fire."

Durga pursed her lips. "The strength of the Yes Curse ebbs and flows based on when you've been asked a question. You wanted to agree to my request. I'm stopping that by speeding it through your system. Don't worry. I have excellent control."

"*Foda-se essa merda.*" The Brazilian swear rolled off his tongue before he could stop it. "How are you doing any of this?"

"I told you. I'm a witch."

"No, *gata*. Where I come from, people who practice *Macumba* dig pits on the beach and fill them with cigarettes and popcorn. Here, witches do fake palm readings and tell me I'll meet my soulmate the next time I drop off my dry cleaning. *This* is something else entirely." Luan wiped his brow, trying to regain control of his situation.

Who am I kidding? That's the definition of this bullshit curse. I have zero *control.*

Might as well go all-in. If *he* were the one seducing *her* at least he'd know what he was headed into.

He smiled with a provocative glint. "Are you going to make me your slave?"

"You're seriously flirting with me? Crap, don't answer that!" Her hand warmed again and his head swam. "Luan, you can't consent to me because you're physically incapable of refusing me. I'm not asking you *anything*."

Her rejection confused him, but he pressed forward, determined to gain back *some* control. "Relax," he reassured her in a silky voice. "I'm a model. I take my clothes off all the time."

"We're not paying in trade."

"Why not? I can't say no to anything you ask. Might as well have some fun with it, right?"

"No."

She was serious.

Luan's throat tightened. Few people ever really let him say no. Most wanted him to flirt *harder*. *Make love to the camera.* Even other models pressured him to share shoots with them or date them, turning aggressive when he declined. One woman had even lost him a few bookings after he'd turned down her advances four times in a row.

Not Durga. She was asking him to back off.

To protect him.

"Lay down."

Her voice caught him off guard, and he tensed, fear sending icy tendrils through his muscles. He forced the sensations aside, putting on his sexiest pout. "You could just ask me, you know," he reminded her huskily.

Durga's eyes flashed. "Down, boy. If you're nervous, say so. I don't like the implication that I'm going to take advantage of you."

"Ouch, *gata*." Luan pouted. "That's not what I meant."

"You really need to stop calling me that."

Luan sighed, toning down his teasing. "Why don't you want to be flirted with?"

"I never said that. I love flirting. But I don't want it when the other person has no choice." She ran her fingers gently through his hair. "You're more than your exquisite hotness, you know."

"Exquisite hotness, huh? So, you do think I'm handsome?" Luan laughed as color rose in her cheeks.

"Maybe."

He'd take it. The remaining tension drained from his muscles, the ice melting into a cool puddle in the face of Durga's genuine concern. She really would protect him. He cleared his throat. "Thanks. Really. But what's the point of all this? You said yourself you couldn't do anything about it."

Her eyes met his and she smiled. Despite his earlier calm, Luan gulped at the sight, simultaneously reassuring and terrifying.

"I said I couldn't pull it off you before. But there are other options for getting rid of a curse."

Three

"I'm going to trace your curse. I can't break it for you, but I can find out who cast it." Durga stood next to the table. "Once we have that, we'll pay them a visit and convince them to remove it."

"And how do we do that?"

"I'll have a chat with them." Durga cracked her knuckles, letting a few sparks of energy fly off her fingertips. "I can be *very* convincing."

Luan nodded, but paled visibly. Little tremors ran through his body and she winced at the sight. Her little show had been meant to reassure, not terrify, him. Durga took his hand in hers, steadfastly ignoring the rising heat at the touch of his skin.

Luan didn't ignore it, though. A knowing smile spread across his face, and he squeezed her hand as she let go.

"These are smoky quartz." She positioned a chunk about the size of her fist by either side of his head. "They'll ground me while I work. And amplify the energy of this one." She held up a smooth blue-green stone with black veins.

"And that is?"

"Labradorite. I need something stronger than the tiger's eye to trace your curse."

She placed it in the center of his chest and goosebumps erupted on his skin.

"You're making me cold on purpose," he accused with a light laugh.

She offered a self-deprecating grin. "It was in a basket on the floor. Sorry."

Luan pouted again. "Promise to warm me up?"

"Ask me when we're done." Her smile faded. "This won't hurt, but it isn't going to feel great."

His deep brown eyes met hers, and his silence spoke volumes: *I trust you.*

Durga nodded. "Close your eyes."

Luan did as she asked, but his breathing sped up, tremors quaking throughout his body.

"Relax."

A laugh burst from him. "I'm half-naked on a stranger's table, waiting for her to go on tour in my soul for a curse that makes me say yes to anything I'm asked to do. And you want me to *chill*?"

Durga's movements faltered, the total lack of flirtation catching her off guard. A tiny crack had formed in Luan's façade and she wanted – needed – to honor that.

She leaned forward and began massaging him slowly. Her hands warmed as she called on her energy and sent it slowly into Luan, pouring it like warm honey through his limbs. He froze for a fraction of a second before relaxing as he grew accustomed to the feeling.

Opening her senses, she pressed more power through him. She could feel each of his muscles as though they were her own and she sucked in a breath, her hands roaming slowly over his torso. He moaned and grabbed her hands in his own and Durga paused, waiting for permission to continue.

Wordlessly, Luan moved his hand with hers, and Durga understood his unspoken request to resume. Together they eased tension from his shoulders, chest, and stomach, their movements synchronous and sinuous.

Massaging Luan while he held her hand and guided her to what he liked was more intimate than she could've expected. She wished they could stay like this, as man and woman, rather than human and witch.

"Durga."

She shivered at the sound of her name on his tongue.

Slowly, she laced the fingers of her right hand through his left. "Let go if you need me to stop."

He nodded. She lifted his other hand and placed it in the center of her chest before resting her left hand on his chest, completing the circle of energy between them.

Durga gasped as the connection took hold. Pure electric heat roared through her, lighting up her nerve endings with potent awareness. Arousal pulsed through the link, and it was all she could do to keep from panting. Under her hand, Luan groaned, the rich sound vibrating against her fingers.

"Luan," she breathed. She needed to know he was comfortable continuing, but didn't know if she would get an honest answer.

She began to pull away, but his hand tightened in her shirt, telling her without words that he understood. That he was okay.

She opened the connection further and moaned aloud at the feel of him. His back arched off the table, a picture bursting on her mind of him doing that again.

With her on top of him.

Was that her thought or his?

It didn't matter. She needed to focus.

Closing her eyes, Durga saw him through her lids as a glowing entity. "Luan," she purred, pouring desire into her words to strengthen the effects of the curse. "Would you take an ice bath with me?"

A dark shadow passed over his form, and Durga pounced, mentally diving into the tangled mass of power.

"Just say when." His answer, the timbre of his voice wrapped her in their embrace, promising to fulfill all her erotic fantasies. She had to fight to hold her concentration.

With unerring precision, she pulled apart the different threads of the curse, sifting through its attachments to Luan, seeking the core underneath. It came into view, pulsing with its own powerful life force.

No. It couldn't be...

"Durga." Luan whispered her name, half-plea. "How deep are you?"

Durga whimpered, uncertain if the raw need in his voice had been intended or not. "Luan," she breathed. "Do you want me to stop?" As soon as the words were out, she froze, realizing her mistake.

"Yes," he answered. His hand tightened on her shirt, and the world tilted under her.

Luan released her, the circle broke, her consciousness toppling back into her body. She struggled to regain her equilibrium, breathing heavily. It didn't even feel like she was standing anymore.

An uncomfortable lump in her chest and a soft thumping at her ear caught her attention. Durga stiffened, realizing she was hearing Luan's *heartbeat*. She was lying on him, straddling his waist, with the labradorite stone sandwiched unpleasantly between them.

She tilted her head to look at him. His head was back, and he was breathing heavily, the rise and fall of his chest making her undulate on top of him.

"Luan?"

He met her gaze, humor glinting in the umber depths of his eyes. His hands slipped to her hips. "I didn't want you to stop."

Luan stood next to Durga in the Warehouse District, holding her hand. He was now fully prepared to accept her abilities were real and though he was still terrified of what she could do, he wasn't afraid of *her*. He knew she'd never hurt him. And after what they'd shared when she searched for the origin of his curse, he wanted *more* of her.

Thinking about the experience instantly had his body hard and ready. It was all he could do not to drag her into the shadows and beg her to use the curse on him any and all ways she chose.

Unfortunately, Durga's attention was solely focused on the door to the building in front of them. She seemed... nervous.

He squeezed her hand and she startled, as though she'd forgotten he was there. "You've done a lot for me already," he told her quietly. "If there's a reason you can't go in–"

She shook her head. "I'm not leaving you like this. One thing, though." Her brown eyes practically glowed in the dim light. "Let me do the talking."

Luan nodded. "Sure, *gata* – Sorry, Durga."

Her eyes flashed again, but she nodded. "Follow me."

Inside, rave music pounded in time with blinking blue and white lights. People moved sensually against each other on the dance floor while others reclined at a bar with glasses of brightly colored liquids. Durga led them unerringly through the crowd to an unmarked black door. The moment she reached for the handle, a blonde appeared at her side. Barely five feet tall, she seemed to have materialized out of nowhere.

Durga addressed her without turning her head. "I'm not here for a fight. I just want to talk."

"You're not welcome here." She gave Luan a once-over, tilting her head back to scrunch her face up at him in disgust. "Especially not with your little human."

A chill raced down Luan's spine. The fact that she'd referred to him as *human* was bad enough. That this pint-sized bouncer thought he was *little* somehow made it far, far worse. At his side, Durga actually *growled* at the other woman.

"Let me pass, Heli. I came empty-handed, but I'm prepared to leave with your hide."

A minute went by. Two. Finally, Heli let go of Durga's wrist and stepped back, palms up. "Don't say I didn't warn you."

Durga didn't bother answering. Instead, she yanked open the door, revealing a tiny elevator beyond. She tugged Luan with her and punched the only button on the gleaming metal wall, her new demeanor giving him pause. The door slid closed and Luan's limbs tingled with their descent.

❧

THEY EMERGED INTO AN UNDERGROUND CAVE. THAT WAS THE only way he could describe it. Electric lights illuminated cratered rock walls pocked with outcroppings and cracks, which extended so far into the distance, they disappeared into darkness.

"Alma!" Durga's powerful shout startled Luan, her voice echoing in the empty expanse. "You worthless, flea-infested scratch post! Get your ass out here!"

Slowly, footsteps pierced the stillness, and Luan did a double-take.

A stunning brunette woman with dark brown skin sauntered out from behind an enormous boulder on the very edge of the lit space. Model-thin and wearing a low-cut, skin-tight red dress, she looked like she'd just walked off a photo shoot. Something about her aristocratic features tickled Luan's memory, but he couldn't place it.

She laughed airily at Durga, tossing her hair over her shoulder, before becoming very serious. "Get out."

"You're an idiot, Alma. What the hell were you thinking, putting a Yes Curse on a human? You're lucky I found him first."

"*Lucky*?" Disgust dripped from her words. "Was I 'lucky' when you and your family sided with the hunters against us?"

"They would've killed us! We were trying to protect the pack–"

Alma waved her off. "We can handle them. As for your human here... He got what he deserved."

"What I *deserved*?!" Luan exploded. "I've never met you before!"

"Luan," Durga hissed at his side.

Alma's brown eyes pierced him. "You turned down my granddaughter, Luz, when she asked you out. You have no idea what it is to be *agreeable*, you stuck-up piece of shit. Well, now you know."

The air whooshed from Luan's lungs. *Luz.* She was behind this? "Luz needs to hear 'no' more often," he seethed. "Your *granddaughter* wouldn't leave me alone! She lost me jobs because I said no! I need to be more agreeable? Your granddaughter needs to be less spoiled!"

"Luan, let me handle this," Durga implored. Luan could tell he was missing something important and that he should probably listen to her. But he'd had enough.

"*What gives you the right*?" He shook with the force of his anger.

A soft hand on his forearm brought him back to himself and Luan turned to find Durga wide-eyed.

"You're actually kind of adorable," Alma purred. "I can see why Luz wanted to play with you. Let's have some fun, shall we?"

"No–!" Durga shouted as Alma turned her attention fully on him.

"Luan, is it?" Alma's voice washed over him, wrapping him in its embrace. His mind instantly cleared of everything but the goddess before him. He nodded, desperate to please her.

"Luan, listen to me..." A soothing voice near his shoulder penetrated the fog, and he blinked in confusion.

"He can't hear you, dear," the object of his affection spoke up. "Would you come here?"

Luan moved without thought. Someone grabbed his arm, but he ignored them, moving toward his goal.

"Would you like to kiss me?"

"More than anything." Luan meant every word from the depths of his soul.

"Luan!"

He hesitated at the familiar voice calling him again.

He shook it off and kept moving, marching toward the only person in the world who mattered. Alma. *My soul.*

Without warning, a cat the size and shape of an enormous panther sprinted past him, knocking him to the side with its muscular body. Luan froze. No! It was going to attack his beloved!

Just before the beast reached her, Alma crouched down, her body rapidly transforming into a similar cat, catching her attacker head-on. They toppled into a tangled mess of fur and roars, the sounds of scratches and thumps reverberating nauseatingly off the cavernous walls.

Luan stumbled forward as the curse released its grip. He turned, desperately seeking Durga, but he couldn't see her anywhere. Panic seized him.

Growling, the two predators broke apart, circling each other. The larger one with darker brown fur swiped at the smaller one, baring its teeth. The smaller one responded in kind before launching itself at the larger one again.

Their movements blurred, and when they stopped a second time, Luan could see the larger panther had its jaws locked around the neck of the smaller one. It thrashed for a few seconds before finally submitting, body going slack.

The victor let go and roared before rising on its hind legs... and *transforming into Durga*.

Luan blanched. Beside her, Alma returned to human form, sitting miserably with her legs tucked under her.

Both were covered in bloody scratches and scrapes. Luan stood perfectly still, rooted in place by sheer terror. Maybe if he didn't move, they couldn't see him.

But they were ignoring him.

"Take it off." Durga's tone left no room for arguments. "Now."

Alma grumbled, but lifted her hand, cupping it toward Luan. He was drawn forward, feet skidding in the dirt as he tried to hold himself in place. Dark black smoke evaporated off his body, sucked in her direction like an oppressive weight sliding off his muscles.

"Luan," Durga said, still not looking at him. "Do you want to sleep with Alma in a freezer tonight?"

"*Hell no*!" The response burst out before he could stop himself.

Nem fodendo! I can refuse something? He held his breath waiting for some magical rebound kick in the ass. But none came.

"Happy?" Alma demanded.

Durga smiled chillingly down at her. "Let's get one thing clear. I didn't kill you just now. For that, you removed the curse. In return for me not telling anyone about this little... scuffle, we'll talk later about my family's banishment."

"Sure, why not?" Alma snorted, but when Durga snapped her teeth, she cowered. "Okay, yes, fine! Just get out."

Durga walked toward the elevator, and Luan took a step back. "Let's go," she said as she passed him.

He couldn't agree fast enough.

On the street again, Durga tossed her head back, rolling her shoulders as though working out a kink. The street was unusually devoid of people, and they walked in silence without passing anyone. A chilly breeze blew and Durga shivered, the movement drawing Luan's attention fully to her.

She was a wreck.

Her black shirt was shredded, the material held together in places by mere strings. The holes in the material revealed deep gashes in her back and arms. A quick glance down confirmed more wounds on her legs were still oozing blood.

Caralho. She bled for me.

Without saying a word, Luan removed his leather jacket and draped it around her shoulders. Durga turned wide eyes to meet his, and his chest tightened as her golden-brown irises filled with regret.

"Sorry you had to see that."

He shrugged. "You got my curse off, and you look like someone decorated you with a pork claw. I owe you." He tried for joking, but the last words stuck in his throat. He cleared it and tried again. "Hey seriously. Do you need a hospital or something?"

She waved him off. "Nah. These'll close up by the time I get home."

They stopped at the street corner, standing in silence under a light from one of the buildings. Both seemed at a loss for words. He couldn't tear his eyes from the horrible slash marks on her soft skin and the deep, sinister shadows they formed under the light.

With a soft sigh, she slid his jacked off and held it out to him. "Well. Good luck, Luan."

She turned to leave and Luan caught her hand. "Wait!"

She lifted an eyebrow in question.

He blew out a breath, releasing some of the tension that had built in him since he'd seen her transform.

"Thank you, *ga - merda!* No wonder you didn't like when I called you that!" He slapped his forehead, eyes wide with shocked realization. "You know what? Screw it. It suits you. You're beautiful and you're a... cat. You're a beautiful cat!" He grimaced. "That sounded much better in my head."

Durga started laughing, the sound drawing him in until they were both guffawing, tears rolling down their cheeks.

When they'd finally calmed down, Luan felt lighter than he had in weeks.

"Seriously, thank you." He smiled mischievously. "*Gata*. Can I call you that now that I know your little secret?"

"If it makes you happy."

"What makes me happy is complimenting a beautiful woman in my language. Not any woman, though," he clarified. "You, Durga. And all your magical witchiness." He paused, reconsidering. "Next time, though, let's go somewhere it doesn't apply to anyone else."

"You want a next time?" Durga gaped.

"Not really."

Durga's face crumpled in confused hurt.

Luan chuckled and drew her into his embrace. "Just wanted to prove to you I could say *no*. Go on, test me. Ask me anything."

She grinned evilly. "Can I put an ice cube down your pants?"

Luan sucked in a breath. "Never."

Durga slid her hands up his chest, wrapping her arms around his neck and fitting her body to his.

He grunted.

"Your turn," she whispered. "Ask me again."

"Will you warm me?"

Durga kissed him and one word filled his mind at the taste of her.

Yes.

About the Author

Lily is an author of contemporary paranormal romance with a hint of mystery. She is deeply passionate about travelling, cultures, languages, and the supernatural. She's lived in Italy, Egypt, and the weirdest place of all, Austin, TX, but she currently resides in the Northeast corner of the US, in an area with more horses than people.

When she's not writing or teaching world languages, Lily relaxes with a great book or movie, especially the original Star Wars trilogy and the MCU movies. Unless it's raining, in which case you'll have to follow her outside to enjoy the best weather there is!

Find out more about Lily's books and her upcoming Elemental Endirim series on her website www.lilykindall.com, and follow her into a world of romance, magic, and mystery for an unforgettable adventure!

The Britches of Addison's Mountie

BY CANDACE SAMS

A Mountie seeking a promotion wants to make a fantastic impression. He takes his uniform to the best seamstress in town only to discover his pants have been *hexed*. When you live in a society where magic is very real and its use is highly illegal, someone needs to suffer the consequences for foiling this cop's chances at improving his life. But who to blame? And, is blaming someone the right response when you've got your own magical secrets to hide?

One

I ***n an alternate reality***
Where magic is real but banned!

"THIS HAS TO BE DONE RIGHT AND BY FRIDAY AFTERNOON."

"Duncan McCloud, how many times have we altered uniforms for you?" Matilde Blackthorne asked as she tilted her head, awaiting an answer.

"Hundreds. But this is special. It's the gala you know. It's probably the second time I've ever worn the serge and, as your measurements show, I've changed since the last time I had it on." he told her, referring to the scarlet tunic and dark pants on the countertop. "A promotion could come from this."

"Oh? What kind of promotion?"

"Head of the *MTF* in this district. It's what I've been working for."

Matilde blinked as if she didn't know what he was talking about. "And what in the world is an *MTF*"

"*Magical Task Force*, of course!"

"I see. One would hardly think such a thing is necessary these days." Matilde rechecked the measurement notes she'd taken and nodded. "I promise, your uniform will be in excellent condition, tailored to the *nth* degree and in perfectly pristine order. In fact, I'll have everything done by Thursday. Since we've just taken your measurements, I can get started right away. For a man who has been our customer for years, I'll make a special effort. Particularly if you'll be chasing down miscreant magical entities in the very near future."

"That would be outstanding."

"With so much at stake, you'll want a final fitting to make sure everything is in order. Come by at...shall we say four o'clock Thursday afternoon?"

"That'd be great," Duncan responded with a firm nod.

Matilde carefully gathered the clothing and put it all back in a special hanging suit carrier. "You'll be sure to give your boots a heavy polish."

"Absolutely. I'll see to that myself."

"Grand then. We'll see you on Thursday. If there are any minor tweaks to the uniform, we'll make them then and you can take your uniform with you."

"You're the best, Matilde."

Matilde present a bright smile. "Thank you, kind sir."

He glanced toward the back of the sewing shop. "Uh, where's Addison?"

"Looking for sequins for ball gowns. Apparently, everyone who is anyone is going to this season's first gala and we've simply been inundated."

"That makes it even more extraordinary that you'd rush the job. Like I said, I didn't know I'd even be invited to this thing but my supervisor gave me a heads up only this morning. I took off work early to bring my uniform to the best tailor in Cauldron City."

"Do put in a good word with your comrades. We can always use the extra business. Rushed or not. New business is always welcome."

"I'll do that. And thanks so much again," he gaily added as he turned and made his way out of the shop.

❧

ADDISON TOOK THE FINAL BOX FROM THE BACK OF HER VAN AND scooted it through the back door, into the main sewing room of the shop. Luckily, she'd been able to find everything on her list, plus a few extras for those who always put off fittings and repairs until the last minute.

Every year, during social season, this same thing happened. It wasn't as if folks didn't know when the party season started but, like people do, they put off what needed to be done until someone *else* had to make up for the shortage in time. That someone else was her and her aunt. Still, business was very good and she wasn't going to complain about a few late nights.

"Ah, there you are."

Addison smiled at her aunt, always wondering how a woman of fifty-seven years manage to look more like thirty. Matilde Blackthorne didn't have a gray hair and her svelte figure still had men turning their heads when she walked down a street.

"What's that?" Addison asked as she glanced at the clearly marked Royal Canadian Mounted Police garment bag her aunt was carrying. The officers who came in with those bags simply referred to the scarlet tunics they sometimes if rarely wore as nothing more than *the serge*. "Not another uniform to repair is it?"

"It is, as it happens?" Matilde carefully hung the garment bag on the *expeditious requests* rack and grinned. "This time, it's for Duncan."

"Seriously? He's going to the gala?"

"Mmmm. Apparently so."

Addie, as she was usually called, sighed heavily and began opening her boxes to put their contents on shelves. "So, I guess he'll be taking someone?"

"He didn't say. I didn't ask."

"Yeah. It's none of our business. I was just wondering," Addie remarked as kept putting stock on the shelves.

"He came in to be fitted this afternoon. Apparently, he only just got the invitation. There might be a promotion in it for him."

Addie stopped and turned toward her aunt again. "Oh, I hope so. He deserves it. He's such a nice person."

"Really? Is that so? And we all know nice people are promoted as District Head of the *MTF*, don't we?"

Addie backed against a counter and stared into the distance. "He...he's being promoted? To *that*?"

"He thinks so, dear. He believes that's why he was invited to the gala in the first place. Clearly, there must be something to his assumption. Not every Mountie in Cauldron City will be going to one of the biggest affairs of the entire year. Only the very most powerful people end up at such functions. And, up until now, Sergeant Duncan McCloud was *not* on anyone's list of influencers."

"But the *MTF*," Addie whispered. "H-He didn't seem the type."

Matilde sighed heavily and shook her head. "My girl, I told you not to be so fascinated by that man. Good looks and stoic bearing notwithstanding, he'll do whatever it takes to succeed. If we've learned anything at all about him over the years, we know that much. And...not to sound terribly cruel... but if he wanted to notice you, don't you think he would have by now?"

Addie didn't respond.

"It's a very good thing he didn't. The gods and goddesses have been looking out for you in that respect," Matilde continued. "You could have easily ended up the partner of a man who'd find a way to throw you in jail if he knew what and who you really were. Men like him don't mix with people like us. Especially now that we know where his ambitions lie."

"I just never though he was that close-minded."

"Addison, you own and run a seamstress shop. We've deliberately made ourselves as innocuous as possible. All so that we can be who we are without getting on anyone's radar. Because of people like him, there are very few of us left—"

'That's not true! Nobody is burning us anymore. They just fine us and lock us in jail if we get out of line."

"And who decides what that is? People like *him*?"

"Aunt Matilde, in the last century witches did plenty of harm. Not all, but *some* did. And their actions are why we hide ourselves now. Ordinary people are afraid of us. Our own Great Uncle Rupert tried to put a spell on the Premier in Ottawa. He turned the man into an outhouse bench before being caught and forced to undo that hex."

"He didn't mean any harm. He was only trying to show the Canadian government what could happen if witches weren't given the same rights as everyone else," Matilde muttered.

Addison slowly grinned. "It *was* funny!"

Matilde chuckled in response. "Yes. And he was willing to spend a year in jail for that prank. But, it was extreme and did do a great deal of harm to all of us."

"There are good and bad aspects to everyone. Maybe the law will see it that way someday. I mean, they leave us alone as long as we register."

"But we *haven't*. You should remember that the next time a well over six foot Grecian profile Mountie walks into our shop and captures your attention, my girl."

"I guess you're right. He's been coming in here for years and never notices me," Addie agreed. "The gods and goddesses have been protecting me against that kind of attraction."

"Count on it. Now, let's get sewing. We've tons of work ahead of us."

Two

Matilde watched as Addison turned off the lights and head upstairs for the evening.

The work was done save for one order. And she had assured Addie that this one order would and must be hers to finish.

Her own apartment was at the west end of the building, Addison's was on the east end. As good as business was, it was better that they owned their own establishment outright and made the entire upper floor into living quarters. This saved on rent. Still, taxes had to be paid and bills for new materials and equipment added up.

With that in mind, she picked up Sergeant Duncan McCloud's uniform. Despite the need for expert craftwork, which she'd done a hundred times, it was the easiest to finish. Easier still because she would be using magic.

As she picked up a needle and thread, intending to make these very intricate first seams with stiches that would mark the way for the machine sewing, it occurred to her that here was a chance to do something for witches everywhere.

For centuries, witches had been hiding from those who would hunt them down, never discerning the good from the bad. If one witch did something wrong, every one that could be rounded up paid the price for that one practitioner's indiscretion.

It wasn't fair and never had been. Nowadays, witches had to register so that they could be checked on and monitored. Like so many others, she and Addie had never put their names on any list, fearing what might eventually happen if they did. This was a situation not applying to all the other citizens of the world. Just witches.

"I shouldn't," she whispered to herself. "Duncan is a nice man. He never did anything to harm us." She shrugged. "Then again, I might keep some unknown practitioner of magic out of trouble if I do what my instincts tell me to." She glanced around knowing the silliness of that covert act as she committed it. Still, there was no sense taking any chances that Addison might see. Her niece would never speak to her again if she knew what was about to happen.

Duncan shouldn't have shared that information about being promoted to the Magical Task Force. Had she not known, she wouldn't have been compelled to do what she was about to do. Thus did she convince herself there was no responsibility on her part.

Matilde thought long and hard, then smiled to herself. She took a deep breath and made the commitment.

"With every stitch I hereby take, history must in time remake. For cruelties that were never addressed, let them now be openly assessed. The man who dons this uniform would be...the next to hunt with impunity. If tracking witches is his aim and harm befalls them by placing blame, let him be the one disgraced, let him be judged in an open place. Let others see him and know the truth, be not deceived by his beauty and youth. I ask all this with humility...to see justice done...So Mote It Be."

She began to stitch with great care.

When she was done, she went to the machine that would make the final alterations permanent.

Where he expected a fitting in which small changes would be made, the entire uniform would fit with such precision that no alterations would be needed. And maybe, in his coming humiliation, he'd never visit their shop again.

She'd seen the way he'd looked at Addison. And Addie wasn't immune to the man's godlike face and build.

The spell she'd cast was for the best. Duncan wouldn't be hurting any witches and any attraction between him and her beloved niece would be prevented.

Duncan looked himself over in the mirror. The fit was flawless. He'd picked up his uniform and, as he had on so many occasions, wondered how anyone sewed so well.

He'd known the uniform was without error when he'd tried it on at the *Stich In Time* shop.

Matilde Blackthorne had outdone herself. Sadly, as soon as Addison made an appearance, Matilde made Addie pick up the phones and take orders. As usual, he had little time to speak to the chocolate-tressed, blue-eyed beauty who, in every aspect, was as regal and lovely as any deity. The first time he'd seen Addison, he'd known she was special.

Sewing and business skills notwithstanding, Addie seemed kind to everyone she met, even under pressure as he'd seen her handle recalcitrant customers in many instances.

How many times could one man show up for shirt fitting or a uniform repair and *not* cause suspicion regarding his intentions?

But there was one problem. It was the issue that kept him from ever asking Addison out.

She wasn't like him. She didn't know what he was and he'd seen the results of mixing one life with another when the world wouldn't accept such a mix.

But that could all change tonight.

Tonight, he had a chance to get that promotion and, along with a supervisor who was more than willing to listen and make changes, he could ask Addison out and the laws would stipulate that discriminating for any reason would not be tolerated. Not on any side.

He actually began to think of a future with the tall goddess-like woman who ran a sewing shop and who had always been so kind to him. Addison was wonderful.

Of course, she could have asked him to go for a coffee. She hadn't. That would have concerned him more but that his own reticence must have put her off. She'd sensed his attraction but had not seen him do more than make polite conversation.

After tonight, she'd know the reason. The whole world would know things could be different. And better.

Twelve hours later, he stood in his bedroom and gazed at a totally different reflection than the happy countenance he'd viewed just that afternoon.

That magic had been used was apparent. That he'd been the victim of it was infuriating.

He knew who to blame and waited until dawn to finally change out of his uniform, taking great care to throw his britches in a bin, to be burned as soon as possible. He changed into a simple black t shirt, jeans, walking boots and a jacket. The confrontation he intended had no place in law enforcement.

When it was eight o'clock and that damnable shop opened, he was out the door of his home at breakneck speed, determined to confront and put right what had been done.

❧

ADDISON LIFTED HER CUP OF COFFEE AND PICKED UP A RECENTLY printed out list of customers to be billed. She almost spilled the hot beverage over the countertop when well over six feet of very muscular, military-looking if civilian dressed Mountie stormed into the shop, slamming the glass door open so wide that it almost broke off its hinges. The look on his handsome face was nothing less than murderous. His cobalt blue eyes almost glowed with fury. For the first time in her life, she felt the world was about to fall apart.

Duncan McCloud wouldn't have entered that way unless something very bad was about to happen. Clearly, something already had and he was out to rectify some serious matter.

"Where's your aunt?" he whispered in a voice so menacing as to command the attention of all the gods and goddesses.

"She's upstairs. I-I was letting her sleep in..."

"Then I'll deal with you *first*!"

"Gods of old, Duncan. What happened?"

"You're both unregistered witches, that's what happened."

She froze and stared.

"Did you think I wouldn't know after that stunt you pulled last night?"

"I-I don't know what you're talking about."

"Yes, you do!"

Addie stiffened. "Maybe you'd better leave."

He slowly nodded. "I can do that. And come back with a team from the Magical Enforcement Unit to make arrests!"

She shook her head. "No. Please...that's not necessary."

"What's all the ruckus?" Matilde bellowed as she walked into the counter area while pulling a robe tightly about her body.

"Duncan is angry," Addie simply claimed as she backed away from the counter.

Matilde lifted her chin. "Don't blame my niece. She had nothing to do with it. By now you're aware of the hex. It was mine and mine alone. But how did you even know magic was being used?"

Duncan put both hands on the counter and glared at the older woman. "Do you know what you did?"

"Unless I miss my guess, you had a very eventful evening."

Addison continued backing away until she was in a position to see both their faces and understand what in the world was happening. She had never been around people so angry and the force of it almost took her breath away. Her intuitive powers were augmented by the rage and made her feel as though she should do something. But what? And to whom? What was going on between her aunt and the man who'd just blurted out that he knew Matilde and she were witches; a man who could lock them away for not having registered their powers as the law required.

She waited to see what would happen before taking any action that might confirm or deny anything.

"You've never put your name on any registry. You aren't on any list. I checked," Duncan proclaimed. "You've made matters worse for yourselves by sewing some kind of incantation into my uniform. *Specifically*, my pants."

"I did," Matilde admitted.

Now Addison spoke up and moved toward the older woman. "*You did what*? Gods, time, and memory...Aunt Matilde, what have you done?"

"I acted. I put a hex into the pants he'd be wearing at last night's gala."

"Why would you do such a horrible thing?" Addie yelled.

"Because she didn't want me to be promoted as head of the Magical Task Force. Isn't that right, Matilde?" Duncan said as he moved closer to the older woman though the only thing keeping them apart now was a counter.

Addison saw, for the first time, how the counter she'd always deemed quite wide before now seemed like a picket fence next to the size of the man standing on the other side.

"Aunt Matilde! What were you thinking? Or were you thinking at all? We don't do such things. We've never used magic to harm anyone. *Never*."

"As powerful as the magic was, I couldn't stop what happened," Duncan explained. "And, as powerful as it was, it still missed the mark."

Matilde jerked her head in his direction. "What are you saying? What do you mean when you say you couldn't stop it? Of course you couldn't. You shouldn't have even known there was magic involved at all," she reiterated.

"First, I got the promotion. But not before putting on a show that will have every supervisor in the entire Province talking for the rest of my life! Second, I knew magic was being used because I'm a witch, too!"

Now, it was Addie's turn to stare in absolute amazement. But that was soon overcome by anger due to Matilde's behavior. First, she had to calm the man in front of her though her senses told her that, as raw as his anger was, he was getting it under control. Her powers of empathy began to sense more to the story that was only going to get bigger.

"Aside from you being a witch...what happened, Duncan. Tell me everything. Leave nothing out. My aunt and I will stay put and listen to every word you have to say." With those words uttered, Addie opened the counter barricade, walked to the front of the store and locked the doors so no early customers could get in. She turned on the closed sign and pulled the curtains shut to hide the showroom and the counter area. Whatever was going to be said, any response to it didn't need to be made public.

Duncan turned to her and she nodded for him to continue. He needed to be heard and her aunt needed to be shut off from commentary, at least for the time being. To make sure the older woman said nothing, Addie held up one palm as a gesture for Matilde to remain silent.

"I arrived at the gala with no problem. After I got there and the dancing started, that was when the shit hit the fan," Duncan explained. "I was sitting with my supervisor and her supervisor when the disc jockey put on a very popular tune that most of the kids listen to."

"What happened?" Addie prodded when he stopped to glare at Matilde.

"For some reason I couldn't explain, I jumped onto the tabletop and all two-hundred, fifty pounds of me got up in my superiors' faces. In my scarlet tunic, pants and boots, I made a spectacle of myself by twerking. And I mean *twerking*."

"On the tabletop?" Addie whispered.

"Right in their faces," he bit out. " No matter what I did, I couldn't stop. The entire assemblage got a great view. I am officially the laughing stock of the entire city and district." He paused. "But I am *also* the new District Supervisor of the Magical Task Force."

Matilde opened her mouth, but Addie loudly shushed her.

"Go on, Duncan," Addie quietly urged.

He took a deep breath, dragged both hands through his thick, military cut hair and began to pace.

Addison felt how he was trying to get himself under control but couldn't fault his anger. She would have throttled someone for doing such a thing to *her*. Witch or not.

To use magic to interfere with someone's life and livelihood in such a way was criminal indeed, but most certainly wrong on every other level.

Witches, the good ones, had one rule. They caused no harm. And harm was harm, the definition was not to be debated. Not ever.

"When the music stopped, I got off the table and walked to the outer foyer of the auditorium with what dignity I had left. My supervisor ran after me."

"And then?"

"She flatly told me that, up to that point, she'd had someone else in mind for the promotion. Her impression of me was that I was a good leader but a little..."

"What? Go on..."

"Uptight. A little too rigid in my thinking. The...*twerking*...actually made her consider me in a whole new light. She said she suddenly realized that, if I could make fun of myself and not take myself so seriously, that I had the qualities necessary for the job. She said there were already too many *'inflexible toads'* in her office. So, she changed her mind about giving me the position, shook my hand and told me that she'd never had so much fun in her life. She said that I'd certainly livened up what had been one of the most boring functions of her entire life."

"I-I don't understand," Matilde began but Addie shushed her again.

"As I've admitted, I am a witch. So is my supervisor, as it happens. But she didn't sense the magic being used or she'd have surely assumed I'd employed some hex to get my new position. But that's easy enough to explain, isn't it Matilde? You only meant for *me* to know what was going on and to be quite unable to control it! You made sure nobody else would get harmed which was the very least you could do, since you thought so little of me as to cast a damned spell in the first place!"

"I think I'm beginning to understand," Addie claimed, "though I'd have never known you were one of us, Duncan."

"I'd have told you if—"

"If we'd been registered as witches, you'd have known we weren't just normal folk," Addison finished on his behalf. "We're so good at hiding ourselves in this age that it's impossible to tell who is who anymore."

"*You? A witch*?" Matilde repeated in awed mumbles.

Addison turned to her aunt. "Some of us have some apologies to make, on a massive level. As for myself," she faced Duncan again, "I can only tell you how sorry this happened to you. I mean to make amends on behalf of my family and our ancestors."

Duncan took several deep breaths, then simply nodded. "There's more to explain. Best to make a thorough job of this, so there's no more misunderstanding, I need to tell you not to register at all. Not now."

Addison simply stared.

"I'm not just angry at Matilde, but at myself," he continued. "I'm every kind of coward, hypocrite and bigot though I'd have not thought those qualities were in my character. At least, not until now."

Addison shook her head in confusion. "Why would you say these things?"

"For the following reasons," he began as he lowered his voice by many decibels. "First, I've always hated that damned registry. Every good cop does. It's a violation of witches' rights. No part of the population should be singled out in such a way. That's why I can't, in good conscience, tell you to go put yourself on that damned list. I was put on the list as a baby and had no say in the matter. Second," he quickly continued, "I wouldn't ask you out, Addie, because I thought you were a regular mortal. As powerful as some of us are, we cannot detect another witch who doesn't want to be detected. Of course, you both know that. And, with all my airs and sanctimony on the subject, I didn't want to date a normal woman even though I work with them without any problem. When it comes to having a close relationship with someone, that seems to be a completely different story. Third, I wanted the promotion so that I'd be one of the very first RCMP officers to directly rebel against the laws now in place. That is to say, I and others holding similar positions, including most of the law enforcement officers in Canada and across North America, have been making agreements, through unions and other sources, not to hold whole witch communities accountable when one among them does something heinous with magic. If a normal human commits an assault, we don't arrest everyone in their family and the same standards should apply to witches. Regarding that, my hypocrisy comes in, in that I wanted the job badly enough that I didn't want to tell my supervisor that she hired me after witnessing the results of a hex! So, all in all, I'm not feeling very good about the lengths I'd go to, to get and keep a promotion and my absolute bigotry in not wanting to date what I believed to be a normal girl. So, there it is, I'm as bad as the rest of the population," he finished as he leaned against the counter and stared at the floor.

Matilde finally spoke up. "How could you and other police officers simply disregard national law?"

Addison held her breath while waiting for that answer.

"The objective was to simply treat witches as we do everyone else. Novel concept right?" He snorted. "The lawmakers wouldn't have any control over it, they'd have to consider doing away with, and purging, the witch registry altogether. If the cops won't enforce their idiocy, then the powers that be will have to repeal it. And it will work if we all stick together. We have poles from the public on our side, by massive numbers. At least most of the population isn't as deceitful as I seem to be."

Addison put one hand on his arm. "If it makes you feel any better, I might have gone out with you, thinking you were a regular human, but I'd have eventually let you walk out of my life rather than tell you I was a witch. There have been cases where mixed witch/human couples were highly discriminated against. By both sides."

"I know," he adamantly told her. "My uncle James is a witch. Forty years ago, he married the love of his life, Joan. She's a regular human. They were denied housing, fired from jobs, and eventually had to settle on a farm up north to get away from the hatred. That's why any bigotry from me is so wrong, egregious, and infantile. I, of all people, should know better! I didn't know I had all this insincere bile in me until lately. And I don't like it!"

"If you and I can see it in ourselves," Matilde softly told him, then we can begin to root it out. "I am so very, very sorry for what I've done, Duncan. I had no right to meddle in your life, even if it backfired. Which I fully understand now."

"What do you mean?" he asked.

"Basically, I worded the hex so that you'd get what you deserved. And you did. You got the job! With a bit of twerking thrown in."

He smiled. So did Matilde.

"Let's go upstairs and get some breakfast. Duncan, you look like you could use some fresh cinnamon buns."

"What I could use is some friends who won't judge me for all the faults I have."

"If you have them so do we all," Matilde claimed. "Now, let's go upstairs and talk some more. There won't be any customers this early after such a big social event. We can spare a little time for a long conversation."

One year later

With the witch registry having been officially banned and dropped, with all its members purged from that list for all time, folks began to get along better. If everyone saw each other as the same, it followed that people were not so quick to judge.

Bigotry still existed and always would in the world, but at least one very wrong issue had been addressed if not totally forgotten.

The law enforcers no longer punished whole covens, families, or communities for what one witch did wrong. Indeed, witches were policing their own populations so that no regular humans had a right to fall back on old abuses.

Addie gazed down at the white handfasting gown she was sewing and smiled.

In Autumn, she and Duncan would be forever united. Matilde had found a lovely spot out in the countryside where the forest would serve as a backdrop to their vows. A farmer had rented them a pasture for the festivities that would follow.

Since Duncan's family was a very large one, she and Matilde wouldn't be so alone any longer. Her own parents, having passed away in an auto accident when she was five, would be represented in spirit. As would all loved ones no longer present.

If there were happier lives, she'd seen none. If there was a more handsome, more delightful future spouse, she'd found none. And if hexes could cause such glorious circumstances, perhaps not all were so bad.

At least with no harm done.

So Mote It Be.

About the Author

After publishing over a hundred titles in the fantasy, science fiction, Gothic, paranormal, and action-adventure genres, **Candace Sams** has received more than thirty awards from various organizations, including five National Readers' Choice Awards. She is also a USA Today Bestselling Author. Her *Tales of The Order*^{TM} series, as well as several other works, have been vetted for movie options.

Candace loves the country life. She lives in a rural area of the US. A plethora of dogs and cats have adopted her. She loves to hear from readers and can be contacted through her website at

www.candacesams.com.

Or on Twitter @CandaceSams. Also find her on Facebook:

https://www.facebook.com/CandaceSamsAuthor/

and find her on Instagram https://www.instagram.com/candacesams5461/

The Witching Hour

BY TAYA RUNE

Heka has arrived to uncover what she can about the Salem witch trials. Now she waits in her prison cell to find out why the witches are dying rather than escaping. She is the most powerful witch in the Seven Planes, but even she can be surprised at times.

The Witching Hour is a stand-alone short story within the Enchanted Underworld Universe.

*

Heka tested the ropes that held her wrists together. There was no chance she was going to get out of the binds—unless she used magic and doing that would defeat the purpose of her being there.

The trial had been swift and pointless. The priest's claims of witchcraft were flimsy at best. Heka had not used any since she had come to live in Salem two weeks ago; instead, she had used her knowledge of herbal law to aid a baby with colic, and to soothe an old grantha's gout.

The witch trials had been happening for the past year in this region, and Heka had tended to stay away. As the most powerful witch in the Seven Planes, she had come to understand that she couldn't save everyone, and the humans were so prolific, that a few killing each other was neither here nor there. But they had hung a total of eleven true witches and warlocks in one year, and it was time to step in and find out what was behind the current spate of lunacy and if it was by chance or design.

The Witching Hour was fast approaching. Heka could feel it building and welcomed it. She had drained most of her power earlier that day in the hope that she would appear weaker to anyone with abilities to detect magic that may be involved in the farcical charades of the Salem witch trials. Once the leylines of the Planes had discharged their energies at two hours past midnight, she would refill her powers to a certain extent, though never as much as when they were in the other Planes. The Human realm was where all creatures from the other Planes were weakest—the witches being the only ones able to perform any great feats of magic since the disappearance of the Druids. And with the current witch hunt going on through Europe, the

Enchanted Underworld's Fae King was holding meetings with the full council to discuss a ban on using all forms of magic on the Second Plane to protect its citizens.

A warm feeling swept over Heka, and she leaned her head against the cold stone wall of the cell. She closed her eyes and enjoyed the sensation as her power reserves refilled in an exquisite combination of pleasure with an undertone of almost pain. It was always disorientating for a moment or two, and far more so on Friday the thirteenth and All Hallows Eve.

A key rattled as it was inserted into the lock of the wooden door, causing Heka to sit up straight and focus. The cell door swung inwards to reveal a small girl, no more than six, terror clear in her brown eyes, and her bottom lip trembling. There was a deep growl from somewhere behind the girl. A cloaked figure moved to stand behind her and placed their hand on the girl's fragile shoulder. A fine bracelet, that almost glowed white, looked out of place on the heavy wrist.

"Move forward," he ordered.

Heka tried to convey to the child, with a small smile and softening of her eyes, that she was no threat. The girl took several steps into the small cell, the man never letting go of her shoulder. Another growl filled the silence, and a massive black dog followed the man into the room. The animal was huge as it stalked toward Heka and came to sit next to the girl. Its eyes the same level as the frightened child's.

Heka's gaze moved from the child to the man in the cloak. He slowly lifted his head and locked eyes with her. She bit back a gasp as she took in the black irises and almost haunted look in the no longer totally human eyes, as who he was registered in her mine, and several things fell into place at once.

"How did you escape?" she demanded.

This brought a haughty, dismissive laugh.

"You are in no position to question me, witch."

Heka looked down to the ropes on her wrists and concentrated for an instant. In a puff of insubstantial smoke, the bindings disappeared and she went to stand.

"One more move and the child dies," the escapee from Hell warned.

Heka stopped and sat back down on the floor, hands up in supplication. She knew this hybrid's reputation from passed down histories and the books locked in the fortress that held the Elven Ingress and the Enchanted Underworld prison. This was the infamous Chaos, once a Druid with enormous power. The man cast into the pits of Hell as punishment for the subversion of the Angel, Arella. The man who was the reason that no new portals could be made—that magic was now forbidden and slowly being forgotten. The man who, if rumors were to be believed, had a hand in the downfall of the Elves.

"What do you want?" Heka asked.

"So many things." He laughed almost manically, and Heka began to wonder if Hell had taken his sanity.

"What do you want from me?" she rephrased.

"That should be obvious. What was stripped of me I now must take from others."

"You are behind the witch trials? You orchestrated this for power?"

Chaos grinned maliciously. "Power, revenge, control, boredom. Pick one."

"How did you find your way out of the Seventh Plane?" Heka knew she was pushing her luck by asking again, but she was hoping for an answer, or at least something she could start to look for once this was over. A tiny thought floated through her mind, which she dismissed quickly. *"If you survive this,"* her mind corrected.

"The witch trials have been incredibly disappointing here in so many ways." He spoke almost conversationally, completely ignoring her question regarding his escape. "The peasants of Europe are truly inspiring with their desire to burn everyone at the stake, and the English have come up with a cruel game of dunking the accused in water until they drown. The fear and hysteria it's causing is marvelous, but all the true witches have now gone to ground. Thought I might try my luck here, but hanging is nowhere near as fun. And for all the claims that there is great power here it all seems to have disappeared too." Chaos shuffled the girl forward. "But you..." He spoke softly, almost lovingly. "Radiate power."

Heka stared up at him, her back straight with defiance. She could blow up this entire room, if she chose, and live through it; but that would kill the girl, and this close, Heka could sense the girl's burgeoning powers. It went against everything she stood for to kill one of her own kind. Heka always had a shield around her, but to include another person plus bring forth the power required to set them free would take more than a few moments to prepare. Heka needed time but was still hoping to find out more from Chaos. She would continue to go along for now.

"Dog," Chaos commanded. "Guard."

The huge black animal stood, its hackles raised. It moved to a position where it stood between the girl and Heka, its gigantic jaw near the child's neck.

"I want you to stand, slowly," Chaos ordered. "The dog will tear her throat out before you can discharge any spell."

Heka did what she was told. With great care to show she was not going to cast a spell, she rose from the hard floor. It surprised her to find that she was about the same height as the former Druid. "Nice pet," she commented sarcastically as the dog continued to rumble at her.

"It's amazing how quickly you can train an animal when you discipline them properly."

For a brief moment Heka felt sorry for the massive beast. "Let the girl go," Heka reasoned. "You really don't need to threaten her to make me comply."

"Why would I let her go?" He laughed that crazy laugh that made Heka's skin crawl. "She will be my first."

"Your first what?" Heka tried to not sound alarmed.

"That is not your concern."

Heka physically bit her tongue to stop from revealing herself. She wanted to tell him exactly who she was and what power she held amongst her kind, and that the child by default would always belong to her. The dog that stood between her and the child growled threateningly, causing the girl to whimper in terror. This just made Chaos laugh.

"Hold out your hand, palm up, and let down your shield."

Heka did what she was told, but instead of letting her shield go completely, she partitioned a section of her knowledge away from the rest. She had been shown how to do this by the Keeper several years ago. Only a rare few had the power and ability to do it. Her secrets were safe, but Chaos would never know that she wasn't giving him everything.

He reached out with his free hand and hovered his palm over the top of hers. Instantly her hand began to heat, and she felt him slowly drain the power she had just renewed at Witching Hour. She now understood this was why he waited and why the witches never escaped or fought back. The threat of the death of the child kept them in check until he drained enough of their power that they had no reserves left and no Witching Hour to renew their strength enough to run.

Heka felt weak, her mind was becoming foggy, and she was struggling to form a coherent thought. She knew the feeling was temporary because of the increasing speed in which he was draining her, but nevertheless, she fought to remain in control of her emotions. She could only imagine how a weaker witch would react to this violation of mind and power.

The sound of his nasty laugh invaded her mind. Her stomach roiled with revulsion.

"You are nothing," he whispered into her mind. "You are not special, unique, or overly intelligent. They don't even trust you to know their secrets."

Heka struggled to understand his words and what he was implying. What secret was Chaos hoping to find in her mind?

The draining of her power was almost complete. It had become a trickle as he siphoned off the last of it. She wanted to pass out but planted her feet and refused to show him her fear at being so vulnerable and weak. Was this what it felt like to be human?

He disconnected their link and her hand dropped, brushing the soft black fur of the dog. A deep rumble came from the chest of the beast. Heka slid to the floor. Her legs were wobbly, no longer able to hold her. Her head spun and she blinked rapidly to remain focused. This was the crucial moment. She waited for his next move.

"If you are the best the witches have to offer than I am bitterly disappointed. You know nothing of importance," he taunted. "Though, I will admit, I feel stronger than I have in years." He sneered at her, revealing black gums. "Well, I shall not tarry. I think Salem has lost my interest. They don't seem to have the heart for killing in the way I had hoped. I am terribly dismayed, to be honest. I will have to work on ways to increase their blood lust. A good war is in order, I believe."

"Why?" she asked, too tired to expound further.

"Chaos. Why else?" His black eyes glinted cruelly.

Heka was now certain he had lost all his humanity and most of his sanity.

"It is time for me to go," he announced.

"Leave the girl," Heka said quietly.

"I beg your pardon?" He began to laugh. "The sheer audacity."

"Leave the girl," Heka repeated.

"Say it again and you die," Chaos warned, his voice ominous.

Heka lifted her head and screamed at him. "Leave the girl!"

Everything happened at once. Heka reached out and grabbed the girl from his grasp, pulling her out of his hand and dragging her down and into her arms for protection. *Now, Nyx,* Heka spoke for the first time with her mind's voice as she dragged the child away from Chaos. Before Chaos had a chance to respond, the black hound launched at him, burying his sharp, large teeth into the thigh. Nyx did not let go, instead he shook his head aggressively. Blood sprayed around the room and Chaos screamed in agony. *Nyx, release*, Heka told the dog. With a final growl, the huge animal let go of Chaos' thigh and stood in front of Heka and the child with his teeth bared, blood now dripping from the sharp fangs.

Heka reached out and placed her hand on the beast. He was her familiar and her companion, and so much more. Nyx stored her excess power. Quickly, she took enough from him to restore her shield and extend it to the child, she now cradled in her arms. With her brown eyes blazing, Heka threw her head back and stared at the wounded half man, half demon. It was a stalemate and they both knew it.

She wasn't strong enough to attack and she wouldn't risk Nyx unless she had to. Chaos was weakened and risked being bitten again if he tried to take the child. Chaos held much of her power, but he obviously couldn't use it, or he would have by now. *Interesting*.

He glowered at her for a moment before he took a step back toward the door. Chaos stumbled and fell against the frame, his hand on his thigh.

"I will find you and you will pay for this," he threatened as he took another step backward.

"Have no fear. I plan on finding you first," she hissed at him. For emphasis, Heka held out her hand and created a fireball, showing him her power had returned. He didn't need to know this was all she had and it was fading fast between keeping the shield up and the fireball burning. "Run away, little demon boy, before I send you back to Hell."

Nyx growled and took a menacing step forward. Chaos, with one final disgusted look, stepped into the dark corridor and disappeared from sight. Heka held the fireball for another few seconds before she deemed it safe to let it fade. She kept the shield in place.

As if released from a spell, the little girl began to sob loudly.

"Shhhh," Heka murmured. Rocking her gently and patting her head. "He's gone, you are safe."

The girl looked up at pointed a shaking finger at Nyx. "Bites," she stammered.

"I promise Nyx won't bite you. He is my friend."

The child looked dubious.

"Can you keep a secret?" Heka asked. Her face serious.

The girl looked from the dog to Heka and back again. "Yes."

"You are a witch."

The child nodded. "That's what Ma said."

"Where is your mother?"

"Went to visit her sister. Da sent her away cause no longer safe."

"Where is your Da?"

"Dead." Her lip began to tremble, and her beautiful big eyes filled with tears. "That man killed him when he wouldn't sell me." She looked at Nyx angrily. "Dog did nothing."

Heka turned the girl to look fully in her face.

"That was my fault. Nyx was told to do nothing but watch."

"Why?"

"I needed to know what was happening and I sent him ahead." The child frowned, confused, and Heka didn't blame her. "Nyx is not a dog. He is my familiar. He stores my power and helps me in other ways. He can also look like a man. Would you like to see?"

Heka secretly hungered for the sight of Nyx in his human form. It had been four long and lonely months without her familiar.

The girl looked dubious but nodded.

"Nyx, you may transform," Heka told the huge animal. He growled his acknowledgment once before he began to shimmer and change shape. The bright shimmering over the form of the dog didn't allow the eyes the chance to watch the transformation. When the shimmering subsided, the dog was gone and in its place was a man on all fours with shaggy black hair, huge brown eyes, and shiny dark skin.

"Hello, my love," Heka spoke quietly.

"My darling, it is good to see you." Nyx moved to sit next to her and held out his hand for her to grasp.

In his human form, the transfer of power was quicker. Heka felt herself return to normal and quickly unlocked the vault she had created for her secrets. She wondered if she did really hold the one Chaos had been looking for.

Nyx looked to the small girl in Heka's arms.

"What is your name, child? He never asked your name."

"Annie."

"I am sorry about your Da, Annie. When Heka tells me to do something, I am compelled to do it, even when I want to do otherwise. I hope one day you will understand and forgive me."

Annie looked at Nyx, her face serious. "I hope so too."

Heka looked at the anguish in Nyx's face and the pain in Annie's and she couldn't face it for the moment.

"I think it is time for you to rest, Annie." She gently spoke a spell and placed her hand over the child's eyes sending her to sleep. Heka looked to Nyx. "We need to leave and find her mother."

He stood and held out his hands. "Here, let me carry her."

Heka gave over the small child and stood. She felt good. Strong and capable with her powers returned. If she didn't have Annie to deal with, Heka would have considered beginning her hunt for Chaos immediately. But she knew there was things she needed to know before she faced the man who was becoming a demon.

Heka brushed off the dirt from her gray skirts and pulled her cloak straight. It had been a closer call than she cared to admit but now she took a deep steadying breath and looked into her familiar's gorgeous eyes. Heka didn't know how he had managed to gain Chaos' trust so quickly in the few months they were apart, and she was almost afraid to find out after the punishment comment earlier. When she had arrived in Salem two weeks ago and she had not seen Nyx and had sent out her thought to find him. He had responded with a simple, Safe. Found him. You get caught. And that is what she had done.

"I missed you," she whispered, lifting her hand to stroke his face.

He looked sad. He was bound to her in ways many didn't understand, but it didn't make it easier when he had to do things that he didn't like. Heka knew the death of Annie's father would be added to the list of regrets that haunted Nyx in his sleep most nights. She wished with all her heart that things could be different, but it was their job to keep to the Enchanted Underworld safe, as well as the witches and warlocks who chose to live on the Second Plane, rather than the Third.

"I am sorry." She held his cheek and stood on her toes to kiss him gently on his full lips. He returned the kiss with tenderness, and a soft growl in the back of his throat.

About the Author

Taya Rune is a writer of romance, a sucker for happy endings, and has a knack for asking people uncomfortable questions.

She is a USA Today Bestselling Author and a finalist for Romantic Book of the Year for the Romance Writer's of Australia.

For a complete reading order and to discover the entire Enchanted Underworld Universe head to tayarune.com While you are there sign up for her newsletter to get all the games, gossip, and giveaways. Start at the Warlock's Lair.

A Witch and Her Wolf

A WITCHES OF VALPORT SPRINGS AND SHIFTERS OF CRYSTAL CREEK STORY

BY KASSANDRA CROSS

While driving home late one night, Bella's headlights reveal a mysterious man by the side of the road. Uninjured, but in need of a ride, he seeks her help following a crash with his motorcycle. Bella's witchy instinct can sense his sincerity, but it also tells her he isn't all human. Meet Baron: not just astonishingly handsome, but a wolf shifter on his way to Valport Springs to chat business with the werewolves in town.

As a dedicated boss babe, Bella is wed to her work. When Baron seeks not only her assistance but also her number, might she finally be ready to risk her heart? Or will she retreat back to her safe world of Bewitching Brews and never see him again?

The drive back to Valport Springs is always a joy. I love the way the sun catches the leaves on the trees, the way they seem to glisten like green magic and gold. Each little vein in them throbs with power, our magical town so full of mystery, energy and the craft. There is sorcery pulsing from the ground up. The roads always seem to light up as I take the woodland bends, guiding me home sweet home...

But not tonight.

After the trades fair ran over by several hours, I find myself driving in the dark. A large storm cloud swirls overhead, which is undoubtedly following me because of my terrible mood.

I flick on the full beams so my headlights shine and light the way. They cascade up the trees, along the huge and ancient pines that run for miles along the outskirts. If you were just passing by, you would never know that deep within these pine woods, there are also secret sequoias. Those giants were planted here by our ancestors hundreds of years ago on our sacred land. It's the very tip of what makes Valport magic. But for me, I love it even more because it's home.

I lean across to turn over the radio. I've been listening to it almost out of range for the last thirty minutes and the fluffy buzz is starting to give me a headache. I blink and yawn as a clearer song kicks in, and I tap the wheel to try and keep myself alert.

It's hard work being a boss babe. Running a business solo has been the greatest, yet most rewarding, experience I've ever had. But these late-night homecomings are exhausting, especially when I know I've got to be up, out, and back at the coffee shop at 5 am. I open the window a crack and feel a blast of cool air rush up against my cheek. I'm approaching the Welcome to Valport Springs sign, so I slow, knowing there's a bend coming up beforehand.

As my headlights cut through the darkness, I jump when they shine on something blocking the road, and a large, shadowy figure emerges from the trees. It waves its arms and I slam on the brakes, even though my instincts begin to kick in with danger.

I'm sure there's an urban legend about a scene like this...

Am I about to be murdered by this crazy creature of the night?

I quickly lock the doors, my engine still turning over and my hand reaching for the stick to knock it into reverse. Magic tingles through my fingertips, my veins coming alive with the power of the elements. My heart longs to harness the energy of the storm, but I know for now that I have to keep it locked inside. This could all be perfectly innocent, and I don't want to annoy the elder witches as they sleep soundly in their beds.

The figure steps out of the shadow of the trees and I see him shield his eyes from the light. I squint, trying to make out his features, but I can already see what's blocking the road. There's a motorbike, lying on its side, the back wheel spinning slowly as if it's only just happened.

He comes closer and I grip the wheel, my heart a raging drum in my chest.

"Hey!" he calls out to me, his face softening.

He's tall, probably around six foot four, with piercing dark eyes and a smattering of stubble. He's clad in thick leather, and he stops to reach down and scoop up a helmet before he takes another few steps closer. I find myself tense, surprised at how handsome he is as my gaze fixes firmly on his.

"Are you okay?" I call out of the crack in the window.

He cocks his head to the side and I see how strong his jawline is, along with a red mark forming on his cheekbone.

"I've been better," he says as he glances back over his shoulder.

"What happened?" I ask, my foot still hovering over the accelerator.

"Took the bend too fast," he says with a wince. "Unfamiliar roads."

I let my eyes glance over him and notice a rip in the leather on his thigh.

"Ouch," I say, biting my lip.

"Yeah, it stings," he half-laughs. "But that's why we wear this stuff."

I nod. If he hadn't, I dread to think what kind of state he would be in.

He's not from our town, and I have never seen him before, but I'm not about to leave him here in the middle of the night after an accident.

"Do you want a ride?" I ask. "I'm heading into Valport, maybe you could see a doctor or something?"

"I don't need a doctor," he says confidently, running his hand through his hair.

He takes another step closer and looks into the window. I feel so small sitting there, it's like I'm shrinking further into my seat as I look up at him.

"But a ride would be great, thanks," he smiles.

I gaze into his eyes and sense something different about him, my witchy instincts kicking into overdrive. This guy isn't all human, I can tell.

"Okay," I say as I press the unlock button on the inside of the door.

He walks around the front and bends down, lifting up the bike and dragging it off into the forest. I watch, half amused, as he disappears amongst the trees before appearing again, strutting towards the car. He opens the passenger side, sliding in next to me. I expect him to groan with pain, but instead, he sits down and sighs.

"This is the last thing I needed," he breathes.

"Ditto buddy," I say with a mock roll of my eyes.

He smirks and I do too, before I press my foot on the gas and we drive on to town.

❧

I PARK OUTSIDE MISTY'S, ONE OF THE ONLY BARS ON MAIN Street still open at this time of night.

"Thanks for the ride," he says, rubbing the tip of his shoulder. "I appreciate it."

I look across at him and marvel at how big he seems, along with how much space he's taking up in this old car of mine. His head is pretty much touching the roof, and his muscular arms flex as he reaches for the handle and smiles at me warmly.

"Are you sure you don't need any medical attention?" I ask, to be polite more than anything.

"I'm fine," he says. "It's the bike I'm worried about. She's unrideable and all alone in the woods," he falters and leans in closer, his dark eyes glinting with mischief. "Do you know any mechanics?"

I bite my lip, trying not to smile. He's too handsome for his own good and I have the feeling he knows it. I feel a heat coming from him, one that tells me I was right about him being supernatural. I wonder if he can sense it in me too, if he feels the forces of the elements flowing through my veins.

"Sure," I say as I turn the key on the engine.

I unclip my belt, get out, and wait for him to follow my lead. He rises from the passenger side and smiles at me over the top of the car. "This place may be the only bar left open at this time, but you can bet your life there'll be someone in here who can help," I tell him.

He smiles and winks, setting off butterflies in my chest. They flutter down to my navel and settle there, teasing me.

"It's a good job you were passing by," he says as I step past him and he rushes up to my side. "You're very helpful."

"I wouldn't get used to it," I say coyly. "I believe in karma so I'll always have time for someone in need, but trust me, I'm exhausted and wish I was in bed."

"Well that option doesn't sound too bad either," he says with a lilt in his voice.

It catches me off guard and I cast a glance at him, hoping that a wicked blush isn't spreading out across my entire face. He smirks back, knowing he's unarmed me with his charm, and I shake my head with a laugh.

"Easy," I warn him. "I know people in here who might be a little *protective*," I raise my brow.

"Oh yeah?" he goads me. "Well good job, because I know people here too."

I feel my brow crease into a frown and watch as he walks ahead, pushing open the door to Misty's and letting out a plume of warm air and the sounds of laughter and music. I can smell the alcohol and the mix of sweat and cologne. He grins at me, beckoning me with his head, knowing he has me on the hook.

He's cocky and arrogant, but it's working well for him. Plus, it's not often a chance meeting happens with another magical being from out of town.

Now, I need to know who this guy is.

We step inside and move through the crowd. It's packed but that isn't surprising for a Thursday, Archer and his guys like to entice the locals with promises of cheap beer and exotic cocktails. One of the local witches even assists on occasion, helping to cook up love potions to give everyone a high they never knew they needed. The last time cocktail night at Misty's was unleashed on Valport Springs, I think the next generation was conceived. It was totally wild in every sense of the word.

My biker guy strides right up to the bar counter and I watch him flatten his hands out across the wood. Big, sculpted hands that send a thrill down my spine as I watch the tendons in them flex. His confidence is powerful, and as a door at the back of the room opens, and I see Archer emerge, I know immediately what is about to happen.

Whether it's witches instinct, or the fact it is suddenly glaringly obvious, I'm too caught up in the moment to tell. But it's clear what this guy is the second I see Archer's eyes light up with recognition.

This cocky mo-fo is a wolf shifter, just like my good friend Archer who owns this place.

"Baron," Archer grins as he strides closer, holding out his hand and pulling the biker closer to him for a big, bro hug. They slap each other on the back and the biker winces ever so slightly, a small hiss escaping his lips.

Baron the Biker. I find my eyes widening, a flicker of enjoyment igniting inside me.

"What happened?" Archer asks him. "You been in a fight or something?"

"I wish," Baron smirks. "Came off my bike just outside of town."

I cross my arms over my chest, feeling myself bristle. I'm intrigued but I'm also tired. Archer looks over Baron's shoulder and cocks his head as he smiles at me.

"Luckily, I had this lovely lady passing by," Baron grins as he turns and his eyes catch mine.

A heat floods through me.

Two wolf shifters staring at me at the same time is the kind of thing that could seriously get a girl in trouble. I take a beat and nod, slowly coming closer.

"I offered to call the medical center," I tell Archer. "But he says he's fine."

"He?" Baron steps around the side of me and re-enters the conversation. "What, so I'm not here now?"

I roll my eyes playfully.

"I'm tired," I tell them with a meek sigh. "His bike is in the woods near Corpse's Curve."

I watch with amusement as Baron's eyebrows shoot up his forehead.

"Corpe's Curve?" he asks with wide eyes. "Well, Jesus Christ."

Archer and I laugh.

"She's messing with you," Archer says, tapping me mischievously on the arm. "Get yourself to bed, Bella. Don't you have to be up at the crack of dawn?"

"I certainly do," I say. "Got to be open for the early risers. Look after him. And, good luck, Baron."

I turn and make for the exit, moving through the crowd quickly, without looking back. But I don't get far before I feel a warm hand on my shoulder.

I turn around to see Baron and his sexy eyes gazing down at me, a wry smile spreading out across his lips.

"I don't usually do this," he says, the smallest hint of insecurity passing over him which is actually pretty endearing. "But, I'm going to be in town for a few days, and I wanted to thank you. I was wondering if I could get your number."

I leave him hanging for a moment, the air between us becoming electric with tension and the magic we both have within us. I know he's trouble, it's written all over his face, but he's also exciting. I know what I want, but the last thing I need is any kind of distraction. A sag of disappointment hits me hard, it kills me to do it but I slowly shake my head.

"Whilst it's a nice idea," I say. "All I do is work. I can't take any time off, I'm a one-woman show."

I smile and turn slowly, internally cursing myself for not just taking a chance for once.

As the door to the bar closes behind me, I rush as quickly as I can back to my car and start the engine. I pull away before I have the chance to see if he's followed me or whether he took the rejection and went looking for someone else to pass the time with whilst he's stuck here in Valport Springs.

He may have been cute and full of magnetic wolf energy, but I've got a business to focus on, and I don't have time for anyone throwing me off my game.

I drive home in the dark feeling kind of deflated, not that I would ever admit it.

One of these days, I swear I'll learn to throw caution to the wind and let myself have some fun.

❧

By the time 9 am hits in Bewitching Brews, I've already served what feels like ten thousand coffees. The people of Valport Springs need their caffeine hit on a morning, and I'm more than obliged to supply. I sit at the counter and take a minute to regroup, the insane early rush starting to quieten down. From now until noon, I can expect a more relaxed environment of moms with their toddlers catching up with friends, older ladies exploring the range of herbal teas I create from scratch in my potion room, and even a small coven of witches who often stop by to support one of their own.

The sun shines outside, and the birds sing, flitting from the hanging baskets of flowers, enjoying the fresh water dripping from the petals after their morning drench. Our Main Street is so picturesque, and the people of the town all help to keep it that way. The committee is so good at making sure nothing is left to become unsightly or neglected, and the flowers are a real sign of that. Stunning blooms of blue, pink and purple sway from the lamposts and on the corners of buildings, making each store pop with color.

I stir my own tea, a magical blend of rose and lavender that I grew myself in my botanical garden and infused with rose quartz to bring a little love into my life. I know I'm being contradictory, especially after last night and the way I turned Baron down. But perhaps I've thought differently since. I went to bed thinking about those eyes and that jawline, the way his wolf called to my witch, and made me wonder... *what if*?

Right on queue, as if the universe was just waiting for me to internally acknowledge it, I sense something change in the air. I bite my lip, my nerves mounting, as my witchy instincts kick into overdrive and I feel his eyes rove all over me.

Baron is close, and he's looking for me.

I sit up straight and stir my tea sunwise, invoking the power of the elements that flow through me and directing my intention.

I want to see him again.

Right now.

A rush of hot euphoria courses through me, my blood coming alive with magic and the satisfying feeling that I've created something good. My senses turn on high alert, my hearing suddenly completely in tune with what is outside, the sound of a pair of heavy footsteps coming closer.

I watch with bated breath as he appears on the other side of the window, a cheeky look on his face that borders on confusion but also titillation.

He knows what I am. It's written all over his face.

We stare at each other through the glass, my heart pounding. He shakes his head slowly with an affectionate grin, his eyes never leaving mine. I gently allow my fingers to let go of the silver spoon, the tea in the cup still swirling like a storm, brewing up our imminent reunion with magical ferocity. The ting breaks the trance like a thunderclap and he is pulled from his daze as he steps back and looks up at the storefront of Bewitching Brews and shakes his head as if he's been in a deep sleep and has just been dropped in a tub of cold water.

I smirk.

I've never tried that particular spell before, but it certainly worked like a charm. When he clocks me through the glass he nods slowly, amusement cresting over him before he reaches for the door and pushes it open wide.

When he enters my airspace, it feels as if every nerve ending has come alive, the tea doing its magical work as well as the intention I know I have running within my soul.

"Should have known," his voice is smooth as butter and deep as the ocean.

He steps towards me, his eyes not once leaving mine.

Even though the cafe is busy and bustling with people, we may as well be the only ones here.

"So," he smirks, "you are a witch."

"What gave it away?" I smile back as I cock my head to the side.

"You mean apart from the fact I was just magically summoned here?" He crosses his arms over his chest and widens his stance.

I bite my lip.

"Sorry about that," I tell him genuinely. "It's just, I wasn't sure how long you were sticking around. For all I know, your beloved bike could be back up and running by now."

"Fat chance," he grins, his eyes glinting. "She's beaten up pretty bad."

I pout on his behalf and he throws his head back and laughs.

"So you want to see me now?" he asks cockily as he takes yet another step closer. "What happened to being married to your work?"

As he says the words he looks up and around, taking in the special details of Bewitching Brews and all I've achieved over the past year. He nods his head slowly, his eyes flitting from one corner to the next.

"Not bad, by the way," he says with a wry smile. "It looks like you're pretty talented too."

"Thank you," I accept the compliment graciously and reach down to lift up my teacup and saucer, pulling the rim to my lips and taking a long, luxurious sip. It gives me more butterflies, the rush of passion flowing through me.

"Maybe I was a bit premature last night," I say with a nonchalant shrug.

"As long as you're making up for it now, I suppose..." he trails off and looks behind me to the shelves behind the counter, stocked high with herb jars and elixirs.

"When Archer told me you were part of the witchy crew here, I almost didn't believe him at first," he says in a hushed voice as he comes closer. "I knew there was something different about you, I just couldn't put my finger on it."

The notion of him putting his fingers on me is suddenly all I can think about, and I have to take a breath to try and break that wicked train of thought.

"And what about you, Wolf?" I say with a knowing smile. "Where did you come from?"

"So you have me all figured out?" he grins. "And you're just taking it all in your stride."

"Why wouldn't I?" I tease. "I've met wolves before. The moment I saw you on the side of the road I knew there was something magical about you, it just took you being on first-name terms with Archer for me to put two and two together."

"I'm from Crystal Creek," he says resting those big, manly hands down on the countertop. "And I was coming here to discuss business with my lupine brothers."

"A biker and a werewolf, that's a new one for me around here."

"A beautiful witch with a sassy attitude but a heart of gold... that's kind of a new one for me too," his eyes still bore into me, making me just ever so nervous.

This guy... I was not expecting him. But now here he is, and I'm having trouble pulling away. It's as if I've been waiting for him to set foot in this town and shake things up for the better.

"So how about it?" he asks, his tone darkening. "Do I get your number or not?"

I bite my lip again, my ability to stay cool, calm, and collected dwindling by the second. The herbal love tea has sent us both into overdrive, I can see his need as much as I feel mine.

"I guess," I say almost in a whisper, leaning in closer to him across the counter. "But only if you promise to use it wisely."

Baron's eyes glint with something animalistic, as if his hunter instinct is kicking in and he's enjoying the chase.

"Yes ma'am," he smiles.

I nod and then I hold out my hand, waiting for him to pass me his phone. When he slips it into my palm, I add my details and then give it back.

"I mean, I could always just find you here," he says as he tucks the phone into his back pocket. "But I have the feeling we'll have some fun on text."

"We'll see," I say with a toss of my hair as I turn my back on him and cross over to the coffee machines.

When I look back over my shoulder he's smiling and shaking his head, knowing he's letting himself in for some trouble with me. But I can tell he can handle it.

He's a werewolf *and* a biker...

That, coupled with being matched with a witch, is going to get hella exciting.

He raises his hand and waves as he backs out of the door, and I watch him go, the full feeling of satisfaction rising in my chest. It's been a long time since I've been on a date, and I'm not sure I've ever felt something like this before. It's a huge step, one I've been needing to take, but denying for so long.

Even after all my protesting, I have the distinct feeling that Baron and I are going to have a lot of fun.

Who would have thought a potential love interest would just show up here in this sleepy little magical town?

Love works in mysterious ways, and some might say, it was written in the stars...

About the Author

Kassandra is a bestselling author of dark and gothic fiction. She loves exploring forbidden love that hurts and creating powerful morally gray antiheroes. Expect monsters, witches, shifters, and psychos falling in love (and lust) amongst deliciously gothic settings to set your wicked little soul on fire.

Read The Witches of Valport Springs HERE

Read The Shifters of Crystal Creek HERE

Join her Reader Group HERE

Get a FREE magical story HERE

Mission: Moon Magic

A TALE OF A CAILLEACH GEALACH: THE IRISH MOON WITCHES

BY R.L. MERRILL

Throughout the history of Ireland, witches have depended on the moon to fuel their magic, but since the turn of the century, their power has been weakening. The High Priestess of the Irish Council of the Moon has dispatched her granddaughter Sally to find the cause. When Sally discovers the United States is planning a new mission to the moon, Fate places a man with classified information in her path. She doesn't count on falling for him, but Commander Tuck O'Brien has some tricks up his own sleeve. Before the night is over, Sally will be forced to choose between her mission...or her heart.

*

If you would have asked me as a young person what I'd be doing with my life, I never would have foreseen that I'd be tending bar at a place with a candelabra made out of animal bones. Neither would I have predicted that me gran would send me out to be a spy, but oftentimes folks get sucked into the family business whether they want it or not. I wanted it, but that didn't mean I didn't grumble about it from time to time.

As I leaned my chin into my fists, resting my elbows on top of the wooden bar, I wondered is this it? The pinnacle of my success in life? I let out a big sigh that no one else would hear, but it helped me release the somewhat childish irritation over my current situation.

"Ay, Gran. What am I doin' here? I miss home." Being the granddaughter of the High Priestess of the Irish Moon meant that when she gave me a mission, I followed orders.

I'd been living abroad in America for some time, sowing my wild oats, dipping my toes in the sea of fish...

Nay. None of that was true. I'd spent every waking moment studying texts, visiting countless libraries, all while trying to find answers for Gran to the problem plaguing every Moon Witch on the planet.

Something was interfering with our link to the celestial body we claimed as our own, and therefore, messing with our magic. Gran sent each of her thirteen grandkids out into the world searching for answers. So far, none of us had found a way to solve our dilemma.

Until the morning I was reading a *New York Times* article while waiting for my nails to dry and saw a route none of us had yet taken.

I rang up Gran and told her what I'd read. She said she'd do some divination and get back to me with a plan. That night, I'd dreamt of her.

"Go to the bar called Witchitas. They're expecting you. The person you need to talk to will be there soon. Meet him. Get him talking, and find out what you must do to be part of his mission."

Witchitas was a pretty cool bar if you could find it, which I did, right on the shores of Lake Tahoe in California. It moved around, apparently, to where it was needed. I didn't mind the work, but I'd been serving beer and ciders to the local clientele—both magical and those unsuspecting humans who wandered in—for three months now, and I was beginning to think Gran needed to cleanse her divination stones, perhaps dip them in Abhainn na Sionainne—The River Shannon—as no person of interest had yet crossed the threshold.

I pulled a pint of dark fruit cider for a customer and was looking through the cloudy window at the parking lot when I spied something interesting. A classic seafoam green and white Ford F150 pulled into the lot towing a vintage Airstream caravan behind it. The driver expertly parked the rig in one of the designated overnight slots in the back row. There were already several campers who'd reserved their spots long-term as the view of the lake from the bar was stunning.

I'd always found those silver tubular travel homes nifty, exciting, and the idea of traveling around, free, with no pesky family members troubling you, was attractive. I likely wouldn't have any time to go off in a caravan for some time, maybe not ever if we couldn't figure out what was going on with our Moon Magic. But it was sure fun to dream!

My heart danced a little jig as a tall, fit guy stepped out of the cab in a flannel shirt and light blue jeans. He pulled a ball cap down low over his brow. A cap with wings on it.

"He'll be wearing the tartan of a Scot, but in his eyes, you'll find the colors of Galway Bay, and he'll have the wings of a bird upon him."

I hadn't expected him to have actual wings, but the rest added up. This guy was my mission. Thank goodness. The sooner I made contact, the sooner I'd have a report for Gran and the council.

The man walked toward the steps of the bar, talking on a cell phone. He took two quick glances back at his trailer and around the lot, stopped in his tracks, had a few more heated comments for the person on the other end of the line, and then he hung up. He took the front steps two at a time, his long legs eating up the distance, and cursed under his breath as he passed me in the foyer of the bar.

"What's 'bullshit'?"

He glanced at me, and his eyes, the color of the waters of Galway Bay, were wide as if he'd not intended to be heard. Too bad for him, me hearing was ten times as good as perfect human hearing. We Moon Witches come from excellent stock.

"Sorry, ma'am. Just had some bad news is all. Pardon my French."

"That certainly wasn't French. And no need for apologies. I hear much worse working here." I studied his cap closely as he stood before me. The wings embroidered on his cap went along with the insignia for the Air Force.

"You fly, do ye?"

His nostrils flared and grunted. "Yeah. Why?"

I shrugged, thinking of a way to keep him engaged. "Oh, just curious. Never flown a plane meself." It wasn't completely a lie. "Always seems so against nature, you know?" I hated fibbing. I most certainly had flown before, though it didn't come as naturally to me as it did to others of my kind.

He seemed quite disturbed by my comment, and I assumed he'd commence mansplaining to me why I was wrong.

"I get it," he said. "It's not for everyone. Helicopters, for example, are absolutely against nature. I've flown jets, and the space shuttle, both of which have solid scientific explanations for why they work."

Interesting. "I see."

The scowl he'd worn when he'd crossed the threshold would have terrified the bravest of folks, but his mood was nearly comical in its crabbiness so I couldn't help myself. I kept poking him.

"Are you one a them soldiers who jumps out of perfectly good airplanes, then?"

"No, ma'am. I flew combat missions. Now I'm in a classified program." He shrugged. "Can't talk about it."

"Oh right, or you'll have to kill me. Fair enough. Have you come to this establishment on a mission or for pleasure?"

He stepped aside to stretch out his back. "A bit of both. I was in meetings today and then..." He trailed off and exhaled harshly. "Forced shore leave starts now."

"You don't seem excited about it?"

He shrugged. "Not here by choice."

"Well, there's plenty to do around the loch," I said, gesturing to the rack of pamphlets against the wall. "Or, if you prefer it, there are the attractions near the casinos. The summer is quite lovely here in Lake Tahoe."

His eyes traveled over the racks, but it was obvious he wasn't into the tourist stuff. "Probably I'll hang out in the trailer," he said, flicking his thumb back toward his Airstream. "Probably work out, get some sleep."

And there it was. Sadness bled from his pores as pungent as curry. His shoulders curled forward, and I knew instinctively I needed to perform an intervention with this man.

"That's rubbish. Forest lands will do you good. Fresh air, you need. And we've got plenty of diversions here at Witchitas, not to mention you should, at the very least, partake of our food and drink."

He glanced inside the doorway at the pool tables, dart board, live band entertaining the dancers, and his nose wrinkled. He didn't seem to be the usual human bar patron.

"What's your name, flyboy?" I held out my hand, intending it to stay there until he shook it.

One corner of his lips quirked and I knew I had him. He reached out a cool hand and took mine. "Commander Tuck O'Brien."

"Irish, huh?"

He shrugged. "Along with some other Northern European blood."

"Hmm. With a name like that, you simply must stay for a Guinness, or perhaps one of our delightful Irish whiskeys."

"So you're really Irish? Like from Ireland?"

I gave him a little curtsy. "Connemara in County Galway. Sally Monaghan, at your service. We've even got a decent Irish stew on the menu. Stay for a bit. We'll have you feelin' better in no time."

He stood a little straighter, noticing that we were nearly the same height.

"You seem convinced there's something wrong with me."

"Your whole constitution says so. You look like ye just lost your best mate, or your pup."

His blue eyes deepened in that moment, opening a view to his soul that he'd kept locked away from the world for ages. He couldn't hide it from me, though.

"How long's it been?" I whispered.

He frowned. "Since what?"

I shifted and bumped him with my shoulder. "Since your wife left you."

He stiffened with alarm and the foyer filled with the scent of ripe onions, strong enough to make my eyes water.

"How'd you know that?"

I shrugged and looked away to allow him a moment to collect himself. My magic allowed me to use my heightened olfactory senses to detect mood and intent in others, and once I got someone talking, they opened to me, blooming like a tender rose. 'Twas me special gift in the Monaghan family. Gran says I was blessed by the goddess.

"A year ago. Today. How did you know?"

"The slightest depression on your ring finger. As if you'd worn a ring for a long time. And your eyes. I'm sure you've heard that the eyes are the portal to the soul, yeah?"

"I guess so. It was supposed to be a trial separation. She filed for divorce two months later. It was final a month ago, and here I am. I'm sure you don't want to hear about it."

"Heavens, no, I don't," I said, chuckling when he gaped at me, aghast. "Only because you obviously don't want to talk about it."

He laughed too. "Old news. But yeah, I'm being promoted and my commander says I gotta take time off before my next assignment. One of the guys lent me his truck and trailer and they sent me this way, said y'all had good fishing and some camping spots. Am I in the right place?"

I smiled. "Indeed you are, Commander O'Brien. Let me pour you a drink and see if we can't find some local attractions to entertain you."

Hope sparked in his eyes, and I knew I'd hooked him. I'd bring him in, ply him with drink, peel back the layers 'til I had an inkling what his mission was all about, and then I'd extricate myself and report to Gran.

THAT WAS THE PLAN, ANYWAY, BUT AFTER THREE PINTS OF Guinness, two bowls of stew, and a game of darts, my shift was over. But not my night. The tipsy astronaut lured me out onto the dance floor and he shed every last bit of the uptight, angry shell he'd been trapped in when he arrived.

Turned out, alcohol took away his inhibitions, as expected, but also revealed a hidden talent for dancing in such a way that had me hot under the apron. The band had long since finished and the DJ had some late-nineties era music playing. Tuck's ballcap was lost somewhere, and his black hair fell into his eyes. I wondered if his current overdue haircut met with regulations. Sweat trickled down me neck and into me bra as I danced with abandon, loving the way this "mission" was playing out.

When George Michael's "Outside" came on, Tuck really let loose. The guy had moves I could barely keep up with, but I was determined to do me best. I had him right where I wanted him. He was ready to open up to me and tell me about his mission—

He slid his hands around my waist, moving right into my dancing space, and the sizzle I felt up and down my spine nearly had me forgetting my purpose. Our hips swayed together; his one hand anchored my hip while the other caressed my back. With his thigh between mine, things were getting downright indecent, and despite my desire to complete my mission, my desire had other ideas...

"Sally?"

"Hmm?"

His lips were against my ear and when he spoke, they brushed my skin, completely destroying any hold I had over my behavior.

"Why don't *we* go outside?"

It took me a moment to register what he was asking. Not that I wouldn't have agreed. I'd have agreed to jump out of an airplane at that point. His fingers dug into the back of my neck and his breath ghosted over my cheek.

Then he started singing to me, and I was a goner.

I took his hand and pulled him off the floor as the song ended and the lights flickered, indicating it was last call. I led him out the side exit, waving to the bar's owner on the way out. This door was closest to where he'd parked the Airstream. I headed in that direction, but he pulled me to a stop.

"Sally, I'm sorry. We don't have to...I'm usually much more of a gentleman than this."

"You're just showing me the Airstream, yeah?"

"Yeah."

"Where we can talk, maybe rehydrate after all that dancing?"

He swallowed hard, his prominent Adam's apple visible under the skin of his delectable throat. "Yeah."

"Inside where the mosquitoes won't get us?"

"Oh, yeah."

"And you can show me what it's like to be up there?" I pointed up to the sky. The moon was a perfect gealach dheirceach—waxing crescent—tonight. My favorite phase of the moon. It was a time for reflecting on what needed tending to on the next full moon. I felt a flutter in me chest, thinking about the last time I was home for a waxing moon feast next to the River Shannon.

"*Oh yeah...*"

Our eyes locked and a faint tinge of garlic tickled my nose. The poor man. He was nervous. Likely he hadn't been with another woman since his wife.

"Don't worry yourself, Commander. I'll take good care of ye."

An hour later, we lay side-by-side, naked under the crisp, clean sheets of the bed in his tidy trailer. Moonlight shone on our glistening skin through the open hatch his mate had custom designed in the roof of the Airstream for the purpose of stargazing. I wanted to kiss the guy for not only loaning the lovely caravan to Tuck, but for designing such a useful, and delightful, amenity.

"What's it like up there? Right up close and personal to her?"

I'd been so carried away dancing with Tuck, and then, well...once we got inside his caravan, all magical maneuvering was strictly on his part. I might've told him I'd take care of him, but the fella's hands were highly skilled. His wife had been one lucky lass.

I hadn't been touched in a sensual manner by a man, woman, or nonbinary paramour in many, many moons, since long before I'd come to America. And seeing as we witches tended to live a wee bit longer than most humans, I'd had plenty of time to frolic in the fields. That prospect hadn't really interested me before, though. Knowing I'd likely be conscripted by Gran and the Council, I preferred to flirt and flee.

Tuck was different, though, and this...thing happening between us was magic in its own way. He may have been put in my path for an important reason, but the moment he kissed me—and could that man kiss!—he immediately became more than a mission, which should have alarmed me.

"Truthfully," he said, his sexy, sated smile becoming serene, dreamy, "it's the most incredible thing I've ever done with my life. All the hard work and sacrifice, it was worth it just to see the moon up close. It's breathtakingly beautiful. Puts everything else into perspective."

"I believe you. The moon is precious, so important. Most folks don't ponder its significance. I can't tell you how wonderful it is to meet someone who feels as I do about her."

He turned to gaze at me and the soft look of adoration, along with the smell of sweet, ripe blackberries, fresh picked from the vines, rang the alarm bells a tad more insistently.

I rolled over onto my back, and gasped. Wonderful. *Right.* At some point, I was going to have to use magic to gain the intelligence I needed from him, but I didn't want to disrespect Tuck in any way. He'd been so gentle, so eager, so...*holy mother of the moonlight*, he was so gifted...

Why, of all the persons to stumble into Witchitas, did Tuck O'Brien have to be my mission?

Tuck brought my hand up to his lips and brushed them gently over my knuckles. "I'd love to take you to the Lick Observatory in the Bay Area. It's probably my favorite of the telescopes, although the images that are coming through from the Webb Telescope, which we launched two years ago, are stunning. We've learned more than we ever have since the beginning of the space program." His smile faded a bit and he looked away, back up to the sky, and he sighed.

"What's wrong?"

"I'd hoped to take another mission up there. One more flight around that beautiful girl." He exhaled and the muscle twitched in his jaw. "The last shuttle mission was twelve years ago, and I don't think I fully appreciated that it would be my first and last trip into space. I thought for sure there'd be more opportunities. Then they scrapped the Space Shuttle program. Now they're starting again with the Brigid mission...and apparently, I'm needed elsewhere in the organization."

Brigid. *That's it.* The article I read mentioned it. I placed my hand on his perfectly sculpted chest. "The bad news earlier?"

He nodded. "Sometimes being good at your job means being rewarded with the thing you least want."

I snorted and it surprised us both. "You've got that right." I *had* to be so loyal to Gran, had to be dogged in my determination to find the fix to our Moon Magic problem. "You *are* good at what you do, but I get it."

If I hadn't been so observant, if I would have missed that *Times* article, maybe I could have crossed paths with Tuck O'Brien in the normal way. We could have met, courted, made something of our out-of-this-world chemistry.

But no. Before the moon slipped behind the Sierra Nevada Mountains, I'd have to dig a little deeper into Tuck's psyche and find out how to get a witch chosen for that next mission to the moon, even if that meant getting him in trouble with his job for giving up classified information. I could make him forget everything, of course, but then, I'd never have this again.

He rolled back to face me, excitement dancing in his eyes like the stars above us, and he pulled me into his arms, my body molding to his once more.

"You sure? Maybe I should try again. I'm not convinced I performed to my full capabilities." The scent of his intention permeated the caravan, a heady perfume of lilies in springtime.

My favorite.

The crisp brush of the hair at the juncture of his thighs against the sensitive skin of mine was a sensation I'd never forget, nor would I give up the memory of his hands grasping my shoulders as he entered me once more, mimicking that hip movement he'd performed on the dance floor, only this time, it wasn't indecent, it was unbelievably hot...and surprisingly emotional.

My heart rode high in my chest as our bodies met. My thighs spread wide for his thick hips and strong legs, we barely created motion that would alert any passersby as to what was going on inside the caravan, but the friction inside of me brought on wave after wave of pleasure for us both, hitting us like the g-force an astronaut would experience blasting off to the heavens.

When we came down from that high, Tuck nuzzled my neck, kissing me as he muttered his appreciation. I knew time was running out before he'd be pulled under by the tides of sleep.

I pressed my hand to the side of his head and closed my eyes as I whispered. "Tell me what I seek to know."

He jolted slightly, but his body was unable to fight the need for rest, and the pull of my influence.

I absorbed all I needed from him, and then let him drift off to dreamland. Maybe, if I was fortunate, a sliver of tonight's experience would remain there, in his subconscious, so we might be together again in some capacity.

I brushed his hair back and kissed his forehead. I asked the goddess for his protection and to wipe his memory of our meeting, but before I considered the consequences of my actions, the words a witch should never utter—unless she's sure of her heart—tumbled from my lips.

Only your name shall I cry out in the night
Only your eyes shall I gaze upon at daybreak
I choose you to cherish and honor
I pledge my hand, heart, and spirit
through this life and into the next.

I slowly extricated myself from Tuck's bed, taking one last moment to admire his bronzed skin, dappled with dark hairs and freckles, and his plump red lips pursed in sleep. His cheek was smushed against the pillow and his hair fell once more in his eyes.

I dressed hurriedly, but couldn't resist one last kiss. I pressed my lips to his, and as I rose, unbeknownst to me until much later, a tear rolled down my cheek and splashed gently on his cheek, the salty water rolling over the laugh lines of his face, over his dimple, and onto his bottom lip. Which would have consequences for us both.

I turned to go and made sure to latch the lock with my influence before trotting over to my ancient Volkswagen Rabbit. I closed the door without making a sound, a feat, really, considering the age of the rust bucket. I pulled out my cell phone and called Gran.

"Tell me," she whispered into the phone.

"Brigid is the name of the project. They are selecting diverse candidates, including women, for a new mission to study the moon. That's it. That's all he knew." My hands shook as I juggled the keys. "I'm done, I'm coming home. I need to be home." Tears spilled down my cheeks as I struggled with the ignition.

"Ah, lassie. Your mission is not complete. I'm afraid ye'll have to stay a bit longer. Your time with the Irish commander is not over."

I gasped as she explained what I would have to do next.

It seemed I'd be meeting Tuck again, only this time, I'd not be his bartender.

I'd be his trainee.

He wouldn't remember this night, but maybe, just maybe, if my magic was strong enough, he'd remember how he felt tonight, and he'd remember my words. Mission: Moon Magic had to be a success. The future of the Irish Moon Witches, and now, the fate of my heart, hung in the balance.

Soon, Commander O'Brien.

The End...For Now...

About the Author

R.L. Merrill loves creating compelling stories that will stay with readers long after. Ro writes inclusive contemporary romance to make you swoon and creepy paranormal to make you shiver. A mom, wife, daughter, and former educator, you can currently find cruising in her Bronco with Great Dane pup Velma, being terrorized by feline twins Dracula and Frankenstein, or headbanging at a rock show near her home in the San Francisco Bay Area! Stay Tuned for more...

Amor Fati

BY NIKI TRENTO

The locals claim his new house is haunted, but Sam doesn't believe in the supernatural.

Living in her ancestral home with only her familiar for company, Elixis is the last of her line. And the clock is ticking. The problem is she can't stand any of the local warlocks.

When a sexy man moves in next door, Elixis is torn between obeying the coven's rules and her own desires.

Fate has its own design, slithering in to take matters into its own fangs.

Will Sam open his mind to the magic of his new world? Will Elixis throw caution to the wind and let her inhibitions go?

One

Sam

Moving out on my own to a small town that is nestled between the concrete jungle and the spacious fields of the country, and far from where I grew up is simultaneously exhilarating and frightening. Nothing *made* me move, it isn't a career move or even to get as far away from my family as possible. Nope. I just need a change.

And what a change it's going to be! For starters, my new house is haunted. Or at least the locals seem to think so. Curious of the stranger in their little hamlet, I'm always asked the same questions: Where are you from? Where are you staying? And my personal favorite; You moved into *that* house?

After a few queries, I learned that the family who lived there before, the Wallgren's, had to relocate their mailbox to the edge of the property because not even the mailman would step foot on their porch. Children would dare each other to see who could get the closest to the door without pussing out.

Their fear is palpable. I can't help but internally shake my head and laugh. I've been there for two weeks now and have not had any odd experiences or heard weird, unexplainable sounds. The only thing that I would categorize as 'out of the ordinary' is the neighbor with the insanely overgrown backyard.

This is the kind of area with mostly cookie cutter houses and a homeowner's association, yet the house next door looks like something out of a fairy tale with a wicked witch that entices children into her oven. The house isn't in shambles by any means, but it has a vibe about it. It is obvious to anyone who has any inkling about architecture that the house is a few centuries old, styled in the fashion of the original colonial homes for those with some money to spend. It is also larger than the homes surrounding it. However, I can't see beyond the spacious yard crowded with plants. In my opinion, it brings down the quality of the property.

As for the owner...I have only caught glimpses of her over the past couple of weeks. Hard to miss her bright red hair as she moves around in the greenery spanning her yard that hides the rest of her from my view. Even if pressed with a gun to the head, I wouldn't be able to say anything more about what she looks like aside from her hair. For all I know, she has an underbite, a crooked nose, and a lazy eye.

Two

Elixis

"Between you and me, Scytalis, I don't know how he hasn't run screaming from that house yet." I look down at the large snake lazily moving between the stalks of the Foxgloves, his shimmering scales reflecting the sunlight in a myriad of colors.

He is either stubborn or stupid. You know how those non-magicals can be. My familiar is older than he will ever tell me, but it shows in his grumpy retorts. He found me while I explored the arboretum with my mother and her coven...my coven, when I was thirteen years old.

"Hmm. Perhaps the ghosts or demons are trying to get a feel for him," I muse, carefully pruning back my lavender. "Demons are known for finding their prey's weakness before wreaking their havoc, so that is a possibility. If it's a ghost, though..." my sentence breaks off when I hear his barely concealed chuckle along our bond.

Whirling around, I give him the 'don't fuck with me' stare. "What is it, Scy?"

Nothing, Elixis. Nothing at all. If I didn't know better, I'd think the ancient beast is smirking at me. Asshole.

Having the lavender needed for my potion, I move to the edge of my yard. The edge that borders the Wallgren's old place. I kneel down and thrust my hands into the soft soil. Being a Green Witch and having a connection to Mother Nature, I can move through the dirt just as easily as if it were water.

The final ingredient is hiding from me, the cheeky bastard. My pinky touches the root and I smile broadly.

"Found ya!" I wrap my fingers around the Devil's Shoestring and measure out three inches before snapping the piece off. Most roots are simple to find, coming to my command, but these little bastards are defiant. Or maybe just playful.

What are you brewing today? Scytalis asks.

"Protection potion for Widow Sabala. The Randall boys are causing trouble for her. Last night, they cracked a window and sprayed it with paint." I shake my head. Ever since their dad took off, they have been like a babbling, bumbling, band of baboons. Widow Sabala has been in that shop since her early twenties, back when the neighborhood was still growing. For the local boys to be so destructive hurts my heart.

The scraping of metal against metal breaks through the peacefulness of my gardening. The new neighbor has returned from whatever errand he went on. I really wish he would fix his damn truck door. That sound is enough to drive a witch wild.

"Howdy, neighbor!" a gruff voice hollers. "Glad I caught ya."

Rolling my eyes, I put my herbs and roots into my apron pockets and dust the dirt from my hands. Stepping through my vegetation, I meet him at the fence, keeping enough distance between me and that house. Damn place gives me the willies.

"What can I help you with?" No doubt the locals told him what I am and what I am capable of. I prepare myself for the inevitable plea of helping him to rid his home of whatever evil resides there.

His eyes widen as I push an overhanging plant out of my way to see him better. Soft, thick lips open and close a couple times like a fish out of water before he finally spits out his words. "Oh! Um... No, I don't need help. I, uh, wanted to introduce myself." He holds a hand out over the wooden fence. "I'm Sam."

Staring at his hand, I debate whether to get close enough to actually touch him.

He won't bite. Be civil. Father Sky knows what your mother would think if you didn't put forth your best manners.

Damnit, Scy. Why'd you have to go and bring my mother into this? I growl along our bond. He snickers.

With apprehension, I step closer, just enough to touch his hand. The moment our skin makes contact, a zing akin to electricity bursts through to my core. I clench my thighs together, feeling heat rise in my cheeks.

I drop my hand, reluctantly, and look away from his warm hazel eyes. "Elixis."

"What's that?" he asks. His tone tells me he didn't hear my quietly mumbled name.

Clearing my throat, I try again. "My name's Elixis."

"That's a very unique name. Pretty."

I peek through my lashes and notice his cheeks are a bit pink, too. He runs a heavy hand through his dark brown hair. Too bad he's non-magical, because holy crow's feet! He is one sexy slab of man! I knew he was a decent looking guy as I peeked at him from my window, but seeing him up close like this...

"Thanks. Umm, I have some work to do. It was nice to meet you, Sam." I slowly back up, using my bond to be sure that I'm not going to accidentally step on my familiar.

"Coffee!" he yells before I get halfway to the house, stopping me in my tracks.

"What?" I smile at his random declaration.

"Maybe we can get coffee. Together. Maybe?" He reminds me of the Randall boys when they were young, unsure of himself.

A date? We've only just met, and he knows not a damn thing about me.

So what? It's coffee. You are acting like he asked you back to his bedroom.

Scy...he's...he's non-magical. It's against the rules.

The snake grunts. *Rules? Rules are made to be broken, El.*

Shrugging, I nod my head. "Okay. Sure." Before he can see the smile that stretches across my face to the point of discomfort, I turn and jog into the house.

Closing the door behind me, I lean against it, my heart racing as I slide to the old wooden floor. "What in the hell did I just do?"

Three

Sam

I sure pegged my neighbor wrong. She is more stunning than any woman I have ever met, and when our hands touched, a surge slammed through me. It felt like I have known the red headed vixen my entire life. The intense need to get to know her, every aspect of her, tugs at my chest. There is something truly bewitching about Elixis. I suppose that's why I blurted out the invitation for coffee.

Being so forward like that is not who I am. My brother, yes. He would have had her giggling and ready to go skydiving within twenty minutes of meeting her. My M.O. is more the 'stay in the friendzone until she is ready'.

Rolling my shoulders, I trot up to my porch, hoping to catch another glimpse of her before she disappears behind her door. All I catch is the whip of red hair trailing behind her before the door slams. I can't help but think that she regrets agreeing to coffee.

As I turn towards my own door, I stub my toe on the ceramic skunk that sits to the right of the entrance. Whoever made it used so much detail that the skunk looks real...until you stub your toe on the fucker. I swear the thing looks like it is smirking at me sometimes.

Flipping the small statue off, I hobble inside. As I stand in my kitchen brewing a fresh pot of coffee, I realize we never set a time to meet, let alone a day. Hell, I don't know if she wants to meet at the coffee shop or ride together.

"Is it too soon to knock on her door to finalize plans?" I ask the open space.

No, a phantom voice in my head whispers. Great. I'm fucking answering myself now. Shaking my head, I return to my task, readying a mug with two sugars and pumpkin spice creamer. I decide I'll go over a little later. I don't want to seem desperate.

Go now, the voice urges.

That wasn't my inner voice. Fuck. Maybe the locals are right...my house really is haunted. Laughing at myself, I pour my coffee. Why would a ghost want to push me out on a date with the neighbor? Get a grip, Sam!

You'll regret it if you don't go now.

"What? Who's there?!" I yell, losing my hold on my sanity.

Go! Before she loses her nerve!

I quickly leave the house, grabbing my keys off the small table just inside the front door. I am losing my damned mind! There is no such thing as ghosts. Especially not ones who play matchmaker!

The sun warms my face as I step out from the shade of my porch towards my truck. I lift my arm to grip the chrome handle and hesitate. Maybe I should man up and knock on her door. What's the worst that can happen?

Slipping my keys into my pocket, I turn to walk down the driveway. Before I know it, I'm standing in front of a wooden door. Ivy and some odd symbols are intricately engraved in the frame and plants hang to either side. My arm seems to move of its own volition as my knuckles rap against the wood.

I suck in a deep breath and let a long, slow sigh escape my lips. Perhaps this wasn't a good idea. What if she is out in her garden again and doesn't hear me knocking? She could be peeking through a curtain and ignoring me. Or she could be in the shower, washing the dirt away.

An image pops in my mind of her long red hair sticking in sopping strands down her back. Water slips down the slope of her breasts as she runs her hands down her taut belly. A fire blooms in my stomach as my dick becomes as hard as stone, pressing painfully against the zipper of my jeans.

I imagine what it would be like to cup my hands around her face and kiss her. Plying her soft, plump lips open with my tongue, demanding entrance. To feel her nails scraping down my back as she begs me for more.

"Fuck!" A sharp pain burns at my ankle, and I look down. The tail end of a snake slips off the side of her porch. And not just any snake...a mammoth of a beast as thick as my forearm.

Four

Elixis

After Sam invited me out to coffee, thoughts of licking whipped cream off his broad chest have me overheated and overexcited. I never thought it possible, but I become so wet that my inner thighs are drenched, causing my dress to stick to them awkwardly. A cold shower is the only answer to my problem. I sprint up the stairs and turn the cold tap on full blast. The chill makes me shiver as goosebumps erupt on my skin. My heated face and the lava flow between my thighs cools nearly instantaneously.

I flip the bar of soap between my hands to bring up a thick lather. Then I run my slippery fingers over my breasts and down my belly, imagining Sam's hands running over my skin, only causing the heat to return.

"Damn. If I don't stop thinking about this guy, I'm never going to get out of the shower." Of course, if he were to join me...

I slap myself across the face. "Get with it, Elixis! You can't have anything more than a friendship with him," I growl beneath the water. Letting the cold water rinse the soap from my body, I make a unilateral decision; the coffee date can't happen. A single, sexy as sin man can only think that I am interested in a lot more than coffee.

Five

Sam

Rushing to my house with a limp definitely isn't a graceful act, but I need to check on my wound and get myself to the hospital.

Bathroom first, then the hospital. I pray the doctors will know if I've been injected with venom and are able to get me an anti-venom without knowing what kind of snake bit me.

Fire creeps up my calf, building in intensity by the second. I barely make it up the stairs of my porch only to fall to my knees at the door. My body crumples as the pain burns up through my thigh.

Fighting against the pain, I keep my eyes open, afraid that I will succumb and end up in a coma. The ceramic skunk appears to be looking down at me. Its violet eyes watching me with curiosity.

My eyelids grow heavy. I can't keep them open any longer. They close slowly.

With a grunt, I open them again.

The skunk's head is tilted to the side.

My clouded mind can't make sense of it as my eyelids droop closed again. Darkness takes hold of me. And this is how I die. Lying on my porch in a house I've barely lived in while a ceramic skunk mocks me just inches from my face.

Six

Elixis

To avoid bumping into Sam, I slip out the side door of my house and walk the two blocks to Widow Sabala's store to deliver her protection potion. After explaining to her that it is as simple as wearing a necklace, I wander the aisles. I shake my head at the foods that non-magicals stuff in their bodies. Things that have more chemicals than letters on the box in them, loaded with sugars and things that are manmade instead of nature based.

Despite not needing anything, I pick up a few random household needs and make my purchase. Most of my food comes from my garden, or from one of the witches in my coven. However, if I don't buy at least toilet paper, I feel that people will be curious about that. I mean...everybody needs to wipe, right?

Walking home, I take stock of my magic and energy. While my magic is coursing through me waiting to be used, my energy is practically depleted. Avoiding Sam at all costs today has been soul sucking. Perhaps an early dinner and bedtime will do me some good. As my GiGi used to say, 'A tired witch is of no use to herself or her coven.'

I kick my sandals off as soon as I cross my threshold. By the time I reach my kitchen, standing in front of the opened cabinet that hides my modern fridge, the idea of eating is less enticing. However, GiGi's words ring through my mind again, so I grab a handful of berries and trudge up the stairs to my bedroom.

"I'm turning in early tonight, Scy. See you in the morning," I call out, although I know he will hear me no matter where he is. Got to love that bond between a witch and her familiar. Placing the berries on my dresser, I slip my spaghetti-straps off my shoulders, letting the thin dress pool at my feet. My arm lifts, intending to pluck up my berries, but then drops back to my side. I'll eat them tomorrow. I'm just too fucking tired.

My bed is unkempt, unlike the rest of my home. It is just how I left it this morning, and it has never looked so inviting as it does right now. The soft bamboo sheets slip across my naked body like a lover's caress. Even my head is snuggled within the soft cocoon.

Sleep takes me quickly.

❧

Greenery surrounds me, plants I barely recognize. This isn't my garden. An animal scurries around, too tall to be Scytalis, but I sense his presence close by. My arms are stretched out to either side of me as I run my fingers over the leaves, buds, and flowers. Instead of soft soil, warm stones cradle my feet with each step. It's then I realize, I am on a path. But to where?

Stopping, I look over my shoulder. The path is gone, the vegetation has grown over it. There is only one direction to go as the stalks on either side of me are far too dense to step through. I try anyway, telling them to part. My attempt is futile. Okay. Forward it is.

I break through, after what feels like hours, to a stoic room. A room? I look up, no ceiling. No walls, either. Yet, the scene in front of me sure looks like a room. A bedroom, to be precise. Starlight from above, plush carpet below, and in the center of it all a large canopy bed.

Sheer, deep green curtains flow in the breeze, giving me cursory glimpses of what lies in the center of the bed. First a foot, large and bare. Then an arm as another curtain sways. The material behaves as a feathered fan, showing a little of its dancer at a time. Though I can make out his whole outline through the sheerness of the fabric, those little peeks are far more enticing. I find myself yearning to see his face...and his manhood.

I chastise myself, "Creeper much, Elixis?"

"You've decided to come," the deep voice behind the curtains says. It takes a moment, but I recognize it.

Sam.

My feet move of their own accord, eating up the ground between where the vegetation stops and the edge of the massive bed—which only seems to increase in size from one moment to the next.

"You are more stunning than I ever could have imagined," Sam says. His voice is thick with desire, seeking me out from within his secluded nest.

I feel heat rush to my cheeks and to my core simultaneously. My thighs quiver as my pussy clenches. What this man can do with just his voice! I can only imagine what he can do once he begins touching me.

"What are you doing out here, Sam? And...where is 'here'?" My second question is little more than a whisper.

"We are wherever you want to be. Come to me, my wicked little vixen." I can hear the smoldering smile in his voice.

Bending, I crawl onto the bed. The green curtains tickle my skin and I realize I am as naked as the day I was born. That's not all...Sam is just as bare as I am. Though, to his credit, he has a bouquet of orchids in his hands covering his most...vital parts.

Heat emanates from his body, calling to my chilled skin. Again, the bed seems to increase in size, though this time, stretching so that where Sam sits with his back against the headboard is further away than it was when I first saw him.

My breasts sway with every movement I make, struggling to get closer to him. The mattress is overly soft, making me feel as though I am struggling through quicksand. My desire for him seeps down my thighs and I become more frustrated.

"Why can't I reach you?" I ask, panic lacing my voice.

"You are holding yourself back, Elixis. Keeping yourself from me. But you don't have to anymore. Come to me, vixen."

Taking a deep breath, I decide that I need Sam. I need him in ways that I can't explain. In ways that would make Serafina Jax, my favorite author, blush! Or maybe she'd encourage me. The coven doesn't need to know that I fornicated with a non-magical. And if they find out...so what. It isn't like I am walking down the aisle to marry him. A good fuck never hurt anyone before.

With my mind made up, I reach out my right hand and grasp Sam's ankle. Lightning blazes through me and I giggle, imagining that I look much like Thor in this moment. A wide smile breaks out across his face, matching my own.

"You did it, little vixen."

His words of praise ignite something deep within and the next thing I know, I'm on my back with Sam's head between my thighs. His bright hazel eyes peer up at me, locking on mine as he slides his tongue along my slit. His teeth graze my clit before it's sucked between his lips. My back arches as I throw my head back. A moan worthy of a top tier porn star escapes my lips.

I have only been with one man—a warlock who was a wham, bam, not even a thank you, ma'am kind of lay. He left me unsatisfied and questioning my sexual orientation. But Sam. Oh, goddess! Sam in just a few words and a handful of tongue twists has set me solidly in the female seeks male column!

Slightly calloused fingers slide into me, eliciting a feral growl from my throat. My hips push upwards, forcing his fingers and his tongue against the soft folds of my pussy. He nips my clit in response as a deep chuckle sends a tantalizing vibration through me.

I look down at his mop of chocolate hair. As if sensing me, he lifts his head. His pupils are dilated, making his eyes more black than hazel. The heat within those honey depths only serves to bring my orgasm even closer to the surface.

He removes his fingers and I pout. As an apology, he swirls a sinister tongue in their place.

And that is all it takes.

My orgasm crashes around me. My thighs and ass are soaked. And Sam is growling like an alpha wolf as he laps up every possible drop of my cum.

Seven

Sam

NEVER COULD I HAVE IMAGINED HOW AMAZING ELIXIS WOULD taste on my tongue. How her thighs would feel quaking around my ears. She is pure bliss. No. She is more than that. She is absolute ecstasy.

I lick up every bit of cum she gifted me before I crawl up the length of her body. Her chest heaves as she struggles to catch her breath, pushing her delectable tits against my chest with each uprising. As she shivers, I cover her with as much of my body as I possibly can.

"I want you to taste yourself," I say, surprising myself with my boldness.

Her neck stretches as she lifts her mouth to mine. Her soft, pink tongue pokes out from between plump lips. Elixis flattens her tongue and swipes it up my chin, then across my lips. A purr vibrating her chest before she sucks my bottom lip between her teeth. My already hard cock turns to granite.

"Fuck me, Sam. Fuck me like your life depends on it," she demands.

I waste no time in sliding my long cock into the deliciously wet folds of her. Entering her with careful ease. Not that I am some Guinness Book Record holder for the size of my dick or anything, but I could be a contender. The thought of hurting her in any way has me moving gingerly to avoid popping her like a freshly blown bubble.

Her short nails dig into my shoulders, her heels into the backs of my thighs. "Sam." Her sexual frustration seeps through her words. "For the love of Samhain! I said fuck me!"

My vixen raises her hips, pulling me fully into her sheath. Our groans of pleasure mingle to create the most beautiful sound known to man as her muscles contract around me. It only takes a second for our bodies to find a rhythm. I feel something creeping down my shoulder and resist the urge to swat it away. A deep inhalation as I slam my cock into her again brings a faint whiff of iron. Blood. My vixen has marked me with her nails.

I dip my head down, pulling the soft fleshy skin where her neck and shoulder meet between my teeth. An eye for an eye, as it were, I bite down. Her gasp quickly becomes a groan as she tilts her head to give me more access. The tang of her blood splashes onto my tongue. She tastes of sunshine and earth.

Licking at the mark I made on her neck, I feel my balls tighten.

"Don't." pant. "Stop." Her breathing is erratic as my thrusts become disjointed.

My entire body quakes. "Fuck, Vixen!" I cry out as I bury my seed deep inside her sweet pussy.

"Oh, Sammmm!" My name becomes a moan on her swollen lips. Her orgasm comes like a demon being exorcized.

Falling to her side, I pull her closer to me and kiss her forehead. "I think I love you, Vixen."

Eight

Elixis

I jerk awake. My body is coated with sweat, the sheets are rumpled on the floor, and my thighs sticky. Talk about a fucking wet dream! I thought those only happened to men.

Sitting on the edge of my bed, I stretch my back before standing. My legs are weak and wobbly, but I force myself to the bathroom. My bladder must weigh about five pounds judging by the pressure and my need to pee.

The cold tile of the bathroom floor awakens me even more. My body temperature feels as though I am on the cusp of a dangerous fever. I turn away from the toilet and turn on the shower instead. I'm freezing and yet hot to the touch. Great. Just my luck to have an incredible sex dream and then wake up sick.

My muscles are sore, and I moan under the hot water. Then suddenly, a sharp pain emanating from where the water hits the base of my neck makes me yelp. In a rush, my dream slams into me.

"No. It can't be. It..." I stumble awkwardly out of the shower and slide over to the sink. Wiping the steam from the mirror with my hand, I turn my head to the side. There, right where Sam bit me in my dream, my skin is red and... "What the actual fuck?" My fingers run along bumpy indentations that look suspiciously like a set of teeth.

Nine

Sam

Crickets chirp nearby, calling me from the depths of my own mind. I open my eyes to see the dark sky just beyond the overhang of my porch.

Expecting my body to be sore and stiff from sleeping on my porch, I carefully pull myself into a sit. That dream was surreal. I can still taste Elixis' sunshine and earthy flavor on my tongue. My hand goes to my thigh where the wet denim covers my softening dick. Damn. I haven't had a wet dream since I was a teenager. My brother would tell me I need to get laid.

A dull throb in my ankle has my memory of the day before rushing to the forefront of my mind. I was knocking on Elixis' door when a snake bit me. The cuff of my jeans is stained a dark red. Bending at an awkward angle, I pull the material out of the way to examine my ankle. Two red marks...not holes, but healed divots, adorn the soft space below my ankle bone.

"How fucking long have I been passed out on my porch?!" Anxiety tears through me as I scream whisper to myself.

Not that long.

Whipping my head around to see who said that my gaze lands on the skunk behind me. The skunk's violet eyes blink at me before it drops to all fours. It seems to roll its tiny shoulders before saying, *Boy, am I glad to be out of hibernation.*

My eyes roll skyward, and I fall onto my back. Hard.

Witch Way to Oz

BY ANNEE JONES

"Welcome to Oz, where your dream of finding true love awaits!"

When Ruby Jayne sees an advertisement for Oz, the newest matchmaking app that is all the rage, she can't help but sign up. After all, ever since she was dumped for the voluptuous server at the local pancake house, she's done nothing but work. Now that she's in the big city for the fashion design competition, what better way than to let loose and explore the town than by going on a few dates?

After completing the required Yellow Brick Road questionnaire and a meet-and-greet video session with her personal love coordinator, Glinda, she's matched with three eligible bachelors.

When Ruby realizes that each of the three is missing something—a heart, a brain, and courage—things start getting a little weird...

One

"Pew." I sat up straight in the king-size bed of my hotel room, accidentally displacing my gray cairn terrier, Toto, who had been sleeping soundly at my feet. Clearly displeased at such a rude awakening, he turned in a circle, pawed the stiff sheets, and settled back down, nestling his furry little head against the side of my leg.

Apparently he hadn't detected the same putrid scent of smoke I did, or at least wasn't bothered by it. Although, now that I was fully awake, I could no longer smell the acrid odor. Maybe it was just a dream, probably induced by the bananas flambe I had for dessert last night. I wasn't used to such extravagant meals back in my little farming town in Kansas.

With a sigh I laid back down and tried to will myself back to sleep, but after several minutes of tossing and turning, realized it was useless. I reached for my smartphone, which I'd placed on the bedside table before going to bed. The display read 4:17am. Great. Only 1 hour and 43 minutes left before the convention center that housed our temporary workspaces for the competition would allow us access. I'd already finished sewing all the custom fashions I'd created for the final runway show, with the exception of one. Something was still off about the dress, but I hadn't been able to figure out what.

In any case, I had some time to kill before needing to get ready to head over for another day of re-working my design, and it was clear I wasn't going to be able to go back to sleep. Not feeling like picking up the paranormal romance novel I'd begun reading last night, I punched the passcode into my phone, figuring I'd waste time scrolling social media like 99% of the rest of the population.

I clicked through several apps, not finding anything that peaked my interest, and on a whim decided to search the store for the newest trending program. Right away, a bright yellow graphic with rainbow-colored lettering caught my eye. *Your Dream of Finding True Love Awaits!* Read the flashing letters.

Seeing as how my last boyfriend dumped me for the perky new server with the double-D's at the local Waffle House, I figured I had nothing to lose and clicked.

Right away, I was taken to another dazzling screen with an image of a beautiful landscape filled with colorful flowers and a winding yellow brick road down the middle leading to a glittering castle in the distance. An instant later, a series of questions popped up.

Follow the Yellow Brick Road! The screen flashed.

Cute. I smiled at the marketing gimmick and began to fill out the digital questionnaire with such details as my name, age, height, job, relationship status, and location.

After I'd answered all the questions, the app directed me to a page of terms and conditions in tiny lettering. I scrolled all the way to the bottom, hit the check box to accept and signed.

Congratulations! Now it's time to schedule your interview with your personal love coordinator! You've been assigned to Glinda, the Good Witch of Love. Just click on the "Ready" button when you're ready for your video session and start being matched with the dates of your dreams today!

I chuckled. I couldn't help but be charmed by the adorableness of it all. Not wishing to be seen without at least putting on some decent clothes and running a brush through my hair, I hurried out of bed and into the bathroom, where I quickly showered and dressed. By the time I finished swiping on a bit of mascara, Toto appeared, wagging his tail eagerly. I bent down and petted him.

"Never one to miss breakfast, are you?"

After opening the curtains to let in some early morning light—what light could reach my 17th floor hotel window in between all the skyscrapers and office buildings that is—I crossed to the corner where I'd placed my suitcase and all of Toto's things and poured some doggy kibble into his bowl. He began munching happily, and I made myself a cup of coffee using the room's single-cup coffee maker. After adding a couple of creamers and a packet of sugar, I retrieved my phone and settled myself into a chair at the small round table.

I stared at the red *"Ready"* button. Should I click? The clock on the nightstand read 5:19 am. Thankfully the hotel was across the street from the convention center, so I had a good 30 minutes, give, or take, before it was time to head over.

I hovered my finger over the screen. Why not take a chance? I tapped.

The screen promptly split and slid to either side, like theater curtains. In the middle was a plump older woman with long blonde hair (was it a wig?), topped by a pale pink fairy hat with a tulle train that fluttered around her shoulders. She appeared to be wearing a matching dress with a pink satin bodice. A huge rhinestone necklace lay against her very tanned, wrinkled cleavage. She'd really gone all out to complete the look with heavily applied sparkly blue eyeshadow, false lashes, and rouged cheeks. And if I wasn't mistaken, the frosted pink lipstick covering her lips was the same shade my mother used to wear about 20 years ago.

"Greetings, dear!" The woman clapped her hands. The rings that adorned each of her 10 fingers clanked together.

"I'm Glinda, your Good Witch of Love, and I'm so happy to welcome you to Oz!"

"Thank you," I replied with a smile.

She glanced at a second monitor at her side, placed at an angle where I couldn't see the screen, and popped on a pair of black cat-eye shaped glasses with crystals glued onto the upper rims.

"I see here that your name is Ruby Jayne, and you are 26 years old. Is that right?"

"It is," I nodded. "My birthday was a month ago."

"Happy birthday," she said, her eyes still on the screen. "And you're a fashion designer, specializing in costumes, and you're here in New York this week for a competition?"

"Yes," I confirmed. "I'm from a small town back in Kansas, and I was selected to be a contestant in *The Best Fashion Designer in America* competition. I've never been to the city before, and I was hoping maybe some local singles could show me some good places to eat on my breaks."

Glinda looked at me over the rims of her glasses. "But you are hoping to find true love, right?"

I could feel heat rising to my cheeks. "Well, that would be nice," I admitted.

She smiled and gave me a wink. "I understand. Don't worry, just leave everything to me."

She typed rapidly on her keyboard, her bejeweled fingers flying over the keys. I imagined her wpm had to be at least 80.

"All right, I believe I've found your perfect match! I've just set you up on a lunch date with Biff Irons. He's 27 years old and owns the most popular gym in New York. You'll meet him for lunch at noon at the Heartbeet

Superfoods Café. It's only two blocks from where you're staying. He'll be waiting for you at the door."

Wow, she was fast. "Okay," I said. I mean, might as well meet the guy, right?

"Let me know how it goes afterward," said Glinda. "Just tap on the button with my photo in the app to reach me."

After promising that I would get back to her, I closed the app and reached for Toto's leash and my purse. "Time for you to do your business, and then me to do mine," I told him. Only six hours to go before I'd meet Biff. I crossed my fingers behind my back as we left the room, the heavy door closing on its own behind me.

Two

The morning wore on. I rubbed my temples and stared at the blue and white checked dress on the mannequin in front of me.

"Why can't I get this right?" I asked Toto, who was lying on the floor underneath the flared skirt, chewing a bone.

He thumped his tail against the floor in response.

"Thanks for trying to help at least," I said, kneeling to give him a scratch behind the ears.

My stomach rumbled, reminding me it was time for me to head to the café for my lunch date.

"Wish me luck," I said to Toto before I locked him in the workroom and left the convention center.

The weather was balmy, and people crowded the sidewalks. I used the map app on my phone and followed the directions to the Heartbeet Superfoods Café. I wasn't sure what I'd been expecting, but the man waiting at the door made me think of an Arnold Schwarzeneggar impersonator from back in his heyday.

He flexed his humongous biceps and smiled. "You must be Ruby. I'm Biff."

I placed my hand into his giant one for a shake and hoped he wouldn't break my fingers.

"Nice to meet you," I said politely. "Have you been here before?"

"Oh yes," he replied, holding the door open for me and ushering me inside. "I picked it out especially."

A young male server with long dreadlocks and Birkenstocks showed us to a table by the window and pointed to a card with a QR code.

"That's the menu," explained Biff.

Interesting. I'd never been to a restaurant where everyone was expected to have a smartphone.

I reached into my bag for my phone and opened the camera, then pointed it to the symbol on the card.

"Wow," I commented, reading over the extensive information that came up. Each menu item was labeled with symbols indicating whether it was Paleo, Keto, Kosher, vegan, vegetarian, gluten-free, organic, pasture-raised, and local, and included complete calorie and nutritional makeup. In Kansas, the whole menu without the added details would have taken up half a sheet of paper.

"I know, isn't this place wonderful?" Biff grinned, showing off dazzlingly white teeth. "I used to be really skinny when I was a kid, but then I started eating organic and working out. And now look at me! I own the hottest gym in New York, and I've won more bodybuilding competitions than I can count. I'll have to show you my calves after lunch."

The server returned to our table with a large pitcher of ice water with sliced cucumbers and lemons floating at the bottom and poured the infused liquid into our glasses.

I lifted mine to my lips and gulped, briefly wondering if there any way I could make a run for it, but figuring Biff would probably catch me before I'd even gone two paces.

After placing our orders—mine for a bowl of broccoli cheese soup and Biff for a roast beef sandwich on gluten-free sprouted wheat—I ticked the seconds off as I listened to Biff drone on about each of his major muscle groups.

When the waiter finally delivered our meals, I took my spoon and began slurping down my soup as fast as I could.

Biff laughed. "I knew you'd love it!" he exclaimed. He picked up his sandwich and devoured half of it in one bite.

Luckily, we both finished eating quickly, and when the server came by to take our plates and ask if there was anything else we wanted, I was ready.

"No thanks," I said, placing a $50 on the table. "Keep the change."

Biff's eyes grew wide. "Wow, big spender, aren't ya? I was gonna get this, but hey, thanks. Glad you had such a great time."

"No problem," I murmured. "I'm sorry but I need to run. Hope you have a wonderful afternoon!"

"You, too," Biff said, waving his giant hand as I slung the handle of my purse over my shoulder and fled.

Three

Safely back at my workspace and in private, I tapped the button to call Glinda. She answered on the first ring.

"How did it go?"

"I'm sorry, but Biff was not a match," I told her firmly.

"Really?" She sounded surprised. "Tell me more. What was the problem?"

I sighed. "Basically he was all brawns and no brain."

"I see." I heard the sound of typing over the receiver.

"Ah-ha!" Glinda said a minute later. "I've got the perfect match for you! Albert Twombly. He's only 25 but he's a genius. He's going to be the next Bill Gates!"

"That sounds promising," I replied. Intelligence was definitely an attractive quality.

"I've arranged a date for the two of you for dinner tonight. Albert asks you to meet him at Made for Mandarin at 6 pm."

"That sounds great," I said. "I love Chinese food."

"Excellent!" said Glinda. "I look forward to hearing how it goes."

I returned to working on the dress. However, despite altering the sleeves to make them a bit puffier and adding tulle under the skirt to give it more volume, I still wasn't happy with it.

"Toto, what do you think?" I asked my dog. He looked at me and panted.

"A blue sash around the waist!" I snapped my fingers and grabbed some blue satin. After finishing the edging and tying into a huge bow, I stood back and frowned.

"This is driving me crazy," I said, running my hand through my long brown hair. Something still wasn't right. However, I was going to be late if I didn't leave soon to meet Albert. I took Toto out for a potty break, and then we walked back to the hotel room where I gave him his dinner and quickly freshened up.

"Wish me luck," I said on my way out. But Toto was too busy with his crunchies and didn't look up.

When I reached Made for Mandarin, I wondered if I'd come to the right place. This looked like any other inexpensive mass market fast-food chain. Surely a man as smart as Albert wouldn't have chosen a fast-food joint for a date?

"Ruby?" A short, obese man with early balding and a sweat-covered brow held out his hand.

"Yes?"

"Hi, I'm Albert," he said, taking a handkerchief from the pocket of his ill-fitting jeans and wiping his forehead. "Sorry, I'm a little nervous," he said with a high-pitched giggle.

Clearly I needed to have another little chat with Glinda.

"This is the best place ever!" said Albert, leading me inside.

"Hi Albert!" said the waitress, an older woman with a perfect bob. "Oooh! Who do we have here? A date?" She clapped her hands. "Has your mother met her?"

His mother?

Albert plopped down at the closest table and shook his head. "Not yet," he said. He leaned forward as I slid into the seat across from him.

"I live with my mom," he said. "I've got the whole basement to myself and have all my computers and gaming equipment in there. Mom cooks for me and does my laundry. I mean, what more could a guy ask for, right?"

I blinked. "Um."

The waitress handed us plastic-covered menus with photos of various dishes. I pointed to the first one. "I'll have that, please."

She nodded and then turned to Albert. "Your usual?"

"Yep," he said proudly. "Mom and I order take-out from here every Friday night," he explained.

"I see," I replied.

The server brought our dishes to us in record time. Then again, it was fast food. And just like any other chain, the portions were huge, the food was overcooked and dripping with grease, and everything was absolutely delicious. Albert and I both ate every bite.

"I'm stuffed," I announced, feeling a little queasy.

"Have a mint," he said and handed me a warm piece of foil-wrapped mint chocolate from his pocket.

"I think I'll save it for later," I replied politely, placing it on the seat beside me.

"Want me to put this on your tab?" asked the waitress, coming by to clear our plates.

"Yes, please," said Albert. He glanced at the square face of his high-tech wristwatch. "Listen, Ruby, this was fun, but I've got to get going. Mom's expecting me home soon. Our favorite show on the sci-fi network is on tonight."

"No problem," I said. We walked slowly from the restaurant onto the sidewalk and parted ways. I waddled back to the hotel and when I got to my room, the first thing I did was grab my phone and punch the button to call up Glinda.

"Albert's the one, isn't he?" she asked as soon as she answered.

"No!" I groaned as the contents of my stomach churned uncomfortably.

"Oh, dear," said Glinda. "You sound a little peaked, honey. Are you feeling all right? Perhaps have a mint."

"Ugh," I said.

"Tell me, what was wrong with Albert?"

"He lives in his mother's basement," I said.

"Oh. Yes, I can see how that would be a problem. In other words, you need a man with more courage, don't you? Someone brave and independent?"

"Yes, that's it exactly," I said, lying down on the bed and propping my feet on a pillow.

"Give me a sec," said Glinda. Again, I heard her fingers typing away.

"Ah-ha!" she said. "I've found your perfect match now! Third time's a charm, right?"

"Maybe," I replied. I had to admit, my faith in the Good Witch was waning.

"His name is Ace. Ace Cheatham. He's a pilot. Isn't that a brave profession? And he's available to have lunch with you tomorrow. Do you like sushi?"

"I don't know, I've never eaten it before," I said.

"Well, you'll have your first chance tomorrow at 1 pm." Glinda gave me the name and location of the restaurant.

"Have a good night's sleep!" She said brightly before she hung up.

Four

I didn't think it was possible, but Date #3 was even worse than the previous two. Ace was not only a half-hour late, but he didn't even bother to apologize. His dashing good looks weren't enough to make up for his overblown ego, either. Not only did he spend the whole date bragging about his astonishing flying feats from his time in the Air Force and how every major airline was waiting to snatch him up, but he openly flirted with the waitress while attempting to play a game of footsie with me at the same time under the table. Even though I found the sushi quite tasty, I pretended it wasn't to my liking just so I could hightail it out of there as fast as possible.

Ace walked me out of the restaurant, then grabbed me around the waist, planted a sloppy kiss on my lips and pinched my butt. "Bye, sweetheart. Enjoy your time in the city."

I may have thrown up a little in my mouth. Heading back to the convention center, I entered my workroom and angrily slammed the door behind me.

Toto immediately ran up and I bent down and lifted him into my arms.

"I'm sorry, I didn't mean to scare you," I told him, nuzzling his furry face. "But I'm pretty sure that was the worst date I've ever had."

Suddenly, there was a loud knock on the door. One of the producers, maybe?

I put Toto back down on the floor and opened the door.

A woman with a green face and long stringy black hair wearing a witch costume flew into my workroom. She pointed a gnarled finger at me.

"Lay off my husband!" She yelled.

"Look, I don't know you or your husband," I said, not sure what to make of her choices of makeup and attire.

"Yes, you do, hussy! I'm Ace's wife and I saw you with him today! You'd better get your greedy paws off him, or else!"

Toto suddenly began to bark, sensing that I was being threatened.

"And don't think I won't come for your little dog too!" She yelled before throwing her cape around her shoulders and stomping back out in a huff.

"What on earth was that about?" I wondered aloud as I closed the door in her wake.

I turned to my dress, determining to forget about the strange intruder and focus instead on completing my final design for the upcoming show.

"Maybe I should try this on myself," I said. I unzipped the dress and removed it from the mannequin. Then I undressed and stepped into it. After fastening the zipper, I moved in front of the three-way mirror and turned this way and that. The blue and white check pattern and ruffled bodice made a pretty combination. But it needed something—a pop of another color. Red would be perfect! Yes, a pair of red shoes!

I went to the boxes of shoes stacked up against the wall and knelt down to search for the ones I was thinking of. I quickly found them—cherry red sequined pumps with a buckle.

I slipped my feet into them, lifted Toto into my arms, and hugged him tight. "Oh Toto," I said, clicking the heels of my shoes together. "We don't belong here, do we? I just want to go home."

Five

All of a sudden, Toto leaped out of my arms, landed on the floor in front of me, and before I could blink, turned into the most handsome man I'd ever seen. He was tall with broad shoulders and narrow hips, and his hair was short and dark, streaked with just the tiniest bit of gray. His goatee was perfectly trimmed, and his bright green eyes sparkled as he smiled at me.

I gasped in shock. "Toto!"

"You mean Theo," said the gorgeous hunk of burning love, who took a step closer to me and wrapped his arms slowly around my waist. I leaned against his chest, somehow feeling that I could trust him. As my body relaxed, so did my willpower and when he bent his head towards mine and our lips met, it was pure magic.

Our kiss deepened, and I began to sense my heartbeat. Or was it his? I couldn't be sure. Oddly, the beating started to get louder.

"Do you hear that?" I asked, pulling away slightly.

"What?" he asked, gazing at me in confusion.

But the beating was so loud now that I could barely hear him. My head was throbbing with the pain of it. I rubbed my temples, but it only got worse.

"Make it stop," I moaned, closing my eyes because it hurt to keep them open. I tried to open them again, but for some reason I was having trouble.

"Help," I whispered right before I lost consciousness.

Six

"She's awake!"

I opened my eyes to the sight of my mother's face hovering over mine.

"Where am I?" I said, trying to sit up.

"Now, now." My father suddenly appeared and gently pushed me back onto the pillows. I gazed around, realizing that I was lying in a hospital bed.

"What happened?" My head was aching and when I reached up and touched my fingertips to my right temple, I found it covered with a bandage.

"Hang on, let me turn this off." My father picked up the remote control on the bedside table and aimed it at the television, where the final scene from The Wizard of Oz movie with Judy Garland was playing at a low volume. He pressed the button on the remote and the screen faded to black.

"Where's Toto?" I asked, still not fully lucid.

My mother laughed. "Oh, that's cute. Arthur, she must have been listening to the show while she was coming to."

My dad chuckled and squeezed my hand. "I think our girl will be okay now."

At that moment, a plump older woman dressed in a nurses' uniform with bleached-blonde hair and skin that indicated she'd spent too much time in tanning beds during her youth bustled into the room.

"I hear Ruby's awake!" she cackled as she checked my vitals. The nametag pinned to her white top read Linda North. She scribbled onto her clipboard and looked at me kindly. "Welcome back, dear. Do you remember anything about what happened to you?"

I tried to think. "The last thing I remember is working in my workroom."

"That's right," said my dad. "You're here in New York for the fashion design competition. You made it to the final."

"A fire broke out in your temporary workspace, and the authorities confirmed it was a case of arson," my mother continued. "Eliza Gulch, who you were going up against in the final round, confessed."

"Oh my gosh!" I yelled. "That witch!"

"She was capable of some dirty tricks, that's for sure." Mom shook her head. "She told the police she didn't think you were going to be there when she set the fire, but it turned out you'd gone back after hours to fix something or other with one of your designs. In any case, you fell when you were trying to get out and hit your head. Thankfully a fire fighter saw you and pulled you out in time."

"Yep," Nurse Linda nodded. "Other than a slight concussion, you only suffered a bit of smoke inhalation and minor burns. You'll be just fine in a few days."

"Great," I said, breathing a sigh of relief. I looked at my parents. "You know, I always thought I wanted to be some big-name fashion designer with my own studio in New York, but after being here this week, I've realized big city life isn't for me. What I really want is to go home to Kansas where I can be just plain ole' Ruby Jayne. Maybe I'll get a dog."

"You'll never be plain, honey," said my mother with tears in her eyes. "You're our beautiful daughter."

"Our pride and joy," added my father, his own brown eyes getting misty.

Suddenly there was a soft knock and the door to my room cracked open.

"Look who's here!" exclaimed Linda. "I think you'll want to meet the man who saved your life."

A tall, handsome man with dark hair streaked with gray and bright green eyes appeared at my bedside.

I gasped. "Theo?"

He laughed. "That's right! Wow I can't believe you remembered my name! You must have heard someone say it at some point. I'm Theo Barnhart, nice to meet you."

My dad clapped him on the back. "This guy not only carried you out of the fire, but he's come to check on you every day for the last five days since you've been in a coma on his own time."

Theo blushed. "I just had to make sure you were going to be okay," he said softly, looking at me tenderly. "Linda's been kind enough to bend the rules to allow me to see you, since I don't exactly qualify as family."

Heat rose into my cheeks.

"When do you think she'll able to travel, Linda?" Mom asked. "We'd love to go home to Kansas as soon as possible."

"I'll check with Dr. Goode," said the nurse. "But her vitals look good and as long as she remains stable for the next 24 hours, I don't see any reason to keep her here."

"Kansas?" Theo perked up. "My sister moved out there last year with her husband and kids. I've visited them a couple times and really like the small-town vibe. I grew up in the city and have been thinking for some time about making a change. Maybe we could exchange phone numbers and next time I come out your way I'll look you up?"

"Yes," I replied happily. "That sounds great."

Linda handed me my phone, which had been lying on the table next to a roll of clean bandages and winked. "Here you go, dear. I've always loved playing matchmaker."

About the Author

Annee Jones is an international bestselling author of romance, fantasy, and mystery. She is passionate about writing stories where dreams come true and love wins!

Professionally, Annee works as a disability counselor where she is honored to help her clients navigate through complex medical and legal systems while rediscovering their wholeness in Spirit.

She also freelances as a professional book reviewer for a major national publication and blogs about books for several publishers when time permits.

Subscribe to Annee's newsletter to stay up to date on new releases, sneak peeks, author parties, and exclusive giveaways: https://www.anneejones.com/newsletter

Find Annee and her books here: https://linktr.ee/anneejones

Oh, No!

BY RUBI JADE

Ten years ago, I placed a hex on my high school bully. I never thought that it would come back and bite me in the butt. Especially when it comes to Jasper–my best friend, roommate, and oh, yeah, the guy I've been in love with since we were kids, starts dating her.

Will my silly mistake cost me his friendship and possibly his heart?

One

Beulah

TEN YEARS AGO, I PUT A CURSE ON MY HIGH SCHOOL BULLY. LET'S just say she made Regina George look like Mother Theresa. One day after another of her abusive tirades, I couldn't take it anymore. In my rage, I couldn't control my magic and took away the only thing I could think of that would ruin her life. Her ability to orgasm.

Yeah, I know, it was an awful, petty thing to do. Especially since I made it so she couldn't even fake it. You know those girls in the pornos that sound like they are giving birth to feral kittens when they cum? Yeah, she sounds worse. And that's what I'm experiencing now, ten years later from my living room couch.

I sigh and smile at the same time, as the sounds of Patricia orgasming from Jasper's room reach my ears, where I sit in our living room trying to read from my spell book. I turn the page and look beside me where my black cat Osiris lies unamused. His ears flicker as I look at him and he blinks at me with his jade-green eyes.

"At it again." his voice is heard in my head.

"Yup," I say out loud popping the p as I turn another page in the book. I look towards the television, which is on, funnily enough, *Sabrina the Teenage Witch*. I lift my right hand, point my pointer finger at the TV, and raise the volume using my magic.

"Oh, Jasper! That feels so good!" Patricia exclaims.

Want to know the kicker about this hex? It only happens if she does something to me, verbal or physical.

That's it.

If she were a decent human, she could be enjoying herself, but since she made a rude remark before entering Jasper's room, here we are.

You'd think after ten years, things would be different but here we are as adults and she acts the same way. Still acting like the Queen Bee as if we were still 15.

Some things have changed, just not for her. Especially Jasper.

I guess he's forgotten how she treated him back then. I guess his dick is the one calling the shots these days. But since Jasper's appearance has also changed, I'm sure that is why Patricia noticed him. He is not the skinny, nerdy kid anymore. He is all man now. Muscular and tall. I don't blame her at all.

To say I'm still in love with my best friend is an understatement. I've loved him since I met him in middle school. I noticed his essence from the get-go. Appearances didn't matter to me. And not just because I was a chubby acne-prone girl back then either.

It's not to say I don't also appreciate the way he looks now. He's definitely grown, but I'd love him even if he was still skinny and 'nerdy' looking.

Patricia cries out again and I wince, hoping my windows will withstand the shrieks. Then things fall silent for a while. I focus back on my book mindlessly looking at a new spell to try out.

That is until I hear her talking behind Jasper's closed bedroom door.

Damn. She's coming out.

"Control yourself. Don't let her rile you up." Osiris says in my head. I just gently nod but he knows I struggle. She pushes all the right buttons to piss me off and she knows it.

The door opens and she giggles as she exits. She fumbles with one of the buttons on Jasper's shirt she's wearing, pretending to button it but I know that's for my benefit. She will leave it unbuttoned so I can see how much more well-endowed she is than I am. I'm a B to her Double Ds.

She spots me and as predicted she drops her hands.

"Oh, Beulah Moo-lah. I didn't know you were here." She places a hand on her chest as if appalled, "If I'd known, I'd have told Jasper to be quieter." She smirks.

I nod in response, not wanting to say anything to give her fuel and turn back to the TV and my book, ignoring her. Of course that won't pass on her account.

She floats over to the kitchen. She has this way of walking that looks like she's ice skating.

She makes a show of getting a bottle of water from the fridge and opening it, taking a small sip then walking back to the adjoining living room where I'm sitting.

"Oh Beulah Mule-a, it's such a pity you don't have something better to do on a Saturday night than to sit here with your cat. Have you thought about finding your own place so you're not cramping Jasper's style?" She narrows her eyes at me but I still don't respond. If she only knew this is my apartment, not Jasper's.

"Oh. I've heard of a new dating app for people like you. I think you should give it a try and see if you can find someone so you're not sad and lonely. What's the name of that app?" She places a finger under her chin, deep in thought. I notice that Jasper steps out of his room behind her wearing only sweatpants. I make no indication that he's there. He crosses his arms over his powerful-looking chest without a sound. "That's right. 'Single Cat Lady' I'm sure you'll find someone special there to take both of you freeloaders in. Jasper is too nice to tell you himself that he's tired of having you here in his house so it's time to leave." She gives me another smirk and takes another drink from her bottle but spills all down her chest. "Oops. Silly me. Let me go clean this up. Maybe Jasper will lick it all off of me," she says wiggling her eyebrows. "Hope not to see you in the morning, you fat cow."

I smirk when she turns around and yelps in surprise at finding Jasper standing right behind her, looking angry.

"What did you just say?" he says in a low but menacing voice.

"Oh, Jasper honey. I didn't see you there."

"Patricia, what the fuck did you call her?"

"I-I was joking!" she stammers.

"That didn't sound like a joke to me. That's my best friend you're talking about! What gives you the right?"

She huffs, stomps her foot, and points at me, "She *is* a freeloader. Why else would you have her living here? And with her dirty ass cat." She gives Osiris a disgusted look.

Osiris hisses at her. I reach over and pet him to soothe him but don't say anything.

Jasper runs his hands through his hair. "Patricia." he sighs and then places his hands on his hips and leans towards her, smirking. "Grab your shit and get the fuck out."

"Jasper!"

"Now." He narrows his eyes at her.

"Fine. You're a terrible lay anyways," she says huffing her way back to his room to change.

"And you sound like a banshee," Osiris says and I snort.

"I'm glad only magical folk can hear you," I say to my cat.

A few minutes later, Patricia comes out of Jasper's room dressed in the tiny dress and heels she had been wearing when she arrived. Her designer bag is in her hands.

She stops in front of Jasper and slaps him across the face. His face turns to the side but he doesn't react. He stays as he is as she stomps out the front door.

"Good riddance," Osiris says and I couldn't agree more.

Two

Jasper

I WALK UP TO THE DOOR TO THE BLUSHING SKULL. THE BELL over the door jingles as I open and enter, holding it open for a patron leaving the establishment.

The Blushing Skull is a witchcraft store selling anything you could want or need. Spells and potions handcrafted by Lala herself. Crystals, books, and even Tarot readings. Like I said, anything you could want or need. Her store is very popular.

Beulah, or Lala as I call her, glances up at me when I approach and gives me a warm smile. "Hi," she greets me.

"Hey. I come bearing gifts." I tell her as I lift the drinks and bag of food.

"Oh, yum." she looks at the logo on the bag and her smile grows wider, more excited. "Are those tacos?" She asks giddily.

"Of course," I say laying the food on the counter in front of her.

"Let me lock up," she says and comes around the register to lock up for lunch. I gulp as I watch her retreating back in that small burgundy mini skirt and calf-high boots. Her top, God her top. It's a bralette thing with a sheer see-through lace long-sleeve top over it where I can glimpse her belly button with the sparkly ring and her breasts pushing up against the top of the bra.

I swallow audibly, glad she's at the door and can't see me. I turn back to unpack the food, hiding my obvious arousal from her.

She comes back around and sits on the stool she has behind the register as she makes a happy sound watching all the delicious morsels I've brought.

She brushes her long moonlight silver hair over her shoulder. It's an interesting color. Silver with hints of lavender. It matches her eyes. They're a gorgeous lilac-silver color. So unnatural and so very Lala. They suit her personality. Her aura.

Those lilac-silver eyes dance with glee as she looks at what I brought her and I smile.

Who doesn't love tacos? But Lala? It's next level with her.

I push them toward her and she thanks me before digging in.

I chuckle and start on my own meal.

Osiris jumps up onto the counter licking his snout as he looks at our food and I laugh.

"Oh, Osiris. Always so food motivated."

He gives me a narrowed-eyed look and if looks could kill I'd be falling over now.

"Now, now. Don't give me that look. I brought you a chicken one." I say pulling out the last taco and unwrapping it. I place it in front of him and watch as he attacks it as if he hasn't been fed in months when I know Lala fed him this morning.

Lala rolls her eyes at him, "You're going to get chonky."

He hisses at her in reply but goes back to eating.

We eat in silence for a bit before I break it, "We haven't really talked in a while. How's business?"

"It's good. It's my busier time of the year with Halloween coming up."

I make a non-committal noise as I continue to eat, knowing it does get busier now until the new year.

"So... how are you?" She asks after a brief pause.

"Eh," I say not looking up at her but rather down at my food.

We haven't really spoken about the incident with Patricia. It was awkward, to say the least after she stormed off. It's been a month since then and I'm happier. Patricia and Lala have never gotten along. I'm not 100% sure why not, but hearing what Patricia was saying definitely helped me understand a lot more.

"I'm sorry, Jas," Lala says, placing one of her hands over mine. The heat that zings through my body at her touch is surprising but not unpleasant.

I look up and catch her eye. "I'm not," I say turning my hand and capturing hers, holding it tight.

"W-what?" she stammers.

"I'm sorry for what she said to you, but I'm not sorry for getting rid of her. I'm happier without her." I say

She just stares at me for a moment. I catch the moment when her expression changes. Her mouth is in a tight line and I can tell she's trying to hold back a verbal lashing. I know her too well.

I squeeze her hand, "Tell me."

"Tell you what?"

"Whatever it is you're holding back. I know you, Lala. Tell me. Give me the verbal whipping you're holding back. I can handle it. And while you're at it, you need to tell me what hex you put on Patricia as well."

When her eyes meet mine I know I've got her.

Three

Beulah

FUCK.

Shit.

Damn!

I take my drink and suck on the straw to give myself a moment to collect my thoughts. He knows. Damn it!

"Beulah?" he questions.

It feels so strange hearing my full name from him. But at the same time, it sends a shiver of pleasure down my spine. I plop the straw out of my mouth and place the cup on the counter. He watches me closely, narrowing his eyes.

Did I just imagine him staring at my mouth?

I stand from the stool, pulling my hand out of his and busy myself tidying up an already clean display, avoiding him.

"I don't know what you're talking about," I say and move to tinker with the display behind the counter.

"Beulah?" he extends my name again. "Tell me," he repeats.

I sigh and grab the trash from the counter and walk to the back room. "Nothing," I say over my shoulder.

He follows behind me and I again maneuver around the space to avoid looking at him.

"Tell him Beulah, or I will!" Osiris threatens from the other room. I turn my head to throw a dirty look in his direction but find Jasper standing in the doorway, his arms crossed, staring at me.

"I heard that. Now tell me everything," he says narrowing his eyes at me.

I don't think he's ever looked at me like that and I take a step back from him. He's intimidating when he's angry.

"N-nothing...bad bad," I say unsure how to tell him.

He arches a brow, "What does that mean?"

I look down and move, unable to stand still and feeling like a caged animal.

Why did I come in here? I boxed myself in. Damn it. Stupid idiot!

I want to bang my head against a wall for my stupidity but I can't right now. It'll have to wait until he leaves.

I stop by my work table and sigh again before looking towards him. "I hexed her ten years ago." I quirk an eyebrow at him. "How did you know I did it?"

He shrugs. "I had a feeling."

Looking at him, I sigh.

I'm tired of this. Tired of hiding how she treated me. He will have to know everything. It's an all-in sort of confession now. So I start telling him everything.

"That-that was so cruel." he manages at one point.

"Well, it's what I lived. And everyone loved her. She never did anything wrong. I was the weird one and deserved to be picked on."

I can't help it. The feelings I'm feeling overtake me and I let out a cry of frustration and turn away from him, crossing my arms over my middle, as if that will protect me from all the pain. Everything that she's done to me. Everything I've felt. Everything I'm about to feel as I tell him everything.

"Are you ok?" he asks. His voice is soft as if he doesn't know how to approach me.

I pace in front of him looking down at my boots, still hugging myself. I need to tell him but I'm not sure how.

"Beulah?"

I stop in front of him, my side to his front and turn my head so I can look at him. The anger has dissipated a bit and I feel deflated. "You don't know do you?" I ask.

"Know what?"

I look at him and examine his face. His handsome, gorgeous, I-want-to-punch-him-in-the-mouth face, and I sigh. I turn my body to face him. "You are so clueless, you know that?"

He examines my face but doesn't respond so I continue. "I love you, dumbass." His eyes go wide and he takes a step backward. I continue, needing to get it all out of my system. "I've loved you since 7th grade. Back when you were nerdy and picked on, I loved you."

"Beulah..."

I lift a hand to stop him from speaking. "And recently, watching you with her. She, who made my life hell. It was killing me."

"What?"

My eyes meet his and flash. "What? You thought just because we grew up that she stopped? You only witnessed what she said *one* day."

"Damn Beulah." Jasper starts again but I lift a finger to silence him.

"No. Just wait." I look at him as I continue, "Beulah the mule-ah. Beulah is a cow name. Are you a cow Beulah? Moo Moo Beulah." His eyes show shock again. "Want me to go on? How they pushed me against lockers and made fun of how I didn't fit in them. Some of the horrible things they did to me in the gym locker rooms. Trust me. It put *Carrie* to shame."

"Beulah, I didn't know."

"Of course, you didn't. I never told you! The shame I felt. The shame I still feel. I like my name. It's witchy and fits me perfectly but they defiled it with their name-calling. They made me hate myself, calling me a cow. Making a poor kid feel body shamed because she was chubby at the time. I had to learn to love myself again. And I do. And then she came back into my life. Because you brought her back into it and can you guess how that's been so far?"

"Hell?" he says in a pained tone, a grimace on his face.

"Jasper... she may have grown up in body form but she has not grown up mentally." I tap my temple. "She's still stuck in high school. She's still making my life hell. Beulah the mule-ah, Jasper!" I step towards him and pound my fists against his chest. His strong, muscular inviting chest but before I lose myself in him I need to tell him everything.

His hands come up and grab me by the elbows, not to push me away or pull me close. More to just hold me up. It's not strong. I could step out of it if I wanted to.

"So what did she do to make you hex her?" He asks softly.

I slowly lift my face to look at him. Tears are on the verge of falling down my face. I muster the strength to open my fists and place my palms flat against his pecs. His warmth seeps through his shirt drawing my hands closer. I resist the temptation to rub my hands up and down his torso and focus on his face.

"One day, she and her minions just pushed me too far. Calling me a fat cow, knocking me to the floor and as she walked away I just couldn't take it anymore. The hex came out before I could stop it. But you know what? I'm proud of myself. I don't regret it." I smirk at him. "And you know the kicker?"

"What's that?" he asks.

"The hex only takes effect if she does or says something bad to me. Truthfully. If she was a decent human and was kind, the hex wouldn't have worked. So it's really her fault."

I step away from him and turn my back. I run my hands through my hair and let out a frustrated breath. "I don't regret it," I repeat to the wall. I close my eyes lifting my face to the ceiling and breathe out. I feel so much better. So much relief washes over me at letting out the confession.

I'm surprised when a moment later I'm being turned around and pressed between the table behind me and Jasper's strong chest. He's got me wrapped in his arms, his breathing is coming in ragged pants and he's looking down at me with an intensity I've never seen before.

"Beulah." the way my name comes out in that tone has my panties sopping. "Beulah," He repeats his eyes going from my eyes to my lips. "You should have told me before."

I absentmindedly lick my lips as I watch his mouth. So close. So close I could- "What part?" I manage to ask.

His eyes crash with mine. "That you loved me."

My breath catches as the tenderness he's looking at me washes over my entire body. I don't know how to respond but luckily I don't have to. Because he continues talking.

"Beulah, I've loved you since forever also."

My heart.

I think I just died.

"I never said anything because I thought you only saw me as a friend. My heart has always belonged to you. Only ever you, my Beulah." he lifts his hand and slowly caresses my face. I can't help but push myself into his touch, wanting to get as close as possible to him.

His touch. His caress.

His thumb rubs up and down my cheek. So tenderly. So full of love it makes my heart want to explode.

"My Lala," he says, then his mouth crashes over mine.

The moment our lips touch, I see stars. Explosions of colors behind my eyelids. There is a tingling in my hands, like electricity on the tip of my fingers. And heat. So much heat, starting in my belly and taking over my entire body.

I lift my hands and place them on his chest like I had wanted to do earlier but I don't push him away. I instead grab hold of his t-shirt and pull him closer. Pull myself closer to him, deepening the kiss. His hands come around my waist and pull me closer to him. Flush against him, I feel his big strong erection pressing against my belly.

A moment later we both slowly pull away enough that we can look into each other's eyes but are still close enough to feel our breaths against our faces.

"W-wow." I manage to say.

He smirks as he stares down at me. Heat radiating in his eyes. So much desire I'm sure is mirrored my own. "I agree." And then his mouth is back on mine, and he's pushing me backward.

My back meets the edge of the worktable and the heat from before ignites even stronger. An explosion of desire overtaking my senses and I groan against his mouth. His hands trail from my hips and down to my thighs and he grips them. Digging his fingers into my flesh.

I gasp in surprise when a moment later he lifts me up onto the table. He spreads my legs open and stands between them. I feel uncertain for a moment since I'm wearing a tiny skirt but this heat.

This desire.

It's overtaking everything. I push towards the table's edge, trying to be closer to him. So that part of me that is itching for attention can be touched even if it's just by his pants. I need the friction. I'm acting like a horny teenager wanting to rub myself against him in any way I can.

He chuckles, removing his mouth from mine. "Calm down. We will get to that."

He trails kisses down the side of my neck, around my ear, and down to my shoulder through my shirt. I want it gone. I want his lips to touch my skin directly.

I trail my hands down his chest to where his shirt is tucked into his pants and pull the shirt out allowing me to move my hands under and touch his abs directly. He steps away and with a grin, pulls it up over his head.

I've seen him shirtless before. Hard not to when we live together, but this time it's different. Usually watching and drooling, ok admiring from afar, but this time I can touch him. Touch him all I want. And that's what I intend to do. I reach to touch his pecs but I'm stopped when he grabs the hem of my sheer long-sleeve top and pulls it over my head as well, exposing my bralette underneath.

"Damn Beu." he groans as he stares at my cleavage. It's not too exposed in this top but apparently, it's enough for him.

He stares at them for a moment longer and then his mouth is over mine again. His tongue makes its way into my mouth. I pull him in closer, the apex of my legs needing attention, so I wrap my legs around his middle. The moment we have contact I moan, loudly. He presses his groin against me and swivels his hips.

"Yes, Jasper. Like that. Please." I moan against his mouth.

He moves his mouth away from mine and to my neck, running it up and down. His stubble scratching deliciously against my skin. One of his hands leaves my hips and he places it between us right where I want him most. He strokes me through my panties and the zap of electricity runs all the way up to my hair.

"Jasper." I moan.

His stroking speeds up and when he moves my panties aside and touches me directly. I almost cum then and there. He must feel it because he pulls away just as I'm about to go over.

"What?"

He grins wickedly at me and slowly lifts his hand to suck on his fingers, staring me in the eyes. I can't look away. It's so hot. I bite my bottom lip and watch him slowly bring his hand back down and back to my entrance. This time he inserts them inside and I buck. It feels amazing. He begins thrusting and I rock against his hand, chasing the release that is so close I can almost taste it. But just as it's about to happen, again, Jasper pulls out of me.

"Jasper!"

He smirks at me again. "Patience." He pulls away and starts undoing his pants pulling out his erection. I can't look away from it. I lick my lips and then catch his gaze. "As much as I'd love that pretty mouth of yours over my cock, I can't wait much longer to get inside you."

"Yes please," I murmur. I lift my skirt up higher on my hips and remove my panties, throwing them aside. I spread my legs open wider. His gaze locks on my exposed opening, glistening as it awaits him.

"Damn, Lala. I wish I could eat that pretty pussy but I can't wait much longer."

"Then don't. We have time later." I say, desperate to have him inside me as I reach to touch the throbbing head.

"Oh no you don't," he says, swiveling his right pointer finger in a circle. The magic hits me instantly, pulling my arms to my side and sticking my palms against the tabletop. I try to move but they are stuck. I look at him as he approaches. After all these years, he's never used his magic on me. Sometimes I forget he's a wizard.

"No touching. I want you like that," he says as he brings his erection to touch my opening. He stops before he enters me and looks me in the eye. "You're still on birth control? I'm clean. Never went without protection. I just don't have one right now." he asks.

"Yes. It's ok. Do it." I reply still unable to look away from where he's so close to entering me.

"Fuck yeah," he says, and with that he thrusts in all the way.

I cry out as he fills me, stretching me so deliciously. "Yes. Fuck me." I try to reach out to touch him, to pull him closer but the magic he used, stops me from moving.

His thrusts speed up and he holds me by the hips. I'm so close.

He pulls out.

"Damn it, Jasper. What are you doing?!"

His only response is that same smirk he's been giving me each time he does it. He slowly enters me again and begins thrusting. This goes on a few more times. Tears are falling down my face at the frustration of needing to orgasm and being unable to.

"How does this feel? Huh? Is it torture?" he rasps as he continues to thrust into me.

It feels unbelievable. I need him to keep going if only I could- "Jasper!" I cry out. "Please, let me come," I beg with a sob.

I'm approaching the edge again. He grabs my chin with one hand and makes me look at him, his expression serious. He kisses my lips hard before pulling away to look at me again. "My Lala," he runs his thumb over my bottom lip. "Cum for me."

It's what I needed. What my body was waiting for. My orgasm washes over me so strongly that I black out for a moment. I cease to exist in time and space as wave after wave of pleasure washes over me. In the distance, I hear Jasper's roar as he reaches his own release. A moment later his face lands on my shoulder and he rasps trying to catch his breath.

"Fuck, Lala. That was-"

"Magical?" I smirk as the bliss of our lovemaking washes over me.

He lifts his head to look at me and smiles widely. "Yes. Magical."

He kisses me tenderly. I'd like to reach up and caress him but can't. His magic still holds me back. When he pulls away our gazes catch. "How about closing the store early today and continuing this at home?"

I grin at him. "Sure. Just release me."

He looks like he's thinking hard about something. "No. I don't think so. I like you like this."

I grin back. "Then make yourself comfy. We will be here a while." I wink.

"There's no place I'd rather be."

“I love you, Jasper.”

He kisses me in response and my heart agrees. There is no place I’d rather be.

About the Author

Rubi Jade fell in love with reading in the fourth grade. It didn't take long for her love of reading to transpire into writing her own stories. When she discovered romance, she never went back, falling in love with the genre itself to the point her writing style changed as well. Her favorites are romantic suspense and that's what she loves to write as well.

Rubi is currently a stay-at-home mom of three and moves around the US due to her husband's job. She currently resides in Montana, USA.

When not writing, you can find her with a book, romance of course, drinking coffee, wine or beer (depending on the time of day), eating tacos, and daydreaming or binge-watching TV.

Sign up for her newsletter at: https://www.subscribepage.com/rubijade

Find out more about her: www.rubijade.com

Follow her on social media: https://linktr.ee/rubijade

There's An App For That

BY HANNAH MCKEE

There's an app for everything now. Shopping, photography, even love.

Gorgeous witch Helle didn't want any of that. All she wanted was to eat some cake after another terrible party. When things go awry, she finds herself transported into a magical land of crashing gemstones and steamy cauldrons.

Kevin is planning the biggest party of his career, but he needs more excitement in his life. He finds it when he opens his phone to discover an app he never downloaded.

Will the unlikely pair work together to escape their fate and save the witch's counsel?

One

WAND TRIP

Helle had never been to a party that she liked. She hated crowds, loud noise, and dancing. Party games have never been her cup of tea. The only thing she ever enjoyed at a party is cake. Yet, for some reason, her parents loved them. They loved them so much that they had a different party to go to every weekend. It didn't help that her mom and dad were both high standing members of the witch's counsel. Because of that, Helle didn't have a choice. She had to make an appearance at every single one.

Today was no different. Helle was at yet another soiree, trying her best to avoid Calvin, her dad's latest assistant. He gave her the creeps, but her dad can't seem to get enough of him. Which was strange, because even though her dad was friendly, he had never taken his assistant's advice before.

As she tiptoed down the hall of her parent's castle in Ravenmoore, hoping to snag the last slice of black forest cake from their latest shindig, Helle overheard Calvin. His commanding tone echoed across the cobblestone.

"You promised me everything, Mr. Crafts."

Helle's ears perked at the name. He was speaking to her father.

Calvin continued. "It's not everything if I can't marry your daughter."

"Helle?" Mr. Crafts chuckled. "That girl has her head up in the clouds. I can't make her do anything she doesn't want to do. And trust me, she doesn't want to get married. Even if you were the most handsome wizard on the planet, she would wait for true love."

"She will marry me," Calvin hissed. "Combining our magic before the blood moon will give me more power than either of us can imagine."

Mr. Crafts began to scream, the sound cut short when a thunderous crack sounded through the hallway.

"Yes, Calvin," Mr. Crafts said, his voice monotone. "Helle will marry you. Tonight."

Helle couldn't control herself any longer. She rounded the corner and stopped in front of the two men.

"You monster!" she shrieked as she jumped in front of her dad. "How could you do this to him? To us? You'll never get away with this."

"Helle," Mr. Crafts placed his hand on her shoulder and squeezed. Helle wiggled out his grasp.

"Dad," Her father's eyes were dull, as if his soul had been removed. "Come back."

"He's not your father anymore," Calvin said. "He's nothing more than my puppet. But you can fix this, darling dear. If you agree to marry me, before the next moon, I will release him."

"I won't."

At her denial, Mr. Crafts removed his wand from the pocket of his robe and pointed it at Helle.

Calvin smirked as he pulled his own wand out of his pocket. "Our marriage is a win-win. I'll be more powerful than any of us can imagine, and you will always be taken care of. You would learn to love me."

Helle shook her head. "Never."

Mr. Craft's eyes widened as Calvin's wand sparked, a bolt of light streaming toward his daughter. She leapt into the air and fired back.

"Excidere!" She yelled.

The men's wands flung out of their hands. As the men dove to catch their magic, Helle bolted down the hall. As quick as she ran, Calvin was faster. There was only one trick she could think of to escape this dreadful fate. If she could flee for the night, she would come back the next day, after the blood moon, and save her family.

"Portalum Evocare," Helle pointed her wand and flicked her wrist to the left, drawing a wing in the air. A large circle of pink smoke appeared in front of me. "Los Angeles."

A sidewalk appeared inside the smoke. Then a busy road next to it, with cars and buses. People formed from mist, real people, as they went about their days. Two men stood beside a large van, unloading enormous boxes from the back. In a few more steps Helle would be safe, lost in a bustling city where nobody could find her. She jumped, her heart pounding against her chest. Her head went through the portal, then her torso and hips. Suddenly, she felt something tug at her feet. Her knees buckled and she tumbled forward, the hard ground knocking every last drop of air from her lungs. She glanced over her shoulder and whimpered. Calvin was floating above her, his usual grin twisted into a menacing frown. Black tar oozed from the tip of his wand, pulling her toward it.

"You will marry me," he growled. "I might not be able to put the same spell on you that I put on your father, but you and your family's powers will be mine."

"No," Helle cried as darkness enveloped her. A single tear rolled down her cheek, landing on the tip of her wand. A pink spark appeared, fluttering weakly until everything turned black. The only thing she heard was a faint beep followed by a peculiar, upbeat jingle.

Two

THINK PINK

Kevin stopped short, the large box in his arms tumbling forward with the sudden motion. He could feel it slipping from his grasp but despite his attempts to maneuver it back in place, it kept falling.

"Dude!" Ryan dropped the curtain he had been carrying and ran to Kevin's aid. "Focus man. Unless you want to break all our equipment."

"You didn't see that?" Kevin said as Ryan helped him secure the large box. "Everything turned pink."

Ryan slapped Kevin's shoulder as he burst out laughing. "You want to use that excuse? Sorry Mr. Bauchman, I broke the photo booth you ordered because the sky was pink? That's what happens at a sunrise wedding."

"The sky wasn't pink," Kevin rolled his eyes. "Everything was pink." He wanted to figure out what it was, but he knew not to keep pestering Ryan about it. His friend had a one track mind, and this wedding had to go off without a hitch. It was their first semi-celebrity event. If everything went right then Dynamic Duo Events would be unstoppable.

"Whatever man, nothing was pink, ok? Now let's get this booth setup."

Kevin took a step then paused. A strange vibration buzzed across his leg. He was about to reach down when he remembered two things: he was holding a very heavy box filled with expensive equipment and he had put his cell phone in his pocket earlier. It buzzed again, confirming what he already knew.

"What now?" Ryan said. "Keep moving."

Kevin grunted as he started moving. The box was heavier than he remembered. "You know, I never thought we'd be planning parties for a living."

"Seriously?" Ryan picked up the curtain and grabbed another box before kicking the van door closed. "All you did was party in college. Now you get paid for it."

Kevin snorted. "This is just another one for the books." He walked up the first flight of stairs, a nervous flutter growing in his stomach as he got closer to the door.

"Right," Ryan smirked. "Another party that just happens to be the wedding for a tech billionaire and his actress fiancée. Your dad helped us land this event, but it's up to us to make it unforgettable. If we mess anything up you can bet that all of Hollywood will know about it."

Kevin pressed a silver button on the wall and the door in front of him swung upon. "That's why we won't let anything go wrong today."

An hour or so later, the wedding was in full swing It was going so well that Kevin decided to take a break. He stepped out of the party and opened his phone. As soon as his screen lit up, a pink light flashed. Music began playing and an app opened.

"Steamy Cauldron," he shrugged. "I don't remember downloading that but I guess it's worth a try."

He started humming along to the perky music. As he did, a male voice began to sing. "In an app's domain, a tale unfolds, a witch entrapped, her story untold. Jealous love, a wicked display, 24 hours for her heart to sway. True love's embrace, her only escape, Or forevermore, in the app's landscape."

"This makes no sense," Kevin said. "What's the story here?"

The screen cut to black and the words LEVEL 1 drifted across the screen in bold, white letters.

"Another puzzle game," Kevin smirked as he ran his finger over the cauldron, forcing the witch to release a beam of colored foam from her wand. When a like color hit the foam above, it drifted off revealing a new pattern. "Typical. At least this witch is hot."

His gaze lingered over the image of the witch on the bottom of the screen. She looked so real. He could make out individual strands of her wavy red hair, which cascaded to her waist from her high ponytail. He grinned when he saw the row of freckles splashed over her nose.

"She is definitely my type. Curvy, but not overdone. She'd be perfect if she didn't look so... sad?" The witch's expression flickered between over the top happy and downright miserable. With each switch there was a subtle pink beam. "Must be a glitch. Still, what are the odds? More pink?"

He shrugged and continued playing. He beat one level after another, each time the witch looked a little more animated. Her green eyes brightened and enlarged, her perfect nose blended into a cute-as-a-button curve. Still, he was drawn to her.

"I wish she was real," he muttered. "A girl like that would never be with a guy like me."

Three

GEMSTONE MADNESS

At first Helle was confused. She had no idea what happened to her. One minute she had been running for her life, the next she was surrounded by vast nothingness. She couldn't see through the darkness. She stretched out her hands and legs, hoping to feel something around her. Her breath caught in her throat when she realized she was alone.

"No," she whimpered, realization pulsing through her as the memories of being pulled into darkness returned. "What do you want with me?"

"Helle, my love," Calvin's voice echoed through her mind. "You can leave this place any time you want. All you have to do is agree to marry me."

Helle opened her hand and called out. "Wand."

Nothing happened.

"Wand," she tried again, a little louder. Still nothing. "Where are you?"

"Your magic won't work here," Calvin said.

Helle was about to respond when she noticed a small bolt of pink electricity forming by her left foot. It was magic.

"My magic," she whispered. "There's still a chance."

She continued, this time loud enough for Calvin to hear. "You may have trapped me, but you weren't quick enough. I'll find my way out of here."

"Silence!" Calvin screamed.

Helle couldn't hear anything else. She sat in the shadows, without vision or magic, for longer than she knew. Time seemed to be still. She counted her heartbeat, but lost track right away from the abnormal beats. It was as if her body couldn't place itself either. Then, loud music blasted out of nowhere, followed by bright colors and a steamy cauldron bubbling to the brim with fluorescent foam.

"I'm delirious," Helle tapped at her temples. "That's the answer. I've simply gone mad!"

She was about to lie down when a dark shadow filled the sky above her. It was unique. Long and flat.

"A finger?" Helle rubbed her eyes. "It is! And behind it is, what? Brown eyes? And a crooked nose? It's a man. I feel like I've seen him before."

Her heart raced as the finger came closer, nearly squashing her face, when it stopped and began to slide. Her arms moved on their own, copying the sway of the finger, until foam began to lift from the cauldron and launch from her wand into the sky above. Gemstones rained down on her as the preppy song blasted again.

This happened over and over, until level twenty-seven. This time, when the gemstones crumbled over her, she flinched. For a split second Helle could move on her own. She wiggled her toes and lifted her arms, twirling in a circle as she examined the way her body glided under her own control. She glanced up, staring at the brown, oval eyes. They were wide with dilated pupils.

"He saw me," she mumbled to herself. "That means... Hey! Hey you!"

The man blinked. "Interactive. I've never seen anything like this before." His finger swiped across the screen then paused.

Helle tried to yell again but was interrupted by the app's jingle. She tried to wave but her arms would not lift. She tried to jump but her knees stiffened, unable to be bent. A new puzzle formed above her as a cauldron popped up from the ground. Her arms went through the motions of the man's finger until yet another level was complete.

As soon as the gems began to fall around her, Helle pounced.

"Yoohoo!" she yelled as the man's finger hovered her. "Down here."

The man paused and glanced at her.

"Hello?" he said, his voice muffled. "Is that you, witch?"

He held the phone away from him, allowing Helle to see his face for the first time. Her cheeks warmed as she took him in. His nose, though still crooked, was balanced by his infectious smile, which was like sunshine breaking into her surroundings, illuminating everything around her. For a moment, she yearned to learn more about him.

"Hi," she chirped.

"Hi, back," the man responded.

A gemstone crashed on Helle's head before she could respond.

"Ouch," she groaned as the gem bounced off her, disappearing once it hit the ground.

Kevin chuckled. "Are you ok?"

"I am....not, I mean. I'm not ok. I need your help."

Kevin's brows furrowed and his eyes narrowed. He appeared to be deep in thought, and Helle felt her shoulders drop. She took a deep breath, calming herself. Even though he wasn't a wizard, this man was on her side. He was trying to come up with a way to save her. However small, Helle knew she had a chance.

"Ok," Kevin snapped his fingers. "You need my help. So, we're obviously moving on to some other kind of puzzle and this backstory is going to be important."

"Pay attention," Helle snapped, trying to hold back the tears welling. "You have this all wrong."

"I've never seen an app like this before," Kevin interrupted. "Usually the graphics are just so-so. And this must have some AI element to it to be interactive."

"We don't have time for this." Helle wiped at the tears rolling down her cheeks. She had to pull herself together. It was the only way to make sure he would understand her, and she needed him to tell her mother what had happened. She cleared her throat.

"Kevin," A voice yelled in the background. "Get over here buddy, I need you."

"Kevin," Helle whispered. "That's his name. Kevin!"

She screamed for him again, jumping and waving when he glanced in her direction. "Kevin! Help me!"

She fell back as his eyes widened and his pupils dilated. "Down here!" she tried.

"Witch?" Kevin said, his finger caressing the screen of his phone, next to her face. She reached for it, wishing she could feel him through the screen. "This isn't real," he whispered.

"It is," Helle said, the tears she had managed to hold back flowing once again. "I promise it is."

Kevin turned white, and for a moment Helle thought he might pass out. He looked over his shoulder. "Give me a minute," he yelled, before turning back to Helle.

"This can't be real," he mumbled. "What's this game called? I need to look this up."

"Dude!" the voice called. "We've got a situation. Get over here."

"I'm coming," Kevin said. He turned his attention back to Helle and squinted before shaking his head in disbelief. "These app creators have really stepped up their game."

"No!" Helle yelled as the phone began to move. She couldn't risk him not opening the app again. "I need you now."

The electricity at the bottom of her foot spiraled up her leg, through her body and into the cartoon wand she held. It blasted through the screen of the phone. All Helle could see was pink, then, her vision returned. Through the screen, Helle could make out a party. It would have been lovely, if it wasn't spinning around and around until there was a wooden floor speeding toward her. A loud bang echoed through the app world as the screen shattered and flickered off.

Helle sat cross legged and groaned as she balanced her face in her hands.

"Stupid," she muttered, consoling herself with deep sobs. "You stupid, stupid girl. You finally found someone who might have been able to help you, and you ruined it. Just like you ruin everything."

She opened her eyes and looked around. It was light, the phone had frozen mid-level, with gemstones still floating above her while the steaming cauldron bubbled below. She turned her head, realizing for the first time that she wasn't just stuck in a single level. It was a complete land, with different rows of gemstones floating in the sky like clouds with different patterns.

"I wonder if I can make it to the final level. Maybe there's a portal there."

She stood and dusted herself off, ready to start a new adventure, when the light that had shot out of her wand began circling in front of her. It spun and weaved, creating a giant cocoon that burst open when the light reached the top. Inside stood Kevin.

"Where am I," he said, his hands trembling as he pointed at Helle. "You! You brought me here."

Four

MESSY EMOTIONS

Kevin didn't know what to do. The girl standing in front of him, who less than five minutes before was just a cartoon character, had wrapped her arms around him, pressed her head against his chest, and exploded into a messy ball of emotions. One second she was crying, the next she was shouting, followed by excited squeals before the triathlon started over. The only consistency was the disappointment in her eyes, which for some reason was directed at him.

"There, there," he said, patting her on the head. He felt like he was the cartoon, mimicking what he had seen in movies.

The witch sniffled as she pulled back, catching his gaze.

"I'm sorry," she said as she wiped at the baby hairs frizzing around her face. Her ponytail had fallen half-way down with pieces of hair completely loose, but Kevin thought she looked even better now. She was real.

Kevin brushed the bangs away from her face, hoping she couldn't tell how nervous he was. "Don't be silly. What do you have to be sorry for? I played this game. I dropped my phone. You didn't do anything. Unless you made the pink flash that- please don't cry."

"It was me," Helle said as she wiped her eyes. "I did it. The pink flash. That's my magic."

With that confession, Helle told Kevin the entire story.

"I know there's a way out of here," she said. "There has to be a portal somewhere. You must have found it on the other side."

"I guess we'll have to find it," Kevin glanced around. "Which way?"

"To the left," Helle pointed. "That's the way the sky turned when each level changed."

The two walked, level after level, to no avail. There was no spark or portal in sight. The more time they spent together, the more comfortable Kevin became with Helle.

"I can't tell if it's been years or minutes," Kevin said as they passed under the words LEVEL TWO HUNDRED FIFTY-NINE. "How much further do you think it is?"

"I'm not sure," Helle replied. She started to climb over some fallen gemstones when her foot got caught.

"Argh," she yelled as she began to tumble. Kevin grabbed her wrist, holding her inches above the ground.

"Don't worry," he pulled her toward him. "I've got you."

Helle blinked and glanced away. "Thank you."

Kevin helped her out of the pile. She took a step and winced. "It's twisted," she moaned, rubbing her ankle. "If I had my wand I could heal it."

"I think I can help," Kevin kneeled in front of her and pointed at his back. "Hop on."

"I don't know if that's a good idea," Helle said. "I weigh more than I look."

Kevin shrugged and pointed. "I'm sure I can handle it."

Helle did what she was told, hopping onto his back and wrapping her arms across his chest. He grasped her wrists, glad that she couldn't see the smile spreading across his face. They continued on, moving through twelve more levels, before Kevin began to stumble.

"I guess I'm a little tired now," Kevin said as Helle slid off him. She landed with a soft grunt and walked to his side. "You look much better now."

Helle's face turned bright red and she flipped her hair over her shoulder. "I am, thanks. I could have walked through the last level, I guess. I just... I don't know."

Kevin stopped so short that Helle nearly knocked him over. "Just what?"

"Um, well, you know."

"No, I don't," Kevin said with a grin.

"You do," Helle insisted. "Or you wouldn't look like that."

"Like what," Kevin asked, pretending to frown.

"Happy," Helle said. She turned to face the next level before Kevin could respond. "Let's keep going."

"I will," Kevin interlocked his hand with Helle's forcing her to spin into him. He caught her, letting her body melt into his. Before she could protest, he kissed her. Her soft lips pressed against his, matching the intensity he had felt for a while. His heart raced as any ideas he had about this being some crazy fever dream vanished.

When Kevin opened his eyes, he and Helle were still kissing, but they were no longer inside the levels of Steamy Cauldron.

"Helle," he whispered, embracing her as she opened her eyes. "We've got a problem."

Five

ALL THE MAGIC WE NEED

Helle opened her eyes to the worst scene she could imagine. She and Kevin were embracing in the middle of a wooden dance floor. A bride and groom ducked behind the large cake table and their guests and vendors hiding throughout the venue, while Calvin floated above them. Dark , smoky clouds filled with lightning and thunder glided around his legs. Kevin's grip tightened around her waist as Calvin pointed his wand at them.

"Relinque!" he shouted. Hands of smoke grew from the clouds, ripping Kevin and Helle apart.

"Wand," Helle yelled. Out of nowhere, there was a small, white puff around her hand and her wand appeared.

"You may have gotten your magic back, but that doesn't mean you can beat me." Calvin let out a wicked cackle dripping with cruel delight. "You're going to marry me."

"Why would she marry him?" the bride quipped from behind the cake.

Without turning around, Calvin pointed his wand and bounced it. The bride flew into the air and dove into her thirteen-tiered cake. She kicked and moved her arms, destroying everything on the table. He then pointed his wand at Helle.

Helle returned the gesture, ready to fire, when Kevin leapt in front of her. "I won't let you hurt her," he yelled.

"No?" Calvin raised one eyebrow. "What are you going to do about it?"

"Kevin," Helle whispered. She lowered her wand, not willing to risk any injury to this man. "Don't do this. He'll hurt you."

"I have to," he said, turning to face to her. Helle's heart raced. She wanted to make him stop, to put a spell on him and send him into hiding where he would be safe, but for some reason, she couldn't. Kevin cupped her face in his hand.

"I know how we got out of the game. It was in the jingle. I love you, Helle. I know you love me too. That's all the magic we need right now."

Helle grabbed his hand and placed it above her heart. "Do you trust me?"

"That's enough," Calvin shouted. He pointed his wand at them and Kevin went flying into the air. He hit the ceiling before dropping until he floated next to the evil wizard. "I don't need to wait for you, Helle. You'll do anything I say, just like your father."

Calvin's wand sparked and zapped as he placed the tip against Kevin's temple.

"Will you marry me, darling," he said with a cackle. "It may sound like a question, but I assure you there is only one answer."

Helle glanced at Kevin, who winked. She turned back to Calvin and bowed her head. "Partiore," she whispered. Her wand split, with one half exploding into small, silver shards.

"What," Calvin said. "Don't mess with me, witch."

"I said," Helle grinned, feeling more confident than she thought she could. "Partiore."

"No!" Calvin gasped. "You can't use that spell. Not with someone you just met."

Calvin turned around. Kevin soared above him, raising a thin wand above his head, small silver shards shooting from the tip. He glanced back at Helle, who was waiting with her wand pointed.

"Expelle," she said, as white glitter blasted at Calvin.

"Expelle," Kevin repeated, silver shards joining with Helle's magic. It worked together, swirling around the wizard until it shrunk him into a small circle and popped.

Kevin used the wand to transport him down, in front of Helle. "Where did he go?"

"He's going exactly where he belongs. His fate is now in the hands of the witch's council. I can't imagine it will end well for him, since my father leads it."

"What about your magic?" Kevin shook his wand, trying to keep his feet from being hit by the sparks. "How do I return it to you and why isn't it pink anymore?"

"You can't," Helle said with a sigh. "When a witch falls in love with a mortal, she is able to share her magic. This spell is rarely done, though, because the magic can't be returned. As for the color, it is very personal to each witch or wizard and can sometimes change when they experience something big that impacts their life. For me...it was meeting you."

"Well...this magic is still yours," Kevin kissed the back of Helle's hand. Her heart fluttered. She knew she had made the right choice. "You'll never need to worry about that."

"We do need to worry about this though," Helle said, referring to the wedding. Though most of the guests were still hiding, the groom had managed to pull his bride out of the wedding cake and was towering over Ryan, who looked like he was either going to punch the groom or burst into tears. "Just follow my lead."

Kevin mimicked Helle's motions and words, until the venue was clean and everything was forgotten with only Kevin and Helle remembering what happened. Soon enough, the dance floor was packed.

"Would you care to join me?" Kevin asked.

"Aren't you supposed to be working this thing?" Helle said with a giggle as Kevin wrapped his arms around her waist.

"They won't even notice," he said, swaying to the sweet melody.

Helle rested her head on his shoulder. "Did I ever tell you that I hate parties?"

Kevin ran his fingers through her hair. "That's only because you haven't been to one with me."

"Well, I really hope the next one starts out differently," Helle said before kissing his cheek. "Though I don't mind how it ended. When this is over, you're going to have to meet my parents. They're going to want to know how we managed to meet and fall in love in, I don't know, under five hours."

"That's easy," Kevin said. "We tell them there's an app for that."

About the Author

Hannah McKee is an American storyteller and novelist. She writes paranormal fiction, women's fiction, romance, and children's picture books. When she is not writing novels, she is writing scripts. An attorney by trade, farmer by hobby, and mother for life, Hannah has learned how to spin a tale and shares that talent with you. You can follow Hannah on Instagram at www.instagram.com/hanadoesstuff. Her debut novel, Of Heaven and Hell, was published in 2020. Her debut children's book, Unicorns Hate Cupcakes, can be found wherever books are sold. She is currently working on its sequel, Reindeer Hate Carrots.

Hexually Vexed

BY EMMY DEE

Lena is the worst at dating. So, when the opportunity to go out with her long-time crush is shoved in front of her, courtesy of her best friend, Piper, Lena can't help but worry. Will she ruin this date, too?

Even with her limited future sight, this gray witch didn't see herself walking out on the hunky donut shop owner. Nor did she imagine she would run into an alpha wolf shifter with impeccable manners.

Is Lena destined to be alone? Or will a girl's night out turn her love life upside down?

One

GOOD THINGS COME WITH HOLES

That absolute shit-stain. I knew he was no good. Not really, but after Piper told me about what she just witnessed, Shane would regret the day he cheated on my best girl.

I told her I'd have this hex brewed up in fifteen minutes, and damn it, I'm gonna get it done!

When I chose the route of a gray witch, my mother was… less than happy. She wanted me to follow in the family footsteps to develop my Sight. But after she saw how naturally it came to me, and how pure and potent my product was, she went from pissy to proud.

Now, she's eighty percent of my business. Her friends are constantly in and out of my shop asking for literally any kind of potion, hex, curse, etc. Her ceaseless bragging has turned quite the profit for me.

It only takes me a minute to brew up Piper's hex. I'm just missing the final, and most crucial, ingredient.

Popping the cork, I "accidentally" add an extra drop or two of essence of self.

Just for potency's sake.

When I ran into Piper Lancaster at that witch's convention a couple of years ago, I knew she was my soul sister. Her brother thinks she's just using me to compensate for her lack of magic, but that's not the case. I can sense she's made for something great. She just hasn't found the tools she needs to unlock that greatness.

A poof of silvery smoke emerges from my mini cauldron, indicating that my concoction is completed. I transfer it to a vial and pop the cork in just as Piper reappears at my front door, donuts in hand.

Bless her poor broken heart.

They say that diamonds are a girl's best friend, but I suspect that this "they" have never tasted donuts. Especially donuts from...

"OMG you brought me Glazed and Confused donuts?!" My mouth waters at the sight of the psychedelic box with a donut smiley face.

"I did," Piper smirks. "I also got you a date with that donut guy you've been lusting after."

"SQUEEEEEEE!!!!" I punch her on the arm and she laughs at me.

"Don't say I've never done anything for you," she says, setting the donuts down on the counter and plucking the vial out of my hand. "And thank you for this. You're my bestie for the restie,"

The shop door swings open and she blows me a kiss before leaving, the door slamming shut behind her.

"Lock up, shop!" I holler at my enchanted door. Even if the jerk gets on my nerves, he's my favorite part of the shop.

Yes, he's a he. I've noticed that he's overly friendly to my female customers and certain males he won't even open for unless I tell him to.

But I wouldn't trade him for the most beautiful regular door in the world.

After properly finishing my closing duties for the day, I restrain myself until I square everything away before indulging in one of the world's best donuts. When I open the box and see "Text Me" written with a love heart and a phone number on the inside cover, I can't hold back my squeal.

I take a picture of the note on the box and grab a random donut, adding the photo to a new text and sending it to Gilbert.

I devour my donut, cookies and scream, one of my favorite flavors, and my phone dings.

Gilbert: Donut girl? Did you eat the cookies and scream yet?

Oh my God, he knows my favorite donut.

Me: Just finished it! Delicious as always!!

Gilbert: That's good to hear! *smile emoji* So... about that date?

Me: Yes??

Gilbert: What time is good for you?

Me: We could do lunch any day, and I'm always free after six!

Gilbert: Lunch sounds perfect! Could you do tomorrow?

I clutch the counter… that's so soon! Am I really prepared? Should I get my hair cut? Buy a whole new wardrobe? Oh my God… What if I mess this up?

I was so excited by the thought of going out with Gilbert that I didn't even think about my bad luck streak…

No. This time will be different.

Me: Tomorrow sounds great!! *smile emoji, thumbs up emoji*

Gilbert: Wanna meet at Louis's Bistro around 11 then?

Me: It's a date!

I can't believe I said it's a date, how cringe can you get? But it doesn't matter. That's the worst thing that's going to happen on this date.

Door lets me out and clicks the lock behind me as I set off for home with a spring in my step and my box of donuts in hand.

I can't believe I'm going on a date with Gilbert Fischer!

Two

FIFTY WORST DATES

I spent the better part of last night preparing for this date. After deciding what to wear, a black sundress with tiny skull flowers and platform sandals, I wound up psyching myself up so much that I didn't sleep.

I was trying to avoid my past bad date experiences, but one by one they flashed through my mind.

The time I tripped on my own two feet and spilled hot coffee on Harry Jones. The time I got choked on a cherry tomato and my date had to perform the Heimlich maneuver only for me to throw up on his shoes. The time I had an allergic reaction to the avocado on my sandwich and had to be rushed to the hospital.

I'm a real fun girl to take out.

I lay in bed until seven, when I couldn't hang on any longer. Then I get up and get ready because if I'm going to be any kind of fun on this date, I'm going to need some coffee.

It's a quick walk to the coffee shop, where I grab my vanilla iced latte with a triple shot of espresso.

My shop doesn't open until nine, so since I'm up early, I take the extra time to organize my current orders and file the ones I've completed this month. I also do inventory, making a list of any ingredients I'm getting low on and noting which ones I have used little of lately.

By the time nine o'clock rolls around, I've got the shop neater and more ready to go than it's been in months. That triple shot may have been excessive.

I help the handful of usual customers and a few new ones that heard of me through the grapevine... taking their orders and promising a high-quality product when they return to pick it up, then I close for lunch.

I'm nervous as I walk the few blocks to Louis's. Throwing up a prayer to whoever may be listening to not let me make a fool of myself.

Gilbert is standing at the end of the little walkway, looking as handsome as ever with his chin-length, wavy auburn hair and his light blue eyes. Just a smile and a wave from him already has me swooning.

I give him a little wave back as I approach him.

"Hi," I say shyly.

"Hi!" His smile is bright as he holds his arm out for me. "You look lovely today. Lena, right?"

I can't stop the blush from creeping up my neck. "Yes. Thank you. And you're Gilbert? You look lovely, too."

I'm such an idiot. I can't believe I said that. He looks handsome; he looks hot; he looks like a god. Anything else would have been better than lovely.

He laughs, and my insides flutter.

"Would you like to sit inside or outside?"

"I'll let you pick," I say, looking away. Nothing too terrible has happened yet. Come on, Lena. You've got this.

"Outside it is then. It's so nice out today," he says, stopping at a table and flagging a waiter down.

They give us a menu and take our drink order before whisking back into the restaurant.

So far, everything is going okay. I haven't made any blunders yet.

I look up from my menu to find Gilbert staring at me. Not in any sort of particular way. It's almost like he's lost in thought.

"Your friend is nice," he says, finally.

"Oh... Yeah, Piper is the best."

While I do think that my friend is great, I can't help the zing of disappointment that runs through me. We're the ones on a date and he brings Piper up.

"She said I'd enjoy myself if we had a date. Quite the wing-woman." His eyebrow quirks.

"Well... are you? Enjoying yourself?" I fidget with the menu.

"Hmm..." he starts, but is interrupted by the waiter.

"Here are your drinks. Have you decided what you'd like to eat? Or do you need a little more time?"

"I'm good if you're good," Gilbert says, making sure I'm ready.

"I'm good."

He nods. "Right, I'll have the number four, with extra bacon please."

The waiter scribbles his order down and looks at me expectantly.

"And I'll have the number two."

They jot that down as well before grabbing our menus and rushing off once more.

"Do you date a lot, Lena?" Gilbert asks, leaning back in his seat.

"Um... no, not particularly."

"Why is that?"

What the fuck? "I don't feel like I have to tell you that." I lean back too, slightly uncomfortable with where this line of questioning is going.

"Fair enough," he says before moving on to his next question. "When did you notice you liked me?"

I almost spit my drink out. "Sorry?" I say, coughing and trying to catch my breath.

"Your friend, Piper, I think you said. She said you've liked me forever. How long is forever?"

"Piper wouldn't..." This is not going the way I imagined it. The easy-going donut shop owner is nowhere to be found. Instead, I find myself on a date with the guy who interrogates murderers or something.

"Why would you ask me that question, and why do you keep bringing Piper up? Do you like her or something? Would you rather be on a date with her?" I push back from the table, standing with my fists clenched.

"I think I'm not feeling well. I'm going to go." I turn to leave, but a warm hand grabs my wrist. Electricity zaps through me and I freeze.

What was that? Gilbert's eyes are so intense they seem like they're glowing.

"Wait," he says, his voice a deeper rumble than usual.

I shake him off, determined to save a little of my dignity. "It was nice sharing a drink with you."

I walk off, squeezing my eyes shut to hold back the tears. So much for the amazing Gilbert Fischer.

Three

WRECKED, VEXED, AND HIGHLY UNDERSEXED

The week after my ruined date with Gilbert goes by slowly. Nothing like time to make you feel worse about yourself.

I should have known better than to expect a date to go well. Especially one I was so looking forward to.

The only consolation I have is that this time, I wasn't the one to ruin the date. I didn't trip, or spill anything, or spit my drink in his face, or wind up in the hospital.

I just ran out because he was asking me some very uncomfortable questions.

By Friday, I must be noticeably upset, because my door wouldn't open for anyone. Even after I yelled at him to let the people in, he remained firmly locked.

"Fine," I grumble at him. "There is something wrong with me, I guess."

Door squeaks his hinges at me.

"Well, what do you expect me to do? My crush turned out to be a real jerk."

He opens and closes himself almost in a pattern.

"Are you...dancing?"

He squeaks his hinges and swings open fast.

"You think I should go dancing?"

Another squeak and he waves back and forth, not quite closing.

"I guess Piper and I haven't been to the club in a while..."

I contemplate going out or sitting at home binging Backyard Summonings and eating chocolate chip cookie dough ice cream. But I guess

Door can sense my hesitation because he swings open as hard as he can and slams himself. A groan creaks through the wood.

"OKAY! I'll text Piper." I say, trying to calm down the door who just became my therapist.

He squeaks his hinges in a satisfied way and then goes silent.

I pull out my phone to text my friend before my door decides to unattach himself from his frame to do more than scold me and she responds almost instantly.

Apparently, she needs to get out of the house, too.

Since I'm getting nothing done today, I decide to lock up early to get ready. Maybe dancing with handsome strangers and my best friend is what I need to forget about Mr. Twenty Questions.

I give Door a pat on the way out and whisper my thanks. He locks up behind me, looking somewhat proud of himself.

As much as a door can look proud.

❧

PIPER AND I DECIDE TO MEET AT THE CLUB. HER FRIEND, JEFFREY, sees me heading to the back of the line to get in and waves me over, unlatching the velvet rope and stepping aside to let me through.

I nod my thanks and head inside. The heady thump of the music already soothing my aching heart.

It doesn't take me long to find Piper. She's at the bar and she looks like she wants to punch the next person who approaches her.

I smile and saunter up to my bestie. "What's got your face looking so sour?"

She narrows her eyes at the four insanely attractive men who are walking toward us. They're talking and laughing amongst themselves and every female within range is stopping to stare at the group.

"I told them to stay at home," she grumps, flagging down the bartender and ordering three shots.

"All of them?" I raise my eyebrow at her and get my answer when she slides one shot to me and quickly downs the other two.

"Damn chica... you've got your hands full." I down my shot and order two more. I give one to her and we clink our shot glasses together before downing them as well.

"So," she says, turning away from the entourage of hot hunky guys to survey the club. "How'd your date go?"

"It was shit." I feel like I need to be honest since she went to the trouble to get me that date when I couldn't work up the courage to do it myself.

"Damn, I'm sorry!" She wraps me in a one-armed hug, and I melt against her. "I know a couple of guys that wouldn't mind roughing him up a bit."

"That's okay," I laugh.

Piper would in fact know more than a couple of people who would jump in an instant to do something she asked. She's a parole officer, and she's quite successful at keeping her parolees in line. It's a gift she has, I guess, but any of the people she's helped reintegrate into society would drop what they were doing in an instant to help her.

"Then let's dance," she says, grabbing my hand and leading me away from the bar to the dance floor downstairs.

The shots we took have already loosened me up, and it's not long before I'm losing myself to the music.

We twist and twirl and laugh, holding our hands up and grinding up against each other. Our revelry is attracting attention.

Two of the guys that followed Piper here pull her away from me far enough that they could dance with her, but not so far that we're out of each other's sight. One of them has blonde hair and a brilliant smile, the other has small horns sticking out of his brown hair. The three of them are moving in sync and it's hard not to stare. I look around for the other two guys, and they're standing on the balcony, their eyes glued to Piper.

Even from here, I can see the heat.

A light tap on my shoulder pulls me from my distraction. A giant of a man with chestnut hair pulled up in a man bun and muscles to spare smiles down at me.

"May I?"

I give him a once over and his gaze darkens in appreciation. "Mmm... Yes, I think I'd like that."

This is exactly what I was looking for to take my mind off of Gilbert.

"My name's Rusty," he leans down so I can better hear him over the din of the music. His breath tickles my ear, and a shiver runs through me.

"Lena," I say back, putting my hand on his shoulder to give me the little boost I need to get closer to his ear.

He's still stooped over. He's just that big.

He stands back up, smiling, and spins me around, placing his large hand on my stomach, pulling me ever so slightly against him.

My hips sway and he matches my rhythm, both of us moving in time to the music. I lift my arms, and he leans just enough that they can wrap around his neck.

His chest rumbles against me, and he nuzzles his nose into the soft space behind my ear.

I hum my approval and he must have heard me because he loosens my arms just enough that he can slip out and spin me around to face him. He replaces my arms around his neck just as the beat picks up.

We grind against each other. Rusty looks down at me with searing heat, and it makes my heart race. I could see this night ending very well indeed.

The music finally slows.

"Do you want to keep going?" He says, voice husky.

It does things to me.

"If you do."

His smile is warm, and he pulls me closer, leaning down to kiss me.

Warm, plush lips brush against mine and then I'm yanked away. Rusty's warmth is gone.

An arm bands firmly across my chest and a growl comes from behind me.

"Stand down, Alpha." I look up to see Gilbert, face flushed with rage, staring Rusty down.

The big man I was dancing with bristles. "What claim do you have on her? She was dancing with me. *Happily,* I might add."

I was happy. I try to pull away from Gilbert, but he holds me firmly in place.

"Let go of me, Gilbert."

"No."

Rusty clenches his fist. It looks like he's ready to throw down, but there's no fighting in the club. It's the one rule everyone follows.

"I think it should be up to Lena to decide." His shoulders are tense, but he unclenches his fist.

Gilbert tenses behind me. Yeah, that's right buddy. You know I'm not about to choose your ass over this giant gentleman that's standing right in front of me.

The arm across my chest loosens, and I step away from Gilbert Fischer.

He sighs, a defeated look crossing his face.

"I just want to talk," he says, looking from me to Rusty. "If you're willing to listen, I'll be up there." He nods at the bar and walks off.

A large hand plants itself on my shoulder. "Are you alright?" Rusty's already familiar baritone rumbles through me and I place my hand on his.

"I am. Thanks to you."

His free hand rubs his neck and his ears tinge pink.

"It was nothing."

I turn, facing the handsome giant, and wrap my arms around his waist, burying my nose in his shirt. He smells of bergamot and a dark liquor and the scent sends a shiver through me. His chest rumbles again, and he wraps his arms around me, lifting me up so that we're eye to eye.

I smile at him, and he smiles back and carries me off the dance floor.

Looking over his shoulder, I see Piper, concern written all over her face.

I give her a grin and a thumbs up, and the concern quickly turns to a haughty smirk. The other two guys who were content to watch before have joined her, and when the next song starts, the five of them start dancing.

When we get into a less crowded area, Rusty sits me down.

"Did you want to go talk to that guy?" He asks, his own concern shining in his amber eyes. He must be a wolf shifter.

I nibble my lip. Do I want to talk to Gilbert? I'd like to know why he felt it was necessary to grill me so intensely about my dating life in the first five minutes of our first date.

"I... kind of do?" I say tentatively. "But if you don't mind, would you come with me? I went on a date with that guy and it... didn't end well. I'd feel more comfortable if you were there."

Which is completely insane. I've only just met this guy. But everything about him screams safety. He feels like coming home to a warm fire and freshly baked bread.

He smiles and the butterflies in my stomach swirl to life.

"Anything for you."

Four

THIS ISN'T A SEX CLUB

I grab Rusty by the hand, his much larger one making mine look like a child's, and lead him up to the bar area.

It doesn't take me long to find Gilbert. Now that I can see all of him, he's hard to miss.

His navy slacks fit snugly to toned thighs and the pale pink button up he's wearing compliments his auburn hair nicely. The top button is undone showing just enough of a tanned chest, and he rolled his sleeves up to show off his toned forearms.

We walk up and his eyes zero in on our intertwined hands. He frowns.

"So, did you really want to go on a date with me, or were you just trying to make me look like a fool?" He glares at me.

I let go of Rusty's hand.

"Of course I wanted to go on a date with you. I was so nervous that I stayed up all night the night before. I was afraid I'd ruin our date like I've ruined every other date before that. But you saved me from that. *You* ruined this one."

"What are you talking about?" He crosses his arm, his glare becoming more intense.

"All those insanely personal questions. Those are not first date questions. And I don't believe that Piper told you I've liked you for forever. She's not like that."

Rusty steps into me, reminding me he's here if I need him.

Gilbert growls, getting up from the booth he's placed himself in. "Back. Off. Wolf."

"No," I place my hand out, stopping Gilbert before he can step closer. "Rusty stays. I've known him all of thirty minutes and I already feel safer with him than I do with you."

Gilbert steps back like I've slapped him.

"I..." His shoulders slump. "I guess I deserved that."

He motions to the circular booth where he sits down once more. "Have a seat."

I hesitate but decide to sit. The way Gilbert is acting is nothing like he's acted at his shop. I feel like I deserve to know why.

Rusty slides in beside me, sandwiching me between the two. I scoot closer to my new wolf protector.

"I'm only sitting because I would like an explanation of this complete one-eighty in your behavior."

"You deserve one."

I can tell he knows that he's quickly losing any favor he had with me. He looks around and then murmurs something under his breath. The noise from the club dampens considerably and I quirk my brow at him.

"I'm fae. Well, more specifically, I'm a fae prince."

I gasp and Rusty grabs my hand.

The portal between the fae world and the human world used to be open, and anyone could use it. But twenty some-odd years ago, the portal suddenly closed and whatever side you were on is where you were stuck.

Occasionally, a fae will slip through, but it's not common, and it's definitely not something that's talked about openly.

"Okay... shock aside... what does that have to do with me, and why you're suddenly interrogating me like I'm some kind of floozy who dates with reckless abandon and sleeps around?"

Rusty's grip on my hand tightens.

"Because... You're my true mate." Gilbert looks away from me but returns his attention to me quickly when I yelp.

Rusty lets go of my hand, an apologetic look on his face, but turns his attention to Gilbert, his lips drawing back in a snarl.

"There's no way she's your mate, fairy, because she's mine."

"Woah, okay, hold up." I scoot away from the wolf. "What now?"

Gilbert scoots up behind me as Rusty scoots toward me in the booth.

"You don't feel it? That feeling of being at home?" He places his hand on my leg, sliding me closer to him. "It's warm and safe."

"I... I do..."

An electric shock goes through me as Gilbert's chest meets my back.

"Did you feel that?" He whispers in my ear. "The electricity. It's addicting, isn't it?"

I can only nod as the contrasting feelings war within my body.

A shiver runs through me and both men rumble with approval. Gilbert places a kiss on my exposed shoulder and works his way up my neck. Rusty wastes no time, leaning in and fully claiming my mouth.

A hand cups my breast, squeezing gently while another runs up my thigh and slides under my dress.

I pull away, breathless.

"Someone will see..."

"I've glamoured the booth," is all Gilbert says before gripping my chin and turning my head to claim my lips for himself.

The hand in my dress, which belongs to Rusty, is daring as a faint rip sounds out and my underwear falls away from my pussy.

My wolf disappears beneath the table and his breath on my legs is the only preparation I get for what comes next. He spreads me wide, pulling me to the edge of the seat before his tongue delves into my core.

Gilbert has pulled my off the shoulder dress down, exposing my breasts, as he takes one of my nipples into his mouth. I lean my head back against the seat, moaning.

This is definitely not what I was expecting to happen on girl's night out.

Rusty's skilled tongue moves up to my clit, and he slips a finger inside me. I squirm from the attention as pressure builds. I'm not going to last much longer.

Gilbert pulls himself off my nipple with a pop, and Rusty stops his feasting. Reappearing above the table.

They were at each other's throats only minutes ago, but now they seem to be in silent communication.

Gilbert undoes his belt slowly while Rusty kneads my untouched nipple. When Gilbert has freed himself, he looks into my eyes.

He's asking if I'm okay with it...

I lick my lips, nodding. This is one question I'm happy to answer. Without warning, Rusty lifts me from behind and Gilbert slides under me, his feet straight out on the bench. Slowly, I'm lowered onto Gil's very erect cock.

I gasp as I go lower until finally I'm completely settled in the fae prince's lap. He groans, resting his head on my shoulder as I ride him. I feel his energy coursing through me, powerful and electric. It doesn't take long until I'm back on the brink.

I guess he can feel it because he picks up the pace, bouncing me up and down, our skin slapping together in a frenzy. He comes, and the energy I felt before feels like it's going to split me in two. This must be the mate bond.

My right clavicle stings and a mark appears. Gilbert's mark.

Before I can find my own release, I'm yanked off the fae. My wolf looking at me like he wants to eat me alive. He lays me on the table, his own pants already undone, a bead of pre-cum drips from his very large, very erect cock.

He gets on his knees, and just like Gilbert, he seeks my permission.

A breathy whisper escapes me. "Yes."

He thrusts into me. It's hard and fast and wild. A yelp escapes me, followed by a moan.

This sex with these two men... it's not for pleasure. This is a claiming. Maybe they're afraid I'll run, but their worries are in vain.

Rusty swells within me, and I squeeze around him. He grunts, spilling into me, filling me with his warmth. I'm almost there, almost found my peak, when Rusty bites down on my left shoulder, marking me as his.

Pleasure spills through me. I shudder through wave after wave of heat and electricity.

Rusty pulls back, bringing me with him as he sits back in the seat. Gilbert scoots over, nuzzling into my neck.

With the three of us like this, everything inside me settles. My own magic weaves itself with the warmth of my wolf and the electricity of my fae.

My world turns over, righting itself when I didn't know it was upside down. Something big is on the horizon. My Sight might not be as great as others in my family, but even I can see it coming.

But now, instead of facing it alone, I'm facing it with my mates by my side.

About the Author

Emmy Dee is a small-town girl from Arkansas. She has her bachelor's degree in general studies but chooses to be a stay-at-home-mom, spending her days wrangling her three kids. (All under five, send caffeine.)

Emmy has always been a firm believer that reading strengthens the mind, but only if it's something that you enjoy. She also loves romance in her books, and her first book boyfriend was Biff Hooper, a side character in the Hardy Boys books.

She's spent most of her adult life trying to find her place in this world, and after writing her first book, she finally felt like she found her niche.

If you want to know more about Piper and her guys, check out A Hexual Misfortune!

https://www.books2read.com/AHexualMisfortune

Or you can check out Emmy's website where you'll find more books, be able to sign up for her newsletter, or stalk her socials!

https://www.emmydee.com

Witch On-Call

BY MK MANCOS

Mara Keel doesn't ask for much out of life; a peaceful existence, a comfortable living, and for her call shifts at the paranormal maintenance office to be quiet ones. Enter Wellington Cross, a man as sexy as he is annoying. His problems become hers as she investigates a peculiar invasion that fills his house with the physical manifestation of a revenge spell. Sparks fly between witch and client when Mara turns her skills to solving the riddle of who sent the spell and why.

*

Gelatinous goo oozed and ran over the lip of the hole, coming up from the depths of dirt and rocks. It slithered up and struggled in an attempt to start across the lawn to the flower beds.

Mara Keel stared down into the six-inch hole and shivered. Man, that thing was gross.

Why was she always the witch on-call when something weird happened in their little hamlet of Reapers' Key? The worst part was that invariably the call into the helpline came from none other than Wellington Cross.

At the moment, he stood on the other side of the hole from her with his arms crossed, dark brow raised as if he graded her on her performance and found it lacking.

Jerk.

She wasn't the one who perpetually had some kind of weirdness befall her home and garden. The man attracted odd like most others did lint.

"Did you dump something here?" Mara opened her kit and started taking out implements of her trade to deal with the problem. Wand. Candles. Blessed salt. Athame

Wellington—Wells to his friends, of which she wasn't one—looked even more offended if that was possible.

Mara returned his stare. She wasn't about to let him or his money and connections intimidate her. Not that he could. She'd vanquished bigger and badder than him.

"No, Ms. Keel. I'm not into playing games."

"I don't recall accusing you of such a thing. I asked if you dumped something in this hole."

"No. I haven't dumped anything."

A belching noise came from the oozing mess as it finally slid free of the lip of the hole and rolled over as if exhausted from the exertion.

Me, too, buddy. Me, too.

"It seems a shame to neutralize it after it's worked so hard to climb out." Mara picked up her wand and drew a few symbols in the air with it. Bright, golden light lit the symbols, glowing brilliantly in the gloaming.

A high-pitched shriek filled the air before the thing deflated and soaked into the ground.

Wellington wasn't amused or impressed. "Is that all?"

"What? Not enough excitement for you?"

"Let's say, I expected more for my money."

Now, she was really irritated. "Why should I expend the energy to create a huge light show for your entertainment when a simpler solution got the job done?"

That brow of his raised again. "Is it, though?"

Oh, if she'd been able to manage it, she'd have ripped his eyebrow off and beat him with it.

"You know? Next time you have some kind of magical crisis here, don't call. Deal with it yourself if you're so particular about the way things are done." She spread salt around the hole and poured it on the ground where the fluid had absorbed into the dirt. "If you do have some kind of magical anomaly, ask the call center who is on for the day and if it's me, wait another twenty-four hours before calling it in."

Mara threw her things back into her kit and closed it. "Good evening, Mr. Cross."

She started away from his house.

It really was a lovely piece of property. The house was a gorgeous, white gingerbread style, with tall pines surrounding the back of it. Along the sides were lovely willows, two weeping figs, and a couple of rowans.

The flower beds were full of the most beautiful blooms that were allowed to grow in uncultivated beds. Their colorful disarray was so breathtaking that it was a complete counterpoint to the horrible personality of the owner who lived there.

Mara let herself out of the little, white gate and started down the front walk. The compulsion to look back at him almost made her turn her head. *Almost.* Not quite. She was stubborn enough to fight herself on that point and win.

Her cat, Matilda, sat on the hood of Mara's car, grooming herself.

"Where did you come from?" She picked Matilda up and opened the door.

The old vehicle was one step away from the junkyard, but still had the spirit—even if the body was failing. Like most of her life.

Still, it was a living.

The on-call center wasn't her sole source of income, though it did help with the necessities. Most of her other money came from those tinctures, balms, lotions, and other such things she made for clients and sold at fairs.

Reapers' Key had turned into quite the tourist town over the past few years. Lucky for her.

After her father died, leaving her alone, she had been forced to economize. His long illness had been tenacious and incurable by means both mundane and magical. She had loved him with her entire heart.

And yes, after having seen the tender and compassionate example he'd set all her life, any man who came into her life had huge, pointy shoes to fill.

Mara glanced over her shoulder toward the house. Wellington stood at the front window looking out at her.

Boy, she was in half a mind to give him the one-finger salute. But then, that would be unprofessional, and she needed to keep this job. Especially if Betsy—her car—decided to go to that big garage in the sky.

She climbed into the driver's seat. Crystals hung from the rearview mirror, warding the entire vehicle in positive energy and protection.

That was about the only thing holding Betsy together.

She set Matilda in the passenger's seat and started the engine. "So, what have you been up to tonight besides spying on me and Mr. Personality?"

A plaintive mew was the only response.

"I'm sure your night was more exciting than mine." As she started away from the curb, her phone rang.

The call center.

"Hullo."

"Have you left the Cross residence yet?"

"I just pulled away. Why?" A sinking feeling oozed up, much like whatever the hell that had been in Wellington's hole.

"Because he just called back. He found the same thing crawling up out of his kitchen sink."

Mara pulled over and placed her head on the steering wheel. This was going to be a long night.

Wellington looked out the window as headlights pulled up to his gate. That rattle trap Mara Keel drove should be condemned by both the DOT and the motor club.

It didn't even qualify as a car on the academic level.

Even from where he stood, he saw the stony expression on her beautiful face. Damn, she was lovely.

And that attitude was like a firecracker going off.

This time, she didn't come alone. A calico cat trailed after her as she stalked up the walk.

Her familiar.

Oh, this was rather unprecedented. He didn't expect the familiar to be in tow. Had she left the poor thing out in the car the entire time she was here?

Disapproval pulled his brow down as he opened the kitchen door.

"I thought we had an agreement?" She stomped up the stairs and into his kitchen, going straight for the sink.

"No. We didn't. You made some arbitrary rule about waiting should I need assistance again. It's unfeasible and dangerous."

She glared down into the drain. "It's gross, but I doubt it's dangerous."

The cat had followed her in and jumped up onto the counter.

Wellington stepped forward in outrage. "Get down from there."

The cat merely sent him a glare from polychromatic eyes and looked into the sink in the exact pose her person did, then hissed.

Mara turned to her familiar and gave her a long stroke down her fur. "That bad, huh?"

The cat hissed again.

"All right, I'll take your word for it."

Mara hefted the bag up onto the counter and opened it. She pulled out the wand and the salt again. This time she also had a little bottle with a dropper in it.

"What's that?" Wellington pointed at the bottle. Looked toxic even from where he stood.

"A little extra protection."

"I don't want it eating my plumbing."

She gave him a saucy look straight up and down. "You should be so lucky."

"Outrageous!"

"Yeah. Yeah." She flapped her hand at him then got to work.

This time, the shriek echoed back up the pipes as it slid back down the drain. Mara turned on the tap and ran water after it then poured the salt.

After that was finished she turned off the water and then took the stopper out of the bottle and poured some straight into the hole. "Don't use this sink. Don't even run water in it for the next thirty-six hours. Got that?"

"What will happen if I do?"

"Your head will shrink like a baked apple and all your hair will fall out."

Aghast, he backed up. "Are you serious?"

She raised a shoulder and put her supplies away. "You willing to risk it to see if I'm lying?"

Truth of the matter, he was damned curious. All magical matters fascinated him. Including Ms. Mara Keel.

Oh, she fascinated him most of all.

She was such a prickly pear.

With an ass shaped like a juicy peach.

Wellington bit his tongue to keep that thought in his head where it belonged. Unfortunately, the cat looked up at him as if to say, "What?" If the feline had spoken, he was sure the attitude would have been similar to her person. Maybe a bit saltier.

"Oh, no."

At Mara's dejected tone, he followed her gaze over his shoulder, turning in time to see a shiny, slug-like creature oozing across his dining room, leaving a wet streak in its wake.

She hurried into the dining room, opening her kit as she moved. He didn't think it prudent in those high-heeled boots she wore. The liability alone should she break her ankle on his property raised his blood pressure by more than a few degrees.

"You realize, you have an infestation," she shot over her shoulder as she came to a stop.

The cat ran through her legs to meet the thing head-on. It hissed. Both the cat and the ooze.

The cat reared back in offense. The word "Nah," clearly in its mismatched eyes.

It took a paw and batted the thing across the room to knock against the china cabinet.

"Stop it. It's getting liquid all over the place." Wellington went to get a mop and some floor cleaner. He shimmied in revulsion.

He'd never be able to eat a meal in there without thinking about how it moved and hissed. The squishing sound that erupted when it made high velocity contact with the wood. Kind of a wet sponge when it hit the sink.

As he opened the cleaning cupboard there was movement from the corner of his eyes. *"Damnitalltohellandback."*

They were everywhere. Infestation? Hell, it was an absolute invasion.

"Mara!"

The sound of her heels clicking across the kitchen floor heralded her arrival.

"Whoa." She stood so close he felt her breath on his skin. Great, not only was his house ground zero for oozefest, but he was about to be tortured by the woman of his dreams.

Not that he'd ever let her know that.

Wellington glanced at her over his shoulder. This close, he could appreciate all the little tan freckles across the bridge of her nose. God, was he a goner for a woman with freckles. He wanted to play dot-to-dot, drawing lines connecting them with his tongue.

"I asked you a question," she snapped.

"What?" Heat rose to his face. "I'm sorry. I didn't hear you."

"How could you not? I'm standing directly at your ear." Awareness came into her eyes and she took a step back. "I'm sorry. That was insensitive of me."

Lost, he said the most unintelligent thing of his life. "Huh?"

Ms. Mara Keel rattled his brains like no other woman he'd ever met. And that was saying a lot.

Wellington was descended from Cupid himself. Women usually fawned over and adored him, which made Mara's reaction to him something of an anomaly.

"Your hearing. If you have hearing loss, then I apologize."

All right, having her say she was sorry was something of an anomaly as well. When he should have corrected her that his hearing was fine, it was his brain examining all manner of interesting things that had robbed him of his attention, he kept his damn mouth shut.

Using the current situation as an excuse, he waved his hand in the general direction of the shelves. "What are we going to do about those?"

"Well, this is quite a different problem then one or two of the little buggers showing up." She left him in the cupboard and headed back into the dining room. When she returned, she had a book in her hand.

"This actually smells of a spell. Not a horrible one, just an annoying one. Like getting a cut every-time you pick up a piece of paper or not finding a parking place close to a store."

"Those are spells?" The thought someone who practiced magic would actually go so far as to create such pointless and annoying spells fascinated him. Confounded, but also fascinated.

"Oh, yeah. So is forgetting to put your garbage out to the curb every week." She flipped pages in the book until she came across what she was looking for. "Ah, here it is."

A smile lifted the corner of her mouth and transformed her face. How was it possible that she grew even more beautiful?

"You've been very naughty, Mr. Cross."

He tried to read the book upside down, but it was written in a language he'd never seen before. "Naughty? How?"

"This is a curse from someone to whom you have broken their heart. A scorned lover in other words." She followed her finger as she read down the page. "Oh, no. This is going to take some time, I'm afraid."

"You mean I have to live with them?"

"Well, it's either that or move to a hotel until you figure out who you've scorned and make amends." She closed the book with a snap. "I mean, I can clear them out, but they'll just keep coming back until you take corrective action."

"All right. Do what you can now, and I'll try to sit down and think about anyone I might have upset recently." Really there weren't that many in the last few weeks. The last significant relationship he'd had wasn't with a witch. It had been a mundane who lived two towns away and moved to Australia for a promotion.

That had been over six months ago.

He went into his home office and sat down at his desk. How was he supposed to remember all the women he'd dated? No, he wasn't a cad. He enjoyed women, and they enjoyed him. Until they didn't.

One of the curses of being born of the Cupid clan. Irresistible to women, but harder to hold onto them. Once he introduced them to his friends, they always ended up pairing off together, leaving Wellington the outsider.

Maybe it would be different with Mara. She didn't seem to take to his charm.

Nope. Odd how the one woman he wanted in the world was immune to the Cupid charm.

MARA WALKED EACH ROOM, PLACING DOWN BLESSED SALT AND brushing the air with a counter spell as Wellington sat as his desk frantically looking through a little black book.

OMG! He really has one of those.

"This is only going to help keep some of the little buggers from springing up. It also won't get rid of the ones already hiding here." She flicked her fingers sending the web of the spell outward to cast in the corners of the room. "I did what I could in your pantry, but you might want to deep clean in there."

He moaned and put his head back, staring up at the ceiling. "This is a nightmare."

"Well, I can't say that I'm shocked, but..."

He spun and pierced her with that laser gaze of his. "What was that? Are you saying I deserved this?"

"Not at all. Just saying I'm not surprised someone decided to lash out.

You are rather—hmmm—how do I put this that is the least offensive?" She stopped and tapped her finger against her chin. "You're a bit on the cold and standoffish side."

A frown marred his brows. "I am?"

"Wait? What? You thought you were open and approachable?"

"Well, yes." He rubbed a hand over his heart. The thought he might not be accommodating clearly upset him.

Mara raised her shoulders. "Not that it matters to me. I'm merely the person who gets called out when your love life goes tits up."

The ghost of a smile filled the corner of his mouth. That little crack in his generally negative persona did weird things to her belly.

Matilda mewed.

Mara looked down at her familiar and nodded. "Oh, all right. I'll get back to work."

The cat sat down and started licking her paws.

Mara worked in silence for a few more minutes, but Wellington continued to watch her with an eagle eye. Not that he'd know if she messed up or used words that constituted no known spells. The fact of the matter was his unflinching regard unnerved her.

"Maybe I haven't been dating the right kind of woman."

"I'd say that's apparent." She dipped her hands into the salt and put it in the far corner of the dining room. Then she straightened and looked at him. "Not that it's any of my business, but what sort have you been dating? Someone who is capable of doing this," she waved her hand to indicate the infestation, "is going to be someone who also threw up a few red flags along the way."

The frown returned, and he glanced down at the little black book open on the desk in front of him. "I thought they were nice women. What kind of flags should I have looked for?"

"Jealousy. Possessiveness. Too eager to please." She ticked them off on her fingers.

"You put too eager to please in the same category as someone who is jealous or possessive?"

Mara nodded. "Oh, yes. Anyone who's like that is clearly not looking after their own needs or they are malleable to change for a partner. You don't want someone like that."

Intrigue lit his eyes. He turned and hooked his elbow on the back of the chair as he watched her. "What kind do you think I need?"

"Someone who will stand up to you for one. Not take any of your shit and attitude. You, my friend, need a challenge." She went back to slinging the spell and, in a few steps, she ended up back where she started. "I'm going to go outside and work this protection on the perimeter of your house. Then the property at large. That will give you three levels of coverage."

He stood from his desk. "I'll walk with you. The ground is uneven in places."

Those weird little flutters trembled in her belly at his chivalry. "If you want. But I can grab a flashlight out of my kit."

Shock rounded his eyes. "You use a flashlight? Not some kind of witch globe or something?"

She laughed. "Not magically efficient. It burns too much energy over a period of time. When I leave here, I might have to go somewhere else and I don't know how much of my reserves I'll need."

He stood in front of her. His gaze roamed over her face and tension coiled in the air between them. Heat shot to her cheeks.

"Well, I better get on with it then." Mara dipped a shoulder toward the door.

Wellington followed in her wake, heightening her awareness of the dark yard. He hit a switch as he walked by and illuminated the outside. It didn't reach a lot of the shadowed corners, but it did help considerably.

"Oh, no." She stopped at the second step from the bottom. The grass in front of them seemed to undulate in the dim glow from the porch light.

A sea of oozing bodies crawled and squiggled over the lawn.

"Wha..." His question trailed off as he gripped the wrought iron hand rail. "I don't even believe...why would...? Ugh..."

Mara turned. "This is really, really bad. Whoever she is, she harbors you much ill will."

"You mean like one of those little guys is going to suffocate me in my sleep?"

She raised her brows. Truthfully, that had never even entered her mind, but now that he said it. "I can't vouch for the safety of you going back in there tonight. If I were you, I'd stay in a hotel."

"Won't the spell follow me?"

"It might. I mean, there's always the possibility." She stared up at him. Wellington was taller than her but standing up on the stair above her made him impossibly so. "Look, some spells are placed on people; others on places. Some, a combination of both. We don't know which this is. It might be confined to location."

"Okay, well, how do we go about determining which it is?"

"We have to find the one responsible. Both the caster and the client."

"And how do we go about that?" He raised his brows as if intrigued by the hunt.

Mara's heart gave a little betraying flutter. Having his full attention on her did weird things to her insides, especially standing this close. "I need to find the beginning of the spell and trace it back to its origins."

Wellington rubbed his palms together. "Now you're talking."

❧

WATCHING MARA WORK TURNED HIM ON LIKE A WIND-UP TOY. Every movement of her body spoke of confidence, competency, and command. If she hadn't used her powers for spell work, she would have made a good battlefield general.

After completing the concentric salt circles, she started at his front gate and hunted for the origins of the spell. Concentration furrowed her brow.

"I don't understand this." Mara parked her hands on her hips and shook her head.

"What's wrong?" Wellington crossed the yard to her. He'd been content to stand on the porch and watch her, but now...no. He had to be near her. Be supportive in any way he might.

She turned in a circle, consternation on her face. "The only signature I can feel is my own. And yours. But that can't be right. You aren't a caster." She raised her brow as if he'd tricked her. "Are you?"

"Me? No. But there are powers. Generations back."

"Ugh. Why didn't you tell me? I'll need to know what kind of powers and how far removed." She started back up the walk and to the house.

The barriers Mara erected had reduced the oozing slugs to only a few here and there. All the others melted back into the lawn, giving the grass polka dots of brown where their acidic bodies had been.

Wellington followed behind her, enjoying the sway of her hips and the determination in her stride. "I don't see what my ancestor's powers have to do with anything."

Once in the kitchen, she turned on him, poking him in the chest with a slender finger. "Because certain abilities can cause backlash and unexpected results. Like mixing two chemicals that are inert if separate, but together.... *Kaboom!*"

"Oh, I really enjoy the *Kaboom*." When his gaze skimmed her face and landed on her lips, he realized he'd said that out loud. His face heated. "I mean, I understand."

"Do you?" She leaned forward into him; hands raised and palms up. as she leaned forward into him. "Because I think I may have forgotten what I was saying."

He wanted to get lost in her eyes. Drown in them. "Yeah. I know what you mean."

When he dipped his head to take her lips, then cat moved between them like some furry chaperone.

It mewed up at them. When that didn't work, it hissed.

Not that Wellington cared. He finally had Mara Keel in his arms where he'd wanted her all along. Her lips soft and warm against his.

The cat hissed again and swatted at his leg with claws out.

"Ouch." He backed up and rubbed his shin. "It attacked me."

Mara glanced down at her familiar with an admonishing glare. "Seriously?"

Another mew. This one punctuated by a low growl.

"Unprofessional?" The questioned accusation came out in a huff.

Wellington realized not only did they share a bond, but they also communicated telepathically. Okay, that was only mildly disturbing.

Then Mara glanced at him and touched her lips. "You're a Cupid?"

Shocked, he did a double take. The cat had ratted him out.

"A descendant. Far back in the line, but yes." Chagrinned, he put his shoulders and palms up. "I don't make it a habit of advertising that fact."

Mara rubbed the middle of her forehead. "This all makes so much sense now."

"How so?" Wellington took her arm and brought her to a small, cozy sitting room where he guided her to the sofa and sat her down. "Explain."

"My family weren't originally spellcasters. We did the other side of work. Curses." She shook her head. "Don't you see? You called me out, I resented it. The feelings feed off the latent power in you and threw little unconscious curses at you."

For all her misery, she looked damned adorable.

Wellington went down on one knee in front of her and held her hands in his. "I'm sorry. I didn't realize we were a bad mix. I've been kind of crushing on you since the first time you came here. Honestly, you took my breath away."

A sigh rattled his windows and shook the house slightly, a breathy wind from a spent spell.

Mara glanced around his shoulder. "They're gone. All of them. The curse lifted."

"That was it? All I had to do was confess my feelings?"

She laughed and pulled him to her by grabbing his shirt collar. "No, Mr. Cross. I had to realize your motive. To know you didn't do this to punish me."

"It's Wells, and I'd never do that to you." He leaned in and took her lips again. She wound her arms around his neck and surrendered to the magic of the moment.

This time, the cat did not interrupt.

About the Author

MK Mancos lives and works from her home on the beautiful, Florida Gulf Coast where she can watch the Blue Angels practicing overhead. She shares her life and home with her artist hubby, Dave and their two daughters. You can interact with her at her reader group on Facebook: Mystic Kat Readers, join her Patreon at: www.patreon.com/MysticKatReaders, or on IG and TikTok as MK Mancos author.

Spilt Milk and Spiders

BY MONICA SCHULTZ

*

Mum is always warning me not to leave the bookshop too late, but I never listen. What's the worst that could happen to a witch? Small town Morglen is known for its suspicious lack of crime, and I have a talisman or two to keep me safe. Turns out the real danger is running into your ex.

Vincent hasn't seen me yet. His eyes are trained on his phone with laser precision. He's sporting a beard that's new since I last saw him, and I hate the way it makes his jawline appear even more godlike. It's enough to unravel the seven years of hard work I've put into convincing myself that Vincent is unattractive and I don't miss him. My face flushes bright red. I'm not ready for this.

I heft the straps of my backpack a little higher and scan the park for an escape. Gerald, my cat-sized spider, squirms inside the bag as I duck behind a park bench and land with a soft crunch in a pile of leaves.

"Beth?"

I hug my knees to my chest. The chances of another Beth walking through the park are admittedly slim, but not impossible. I lean my head against the bench. Who am I kidding? The only other Beth in Morglen is sixty-five and spends every night glued to her couch watching re-runs of *Friends*. I take a deep breath and peer over the bench. Vincent stares at me like I've lost my marbles.

"Oh, hi, Vincent. Didn't see you there."

"What on earth are you doing?"

I pluck leaves out of my waist-length, chocolate brown hair and wave them at Vincent. "Just collecting a few samples for the shop's holiday display."

There's only a street light illuminating Vincent's face now that he's put his phone away, but I can still see his thick eyebrows twitch with disbelief. It's the same look he gave me when I told him I wanted to stay in Morglen. The look is an Oscar worthy performance compared to the stone-faced silence he offered me when we agreed that all long-distance relationships end in heartache.

"So... What brings you back to boring old Morglen?"

"Trinity's wedding. I'm a groomsman, remember?"

I squeeze my eyes shut. How could I forget? When Trin asked me to be her maid of honour, I knew I would get stuck with her big brother in the wedding party. Somehow, I let myself believe Vincent would be heartless enough to pull out at the last minute and save me from any awkward situations.

"Of course, but that's not until next week."

Vincent shrugs. "I wanted to surprise Trinity. It's been so long..."

Silence stretches between us until my brain is screaming for me to flee the awkward small talk. But my body doesn't listen. My legs have grown roots and my starving eyes are consuming in every inch of Vincent just so I can torture myself with the details later.

"So... Have you been back in Morglen long?" I force myself to ask.

Vincent runs a hand through his dark hair, his fingers snagging on the curls. "Just arrived, actually. I thought I might grab a coffee."

"A coffee?"

Vincent crosses his arms over his chest, immediately defensive. The motion is enough to make his biceps bulge in a way that is dangerous for my heart.

"Excuse me for being jet-lagged," Vincent drawls.

I drag my eyes away from Vincent's arms. "Aren't you forgetting something? Shoebill closes every day at three."

"Oh. In Oxford, there are a couple of wizard-owned cafes that stay open until midnight. It's where I started tutoring. During my PhD, I practically lived in those shops."

I roll my eyes. "Sorry we don't measure up, *Doctor* Thorne."

"Beth, you know I'm not that kind of doctor."

I stare at the ground and wish I could let Gerald out of his travel bag. I'm not sure if I want him closer for comfort or just to scare Vincent. A smile plays at the corner of my lips at the memory of Vincent's scream when a huntsman got into the bookshop. He always claimed it just surprised him, but Vincent never sat in that particular reading nook again.

"Fine." Sick of my silence, Vincent holds his hands up in defeat. "I'll see you at the rehearsal dinner, Beth. I'm sure they have something instant at the motel."

I've imagined meeting Vincent again a hundred times since our mutual breakup, but none of them ended like this. The dark circles beneath Vincent's eyes remind me of the sleepless nights we stayed up studying for our final exams and the mochas we drank together. Nothing beats Shoebill's coffee, but my little barista station at home is still miles better than the ancient sachets from the motel.

"Wait, Vincent."

Vincent turns on his heel, already halfway across the street.

"Come back to my place instead. I'll make you a coffee. Promise no Nescafé."

"Your place? You moved out?"

Vincent's eyes run the length of my lanky body, and I fight the urge to blush. I scoop my hair over my shoulder, covering my flat chest, and clear my throat. Vincent always claimed to be more of an ass guy, but I've seen the busty blonde from his travel selfies.

"Yeah, not long ago."

"You wouldn't mind me coming over?"

"Sure, why not?" My voice comes out all squeaky and I fight to lower it to a more normal octave. "We can do that, can't we? We're still friends, right?"

Vincent re-joins me beside the park bench and knocks his shoulder against mine. The touch sends electricity shooting through my body. I chew the inside of my cheek and tell my heart to shut it. He's just a friend now. A friend that will leave again.

"Sure," Vincent says. "We're friends."

MAYBE I SHOULD HAVE WARNED VINCENT ABOUT THE MESS. Excess stock from Fowler's Book Nook is piled around my living room and on every available surface. I snake my way through the stacks of books and into the kitchen, ignoring the disapproving air that is radiating off Vincent. It's not my fault that Dad always orders extras of everything, *just in case.*

Vincent runs a finger along the top of a book and grimaces. "You know, there are spells that could help with the dust."

I switch on the barista station. Vincent, of all people, should remember how terrible I am with spells. Mum and Dad don't practice their magic to help blend in with the more mundane residents of Morglen. Without their guidance, my magical growth was stunted. But I can make a mean latte. I focus on the little machine that is the pride and joy of my townhouse.

"Do you still take your coffee with two sugars?"

Vincent leans against the kitchen bench and makes an affirmative grunt.

"Is almond milk ok? I know you prefer oat, but..."

"That's fine, Beth. Don't worry about it."

I rummage through the fridge for the milk. As I bend, Gerald wriggles inside the backpack. His legs prod at the zipper, urging me to release him.

"So, um... have I told you about Gerald yet?"

Gerald squirms again at the sound of his name, and I know I can't take too much longer to warm Vincent up to the idea of a pet spider.

Vincent screws up his nose. "Gerald? Who calls their kids Gerald these days?"

"Well, Gerald's not exactly a kid."

Vincent shoves himself off the kitchen bench and stalks into the living room. "I'd rather not know about him, Beth."

I follow Vincent, his latte in hand. "But you really need to meet. And you'll like him. I hope. First impressions might be a little rough, but I promise he won't bite."

Vincent accepts the offered drink and perches on the edge of the couch. The heavenly scent of a fresh brew makes my mouth water, but I'll be up all night if I drink anything but decaf now.

"Did Trinity tell you I've been seeing someone, too? Her names Clara. She studying neurology."

My cheeks burn. I'm tempted to abandon ship and hide beneath my quilt now. Screw the latte. Vincent can let himself out.

"She's just one of the witches I've met since moving to Oxford," Vincent continues. "The magic community is so much larger in England than we thought."

My mouth opens to boast about my own life in Morglen, but everything I've done in the last seven years pales in comparison to Vincent's grand adventures. Maybe I do need a drink. I back away from Vincent and trip straight over a pile of books.

"Beth! Are you ok?"

"Couldn't be better," I mutter from the floor.

Books are scattered in every direction, but at least I didn't flatten Gerald. Vincent's lips tighten as he fights back a grin. My eyes narrow.

"Don't you dare laugh at me."

Vincent raises his mug to hide his smile. A snort of laughter escapes before he can rein it in.

"It's just that it wouldn't be a problem if you used your magic to shrink them."

Anger stirs my dormant magic to life. It buzzes beneath my fingertips, begging me to make Vincent feel a fraction of the embarrassment he has put me through tonight. Images of Vincent stubbing his toe or tripping over a shoe lace run through my mind. Or even better; spilling hot coffee all over his nice chinos.

A wicked smile flickers across my face. "I'll show you magic."

Gerald pokes me in the ribs to get my attention. Guilt twists my stomach, but it isn't enough for me to release him just yet. Vincent needs a taste of his own medicine first. With a flick of my wrist, I let loose.

In a rush of heat, the magic leaves my body. I shiver without its warmth, but the result is worth it. Vincent swears, coffee drenching his legs. He stands, reaching for a nearby tissue box, only to stagger into the arm of the couch.

"I think I'm going to be sick."

I abandon Gerald's travel bag and struggle to my feet. The room spins as I stand. I reach out to help Vincent, but he's already stumbled away.

"The bathroom is to the left!" I call after him, too weak to chase.

Coffee drips off the couch and puddles on the linoleum floor. I blink stupidly at it. The almond milk tasted fine this morning. With slow movements, I mop up the mess. The couch is almost dry when a crash from the bathroom forces me out of my stupor.

"Beth Fowler, what have you done?!"

My stomach sinks. I run to the bathroom, my face paling when I don't immediately see Vincent. His clothes lay in a heap on the floor, Gerald perched in the middle of them. *Gerald*? I stare at the spider in front of me. It's the size of a cat and covered in thick fur, but it's not Gerald's light brown fuzz. Vincent's black curls cover the spider's long legs.

"Oh no."

"You better explain yourself," Vincent says, his voice full of barely leashed fury.

"It was an accident."

"Beth! I am a *spider*! You know I hate spiders!"

"I promise I didn't mean to. I just wanted to make you spill your coffee."

"My coffee!" Vincent shouts, his mandibles flicking with each syllable. "A child could do that."

I wring my hands and search the white-tiled room for answers. "Can't you turn yourself back?"

Vincent climbs out of the pile of clothing, off-balance in his new body. Once on clear ground, his eight eyes shut against the bathroom light. I hold my breath and pray Vincent still practiced magic while at Oxford.

"Nothing. My magic isn't there. You'll have to do it."

I sway, my lungs deflating as all hope leaves my body.

"I don't know if I can."

"You better damn well try, Beth. I'm not staying a spider."

I chew my bottom lip. "Let me get Gerald first. He might help calm me."

The pitter patter of Vincent's feet follows me as I step over fallen books. "Gerald? Are you serious? I'm a freaking spider, and all you can think about is your new boyfriend?"

I almost drop Gerald's travel bag in surprise. "Boyfriend? Vincent, Gerald is my pet spider."

I unzip the bag, and Gerald immediately scurries out. His fur is a little crumpled after so long in the bag, but he quickly shakes it out. Vincent freezes at the sight of him, terror filling his eight eyes.

"Beth, I don't want to alarm you, but there is a giant spider on your shoulder."

I laugh and scratch Gerald under his ticklish front leg. "Hate to break it you, but you're also a spider."

"That's different! I can talk. Wait. Can he talk?"

"No. He's just a regular spider. Just bigger. And cuddlier."

"Do I even want to know how you ended up with Gerald?"

"Let's just say I made a mistake while trying to save a stray cat from choking on a huntsman."

Vincent shudders, each leg trembling. "Enough said. Can we try to change me back now?"

I nod and squeeze my fingers together, feeling for the magic. Emptiness greets me. The constant hum of life that usually flows through me is silent. Tears well forth.

"Oh God. I think I used it all up."

"Okay. Don't panic. It's not gone for good. You're just tired."

"What are we going to do?" I wail. "The wedding is next week. Trin is going to kill me."

Vincent crawls up to me and slams a paw against my shoe. His new claws prick me through the canvas and jolt me to my senses. I wipe away my tears with the palm of my hand.

"You're not telling Trinity. You know what she's like. She'll flip her lid if she finds out."

Vincent paces the length of the room, weaving in and out of various piles of books. The steady tempo of his feet is enough to make my eyelids droop with exhaustion. I flop onto the couch, Gerald cradled in my arms.

"Here's what we'll do." Vincent pauses atop of a fallen book and waves a leg in my direction. "You'll get some rest. Your body will recharge while you sleep, so that hopefully you'll be strong enough to change me back in the morning."

"What will you do?"

"Think. Sleep, maybe? Do spiders even sleep?" Vincent looks at Gerald with a mixture of suspicion and disgust.

"Yes, of course they do."

Vincent's head bobs up and down in the imitation of a nod. "Well, goodnight then. I hope you don't mind if I insist Gerald stays in your room?"

A wan smile brushes my lips. "No problem. Sorry, by the way, Vincent. I promise you'll be human again soon."

❧

THE BOOKSHOP IS QUIET THIS MORNING, THE ONLY SOUNDS coming from Dad's shuffling feet as he slowly stocks the already full shelves. I chew the cap of my marker and contemplate my handiwork. The sign isn't as pretty as Gerald's engraved plaque, but the message is still clear. *Don't pat the cat.*

I stick the sign to a nearby shelf so it overhangs the cushion I've assigned to Vincent for the day. Like Gerald, Vincent is within patting distance of my desk, but I'm sure he would rather have Clara stroking his fur.

Vincent's eyes blink open, breaking the feline illusion. "Any ideas yet?"

I slump in my seat. My magic returned overnight, but the only change I could manage in Vincent this morning was to give his fur frosted tips.

"No. And close your eyes, someone will notice you."

"We're at the back of the store. No one comes here except family, and your parents are both blind as bats."

"They're not *that* bad."

"Oh yeah? Wasn't it your mum who went full Karen mode on Rob's Pizza because she thought they had delivered just the dough without toppings?"

I giggle at the memory. "She didn't have her reading glasses on when she opened the box. How was she supposed to know it was upside down?"

Vincent chuckles, the sound filling me with a warmth I had almost forgotten. I shift my attention back to my spreadsheet. The last thing I need is to catch feelings again now that Vincent has moved on to someone new. Clara. She's probably the type to explore the world with Vincent, instead of insisting her happiness is right here in Morglen.

"So, what do you work on back here?"

I tilt the screen so it faces Vincent. "The store's finances, mostly. Things like stock-take and tax records."

I click through a few programs I've set up to make the management of Fowler's Book Nook easier. The brightly coloured systems are the only reason the store stays afloat outside of the tourist season.

Vincent shakes his head. "Why are you still here, Beth? You have so much potential and yet you waste it on the Book Nook."

I grit my teeth and close the programs back down. "Fowler's Book Nook is not a waste of my time."

"Beth, those programs are ingenious. You could be out selling them to multi-million-dollar businesses. But you're here. In Morglen."

"Not everyone needs to chase the biggest and shiniest dream, Vincent, just to feel something."

Vincent jumps off his cushion and onto my desk. I flinch away from him, shoving aside my chair.

"Look, I'm happy here. I'm not you. I may not understand your desire for travel, but at least I've always respected it."

Before Vincent can rehash any of his same old arguments from seven years ago, I storm off, swiping angrily at unbidden tears. I weave through the bookshelves, hunting for an aisle too full for even Dad to touch.

"Beth?"

I look up just in time to see Trin's smiling face before I run into her. Trin staggers back, rubbing the spot on her forehead where my shoulder collided.

"Sorry, Trin. Are you ok?"

Trin shakes out her wild curls and laughs. "Don't worry about it. I'm fine. Did I hear you talking to Vincent? Is he here already?"

I force a smile, glad that Trin is too busy looking between books for her big brother to notice my red eyes.

"You know me. I've just been chattering away to Gerald while I work."

"You sure? I could have sworn I heard someone else? It would be great if he were here. Mum is driving me up the wall, and Vinnie has such a knack for conjuring florals."

"I could help. I conjured some of the fall leaves for our holiday display last year."

Trin scrunches up her nose and glances over my shoulder one last time.

"Don't worry about it. I'm sure I can rope Paige into helping."

"Paige? As in your sister?"

Trin shrugs. "Why not? She should have some responsibilities as my bridesmaid."

The urge to argue that Paige is only sixteen is on the tip of my tongue, but I keep my mouth shut. I have no right to be offended while Vincent is stuck in the body of a spider. Shoving aside the sting of rejection, I put on my best customer service face.

"So, what can I help you with? You don't need a book, do you?"

Trin pulls out her phone and swipes through photos of blush pink dresses.

"You have to settle the debate. Which one should Mum wear to the rehearsal dinner?"

"Let me see them again."

This time as Trin swipes through the dresses, I steal glances at her face. On the third photo, her hazel eyes fill with longing.

"That's the one." I point at the phone before Trin can swipe to the next.

Trin's face lights up. "I knew you would agree! Mum liked the first one, but it has too much of peach for the bridal party."

"You know, she wouldn't wear it if you just told her that."

Trin rolls her eyes. "Yeah, but then people might accuse me of being a total bridezilla. Thanks for understanding, Beth."

Trin squeezes me in a quick hug before she darts out of the shop. The bell above the door chimes on her way out, but I can still hear Mum snoring at the front desk. At least it's not busy today. With a sigh, I head back to my corner of the store. I might as well get some work done while I wait for an idea to strike.

"That wasn't fair of Trinity," Vincent says.

I flop into my seat. "You heard that?"

Vincent shrugs, four front legs lifting above his head. "Apparently, spiders have sensitive hearing."

"You would've said the same thing."

Vincent crawls over to my keyboard and forces me to look at him.

"Maybe before, but I've seen you in your element today, Beth. You're right. You've got exactly what you want here. You might not be the best witch-"

"Hey-"

"But you're happy. I can see that now. And I can't say the same thing about me in Oxford. When I got Trinity's wedding invite... well, the only time I've felt more jealous was last night when I thought Gerald was a man."

"What's Trin have that you don't? She's always gushing about your adventures across Europe during the summer breaks."

"Don't get me wrong. I love travelling, but I don't want to backpack forever. I'm ready to settle in one place and start a family."

The flutter of butterfly wings in my stomach leaves me breathless, but I'm *not* catching feelings. This isn't about us or the pregnancy scare we shared at sixteen. I frown at Vincent.

"What about Clara? Does she want kids too?"

Vincent looks away. "Clara's not my girlfriend. She's part of my *Dungeons and Dragons* group. I just wanted to make you jealous."

"Oh."

This time I don't try to drown the butterflies. A blush creeps up my neck as I hunt for the right thing to say. My mouth opens, but nothing comes out. How do you tell a person you've thought about them every day for the last seven years? I chew the inside of my lip as the air of possibility turns into an awkward silence.

Vincent clears his throat. "Anyway... Let's go get lunch. Maybe you'll feel even stronger. Besides, I think I have an idea."

WE SPREAD THE LUNCH FROM SHOEBILL ACROSS THE LOW TABLE in my living room. Vincent cradles his coffee on the couch, adjusting the position to a standard only he can see. I smile behind the pastry I'm nibbling on. Even as a spider, Vincent remains a perfectionist.

"This is either going to make a gigantic mess or I'm about to be human again."

"The townhouse is already a mess."

Vincent shoots me a terrifying grin full of sharp teeth. "Looks like I'm about to be human then. You ready?"

I nod and put down my food. Warmth tingles through my body as I summon magic to the surface. I squeeze my eyes shut and picture Vincent drinking his coffee without spilling a single drop. The plan is simple. Same spell, just in reverse.

"Remember to breathe, Beth. You've got this."

With my eyes closed, it's easy to imagine Vincent's voice coming from his human lips. I take a deep breath and force my body to relax. The magic hums at my fingertips, ready to obey. I open my eyes and flick my wrist, letting sweet memories of every kiss we've shared guide my thoughts.

Fur explodes through the living room, blinding me. As the fluff settles, I glimpse the unharmed coffee cup moments before Vincent's silhouette appears. I squeal in delight and dive into his arms. Warm skin greets me as Vincent wraps me up in a bear hug.

"You did it, Beth."

I snuggle in against his naked chest, my body instinctively knowing where I fit against him. Wait. *Naked*? I reel backwards and stare at the ceiling to keep myself from stealing a glance.

"I'm so proud of you," Vincent says, oblivious to his nudity. "How did you do it?"

My face turns from pink to scarlet faster than I can think. "I thought about how I would kiss you if the spell worked."

Mortified, I clamp a hand over my mouth. Vincent closes the gap between us. His breath tickles my neck as I continue to make steady eye contact with the ceiling.

"Then why don't you?"

I finally look at Vincent. The frosted tips I gave him this morning look ridiculous against his black hair. I roll a curl between my fingers, toying with the silky texture. Vincent leans into the touch, cradling my hand against his face.

"I've missed you, Beth."

The honesty is all I need to let my lips tell Vincent how much I've missed him too. Vincent kisses me like I'm air and he's suffocating. My hands get lost in his hair as he lifts me onto the couch. Vincent covers me with his body, and I'm shocked by how hard he is already.

I break the kiss, my heart beating so fast that I'm worried it might break again.

"Stay with me this time?"

Vincent's eyes glaze with need, but he sits up to give me space. My breathing is ragged as I watch him process the question.

"I'm sure Morglen State High could use an overqualified history professor."

"You mean it?"

Vincent traces the outline of my lips with his thumb. "From now on, I only want to be where you are."

Waking The Witch

BY KATIE BALDWIN

Aisling O'Brion woke up the morning of her twenty-fifth birthday and felt awful. Unfortunately, waking up with the worst hangover ever wasn't the most upsetting part of her day. She thought she saw ghosts during her rounds as a resident at St. Albans Sanatorium. Was she losing her mind? Luckily, her friend and secret crush, João Magalhães, was by her side to keep her calm and somewhat rational. But it turns out there's nothing ordinary about the handsome João. They share a secret heritage that's about to change everything in Aisling's life. But can they share even more?

One

S*eptember 1993*

AISLING O'BRION WAS GOING TO BE LATE. EVEN HER CHERRY RED 1987 Ford Taurus couldn't magically transport her to the sanatorium in time. Having a viewing party to check out the new show, *The X-Files,* seemed like a good idea last night. Now, hungover from too many glasses of wine, she didn't remember even watching the show. Through her hazy memories, she did remember staring at her friend and secret crush, the gorgeous João, like he was an angel sent by God. So embarrassing.

She groaned and turned up the volume on the radio. "Heart-Shaped Box" by Nirvana was such a killer song. She rolled down her window, letting the wind whip her curly red hair as she howled with Kurt Cobain. Yeah – it hurt her head a bit, but it was worth it. The moody music was a brief respite from a crappy morning. Her head was heavy, and her tongue felt like it was wearing a fuzzy sweater. She was simultaneously cold and sweating, and her stomach pitched and lurched.

Why did she have to have the worst hangover on her birthday? So not fair.

Then to make matters worse, her parents insisted on seeing her tonight. She loved them like crazy, but why were they being so weird? Yes, it was her twenty-fifth birthday, but she planned to go home over the weekend to celebrate with them. But no—they *had* to see her tonight. After last night, all she wanted to do was sleep for hours. They'd insisted on driving two and a half hours to Radford from their Charlottesville, Virginia, home to take her out for dinner. Ridiculous. It didn't make sense.

She turned left onto the long winding road leading to St. Alban's Sanatorium. Despite her pounding head, she couldn't help but gaze in awe at the looming historic building as she made her way toward the lot. Originally a boy's school, the building had a reputation for being haunted – which was ridiculous. Sure, it was creepy. But it was built in 1892, and the old brick building showed signs of age, allowing people's imaginations to run wild. Yet there was something majestic about the classical revival building. It harkened to older, more elegant times. She loved doing her clinical training within the historic walls.

Speaking of work, she would shake off this hangover and do her job despite feeling the nasty effects of too much drinking. She hadn't come to Radford University to curl up in the bathroom, waiting for the nausea to end. No. She was here to take the next step in becoming a therapist. And she would maintain the course despite her queasiness.

She took a deep, focused breath and stepped out of the car. And there, to her chagrin, stood João looking perfect, which irritated her because he'd had more to drink than she did last night. But he looked non-the worse for wear after last night's drinking.

To be fair, she typically found him to be the *very opposite* of irritating. They had become good friends since starting graduate classes together. It seemed apparent to her that they were both trying to figure out whether to date or remain friends. At the very least, she leaned toward having one night with him.

"Poor thing. Too much wine last night, eh?" João said in that silky voice of his that made her think of smooth whiskey and sex. He wore a brown and cream plaid shirt over a faded Alice in Chains concert T-shirt. A pair of well-worn button-fly jeans clung to his body in a beguiling way. *Yum*. The black high-top sneakers were the cherry on his perfect outfit sundae. He was wrong if he thought he was pulling off the "grunge" vibe with his messy hair and outfit. He was a male-model version of the look. A little too clean and coordinated to be accurate. And she'd bet actual money the light scent coming off him was Obsession for Men. She'd often imagined all those grunge bands smelled like a combination of cigarettes, body odor, and patchouli. He smelled like a dream.

"Good morning to you, João. And yeah, I had way too much wine." Aisling growled and made every attempt to move past him without smelling his intoxicating cologne.

"Why do you look pissed at me?"

Aisling turned and glowered at him. "How are you...I don't know... so perfectly dressed? And did you iron your clothes?"

João tilted his head to the side. "You're mad because I took the time to iron my clothes?"

"I'm mad," She said as she began to walk quickly away from him and up the stairs toward the sanatorium, "That you look smokin' -- like a frigging model, and I look like the creature from the Black Lagoon." He had an extra glow these past few days, which, truth be told, she found even more attractive. But she wasn't going to tell him that.

❧

"You think I look hot?" His smile was deeply self-satisfied, and that irritated the shit out of her.

Damn it. She hadn't meant to say that part out loud. "Never mind that."

"You look beautiful as always, Aisling."

She turned, somewhat mollified by his compliment. "Thank you. I feel like death on toast."

"Maybe you should go home and rest."

"I can't," Aisling said as she opened the door to the building.

João looked intently at her and said, "When is your birthday?"

"Today is my birthday; why?"

She ignored a weird look of concern on João's face as she walked inside.

Man, it was cold – it felt like the frigid air seeped directly into her bones. The building was always cool, but it seemed downright blustery today. And why was her whole face tickling like she was about to sneeze? Her body was her enemy today.

"What's wrong?" João asked, his voice showing more concern than it should, given the circumstance.

"Nothing," Aisling said, giving him side-eye. What was up with all that protective tone in his voice?

When she turned to walk past the vestibule into the hallway leading to the doctor's offices, she thought she saw movement. But no one was there. She paused and felt João halt behind her. She was about to turn and give him another glower when movement caught her eye. There *was* something there. But her brain couldn't quite make sense of what she was seeing. Three young boys dressed in little suits with starched white collars, ties, and short pants stared at her sadly. They looked like the boys in the old-timey photos in the parlor from when the place was a preparatory school for boys.

All at once, she felt despondent and couldn't figure out why. It was like the boys were communicating their emotions to her. And if that wasn't creepy enough, she could see right through them. So, either this was the worst hangover ever–or she was showing signs of schizophrenia. Ghost visions due to overindulgence of alcohol or mental illness? She didn't care for either reason, which made her stomach roil.

The other thought – which she quickly dispelled – was that she was seeing ghosts. But she didn't believe in the paranormal. She believed in *science.* Yet there they were. Ignoring her belief in science. *Ugh.* This day sucked.

She focused on what she could understand. There was no history of schizophrenia in her family—but that didn't mean she couldn't have the disease.

"Aisling?"

She grunted at João and continued to ponder her potential mental disorder as they went to Dr. Miller's office to start the day.

On the other hand, the completely illogical paranormal side, if she knew anything about hauntings, was that spirits tended to haunt places where terrible things happened. The history of St. Albans, when it was a boy's school, was...not good. There was a lot of documentation of violence and bullying. These three boys looked like they'd been through some nasty shit. One particularly horrible story was about a slight boy who was used as a football by the older boys in the school. He was so severely beaten that he ended up dying.

"What's going on with you?" João asked as he gently touched her shoulder.

"This hangover is the worst ever." She said as she tried to keep her eyes on João, but one of the boys beckoned her to follow him down a hall that had been closed off for several years. The building was over one hundred years old and desperately needed repair. Unfortunately, the owners decided it was cheaper to build a new building than spend the money to upgrade this one. The inner workings of the sanatorium were in the process of moving right next door.

"Don't follow him," João said quietly.

Aisling turned and, to her surprise, found her friend staring at her with a look so serious she didn't know whether to laugh or run from him.

"You see them?"

He nodded.

"What time were you born, Aisling?"

"Six-thirty in the evening. Why?"

João shook his head and swore in some other language. "I knew you were one of us, but I didn't know your change would happen today."

"What. The. Fuck are you talking about João?" Aisling asked, eyebrows raised.

They stood outside Dr. Miller's office – thankfully, he, too, was running late- so there would be no lecture about tardiness.

He ran a hand through his hair and sighed. "I'm from the Brazilian clan. My birthday was two days ago."

"Clan? Dude, are you sick? You stopped making sense – like ten minutes ago." Aisling whispered.

João closed his eyes like he needed to be patient with her.

The hell?

"You are from Clan O' Broin. And today is your change. Aisling, you're a witch."

Her mind began to race as the words *clan* and *witch* swirled around her brain. Something about those words rang true, but she didn't know why or how. And more importantly – being some mystical creature was not in her science comfort zone.

"What the hell is going on? Are you punking me? Because not today – do you hear me? I can't handle it today." Aisling yelled.

And that—while the oddest conversation that had ever occurred in Aisling's life was going on—was when her clinical supervisor, Dr. Miller, approached the group. "You're late. We have rounds. Let's go."

João glanced at Aisling as they donned their lab coats and moved quickly to keep up with Dr. Miller. "When I first met you at orientation, I knew you were one of us, but you didn't seem to know anything. How is it that you don't know who you are?"

She arched an eyebrow and said with as much bravado as she could muster. "I don't have any idea what you're talking about. And frankly, I'm tired of saying the same thing repeatedly to you. I think you might need some help."

She hoped she was giving the impression of an intelligent woman of science. While in reality, her carefully crafted world was spinning on its axis. Her pulse was racing; her palms were wet with sweat. Today might be her birthday, but it was likely the day she would be institutionalized.

She would have to forgo a nap later today to go to the University's medical offices to look into a therapist. João wasn't the only one who needed help. She could see ghost children floating around the damn building. Explain that, science!

Something was not right in her world.

Much to Aisling's chagrin, the rest of the rotation continued to be peculiar. Ghosts persisted in floating around the sanatorium. Each time one appeared, João would acknowledge them with a nod. Meanwhile, Dr. Miller acted like no sad old-timey boys were following them during their rounds. So, it seemed that Aisling and João were sharing a delusion. While she found João extremely attractive, she didn't want their connection to be – insanity.

As they walked into their first patient's room, Aisling made a mental note to review the signs of schizophrenia in her Diagnostic and Statistical Manual of Mental Disorders. It couldn't hurt to come to therapy prepared. Despite the cryptic "witch' discussion with João, she was pretty sure something mental was happening. Although if she remembered correctly, one of the main first symptoms was a lack of interest in personal hygiene, *not* visual hallucinations. She was nothing if not a fanatic when it came to hygiene. But there were likely other symptoms to consider.

And then there was João. She surreptitiously eyed him to see if he looked unkempt or smelled like he hadn't showered in a while.

A cursory scan didn't highlight anything of note. He still looked like a male model.

She couldn't help sniffing him a bit to ensure he wasn't showing signs of schizophrenia. My God, the man smelled yummy. Which meant she had to cross the hygiene issue off both of their lists.

"Did you just sniff me?" João muttered under his breath.

"No!" she said too loudly, a blush heating her face.

"What is it, Ms. O' Broin?" Dr. Miller said as he gave her a stony expression.

"Nothing, Doctor. Sorry to interrupt."

Dr. Miller shook his head and continued to review the symptoms of their latest patient.

João frowned at Dr. Miller, "He shouldn't be a psychiatrist. He has no bedside manner whatsoever."

Aisling smiled. It was sweet that João was protective. He was so different from most men she knew. He was kind, not caught up in being overly masculine, and intelligent. His only weakness was that he was aware of his good looks. His ego was way too large for his head. He was around six feet with a trim build, all standard hot guy stuff. But it was his warm, sensual brown eyes and whole Brazilian sex god aura that was alluring. His beard and black curly hair were meant to appear messy, with an "I just woke up from wild sex" energy. It was cute how hard he worked to look like he didn't care about his looks.

Wait. Was she staring at him again? What was the matter with her? When did she start sighing over men like a teenager in a 1950s movie? Why was this day the absolute worst? Aisling groaned, which drew the attention of the smoking-hot João.

She turned away from him to focus on their patient. But she could feel his eyes on her. And holy hell, her body was intensely drawn to him, like a magnet. She'd always found him attractive, but now she wanted to strip him and bone the living hell out of him. STAT. What the hell was going on? Who gets all hot and turned on while simultaneously wanting to vomit?

Focusing on his problem areas could help. João was a few nuggets short of a Happy Meal. Just because they could both see hallucinations didn't mean they should be *acknowledged*. But he certainly didn't get that memo as he continued to smile at figments of their collective imagination. What a wack job.

A chubby little ghost waved at her from the corner of the room. He couldn't be more than eight years old. Aisling closed her eyes. When she opened them, the damn specter was still there. João glanced over at Dr. Miller and found him preoccupied, crouched in front of the boy, and began speaking softly to him. Aisling couldn't hear what they talked about, but she could see that whatever João said positively affected the boy. His little ghostly eyes lit up, and a shy smile appeared on his lips.

João stood up and beamed at the boy, who gave him a huge grin and vanished.

"I think he crossed over." João nodded.

Yep—this guy was nucking futs.

Two

João Magalhães tried to cover his grin when he watched the beautiful Aisling roll her eyes at him. He'd never met a witch who didn't believe in the supernatural. And P.S. *She* was supernatural. Or at least she would be at some point today once she shifted into her magical body.

João shuddered as he thought of what was ahead of her for the day. He had shifted two days earlier. It had been awful. He'd driven home to meet with his family and other members of the Magalhães coven for the ceremony. He'd planned for this night for years. He'd made contingency plans in case he didn't survive the shift. It was a sad truth that many didn't live through the painful change from human to witch. And he wouldn't leave this world without letting everyone know he loved them.

If he were to die, he would do so with no regrets. But he *had* survived. And while he looked the same as the day before his change, his aura, which had always been a bright orange, was now a deep violet. It made sense; the goddess had bestowed on him the gift of sight, healing, and speaking to the dead. So, a violet aura was on par with that new part of him. His older sister had foretold his gifts when he turned fifteen. Once he knew, he mapped out his life to be of service to the world at large and his coven. One moment in the vision still perplexed him. He knew he would somehow be connected to the witch that would shape their future. He desperately wanted to learn more about this part of the vision, but the goddess had been coy. And he was not one to push a deity. It simply wasn't in his nature.

While the Magalhães clan was one of the smaller witch covens in the world, they were known as gifted healers.

His grandparents had moved from Recife, Brazil, to Richmond, Virginia, in 1963, just before the 1964 Brazilian coup d'état, which brought about a military dictatorship in Brazil that lasted twenty-one years. Witches were definitely on the military regime's targeted list. They wanted to use them to locate anyone who was against the government. To be used as a weapon went against the Witches' Creed to *harm none*. But they wouldn't have been given a choice without his grandmother, his Avozinha Roberta's prophetic gifts. Many members of the Magalhães clan left Recife in the dead of night because Lemanjá, goddess of the sea, gave Avozinha a powerful warning to the coven to leave the country immediately. But not all of them heeded the sign, and those who remained in Brazil were forced to work for the military regime. Once their gifts were no longer helpful, they were summarily executed.

Since then, the shift to witchhood has been a celebration in his clan and a moment to memorialize those who died during that dreadful period in Brazil's history. But it was also a time of trepidation for the parents of those shifting.

His family had wept joyfully when he woke up—very much alive—from the ceremony. It had been brutal, like the worst stomach flu of his life, followed by nightmare-like hallucinations and shooting pain that caused his body to flex to breaking. So terrible was the pain that he had passed out. But he was here and ready to begin his new life as a witch. And his new supernatural instincts were very drawn to Aisling. Not that he hadn't found her attractive before; he certainly had. But now it was a yearning deep in his stomach to be with her -- always.

He now knew his life was somehow tied to the redheaded witch who didn't know who she was. But he wasn't sure how. He only knew that Aisling was, for want of a better word – his – of that, he was positive. But she would have to accept herself.

Aisling seemed intelligent and kind. Given how her green eyes softened whenever she spoke to patients, she followed the witches' path despite being unaware of their existence. But that wasn't her only allure. She was a pretty woman. She looked like a dancer, willowy and graceful. Even in a tartan skirt, black tights, and a black mock turtleneck, Aisling looked like she was about to go on stage and perform the Pas de Deux.

The O' Broin clan was mainly known for their gentility and grace. They had the best green thumbs in the world. But each witch, no matter the coven, was also given a psychic gift, and Aisling appeared to share his ability to see the dead. As he watched her lightly press a hand to her stomach, her face scrunched in pain; he knew her change was only hours away.

"Are you okay?" he asked gently.

"I think I have a stomach bug or something."

"It's something," he muttered.

"What did you say?"

He gazed around the room and found Dr. Miller distracted with another resident. So João gently cupped her elbow and escorted her to the window. "I know you won't believe me, but you don't have a stomach bug."

"Don't start that again."

"If you were born around six thirty – your shift has begun."

Aisling rolled her eyes.

João took a deep breath. He found her disbelief ridiculous. Especially now when she was seeing ghosts. "When are your parents coming?"

She placed her hands on her hips and scowled at him. "You're nosy."

He returned her scowl until he received another dramatic sigh from the little witch.

"They'll be here around four-thirty. They were supposed to be here last night, but my brother was in a car accident."

"Is he okay?"

"Yeah. But he had to stay in the hospital overnight. I told them I would see them this weekend, but they were weirdly insistent on coming here for my birthday."

"Trust me, Aisling; you want them here for what's about to happen to you."

"Please stop with all that, okay?" She asked, leaning in so her alluring scent mesmerized him. She smelled of sunshine.

"So, after your rounds, they will meet you, right?"

"Yes, João, they're meeting me at my apartment for dinner."

"I know you don't believe me, but please listen to my advice. When you leave here, make sure to fill your largest thermos with water, wear loose clothes to your cere...um, dinner. And I'd suggest putting your hair in a ponytail or away from your face."

Aisling began to laugh. "That's pretty random."

João didn't return her smile but poured as much gravitas into his gaze as possible. "Maybe, but you should listen to me."

All he got from the witch was a dainty snort. He groaned inwardly. She was not in the slightest bit ready for what was happening. What were her parents thinking? He'd heard rumors that the O' Broin clan kept the truth about who they were from their children. In the 1950s, they had a devastating number of suicides of young witches before they went through the change. Their members dwindled to four hundred. While that was terrible, to João's mind, they'd overreacted, and now Aisling was woefully unprepared for her change.

She paled suddenly and clutched her stomach. The pain was growing. He needed to get her out of there.

"Breathe through it, Aisling."

She scowled at him. "I'm not giving birth." Then another wave of nausea hit her so hard she clutched at the window ledge.

"That's it—your change is happening." João turned to Dr. Miller. "Excuse me, Doctor, but Aisling isn't feeling well; I'm taking her home."

"No, you're not." She was working up to another epic scowl when she went completely pale and fainted. João grabbed her just in time to stop her fall to the ground. He lifted her into his arms and began to walk away.

"Christ..." the doctor muttered, utterly unsympathetic to his student's plight.

João muttered in Portuguese, "How are we supposed to help people when our example is this subpar psychiatrist?"

Thankfully Dr. Miller didn't speak Portuguese.

He rushed down the stairs of the sanitorium and placed the unconscious Aisling in his car. Taking a deep breath, he began to connect to the goddess. Somehow, he needed to reach her parents right now. He prayed the goddess would help him.

Three

Aisling woke up and knew two things. She was in a moving car. And the pain she'd experienced before was nothing compared to what was happening now. The nausea was brutal, but the cramping – so much worse than menstrual cramps – made her shout. Her body felt like someone has taken a hammer to every bone. Never in her life had she experienced this torment.

She looked up to find João driving as Alice in Chains' song "Got Me Wrong" played quietly in the background. The weirdest thing was not that she was in a car in the worst pain of her life. No. It was what she saw coming out of the speakers. Musical notes floated around the car like someone was blowing bubbles shaped like the exact composition of the song. She felt like she was tripping. It was beautiful and terrifying. It was like she was witnessing her steady decline into mental illness.

Pain gripped her body so intensely that she cried out.

"Do you see musical notes?" She asked, trying for some semblance of calm.

"Shit, you're seeing things?" João asked, and the car's speed increased. "We'll be at the lake house in twenty minutes."

"Lake? Why?" Aisling asked as she panted.

João glanced at her briefly, his eyes dark with concern. "We're meeting your folks at Claytor Lake. Thank the Goddess; your mother is a telepath," João muttered. "She felt your pain and connected to the closest witch. I wasn't getting anywhere trying to reach out to them, so I'm grateful she found me."

"A telepath? My mom isn't into that stuff," Aisling wailed as she clutched her stomach.

"So stubborn, even with all the pain she's going through," João murmured.

"I...can you please help me? Why does this hurt so bad?" Aisling said, grabbed a used take-out bag from the car's floor, and vomited in it.

"Fuck this," João said as he pulled the car over.

João picked her up and placed her in the back seat. He went to the back of the car and returned with a blanket. Then he eyed Aisling with concern. His brown eyes assessed her from head to toe.

"Aisling, I'm gonna cover you with this blanket. Then please put your head on my shoulder and listen to my voice."

To her surprise, his voice soothed her, almost like he hypnotized her to relax. That was nice.

When he entered the backseat, she smelled his cologne as he wrapped his arms around her. "I know you're scared, but you're strong. You can get through this."

Her only response was a soft hiccupy cry. He wrapped the blanket around her. It smelled of grass and bright sunshine and calmed her even more.

"Aisling, I need you to say you're strong."

"I don't f...feel strong."

"I know," he murmured, "I didn't either. But the first moment I met you, I knew two things. Can you guess what they are?"

"No."

"I knew you were strong and the most beautiful girl I'd ever seen."

"Yeah, I'm a hottie covered in an old blanket with vomit on my face." She gave the best scowl she could muster under the circumstances.

João laughed, lightly brushing his fingers across her face, "There's no puke on you."

"I can't believe you're making a pass at me right now," she muttered.

"I'm distracting you from your pain."

"By pissing me off?"

João shrugged. "Whatever works."

The pain came back all of a sudden. It was so fast and all-encompassing that she barely had time to take a tiny breath before she howled in shocked agony. The pain radiated throughout her body—not one muscle was given a reprieve. Then everything went black.

Four

João opened the cabin door and walked into the open room with an unconscious Aisling in his arms. It was like walking into a TV log cabin. Very rustic, with an old pot belly stove in the corner. The furniture was sparse – a small table with two chairs, a bathroom, and a cot in the corner. And thankfully, the fire was lit. Aisling was shivering.

Then he focused on the man and woman, presumably Aisling's parents, staring at him with horror and concern.

"I'm João from the Magalhães Clan." He gently placed Aisling on the cot and covered her with the blanket.

They nodded, and the man stepped out with his hand extended. "My name is Finn; this is my wife, Maeve."

"How are her symptoms," Maeve asked.

As if on cue, Aisling began to scream.

"My baby," Maeve moaned and fell to her knees by the side of her daughter's bed.

"Why didn't you tell her the truth?" João asked the man.

Finn's eyes filled with tears. "The clan decided to let the young live their lives as humans until such time as they either became a member of the clan or died."

"You aren't telling me something," João said cautiously.

Maeve faced him, "We believe that she may be the One."

João's mouth dropped open. "The one who saves us from the second burning times?"

Finn nodded, "Unfortunately, that means her shift may be a lot worse than normal."

"Why do you think it's her?" João asked.

"The goddess told us she's in our line. We've known for centuries that she's coming. She will become a witch when human minds begin to fear witchcraft again." Finn said.

"All signs point to humans being overly concerned about evil and witches. In many ways, it's worse than the satanic panic of the eighties. When that happens..." Maeve began.

João scrubbed his hand over his face. "When that happens, humans will slaughter other humans and witches alike. Just like before. We need to do everything we can to save Aisling."

"The goddess told us she was coming soon. But as you know, time means little in that realm. We'll do whatever it takes because she's our daughter, and we adore her." Maeve said softly as she gently finger-combed Aisling's hair.

"If it's Aisling, it's been foretold that she will present herself to humans as a witch and eventually, through her gifts of empathy and kindness, transpose the fear to respect and love," Finn said quietly.

João gazed at Finn and Maeve. "If her shift is worse than mine, she's in for hell. I just went through it and...I'm lucky to have survived."

"I can take some of her pain," Finn said. "I was planning on doing that tonight."

Maeve shook her head. "I don't...my gifts are mostly telepathic and psychic. That's why I could contact you."

"I can keep her calm with my voice," João said. "You may be able to reach her when she's unconscious, right? Isn't that part of a psychic's ability?"

Maeve brightened, "It is. Yes."

João nodded, "Then, between the three of us, we should be able to get her through this."

Aisling moaned, and João kneeled by her bedside and closed his eyes. "Aisling, hold onto my hands. We will stay connected like this for the rest of your change. I'll be with you every step of the way."

"Where's Mom?" She moved her head as she searched for her mom. "This guy is crazy. All he talks about is witches and stuff. Can we go home, please?"

Maeve whimpered a bit and then gently touched Aisling's cheek.

"He's telling you the truth, baby," Finn said as he knelt next to her mother on the other side of the bed. "We are witches. Descendants of the goddess Danu. We were brought to this realm to heal and bring cohesion to a chaotic world."

"No." Aisling shook her head until another spasm hit her. "Oh God!" she screamed.

"The hallucinations will begin soon," Finn murmured.

"Hallucinations? I think they've already started. I saw little boys at St. Albans this morning," Aisling panted.

João eyed her parents. "She has the gift of speaking to the dead. Were you aware?"

"Yes," Maeve said softly.

"The boys weren't hallucinations, Aisling," João said, "They're trapped there. One of our jobs as witches is to help them pass on to the Summerlands."

"Do you see what I mean? The Summerlands? What the hell is that?" Aisling groused, her face red and covered in sweat. "He speaks in nonsensical words."

"That's enough, Aisling," Maeve said in that tone only mothers can use. "João is not lying or using any made-up words. The Summerlands are our word for heaven."

"Mom," Aisling pleaded, "Can we please go home now?"

"I'm so sorry, baby," Maeve said and kissed Aisling's heated forehead. "But we have to stay here. You must go through this change. Remember when you were young and had that imaginary friend called Edgar?"

Aisling's lips puckered, but she nodded.

"Edgar was your great-grandfather on your mother's side. He protected and played with you when you were young," Finn said quietly.

"A g...ghost?" Aisling whispered.

Finn nodded. "Your mom could see him too."

"Even human children can see spirits. And you stopped seeing Edgar around ten years old." Maeve said.

"This is all real?"

"Yes, my darling," Maeve whispered.

Aisling closed her eyes and whimpered. Then her bright green eyes turned to face João with steely determination. The witch was ready for war.

"You just went through this; what is next on the torture agenda?"

João squeezed her hand. "The hallucinations will get *dark*."

"Great," Aisling sighed.

Five

As if he called the darker images with his words, Aisling's world went dark. She couldn't see her family or João but heard bells ringing. Not sweet bells like Santa's sleigh, but grave bells like the ones affixed to the top of a coffin with a string inside so that if a "dead" person woke up buried alive, they could call for help.

She wouldn't even know about the damn grave bells, but for a horror movie, she saw as a teen. Ever since she saw the damn film, she'd been haunted by the idea of being trapped in a grave with only a bell to let those above ground know she was alive. It had become her biggest fear. And now, it appeared, she was buried alive.

Aisling tried to reach out her hand to grab the string that would ring the bell, but she couldn't move. Taking a deep breath, she thought about the problem. What was a tribulation without testing a person's ability to resolve their issues? She could be rational; she knew she was in a cabin in southern Virginia. But a tiny voice inside screamed to get out of this box. Then the chilling sound of the bell rang again.

. Where was it coming from? An image came to mind of her mother trapped in another coffin. Panic on her face as she yanked on the bell over and over to no avail. Somehow it knew that what she feared most was her loved ones being trapped. The next vision had her father trapped in a coffin, then her brother, and finally João. She knew it wasn't true – they were all safe in the cabin, but the cloying scent of decay was overwhelming. And she feared that soon her mind would accept this vision as reality.

She couldn't see or move. She was trapped. And despite her rational mind, she let out a scream.

João's voice came from somewhere within the coffin. "Take a breath, Aisling."

"You are all safe, right?" she said, her voice shaking.

"We're all here and safe," Came Maeve's voice.

"Aengus?" She said, hearing her voice strain in fear.

"Your brother is home with Uncle Connor."

"Where are you right now, Coração?" João asked.

"I'm buried in a coffin. Get me out, João!"

"Baby," came her mom's soothing voice, "You aren't buried alive. You're safe."

"You must figure out how to escape, sweetheart," her father said. "The goddess told us you would have the gift of sight, mediumship, healing, and astral projection."

"Well, that's super, Dad. How does it help me?"

"Take a deep breath," João said.

"It smells like death in here," Aisling muttered.

"Ignore that and focus on your breathing," João ordered.

"Easy for you to say, João."

She heard his chuckle, and that lightened her mood a tiny bit.

"Did you ever play, 'light as a feather, stiff as a board'?" João asked.

"About a million years ago."

"Good. I want you to be perfectly still and begin to see yourself as light as the wind or a feather. The goal is to force your imagination to become your reality. You will shift through the coffin because you demand it to be so."

"This is stupid."

"But you'll do it," her father said in a warning voice he hadn't used on her in forever.

"How come you're so good at this? Didn't you just shift or whatever?" Aisling asked.

João chuckled, "Yes, I just shifted or whatever. But one of my gifts is the ability to hypnotize with my voice."

"That has to be wildly successful with women."

"I would never use my gifts that way."

"You don't need to when you're already such a snack."

More laughter from João. "Are you ready to begin?"

Aisling shook her head but did as instructed. She even murmured the chant "light as a feather, stiff as a board" repeatedly. Nothing.

"It's not working," she heard herself whine. Damn, if she survived this, she'd be embarrassed about that.

"You don't believe you can do it," João murmured. "This must be your test. Yes, it makes sense. I've never met someone so set on science being the only option. You never left any room for the mystical. Your trial is about your belief system. Mine was different because I already knew who I was."

"What was your trial?" she asked. The more he spoke, the more connected she felt to him. It was soothing.

Big sigh from the hunky man. "My hallucinations were about my looks."

Aisling snickered. "You saw an ugly guy in the mirror, didn't you?"

"Yes, I did, and I learned I rely too much on my physical self. It was a lesson I took to heart. But for you, sweet Aisling, your trial focuses on your need to believe entirely in science and not in anything remotely paranormal."

"My parents never mentioned...."

She heard a sob from somewhere on her right side. Her body was still stuck in the coffin, but her mind was free to listen to her family.

"We were so afraid you'd learn about your heritage and ..." Her mother began to wail.

"Aisling, we never told you this, but your mother lost a sister. Her name was Aislynn. Their parents broke the rules and told both children they were witches when they were young. Maeve watched her sister's fear consume her. She decided to end her life as the change occurred. She couldn't handle the hallucinations."

"Am I named after her?" Aisling asked.

"In a way, yes. I wanted my big sister with me," came the soft, whispered voice of her mother.

The words soothed her in some way she wasn't expecting. Knowing that she honored her mother's sister gave her strength. She resolved to use that strength to survive this nightmare. She would survive this ordeal to honor her Mom and her sister.

"Mom, I won't give up."

"Then get out of the coffin, Aisling. Focus your mind and leave. Now." Her father used that stern voice that had made her quake in her boots as a child.

Aisling closed her eyes and pictured being light and rising in the air. She was floating past the coffin, above the earth where she was buried, and into the sky. And still nothing. Her rational mind wasn't buying any of this. Part of her still believed this whole thing resulted from a bad hangover. But with dawning clarity, she became aware that she had always stubbornly pushed away anything she feared. She held onto her perceived reality, ignoring anything that didn't fit into her well-crafted belief system. Now she needed to break down that system to survive the night.

A memory crept into her mind. She'd awakened on a night when there was a full moon. Her parents, along with others, danced around a fire. There was such joy on their faces. And within the fire, she'd seen the shape of a woman.

The goddess.

It had always been there – that memory. But she tucked it away, refusing to believe in something she didn't understand.

That was her weakness.

Then she heard João begin to murmur in the most comforting voice she'd ever heard. "You are incandescent. You are filled with gifts from the goddess and your kin. You are mother, maiden, and crone—you are light and dark. Your soul contains aspects of earth, air, fire, spirit, and water. You are stardust. Now, sweet Aisling, rise."

And she did. Aisling floated above the graveyard and flew toward the cabin, where she knew her parents, and João were waiting for her.

She opened her eyes and found that the whole place pulsed with life. Tiny fairies were in the fire, and magic filled the air in various shimmering colors. It was like a concert light show but so much more impressive. She grinned. "I did it! It's over, right?"

Her mother cupped her cheek, "You finished the trial, yes. But the transition is yet to come."

"Well, shit," Aisling muttered, then threw up on João.

Six

João breathed a deep sigh of relief as he showered off the remnants of Aisling's vomit. She'd survived. Thank the Goddess.

After a large glass of water, she slipped immediately into a deep sleep. He remembered that he'd drifted to unconsciousness after his trial as well. And the sense of peace that he'd experienced was overwhelming. His big brother Roberto had picked him up like he weighed nothing and tucked him into bed. João's only thought was that he'd survived, and then —nothing.

Now that he was clean and dressed, he padded over to the bed to watch Aisling as she slept. The peace he'd felt that night echoed on her face. Her mouth was slightly open; the redness from the brutal pain was gone allowing her milky white skin to shine.

"That was brutal," Finn said, startling João.

"Yeah."

"You know that you're connected to her, yes?" Her father asked, a look of discomfort on his face. No father wanted to think of their daughter as a sexual creature – not even witches.

João gazed at Aisling's father and nodded. "Yes, sir. We belong to each other."

Finn grunted and reached out to give his unconscious daughter's hand a gentle squeeze.

"She did it, and now she can rest," Maeve said softly from the door.

"If she's the one, she'll need to learn everything there is to know about being a witch. She has a lot of work ahead of her." João warned.

Maeve stared at her daughter. "She'll be ready. We'll make sure of it."

One month later

João put his coffee cup down and frowned at the door. It was nine in the morning—who was knocking so aggressively at his door?

A quick check of the peephole made him grin. It was Aisling. They'd spent the last month getting to know each other better. Sex was a big part of that, but not the only connection. They found that they both loved old movies, especially old horror movies. They loved animals and were both passionate about music. They'd become friends the moment they met, but now they both knew they were destined to be much more to each other. And the connection was both thrilling and comforting.

"Hey! How are you f..." he began.

Aisling grabbed his face and kissed him hungrily. Shocked but not one to question a good thing, he responded in kind, licking into her mouth. Her taste was delicious, like sunshine and cherries.

A sexual fog was sliding over his body and mind. He had maybe a few seconds of common sense before his desires took over. And the one thing he didn't want was to give his neighbors a show. Especially since it was likely that Aisling would be his wife. He tugged her inside and moved them into the living room, where the curtains were closed.

"Let's go to bed," she whispered, giving him a wicked grin.

Her seductive voice sent shivers down his body. She was always rushing him. He wanted to take things much slower this morning. "We're going to stay here a while. Maybe make out on the sofa," he muttered as he toyed with her curly hair.

"Why?"

"Because I want to take it slow."

Aisling's eyebrows raised, and she shook her head. "Who said you were in control?" Then she pulled his shirt open, ripping off several buttons.

He stared at his ruined shirt, mouth agape, as buttons bounced on the floor. This woman looked sweet, like a maiden, but he should have known better. She was a witch with a witch's fiery desires. And he wanted to be consumed. "Damn, woman."

"Let's go to bed!"

"Yes, ma'am." He picked her up and strode to the bedroom. A combination of arousal and contentment filled his soul.

"Kiss me," his sweet witch demanded once they were in his room.

He smiled. Oh, he was going to kiss her. Everywhere.

He grabbed her around the waist and pushed her against the one wall free of paintings. "Wrap your legs around me."

Her pupils dilated as her long legs wrapped around him. He pressed his length against her heat and gently rocked as he thrust his tongue into her mouth.

As they kissed, energy built around them; like a whirlwind, it captured and spun them around. It was more than the heat of two bodies coming together—so much more. It was magic. And that was when he realized they were floating at least two inches off the ground.

"Fuck!" he yelled as they fell to the ground.

"Were we—?"

"Yeah," João muttered, "We were floating."

Aisling stood up, shimmied out of her panties, and said, "Let's see what happens when you're inside me."

LATER, JOÃO WOKE UP WITH A SMILE ON HIS FACE. AISLING WAS sleeping beside him, her soft body keeping him warm—or somewhat *overheated*. He was a lucky man.

"Stop smirking; it's going to give you wrinkles," Aisling muttered in a soft croak.

"You were very..." João started.

"Horny?"

"Yeah."

"Complaints?

"Fuck, no."

Aisling sat up; the sheet drifted down to showcase her gorgeous breasts. "I think we made a baby."

João felt the color drain from his face. He still had two years to finish his education—a baby wasn't part of the plan. Then as if puzzle pieces sifted together in his mind, he remembered a part of his vision on the night of his trial.

He would be connected to the witch who would save them. But the goddess had a larger design for him. To be that special witch's father.

"Aisling, you aren't our savior."

She nodded and squeezed his hand. "I know. It's our daughter, Morgana." I had a dream last night, and the goddess told me."

"So, Miss Science, now you're having chats with the goddess in your dreams?"

Aisling laughed, "Yes. Don't give me shit. My parents hid my true calling from me."

"Are you mad?"

"At them? No. I loved being a human girl. And I'm glad I got to experience the innocence of being just human."

João gently kissed her. "We need to get handfasted."

Aisling laughed, her green eyes bright as a summer day. "Yes, my love."

João looked up at her, his heart in his throat. "You love me?" He hadn't even thought the word in his mind, not ready to consider his feelings for Aisling. But he knew. This all-consuming feeling—needing to be near, touch, and laugh with her—could only be one thing. Love.

"I knew when I could hear your voice while trapped in my vision. I knew you were the one," she said softly. "But," She added as she pressed her lips to his, "I think I need to show you how much."

João kissed the corner of her mouth. "Say it."

"I love you, João."

"Eu te amo, Aisling."

"You must mean it if you said it in Portuguese."

"I do." He nuzzled her neck. "Now, let's get back to you showing me how much you love me," he growled.

About the Author

Katie Baldwin is an award-winning author who loves Rock & Roll, rescuing dogs, and a good strong latte. By day she is a mild-mannered researcher at a well-respected university. By night she writes kissing books that are sometimes spooky! When she is not pacing her home and working out dialogue in her mind, she is reading Romance, Horror, and Mystery books by her favorite authors. She can be found on Facebook and Instagram, waxing eloquently about her love of canines and all the books. Check out her website for other interesting facts.

Graduation Day

A 'VISIONS OF WOLVES' PREQUEL

BY KATHERINE ISAAC

After years of hard work, it's finally time for Christina and her friends to graduate from Bishop University and start her life as a fully trained witch. But while focusing on appeasing the expectations of her uptight family, an encounter with two wolf shifters may throw all of her careful plans into disarray.

Part 1 - The Witch

"Christina Montgomery."

Polite applause surrounded me as I walked across the stage, my robe swishing around my legs while my father's words repeated in my head on a loop.

Head up. Shoulders back. Take your time. Smile, but not like you're thankful. You deserve this, and they should be grateful to have the honor of handing another Montgomery their diploma.

The knowledge of my family's presence did nothing to relax me as all eyes in the room followed me on the quick journey from student to graduate. My family always made me nervous, especially in public settings, but today was worse than usual. Today was the culmination of years of hard work. Yet somehow, I knew that deep down, it would still leave me feeling inadequate. I knew I'd need to prove myself again, outside of an educational setting.

Graduation was only the beginning.

I shook the chancellor's hand firmly, but not not tightly, just as I'd been told to. Then I paused for a moment to allow the perfect angle for the photographer to capture my perfectly rehearsed smile. My eyes stung from the stage lights, but there was no way I'd allow myself to be caught blinking in this moment. Or, at least, there's no way my sister would let me live it down.

As I delicately took my rolled up diploma, a loud "whoop" rang out from amongst the line of students behind me. Snapped out of my mantra, a true, joyful smile slipped over my face.

It was Cordelia, my roommate and best friend of four years. Even with my advanced divination magic, I could never have predicted how close we'd become during our time at Bishop University. Once I'd let her in–and stopped acting like an awful, spoiled little witch–I could truly relax around her. She understood the pressure of a powerful family name and needing the escape.

It wasn't until I'd stepped off the stage and made it back to my seat amongst the other fresh graduates that I could see how badly my hands were shaking. Hopefully, my guests in the audience were too far away to have seen it.

At least the worst was over. I could finally breathe a little while I watched the rest of the ceremony. Then I'd just need to survive the networking event for graduates and their guests. After all, it was rare to have so many prominent witch and shifter families gathered in one place. Hopefully, the Montgomery's would quickly have their fill of bragging to other witches and make an early exit. Then I'd be safe.

With any luck, I'd be able to slip away early to celebrate with Cordelia and the guys. It would be nice to actually enjoy this day, at least a little.

The ceremony dragged another hour before we could file out of the university's grand hall, return the rented robes, and gather in the courtyards. Arches covered in entwining white roses decorated the already extravagant campus lawns, creating small areas for families and groups to gather in more private celebrations before joining the larger party in the center.

The sweet reprieve of being lost in a crowd, completely hidden from the prying eyes of my family members, was short-lived, as I spotted my sister waving me over from next to the drinks table with my aunt and father.

"Here we go." I muttered through gritted teeth, the fake smile plastered across my face already making my cheeks ache. Biting the bullet, I joined them, "So glad you all made it!"

My father broke away from his hushed conversation with my aunt Rose and gave me a curt nod. He wasn't much of a hugger on his best days, but at least he wasn't looking at me any differently to how he looked at Fiona on her graduation. His neutral expression told me that I'd met expectations. I'd take the win. Asking for more than that was like asking for a pet capybara who crapped rainbows.

My sister, Fiona, embraced me with light hands on my shoulders, giving me an air kiss on each cheek. She still hadn't grown out of the pretentious habits she'd picked up during the two months she'd spent in our sister-coven in France with our cousins. It was traditional, in our covens, to visit around this age, or once we'd reached a certain level of witchcraft. Now that I'd graduated, I was just a few days away from getting on a plane to stay with them myself.

I'd already made Cordelia promise to hex me if I started using every conversation as an excuse to remind people of my privileged French adventures when I returned. She agreed to it way too eagerly.

My aunt passed me a glass of red wine and quickly started telling me about the families they'd been sitting next to during the ceremony. I knew the students they were related to, but couldn't get a word in to contribute to the one-sided conversation. All I could do was sip the wine and nod. And I was quickly running out of wine.

"Anyway, it was such a long flight to get here and the ceremony was so draining." Aunt Rose sighed, "We really just want to chat with a few friends and head back to the hotel to rest."

Fiona massaged her temple with one hand, suddenly looking exhausted by merely having to exist in the moment. Same.

"Yes, we'll have to catch up properly at lunch tomorrow, before you head to France." My father mused, downing the last of his wine.

"I'm sure you'd rather be spending this afternoon with your friends, after all." Rose suggested. She couldn't have been more right.

With a swift farewell, and more uncomfortable air kisses from my sister, I stepped away, before turning on my heel and swiftly maneuvering through the crowds. It was strange to see so many covens I recognized in one place. But what was stranger, or at least more frustrating, was how the majority of covens only spoke those they considered to be at their level.

After all, it wasn't just witches that graduated today. Bishop University may have been founded as a safe space for witches to practice their craft, but all kinds of supernaturals attended these days. Pretty soon there would probably be more shifters, fae, and other supernaturals in classes than there were witches. That would really shake things up.

As I made my way back towards the university's main building, eager to get to the meeting point I'd arranged with Cordlia and the others, I spotted several shifter friends I'd made over the last four years. Each was surrounded by people I assumed to be from their packs. They looked so happy celebrating together, so very different from my family.

I stumbled as a body bumped my shoulder while passing by me. The stranger apologized gruffly and I waved them away, no harm done, everyone was rushing around in celebration. But as I climbed the steps to the main entrance, my heels clicking against the polished stone, something inside me urged me to look back, like I was suddenly missing something.

Steadying myself with a hand on a stone column of the entrance's archway, I turned for a quick glance. Looking down the steps, my gaze immediately focused on two men staring up at me, and the hundreds of people surrounding me suddenly disappeared into the background.

Even from my vantage point, they both seemed impossibly tall, though one was somehow bigger than the other. While the taller one was broad, the other was lean, like a swimmer.

I couldn't look away. My breath hitched and I gripped the column beneath my hand, mentally praying they would look away first.

Both of them sniffed the air and their nostrils flared. The larger of the two snarled animalistically, his gaze darkening. His lip curled, showing bright white teeth that made my stomach drop. Had I done something to offend them? I'd never even seen them before. But the way they were glaring... They knew me, somehow.

Their mouths moved as they said something to each other, their eyes never leaving me. I couldn't hear what either of them were saying, but I could read their lips clear as day when they eventually growled out one word in synchronicity.

"Mine."

Part 2 - The Wolves

The classroom door clicked shut behind me and I carefully flipped the lock to minimize noise. Once I lowered the blind, fully shielding me from the hallway, I let out a shaky breath and ran my fingers through my hair. The movement ruined my perfectly styled hair, but that wasn't important right now.

Who the hell were those men? I didn't recognize them, so they were probably family members rather than students. It gave me an advantage in hiding from them in the university, but I knew they'd find me eventually. They were shifters, wolves, most likely. With their sense of smell, I wouldn't be able to outrun them for long.

"Mine."

Why would they say that? And why was my heart pounding in my throat?

When it came to terms like 'fated mates', I knew the basics. Soulmates. An unbreakable bond. Destined to be together despite all obstacles.

A claiming of hearts, souls, and bodies.

I thought it was romantic when I first heard of it. Having your perfect match picked out by the universe, what could be more perfect?

But now that I was faced with the very real possibility of being thrown headfirst into one of those bonds, I was terrified. This wasn't supposed to happen to me. I was a witch, a *Montgomery*.

I'd heard from friends that it was rare for a shifter to find their fated mate. Rarer still, for their mate to be a non-shifter.

Rarer *again*, for the bond to include more than two people.

When my father dropped me off freshman year, he told me, "every Montgomery excels past the ordinary at Bishop." Somehow, I doubted this is what he had in mind.

Two sets of rushing footsteps echoing down the hallway pulled me out of my panicked thoughts. The classroom I'd chosen as a hiding place was on the second floor, so I supposed I could jump out the window in a worst-case scenario. Though I prayed it wouldn't come to that.

Please, just leave. Leave so I can forget this ever happened.

Yet a small part of me wondered, what if they found me? And that excited me.

The door handle rattled, but the lock stopped it opening. I quickly flattened my body against the wall alongside the door, using a bookcase as cover, and held my breath. I had seconds, at best, before that door gave way.

The window tempted me again. A quick spell would help me stick the landing and I'd be fine. I just needed to choose whether to jump, or not.

Voices growled from outside the door. Last chance to jump.

One shove had the door slamming open against the wall. I muffled a gasp by covering my mouth with both hands and squeezed my eyes shut tight. It was too late to run, but maybe if I didn't look at them, I wouldn't be so hypnotized by them.

My blood pounded in my ears, making me lose track of how far into the room my predators were. I tried not to breathe too loudly beneath my hands, on the one percent chance they missed me in my awful hiding spot. But I had no such luck.

A brush of skin against my hands shocked my eyes into opening wide. The larger of the two–Muscles, I decided to call him in my head–gently nudged my hands down away from my face. He knelt down to my height as other hand caressed my cheek, slowly, like he thought he'd scare me away again.

The touch of his hand seared into my skin like a brand, but I didn't want to pull away from it. Looking at him up close, I couldn't believe how handsome he was. Green eyes stared back at me, like he was seeing daylight for the first time. He was wincing like looking at me burned his eyes, but he still couldn't look away.

I moved before I could overthink it. One step forward had me in his arms as my lips crashed against his. I gripped his dark hair, holding him as close to me as possible so I could inhale his spicy scent. It was intoxicating.

A blonde head moved into my peripheral vision as we kissed, and I slowly pulled away to look at him.

He moved towards me cautiously, eyeing me up and down. His pale eyes were wide. I couldn't tell if he was nervous, in shock, or some mixture of the two. But when he reached his hand out to touch my shoulder, I felt complete, somehow. Like my lungs finally had enough air to fill them.

Muscles moved behind me as Blondie leaned in and kissed me deeply. It forced me to lean against Muscles, like a solid wall of heat that had my panties melting down my thighs.

He leaned down and growled in my ear, "Let me taste you, little witch."

I nodded, not breaking my kiss with Blondie. I was pretty sure all thoughts were now exclusively led by my screaming need to feel the two of them as closely as possible.

Muscles scooped me up, bridal style, and carried me over to the professor's desk at the front of the classroom. He smirked, showing those bright white teeth again, "Perfect."

Blondie swiped his arm across the surface, dramatically shoving papers to the floor, leaving space for Muscles to deposit me between the two of them. I parted my knees at the edge of the desk and pulled Muscles between them to kiss him again. He ran his hands up my body, cupping my breasts and rubbing his thumbs over my nipples, making me squirm in his grip. After a few moments, he pushed me down to lie against the wood and lifted my dress up to my navel.

He kissed along the waistband of my panties as he spoke, his eyes never leaving mine and his hands stroking over my thighs. "You're so fucking beautiful. Will you take him in your mouth while I lick you?"

Blondie stepped up to the side of me and I stroked my hand over the hard bulge in his trousers, squeezing lightly. "Please."

"Oh, fuck. She begs." Blondie moaned, his eyelids fluttering under my touch.

A rip and breeze between my legs told me my panties were now nothing but scrap, but I quickly stopped caring as Muscles' hot tongue slowly licked up my pussy. He pulled my legs over his shoulders and closed his mouth over my clit, sucking lightly and sending shockwaves up my body. Then he started eating me like I was his last meal, and my legs clenched around his head.

I turned my head towards Blondie, who already had his cock out, hard and waiting patiently. Leaning in, I brought the tip to my mouth but paused for a moment, looking up at him with needy, half-lidded eyes. "Touch me?"

"Abso-fucking-lutely." Blondie caressed one hand over my breasts and stroked my hair with the other, as I finally took him into my mouth.

My hand stroked what my mouth couldn't reach at the awkward angle, but hearing Blondie's breath stutter as he touched me gave me a sense of power magic could never give me.

Sounds from the graduation parties outside were steadily getting louder, filtering into the classroom we occupied. They were almost in full swing and I should've been out there with them. My family was probably still down there, too. But instead, I was spread open on a professor's desk, with one stranger between my legs and another in my mouth.

And I'd never felt more alive. More like myself. Not who I was always expected to be.

My orgasm crashed into me like a surprise wave pulling me under. For a moment, I couldn't breathe, and not just because of Blondie's dick in my mouth. He graciously pulled out to make sure I was getting enough air, while Muscles licked and sucked me through the most intense pleasure I'd felt in my life.

As I steadily came down from the high, Muscles gave me one last long lick that made my thighs twitch around his head. He grinned as he untangled himself from my legs and kissed down my leg, motioning for Blondie to take his position between my legs.

"You should fuck her first." He said, reaching down to adjust himself in his jeans.

Blondie chuckled, "Yeah, don't wanna break her on round one."

Break me?

I looked down to Muscles' crotch as they switched places and *oh, my gods*. Yeah, I definitely needed more of a warm up before attempting that.

Blondie's lips captured mine in a kiss that had my toes curling. "Don't worry, princess. I'm going to take such good care of you." He rubbed his length along my entrance and his kisses moved down my neck to the crook of my shoulder. "And then, when you're ready, I'll leave my mark right here."

My breath stuttered. What did he just say?

Muscles kissed along the opposite side, nibbling the same spot like a mirror. "Then I'll leave mine here, and everyone will know you're ours."

Everyone. Ours.

"W-wait, stop." I sat up suddenly, pushing them away from me. "I can't... I can't do this."

"Hey, hey, it's okay." Blondie pulled me up off the desk, taking my place on the wood as he cradled me against his chest, warm and comforting. I'd never felt so supported in an embrace before. "We can take this as slow as you need to. There's no rush."

Muscles moved in against my back, holding us both in his arms and placing a feather-light kiss against my temple. "He's right. We can take our time. We have forever together."

Forever. Of course, Muscles and Blondie wanted forever. I didn't even know their names. I could never give them the forever they wanted.

My hand moved to touch the ornate silver locket I wore around my neck. It used to belong to my mother, but now it was filled with a powder gifted to me by my friend and extraordinary alchemist, Ellis. I clicked the top, carefully releasing the powder into my hand.

Pulling out of their embrace, I hopped down from the desk and took a moment to pull my dress back down before turning to look at the two men. My fated mates.

"Are you okay?" Blondie asked, giving me space. "Do you wanna sit down or I could go downstairs and get you a drink if you want."

He was so sweet. My gaze flicked between him and Muscles, their expressions confused and concerned.

"I'm sorry." I said sincerely. I knew this would hurt them, but I had to do it.

Muscles' brow furrowed and he took a step towards me. "For wha–"

I blew the powder into their faces, a small blue cloud bursting from my hand as I ran for the door. The powder took immediate effect and I heard their bodies thump against the floor. It was a rare concoction, powerful enough to knock out a fully shifted dragon if needed. Ellis made it two years ago when he was afraid for Cordelia and I walking alone. I never thought I'd ever actually use it on someone.

I had to get away from the university, but I needed to be smart about it. First, I needed a glamor to mask my scent from them. Pulling out my phone, I quickly fired off a text to my friends' group chat. They'd be able to help me with it and then it was straight to France for me. I was already packed, so I'd use my savings to fly out tonight. I doubted my family would miss me at lunch tomorrow, anyway.

With the glamor and distance, I'd have a good lead if they decided to come after me. Combined with my divination magic, I'd be able to stay ahead of them as long as I needed.

But if I ever saw them again, I didn't think I'd be able to resist them.

Or that I'd *want* to resist them.

Thank you for reading *Graduation Day: A 'Visions of Wolves' Prequel*. This story will be continued in the full length novel, *Visions of Wolves*, available to pre-order now.

If you'd like to read about what's next for Tina's friend, Cordelia, her series will soon be starting with *Demon Unleashed*, book 1 in the Eclipse trilogy.

About the Author

Katherine Isaac lives and works in Wales, with her beloved cat-son. Growing up surrounded by mythology and history has fueled her love for epic stories of magic, mystery, and romance.

She is happiest with her nose in a book, pinned down by a cat, or surrounded by nature; whether that's lying on the grass or diving in the ocean.

Katherine describes herself as an eternally sleep-deprived pixie, with the mouth of a sailor and too many characters living in her brain.

Join Katherine's Facebook Readers Group to be part of the discussions and enter exclusive giveaways!

Sign up for Katherine's newsletter to stay up to date on all the latest news!

www.katherineisaac.com

Scaredy Cat

BY KIT BLACKWOOD

Melinda Harper *is* a witch and has the cat familiar to prove it.

When Chester Foley kidnaps Melinda, puts her familiar in danger, and plots to unleash chaos, Belinda steps up.

It's what any decent human being would do, especially if they love cats.

What happens next changes her life, but it isn't easy.

But then, if magic were easy, anyone could do it.

Blood in the Rain

I warned Melinda that nothing good would come of her letting Chester in her life, but she didn't listen.

"I don't know why you dislike him so much."

Because he's not a good person, I thought, but I didn't say it out loud.

"Not everyone likes cats," she added, as if apologizing for that character flaw was going to somehow make me like him more.

I get it. The state of Washington has one of the better gender balances in the country; but factor out men who prefer men and men who are outside the age norms for her—she's 43—and the pickings are slim. Finding an unattached, forty-something straight male magic worker was like bagging a unicorn.

"You should go out with Bree," I suggested. "She's really cute and she likes you."

"She's adorable," Melinda said, "but I'm not bi-curious."

"Except for that time in college when you dated Steffi for a whole semester until she broke your heart by running off with her brother's best friend."

"That was more than 20 years ago," she said. "It's unkind of you to remind me how unlovable I am."

Melinda can be a drama queen at times.

"You know that's not what I meant," I said. "Chester just doesn't deserve someone as awesome as you."

It's not that I'm a snob. He was handsome enough if you liked the bland type, and he could also be quite charming when he wanted to be. Even I thought he looked great in a tux. I'm sure he could have been a very successful male escort if he'd put his mind to it.

My problem with him was that he was so monstrously entitled, self-involved, and narcissistic. For him, magic was all about what it could do for him.

I'm not saying all witches are humanitarians, or even nice people, but I don't think Chester had ever lifted a finger to do a good deed or make someone happy. He certainly didn't try very hard to please Melinda. And that hurt me. Melinda's mission in life was to heal people, mostly without them even knowing it.

In fact, that's how we'd met. I'd been crossing the street when a car clipped me, breaking my leg and sending me sprawling. I was in shock as a group of pedestrians stood there staring, but she rushed over and put her hand on my back. I felt warmth flood all through my body, then concentrating on the break in my leg.

For a moment, the heat was so intense it was painful and then the next minute, the pain was gone, and my leg was just fine.

We've been besties ever since. Twenty years now.

I suppose I'd have grown to tolerate him in time, if only I hadn't been sure that he was out to exploit her in some way.

Melinda's kind of a big deal. True healers are rare, and even some of the big witch families in Seattle—the Alcantaras, the Liangs, the Johnsons—don't have one. For Melinda, her ability was a blessed gift. For Chester, it was a commodity.

I tried to tell her that, but she wouldn't listen. Worse, she even suggested that I was jealous.

"I'm not jealous," I told her. "I'm worried about you."

The disagreement seriously strained our bond, so I quit talking about it. Unfortunately, Chester was just biding his time, and when the moon was full one September night in the middle of the festival of Mabon, he struck.

HIS PLAN WAS CRUDE BUT EXECUTED FLAWLESSLY.

The first thing he did was lock me out of the house I shared with Melinda, and then put a spell on all the doors and windows so I couldn't get back inside.

I might have been able to climb the big tree in the yard and get in through the attic window, but I'm deathly afraid of heights. I got stuck in a tree when I was younger, and the paramedics had to rescue me. It was embarrassing.

And because it was a cold and rainy night, Melinda had drawn all the blinds against the weather and had a nice, cozy fire going in the downstairs sitting room.

I couldn't see inside, and the fire's elemental aura kept me from sensing anything either. I circled the house a few times, but the supernatural seal was solid. Afraid I'd get hypothermia if I stayed out in the rain too long, I retreated to the street and took shelter under a car that was parked in front of our neighbor's house. All the houses on our streets had attached garages, but David often had visitors who stayed overnight. I figured I'd be safe under the car until morning.

Safe, perhaps, but not comfortable. It was raining so hard, water was rushing down the street like a river, and I was soaked and shivering by morning.

And just when I felt like I couldn't get any more miserable, the car's owner exited my David's house and spotted me hunched beneath her Toyota Camry.

I expected her to just get in the car and drive away, but it was my bad luck that she was a cat lover who had spotted me.

Before I knew what was happening, she'd dragged me out of hiding by the scruff of my neck.

I flailed and raked my claws, connecting with her arm and her chin as she wrapped me in the hoodie she'd been carrying.

Once she had me mummified in a velour cocoon, she buckled me into the passenger side seat of the car so I couldn't escape. Then she cranked on the heat, which I appreciated, even if I was terrified of what might happen next.

"Poor kitty," she crooned.

As she drove me toward an unknown fate, I could at least take satisfaction in knowing I'd drawn blood.

Meeting Matilda

It had been nearly three months since my cat Olivia died and I was still mourning. My mother had rescued her as a kitten from the parking lot of a supermarket where she was dumpster diving, and it was the luckiest day of her little kitty life. Although Olivia was technically my mom's cat (dad mostly ignored her), she'd been mine ever since the first night she slept on my bed. She'd been my constant companion for 22 years, taking me through school and college—I lived at home while going to UWA—and through my first jobs and my first real heartbreak. She'd kept me sane during lockdown.

When she died, I grieved so hard for her I didn't think I'd ever be able to even look at another cat without breaking down in tears. But one day, I was lazing in bed, scrolling through my socials, and clicked on a video someone had posted of their adorable tuxedo cat, and I realized how much I missed having a cat in my life.

And as all cat lovers know, the minute you put that intention out into the universe, the universe obliges.

And so, on a Saturday in early October when the fall foliage was at its peak, I met Matilda.

It was the perfect day to go in an adventure. After a cruel summer, the days were getting cooler, and the nights were cooler still. A recent rain had washed all the city smells away, so the air was crisp and fresh.

I packed a sack lunch and biked out to Gas Works Park to eat it. I've lived in the city my whole life and I've never lost my fascination for the place. Long before people were pinning photos of abandoned places to their

Pinterest boards (I don't judge, I have more than dozen boards myself), the "life after man" juxtaposition of nature and machinery captivated me.

After I ate lunch, I cycled back to my apartment, but then I saw a sign on the little mom-and-pop market on the corner advertising a sale on their house-made pot pie, and I just had to stop.

Chicken pot pie sounded like exactly what I wanted for dinner, so I went inside to get some, alone with a four-pack of Rachel's caramelized pineapple ginger beer, which is nectar of the gods.

I was coming out of the store when I noticed a gathering outside Reads on Reid Street, the indie bookstore that anchored the short street. Figuring they were running one of their annual outdoor sales, I put my groceries in the bike's basked and wheeled over to see what was going on.

"Hey Belinda," John said to me. I buy something from the store almost every week because they take books in trade, and I always seem to have a surplus. John works for the university's forest science unit, but when he's round, he helps out at his parents' store.

"How are you today?"

"Couldn't be better," I said.

"Yes, you could," he said, and it was such a random answer that I stopped in my tracks.

"How's that?" I said.

"Adoption day."

He pointed out the small adoption fair that had set up right in front of the store. There were enthusiastic young shelter volunteers standing by to act as carnival barkers to entice the unwary into getting close so they could reel them in. the biggest crush of lookie-loos was outside a carrier containing the largest cat I'd ever seen, a huge animal with dark gray fur."

"That is a chonky cat," I said to no one in particular.

"He's half Maine Coon and half Russian Blue said a volunteer.

"She's beautiful," I said.

"Would you like to hold her? She's very friendly."

"No thanks," I said, too smart to fall for that trick.

I noticed a couple of hopeful dogs—an old Westie wearing a bandana, a couple of poodles, and a corgi. *Dogs*, I thought. *Not interested in a dog*. I love dogs, but they're expensive to own. My best friend Jana has a sweet little long-haired doxie and she spends most of her disposable income on Gadget's medical care. Gadget has had tooth issues since she was a puppy and now, as an adult, she has 42 teeth, and every single one of them seems to have a problem.

"I'm not in the market for a pet," I said to John, who seemed to be following me.

He just grinned. "Sure, you are," he said. "Olivia would want you to get another cat."

I didn't remember talking to him about Olivia, but to be honest, I'd been so upset when she died that I was probably blurting out my tale of woe to total strangers. My boss sent me a pet sympathy card and Mom had brought over all my favorite comfort foods—mac and cheese, tuna casserole with potato chips, turkey chili—and I took a break from social media because I didn't want to stumble across an old picture I'd posted of her.

"Olivia's a tough act to follow," I said to John.

"When the owner is ready, the cat will come along." And then when I looked unconvinced, he added. "Everyone who takes a pet gets a free book," he said. "And someone just traded in a copy of that Mary Kupicka book you've been looking for."

I stared at him. "You are pure evil," I said.

"Hey, it's a win/win," he said. "The shelter and I both get rid of excess inventory."

Right then, an older woman came up to him with a couple of books in her hand, so I left him to do his job. And I figured, *what harm could it do to just look around*?

And Matilda was the first cat I saw.

She was in a cage all by herself looking absolutely terrified. She was a large ragdoll, her blue eyes wide open and wary behind her racoon mask. I couldn't tell how old she was, but I estimated somewhere in her young adulthood, maybe eight or nine.

"Why's she in the cage by herself," I asked the friendly young woman wearing a t-shirt that said, "No pet left behind."

"She's timid," she said, and as expertly as a con woman who's just spotted a potential mark, she began her spiel.

"She was found abandoned in West Seattle. She's not micro-chipped, but we can get you a discount on that."

"She's beautiful," I said, "but I'm not really looking for a cat."

And I was going to keep moving but right then the cat stretched her paw through the wires of her cage and put her paw on my hand.

And as clear as day, I heard someone say, "Take me home."

I looked at the cat.

She looked at me.

"Wow," the young volunteer said. "She hasn't done that before."

She started fumbling for a sheaf of papers. And I really, really, really wanted to just walk away, but I found myself stroking the cat's soft head without really meaning to. And of course, she started to purr.

"She likes you," the volunteer said, searching for a pen.

"She could just be self-soothing," I said. "Cats do that when they're stressed."

The volunteer just looked at me. "Are you kidding? That cat picked you, out of all the people who're here."

To be honest, "all" wasn't really that many. The adoption event was blocking the sidewalk, so anyone who needed to get into the market, or into the drug store on the other side, pretty much had to walk a gauntlet of animals. And of course, they all stopped to look at them, the most pleasant kind of window shopping.

"I just need your driver's license, phone number and email address," the volunteer continued. "And there's a $30 rehoming fee."

"Which we'll waive," John said, appearing at my side with the copy of the afore-mentioned Mary Kupicka book."

"We will?" the volunteer said.

"Yes," he said. "As a longtime patron of Reads on Reid Street, Belinda has built up a store credit of $43."

"That's for books not cats," I protested.

But the young volunteer was already popping open one of those cardboard cat carriers.

Resistance is Futile

I knew I had made the right choice when Belinda brought me into her apartment and apologized for it being kind of a mess as if she was talking to another person. The place was actually quite clean, but there were tell-tale signs she'd been cohabiting with a cat for a long time—scratches on some of the chair legs, a cozy granny square quilt that was threaded with soft gray fur.

It wasn't a very big place, but she had filled it with her essence but not a lot of objects.

I couldn't really see much from the carrier, which she set down in the living room long enough to fetch an old litter box from wherever it had been stored and come back in and show it to me.

"I know cats don't like sharing litter boxes, but if you can manage for a bit, I'll go out tomorrow and buy you a new one."

She let me out of the carrier, then showed me a tiny laundry room where she put the box under a window with a screen, and then poured it full of stale pine pellet litter she must have had left over from her old cat. Poor girl. She might think she wasn't ready for a new cat, but someone who kept old cat boxes and litter, just in case, was overdue for a new cat.

"That's not necessary, Belinda," I said. "I won't be here that long."

THE LOOK SHE GAVE ME WAS PRICELESS.

"It *was* you talking to me before." She was surprised, but not alarmed.

"I needed you to spring me from the shelter."

"Where's your owner," she said, which honestly was not the first question I expected her to ask.

"I must say you're taking this rather well," I commented.

"I read a lot of fantasy," she said.

"I'm a familiar," I said. "Do you know what that is?"

"Yes."

Good, I thought. *That will make this simpler*. "My companion is a witch named Melinda Harper. She's been abducted by a witch named Chester Foley."

"Where did he take her?"

"I said 'abducted,' not 'kidnapped.'" I could tell from her reaction; she was a little taken aback by my tone. "There's a difference," I said.

"Okay," she said warily.

"He's holding her in our house, and I need to help her before he uses her power to do something terrible."

"Like what?"

I blew out a frustrated breath. "I'm not sure. But she has the ability to heal people with her mind, which means she can also hurt them."

I could see she was turning the concept over in her mind.

"Where is Melinda right now?"

"At our house." I reached out my paw and touched her hand, transferring a mental picture of our quiet little cul-de-sac to her.

"Looks quiet," she commented. "It won't be easy to approach the house without him seeing us coming."

"You'll help me," I said, trying not to let my extreme relief show.

"Of course, I will," she said.

"You're a good person Belinda."

"How do you know my name?"

"I heard the bookstore guy say it."

"What's *your* name?"

"Matilda."

I expected her to say, "like the Australian song," but she surprised me. "Like the Empress Matilda?"

"Yes," I said. I was about to say something else when suddenly a car backfired on the street, and I flinched.

"It's okay," Belinda said. "That's just Jeremy coming home from work. He can't afford to fix his muffler."

"I don't like loud noises," I said, going all floppy on her lap the way ragdolls do.

"Loud noises are scary," she agreed. "

I started to purr, because it's an automatic response to being petted in the right way, and also because I felt really safe.

"Does she have any friends who could help us?"

"It's complicated," I said, hoping I didn't sound too disloyal. I love her to death, but Melinda's her own worst enemy sometimes. And most of the people in her coven are frenemies.

"So basically, we're on our own."

"Pretty much."

"Can you manipulate other people the way you did me at the adoption fair?"

She didn't sound mad, just curious. "To a certain extent," I said, "but it works better with people who aren't witches."

"Like me."

I just nodded my head. I didn't want to make her feel bad for not having witchblood. It wasn't her fault.

"That'll be helpful," she said.

"What are your skills?"

"I'm a lab tech," she said. "If you need blood drawn or urine sampled or a wart burned out, I'm your girl."

I didn't see how that could be remotely helpful, but I figured if we could get inside my house, I could do the heavy lifting.

"And I have an idea how to get into your house."

It's in the Blood

My idea was that I would dress up like I was coming to a dinner Melinda was hosting, carrying a bottle of wine and Matilda in a tote bag. After he opened the door to me, I was set the bag down and Matilda could slip out. It wasn't a perfect plan, but it was the best I could come up with on short notice.

While Matilda was doing a pretty good job of keeping things together, I could tell she was really tense because she was thumping her tail.

"It's going to be okay," I said, not really sure if that was true or not, but I hoped that I wasn't about to get us both killed.

"I'm really scared," Matilda admitted.

"Me too," I said. "Do you need to use the litter box before we go?" I'd peed about six times, even though I hadn't drunk any water.

"I'm good," she said.

HALF AN HOUR LATER, DRESSED IN A CHUNKY SWEATER DRESS I'D bough on Etsy, and a pair of ankle boots I could run in, I was sitting behind the wheel of my car, parked down the street from Matilda and Melinda's house.

"Okay," I said. "Time to get into the tote."

"What if he senses me in the tote?"

"My tote has RIFD blocking built in. I think that could help."

"Okay," she said, and jumped into the tote, settling into the bottom.

I locked the car and came around to her side, opening the door and grabbing the bottle of wine in the wine bag I'd picked up from the mini market. I picked up my tote as well and slung it gently over my shoulder. "You okay in there?"

"I'm fine," Matilda said.

"Here we go," I said, feeling the strongest impulse to say, "Let's rock and roll" like we were in an 80s action movie.

I RANG THE DOORBELL AND SUMMONED MY INNER EXTROVERT when Chester opened the door. Matilda had described him as good looking, and she hadn't been exaggerating. He looked so perfect; he could have been generated by AI.

"Hiiiii," I said, adding a slight upward inflection at the end as if I'd started to ask a question but decided not too at the last minute. "I'm Belinda. I'm so sorry I'm early—I always hate it when guests show up early and I'm still in the kitchen—but there was almost no traffic, so here I am."

I looked toward the kitchen expectantly, to draw his attention while I sat my tote back on the beautiful slate tiles of the foyer.

I didn't even hear Matilda slink out.

Chester started to turn back, and I handed him the wine bottle. "I hope you like Merlot," I babbled, "Melinda told me she was making brisket."

Chester looked at me, rather bemused.

"Melinda's not home."

Okay, I had to give him points for quick thinking.

"What?" I said. "No." I grabbed my phone and pretended to check a text string. Landing on a particular text—it was one from my mother asking me to pick up some ice cream if I was coming over to watch Ted Lasso with them—I pretended to look chagrined. I looked up at Chester and summoned every ounce of acting talent I had. "I can't believe I've got the wrong night."

I was playing what my father called "the bimbo card" with all my might. "I feel so dumb," I said. He started to hand me back the bottle of wine.

"No," I said, "please keep it. I'll get another one for next Saturday."

I started to turn away, but then turned back. "I'm so sorry to have bothered you—" I left a space for him to tell me his name, but he didn't rush to fill it in.

"Anyway, have a good rest of your night."

I was just about to ease my way out of the door when I heard Matilda yell.

"Belinda, we need you."

Without even thinking, I grabbed the tote bag by the straps and swung it around to hit Chester full in the face. Matilda had brain-waved me the layout of the house, so I knew just where to go, the master bedroom on the first floor.

I arrived to see Matilda trying to drag an apparently comatose woman across the floor. Considering the cat probably weighed eleven pounds and Melinda was around my size, she wasn't making much headway.

I turned around and closed the door, which had a lock on it. I engaged the lock and turned back to Matilda. "Is there another way out?"

"The bathroom has a window that opens out into a deck."

"Lead the way," I said, picking Melinda up in a fireman's carry, and thanking fortune that I knew how to do that without throwing my back out. But I wouldn't be able to carry her far and if we had to go uphill, it was going to be tough.

We made it all the way to the end of the deck before Chester got close enough to hit me with a fireball. It felt like every molecule in my body broke down into its component atoms for a moment and before re-materializing, like I'd just beamed up to the starship. *Enterprise.* It hurt a lot.

But now that Melinda was out of the house, she was starting to revive.

I saw Matilda put her paw on Melinda's shoulder as the witch threw her own fireball, which looked more like a neon purple thunderbolt.

Chester...disintegrated into glassy black shards.

A moment later, I collapsed, hitting the deck hard enough to break my arm.

Melinda was there immediately, putting her hands on either side of the break and pressing. There was heat and pressure and then, relief. "Flex your arm," she said, and I did.

"It feels better than new," I said.

"It is," she said. "You don't eat enough dairy, so I boosted your bone density."

"Thank you," I said. I looked over to where what was left of Chester was starting to drift over the edge of the deck, picked up by the winds. "Is there anyone we ought to call?" I asked. "The police? Someone to smudge the house? Somebody?"

I could feel my voice getting a little shaky.

"No," Matilda said briskly. "We'll sort it out if necessary."

"Well," I said, getting to my feet. "I guess I'll leave you to it."

"Would you like to stay for dinner?" Melinda asked. "I'd hate to waste that nice bottle of merlot."

I hesitated, not wanting to intrude on her reunion with Matilda.

"Melinda needs friends," Matilda said. "And so do you. Stay for dinner."

So, I did.

And as I was parking my car, I heard a plaintive little cry coming from under one of the hydrangea bushes that marked out the perimeter of our apartment parking lot.

Investigating, I saw a small, bedraggled, orange tabby kitten sitting beside a parked Kia and meowing so hard I could see her ribs moving.

"Who are you?" I asked and she turned toward the sound of my voice.

I really don't want another cat, I thought. But as the kitten crept toward me, I knew that resistance was futile.

It was cold in the parking lot, and it was probably going to rain.

"Do you want to come home with me," I asked, because I'd always talked to my cats like they could understand me.

And as if this cat understood me, he came right up to me and rubbed against my ankle. I scooper him up and he attached his sharp little kitten claws to my dress.

"At least his fur matches the dress," I thought.

"Let's go home," I said to him.

About the Author

Kit Blackwood is the para-cozy pen name of *USA Today* bestselling author Katherine Moore. She was born in Washington, D.C., and brought up on Army posts in the U.S. as well as Europe. An inveterate traveler, she is currently a digital nomad living in Portugal. To stay informed about new releases, get access to exclusive content, and participate in giveaways, sign up for her newsletter here. http://kattomic-energy.blogspot.com/p/blog-page.html

A Full Moon

BY CARA NORTH

Maybe the spell got it all wrong. There was no reason the mate June requested to appear in her life would be the one person who broke her heart. Asher was young and stupid the last time he saw June, but now, he was grown and wanted a second chance.

June blew out the candle and exhaled. She was filled with hope rather than desperation. Well, she was filled with both, but her mother's dying wish for her to find someone to help be balm to the grief was not a request June took lightly. Of course she needed support. Her mother was everything to her. Breast cancer had taken her away from June, but also given them a few final months to put everything in order. Everything but the loss, which nothing could prepare her for.

It had been a month and on the full moon, as directed, June performed the ritual to call forth her true love. Her mate. The one who would help to bring new meaning and purpose to her life. Not that she had a terrible life or needed someone in it to feel fulfilled, but her mother was right, she was lonely. June never liked being alone for long and never had to. Her friends were amazing and made things as easy as possible for her, but they couldn't leave their own romances and family obligations to live with June.

The next day, she met one of her oldest friends for breakfast. Sherice looked like she needed a nap but was wearing clothes indicating she was on her way to some workout once this meeting was over. June said, "Please tell me you are on your way to yoga or some meditation class you can fall asleep in."

"Kickboxing." Sherice winked and then smiled at the approaching server. "I'll have a green juice and toast with a side of strawberry preserves."

The server looked at June and she said, "I want the hungry man and tea please."

"Coming right up." The server walked away.

June asked, "How do you do all this?"

Sherice was fixing her natural curls back into a ponytail. "Do what?"

"Two kids, kickboxing, volunteer, part time job at the clothing store." June waved her hand around. "All of it."

Sherice laughed. "Well, kickboxing is what helps me do all the rest for sure. I can take out all my frustrations in that workout and then be a relatively civil person the reset of the day."

June's face must have said it all because Sherice cracked up and said, "You could use some kickboxing or...yoga in your life to help with the stress. At least until some *hungry man* decides to place an order for you." She pointed her painted nail at June and winked.

June shifted uneasily in her seat and said, "I did it."

Sherice pulled up short and whispered, "Shut up. You did not."

Once expression from June's face and Sherice gasped. June said, "It's time, right?"

"Yes!" Sherice was not quiet about that declaration of agreement. Several other patrons looked their way. They both laughed as the server brought them their drinks giving them speculative looks the whole time. They giggled when the server headed to another table. Sherice picked up her juice and said, "Yes. I agree. It is time. So...when should we...expect?"

June shrugged. "I'm on the basic level. I'm not really expecting much. We practiced the craft more for bonding and a spiritual code between us. It's not like we belonged to a coven or anything."

Sherice considered her a moment longer and said, "Well, when Tia is older, you can teach her. I have a feeling she's already casting spells on her father since he can't seem to refuse that child anything."

"He spoils them both." June pointed out.

"True." Sherice sighed. "And me. But still. I am pretty sure that one is one temper away from the dark side, so...you know. I want to keep her on the light side of life. Positive vibes only."

"That what they teach you in kickboxing?" June snickered. Sherice glared at her. "Uh, hu. Comes by that temper naturally. Maybe instead of some gardening and card reading, she should explore some toddler tumbling or one of those dance classes."

"Maybe both?" Sherice smiled. June nodded. Of course, Sherice would come over and learn from June's mother, so it wasn't like she didn't know what the fundamentals were. "I'll come too. Refresh my learning and then we will form our own little coven. A family one."

That made June smile. They were always more like family than just friends. This many years into their lives it was assumed. Tia was June's goddaughter after all. Not through the church, but through her parents' will should something happen to both of them. That reminder made June shiver inside. She would love her besties children for sure, care for and raise them as her own, no doubt. Still, she would rather Sherice and Ty stay alive. She didn't want to lose any more people in her life. Not for a long time.

After breakfast and more conversation about the kids, work, and a little more witchcraft, Sherice went off to kickboxing and June went home to work. It was getting harder each day to remain indoors for extended periods of time alone. This online job had been a gift in the beginning because her mother was dying, and it allowed June to have a job and care for her mother all in the same space.

Now, without conversation, a reason to check on her mom, a timer that was set for medications, the house was too quiet. The silence was too distracting. It didn't take long for her to move away from the computer and on to other tasks. The house was spotless by the time the sun was setting.

As she carried out the trash, she heard a whistle.

Just a sound and her body stiffened because no matter how long it had been, she knew the only person who ever did that upon seeing her was back in town. She turned and looked at the guy who had broken her young heart when they were in high school.

"So." Asher waved and walked forward to the gate at his mother's front yard. He leaned on it rather than opening it.

"So." June ceremoniously wiped her hands together in that clapping way people did when finished with something. Then she smoothed them down and over the jeans she was wearing. It was difficult to ignore how good he looked. As a man, all the features that were just a tad awkward back then, the long arms and legs seemed to have settled along with a much wider, more muscular chest if that t-shirt was any indication. And the legs. The jeans looked well worn in too many of the right places.

He cleared his throat and she realized she was simply ogling the man right there to his face without any discretion. Her head snapped up and her eyes met his. He did have the most beautiful, golden-brown eyes that caught just so in the light to make them...glow a bit. She stared, wordless, waiting.

"I'm." He cleared his throat again.

"You're sick? You sound like you need a cup of hot tea. Add some honey and lemon. It should help." She thought his mother should be taking care of her darling, perfect son. She sure bragged about him enough through the years June would leave the room if their mothers were talking and Asher came up.

He shook his head and said, sincerely, "No. I." He sucked in a breath. "June. I'm so sorry to hear about your mom."

"Thanks." She forced a smile and then turned to walk back into her house. They did not have a fence around their yard. Asher's family had always claimed every inch of their property line with that chain link fence.

Other families had too, but those other families had pets or rambunctious little ones who benefited from that limitation of freedom. June remembered when the family three doors down let them play kickball in the front yard and Asher almost got hit by a car. He had reacted so quickly and jumped back that he only sprained and ankle.

She slowed as her feet took the steps to the porch that led to the front door. Thinking about it now, he was entirely too fast for a kid his age. How did he know to do that?

As her hand reached for the screen door handle, she watched another hand move past hers and it held the door closed. The scent hit her next. Like home and hell, the blend was potent, spicy, and all Asher.

She looked up at the man holding her door closed and started to speak, but Asher moved his arms around her and pulled her into a hug as he said, "It's okay, June. It's all going to be okay now."

How long had she needed to hear that and believe it? Even if he was lying, it felt like the truth in her heart. She reluctantly embraced him, with each surrender of muscle to the movement, the emotions rose higher, threatening to capsize the carefully tethered ship that she stored all of the grief, the pain, the loss of everything from her favorite pair of shoes when she was nine to the man holding her in his arms right now.

Once the first tear took the leap from her eye to her cheek, it was over. The flag of surrender barely had a chance to raise before everything just toppled over and came flooding out of her. As her knees buckled, Asher lifted her up, easily despite her full figure, and carried her inside the house. He didn't set her on the couch. Instead, he held her as he shut the front door and then made his way to that seating and settled in the middle of it, still cradling her like a babe. Rocking, listening as she poured out gibberish between hefty sobs and nonsensical gasps. He reached for then handed her a box of tissues from the end table.

❧

June awoke to an interesting thumping sound in her ear, but since her head was also pounding it took a moment for her to realize they were two distinctly different sounds. Crusty, dry eyes dared to open. Once they had, she wasn't sure if she was in fact awake. The shifting body beneath her moved so they were on their sides, and she was looking up and at the most breathtaking creature she had ever known, Asher.

He didn't quite smile but he did push her hair to tuck a lock behind her ear as he asked, "You want breakfast?"

She blinked, the dry eyes making that motion worse. "Um."

They were both fully dressed.

He said, "You fell asleep."

She pushed up and realized how much her head hurt. "Ouch."

"You need some water." He handed her the glass and that was followed by the pills he pulled from the bottle that was next to the water. "Figured you would need these."

She took them and found a word once most of the water was gone. "Thanks."

He shifted to sit fully facing her and reached for the empty glass. After putting that on the nightstand he said, "June, I love you. I've always loved you. I thought I had to get away from here. Thought a girl like you deserved more than what comes with a guy like me."

She touched her forehead and asked, "What are you talking about?"

"Last night. You told me how I broke your heart. I broke mine too. I just...didn't know what else to do." He rolled his shoulder and looked at her. "I'm...different. You know that, right? Knew that on some level when we were kids. I knew you were something special, but I just didn't think you were my kind of special."

"Wow. I guess that trade school didn't offer much for bedside manner, huh?" She got out of the bed and practically stomped out of her bedroom. He followed and leaned against the doorframe of the kitchen entrance. She pulled down a new glass and filled it with more water.

Asher said, "You know I didn't go to a trade school. I went to learn the family trade. You know what that is, right?"

She shook her head and denied all the words trying to throw themselves out of her mouth and at him. Wolf, werewolf, shifter, paranormal, creature, other, something...

He snorted a laugh and said, "Yeah, you know exactly what that is. And I knew there was something about you...I just didn't know what it was then. I was too young. So were you. But you're a witch. I can smell the magic in your blood. You can sense the wolf in mine. We've always known, but didn't really understand anything."

"That's preposterous. There is no such thing." She was in some stage of denial even if she acknowledged it was only a few nights ago she was casting spells under a full moon.

"I heard you calling for me to come home, June." He stalked forward. "As if you were standing right next to me, but I was on a motorcycle going seventy-five with four other guys from the pack. I pulled off at the next exit and headed home without even telling them where I was going. I felt the break from them. Felt the pull toward you. This is home now. This is my pack. You, us, the family we will make. The—"

"Hold up." It was everything she thought she wanted when she was seventeen. Hell, it was everything she asked for under that moon. It was also just coming from the last man she ever thought would be giving it to her, but he wasn't asking. He was telling. "Don't you even want to hear what I have to say about all this?"

"I heard you. Loud and clear in my head when you called for me. All last night when you poured out your soul and sifted through it. I know, June. I know you doubt your heart right now. You said you would. I won't. Not again. I'm yours. You're mine, so...if you need to start at square one and...I don't know, go out for dinner and a movie, then...it's a date."

"A date?" she was flabbergasted.

He smiled, licked his lips and said, "Yeah. A date."

"Well I uh—" She looked around the kitchen. "I need to eat."

"Have a seat." He pointed and she took the glass of water with her to sit at the table. "I'll catch you up on my life since you did a pretty good job of filling me in on yours."

Asher made her breakfast and filled her in on life as part of a pack of unmated wolf shifters. They all worked construction and other manual labor jobs to help keep them physically fit, challenged, and as a means of burning through some natural energy. Easy to move around with, easy to leave should someone need to pack up and roll out. She asked questions and he answered. It was the easiest conversation she had with a man and June had to admit to herself, he looked right at home in that kitchen. Like he had never left.

When it was time for her to start her online work, she said, "Stay."

"Okay." He smiled. "You have to work?"

"I'll take a personal day. I just..."

"Come here." He moved forward as she moved toward him.

The embrace was everything. He kissed the top of her head and said, "I loved you all my life. You know that, right?"

She nodded. "I've loved you all my life, too."

His lips met hers for the first of a thousand kisses to come. One, two, four more and she didn't care that they hadn't even been on their first date yet. She wanted to be as close to him as possible. Pulling at his clothes, he asked, "You sure? We haven't even been to the movies yet."

She snickered and said, "I know. I can't wait for the lights to go down, the previews to begin, and—"

"The torture?" He laughed as he lifted her into his arms, wrapping her legs around his hips before carrying her to her bedroom. "You used to torment me."

She nodded. "It seemed to work."

"It always worked." He nuzzled her neck. "Everything you did worked. All the time. Even when I was away, I'd dream of going to the movies with you. Remember how your hands felt on me. Your mouth. God, June. I needed you then. I need you now."

"Then have me." She whispered against the shell of his ear. "Now and forever. If I'm yours, then claim me and never let me go again."

It sounded a lot like a growl, but that only made her shiver in delicious anticipation for what he would do. Asher moved with restraint at first and then, slipping into her as she cried out his name, he began to lose that control. Later, as they fell into declarations of love and the orgasmic bliss of their reunion, Asher said again, "I love you."

June looked into his eyes, practically glowing back at her, and said, "I love you too."

❧

ALMOST TWO YEARS LATER...

"AJ!" June called to the miniature Asher jumping from the couch to the chair.

"Oh, boy. You are in trouble." His grandmother from across the street winked at him. Then she moved to June and indicated she wanted to hold the baby. "This is my princess right here."

June snorted a laugh as she gave her leaping son a sandwich and sent him to the kitchen. "She wants to do whatever he does and that means she is almost already walking."

Asher arrived and smiled as he greeted his family. "Oh yeah. She's going to be something else for sure."

"Dad!" AJ called and Asher kissed June on her forehead and headed toward his son.

"What time is everyone arriving?" Asher's mother asked.

June smiled. Everyone was Sherice and her family. As her mother-in-law passed to enter the kitchen, June said, "Anytime now."

Instead of following right away, she went to the bookshelf and put her hand on one of the most special tomes she had. They were starting the summer off right, with a family, food, and lots of fun. Her mother was no doubt looking down on them and smiling. June looked up to the shrine on the shelf and said, "I love you too, Mom."

About the Author

Cara North writes in a variety of romance genres. To learn more about the author, her various pen names, and what project is up next, visit www.creativewritingwithdrnagle.com

A Spell Of Trouble

BY TL HAMILTON

A potion for luck.

An elixir for youth.

A spell for trouble.

Willa lives a quiet life, away from witch society, under the watchful eye of her snarky cat familiar, Maverick. By day, she sells the best homemade skin products in town. By night her dreams are haunted by her shadow lover.

Though she may be a work-in-progress in the potions department, she's determined to find her nightly visitor and begin to build her coven.

Even if it means improvising a summoning spell.

After all, what's the worst that could happen?

One

That night, he came to me again.

Shrouded in the darkness of a dreamscape I knew well, he stalked me like the prey I was in this nightly game of cat and mouse.

A ghostly touch glided across my lower back. Another on the nape of my neck. I shivered in anticipation as his touch became more bold, moving in for the final approach.

My shadow lover.

"Are you ready to sing for me, Bluejay?" His voice danced over the sensitive shell of my ear, the growl of need behind it making my lower belly heavy with want.

"Yes." My voice was little more than breath as my clothing slid to the floor in long, teasing strokes.

I squinted into the darkness, hoping I could catch a glimpse of this man that haunted my sleep. His deep chuckle ran straight to my core, and I squeezed my knees together even as I wanted to curse him. Not like a hex... okay, maybe a little one because this game, while enjoyable, was getting old. I felt as though I knew him at a spiritual level. This was someone I was meant to meet. Someone who would change my world.

If only I could find him in my waking hours.

"On your knees, Bluejay. Be a good girl, and I'll give you exactly what you want."

"And what would that be?" I asked, resting a hand on my hip and wondering how well he could see me.

"My fingers." A firm touch traveled the length of my sternum before retreating.

A warmth at my back warned me of his movement before he tugged my head to the side to expose the vulnerable column of my throat.

"My tongue." I clenched my jaw to keep still as he traced a tickling path from shoulder to ear.

"My cock." A powerful arm wrapped around my stomach, holding me in place as he ground an impressive erection into my ass. The fabric of his pants was a barrier that I wanted gone. In the waking world, I could spell them away with a wave of my hand. But here I had no control.

"Please," I groaned, pushing back into him as he snaked his free hand up my front and plucked at my nipple.

"You beg me so nicely, little witch. Tell me what you want from me."

"Your name."

He hummed.

"I don't think you've earned it."

I cried out as he pinched me hard, the noise fading into a moan as that hand on my hip dipped between my legs and stroked the length of my slit.

"What should I do with you tonight? Make you crawl to me? Perform for me? Choke on me?"

With one hand stroking back and forth through my increasingly slick folds, his other left my breast and came up to circle my throat.

"I think I'd like to take your breath away." His voice was nothing but gravel in my ear, and the whimper that escaped my throat in response was something I hadn't thought myself capable of. Circling my clit once, he grasped my hand and put it where his had just been.

"Keep going, but do not make yourself come. On your knees, little witch."

My breath hitched as I sank to my knees, concentrating on moving my soaked fingers in circles over my hyper-sensitive flesh.

"Open." At the warm press on my lips, I loosened my jaw, allowing his silky flesh to slide over my tongue. The salty tang of precum made me hum in pleasure around his girth.

A gentle hand pushed my hair back from my forehead and I wished I could make out his features. Just a little.

"Good girl. Take all of my cock. Do you like my taste, Bluejay? Does it make you wet?"

It did, in fact, make me very wet. My fingers slid easily through the mess he was making, and I fought to slow myself down. He said no coming, and I was determined to do as I was told.

My nose brushed against soft curls as he hit the back of my throat. As though reading my mind, he withdrew all the way and guided my chin to the heavy sacks below.

"Lick, little witch." I sucked the soft flesh in, inhaling the musky scent that was uniquely him as I worshiped each side.

His groan echoed through the darkness. *Show me who you are*, I silently begged, feeling bold as I ran my tongue back over his perineum and was rewarded with a fist in my hair.

"Use your hand on me, little witch," he growled. "You're going to get me nice and wet, then if you're a good girl, I'll let you taste yourself on me."

I was so close to the edge.

If he'd told me to do laundry, I could probably have come in a screaming mess. With the greatest reluctance, I moved my hand to his cock and stroked a little firmer than necessary, covering him in my moisture.

"Fuck, you're such a good girl. Take me in your mouth. Taste us and then I'll feed you my cum."

With less coordination than he'd shown before, he thrust into my mouth and I felt the stirring of magic at the taste of our combined essence. I loved this part of our encounters because it reinforced the belief that I would find him. Soon. He wasn't the only man out there for me, but he was the first that I'd found. Kind of. One day, I would build my coven and we would live happily.

"Come back to me, little witch. You're mine right now. No wandering off. Are you ready? I want you to swallow all of me."

With a low groan, the flesh in my mouth swelled and stream after stream of salty cum flooded my mouth. Swallowing quickly to make sure I didn't miss a drop, I let my hand fall back to my poor, neglected pussy and began working myself in earnest. I was so close I could feel the orgasm rising in me.

"Let me look after you," he whispered, replacing my hand with his own.

"Yes."

The feeling built as he plunged two thick fingers inside of me.

I was so close...

Two

Three lines of searing pain lit across my right cheek and I sat bolt upright in bed, confused and really pissed about the orgasm I'd just been denied.

"Good, you're awake. I wish to go outside."

I glanced out of the still dark window, then back at the bane of my existence.

"You aren't allowed out when it's dark, Maverick. Mrs. Maguire knows you ate her cockatiel. If you get into her aviary again, I'm not giving her a forgetful jinx. She almost burned down her barn last time."

Cats, in general, are great at making their owners feel stupid, but when that black cat is also a familiar, gifted from a witch's narcissistic mother, and the witch in question couldn't brew a potion if her life depended on it? Let's just say Maverick could say more with a sneer than humans could in a dissertation.

"Forget it. If you need to relieve yourself, use the kitty litter."

"You impudent little witch, I would not lower myself to use that disgusting sandbox. Do you remember the last time you cleaned it?"

I groaned, wishing more than anything to go back to sleep. Maybe I could spend some more time with my dream lover. I loved when he pulled my hair and called me Bluejay.

"Willa! Are you listening to me?"

"I cleaned it last night, before bed, for the express purpose of avoiding this conversation. The litter box is clean. Use it and let me sleep."

"If you were more practiced with your jinxes, there wouldn't be a problem with me eating when I'm peckish. I'm practically wasting away here."

"There's kibble in your bowl."

"I poured it out. It was beneath me. I'm a hunter, Willa. You may not understand that with your substandard magic practice, but we predators need to keep sharp."

"Mav—"

"I am fierce, and I am mighty. You can't keep me..."

Reaching into my nightstand, I pulled out a mouse toy I'd been keeping for emergencies and hurled it out my bedroom door. Like a shot, Mav took pursuit, bouncing off the doorframe and skidding down the wooden floorboards of the hall.

With a deep sigh, I flopped to my back and stared up at the cheap glow-in-the-dark star stickers I'd bought on a whim from a human store. Waving my hand idly, I watched as the spell took hold. Each star brightened as they detached from the ceiling and spun above my head in a dance of light and color. The beautiful display was little more than a parlor trick, but I found comfort in the movement. Much the same as I did when I looked up at the actual stars.

Breathing deeply, I tried to find the relaxation that would send me back to sleep, perhaps back into the arms of my lover to finally finish what we started, but as the spell faded and the stars returned to the ceiling, I resigned myself to an early start for the day.

The house groaned and settled around me as I padded barefoot down the hall, past Mav, who was in the process of gutting the fabric mouse, and into my apothecary.

Some witches were part of elite society, their powers giving them easy access to fame, politics, and the highest echelons of humanity. And some used the back of their house to make skin care products for humans.

I fell into the latter category.

When I was young, my mother had held great plans to make me the next *her*. A mirror image of the grandiosity of her being, only... not quite as grand because Mother hated competition.

When I accidentally turned my baby sister into a guppy with a teething spell, I was told witches grew into their power.

When I flooded Mother's favorite sitting room with a rain squall while trying to brew sunshine in a bottle, I was told my men would balance my powers. That was what covens were for. I just had to wait to find them.

When I brewed a concealment potion to get out of my sister's ascension party and accidentally made the manor disappear, I was given Maverick as a babysitter and told some time in the human world would do me the world of good.

The joke was on my family, though. I quite liked my little cottage, and running my own business gave me purpose.

Humans came great distances to purchase creams and elixirs that promised bright, youthful complexions.

If only I could master the combination of poultice and potion. Unbeknownst to Maverick, who was a right sourpuss when it came to my learning experiences — which he insisted on calling failures, the jerk — I had been working on an age defying cream with just a touch of a youth charm in it. I'd been over and over the spell until I knew it inside out and was sure this was it. This would be my first successful potion. Checking the hall once more, I grinned at Mav's butt wiggle as he pounced on the remains of the mouse toy. He was almost cute when he didn't know he was being watched.

I pulled the door closed and turned to my workbench, mentally ticking off each of the ingredients lined up in little glass jars.

It felt very *Practical Magic* casting spells in my nightgown at midnight. All I needed was Sandra Bullock, Nicole Kidman, and margaritas. Damn, now I wanted a margarita.

Pushing the thought aside, I heaved my small cauldron into the center of the space and began adding ingredients one at a time. The potion swirled pleasantly, casting a lovely glow that looked like sunrise on a summer morning.

"It's working," I whispered, awed by the beauty of the spell.

All that was left was to set an intention and bottle it up. Finally, my luck was turning. I was going to show Mav he was wrong. I wasn't a screwup, I was just getting the hang of...

A drop of darkness swirled in the center of the concoction, spreading through the liquid in spikes of midnight blue.

"No. Nononononononononono," I muttered, holding my palm over the cauldron in the vain hope I could stop the spread by sheer will alone.

"Don't you dare."

The potion swirled into a vortex, the beautiful sunny color swallowed by the inky darkness so completely that I wondered if I had imagined its existence in the first place.

It reached the top of the cauldron and continued to rise, supported by its own momentum as it swirled faster and faster.

Shit. The last thing I needed was to take out my shop with a tornado of youth potion.

In a desperate attempt to stop the destructive force, I cut my hand through the funnel of potion, karate chopping the stupid spell into submission.

Two outcomes followed. One good, one... not great. At all.

The vortex collapsed in upon itself as I made contact with it, my arm interrupting whatever momentum the spell was working under. Unfortunately, being under said vortex at the moment of collapse meant that everything that had been swirling came to a stop on top of me. I gasped and sputtered as the potion soaked me from head to toe, dying my white nightgown blue.

"What was that?" Maverick was outside the door, clearly alerted to my screw up by some innate sixth sense that told him Willa needed to be judged.

"Nothing," I called, spitting potion and slip-sliding across the room to where I kept a mop and bucket for these exact reasons.

"Willa. Open the door."

"It's fine. I'm fine. Everything's just...Ow!" Between one step and the next, my feet went opposite directions. One straight into my large cast iron cauldron, and the other into the mop, which toppled unceremoniously onto my head.

From my sprawl on the floor, I watched in misery as a dark puff of smoke seeped underneath the door and solidified into a black cat who somehow managed to convey his utter disgust with the state of me and my workshop with nothing more than the lift of his paw.

"Stop judging me. It almost worked this time," I grumbled, using the mop as a crutch to climb to my feet.

"Are you aware your hair is blue?" Maverick asked with a sniff.

"What...?" Turning so fast I almost slipped a second time, I came face to face with my reflection in the antique mirror over the hearth. He was right. My once ice blonde hair had transformed into a soggy blue mess, reminiscent of the Cookie Monster. The only sign of my old color was a single strip of white in the front.

"Another failure for the books," Maverick said, turning back into smoke with the swish of his tail and disappearing under the door.

"Go eat slugs, Maverick," I called after his snooty butt.

"I would if you'd lift the wards on the doors and windows," he called back.

Not a chance, cat.

Three

Cleanup took a disproportionate amount of time, considering the mess had happened in mere moments, and by the time I jumped out of the shower, my hair hanging in vivid blue coils around my shoulders, I had to hustle to open my shop on time.

Mrs. Maguire was first through the door, keen to browse the new candle selection that had finished setting the day before. She stared a little too long at my hair before carefully commenting that sometimes a change was as good as a holiday.

I smiled politely, quietly wondering if I should have let Mav out this morning, if for no other reason than Mrs. Maguire wouldn't be in amongst my hand creams, silently judging me.

Father Mason was next through the door, and I heard Mav's snicker a moment before he sprinted across the floor under the priest's feet. The old fool quickly made the sign of the cross, muttering some prayer or another under his breath, and continued toward the front counter where I was sorting essential oils.

"Good morning, Willa. I didn't see you at church yesterday."

"Good morning, Mason. You didn't. And you won't see me there today, either."

His gray brows drew down until his face wrinkled like a shar pei.

"When will you turn away from this devil worship and come back to the light? We are all God's children. He will accept you in his infinite love."

I cocked my head as Mav jumped up beside me. "And yet, you won't accept that I've told you countless times I'm wiccan. I believe in the goddess *and* the god."

I didn't mention I'd met the goddess and could vouch for her existence, while his God was an unknown entity to me.

"I strive to save your immortal soul, girl. Don't think I'll give up on you, even if you have given up on yourself."

Maverick took the opportunity to bat a bowl full of garlic oil on to the priest's robes, blinking innocently at my grunt of annoyance.

As *Father* Mason wheeled toward the exit, no doubt planning his next approach to save this evil sinner, I raised a brow at my feline familiar.

"Oops," he said with a lift of his tiny shoulder.

"I don't suppose you want to clean that up, do you?" I asked, already reaching for the mop and bucket I kept close for these exact occasions. Maverick liked to knock things over. A lot.

"My next familiar is going to be a dog," I muttered, making quick work of the mess.

"That is offensive."

"You're offensive."

"What's this?"

I checked over my shoulder to see Mav in my notebook. "That's private."

"What is it?"

Snatching the book away, I cradled it to my chest, scowling at the little snoop.

He blinked his yellow eyes at me, clearly uninterested in moving until I'd answered his question. Damn it.

I cast my eyes around, hoping for a distraction, but there were no patrons and the shop floor was as orderly as ever.

If I told him, he was guaranteed to tell my mother, and the last thing she needed to hear was that I planned to summon my shadow lover.

"Show me," he demanded, flexing his claws.

"It's none of your business."

"You seem to forget, I'm your familiar."

"You're my mother's spy."

Maverick growled at me. Literally growled.

"Show me the spell, little witch. Now."

Looks like it's now or never.

Once my mother knew of my plan, my time would be up. Summoning wasn't necessarily frowned upon, but with my track record for potions, I'd been put on a tight leash when it came to creating my own spells. I had to cast this now and hope like hell I had it right, or I was going to be doomed to nightly visits from a hot as sin shadow lover who always got me *this close* before I woke up. I wanted my orgasms, damn it. Okay, fine. I also wanted to know the man behind the darkness. He was real, and he was mine. I knew it.

With a deep breath, I centered my focus and began to move, casting a circle and calling the elements before I set my intention and chanted the words I'd written and committed to heart. As I paced out the spell, darkness descended on the shop, a shadow as thick as that in my dreams. Golden threads of light spread from the point where my feet connected with the floor, twisting and flowing in an intricate knot of magic.

Please work.

Raising my hands over my head, I lifted the knot, casting my intention into the universe and begging they answer my summons.

Find me.

The jingle of the bell over the shop door caught me by surprise. Whirling, I released the power and watched the shadow, the threads of magic, and with it, my hope, fade to nothing.

"Impressive," Mav muttered, jumping from the counter and sauntering through the back door as the customer came into view.

He was tall with blonde hair pulled into a knot on top of his head, and a beard that made me wonder if vikings still existed. Ocean blue eyes narrowed on me briefly as he crossed over where my spell had dissipated only moments before.

"Hi," I said, stupidly. Summoning spells didn't work that quickly, did they?

The viking grunted, his eyes flicking up to my hair before settling back on me.

"I need some face stuff for my wife."

My heart dropped into my shoes. Of course, the spell hadn't worked. This poor random dude had wandered into my shop and instead of helping, I just gawked at him like a toad. Admittedly, I was sure most of the female population would gawk with me. The blue jeans wrapped around his thighs fit him like a second skin, and I wondered if I could subtly slide in behind him to check out his ass. A black shirt stretched over his chest to complete his outfit. The man was built. And gorgeous.

Stop drooling, Willa.

"Oh, sure. Over here."

I showed him the wall of cleansers and scrubs, and advised him to add a moisturizer if he knew her skin type. As I worked, Mav reappeared and took up his usual position in the window. Warming his cold heart with the sun's rays, no doubt.

When the viking had made his choices, we wandered back to the counter, and I rang up his purchases, unable to shake the feeling we were supposed to meet.

Leave him alone, Will. He's married, remember?

"All done. Have a nice day," I said, giving him my best professional smile.

"Thanks, Bluejay," he rumbled.

I froze.

"What?"

"What?" He looked equally confused for a moment before his lips kicked up into the barest hint of a smile.

"Because of your hair," he said, tucking his hands in his pockets and taking a step backward.

I touched a strand, glancing down in surprise. Still blue.

The explanation should have placated me. Just a coincidence, right? Except that the nickname, spoken in that voice, was one I would know anywhere.

The bell's jangle shook me from my thoughts and I noticed his bag of products was still on the counter.

"Hey, wait!"

Sweeping it up, I rushed through the door, catching his arm as he hit the footpath. The shock that passed through me was so painful, it almost knocked me over. I flexed my hand, wanting to dissipate the feeling as he turned and gave me a view of something that shouldn't exist. Around his throat, an intricate red web was woven in malicious lines of magic. No wonder it had hurt me. The point was to let other magic users know to keep hands off.

In a stupor, I held up his bag. "You forgot this."

He nodded and accepted it without the slightest hint he'd felt the impact of the spell, then headed down the road without a backward glance. Unable to look away, I waited until he disappeared around the corner before I wandered back inside.

"That was an unexpected turn of events," Maverick hummed as I let the door fall closed behind me.

"It was him," I muttered, ignoring Maverick's snark.

He stood and stretched, his hackles standing up all along his spine, before he jumped down from the windowsill and followed me deeper into the shop.

"You're in a great deal of trouble then, little witch, because that man was under a witch's thrall. A powerful one, by the look of it."

I glared at the unhelpful furball.

"Thank you, Captain Obvious."

This was going to require research. Research, and lots of caffeine.

I turned on my heel and backtracked to the door, closing the shop for the day despite the clock reading barely ten A.M. An urgency that I couldn't explain gripped me, coaxing me to hurry until I was all but running through my house toward the library.

I'd found him, but someone else was keeping him from me.

That was going to change immediately.

Pulling my grandmother's grimoire from its pedestal, I prayed she had a spell powerful enough to break the enchantment I'd just felt, because I really didn't feel like getting zapped again.

"You aren't supposed to touch that. What do you think you're doing?" Mav asked from the doorway. Damn snitch was probably gearing up for a trip to my mother's house to report on Willa the screw-up.

"I'm going to save that man and find my coven."

In true cat fashion, Mav presented me his butthole and stalked out the door, but I thought I heard him mutter something as he passed out of sight.

If I didn't know any better, I'd swear he said, "It's about damn time."

***

That's all for now, but Willa will be back, with Maverick in tow, to track down her coven. Starting with her shadow lover in A Brush of Magic!

About the Author

TL Hamilton hails from Melbourne, Australia, where she lives with her hubby, two little boys, Arlo the wonder pup, and Hugo the turtle.

The consummate daydreamer, TL writes all over the romance spectrum from romcom right through to the dark, gritty hold onto your seats drama. Regardless of the story, you can guarantee you'll find relatable characters and steamy bedroom times between the covers of her books.

You can find TL in her reader group, TL's Dreamers on Facebook https://www.facebook.com/groups/tlsdreamers

Or join her mailing list for updates on her latest releases

https://www.subscribepage.com/g5g7y5

Also by By TL Hamilton

Paranormal RH

Moonlit Alexandrite - https://books2read.com/moonlitalexandrite

Moonlit Alexandrite: Crafty Seductions - https://books2read.com/CraftySeductions

Jacinth - https://books2read.com/Jacinth

Contemporary RH

Where in the world - https://books2read.com/whereintheworld

Contemporary MF/Sports Romance

Target Me - https://books2read.com/TargetMe

Kicking it with the winger - https://books2read.com/kickingitwiththewinger

Split - https://books2read.com/SplitPerfectStroke

Shatter - https://books2read.com/ShatterPerfectStroke1

Shock - https://books2read.com/ShockPerfectStroke2

Ataraxia

BY T.S. SIMONS

Meredith is a strong, independent lawyer reeling from a personal tragedy when she encounters an inexplicably compelling man at a highland estate in Scotland. As they are forced to spend a single stormy evening together, she is tormented by flashbacks from her past, making her question everything she thought she knew. As the truth slowly reveals itself, Meredith is devastated to learn she is the subject of a multi-generational hex that threatens her future. Can she achieve Ataraxia, a state of freedom and tranquillity, in time to break the curse?

"Fucking cheating asshole!" I raged, slamming on the brakes as the obscured stop sign flashed into view through the mist of torrential rain. Nothing was visible; the world outside was shrouded in fog. Rain thundered against the windscreen with such force that it threatened to shatter. Turning off the main road onto a random country lane, the tree branches grazed the car in places.

"Ugh." My neck jolted from another pothole, the size of a small suburb. The haze almost entirely obscured the road. Typical dour Scottish winter weather, though it fitted my mood perfectly as I continued to seethe. I had nowhere to go. I was running, putting as much distance between myself and that scene as possible.

"Why did you believe that fucking asswipe cheating *loser,* Meredith?" I ranted, straining to see through the fogged-up windscreen. "You are a strong, independent woman who takes no shit. Why do you have no damned self-respect?" The car slid sideways in the mud, and I accelerated through the slip, recalling my advanced driver's training.

"Breathe. Focus," I instructed myself as I hurtled down the narrow Scottish lane at breakneck speed. Fuck knows where I was going. The motorway had pissed me off, happy families drifting along preparing for the Christmas holidays. I needed speed and isolation. Driving was one of my emotional outlets, and I was less likely to get booked for speeding away from the main roads.

"Fuckkkkk," I screamed as my white Audi slid in the wet, unable to gain traction. Frantically, I pumped the brakes, but the car slid uncontrollably through the mud into the rear of the black Range Rover stopped at the intersection. The impact of the crash slammed my head into the steering wheel as the airbag deployed, and my ears filled with the sound of shattering glass.

ααα

"You are awake. Good." The deep masculine voice was warm and alluring, like liquid chocolate. It was a statement, not a question. Lifting a hand to soothe my pounding head, I moaned as I touched my swollen forehead.

"Yes, you have sustained some bruises," the low, educated Scots voice continued soothingly. "Concussion. But nothing serious. You are safe."

My head was thumping, and I struggled to focus, but something about the room's scent alerted me that this was not a hospital. It was musky, with the faintest scent of dust and spice, not a hospital's clinical, sterile smell. My partner Ben, the reason I was driving in the rain, was head of radiography at the largest hospital in Edinburgh. After five years, I thought I knew him. We had met at college and had fallen into a relationship in our second year. We had spent many hours exploring secret nooks of his various hospitals to engage in his kink for sex at work. The x-ray room, the doctor's lounge, and even the morgue. Memories of the smashing windscreen morphed into one of Ben's boyishly handsome face, mid-orgasm, his cock embedded in my boss Susy. Her bottle-blonde hair was uncharacteristically unrestrained, and her hair spilled across my favorite purple sheets. Shaking myself slightly to dispel the image, I groaned as my broken head rattled and shards of pain pierced my eyeball, white light flashing behind my eyes.

"Drink," the voice urged, holding my elbow and supporting me to sit.

Forcing myself to lift my head, I cracked open my eyes to see the proffered glass. That tiny slit of vision was enough to make me bolt upright in alarm.

"Where am I?" I croaked, my voice rusty as I took in the dimness of the surrounding room.

"My family home."

Cautiously, I assessed the glass I held, desperately thirsty. *Had he poisoned it? Slipped sleeping medication into it?* My legal training and years of working on gruesome cases, many of which involved sexual assaults of young women, made me overly cautious.

The low rumble radiated around the richly appointed room. "Had I wanted to harm you, don't you think I would have done that while you slept?" The face attached to the voice entered my fuzzy view as he plucked the glass from my hand and sipped, returning it to me with raised eyebrows. A challenge.

Observing his handsome profile, I sipped from the weighty, expensive crystal, searching for a sign. He was my age, mid to late twenties, but his elegant manner of speech made him appear much older. Styled dark hair framed emerald green eyes and a classically handsome chiseled jawline. Damn, he was hot in an old-school Hollywood gentleman way. His facial expression gave away nothing. No hint of who he was. Where I was. My brain raced, wondering how to get out of here without offending this man.

"My phone?" I asked politely as my thoughts reassembled themselves. "Where is my phone?"

He handed it to me from the small lamp table beside the couch, shattered beyond repair. Tapping at the screen resulted in a shard of glass embedding into my fingertip, making me wince, but I refused to cry out. I didn't need help from any man.

"Here," he took my icy hand in his larger one and, using a well-manicured fingernail, deftly flicked the fleck of glass without the slightest hint of emotion. His hand was warm and compelling.

"Do you have a phone I can use?" I asked, pulling away from his touch, despite not wanting to.

"Who would you call?"

My heart sank. Was it that obvious I was alone? My parents passed nearly fifteen years ago, my mother of cancer when I was ten, and my father only a year later, leaving me in the care of my older sister. When she married, her whole life revolved around her husband and children. After her twins were born, she rarely made contact. A birthday or Christmas card would occasionally arrive in the mail, but any plans I made were always canceled at the last minute with some flimsy excuse. Eventually, I gave up trying. It was clear I was a reminder of her past life.

Acquaintances, colleagues, I had many of those. People I could call to drink with, attend a party, or go to an event. But as a lawyer in Edinburgh, and English to boot, did I have any genuine friends? Anyone I could genuinely trust? I thought Ben was my soulmate. Fool that I was.

"A mechanic," I replied staunchly, raising my chin defiantly. "Possibly a panel shop. The faster I get my car fixed, the sooner I can be out of your way. I must also call my insurer and compensate you for your damage."

My companion beckoned and moved slowly to an oversized window, dressed in expensive heavy velvet drapes. The timber cross beams of the window were dark walnut, and the windowpanes were small with original glass, complete with tiny imperfections. This was a period home, no doubt, and an expensive one. Thrusting back the heavy quilt, I staggered to the window in my bare feet, realizing I still wore my blood-spattered pale blue linen dress. My blood, by the look of it. It took one glance to see why he was beckoning me. The dark, wild storm continued to rage outside, barely concealing the spectacular view of mountains and streams beyond. But the view of my beloved TT lying in the driveway below, a crumpled heap smashed beyond repair, made my stomach sink.

"Perhaps a taxi," I sniffed, trying not to show my disappointment.

"When you are well, I will take you anywhere you want to go. We are in a dead spot here. Cell phones do not work, and the storm took out the main line when a tree fell across the road. It will be restored. But not until the crews can get through."

Where did I want to go? My heart lurched, hitting my ribcage with a resounding thunk. Besides no longer having a vehicle, my house was no longer my home. My job, well, how did I return there? Even if I had no self-respect, Ben loved mirrors, being able to watch himself from all angles, and Susy had undoubtedly seen my face as I walked into our bedroom. The weather had unexpectedly turned cold, and I had planned to drop home to grab a warm jacket before returning to the office for the afternoon. While Susy had been on hands and knees, the mirror behind would have displayed my horror, tears blinding me with a view of my boss that no one should ever see. Not to mention the lamp I hurled at them on my way out. No, I would need to find a new car, home, and job. Fucking brilliant. Go for the trifecta Meredith. Ooh, new partner too. I was done. I had caught him cheating once before, but he had sworn it was a mistake and begged forgiveness. Stupidly, I had believed him. But shagging my boss in our bed was a new low. What were four shitty events called... a quadfecta? Was that even a word?

To cover my trauma, I assumed my cool lawyer facade. "I am Meredith." I offered my hand, which to my complete astonishment, he kissed.

"Thomas," he replied equally formally. "At your service."

Inadvertently, I flinched, then realized my reaction was rude. Perhaps he was from continental Europe, where hand kissing was more commonplace. In my line of work, handshaking was the norm, although I had worked with clients and colleagues who kissed. More so, when I worked in London, people were slightly more reserved here.

Before I could respond to his antiquated manners, he glided gracefully out of the room, his black hair just grazing the collar of his tailored black shirt. He ducked his head slightly through the doorway, betraying his significant height. Relief swept through me, finally feeling comfortable enough to poke around the room, shivering slightly from the damp cold.

Hand-cut gray stone walls along the ran house perimeter, decorated with tapestries, oil paintings and stuffed animal heads. A manor house or perhaps a hunting lodge? Despite the roaring fireplace at the other end of the room, rich furnishings, and muted antique rugs, the room had a lingering chill, and I wrapped my arms around myself.

The floor-to-ceiling bookcase that ran the length of the far internal wall caught my attention with a faint buzzing, like a bee trapped in a box. I closed my eyes to focus; it was almost indiscernible. Perhaps a bug caught somewhere? It was irritating, not intrusive exactly, just enough to be annoying. As I crept across the enormous room towards the bookcase, the volume steadily increased until it was almost deafening. A loud buzzing sound, now almost like a helicopter. What kind of insect made that much noise? I shook my head slightly. Maybe there was nothing there at all. Had he drugged me? Through the haze in my head, I tried to focus and determine where the sound was coming from. Was I going mad? Slapping my cheek to reassure myself I was awake, I was confident it wasn't me. Could this be some form of surveillance device? Squinting through the roar of high-pitched static now piercing my already sore skull, a large leather-bound black book with faded gold lettering on the spine drew my attention. Scanning the shelves, it looked like so many others, but that one... there was something about it. I stared at it, fascinated. It was worn and well-handled. The black leather cover was cracked and peeled in places. While it looked like the surrounding titles, that one compelled me. Straining my eyes, I squinted to read the text as it drew me in, pulling me toward it. I needed to touch it. I ran my finger along the cracked leather spine, and the world went dark.

❧

Awakening a second time, I was in his arms, his eyes glistening in the firelight.

"Mariette, my love. It is you. I thought... I dared to hope it was. But you look so different. Never did I dream you would return to me as a redhead!"

Safe in his arms as I regained my senses, my body relaxed, finally at peace. I knew this man. Trusted him with my life. Nothing could harm me. My stomach jittered, and a warm flood of emotion rushed through me. Then my brain kicked in, and my eyes flew open. No. He was a stranger. Handsome, but nonetheless, unfamiliar. But my body screamed otherwise. I loved this man. I knew that beyond any shadow of a doubt.

"Tom?" I whispered, unable to believe my eyes or what I was saying. I fought to keep my thoughts straight, pulling away from him, but his grasp was tight, holding me to him like I was a previous object, and he couldn't bear to let go. I struggled. *No, I was Meredith. Attorney, bitch, and sometimes pilates advocate. But I wasn't. I was his wife, his soul mate. Fuck.* I shook my head and recognized the mistake a second too late as I cried out from the pain.

Tom relaxed his hold on me temporarily, balancing me on his lap.

"Here." He handed me two white tablets from the small table, and this time I didn't even flinch before downing them and gulping the glass of water he passed to me.

"I don't understand," I wheezed through a tightened throat. "Who are you?"

"You know. Think, my love, think. What do you remember?"

"I...I can't," I stammered, fighting against the whirlpool of thoughts threatening to drown me. *How could I possibly know this man? I had met him only today.* The full moon outside indicated it was now night, but I didn't think I had been unconscious for long.

"Tell me," I pleaded, and pain crossed his face.

"I can't," he replied, his voice strangled.

"How long have I been here?" I asked, desperate to get my head straight before addressing the emotion threatening to tear me in two.

"Only a few hours," he whispered. "But in my heart, a lifetime."

"What the fuck are you on? You don't know me." Cranky at my swirling emotions, I yanked away, his face breaking. God, he was gorgeous. Chiseled features and brilliant green eyes betrayed his adoration for me. Guilt twinged at my chest from causing him pain.

"Who are you?" I tried again, desperate to get my thoughts straight.

"No, you need to remember," he pleaded. "Please, Mariette."

"Stop calling me that," I snapped. "My name is Meredith. I am an attorney. And I swear, if you do not get your hands off me this fucking second, I will break you."

The pain etched into his face from my words was evident, but I was fuming. *What had this fucker done to me?* My head was swimming with images of people and places I had never seen.

"I don't know who you are," I snarled, "but I am not who you think I am. What did you do? Drug me? Is that the only way you can get a woman to be near you?"

"No," he whispered, his Scots accent becoming more pronounced. "I would never harm you. Ever."

"Then you will let me go," I announced haughtily.

"I cannot," he whispered as he wrapped his arms around me. Strong, muscular arms. "I have waited far too long."

Placing both palms on his chest, I shoved him as hard as I could, but the recoil threw me backward, electrified. I gasped as a memory blinded me. That chest, rippled and hard. And *mine.*

"What? What do you remember?"

"You. Us." I whispered, unsure I had seen what I thought I had.

"You remember. What else?"

"Nothing." I shook my head. This wasn't real. I was going mad.

"Think, my love. Who am I?"

"Tom," I answered automatically. "You are an academic."

Tom nodded. "A historian. What else do you remember?"

Closing my eyes, I tried to focus, but it was the emotions that swept over me in waves. Love, passion, this man was my best friend, lover, and confidante. He was my partner and my home.

"Why were you near the library?" he questioned softly.

"I heard a buzzing noise. What was that?" I asked.

"Your ring. It called you."

"Ring?" I stammered, dazed.

He lifted my hand. On my left ring finger was an antique rose gold ring, an enormous pear-shaped diamond in the center surrounded by smaller diamonds that radiated down the band. Turning it to let the light catch the facets, I knew this piece intimately. It was *my* ring. Only I had never seen it before. Blinking hard, I tried to get my thoughts straight. No. I was Meredith Martin. I wasn't married – to this man, or any man. But I *was*. I was his.

"It was in the book?"

Tom nodded.

"Why?"

"After...." He choked that sentence off. "I carried it for many years, but eventually, I placed it in our wedding album, praying we would be reunited one day. Seeing it was torture, a reminder of my loss. I never dreamed..."

"Reunited?"

"Please, my love. Try," he begged.

Closing my eyes, I inhaled his scent. Masculine, secure. A vision of him in a tailored grey suit, waiting for me at the bottom of the stairs as I swept down in a long, flowing white dress, my hair pinned up with flowers. He beamed at me, adoration radiating from him as I neared him. The room was filled with the scent of flowers. I knew. My heart belonged to him.

"Our wedding," I whispered, primarily to myself, as the floodgates opened and memories surged of Tom and me together. "I remember our wedding."

His lips crashed into mine, powerful and demanding. With that connection, all resistance melted. I was his. There was no doubt in my mind. We were a pair. Bonded. His kiss was magnetic, and my body yielded to his touch. Not breaking the seal of our lips, his hands stroked my hair, running his fingers through the masses of auburn curls that tumbled to my shoulders. I wanted this man, craved his touch. My arms reached around and ran down his back, firm and assertive, unable to let him go. Logic tried to get the upper hand at several points. He was a stranger, and I wasn't a one-night stand kind of girl. But my heart knew better. I was his, now and forever. The more we touched, the more I remembered about our life, our passion for each other.

"Take me to bed," I murmured.

Effortlessly he scooped me up, and I was weightless, being carried through the enormous stone building, breezing past paintings, tapestries, and artworks. My head spun as he held me against his chest, murmuring to me using words I barely understood. I couldn't focus on my surroundings as we swept down hallways and around corners. He stopped and lovingly laid me on an enormous four-poster bed with burgundy drapes hanging from the top. I knew this room; it was *our* room. My dresser, my art. That familiar view. But before I could focus on my surroundings, he was beside me, caressing my waist, kissing my neck and the tops of my breasts. My eyes closed in bliss as I allowed him unfettered access to my body. Never had I felt so worshiped and cherished as I do right now. My heart quickened as he returned to kiss my mouth and effortlessly slipped the dress off my shoulders, pulling it off in one quick sweep, revealing my matching emerald green bra and panties.

He gasped as he saw me, confirming his approval, but didn't pause in his work, kissing my stomach and down my legs. He could have done anything to me, and I would have let him. My body belonged to him. My mind was no longer in control. As he returned to my head, I slipped the shirt over his head and ran my hands down his chest, using my fingertips along every definition and curvature. I knew this body. I had touched it so many times.

Inadvertently I shivered, and he deftly rolled the heavy quilt back, slipping me underneath with one powerful arm.

"How?" I gasped. My mind was still battling with my body. *Was this just a rebound? Revenge for Ben's betrayal?*

"Later," he murmured, slipping out of his pants and throwing the quilt back over us to ward off the chill in the air. "We don't have much time."

Don't let your brain take over. I pleaded silently as this man kissed and stroked every inch of my body, evoking feelings I had never experienced. It was the strangest mix of emotions, my body screaming that I knew him, but logically knowing I didn't. I wanted to pull away, to run, but I couldn't. The memories were flooding back hard and fast, the old and the new weaving a complex tapestry in my mind of both my lives. As he touched me, I felt vulnerable, but oh, so aroused. He paused, staring into my pale green eyes with his emerald ones, and I knew he was asking for consent. I should run, I knew. Tell him no. Get out of here. But where would I go? I had nowhere to go. No home, no partner, and no job. *May as well get a good night's sleep...*I thought as my hands stroked his broad, muscular back, urging him to take me.

"It isn't enough," he whispered. "You must say the words."

"What words?" I wanted to say, but they were already on my lips, our wedding vows, our pledge to one another. "I am yours, always and forever," I whispered. "We are one body, one soul, one heart. You are my guiding light, and I am yours."

As I spoke the final words, I felt his hardness enter me, and a gasp escaped as he filled me, fitting together like nothing I had ever experienced. We merged, becoming one, and heat filled me with a powerful electric charge, a sense of lightness glowing through me as we surged together toward a mutual climax. Like a fever breaking, the glass shell shattered, and I recalled every detail of my past with crystal clarity as we cried out in ecstasy together and clung to each other.

"I remember!" I panted. "You. Us. Our home. What happened?"

Tom rolled off me, settling himself on his pillows, and gently curled me towards him, my head resting on his shoulder. His arm wrapped around me, and as I felt his heartbeat beneath my cheek, I had never felt so safe.

"We have time now. I apologize for not telling you before, but it was nearly midnight. A hex was placed on us. We have spent a hundred and twenty-five years apart. We have endured immense pain. But never again."

"A hex?" I asked, staring up at him. "Why?"

"Do you recall the marble statues my grandfather took from Greece before I was born?"

"From the Parthenon?" I asked slowly as memories of my two lives intertwined into cohesion. "Shit, you mean the Elgin Marbles?"

"I do. Do you recall them?"

"Not only do I recall the grief they caused, but I am now part of the legal team trying to repatriate them to Greece."

"I am pleased. They have caused too much pain."

"Remind me," I asked, not trusting my memories.

"My grandfather, Thomas Bruce, the seventh Earl of Elgin, was accused of taking them from Greece between 1801 and 1805 while serving as ambassador to the Ottoman Empire."

"Didn't he?" I furrowed my brow.

"Not exactly. He recognized their historical value and engaged artists to replicate them. Draw them. The actual removal was ordered by Philip Hunt, one of his representatives. But my grandfather defended the actions. At the time, he genuinely believed that he was doing the right thing, protecting them. He valued antiquities and thought the Ottoman officials were not protecting them. He believed they would fall into Napoléon's hands. Possibly he was right." I felt the shoulder shrug slightly from beneath my head.

"That's right. But what did that have to do with you, with us?"

"One day, as I left the university, an elderly woman approached me. She was bent over, filthy, and dressed in shabby black clothes. Rags really. She was hysterical, demanding I return the artifacts to the Greek people. She kept hitting my chest, ranting that we had angered Hecate."

"What did you do?"

"She was unintelligible, mixing up English, and what I later learned was Greek, but at the time, I admit, I just thought she was crazy."

"Why?"

"They weren't ours by then."

"That's right. They had already been gifted to the British Museum by then. Your family was ashamed and rarely spoke about it."

"My grandfather only had them for a few years before the British government purchased them and donated them to the museum. I tried to explain that to her, but she flew into a rage, screeching at me that the sins of the fathers would be passed on to the son. I tried to tell her I had no control over the marbles, but I couldn't tell if it was that she didn't understand English or didn't care. That was my mistake. Rather than trying to negotiate, I dismissed her, which I have regretted every day for a hundred and twenty-five years. It was cold and dark, and I was desperate to get home, so I wasn't as patient as I should have been. As I tried to leave, she grabbed my hand and started chanting and waving her gnarled finger at me. A curse I soon came to realize."

"A curse?"

"Hex, technically. She was a sorceress, a Daughter of Hecate, and had dedicated her life to the return of the artifacts. When I arrived home, I found you lying on the floor, your eyes and lips as black as ink, which tore my heart out. It was my fault. I should have listened to her. After that I spent many years searching for ways to break the hex to learn more. I devoted years to researching the Parthenon and Acropolis and studying Greek mythology to lift the curse.

"You haven't changed," I stroked his face. "You are exactly as I remember. But why kill me?"

"The hex was two-fold. Because the statues were taken from her people, she took you from me in retribution. She cursed me to roam the earth, waiting for you, as they wait for the marbles. She ranted at me, then disappeared. Immediately, I was filled with a dark sense of foreboding. I rushed home and found you. You were condemned to be born over and over until the day we could be reunited. But we had only one day in each quarter century. If we did not reunite on the winter equinox in the twenty-fifth year, we were determined to live apart for another quarter century, for eternity. I was unable to love another, unable to die. Cursed to live a half-life, seeing your face everywhere, destined to go mad, pining for the love we once had, but lost. You were cursed to be reincarnated but only live to twenty-five. If this date passed, and we had not reunited, you would die, only to be reborn and repeat the cycle."

A knife pierced my heart. "I am twenty-five, and it is the equinox today. You mean, I would have died tomorrow?"

He nodded, not speaking. My heart ran cold at the thought that this was predestined.

"So I will live?" I asked softly, scared of the answer.

"Now that the curse is broken, you will."

"What broke the curse?" I asked, running my finger along his jawline.

"We needed to achieve a state of *ataraxia*. It was the one word I remembered from what she was ranting at me, and that concept sustained me for all these years."

"Ataraxia?" I sounded out the strange word.

"Serenity, one might say bliss. For many lifetimes, I have waited for us to be reunited. We needed to meet, and if we could achieve a state of ataraxia and serene calmness, we would find each other again. A Celtic Druidess helped me research the hex for many years before she passed. She taught me that the symbols of our marriage would call to you. That was why I placed you in the study, near your ring, praying it was you. She told me meaningful objects hold as much power as words, but that a moment of shared bliss would be the key to breaking the curse."

"Does that mean you will age now?"

"That is my wish. I have searched the world and visited many places, but I long for simple things. You. Us. I wish nothing more than to spend every waking moment with you. We are together now. Neither of us will want for anything ever again."

"I need to call my office," I said, sitting up. "I have a job. A life. Cases I am working on. People who will worry about me."

"Do you?" His eyes held mine in his gaze.

What did I have? Ben and I were done. Susy had ensured that my career with the firm would be over, especially after I had thrown the lamp at them, hysterical, as he fucked her in my bed. My car was totaled. The lease to our apartment was in Ben's name. My sister, well, all she cared about was herself. Everything I owned was just stuff that could be replaced in a day. I knew, beyond any doubt, that this was the man I had waited my life for.

"I am yours. Always and forever."

About the Author

T.S. Simons is a Scottish/Australian author living in the alpine region of Australia. She believes in integrity, sustainability, and community in a world where we place greater value on possessions than people. She enjoys posing philosophical questions that make readers think and reflect on the world we live in.

She holds Bachelor's and Master's degrees, qualifications in governance and management, and is an accredited company director. She is an Australia Reads Ambassador and enjoys reading, traveling, mythology, and snow skiing while attempting to live sustainably with her partner and children. She is owned by a Standard Schnauzer, fox-red Labrador, and three rescue cats who co-manage her household.

Her published works include the acclaimed science fiction romance Antipodes series, and science/adventure-based 45th Parallel series, all available in e-book, paperback, and on Audible.

You can follow her at www.tssimons.com, www.facebook.com/tssimons1, or www.instagram.com/ts_simons_books

Stained Fate

BY SALEM CROSS

As a Fate Witch, Esmeralda Vocco knows better than most not to try and outrun destiny. Still, desperate to delay her own grizzly fate, she attempts to flee.

Dimitri is not just a vampire, and a sworn enemy of witches, but also a longtime lover. His insistence for Esme to stay is strange for the playboy vamp. Her feelings threaten to lead her astray, but she knows she can't wait around for a vampire who has no intention of settling down, not when her life is on the line.

Can Dimitri set the right tone for this important conversation and convince Esme to stay? Or will her fear of the fate that awaits her win out and pull the two of them apart?

*

Bright, iridescent colors overwhelm my sight, stealing the ability to see anything except for the passage of time. But while I catch glimpses of moments, they flash by much too quickly, warped with too much saturation of color to be anything but smeared images. Although my mind can't keep up with what it's seeing, my hands move, taking on a mind of their own. My fingertips caress sharp edges of colored glass, lift tools, and weld. While hundreds upon thousands of other people's fates fly by, my hands move to create a stunning and intricate piece of art, infused with magic, that captures just a single moment of someone's life.

As I work, I struggle to remember to breathe. Remembering that my body is standing in the present day while my mind is stuck in the future is both a challenge and draining. I take a deep breath in through my nose, and then slowly let it out through my mouth.

The colors begin to dull. At the same time, my head starts to throb and the sound of magic humming beneath my skin grows more obvious. Usually I don't hear it at all. At least not until I'm too tired to maintain this level of concentration.

As if to confirm I've burned myself out, the lights and colors blink out abruptly. The halt to the flow of magic is jarring. Gasping, I reach out to catch myself on the edge of the table as my knees buckle.

"Woah, careful now. You don't want to hurt yourself, Esmeralda."

A pair of hands land on my hips to help brace me. I tense in alarm. No one should be here in my converted silo, let alone on the third floor that houses my art studio. I make it a point to keep my front door locked while I use my magic. Just as my heart skips a beat then starts a mad dash to escape from my chest, I recognize the voice and the hands. I blink the room into focus as I relax a little.

"Dimitri?"

Other than the deep chuckle that vibrates through his chest, my back might as well be pressed up against a wall. With no heartbeat or reason to breathe, Dimitri is all but made of stone.

"Who else would it be? Do you allow other vampires that I'm not aware of access to your place of solitude?" There's a perpetual sneer in his voice that I once found unattractive, but over the years, I've learned it's not always from contempt, it's just how he talks. Now I find it, and him, appealing.

With a shaky breath, I move to step to the side and out of his grasp.

"And where do you think you're going?" he demands, his grip tightening as he forces me to turn around to look up at him. I suck in a shaky breath and hope he takes the gesture as me still reeling from spell casting and not from how he steals my breath away.

Blessed with immortality, Dimitri has stopped aging somewhere in his mid-thirties. His dark hair is swept back as usual, locked in place with some type of gel. Amusement causes his matching dark brows to rise as his black eyes lock onto my face. His pale skin doesn't completely erase his heritage, leaving some of the golden hue of his unknown ancestry in place. He's tall and fairly muscular. I wouldn't put it past him to have been a farmer or some type of tradesman back when he was alive.

Contrary to popular belief, people don't automatically become beautiful once they've been turned into a vampire. So for Dimitri to be as handsome as he is, he must've stolen just as many hearts when he was human as he has now as a vampire.

His mouth curves into a cocky half-smile, telling me I've fallen into his vampiric thrall and am staring openly. Heat creeps into my cheeks as I reach up and push against his chest.

"Some space to breathe *please*."

My pushing is half-hearted. Even if I used my full strength, Dimitri wouldn't budge, what with his vampire strength and all. Nevertheless, Dimitri drops his hands from my waist and takes a small step back.

"Are you sure you can stand? I would hate to see you end up on your knees."

Free, I immediately move a few feet away, toward the sink, to put space between us and snort, "I'm sure *that's* a lie."

I *know* it is, because when I am on my knees for him, he's usually purring like a kitten and cumming hard. It's one of his favorite positions for me to be in. My heart flutters again and heat pours into my veins. It's slow moving.

My body is tired after working and magic casting, but just its presence tells me I'm in trouble.

"It's definitely a lie but I'm just trying to be a gentleman," the vampire assures me, lingering by my workstation. "I think you've outdone yourself this time with these pieces."

I finish rinsing my hands and then turn to look out the partially open window. It's dark out yet, but what time is it? I need to start preparing for my departure. Brushing off the sense of sadness that threatens to well up in my chest, I force my attention back to the vampire in the room with me.

"Have I?" I move back toward him. I tell myself it's to admire the pieces of artwork, not to be closer to the handsome vampire, and that's somewhat true. While I cast magic, I can't see what my hands are doing. The artwork is just as startlingly beautiful for me as it is for the patrons that come into my shop to view them.

Stopping beside him, I stare down at the four stained-glass window hanging pieces. I had time to make four? Huh, the internal demand to get this artwork done tonight had ridden me hard all day. I suppose it was because four future patrons really needed a glimpse into their fate. Staring at the art, I smile. They are equally as beautiful as they are unique. I reach out and stroke the one closest to me, created with an array of pink, red, purple, and yellow glass. In the center of it is a dull gray rose. The dark rose is in such contrast with the rest of the vibrant piece that I frown, curious about its meaning.

The majority of the time, I never learn how my art correlates to an individual's fate. I think most of the time my patrons don't even realize what they buy is specifically made with them in mind. They simply walk in and find their fate, like a moth to a flame, and purchase it thinking it's just art. What I do is both rewarding and a curse because sometimes their fate isn't beautiful despite the artwork that may say otherwise.

What does this dark rose signify? I hope it's nothing bad.

"How you manage to create such masterpieces while never actually looking at what you're doing will forever astound me." Dimitri's unusual praise pulls me out of my thoughts. "I watched you for an hour, mesmerized by your skill."

An *hour*? Man, I really need to be more aware of my surroundings. And maybe stop inviting vampires into my house.

"Forever is a strong word in your case." I turn and lean my hip on my worktable and cross my arms over my chest to stare up at his profile. "What are you doing here tonight, Dimitri? Isn't your coven having some sort of celebration this evening? I'm sure you'll be missed. If the others find out you're here—"

"They won't." His sharp answer surprises me as he turns to face me. "I'm always careful when I come to call, you know that."

I do. But given the history between vampires and witches and the budding tension between our races at the moment, I find myself a little nervous in the presence of my occasional lover. His coven just barely tolerates my presence in their small town, located in the foothills of the Carpathian Mountains. Thankfully, my magic isn't a threat to them, or I don't think they would be as lenient.

"In any case, the party is over. Most of them are blood drunk or curled up in their coffins already."

I roll my eyes. Vampires do not sleep in coffins.

"Over? What type of vampires call it quits before sunrise?"

"Sunrise is about a half hour away. And not all of them are down for the evening. Some are still enjoying some delectable physical activity to keep them entertained a bit longer." He reaches up and skims the back of his index finger down my cheek, his smile becoming hungry. Any other time, I'd probably end up swallowing hard and leaning into the handsome vampire before me. Tonight, however, his words douse the warmth gathering beneath my skin.

"*What?*" I jump back in surprise and glance back out the window. Now that I'm actually looking, the sky does seem much brighter. "Oh no! I didn't mean to work through the night. I need to clean up and—"

"Pack?"

"Yes! And then I have to—" I pause, turning to look back at Dimitri. "Wait, how did you know I have to pack?"

I've been extremely careful over the past week to casually get rid of my belongings. Donations have been made in small trips to various shelters as I clean my silo out. I've tried hard to not draw much attention to my departure.

"So the rumors are true." His arrogant smile melts away and tension begins to gather in the room. "You're leaving."

I open and close my mouth, unsure about his sudden change in mood. While I trust Dimitri, vampires tend to lash out when moody.

"Just for a while," I assure him. "I want to travel a bit, to see the world."

Unable to stop myself, my eyes dart to the tall stained-glass window I created two weeks ago that's now covered with a dropcloth. My stomach sinks and my heart slams against my chest. Banishing the rising dread, I look back to Dimitri and take a step toward him.

Dimitri watches me closely. "Hm, and you didn't think to let me know that you are leaving? I'm hurt."

I want to laugh. Let him know? How? It's not like I have his number, nor does he have mine. We certainly couldn't write letters given they would undoubtedly be intercepted by others in his coven. In any case, he doesn't give me the same courtesy.

"Given that you disappear for months at a time, *all* the time, and never tell me when you'll be back, I didn't think it would be a big deal."

"That's different."

Rolling my eyes only causes my attention to fall back to the covered piece of art in the room. Forcing myself to look away, I nod mockingly.

"Sure it's different."

Suddenly, Dimitri is there, in my face, having moved the short distance between us in less time than it takes to blink. His hand comes up to grab my chin so he can tilt my face upward. Though his eyes are black, there's an eerie light burning in their depths.

"I leave to hunt and to be the political voice between covens. You're leaving for what purpose? *Fun*?"

The way he says it causes me to bristle. "I can't go have some fun in other parts of the world?"

"No."

At his quick and certain response, I laugh. "Why not?"

His hold on my chin loosens a bit.

"Because you'll forget about me. You'll find another small town to settle down in, just like you did here and *forget* about me." Some of his teasing nature returns as his hand covers his heart. "I can't have that."

"Me? Forget *you*? *Never.*" As if I could forget about the vampire who makes me daydream about a life I could never have. One where I settle down, have a few little baby vamps to swaddle, or however you take care of a newborn vampire, and have him by my side. "But *you'll* forget about *me* soon enough. It's not like I'm the only plaything around here. I'm sure you have a harem of vampiresses hidden around here somewhere."

It's a well-known fact that vampires are notorious rakes. Our times together, while absolutely the best sex I've ever had, are far from the passionate embrace of two people in love. While, I admit, I may have some underlying feelings for Dimitri, I've all but quashed them knowing that trying to pursue a relationship would end up with me brokenhearted. I cherish the moments when he comes to me, as dirty and animalistic as they are, and try not to want for more.

"A harem?" Dimitri's brow raises, and for a second, that burning light in his eyes diminishes as amusement takes over. "Are you trying to flatter your way back into my good graces?"

"I don't need to flatter you, you big mosquito. Your ego is the size of this country. Nothing I say will hurt your feelings." I reach up and grab his shirt with both hands, enjoying how close we are to one another. I've never felt so scared and secure as I do in the arms of this handsome predator. "But if flattery will get me *something* from this random, late night conversation, then I may stroke it a little more... Along with other things."

Dimitri's answering smile is short lived. "Your words hold more power over me than you realize."

"Why? Because I'm a witch and I could cast a spell over you?" That's not how it works, at least not with the type of witch I am, but I tease all the same.

Dimitri's hand on my chin slides down to my neck. His fingers wrap around my throat, his thumb landing on my frantically racing pulse. The serious expression on his face isn't like the Dimitri I know. I'm so used to the playful rogue, whose smug smile and twinkling eyes steal my breath and chase away my sanity.

"Don't go." His words are little more than a whisper.

I *have* to go. I can't stay with what I've seen waiting for me if I do. Two weeks ago, I created my most stunning piece of stained-glass art yet. But I knew the minute I came to and looked down, that the gruesome fate depicted was for none other than me. Fate Witches only see their fate when their time is nearly up. And the image I created while I was casting my magic? I force myself not to look over at the covered artwork as I suppress a shudder. The blood and the gore in the image were enough for it to be frightening. But it's the man in the dark cloak in the background that solidified my decision to run.

Not that one can outrun what destiny has in store for them, but still... A girl can try.

In an attempt to hide my trepidation, I rock forward onto the balls of my feet and skim my lips against Dimitri's cold ones.

"Why not? Don't tell me you'll miss me." I press my lips lightly against his, loving and hating the way my heart swells at the contact. It's not wise to fall in love with a vampire. Especially not *this* one.

To my delight, Dimitri's hand disappears from my neck to meet the other in a grip on my hips. With ease, he picks me up and spins me around. I giggle, my legs wrapping his waist as my arms come around his neck. He dips me playfully and nips at my collarbone.

"Is me missing you so hard to believe, *witch*?" he teases.

Straightening, he carries me over to my work-table and sits me down, far away from my four new window hangings and all the sharp pieces of extra glass. He steps between my legs, keeping close to me.

I meet his gaze and smile, even as my heart twists in pain. "Yes."

"First flattery and now you try to wound me? Do you really believe I think so little of our friendship? That I do not crave your company?" Dimitri flashes me a toothy grin, clearly ready to let go of whatever moodiness had struck him just moments ago.

Friendship. It's a loose term for what we have and not at all accurate. His comings and goings are so unpredictable that sometimes I think I made the vampire up. Even when he's here, he's not for long. Occasionally, I'll get a night long of mind-blowing, panty-melting, life-changing sex. But other times, it's just a quickie. A few words exchanged, an orgasm or two, and then he's gone in the night's breeze.

"With how time passes for a vampire, you won't even notice I'm gone." I force myself to smile and add a bit of teasing to my voice, hoping to god he doesn't hear the hurt I'm currently trying to hide. "But since you're here, I know how to keep your attention for the time being."

My eyebrow wiggle causes my vampire to laugh. The sound is a bit off though.

"Esme, are you trying to seduce me while I'm trying to have a serious conversation with you?"

"We don't have serious conversations, Dimitri."

He reaches forward to cup my face between his hands. Lowering his head, his lips crash down onto mine. The minute he kisses me, my thoughts scatter. I can't stop from leaning into it. Unfortunately, Dimitri breaks the kiss, keeping it brief and looking utterly unperturbed. I bite my lip to keep my moan of despair tucked away.

But Dimitri knows what he does to me, to an extent. He knows how much I love drowning in his kisses. His smug smile is back as he straightens.

"I'm trying to have a serious conversation with you now, Esmeralda."

I shrug. "Hm... Try kissing me again, and then I'll tell you if we're on the right track to a true conversation."

"I can do that."

His lips are back, and this time the kiss is hungry. I part mine so he can deepen it, and Dimitri doesn't hesitate. His tongue slides into my mouth and collides with mine. I reach up, grabbing his shirt again and pulling him into me. His hands come up and slide into my thick, wavy hair to pull me closer to him. I scoot my hips nearer to the edge of the table, needing to feel more of him. When he leans his own forward, I can feel the hard length of him right at the junction between my legs. The heat that had begun a sluggish crawl through my veins is now blazing through me.

Just as I start to grind against my vampire, Dimitri pulls away again.

"How about now? How's the conversation going?"

I laugh, the sound breathless as I stare up at him. "It could be better. Maybe if we get to the crux of the matter?"

"Oh, I see. You'd think at my age, I'd learn how to have a proper conversation with a woman." Dimitri shakes his head, feigning disappointment. "Let me see if I can get it right this time."

When he moves, it's with his supernatural speed. My clothes are yanked off first. The gasp I let out is cut off as he moves again, picking me up and rearranging me so swiftly that I'm on my hands and knees on top of the table with my butt straight up in the air before my clothes have a chance to hit the floor. Adrenaline and excitement collide inside me. They're swiftly followed by humiliation.

"Dimitri!" I start to turn around, embarrassed at how exposed I am like this.

He grabs my hips to still me.

"Don't interrupt a man when he's trying to make a point, Esme."

I'm about to mention that no point has been made but my words turn into a howl that echoes around the circular room and up into the metal dome high above us as his mouth latches onto my core from behind. *Oh*! Going back and forth from my clit to my weeping pussy, Dimitri licks and sucks. How well he has come to know my body is showcased now as he eats me out. When his tongue dives into me, my hips push back for more. My breathing becomes erratic, and when I close my eyes, it's not from my magic that colors dance behind my eyelids.

My legs begin to tremble. I'm close, oh dear heavens, I'm so *close*. But it's like Dimitri knows it and is purposely keeping me on the edge.

"Please, Dimitri. I need this!"

He pauses, but his face never leaves between my legs.

"Tell me you won't leave." His tongue slides through my folds all the way to my asshole where he circles and probes it. After a few seconds he pauses to demand again, "Tell me, Esme. Tell me that you'll stay here, and you won't leave."

I shake my head, my body shaking. Dimitri hums. It rings with disapproval. His mouth returns to my pussy where he continues to devour me. I cry out as his ministration becomes more demanding. A hand comes up to grab my thigh while Dimitri's other one dives between my legs to help his tongue drag out my pleasure. My eyes cross and I stop breathing altogether as my body tenses. I push back into his face just as the tension in my body snaps and my orgasm comes barreling through me.

"*Dimitri*!"

He continues to lick and suck until my orgasm begins to subside. Just as I let out a contented sigh, his fangs sink into my labia. The scream I let out is nonsensical. My body convulses as pleasure and pain meet together at a peak inside of me. It's too much at one time. My hands give out from underneath me as I collapse onto the tabletop. Even when Dimitri pulls away, my body continues to tremble and shake.

I allow my hips to fall to the side with a satisfied moan.

"Hm... It looks like this conversation went well. Are you going to stay now?"

My laughter is soft. I throw my arm over my face as my body shakes from it. "Why do you want me to stay so badly?"

"Because you are a tolerable person. It's rare to find these days."

I pull my arm away from my face and sit up slowly. Batting my eyelashes, I smile up at him. His pompous smile slips away as he homes in on my change of direction.

"Dimitri, my fanged friend, want to finish this night off properly? As a last hoorah?" I reach up and grab a fist full of his shirt. "I know *I* would love to appreciate you one more time."

He flashes me a grin, but it doesn't reach his eyes. How strange.

"Why are you being so emotional about this?" I demand. I shift so I'm on my knees, making me eye level with my vampire. "Dimitri, seriously, I don't get it."

While we're not close, I feel like I know him enough to be able to tell that this is out of character for him. Where is my egotistical vampire?

He reaches up to hold my wrists. For a moment he says nothing, his grin slipping as he stares at me.

"I don't come around often in an attempt to protect you, Esme. You know that, right? I can't have the others realizing that I'm smitten with a witch. At best, they'd chase you out of town. At worst, they'd kill you thinking you've put a spell on me."

As if *I* had the power to cast a love spell. Ridiculous. But my attention narrows to the word *smitten*. I'm not sure if that's true, or if this is just a rare, sweet moment from Dimitri, but I hold the world close to my heart.

"Don't leave, Esme. Stay..." His throat convulses as if he wants to say more, but he stops and shakes his head.

"I'll miss you." It's only a small concession. If I say anything more it will sound like I'm in love, and while that may not be far from the truth, it's irrelevant now.

For a quiet moment, we stare at each other. I will Dimitri to sense what I feel for him and how desperately I wanted more for us. But I'm not a witch that can influence moods. And he doesn't receive my heartache.

Dimitri breaks the moment with a heavy sigh. His familiar smug smile returns before he swoops down and plants a quick kiss on my lips. When he pulls away he says,

"Let's get to that 'last hoorah' fucking, shall we?"

Without another moment of hesitation, he picks me back up by the waist and carries me across the space, over to the pile of drop cloths and towels.

"No, no, no! They're dirty—"

"Just like you're about to be."

When we get to our destination, he unceremoniously drops me. I yelp as

I land in the soft pile. Before I can sit up, Dimitri's naked. My eyes sweep up his muscular form, starting at his thick thighs and moving up. My pause is long and appreciative when I get to his straining, veiny dick. He's well endowed, something he's probably heard a lot in his lifetime. I lean back on my forearms and spread my legs, giving him a coy smile as I make the trek the rest of the way up to his face. Dimitri's sneer returns full force.

"Look how wet you are for me, witch. It's like staring at the milky way, but this sight is much more breathtaking."

Suddenly, he's on top of me, his mouth crashing down on mine. This kiss isn't swift like the others. It's ravenous. Demanding. Practically possessive and wholly hot as hell. I kiss him back, desperate to hold onto this moment. There will be other vampires in my life. Other men who will find me attractive enough to bed me. But none of them will be Dimitri. I won't let this last night go to waste.

My legs come up and wrap around his hips, positioning his erection right at my entrance. Rather than surge forward, however, Dimitri pulls his mouth away and sits up to rock back on his heels. He grabs my legs, yanks me closer and flings them over his shoulders like it's nothing. Maybe to him, it isn't. I gasp in delight as he notches the head of his erection at my entrance. Rather than slide home right away, he jerks his hips back, pulling free of my body and slides through my folds, running his dick over my leaking arousal. My over-sensitized body shudders. I let my eyelids slide halfway closed as I stare up at the vampire.

"Tell me you'll at least come back," he demands.

I don't want to make promises I can't keep. My eyes dart to the piece of covered artwork and my heart rate spikes.

"Why do you keep looking over there?" Dimitri pauses, his head twisting in that direction.

Shit. I don't want him to see the stained glass window. If he sees it, he might reconsider our whole arrangement and view me as a threat. That could lead to him reporting back to his coven who, in turn, might hunt me down faster than whoever the man in the dark cloak is. Using his distraction to my advantage, I tilt my hips. The movement forces Dimitri's erection to slip deep into my body. I groan as his dick stretches me gloriously. It has a gentle curve upward, stroking just the right spot to make my pussy clench tight around him.

Dimitri's head drops back down so his eyes land on me. He sucks in a sharp breath. I try to roll my hips, but in this position, with my legs up, it's hard to do much. My vampire chuckles before he takes over. His hard thrust is both wonderful and intense.

I bite my bottom lip to keep from crying out.

"*No.*" He lunges forward, his hands falling to either side of my face as he takes my mouth with his. In this position, where I'm practically folded over onto myself, Dimitri can't get any deeper. My loud cry of delight is eaten up by Dimitri, who devours it as his hips rock back then forth. He pulls away only inches to growl, "If this is our last time, I don't want you to hold back. I want to hear it all."

My heart twists before expanding tenfold.

Dimitri tilts his head to the side to kiss along my jawline and then down my neck, all while thrusting in long, deliberate strokes. When his lips meet the junction between my shoulder and neck, he strikes. I'm used to the occasional bite during our passionate sessions. At times, it's almost as if Dimitri doesn't even realize he's made the conscious decision to do so. Those bites are shallow and teasing. They consist of a short sharp burst of pain followed instantly by a short wave of pleasure. All that had been intensified when he bit me earlier this evening in such a sensitive area.

But when his fangs sink into my skin now, it's nothing like what I'm used to.

This bite is deep, avaricious, and skin marring. I open my mouth to scream in pain, my hands coming up to push at his chest. But then pain melts into a different sensation. My blood boils and my heart slams against my ribcage as the ache shifts into a soul-searing pleasure. The scream lodged in my throat turns into a hearty moan, loud and unabashed. I don't even realize that I'm cumming, the ecstasy is so all-consuming, until Dimitri dislodges his mouth from my neck. My entire body spasms and stars dance in front of my eyes.

Just as the pleasure starts to fade, Dimitri bites me again. This time his mouth encompasses nearly my entire right breast. The pain returns only to fade away, leaving me to drift in a sea of unexplored pleasure. Has he been holding out on me this whole time? The nerve of him. Maybe I'll lecture him later. Or maybe I'll just float away on this tidal wave of bliss.

I think I'm screaming, but I'm not entirely sure on the matter. All I know is that as Dimitri repeats the action over and over, marking both breasts, parts of my arms, and the other side of my neck, I'm the happiest I've ever been. At some point during his vicious love making, I swear I taste copper in my mouth. A spicy heat follows behind it as it trails down my throat. It heightens my orgasm to a brand new level, the next wave of ecstasy causing my mind to go utterly blank, and all I can do is savor the hard convulsing of my body.

When he stills, finding his own release while I milk him dry, he does so louder than I've ever heard him before. The hard jerk of his cock spurs on aftershocks of my own orgasm. With a huff, he collapses half on top of me, half in the pile of fabric.

We lay like that for only a few minutes before he sits up and withdraws his softening dick. Blood is smeared across his mouth, emphasized by the white of his teeth as he grins down at me.

"You'll come back now." His voice is a bit deeper, almost growly.

"Oh yeah? You think so?"

Dimitri doesn't answer, but the victorious grin he wears shifts to a feral one. If I didn't know him, I'd be a little scared. But I do, so my heart doesn't race in trepidation and my body remains relaxed.

I sit up next and look down at myself. The blood covering my body is a little concerning, but all his bite marks are already healing. Soon they'll be gone. Or, at the very least, leave thin scars. Suddenly Dimitri's head jerks to the side, toward one of the thin stained-glass windows.

"What is it?"

"I need to go. Sunrise has come and gone. If I don't get back soon..."

Most of the newer generation vampires can't handle sunlight. Dimitri's an older vampire, meaning he can last in the early morning rays. Anything past a certain point, however, and he'll crisp up real quick.

"Go, Dimitri."

He turns to look at me, his eyes searching my face. "Where are you headed?"

"I don't know. Wherever my van can take me." It's the truth. I don't have a location planned. It's both for my safety and for those around me. If someone is coming after me, then the fewer people know about my whereabouts, the better.

"You'd tell me if you were in trouble, right?"

I nod, not willing to lie outright to him. It's not like Dimitri could help me if he knew the truth, so why worry him?

Rising to his feet, he grabs his clothes and slips them on.

"Go have your fun, witch." His smile is *almost* soft.

"I will. Go before you turn to ash."

His eye roll is the last thing I see before he takes off, moving so fast I don't see him exit the room. I wait only a heartbeat later before I'm up and moving. It's time to pack.

Then I need to get as far away from here as possible.

About the Author

Salem Cross is a paranormal why choose romance author. By day, she's a writer, by night she occasionally turns into a majestic unicorn and stabs little kids with her horn when they get too close. Sometimes, when the mood strikes, Salem will blurt out random song lyrics that will most likely be wrong, but that she will still sing confidently while in tune. Unsure what to do with her hands during a conversation, she will hold them up above her head and leave them there until said conversation is over. Also, she bites, so watch out for that. For more books by Salem Cross follow the link below:

https://linktr.ee/salemcross

Enchanted Tides of Love

BY JAYSIC KAE

What's a witch got to do to have a normal life in this town? Cast a hex or two? Ravynne Crane tried to lead a simple life but sometimes Karma wouldn't let that be. When Isabella Monroe walked into her shop it changed everything. Her request would send her on a path to meeting Adrian Breckington and nothing would be the same again.

One

Ravynne Cane ran the family business in the beautiful coastal town of Moonhaven. They sold crystals and other new age items but sometimes she was asked to cast a spell or two. Most were harmless but sometimes she had to think twice about casting a hex. Those were the ones that took the most energy out of her and could be the most dangerous.

Ravynne was taking inventory in the back of the store when she heard the light tingling of the front doorbell.

"Welcome to Silverlight. How may I be of assistance?"

"My name is Isabella Monroe. I'm looking for Ravynne Cane. I have a problem that I need to deal with."

"What kind of problem? "

"The problem is that I recently broke it off with my boyfriend and I have an important social event coming up and if I don't find a solution, I am afraid he might create problems for me and the rest of the attendants. I must speak with her directly as this situation needs to be kept quiet and there are too many eyes and ears out in society who would love nothing more than to make my life a front-page story."

"Well, I don't know if she would feel comfortable helping with a problem that had to be kept secret. Too many times those secrets still come out and if it backfires then she would be caught in the cross hairs and that would not be good for her business or her reputation."

"I don't really care about her reputation. I am trying to protect mine and she is the only one that I will discuss the details with. Now would you please fetch her for me or do I have to go above your head to see some results."

"No, that won't be necessary. I am Ravynne and I'm not sure I want to help you. You are carrying a lot of negative energy. Now I will have to recharge the store's aura. Now if you would be so kind and tell me what your problem is and what you need as far as my expertise then I will gladly listen, but I cannot guarantee that I will perform this favor."

"I need you to put a hex on my ex. I need to find a way to stop him from appearing and destroying everything that I have done. I need him out of my life for good so that I can move on."

"To do the kind of hex that you want will take a lot of ingredients and time. It will be costly not just in the monetary sense but in the human sense as well. Are you sure you want to go through with this?"

"Yes, I will have all the information you need by this afternoon. I will have my PA bring it by to your shop before five o'clock. I expect an answer by the end of the week."

"No one can predict if all will go smoothly that is up to the Goddess and if the forces of nature, but I will let you know my answer by the end of the week along with a price. I should be able to gather the necessary ingredients by the following Monday."

"Very well then, I will leave you now."

Later that evening, just before Ravynne was set to close the shop a young lady walked into the store. Her hair was long and straight as a stick and a mousy blonde. She had on glasses that were too big on her and she kept pushing them up on her face. Her clothes were two sizes too big, and she seemed afraid of her own shadow.

She stood by the front door and nervously looked around.

Ravynne approached with a calming smile.

"Hi, I'm Ravynne, owner of this shop. Can I help you find something specific?"

"Uh, no. No thank you. I am supposed to drop off an envelope for you from Ms. Monroe. She said it had to be delivered to you tonight. I'm sorry I didn't bring it sooner, but traffic was bad and then I got lost trying to find your shop."

"It's quite alright. Not too many people come this way. Could I fix you a cup of tea to help with the chill?"

"Um, no thank you. I'm fine. I just wanted to make sure and drop this off to you before I went home. My cat, Elvis, gets very agitated with me if I am five minutes late with his dinner."

"Ha ha, I know that feeling. My cat, Minerva, is a diva. If her food is not in the proper dish and set out in time she will meow until it happens. I'll take the envelope and let you be on your way."

Ballari handed the envelope to Ravynne and pushed her glasses up. She then turned to open the door and walked back outside into the rain.

"Wait. What's your name? Do you have an umbrella or something to keep you dry?"

"Oh sorry, my name is Ballari. No, I will be fine. I'm going to just run to my car that is up the street and then I park in a garage so I should be fine getting out."

"Ok, thank you for bringing this in such nasty weather. Drive safe and thank you again. If you ever want to come and look at the shop and see what I carry you are more than welcome to come back."

"Thank you, if I ever have free time, I might just do that, but Ms. Monroe has me running everywhere. Well, I best be going. Elvis will start his nightly grumble in a couple of minutes, and I need to make sure I am home before the neighbors complain."

"Have a good night and say hello to Elvis for me."

Ravynne laid the envelope on her desk in the office and went about her nightly closing duties. After she was done, she grabbed her purse and keys and headed home for the evening.

Later that evening as she was getting ready for bed, she had a strange feeling come over her.

It was as if someone was walking over her grave and she wasn't sure what to make of it.

She figured she could consult the cards in the morning if the feeling didn't go away.

She climbed into bed and Minerva settled in her usual spot on the right-side pillow and Ravynne closed her eyes and tried to sleep.

Three

The next morning Ravynne got up and prepared for her day. She made sure that Minerva had everything she would need while Ravynne was at the shop. She stopped at the local coffee shop, as she did every morning, and pulled her car up into the first available space.

She went inside and ordered her usual chai latte with a splash of extra cinnamon and a little bit extra milk. She had just taken her first sip when she ran into a brick wall and her entire tea splashed down the front of her dress alongside the "wall".

She backed up quickly. A very tall muscular male stood before.

She gathered herself and was ready to unleash all kinds of holy hell at him when she looked up into his face and saw his eyes.

They were the purest emerald green she had ever seen, and it reminded her of a cat.

She stood still for a moment and gathered her thoughts.

"I'm quite sorry for the run in. Are you alright? I hope I didn't ruin your clothes. If you send me the bill for dry cleaning, I will pay for it."

"There's been no damage done and these are wash and dry so no dry-cleaning bill will be needed. I wanted to make sure you're okay. I'm sorry for running into you like that. I have a bad habit of not watching where I'm going. I just moved here to Moonhaven six months ago and I still feel like it's my first day in town."

"Oh, I know that feeling. I have lived here my entire life, but I still feel as if it's my first time here. I look around and there is always something different to see. As if the town changes itself without our knowing. I'm glad you're okay and again sorry about your clothes.'

"It will be fine. I will just run back to my place and change and throw these in the wash right away so that they don't have a chance to stain. Please let me get you another drink since it was my fault that you spilled yours in the first place. Can I run you somewhere to change your outfit?"

"Oh no, that's not necessary. My shop is next door and I have an extra change of clothes there and I'll just come back later and get another tea. I must open my shop in the next ten minutes, or my regular customers will think something has happened to me and will send out a search party."

He laughed and extended his hand out to her. "My name is Adrian. Adrian Breckington. I just opened the bookstore at the end of the block."

"Oh, you're the new owner of the Bell Book and Candle shop. Ms. Mirabelle was a wonderful owner, and it was just so sad when she passed. Well, it was nice to meet you Adrian, but I do have to go. If you decide you want to dabble in some new age stuff, I'm two doors down from your shop. Again, sorry for running into you like that. Have a nice day."

"You too, I didn't get your name."

"Oh, I'm sorry I'm Ravynne Cane. I own the crystal store."

"Have a good rest of your day and I will try to make sure not to surprise anyone else by being a wall."

Ravynne laughed and headed out the door with what was left of her tea.

She had a strange sensation come over her as she left.

She figured she would consult the bones once she got back to the shop, and it was quiet for a few minutes.

She knew that Gladys would be on her doorstep any moment and if she didn't hurry, she wouldn't hear the end of the questions that were sure to come from her being late.

Four

Ravynne arrived at her shop and just as she had predicted Gladys was waiting for her at the front step.

"I'm so sorry for being late Gladys. I hope you haven't been waiting too long. I got stuck at the coffee shop."

Raven unlocked the door and went to put her stuff behind the counter and then turned around and waited for Gladys to make her purchases. She went back to the office and grabbed the folder she had received yesterday.

As she picked up the folder, she had that strange feeling again. But before she could open it and see what was inside. Her front door rang again. So, she headed to the front to help the next customer. But it turned out it was Isabella.

"Good morning, Isabella, what can I help you with?"

"I was just checking to make sure you got the envelope from my assistant last night."

"Yes, I haven't had time to look at it yet. That was the plan for this morning."

"Very well but don't take too long. I do not have much time."

"I already told you that I would have it done before you by Friday, as promised."

"Then I'll leave you to it, but please hurry up. It's important that it gets done. It can ruin everything that I have worked for."

"I assure you it will be done as soon as it's possible. Now if you don't have anything else for me. I do have a shop to run. I will look at the folder as soon as I can."

"Thank you, I guess I will talk to you later I'm just worried that something is going to happen before you can get to him"

"Nothing will happen to your event."

Ravynne finished getting the shop open and then at lunch time she decided to close down for an hour and took the folder with her in hopes of reading it while she ate.

She felt some connection with Adrian, but she couldn't figure out what it was exactly.

At three thirty her shop bell rang, and she looked up to see who had come into the store.

She let out a soft gasp when she saw that it was Adrian.

"Why hello there. What brought you here into my neck of the woods? Did you get tired of reading all your books?" she laughed.

"No, the books are still waiting to be read. I decided I'd bring you tea since you didn't get a chance to enjoy yours this morning. My shirt, thanks you, thought it tasted pretty good."

Ravynne just shook her head and laughed. She walked over to Adrian and took the cup out of his hand.

"Thank you for doing that. I was fine without my tea but now I think I need it. I appreciate the gesture. Is there anything else I can help you with or are you just on a tea delivery?"

"No, I'm just a delivery boy for the day. But while I'm here I'd thought I'd look around your lovely shop."

"Feel free to look around. If you need anything or have any questions just ask."

"I don't mind the company, but I know you're busy. So, I'll just mosey around here by myself."

Adrian turned towards the back of the shop and started to look around.

Meanwhile, Ravynne headed back behind the counter and grabbed the folder.

Just as she was about to open it the bell rang again.

She looked up to see who had come into the door this time. She really wished it hadn't rung, she wanted a chance to talk to Adrian and look at the folder to see what was inside.

"Did you find everything that you needed?"

"Yes, thank you very much. I just love coming in here. I feel so much calmer when I step inside. I needed some more of those candles you recommended so that's why I came in today."

"I'm so glad you liked them. I will make sure to have plenty on hand for when you need them."

"I appreciate that." The customer paid for their things and then walked out the door.

Ravvnne put the credit card receipt into the drawer and looked around the shop for Adrian. She found him over by the gems and crystals.

"Have you found anything that you like?"

"Oh, it's all amazing here. I didn't realize that there was so much related to healing and nature."

"Oh yes, if you just pay attention nature will lead you in the right direction ninety percent of the time."

"Well thank you for the lesson. I guess I better get back to my shop before all the books walk out in protest." Adrian laughed.

Ravynne watched as he left the store and felt as if a piece of her had left with him.

This time she was able to open it and nearly fainted.

Inside the folder was a picture of Adrian.

"Oh, my goddess. No, it can't be him. Why did it have to be him. What am I going to do now? I don't think I can go through with the hex. What am I going to tell Isabella?"

She stood there for a few moments and read through the notes that had been included with Adrian's picture.

The notes made it sound like he was a horrible person but from what Ravynne could see from is aura he was good and not evil.

What had he done to Isabella to make her hate him so much? Ravynne knew she had to get to the bottom of things before she made the decision of whether she would follow through.

Five

Ravynne decided she needed to talk to Adrian before she gave Isabella her decision.

"Thank you for calling Belle, Book, and Candle. What adventure can I send you on today?"

"Uh, adventure? Well, that depends on your answer. This is Ravynne."

"Hello Ravynne. I would love to go on an adventure with you. How about a trip to dungeons full of dragons? No, castles with princesses locked in the castle. No, that wouldn't be your thing either. Oh, I know how about a trip to a magical academy."

Ravynne gasped at the last statement. *Does he know?*

"Ravynne, you still there? Did you take a trip by yourself already?"

"No, no I'm still here. Sorry I had to think about which adventure I would like. Anyway, I wanted to see if you had time for some coffee this afternoon."

"Oh ok. How about instead of coffee we do an early dinner?"

"How about five? I close the shop then and it won't take me that long to walk down to Bumberloos."

"Sounds great. Ok, Bumberloos at five then. I'll see you then."

Ravynne hung up the phone and let out a deep breath.

I hope this goes the way I want it too. I am afraid it is going to go downhill, and I won't be able to make it back up.

Adrian is a great guy, I trust it with my bones but what if I am wrong, then what? I hurt someone for no reason and Isabella gets her revenge but to what advantage?

I need to tell her that there can be ramifications from casting this kind of hex. Maybe I can change her mind after I talk to Adrian.

She made her way down to Bumberloos. She saw Adrian standing by the front door.

"Hi. Thanks for meeting me on such short notice."

"It's no problem. Let's head in and see if we can have a table in the back where it will be a little more private. You know how it is living in a small town. Everyone knows everything about everyone."

Ravynne grimaced. She knew the truth to that statement all too well.

Even though her family had established Moonstone there were still some who looked down their noses at what her and her family represented.

The hostess led to them a table in the back that was by a window.

Ravynne took the seat on the right and Adrian took a seat on the left. The hostess set their menus down and left them to talk and decide what they wanted to do.

After they ordered Ravynne nervously picked up her glass of water and took a drink trying to prepare herself on how she would ask Adrian about Isabella.

She carefully set down her glass and for a moment she thought she would spill it due to her hands shaking so badly.

"Uh, the reason I asked you here for dinner was to get to know you better but also I have some questions and I'm not sure how you are going to feel about them."

"Ask away, I'm an open book. Yes, I have done things in my past that I am not proud of, but I would like to think that I am on the right path now."

"Do you know Isabella Monroe?"

Adrian paused for a moment the look of fear in his face.

"Yes, I know her. She and I dated for a few weeks when I first moved here. When things weren't going to work out, I was a dick to her, and I regret that now. What does Isabella have to do with us and dinner?"

"She came to see me the other day and wanted to know if I had met you yet and also to warn me that you weren't a nice person."

"Oh, I'm sorry. I will admit that I wasn't very nice to her when I broke it off with her, but she wanted to move things quickly and I wasn't ready for that. Plus, she had to be in control of everything we did, and I just couldn't do that anymore. I tried to tell her in a nice way that I wanted to end it, but she wouldn't listen, so I had to resort to drastic measures so that she got the point."

"What did you do? If you don't mind me asking?"

"No, it's fine. I'm not proud of it but I just decided to block her number. I also avoided her around town. If I saw her on the street, I made sure to go another direction or hide inside some store until she walked past. I know I should have just confronted her and got it taken care of, but I wasn't sure how she would react to that. I wasn't proud of what I did. I regret it now and I should have talked to her."

"Well, I guess I can see where you were coming from. I know she is difficult to deal with. I had my issues with her in just the few minutes I dealt with her. Okay that answered my question. I didn't think you were this bad guy that she said you were. I feel better now."

"I'm glad to hear that. Now, I can enjoy my dinner and not have to worry about some hatchet flying at my head." Adrian laughed.

"No, my hatchets are firmly locked in the safe in my shop. You're safe. Now as to snakes that could be a different situation."

Ravynne and Adrian enjoyed their dinner and as they left the restaurant, they decided to walk to the cliffside where benches had been placed along the way so that people could sit and enjoy listening to the waves crash up against the rocks and just stare at the stars and the moon that hung in the sky.

As they sat down on the bench Ravynne felt Adrian's arm circle behind her and she stiffened for a moment. She was still conflicted about what she had read and what Adrian had told her.

She finally leaned back into the crook of his elbow and closed her eyes for a moment and then turned her head to lean towards him.

She kissed his check and then looked back onto the water wondering what she had done.

She then felt a hand on her face, and she turned to look at Adrian sure that she would see disgust in his face, but she saw nothing of the sort. His eyes were shinning with interest, and he slowly leaned in to kiss her.

She always thought that the sparks flying was just some romantic trope from the books and the movies but in that moment, she felt that they were true. It was as if the other half of her soul had appeared and wasn't leaving anytime soon.

"Wow." Ravynne whispered.

"Ditto." They smiled at each other and then Ravynne laid her head on his shoulder, and he curled his arm around her while they stared at the sky.

After a while they became chilled and decided to walk back to her shop since that was where she left car earlier and she needed to get home to take care of Minerva.

"Thank you again for a lovely evening and thank you for being honest about what happened with you and Isabella."

"You're quite welcome. I'm glad I could be honest with you and give you my side of the story. I will leave you here for now my fair lady, but I hope to see you tomorrow. Maybe this time we meet at the coffee shop, and we don't have a recurrence of the coffee spill?"

She laughed and nodded her head yes. She pulled her car keys out of her purse and started to walk towards her car.

She got inside and saw that Adrian was still standing on the sidewalk making sure she got to her car safely. She started the engine and waved goodbye to him.

Six

The next day Ravynne woke up with a heavy heart. She genuinely liked Adrian and she wanted to see him again, but she had promised Isabella that she would perform the hex.

Now she had to figure out a way to tell Isabella that she wouldn't do the hex and that she thought Adrian was truly a nice person.

She got dressed and drove over the coffee shop.

She pulled up and saw Adrian sitting at a table inside with two cups already on the table.

"Good morning. I see you already ordered. Should I come back another time since you seem to be waiting for someone?"

"Ha ha, funny. No, I went ahead and ordered your latte since I figured you would be here any second."

"Well thank you kind sir. How was the rest of your evening?"

"It was fine. I went home and fed my cat, Artemis and then went to bed. You?"

"Almost the same except for my cat's name is Minerva. I did not know you were a cat person."

"Well, he sort of found me when I first moved here so he decided to keep me." he laughed.

They drank their prospective drinks and then got up and headed out the front door. Adrian walked Ravynne to her car and leaned in to give her a quick kiss.

She had barely gotten inside her shop and had the lights on when she heard an angry voice behind her.

"What in the hell were you thinking?"

"Excuse me?"

"I thought I told you to put a hex on him and yet I see you locking lips with him this morning at the coffee shop. What in the hell is going on? I thought we had an agreement."

"Good morning, Isabella. I was just getting ready to give you a call but now you have saved me the trouble. I am not doing the hex. I have gotten to know Adrian and he is nothing like what you portrayed him as. He explained what happened and that he is truly sorry for the way he treated you."

"Oh, is that what he told you?"

She stormed out the door.

Ravynne stood still for a moment breathing in and out deeply to calm herself down before she called Adrian to let him know what had happened.

LATER THAT DAY RAVYNNE MET UP WITH ADRIAN AND explained what had happened with Isabella.

"She's determined to see you ruined but I am not sure how to fix the situation now. I can't go through with the hex like she asked me and if you don't want to see me again. I understand."

"I'm okay with what happened and just so damn glad you didn't follow through with the hex. I don't think I would like where it would take me. Let me try and talk to her again, maybe she will listen this time." Adrian said.

"I doubt it but give it a try. I hope she understands this time and lets it go."

Adrian nodded his head yes and headed out of the restaurant to talk to Isabella.

Adrian pulled up to Isabella's house and took a deep breath.

I hope this works. I really like Ravynne, and I don't want to see anything happen to her and I know Isabella has a mean streak a mile wide.

He got out of the car and rang the bell.

Ballari, Isabella's assistant, answered the door.

"Mr. Breckington, what are you doing here? You know Ms. Monroe is still furious with you and if she sees you it's going to be hell to pay."

"I know Ballari, and thank you, but I must speak to Isabella."

"Alright. Give me just a minute and see if she will see you. I hope for your sake and mine that she's in a decent mood."

Five minutes later the door opened once again, and Ballari waved him in.

"She's agreed to see you but she's none too happy about it."

"It's okay. I've dealt with this mood before."

"Good luck then, you're gonna need it." Ballari whispered.

Adrian walked in and saw Isabella sitting behind her desk.

"Good afternoon, Isabella. I decided to come and talk to you myself and get everything settled. I know I treated you badly before and I want to apologize for that. Please let this drop and everyone get on with their lives. You will be much happier and so will the rest of us. I am sure there is someone out there who is just perfect for you, it's just not me."

"You hurt me badly, Adrian. I don't know if I can ever forgive that, but I was at fault too. I will call Ravynne, myself, and apologize for the way I acted. I hope you can find what you are looking for."

"Thank you, Isabella, that's all anyone can ask for. I just want the best for you, and I know it's not me."

Adrian left her house and headed back to Ravynne's shop to tell her the news.

Seven

Adrian arrived back at Ravynne's shop and went inside.

"I talked to her, and everything is fine. We got the situation taken care of and she agreed to leave us alone."

"Oh, thank the goddess for that."

"It wasn't easy, but it had to be done." Adrian said.

Ravynne leaned over to kiss him, and they embraced for a long time until the bell over the door sounded.

"Well, I guess that's my cue to get back to work. I will see you later then?"

"Definitely, Bumbaloos at six?"

"Sure."

Adrian walked out and Ravynne got back to work.

About the Author

Jaysic Kae is also known as JK Lycke and Jasmine Skye. This is her first paranormal story. She usually writes romance but likes to dabble in other genres.

She lives in Texas and keeps busy with work and newfound hobby of crochet.

She can be found on Facebook as: Author, JK Lycke

Tenacity

BY J.E. FELDMAN

Middle-aged Mara runs her own coffee shop downtown where human customers aren't allowed. When one slips past the wards and sees Zeni, her Faerie assistant, things go south. Religious fanatics kidnap Zeni and burn the shop to the ground. It's the witch trials all over again.

With the help of her handsome boyfriend and a fellow shop owner, will Mara be able to save her friend in time?

*

"Your shop is haunted."

I pause mid pour with the coffee pot suspended above my customer's cup. I opened the doors half an hour ago and am still blinking sleep from my eyes. It's too early for this.

He seems too well-dressed to be a crazy person in a smart, black business suit while toting a briefcase. His dark hair is slicked back and not a hint of stubble is on his handsome face. But I've seen all types come into my shop during the last twenty years. Crazy comes in many forms.

I finish pouring his coffee, snap a lid onto it, and push it across the counter toward him. "Have a nice day!"

He slaps his hand down, causing me to jump. "There's a naked ghost *right there*." He points over my left shoulder.

My eyes widen and I turn slowly. A petite, feminine figure about three feet tall floats near the upper shelf. She's not quite human with wild, white hair like a fluffy dandelion and solid black eyes. Her dark moth-like wings flutter slightly to keep her aloft. Her caramel skin matches the color of her jumpsuit perfectly, making her appear naked at first glance. Her long arms are wrapped around the jar of chocolate covered coffee beans.

Her gaze flicks from the customer's to mine and she mouths, "He sees me!"

How *can* he see her? A human wandering into my shop means something is wrong with the warding. It's best to feign ignorance.

I turn back to the customer. "It must be a trick of light."

The businessman shakes his head vigorously. He opens his mouth to continue when a hand lands on his shoulder. We're joined by my handsome regular. Sam's blond hair is a bit messy from the wind today. His blue eyes sparkle as he shoots me a wink.

"Good morning, Mara."

My heart always skips a beat when he says my name. Like I'm some teenager instead of a middle-aged woman. "Hi, Sam."

To the man, he says, "We see all kinds of things before our daily dose of caffeine." Picking up the man's cup, he hands it over and gently steers him toward the door. "Make sure to chug that before work. Have a good day."

The bell rings softly as the man leaves, brow still furrowed as he looks over his shoulder. Sam stands and waves until the customer finally walks away down the sidewalk. Brushing off his hands, Sam returns to the counter.

Grateful for his intervention, I say, "Your usual?" He nods. "On the house."

"No need for that," he smiles, retrieving his wallet. He places the exact change on the counter and drops an extra couple dollars in the tip jar. "Are you free this Saturday?"

If my hands weren't busy preparing his mocha latte, I would've slapped my forehead. I forgot to respond to his text yesterday. Our first date was last week and I'm worried he'll think I'm not interested.

"I can make time. Zeni can manage the shop for a few hours."

"Or another day," Sam offers. "Afterall, she let a human in here."

The dandelion-haired fairy makes a face at him as she flies over with a tray of dirty cups.

"How *did* you let one in?" I demand.

There's a clatter as she moves the cups to the sink. Tucking the now-empty tray under her arm, she shrugs. "Must've slipped past the ward."

Shooting her a glare, I pour his latte into a to-go cup. "Can you handle the shop for a bit on Saturday?"

Zeni's black eyes twinkle. She's been asking for more responsibility for weeks, but I've been putting it off. Mostly since I'm a workaholic. Taking days off leaves me with the tedious task of finding something else to busy myself with.

She salutes me. "Leave it to me!"

Slipping a heat sleeve onto his cup, I hand it to Sam over the counter. "Saturday it is," I smile.

❧

"That was a nice outing," I tell Sam, a little breathless as we return to his car.

After treating me to breakfast, he suggested we visit the riverwalk to see the latest changes. New art installations had been strategically placed along its length. From murals to monstrous sculptures, they gave me some ideas on how to update the shop's look.

He holds the door for me. "I have more date ideas, if you're interested."

"I'd like that," I say softly.

His cheeks redden as he shuts the door. He climbs in and drives back toward my shop.

My eyes widen as tendrils of thick black smoke stretch into the sky. I trace it to the general area of my business and my stomach twists. When we reach the street, it's blocked off by fire trucks and cop cars.

"It can't be," I gasp, launching out of the car. I stumble along the sidewalk as Sam calls my name. Pushing through the gathering crowd, I'm unable to go further because of the road blocks.

Glass litters the street in front of my blackened storefront and multiple firefighters battle the remaining flames. My breath whooshes from me. On trembling legs, I prepare to launch over the barrier. A firefighter throws an arm out and stops my progress.

"That's my store," I shout over the sirens.

"Don't worry, ma'am. We got everyone out," he says.

I sag with relief just as Sam materializes beside me. He wraps an arm around my waist to help support me. But just as quickly as the relief came, it vanishes. He said *everyone*, but what about Zeni? The average human can't see her. What if she's still trapped inside?

"It's going to be okay," Sam says. "The shop can be rebuilt."

The firefighter shakes his head. "This place is too far gone."

"Then you'll find a new place."

Anything else Sam says is drowned out by the firefighters finishing putting out the flames and cleaning up the glass from the road. It seems to take an eternity before they finally let me near enough to the building to see better. Everything is gone. The shop is nothing more than a gaping black hole filled with ash. Even if the firefighters would let me inside, I'd never manage to find Zeni's small bones amid the debris.

"Mara, there's a camera across the street. Let's ask for an extra copy of the footage," Sam says.

He gently leads me to the cabinetry shop across the street. Their windows are now coated with a greasy-like film from the dark smoke. There's a chime as we step inside and the plump, elderly store owner rushes forward with arms spread for a hug.

"Oh, Mara! Are you okay? So sorry about your shop," Mark says. The smell of sawdust is overwhelming as he envelopes me in a brief bear hug.

"Still in shock," I admit, awkwardly patting him on the back. "We need a copy of your camera feed," I say as he finally pulls away. My hands briefly twitch with the urge to brush myself off.

"The cops already took it," Mark says. My heart sinks before he shoots us both a wink and jerks his head toward the back room. "But I keep copies just in case."

I sigh with relief as we trail after him. As an ex-con, it's predictable for Mark not to trust the police. He locks the door behind us and has me sit down at a desk with multiple computer monitors. With a few taps, he pulls up the video of my shop and hits enter. I unconsciously lean in closer as I see myself leaving the shop in Zeni's hands for the day. Mark presses another key and it skips forward until he slows it down again.

"This here is the part that's interesting," he declares.

A few men stand on the sidewalk in black suits. It tickles my memory of the man that threw a fuss in my shop earlier in the week. They enter as a group and a couple of customers leave soon after, glancing over their shoulders with agitation. Had they been ushered out? A couple of minutes later, one of them comes out with a bag thrown over his shoulder. Whatever's inside is struggling to get out.

"Zeni," I gasp. They step out of the frame and I crane my head as if seeing around the monitor will help. "Where do they go?"

Mark uses the keyboard to bring up another camera angle. It shows the man opening the back door of a black van and tossing the sack in. I wince for Zeni's sake at the treatment. At least she's alive. When the suspect turns again, I recognize him as the dark haired customer from this morning. I clench the arms of my chair as he climbs into the vehicle and shuts the door.

Mark flips back to the shop view and it shows the other three men leaving. Shortly after, smoke can be seen through the windows. Clearing his throat, he pauses the video. "There's no reason for you to watch it go up in flames. You've already seen the aftermath."

I nod, rotating the chair to face Sam. "The customer you escorted out this morning. It's him."

He nods. "I noticed. And that van they used. It belongs to the First Methodist Church on the other side of town."

I stand quickly, nearly rolling over Mark's foot. "Let's go."

"Hold on, Mara," the store owner says. "You can't run off to handle that on your own."

I shoot him a tight-lipped smile. "Like you, I have a history. I can handle this."

"Don't worry about us," Sam adds. His hand presses against the small of my back as he guides me to the car.

The ride to the church is silent. As we pull into the parking lot, it's hard not to notice the black van parked near the entrance. I fling my seat belt off as Sam stops the car.

"Stay here," I say, slipping out before he can protest.

"Mara," he hisses, gravel crunching as he hurries around to join me. "It's too dangerous. Let me go first."

I hesitate, but time is of the essence. "There's something you should know before we continue dating. I'm a witch." I pause to allow him the usual reaction of disgust. He simply nods and I stutter over my next words. "My entire bloodline is powerful, so I'll be fine."

Sam reaches for my hand, lacing our fingers together. "My father was a warlock. My siblings and I didn't inherit any magic, but I'm familiar with the world." As my eyes widen, he gives my hand a comforting squeeze. "I have no doubt in your abilities. You shouldn't have to face it on your own, is all."

"But what if you get hurt?"

"Nonsense. Let's save Zeni." He tugs me up the front steps.

The quiet interior is broken by the massive door creaking as we enter. Pews line the aisle that cuts through the heart of the church. Beams of light stream through the stained glass windows, leaving a kaleidoscope of colors to brighten our way. We cautiously look around, but no one is in immediate view.

"Let's check the back rooms," I say, climbing the few stairs to the podium. I head for the stage door that leads into a hallway. This is where the staff offices are. As we move along, loud voices come from further ahead.

"I said *not* to harm her," a familiar male voice barks.

Fists clenched, I hesitate outside to listen in. Sam tries to position himself to move inside first, but I don't budge.

"A few bruises will heal," another male whines.

"It's unnatural. We're doing the world a favor by doing this," a third chimes in.

"Just let me go," Zeni's weak voice pleads.

The first man laughs cruelly. "You're not leaving alive." There's a smack of flesh hitting flesh.

I grip the handle so hard, it almost breaks as I twist it. The door crashes against the wall as I slam it open and step in. Two men stand around Zeni while a third sits in the nearby corner. Raising a hand, a surge of energy zips in the duo's direction and knocks them away from her. With wide eyes, they crumple against opposite walls of the small room.

Zeni looks worse for wear with red-rimmed eyes and bruised cheeks. Her bodysuit is ripped around her shoulders and arms. It looks like they tried different ways to bind her. From experience, I know how crafty and resourceful she can be. Nothing can hold her for long. She sags with relief when she sees us.

"Help her up. I'll deal with them," I growl at Sam.

While the two men groan on the floor, I face the one still sitting. It's the same man from earlier. His slicked back hair is slightly out of place and his hazel eyes are narrowed at me. A cigarette is in his hand, but he has no visible weapon. I block his view of Sam and Zeni with my body.

"Why?" I demand.

The man's shoulders heave with a drawn-out sigh. "As priests, it's our job to rid this world of abominations."

I scoff. "You should have begun with yourselves then."

A muscle in his jaw twitches. "How do you figure?"

"The most bloodshed has come from religious fanatics," I say, hearing Sam mutter words of comfort to Zeni. He hovers just behind me with her in his arms. "Take her to the car."

"Come with us," Zeni rasps.

I shake my head. "I have unfinished business here."

"Please," Sam says.

"Go!"

Frowning, he carries Zeni out and they disappear down the hallway. By now, the two men have risen shakily to their feet. Limping, they block my exit.

"What should we do, boss?" the taller asks.

He scoffs and reaches into his suit, withdrawing a gun. My body reflexively tenses at the sight of it as my heart seems to stall. The horrible night from childhood flashes into my mind's eye. Of Mother shoving me into a closet and ordering me to be quiet. To not come out no matter what I heard or saw. If I had followed her instructions, I wouldn't have seen Father shoot her multiple times. My grief wouldn't have released a magic blast that set our family home on fire, ultimately killing him and destroying any evidence. Thankfully, I was sent to live with my maternal grandma after. Otherwise, my paternal grandparents may have killed me too. Witches were still hung or murdered thirty years ago.

I shiver as a cold sweat creeps along my brow.

He notices my balking reaction and slowly levels the barrel in my direction. In those few seconds, multiple scenarios race through my head. If I heat up the gun, it will misfire on its own even if he doesn't drop it first. If I attack him, the gun will discharge since he'll reflexively pull the trigger. There's not a shield strong enough to stop a bullet at this range. Nothing in this room is thick enough to use as a barricade.

I raise my hands in the universal sign of surrender. "Let's talk about this."

He laughs, uncrossing his legs to lean forward in his seat. "You were confident just a few minutes ago. All it takes is a gun in your face to make you compliant? Maybe I didn't need to go through all of this trouble after all."

I swallow hard. As I open my mouth to speak, the faint sound of police sirens reaches our ears. It steadily grows louder as he jolts out of his seat.

He brandishes the gun at me while I try not to flinch. "When did you have time to call the cops?"

"It wasn't us."

He scoffs, running his free hand through his hair. "No matter. They'll take our word over yours. These cops come to church every Wednesday and Sunday."

"That doesn't make them loyal to you," I point out.

"They believe in the Lord and that witches should be annihilated if they can't be purified." He takes a step towards me, grinning when I move away. "There'll be nothing left of you to purify once they get in here."

Two shots ring out and both men blocking the doorway drop with yelps. Blood seeps from their lower legs, staining the carpet with red droplets. They wail and rock until someone approaches and orders for them to get against the wall. My mouth drops when they enter the room.

"Mark?" I gasp.

"Hey, Mara. I waited a while before calling the cops. Wanted you to have a chance at 'em first," Mark winks. He scans the area, quickly gauging the situation. "Put the gun down, bud. Then we can talk in a civil manner."

The man scoffs. "You're not a cop. Nothing but a vigilante."

Mark makes eye contact with me and gives a slight jerk of his head. With wide eyes, I nod while he continues. "Do you always label something at first glance?"

"They must because why else would they burn down my shop?" I demand.

"You're a witch!"

Mark clears his throat. "Ephesians 4:32 says to be kind, compassionate, and forgiving to each other, in the same way God forgave you in Christ."

In a shrill voice, the man says, "Matthew 10:8. Drive out demons. She and that creature are *demons*."

"Ah, there's no curing you then," Mark says. His sad, defeated tone sends a surge of adrenaline through me.

If I blinked, I would've missed his signal. I drop into a crouch, shielding my head with my arms as a blast rings out. There's a loud thud soon after. I chance a look and find the dark haired man on his side. A final breath wracks his body before the light fades from his eyes. The same way Mother had looked, except with less blood this time.

Bile rises in my throat and I heave up my brunch. Tears stream down my face unbidden until I finish. Shouts come from down the hallway and Mark complies with their orders. The police officers have him pinned and cuffed by the time I compose myself.

"No, let him go," I plead, swiping away my tears.

An officer gently holds me back while they lead Mark out. "It's just protocol. We have to investigate what happened."

"He saved my life." My voice cracks. Some witch I am. Can't even protect myself without locking up from PTSD. Now Mark's life will be changed forever too.

"Come on," the officer says, leading me out of the church.

Sam is pacing outside, demanding that he be let inside. He rushes to my side the moment he sees us. "Are you hurt?"

I shake my head and he pulls me into a tight hug.

"Sir, an EMT should look over her to be safe. Then we'll need to take her in for questioning."

"Of course," Sam says. He goes to pull away, but I cling to him.

"Is she safe?" I mutter, hoping the officer doesn't overhear us.

"Yes."

"Thank you." I pull away and he gently brushes loose strands of hair away from my face.

"Everything will be okay," he says.

I nod and force a small smile.

AFTER AN EXTENSIVE INVESTIGATION, MARK IS CLEARED OF murder charges, but is put on probation due to his criminal history. I assure him that once I open my new shop, he'll have free coffee and muffins for life. In the meantime, I bring him homemade dishes three days a week.

Zeni physically recovers well, but she has PTSD attacks every so often. With a few rounds of discussions, she returns to the Fae realm until further notice. It's incredibly lonely without her, even though Sam tries to fill the void with dates. The weeks pass by and a large chunk of my savings are used up while I hunt for a job to get back on my feet.

The day starts like any other. Downing a cup of coffee, getting dressed, and heading out the door with a lasagna for Mark. That's when I see Sam's car parked in the driveway behind mine. He casually leans against its fender, but perks up immediately when he sees me.

"Hi, sweetie," he says, planting a quick peck on my cheek.

"Hi! What are you up to?"

Sam grins broadly. "It's a surprise. Can you spare some time?"

I raise the tin casserole dish. "I'm on my way to give this to Mark. Do you mind if we stop by his store first?"

"Not at all. It's on the way." He takes the dish then holds the passenger door for me.

We arrive at Mark's cabinet shop a short time later. There's more cars along the block than usual for a weekend. The bell dings softly as we enter and I wave to Mark who is with a couple of customers.

He smiles and excuses himself to come over. "My favorite couple. How are you?"

"Oh, you know. The usual." I hand over the dish. "Lasagna made from scratch."

"My favorite!"

"Hope you made one for us later," Sam says with a gentle elbow nudge.

"Of course," I laugh. "It looks like you're busy at the moment, but I'll stop by again on Monday."

Mark nods, giving Sam a wink. "Maybe sooner than that."

I glance between them, furrowing my brow.

"See you later," Sam says, wrapping an arm around my waist and guiding me out of the store.

"What was that about?" I ask.

Sam clears his throat and takes my hand. "How about we take a walk?"

Narrowing my eyes, I let him lead me down the sidewalk. It's not long before we reach a storefront. The sign is covered with a white tarp and there's no signage on the windows yet. I tug Sam to a stop.

"I didn't know this space was available. I wonder what business is moving in," I comment.

"It's a coffee shop," he says. He moves toward the door and opens it.

"What are you–"

"Let's check it out."

Before I can protest, he steps inside. I glance around to see if anyone's watching, but there's no one else in the near vicinity. With a sigh, I follow.

"Sam, we shouldn't–"

"SURPRISE!"

I nearly jump out of my skin as the lights are flipped on and a roomful of my old customers shout the greeting as they pop up from behind the serving counter. Chairs and tables are aligned in neat rows around the shop with a handful of empty bookshelves along the back wall.

Tears well up in my eyes and I press a hand over my heart. "What's going on?"

Sam comes over and wraps an arm around my shoulders. "This is your new shop. We all chipped in to make it happen."

"You're kidding!" The tears spill over and I hurriedly wipe them away, fighting to compose myself. "It's too much."

"Nonsense. If anyone deserves this, it's you," Sam insists. Everyone nods in agreement. "Take a look around," he urges.

Still brushing away tears, I head for the counter to check out the new equipment. It looks used, but it's newer than what I had before the fire. There's more cabinet space and the sinks are larger too.

"Do you have everything you need?" Sam asks.

I nod with a sniffle.

"Am I late?" Mark's voice comes from the doorway.

"Just in time for the best part," Sam calls.

I gape at them. "There's more?"

Grinning, Sam points over my shoulder. I slowly turn and notice the small figure floating at eye level behind me. I'd recognize those wild white locks anywhere. Zeni's dark eyes are damp with emotion. With a cry, I lurch forward and pull her into a bear hug.

She clings to my neck for a few seconds before patting my shoulder. "Can't. Breathe," she gasps.

I slowly release and hold her at arms' length. "I can't believe you're back! Are you doing better?"

Zeni smiles. "Much better."

"Are you visiting or..." My voice trails off.

She scoffs. "You can't run this new shop without me. I'm staying, of course."

More happy tears stream down my face as I pull her in for another hug. This one is shorter than the last as she squirms to escape. I dab my face with my sleeve and repeatedly thank everyone in the room. They gradually filter out after promising to come support me on opening day.

Mark is the last guest to leave, leaning in to whisper conspiratorially, "All of this was Sam's idea." With a wink, he leaves.

Turning to Sam, I give him a tight hug. "Thank you for everything."

"You're welcome," he murmurs. He leans back slightly to then press his lips against mine.

I stand on tiptoe and wrap my arms around his neck as the kiss grows heated. Zeni clears her throat loudly and we reluctantly pull apart.

"Let's go home," she says, hovering near the door.

With a bashful smile, Sam hands me two keys on a small coffee cup keychain. As we exit the shop, I use the key to lock the door securely. My heart swells with unbridled joy at the bright future ahead of us.

About the Author

Since a young age, J.E. Feldman's fascination with the written word led her to a career of fiction writing, journalism, and editorial pursuits. She has crafted more than 300 publications over the last ten years.

When not penning the next novel, Feldman focuses on mentoring authors and raising money for charity. The literature world is merely one facet of her life.

Feldman haunts car shows, anime conventions, medieval fairs, and whatever else catches her attention. She enjoys road trips ripe with history, crocheting blankets for the homeless, and can be found reading in cramped bookstores.

Visit www.JEFeldman.com to learn more.

If you enjoyed *Tenacity*, you'll love *The Witch Hunter Chronicles*.

Ace of Cups

BY ANGEL W. SMITH AND COLLA TRITI

It really should be an easy life, dancing through her own existence; her toes in the dirt with her soul flying alongside her hands overhead in the wind. At least, that's what it would have been if she stayed put, living out in the country instead of chasing the love of her life into the city.

It really should be an easy life, dancing through her own existence; her toes in the dirt with her soul flying alongside her hands overhead in the wind. At least, that's what *it would have* been if she stayed put, living out in the country. Desiree moped about it for the umpteenth time that day, let alone the past eight years since.

Her problem? Her romantic heart...

She'd chased the love of her life into the city, dodging emotional hellfire, and dishing it to others under her breath whenever warranted. Des frowned, accepting that she most likely had gone too far, but *The Fates* hadn't been replying to her spellmail, he'd been all too oblivious to her moves and *just* forget the spells she'd used for his attention alone.

Ben was just... unreachable.

Eight, *almost nine years* had passed and all Desiree could feel was that overwhelming sense of doubt when she happened to cross paths with him.

Oh, that doubt was hell too...

Maybe it was her, the treacherous thought weaseled its way into her head. Maybe she wasn't good enough or even *on* his level... because there was *that* to consider. Magic wielders came from all over, all of which were marked by their performance abilities, to which she had none. No scars or burns except for one that couldn't even be considered a true injury. Except as one to her ego: dropping an overcharged wand. Good witches didn't even use wands... gah. What was her deal?

Actually, she knew what her deal was, Des complained inwardly. It was that tree of a man she wanted to climb and the people that got between her and her goal.

Except, eight years really does a number on the heart, she thought as she picked through new plant arrivals at the local garden center. Years ago she would sift through them for their properties, adding elements here and there into her spells. Des used to make potions, spot dabs, and fragrance spells that went unnoticed by her hunk. They drove the general public wild, *or* mad depending solely on her mood that day.

Today though? Today she's just plain exhausted looking over colors of foliage she'll use to eventually paint out her tarot cards with. At least it would be one last excuse to try to get his attention.

"My muse left me," her own voice echoed back in her head. "If you're willing, I'd pay handsomely for your time."

Desiree shook off the anxiety building in her gut while she waited for Ben's answer. He stared at her long and hard before relinquishing his time to her, perhaps out of pity. It wasn't a card she was used to pulling, but it worked!

Ben took out his phone and tapped out her requirements and address, expecting him to do the same. All he asked for was that there would be refreshments and plenty to drink. Not once did he ask about the specifics of her payment though...

It still struck her as odd, but with only hours to go before her *date* with *him*, Desiree pushed herself to focus on her set up. Each passing moment began to harp on her nerves. This was it, her last time to reach him, closed off in her space... It was almost too much to take in and not enough all at once.

Desiree collected her plants, paid, then returned home, flicking out spells left and right to assure herself she'd be home with time to spare. All of which were only considered minor inconveniences to those who took the brunt of them. Her neighbors on the other hand? She hushed *them* with entertainment, naps and timelapse spells.

"There would not be *one* reason not to land Ben tonight. Not one!" Desiree assured herself as she made her way through her apartment door. The bland, uniformed hallway took a new shape as she crossed the threshold. Where once there was chipped paint and mold from lack of care all around her, there was now a shelved garden to greet her. Ferns, succulents, hanging ivy and a handful of stones she'd found around set the scene.

It gave her energy, stability and of course, spell power.

Desiree set down her new collection on the tall table to her right. What was usually a catch all became her designated preparation stand. Above it, racks held various supplies, each dedicated to this evening's activities.

Her studio apartment, while small, entertained a large enough space for a sitting room decorated with a low coffee table cut from a giant geode, one of her favorite pieces. Around it, a couple of oversized armchairs offered comfort to anyone she brought up with her. Des snorted at the thought. They held books and groceries, if not herself.

The room stretched into the kitchen, the flooring not exactly clear on its change had Desiree constantly redecorating with her floating island. There she wisely decided to begin putting out her first round of platters. Cheeses, fruits, nuts, veggies and dip decorated the quartz island. To her right against the wall, she had her dry bar set with wine, bourbon, the local brewery's autumn craft beer and of course, plenty of water.

Just to the right of it was the world's smallest kitchen along the wall, followed by her kitchen table that looked out into the apartment building across the way. Her bed, hidden behind yet another wall of foliage, folded up, tucked away to give her space with him. Desiree checked her phone before double checking her bathroom just beyond what could be considered her bedroom. Toiletries were set within arms reach, a copious amount of towels stacked beside the vanity, and above *all* it was clean. The shower, the toilet, even the floor sparkled.

Desiree was set. If anything, he'd remember how well he was taken care of. Maybe it would be enough to come back, she thought.

A feather light tapping rattled its way through her home.

He's here!

Desiree fought herself not to shriek, her thrill still bubbled up her throat, making it hard to remove the grin that spread across her face.

"I'm coming!" she called back as she hurried to the door.

Desiree peered through her peephole, unlocking the door as she did. Beyond that hunk of wood and metal was the man of her dreams, holding what looked like a bouquet of flowers.

For her?

As she pulled the door in towards her, opening it to him, she couldn't help but marvel up at him. Her tongue swept out to lick her bottom lip.

"Hi Ben," Desiree desperately tried not to sound breathless.

He was just so tall, so broad, *so handsome*... it was a lot to take in.

Almost there, she thought to herself. In. He needs to come in...

"Hi Desiree," Ben replied quietly, pushing a bouquet of wildflowers into her hands.

"For me?" Desiree couldn't help but smile wider.

"For um, whatever you use them for," he tentatively looked around as if her home was a trap.

"Comfort mostly," she replied, watching him. "You're welcome to come in if you still want to do this."

Ben seemed sheepish all of a sudden, looking around past her for evidence that he would be fine.

Her heart hurt to see it. Maybe this was way too far out of his element and she should just...

"Yeah, I mean," he shook himself out of it. "You said you had someone drop out."

"Right," she replied. *That is what she said.*

"I'm told witches have to produce a deck at least once a year to line up with the stars or something," he added as he stepped inside.

His wide, dark brown eyes met hers earnestly as he spoke. His brow furrowed as he tried to remember random facts from wherever he pulled them from, making his thick, plump lips thin while deep in thought. His closeness gave her all the time in the world to map his moles that dotted his skin as if he himself was an uncharted zodiac.

She could stare at him forever.

His beautiful dark hair, set in waves around his ears, hiding them from her too. Idly, she wondered just how much of him he'd allow her during their session, while he continued nervously spouting more hearsay.

"Yes," she answered. "It's a part of my practice and I'd like to make sure this one speaks to me the way the rest do."

"Are there really like, eighty cards?" he asked, preparing to take off his jacket.

It was an absolute struggle not to stare but there she was doing her best to give an answer.

"Seventy-eight."

Ben cleared his throat, nodding as he did.

"And you need all of them tonight?"

... *And you,* she wanted to let slip.

"It would be ideal. Kind of a huge project though. I understand if you..." Desiree's mouth ran dry as he removed his jacket fully, draping it over one of her chairs.

"That's a neat table," Ben made small talk as he removed his t-shirt, and turned to ask where she wanted him.

... *I will literally take you anywhere.*

"Here's good," Desiree's answer seemed to climb in volume with her nerves. "The theme is natural beauty."

Desiree watched Ben's Adam's apple bob as he took in the scene around him. Her paints aligned with spells which could be overwhelming for those who were non-practicing magical types.

"It won't hurt you," she couldn't help but promise. "It actually feels nice."

"You've done it to yourself?" he couldn't believe her.

"In desperation. Yes," she replied. "Not even spills are painful."

Ben frowned, unsure once more.

"Can I show you?" Desiree curled her hair over her own ear as she asked, matching his nerves.

Ben nodded, his attention super focused on her.

Desiree slowly closed the door, joking about how her neighbors simply *did not* need a show, before locking them in. After, she dropped the shoulders of her long shawl, then pulled her blue camisole over her head to match him, besides her bralet.

The atmosphere quickly gained a charge. Despite how she still held his flowers, Desiree felt bare to his heart. Exposed. Unsure. Raw.

Regardless, she had to find her tongue. She had to start speaking or the fear of being rejected by him would burn through her desire to go on.

"Succulents," she waved over the doorway, "Are used as a base. They give a healing element that grounds the spell."

Desiree felt his gaze move from her to the various colored plants and thicknesses, trying to figure it out.

"And the ones I gave you?"

"They're wildflowers, so each has their own exotic flair," she hummed, picking up her spell brush.

She waved it carefully over a blue cornflower, first through the center and out to each petal before swiveling it into a small pallet. Its contents piling together in a premade collection of succulents prior. The action supplied more than she needed for a test sample.

Desiree dipped her chin to her chest to watch herself swirl the spell over her heart. She made a tight coil that surrounded itself once, then a small wave, one to the swell of her left breast, then to her right, hidden by the front clasp of her bralet.

As she looked back up at Ben under her lashes, she could see just how affected he was by watching. His eyes dilated, his deep inhales and full exhales held her attention. He *liked* it.

"What does it feel like?" he asked softly.

"Feels featherlight, like freshly weaved cotton fluttering in the wind," she shivered. "One of my favorites."

"Can I try?" Ben asked gruffly, trying to hide his intrigue.

Desiree nodded, handing him the loaded spell brush.

"Do it for me," he stopped her. "Like you will for this session."

Desiree raised her eyebrows, surprised he still wanted this. She applied his with the same symbol reaching down between his pecs. Her bottom lip protested as she bit down on it for purchase, holding Desiree to this world, rather than floating away in her fantasy land.

"Oh," Ben exhaled.

"Good oh?" Desiree leaned in, hopeful.

"Good," Ben strained. "Do they all feel like this?" he asked almost breathlessly.

Desiree pressed her lips into a thin line as she shook her head.

"Each has their own signature," she paused, checking for his attention. "I can warn you, or we can avoid some if you tell me what you don't like now."

Ben returned the gesture.

"No. Do it," he whispered. "Whatever you need."

Desiree was going to die from her inward wishes alone. What she needed was his energy sapping all of hers with that gorgeous body of his.

"O-okay," she hesitated. "How comfortable are you in your own sin... I mean skin?"

Ben's eyes went wide.

"Your whole *form*," she hurried out of her as if there wasn't a wish in her heart that he was the one. Then, "I need it. All of you... for this."

His thumb flicked the button of his jeans carefully, as if he heard her wrong.

"Something tells me that there's more to this that you're not telling me," Ben's attention roughly took a turn.

Blush crept over her cheeks and the bridge of her nose while she stood there in front of him, committing the glory of *him* to her memory.

"How do you figure," she asked coyly, gathering jars to place on the table.

"Besides this pretty little mess of pink that *I* haven't drawn on you?" Ben replied. "I'm pretty sure..."

"It's a full body procedure," she huffed. "Have you seen the dick? I mean *deck*?

Ben's chuckle seized her. The deep baritone laughter shot through her in ways she couldn't recover from.

"Gods of MERCY! THE DECK!?"

"What kind of *deck* is this?" Ben teased, feeling more courageous than normal. "Certainly not one with dicks."

Desiree shook her head. She was never going to live this down! There she was half bare to the only guy that could ever matter in her life and they were now talking about dick decks, like it was a thing.

Ok, so what if it was? It wasn't like she needed to be talking about it with *him!*

Desiree groaned, dipping her head back between her shoulders, exposing more of her chest to Ben in the process. Reel him back in, her hindbrain proposed. This playful side was fun and all but it wasn't at all what Ben portrayed over the years. Was it her?

"Is that what you want?" Desiree cracked, unable to remain focused. "An entire seventy-eight cards dedicated to your member?"

Ben's laughter quickly ebbed.

"It would be hard, but doable," she conceded, thankful for not having to listen to a *'that's what she said,'* retort.

"If that's," Ben cleared his throat. "If that's what you want."

Something about the way he said it was earnest, as if he was trying to give a little more. *What exactly was in that cornflower?*

"What *I* want is an entire representation of you in my deck. Not just your dick," she wheezed out as she waved her spell brush in his general direction. "Even though this would be a part of my personal collection, not for the general public."

Ben padded his way up to her, closing the space between them.

"You want me *privately*?"

Is that what she said?

Ben curled his finger underneath her chin, carefully forcing her head back up to get Desiree to look him in the eye.

"Is that what this is?" he asked again, void of any kind emotion.

Desiree couldn't help herself. Years. It took her years to get him here. Denying him his answer would send Ben away... And lying about it surely wouldn't save her from herself either.

"Yes," she whispered. "It's true."

Ben's jaw worked as he stared into her eyes, looking for more.

"You barely noticed me," Desiree pouted.

"Barely?" Ben echoed.

"Yeah Ben," she pulled away from him. "I've tried everything to get your attention, but nothing worked. But *this*? This silly little mark finally got your attention? I'm not buying it."

"I haven't *exactly* been all together, if that makes sense," Ben rushed out, surprise written all over his face.

"It doesn't," Desiree deflected, to which she'd realized herself. "I mean, I guess. It's just that – almost nine years, you're saying, you've been detached from yourself?"

Ben's lips parted, ready to reply but no words followed.

"I mean, I get it," Desiree did her best to accept her place on the outskirts of his existence. "Life is tugging me around too but *I still made* the time for you."

"How would you have me prove it? Ben interrupted, still on his own path.

Did he not hear what she just said?

"I don't know?" Desiree shook her head, looking up at the ceiling as if it would give her answers. Her hands flew up to the pasty flat heavens above her, spell brush in hand, then realized herself.

That's it!

It would be a long shot, she thought to herself, but she could do it if he was still willing.

"It looks like you figured something out..." Ben murmured curiously.

"Do you trust me?" Desiree asked, looking up into his dark brown eyes.

"I wouldn't be here if I didn't," he assured her, his attention clear.

"Go eat," she nodded over to the kitchen spread. "This is going to take a lot of energy."

DESIREE COULDN'T HELP BUT HYPERVENTILATE A LITTLE WHILE she sorted out her predicament. Blindly, she prepared body spells to rectify Ben's supposed situation instead of raising a new deck with him. It would just have to wait.

Instead, Desiree pulled up chamomile to calm him through whatever anxiety he might face, calendula for treating wounds, lemon balm to weave in happiness, and coneflowers to boost his natural ability to find himself. The wildflowers he brought could act as spices, getting his blood moving; ready to move, instead of becoming a sack of potatoes afterward.

Truthfully, Des found herself not caring what he wound up as, so long as he decided to be hers. Next to aid her was her favorite deck to lay out on her geode table. A few tealight candles are added for light instead of her recessed lighting overhead. The action alone draws him near once more.

Desiree steadied herself despite how riled up she felt inside. Secretly, her attention flicked back down to the button on his jeans. Her mouth went dry as she proceeded to instruct Ben.

"Those need to, um," she nervously suggested that they had to come off.

"You too?" Ben joked, clearing his throat when she didn't budge. "I mean, yeah, ok."

Ben peeled off his shoes first, then shucked off his pants leaving him in his dark briefs and socks.

"Better?" he asked.

"Oh yes, better," she mumbled to herself, then sank down towards the colorful table. Crystals within the center glinted, their light and shadow flicked their attention to her deck and the collection of potions she lined up for him. "So much better."

Ben kneeled next to her, watching her work. She fanned out cards from her deck then asked him to pick ten for himself. Carefully, he selected each of them as if he knew just how meaningful they were. Desiree proceeded to place the cards out in front of her, allowing him to tell her which was first all the way to the last. She purposely spread them in front of him in three columns, each card very specifically laying in its place with the one he claimed was the fourth laying across the third in the center.

"You said you were detached from yourself," Desiree murmured, kneeling beside Ben at the table. Her spell brush swirled in her first healing pot, "Flip the first one over," she added as she took his chin in her hand to keep him still as she softly slid the balm over his forehead, close to his hairline.

His shiver was slight, but noticeable, making Desiree do the same.

Here we go...

"This is your past self: Four of Cups," Desiree explained. "It means that back then you needed to shut out the world around you to figure yourself out."

Shit.

"Yeah," Ben agreed. "A lot of shit hit the fan. I'm not proud of my actions either."

Desiree nodded, incapable of speech as she pointed to the next card. Still, she held him in place, adding more of the calming solution above his brow and under his eyes at his cheek bones.

"Next is your current self: Hermit."

"That sounds awful," Ben groaned, running his fingers through his hair instead of scrubbing his face.

"*You* picked them," Desiree tried to deflect.

"They're *your* cards," he interrupted, smiling sappily in her hand.

"Uh huh," she snorted, warning him not to move. "That one is basically exactly what you've been up to over this stretch."

Ben cocked his eyebrow up in challenge.

"You know you have," she replied, painting along his jawline. "This is weird though. Usually a reading is between the lines, where the recipient has to reflect on it."

"Maybe that means you should have just believed me when I said I was busy," Ben teased, masking the way he intently watched her.

"*Maybe* it's more for me than it is you," Desiree tilted her head, slipping the third card out from underneath the fourth, then turning the fourth over with it.

"What's it say," Ben changed his position, wordlessly angling his neck toward her as she intentionally marked his skin.

"The third is the Eight of Pentacles. Basically regarding my spiritual path; my choice in these arts. And, fuck you, *Ace of Wands*," Desiree swore.

"What?" Ben chuckled, his grin stretching all the way across his face as he did.

Gods, he's handsome and above all else, needed to be hers.

"My cards just said I needed to get off my high horse and learn something new," she replied.

"Rude," Ben supplied as she perched herself on the side of the table beside their reading. Desiree shook her head, leading his down into her lap.

"You're m-a big guy," she insinuated, explaining she needed access to his shoulders and back. "It takes the pressure off of my knees like this."

Ben hummed there against her lap, comfortably. It seemed the first line of anxiety relievers were helping.

"The fifth one is all you," Desiree murmured.

"How do you know?" Ben questioned.

"It's a family card and I don't have a biological one," she deflected.

"That's something we'll get to the bottom of," he whispered, pressing a kiss onto the fabric of her leggings. *Damn that material,* she wanted to scream.

"Another time," she agreed as he reached past her, his warmth comforting her as he flipped over the card.

"Judgment?" Ben read off of the card itself. "That makes sense, they're always judging me."

"That's not what it means," Desiree sighed, brushing his hair back and away from where it hid his eyes. Before he could question her, she added, "It's supposed to mean you've had a spiritual awakening with either them or yourself. It could be either getting easier to communicate or maybe stand your ground with them. It's something that's changing your tides with them."

Ben disagreed, assuring her that things were just complicated. "Next one?"

"Next is about your personal issues: Five of Pentacles. Basically the need to let go of material goods."

Ben sighed, "I guess, but how do you show you've "made it" if you can't show off what you've accomplished?"

Desiree understood that one all too well. Having her limited supply, her spell brush in hand, gently tracing its way down his back as she held the back of his neck sweetly. "I can't honestly sit here and judge you based on that alone, nor this reading."

"Oh?" Ben asked. "I thought that was what you guys did."

Desiree huffed, "No," she paused, waiting for him to look up at her. "My conscience," she reached across the spread to number seven: The Lovers. Ah hell, cards..." she warned them as she reached across the way to number eight: The Devil."

"What?" his attention barreled down onto the devil card.

Desiree placed the stick of her brush behind her ear, letting the wet brush dribble onto her from its perch. She inhaled deeply as she asked him to stand with her. All the while she promised to burn the two cards that surfaced. How utterly embarrassing!

"It's all in the way you look at it," she wanted to wave him off but oddly could sense his degrees of concern building. "The lovers, Ben, to me," she rolled her eyes back, trying not to make eye contact with him as he stood in front of her for fear of crippling embarrassment, despite still being topless in front of the man of her dreams.

What if he *didn't* accept her? *Gods*, was that her heart seizing in her chest at the thought? Ugh!

"... To me it's my infatuation with you," she swallowed thickly, trying desperately to keep her eyes from brimming with tears.

Ben seemed to only be able to echo his chorus of questions, making it harder to elaborate.

"I've, or at least I thought I loved you since the first time we met, as kids. I guess," she rambled. "That's why I'm here, actually." Before long Des' life story came tumbling out of her. "I figured this was my last time to reach you–"

Before she could make sense of her surroundings, Desiree felt the soft embrace of Ben's arms around her as he cradled her in them.

"Tell me again," he begged, his tone urgent. "Tell me you see me." His body against hers felt tense yet soft and warm, exactly where she'd always dreamt of being.

"I'd tried so hard," she gasped against his bicep as he pulled her only closer as if she was treasure. "For so long..." Desiree trailed.

"And the devil? Would he have stopped you?" Ben worried, pulling her back into view. His eyes searched hers, begging for answers. Anything. Love? Real love? Care from her needy secrets? It seemed all too abrupt to take in, like Ben had stitched himself back together.

"It's lust, Ben," on her exhale his lips crashed against hers. His kiss consumed her as if he'd never get another chance to live this life; to hold her breath as his own.

All at once, she reached for Ben, trying to find purchase on his spellbound skin. She could feel his smile bloom across her lips and the dreamy way he promised she was his tower, his turning point; her truths, sweet and purely debased, as he bent forward to lift her into his arms.

"Wrap your legs around me, beautiful," he murmured against her lips.

Ben's strength supported her easily as if she weighed nothing, making her yelp in response. She held him tightly against her while he pivoted, looking around for her bedroom.

Desiree gasped as the bulge in his briefs began hardening, practically reaching for the apex of her thighs when she dove back in for another kiss.

He couldn't know how desperately she wanted him, how devastated she'd be if this were all a dream.

"Bed's in the kitchen," she ripped her lips away from his, her breath heaving out of her, needy for all he'd give.

Ben grunted, leaning forward to swipe up the last two cards. He showed one, "The Empress." Drawing this card meant her stars aligned; this was real!

"Means," she trailed kisses along his jaw, "I care... about you," she tried answering. "Always. Yours. If. You'll. Have. Me..."

"Planning on it," Ben groaned as he rushed through the kitchen, her heated core roughly slapping against his hardening erection as he went. There was little time to think, little time to react if not to his fevered state.

She hadn't even played with the spells he'd brought. Their properties, while for fun, would only mask his flavor. They would tempt her past what she knew: The Devil's card flashed behind her eyes. She couldn't. Not when he has been the only one for her; the only one she's craved.

Desiree shook her head, her spell brush marking her own auburn waves as it tumbled out behind her hair. She could feel Ben reach for it, his hold on her switching to one arm as if she'd lost a piece of herself.

"All I need is us," she replied truthfully, full of trust as she reached behind her to pull out her bed from where it was tucked away.

"Us," Ben repeated against the shell of her ear, as his reach followed hers. "You're sure about this? About me, Empress?"

"I own what I said," Desiree assured Ben as they both helped settle her bedframe to the floor. "My feelings are mine."

"And the cards?" he questioned, lifting his eyebrow to her as he watched her lay back onto her pretty green bedspread.

"... Are guidance," Desiree whispered, pulling Ben down to her with her legs, still wrapped around his torso.

Ben smirked, "You wanted *my* guidance?" he asked ever so inquisitively as he crawled over the top of her. His arms bracketed her in creating a safe haven she could only dream of, fortified by *him!* Ben rocked forward to plant a kiss on her lips while grinding against her.

"Oh!" she moaned dreamily. "Only yours..."

The drag of his heat against her own made her buck against him.

"Nuh uh," Ben teased, gripping her hip playfully. "You said you wanted mine..."

Ben's face lit up as Desiree realized he intended to give her exactly what she was after.

"Give it to me then," she grinned. "I want all of you, forever."

"... forever." Ben hummed.

About the Author

Angel W. Smith is an avid reader of all things romance who lives just outside of Washington, DC with her husband and two boys. Her love for writing started with all the devotion of a fan fiction writer desperate to rewrite the stars of her favorite dyad. Writing as HisAngel910 on AO3 led her to another author with the same desires. Colla Triti, also known as LostInQueue on Ao3 has been writing since 2018, focusing previously fanfiction. She's incredibly thankful for the friends she's made along the way, which absolutely includes her co-author, Angel W. Smith. The pair have written several stories together as well as their own independent works. Works from both authors can be found here: https://lostinqueue.wixsite.com/my-site/projects-8-1 & https://angelwsmith.wixsite.com/my-site

Awakening Her Powers

BY K.R. HALL

One

We are not alone on Earth. Magic exists everywhere. At one time, witches, wizards, and other supernatural beings lived peacefully among humans. A war between humans and magical beings nearly destroyed the world.

The High Council of Magic gathered the remaining magic-born beings and fled to Thibodaux, Louisiana. A gateway was created to seal away the magical world of Aldea from humans. It has been closely guarded for over three thousand years and over time, humans have forgotten it.

Witches and wizards dress in ordinary clothes and look like humans. They live in typical houses and work everyday jobs. The children go to school and have friends. A wizard's eyes had swirls of gold, and witches had silver swirls in theirs. They come into their powers when they are thirteen. At age twenty, they aged slower and often lived nine hundred years. They didn't show signs of aging until the last seventy-five years.

Briana Foster was a witch, except she had no magical powers. She was picked on at school when her powers never manifested. She was teased for being short. She was only 4'10". The kids called her a disgrace and a good-for-nothing. She tried ignoring the taunts. If they knew she was upset, they'd only tease her more, reminding her she wasn't one of them.

"Why won't they leave me alone?" she cried.

"They are jealous of your sweet nature, so they pick on you so much," her father, Calvin, replied.

Her siblings, Melody and Ned, stood up for her. Her mom, Grace, refused to acknowledge anything was wrong.

At age nine, Calvin's job moved them to another city. Briana prayed that she wouldn't be taunted and would make friends. She was so nervous when her mom registered her that she threw up on the front steps.

Over the summer, the family moved to a new school district. Briana was helping unload the moving truck when she spotted the boy next door. He was tall with short black hair and wore glasses. He reminded her of a computer geek.

"Hi, I'm Briana."

"H-hi," the boy squeaked. "I'm Liam."

Wizard Liam Ward felt the first hints of the mate bond when he was eleven and Briana's family moved in next door. He was too young to understand the mating pull, but he was drawn to Briana. Her black hair came to her shoulders, and her blue sapphire eyes pulled him in.

Liam hated that she had been teased and bullied throughout their school years because she had no magical powers. He watched her from a distance because he was shy.

❧

High school

Briana was in a math class standing in line to ask the teacher a question. Suddenly she cried out with alarm and pain. A boy behind her took a ruler and slammed it between her legs. He was a football player, so his punishment was being suspended from playing the next football game. The boy's teammates and cheerleaders started calling her names each time they passed her in the hallways. Briana was desperate to get her powers but had no idea how.

When he heard about the ruler incident, Liam decided to step in and help her. If the school knew they were dating, he was sure they would stop harassing her. After school, he followed her to the bookstore.

"Briana, right?" Liam asked as he stood beside her. He glanced at the book she held; it was an old issue of Grimm's fairy tales. "Is it any good?"

"Not interested." Briana returned the book and walked to the next aisle, failing to keep him at bay.

He followed her as he tried to project soothing comfort to hurt her. When Briana glanced at him again, he could tell she still wanted to run. She turned her gaze away, hoping he would disappear by not acknowledging him.

"I'm meeting some friends for pizza," Liam said, moving closer. "You want to come?"

"Just because we live next door to each other doesn't mean we have to be friends." Briana stepped sideways, putting more distance between them.

"Maybe another day," Liam said.

"No."

"Can I call you sometime?" Liam asked.

"No. I've heard about your reputation. I'm not interested in being another notch on your bedpost," Briana replied as she moved to leave the bookstore.

"Here's my phone number," Liam said, shoving a piece of paper into her hand.

"I won't ever call."

"I'd like to get to know you."

Liam watched Briana leave. She didn't run, but she wanted to. He could feel her fear, like the thrumming heart of a startled animal. Liam looked older than his actual age of sixteen. He wasn't used to people running from him, especially girls.

"I don't think she likes you," Ryker Hayes said, interrupting his thoughts.

"She will," Liam said, stepping outside. "I've dreamed about her. She's the one."

❧

Briana was frightened and just wanted to go home. She panicked and ran for a block after she turned the corner.

As she neared her home, Briana stopped running. She needed to calm herself so she wouldn't arouse suspicion in her family. She concentrated on the sound of her feet hitting the pavement, the cars driving by, and the loud music as she rounded the next corner. She spotted a few girls that she recognized from school.

Briana started to walk past the girls. One of the girls crossed her arms over her chest, shaking her head as she moved to block her and forced her to stop. Somebody shoved her from behind, and she stumbled, trying to grab anything to stop her from falling. It was useless; she landed on the sidewalk on her hands and knees. Hot tears stung her eyes as the pain shot through her body. She fought back the tears; she wouldn't give them the satisfaction of seeing her cry.

"You are the clumsiest witch," Evangeline laughed.

Briana managed to stand up and brush off her hands. She stepped away from the group, backing up a few steps before turning around to continue home.

When Liam learned about the incident, he was enraged. From that day on, he walked her home.

❧

College

Briana lifted her hand to knock. Before she could, the door swung open, and Liam stood in the doorway, grinning. He stepped aside, holding the door open.

"Hi," Briana said.

He gets sexier every day. Liam had grown into a fine young man. He stood there, wearing a T-shirt and jeans, showing off his well-defined muscles.

"Are you going to come in or just stand there?" Liam asked.

Briana blushed, stepping over the threshold. She always felt better around him; he made her feel more confident. Liam was the epitome of calm. She followed him to the kitchen and sat at the table while he grabbed sodas from the fridge. He handed her one and then sat down across from her.

Briana sipped her Coke. She started hanging out with Liam during their senior year in high school, giving in to his asking her out. They went to the same college. Last summer, she began having crazy thoughts about them together. She thought about giving in to Liam's flirting but was too afraid. She was interested in sex but was a virgin.

"Do you want to talk about what's bothering you?" Liam asked.

"I don't know what you mean," Briana said, trying to be evasive.

"Please tell me what's going on?" Liam asked.

"I just can't," Briana whispered.

"Come on, Briana. You look worried lately. I'm worried about you."

"When we graduate from college next week, I'm going to the human realm," Briana said.

"Why?"

"I need to live someplace where I'm not harassed every day. With no powers, I can blend into the human realm easily."

"Is somebody threatening to hurt you?" Liam reached for her and tugged her over to sit on his lap.

He tucked her head under his chin, holding her securely. She didn't resist. He held her all the time now that they were dating. Liam stroked her hair, running his hand down the length of it and onto her back.

"No. No one is threatening me. I have researched how to get my powers back. Some of the ingredients that I need are in the human realm. If I could stay there, I could try different potions and spells to awaken my magic. It will be okay if it doesn't work because none of them know I'm a witch. I would be safe there."

"Then I'm going with you," Liam said.

"You can't!" Briana said. "All your life, you wanted to be an enforcer for the High Council. If you were to give that up for me, you would resent it and eventually resent me."

"No, I wouldn't," Liam argued.

"You would. We both know it," Briana said. "Not right away, but eventually, you would resent me. And I can't live with that."

"Promise me you will not leave without me. I couldn't stand it if we weren't together," Liam begged. "I love you, Briana."

"I love you too, Liam," she whispered.

Two

A month after graduation, Briana went through the gateway from Aldea into the basement of the general store in Laurel Valley Sugar Plantation in Thibodaux, Louisiana. She had saved money for the last four years. She brought nothing with her, planning on buying what she needed after she found a job. She wanted to tell Liam where he could find her but feared he would talk her into staying.

Briana took a bus to New Orleans, where she found a job. Her tiny apartment was just outside of the city in Estelle.

Every day for the last year, Briana feared someone from Aldea would find her. She hoped Liam would show up; she was disappointed every day he hadn't. Briana had made some friends and had turned down a few dates since her heart belonged to Liam. She was still no closer to finding a way to restore her magic. Sometimes when she felt down on herself, she wanted to return to Aldea, to Liam. She refused to return a failure.

Briana's older sister, Melody, helped smuggle a scrying mirror out of Aldea so that she could keep in contact with her family. They didn't know where she lived, so they couldn't accidentally let it slip. Briana had taken self-defense classes and installed a state-of-the-art home security system to make them feel better about her being alone. Her family wanted her to be happy but thought she would be safer with Liam.

Briana longed to return home to watch fairies frolicking in the gardens and dragons lurking in the forest. She looked to the sky, searching for even a wisp of a cloud, but couldn't see anything more than a brilliant blue sky. She kicked at the long blades of grass sprouting between the cracks of the path that led up to the side of the apartment as butterflies darted around her through the peaceful late summer afternoon.

Briana threw on a T-shirt, jeans, and tennis shoes. Ten minutes later, she was in her Jeep and heading to work. She always drove just a little too fast down the winding gravel roads back in the bayou, but there were rarely other cars on this road, and the gravel certainly wasn't going to hurt her well-worn vehicle.

❧

For eight months, Liam searched for Briana. How could she have left him? He knew they were soul mates, but with her powers gone, she couldn't tell. He discovered she left when he arrived home after his first four months at enforcer training. By then, she was long gone, and her trail was cold.

For the first few months, Liam searched for Briana in Thibodaux, Morgan City, and the surrounding area. This was the last summer to search for Briana. He had to report for his first assignment as an enforcer for the High Council of Magic in September.

Liam returned to Aldea to get a search potion from his friend, Miles Knight, the night before.

"It's been a year since she's been gone, and I can't find her. I need a strong tracking potion," Liam explained.

"We had a shipment of tracking potions arrive on Monday," Miles replied as he moved about the store. "Kendra, have you seen the shipment of tracking potions?"

"Yes," Kendra replied as she exited the back room. "Zane unboxed them, putting them near the scrying mirrors."

"Thanks," Miles said as he headed to the front of the store with Liam close on his heels.

Miles searched the pile of orbs, smiling when he pulled out a hot pink one.

"This is the strongest one available anywhere," Miles explained. "You break it open, and a hot pink trail will lead the way."

"Is there an incantation I need to say?"

"No incantations needed. The trail will begin to fade within ten minutes, so be sure you're ready to follow," Miles replied.

"Thank you, Miles," Liam said.

Liam paid for the potion, then headed to the portal and his Jeep, waiting in Thibodaux.

Liam sat in his Jeep with the engine running and dropped the orb. The orb shattered, and a hot pink trail started quickly. Slamming the door, he followed the path. He followed the trail to New Orleans, stopping at a cluster of apartment buildings.

Liam parked and looked around before exiting his vehicle. He noticed that the trail ended at the door to one of the buildings. He tried to open the door, but it was locked. The apartment numbers with names and buttons were listed on a wall beside the door. He spotted Briana's name, pressed the button, and waited.

Frustrated that Briana wasn't home, Liam returned to his Jeep. He saw movement out of the corner of his eye and turned. He saw a woman leaving the building with a small dog. She didn't pay him attention, so he slipped inside before the door closed.

Standing outside Briana's apartment, the tension he had been carrying for eight months eased a bit now that he knew she was alive and where she lived. Liam placed a spell over her door to tell him when she returned.

Liam headed back to his Jeep and drove down the road, scanning the sides as he went, just in case he spotted her. Liam had gone about half a mile when he rounded a curve and saw Briana walking the road ahead. She turned around to look, and the relief on her face was apparent, even from that distance.

"I'm glad to see you," she said as he pulled beside her. "Oh, Liam!"

"Briana, I can't believe I found you!"

He stepped out of the Jeep and gently gripped her arms, checking her up and down.

"What happened? Are you all right?" Liam asked.

"I'll be okay," she said. "I swerved to miss running over an animal and crashed my car into a tree. I have an enormous headache, and walking in this heat isn't exactly fun. I don't think it's anything serious."

Liam tucked her hair behind her ears. She had a goose egg on her head, likely the cause of her headache. It was going to take more than Tylenol to fix it. Liam tried to keep his facial expression neutral, but his senses were on high alert.

"We need to get you to a hospital," he said. "Someone should take a look at you, just to be safe."

"No, thank you. I'm sure I'm okay."

"I'll take you home so you can shower and change, but then I'll use my magic to heal you," Liam insisted.

"Okay, you can use your magic after I shower and clean up," she sighed.

As she climbed inside his Jeep, Liam took a peek at her firm, round bottom, every curve clearly outlined in her jeans. His mind was overflowing with ideas on things they could do together once she was better.

Three

Liam Ward was the hottest guy she'd ever seen. His eyes could see into her soul. His jaw had enough stubble to cause the best friction on her inner thighs. Her body's reaction to him confused and scared her. Sure, it had been long since she'd seen him, but that was no excuse to throw herself at him. Especially when she couldn't afford distractions. Briana was sure she was close to finding the potion to awaken her magic.

Briana was opening the door as Liam pulled into a parking spot.

"You okay?"

"Yeah. I want to get out of this mugginess and change clothes."

"After you get cleaned up, I'll heal you," Liam said, following Briana inside.

"There are cold drinks in the fridge; help yourself. I'll be out of the shower in a few," Briana called over her shoulder as she headed into the bathroom.

❧

Briana was rinsing her hair when Liam's image popped into her head; he was naked and hard. She wondered what his hands would feel like on her skin. She imagined kissing him. Would he bite her lip?

Briana stepped out and dried off. She pulled her hair into a ponytail, then quickly dressed. She left her bedroom and headed to the living room. She was startled when she saw the raw need in Liam's eyes as she entered the living room. His leg was crossed over the other, blocking her view of his dick.

"Oh. My. God. Please tell me you didn't hear me?"

"I will never lie to you."

"Kill me now," she muttered.

"We're both adults, Briana. I'm glad you're still attracted to me after all this time," he chuckled. "Come sit beside me so I can fix the lump on your head and heal any concussion."

She shuffled to the sofa and sat close enough he could place his hands on her head to heal her.

"I have a confession," Liam began. "I used to dream about my mate as a child."

"Oh. I've heard some magical beings can dream of their fated mates," Briana said. "Have you found her?"

"Yes, I have. I met her when she moved in next door."

"Me?" Briana squeaked.

"Yes, you," Liam smiled.

"Why didn't you ever tell me?"

"When we first met, I didn't understand about mating. As we got older, you were so shy because of the taunting and bullies. You began to withdraw from everyone," Liam explained.

"I didn't know we were mates," she whispered.

"I know. Why do you think I kept asking you out?"

"But your reputation?"

"Is that why you always said no?" Liam asked.

Briana nodded.

"Lori Halsey was mad when I turned her down. I told her I found my mate and was waiting for her to come to me," Liam explained. "She began the rumors. I thought I had put a stop to them before you heard."

"I heard."

"I'm sad that you believed them. We lived next to each other; I thought you knew me better than that," Liam said sadly.

"Liam, I'm sorry. I had people pretend to be my friend and come home with me, but they immediately hung out with Melody and Ned. Some pretended to be my friend to later mock me and belittle me when they discovered I had no powers," Briana cried. "It wasn't hard to believe you would do the same."

Liam pulled Briana onto his lap. He ran a thumb along her jaw, sliding his other hand into her hair, and brought her beautiful face to his. He paused, waiting to see if she would meet him the rest of the way. Sure, they had dated and had been in love, but a lot could have happened while they were separated.

Briana leaned in, lightly brushing her lips to his. As she wrapped her arms around his neck, Liam deepened the kiss. They explored each other's mouths. When she moaned, he drew her closer to his body.

"Briana, I need you," Liam breathed against her mouth.

"I've waited so long for you, Liam. Take me to bed," Briana purred.

❧

BRIANA WATCHED LIAM AS HE WALKED DOWN THE HALL AND couldn't help but notice how his jeans hugged his ass. Her eyes traveled up to his broad, muscular shoulders, and then her gaze roamed down his arms to his hands. She wanted him badly.

Liam stopped to look at her.

"You sure?"

"Yes...Yes, I am." She pulled his head down for a kiss.

"You keep that up, and I'll have to drag you off to have my way with you," he said against her lips.

Briana didn't need any further enticement. She broke out of his hold and ran the rest of the way to the bedroom. She released a squeak when she entered the room and found Liam standing before her. He'd teleported.

"Cheater," she laughed.

Liam pulled his shirt out of his waistband and unbuttoned it, giving her access to his bare chest, where she placed her hands. She pressed a kiss over his heart. Liam sucked in a quick breath as Briana ran the tip of her tongue up his chest.

She slowly ran her hands over his pecs to his shoulders to slide his shirt from his arms. She walked him backward until his legs touched the bed and gave a little push. Liam fell into a seated position.

On her knees in front of him, she removed his shoes. Then ran her hand up the inside of his thigh to his cock. His leg muscles twitched under her hands, and she loved how he reacted to her touch. The way his eyes almost glowed with passion. Her hand cupped him through his pants. Liam pressed into her palm, moaning. Briana unbuckled his belt and unbuttoned his pants.

"Wait," he said, stopping her hands.

He removed his belt and set it beside his shoes. Then rose to slide his pants down.

Briana ran her tongue up his thigh. Liam's soft curse brought a smile to her lips. She craved his touch and needed him over, under, and inside her. She grasped his hard length in her hand and stroked him several times before she licked from base to tip and then took him into her mouth. She made slow strokes with her tongue as she sucked him and knew the moment he teetered on the edge of release.

Their eyes locked. The gold in Liam's brown eyes was so defined that the irises almost glowed. He took hold of her arms and pulled her up to capture her lips with his.

"I wasn't done," Briana pouted.

"You are," Liam replied, pulling her dress over her head.

Heart pounding with anticipation, Briana laughed softly and slipped off her panties. She moved closer and straddled his lap.

She gasped when Liam's mouth covered her left breast. His fingertips raked down her back, over her ass, and pulled her closer to him. Fingers sliding around the curve of her rear to her center, he slid two fingers inside her. Briana moaned as he moved them in and out while rubbing her clit with his thumb. She had lost all control. He picked up his pace until an orgasm cascaded over her.

Liam captured her mouth, thrusting his tongue inside. Briana rubbed her sex on Liam's throbbing shaft between them. Aching to have him inside her, she rose so her entrance was over his head and lowered herself to take him inside.

She moved her hips in a steady rhythm. She loved how Liam made her feel. They were one, connected like two perfectly fitted puzzle pieces. The air filled with their magic, and it only got more intense as they moved closer to their climaxes.

It felt too good to be loved the way Liam loved her. He didn't have to say the words for her to know it. Their growing connection broadcasted their feelings to each other. They were bonding. Each time they touched, kissed, and made love, their link would strengthen.

Liam took hold of her hips and picked up the pace. Briana matched his thrusts until they both cried out in release. Briana collapsed against Liam's chest.

"I love you," he said, kissing her forehead.

She gave him a wide smile as her heart swelled.

"I love you, too," she said against his lips. "I want to spend every day for the rest of my life with you."

"Okay," he said, smiling like he had just won the lottery.

Four

As she had done every day off from her work, Briana went to the St. Louis Cathedral. Practitioners, Tarot cards, bone readings, palm readings, astrologers, and almost every supernatural practice on Earth, set up their tables and tents in the early mornings and stay until the wee hours.

Following her intuition, Briana visited many stalls to find someone who could restore her magic. She tried many of their potions and spells, but as of today, none had worked. This time, Liam was with her.

Madame LaPomeret reminded her of the character Tia Dalma from the *Pirates of the Caribbean* series.

"Divination speaks to the cosmic need for profound love, health, and happiness," Madame LaPomeret said. "Bone throwing is the oldest form of divination."

"I haven't experienced that before."

"I will throw these ancient bones on the table, but the ancestral spirits control the pattern. I interpret what the bones say," Madame LaPomeret explained. "Timelines from your past, present, and future may be exposed. My divination bag includes, among the bleached bones, a dried alligator paw, great-grandmother's hair comb, a piece of bark from an oak tree from Bayou Métairie, and a lock of your hair."

Madame LaPomeret handed Briana a pair of scissors.

"Liam, would you cut it for me?" she asked, holding her hair.

Liam snipped a small strand of hair, then handed the hair and scissors to the woman.

After an invocation and smudging, the woman laid out the cloth in which the bones were wrapped. The casting cloth was embroidered with a circle that was quartered and painted with symbols.

"My ceremonial bundle has been created in the ways of the ancient healing art. Each of the seventy bones is the home for a particular spirit and their unique gifts," Madame LaPomeret said as she cast the bones onto the cloth.

Briana squirmed while Madame LaPomeret looked over the fabric.

"You have a blocking spell on you," Madame LaPomeret said.

"I have a blocking spell on me?" Briana asked.

"Who put a blocking spell on her?" Liam asked at the same time.

"I don't think those are the questions you want to have answered."

"How do I remove a blocking spell?" Briana asked.

"Better," Madame LaPomeret smiled. "Binding spells are black magic. You will need to perform the ritual precisely as I instruct you."

"May I record your instructions?" Briana asked.

"Normally, I would say no, but given the situation, I will allow it."

"Thank you," Briana said, pulling out her cell starting the recording.

"You will need the following: one white plate, a photo of you, Dead Sea salt, rosemary, lavender, verbena, red thread, black thread, holy water, and eight black candles," Madame LaPomeret said. "And this talisman."

The talisman was a gray stone with astrological signs and magical words.

"Thank you," Briana said, accepting it. "Where can I find Dead Sea salt?"

"The New Orleans Pharmacy Museum. Mention my name, and you will be taken to the witch pharmacy."

"Okay."

"First, light the candles, making the sign of a cross while asking the universe for protection. Pour a couple drops of holy water onto the plate while saying, 'In the name of Mother Earth, Mother of the Universe, please bless me in the protection of the higher energy above me.' Next, put your photo on the plate and walk around it three times.

"Place both threads around the photo as protection; red symbolizes protection against evil eyes and sorcery, and black protects against negativity. Place the talisman next to the photo.

"Pray to the universe for help and guidance while dropping seven drops of holy water onto the plate. Pray in the morning and night for seven days, lighting one candle daily and sprinkling the seven drops of holy water. On the last day, take a bath with rosemary, Dead Sea salt, verbena, and lavender," Madame LaPomeret explained.

"Thank you," Briana said. "Will that awaken my powers once the binding spell has been lifted?"

"No. You will need to say this spell while in the bath. 'Goddess of Love and Light, I ask you to awaken my powers this night. By the power of the stars above, so mote it be.'"

❧

A MONTH LATER.

"DO YOU LIKE IT?" LIAM ASKED.

"It's amazing," Briana whispered.

He glanced at the falls. Three cascades of sparkling blue water fell into a pool. Masses of flowers and butterflies surrounded them.

"Is the water cold?"

"No. That's the thing about these falls. They're naturally heated."

He helped her sit on the bank's edge, where she took off her shoes and soaked her feet in the water. She glanced up at him smiling.

"Come, sit with me."

He sat beside Briana. Sitting in Aldea by the falls with her felt right. Liam took his shoes off and dipped his feet in.

"Feels good, doesn't it?" Briana beamed, leaning into his chest.

"It's perfect."

Having Briana in his arms and knowing she was the woman he wanted was better than anything he'd ever experienced. She raised a hand, curling it around his head, pulling his face to hers. She swept her tongue over his lips and drove it into his mouth with an enthusiasm he found irresistible. She pulled back from their kiss, panting. Her eyes were hazy with need.

"That's sexy."

"What?" Liam asked.

"That growling," she purred.

The scent of her desire thickened around them.

He leaned into her, laying her on the grass. Liam kissed her hard, plunging his tongue into her mouth. Briana met his ravaging kiss with her own hunger.

THE END.

About the Author

K. R. Hall started her journey as a reader but quickly learned how much she enjoyed everything about romance, so Karen picked up the pen in 2017 and hasn't looked back. Writing various genres, paranormal romance is her go-to; however, she has a few mysteries and contemporary romances under her belt.

K. R. Hall's favorite books involve characters that aren't perfect and have room to grow or a good mystery you can't quickly solve. She keeps this in mind with each new book and enjoys creating complex worlds where the characters take the stage.

When K. R. Hall is not creating fantastic new worlds for readers to get lost in, Karen enjoys spending time with her husband and two rescue dogs, Sammie and Jake.

Pick up a copy of one of K. R. Hall's books and fall in love today!

https://krhauthor.wixsite.com/krhall

A Cup of Fate

BY AURELIA FOXX

When Lizzy's latest magical mishap impacts the very cute guy at her favorite coffee shop, mayhem and mischief ensues. Lizzy will have to find out how to fix her mistake, and what to do with the conflicting feelings she has for the victim of her witchy mistake.

Nora picked up my Tally Wag Cafe travel mug and it felt like time was suspended for a moment. Felt like being the important words here. I was nowhere near the level of a savant witch who could flex time. Let's be honest, some of the 10 year olds I had been put in class with had more control and mastery than me. I guess my lack of skill came with the territory of only finding my magic and witch ancestry at twenty-five years old. Something I'm told is virtually unheard of. Yet, even after months of training, I was still a miserable fuck up. It was hard not to be discouraged.

Nora lifted the lid and brought the travel mug up to her nose. She sniffed it. Her expression gave nothing away, and a traitorous nugget of hope bloomed in my chest. Not an outright rejection. Progress.

Something had felt right about this potion. I had tried and tried last night, determined to get it right. Batch after batch of failed attempts found their way into my toilet.

Then, around midnight, I had made this last batch, the one currently in Nora's palm. I knew this was the last one I would be able to muster for the evening. So, I took some time to center myself and I put in everything I had left. When my magic left me, there was a different feeling to it, and as I finished the last steps of the potion, the bubbling and smoky haze clearing, I had felt something akin to peace. It had felt right.

Nora dipped the tip of her pinky finger in the potion and took a lick. Her eyebrows bunched and a second later she reached into her purse, uncorked a vial I unfortunately knew all too well by now, and took a swig.

My whole body drooped in my chair as Nora closed my travel mug and placed it on the edge of our small circular table.

"It was better," Nora assured me with a small smile. She patted my hand like an elderly grandmother might do to reassure her grandchild. Nora was technically only a year or so older than me, but nonetheless it had the same comforting effect.

I still wasn't sure why Nora had taken me on as a student when no one else would. All I knew was that I was glad she had. She had become something akin to a sister to me. It was crazy to think those words when we hadn't known each other long. Still, whatever the reason, weird codependency, or something more magical and fated, it was true.

"Better but still awful?" I asked.

"No, I really mean it this time. It was better. For a second, I thought you might have actually done it. But then..." She paused, worrying her lower lip as her eyes became unfocused. She was lost in thought for a bit, before she turned back to me, a half-smile on her face. "I don't exactly know what's wrong with it. It just didn't feel or taste quite right; something felt slightly off. I'll have to do some tests in my brew room to pinpoint exactly what went wrong."

I glared at the travel mug now placed on the table between us. I had been so sure I had gotten it. Seemed my intuition was as defective as my potion making skills.

A heaviness settled over me and I felt my previous blossoming hope shrivel up and die. I pulled my chair back abruptly, wincing at the loud scraping sound on the coffee shop's floors.

"I'm getting another coffee," I announced. This felt like a two-coffee day, maybe even a three-coffee day.

Nora grabbed her purse from beside her and stood up. Her chair was perfectly quiet as she pushed it back. "I could go for another one too."

We both made our way back to the ordering line. Luckily, we weren't there at rush hour and within less than ten minutes, we were on the way back to our table, hot drinks in hand. It was warm enough in the shop, but the crisp fall air from outside called for cozy drinks and small pastries. The thought now in my mind, I was debating going back to get a small pastry when I ran right into a wall of muscle.

I quickly put my coffee down on the nearest table, which just so happened to be ours, priorities, and then bent down to pick up whatever had been dropped.

Books, pens, and a notebook were quickly snatched up by me, and the person I ran into. As I straightened, my gaze focused on who I was going to have to apologize to. Our eyes met and I froze. A pair of brilliant emerald, green eyes stared back at me, and I was instantly drawn to them, so much so that I believed for a moment that magic was pulling us to one another and keeping us locked in a heady staring match.

Someone called out an order in the background, and I jolted slightly. I yanked my gaze away from the stranger and quickly took in the rest of this man. Slightly wavy blonde hair, firm jaw line, and muscled chest, arms, legs.

The man positioned the items he picked up in a neat pile in his arms, before smoothing his crisp white dress shirt and navy-blue dress pants. He turned his gaze to me.

"Thanks for helping," he said, giving a meaningful look to his items still in my grip.

I blushed, all but shoving his things at him.

He chuckled as he grabbed them and positioned them neatly with the rest of his pile.

He then reached for his coffee which he seemed to have also placed on our table when we collided. His fingers were mere inches from it when the urge to say something, anything, came over me.

"Sorry for bumping into your body—uh, I mean you," I blurted.

Nora chuckled behind me, and I turned to level her with a glare.

When I turned my attention back around, the guy was smirking. "It's OK, me and my body weren't hurt." He winked at me and finished picking up his coffee.

I watched him take a step, pausing to sip his coffee, and even though I'd already made a fool of myself, part of me didn't want him to go. I didn't know why I didn't want him to go, or what I wanted from him if he did stay, all I knew was that him leaving so soon felt wrong.

"Hey," I said. Making him pause and turn to face me. "Do you come here often?" I stilled, that was the worst pick up line of all time. With a mental kick to whatever stupid neuron fired that gem, I continued. "I mean,.." My eyes snagged onto his travel coffee mug, the same as mine. "I see you have a coffee mug from here, so that probably means you come here a lot, and if you do, well... maybe we can meet again,if you want..."

He caught my gaze, which was flitting between his coffee mug, the floor and somewhere over his head. A jolt of something zinged up my arms as our eyes locked once again, the green of his irises seeming to glow brighter for a moment.

"Do I want to meet up with you?" he said, his voice a little off. "That is only my wildest dream, my one true wish. Oh, how you bless me."

I blushed with both embarrassment and anger at his words. He didn't have to be so sarcastic about it. Who had I been kidding? He's way out of my league. Just another stupid mistake to add to my mountain of failures.

"Message received." I said, through gritted teeth. Then, I turned to Nora, "How about we have our drinks back at your house?"

Nora nodded as she made a move to follow me, but, she stopped, staring at something over my shoulder.

I followed her gaze and saw that the guy was still there, staring at me. Anger rushed through me. I had gotten the gist of his rejection; he didn't need to stay to see how his sarcastic remark would affect me.

I opened my mouth to tell him off—screw the high road—when I felt Nora's hand rest on my shoulder. She gave me a small head shake.

I lifted an eyebrow at her in question. Nora was usually the first to tell me to stand my ground and not let people walk all over me.

"We need to go," Nora simply said, quickly picking up all her things. "Now,Lizzy" she urged as I stood there, momentarily frozen in confusion. I didn't question her. I wouldn't, not when she looked like she did now. It was the same, 'I mean business' expression she wore when one of my spells or potions was about to go way wrong and she needed my full attention.

I quickly gathered my purse, my failed potion in my to-go coffee tumbler, as well as my new coffee and followed her out the door.

A few feet towards the parking lot, I asked her what was going on.

"That guy you were trying to flirt with," she said, looking behind and speeding up in response to what she saw. "Well, he's following us."

I tried to look back, but she tugged me forward and to keep my balance I had to abandon that pursuit.

"Don't look back," she ordered sternly. "Something is off, either he found out what we are and he's messing with us, or... well, I don't know. He's looking at you like you hung the sun and the moon, and I don't think he's faking it. No ones that good of an actor."

"He's what?" I asked shrilly.

"Look, babe, you know I love you, but what you did back there wasn't top notch flirting—totally cute, don't get me wrong— but not enough to make a man look at you the way this man is looking at you. Even the sexiest woman alive would have trouble making a man she met for the first time look at her the way that man is looking at you."

An involuntary shiver ran up my spine. I had no idea what was going on, but either scenario Nora had proposed was not bad.

We took a sharp turn around the building and quickly walked towards Nora's pedo van, at least that's what I called it. She called it Norman.

It was a slightly rusted large white van. The kind people would turn into a tiny house on wheels. In Nora's case, it was more of a tiny tea parlor and potion studio on wheels. Nora was a total nerd and granny at heart. She liked to be able to have a comfy couch, and her nerd den at hand always. I won't lie, it was kind of awesome, you would never guess from the outside what the inside held. As my favorite sci-fi show would say, it was bigger on the inside. Yes, I was a total nerd too, but I embraced it.

We rounded the side of the van and Nora got into a fighting stance. Her hand hovered over her purse like it was a gun in one of those old west cowboy showdowns. Knowing Nora, what she had in that purse could be just as debilitating as any gun.

"What do you want." Nora said to the man approaching us.

I felt severely under-prepared with a coffee in both hands, a purse without any cool potions inside, and my best fighting move being a crotch kick.

"Beauty, why did you leave?" The man called out as he jogged to us. "You didn't allow me to look at your gorgeous lips and firm butt long enough! You must have been carved by the gods!"

"Ummm..." I didn't know what to say. He didn't exactly have full on creepy stalker vibes, which was way weird because the way he was speaking about me was full on Looney Tunes.

"What do you want?" Nora asked again, this time with more force. Her hand was now inside of her purse, which was bad news for this guy, but made me feel somewhat better...

"Only to admire your friend." He looked at me adoringly. "I'm a scientist. It's in my nature to observe and discover the magical and beautiful mysteries of life. Please allow me the honor to bask in your magical, godlike presences. To learn what you truly desire and make it happen. To..."

Three things happened then, all within seconds of each other. The man took a step toward me, reaching out, as Nora pulled a tiny vial from her purse, and at the same time, the man tripped on his own feet, his coffee spilling from his travel mug. Everything else fled my mind as my attention zeroed in on the sparkling pink liquid that fell from his travel mug.

Pieces started to fit together in my mind. Identical travel mug, screwed up witch, messed up potion. My heart nearly stopped when the final piece clicked in place.

"Stop!" I yelled. It was meant for Nora and whatever potion she was about to chuck at him, but it effectively stopped him too.

He looked stricken, like a puppy who was just hit. "I'm sorry. I was too forward. Of course, you don't want to be touched. Please forgive me, I'm a moron. I'm not worthy of..."

I cut him off. "Give me your travel mug."

His face lit up and fuck it, it was adorable. He handed the mug to me as if it was some kind of crown jewel.

"Of course! Anything for someone as wonderful as..."

I ignored whatever he was saying and turned to Nora.

"My potion," I said, lifting the mug I took from the guy. "His coffee," I said, lifting the mug I had been carrying.

I thought Nora would look worried, but instead she relaxed and let out a laugh. A laugh!

"Oh! That makes sense! One second." With that, she left me alone with the guy and climbed into Norman.

I was still processing the whiplash of the situation and feeling slightly stunned. The guy, not so much. He got up close to me.

"Are you liking my coffee?" he asked.

"Umm.." I looked at him, then to the open door of the van, then back to him.

"Ya, it's great."

"Then why aren't you drinking it?"

Fuck. Fuckity fuck, fuckers. I mentally urged Nora to come back fast, assuming she probably ditched me to get some kind of antidote. At least, that better be what she was doing.

"What's your name?" I asked, trying to distract him.

"I'm Dorian, gorgeous. What's your name?" He was giving me full on smolder eyes and, even though I knew it was my potion causing this, my love potion, heat rushed to my cheeks.

"Lizzy," I said honestly.

Mentally, I was berating myself. A love potion was supposed to be an easy one. The type of potion I was told young witches would fool around with. You couldn't make someone love somebody else, that was beyond the scope of any magic. Love itself was too powerful a magic to ever be truly reproduced. But you could make a potion that made someone adore you, in a non-sexual way. Which was the one I had attempted.

It was completely harmless. Or at least, it should have been. Magic wasn't only about saying words and mixing ingredients. Magic had a spirit, a life of its own. The intent behind magic casting helped shape the magic. Similarly, magic left a mark on the person who wielded it. Which is why many dark magic users turned nasty themselves. The darkness of their intent as well as the spell created poisoned them inside and out.

Because of this magical rule, an adoration spell made and used without any ill intent, or for playing a prank, would dissipate if used for opposite reasons, like coercion or control. It was kind of like the witch made a promise when creating the spell, the magic was created with that promise in mind, and when that promise was broken, so was the contract the witch made with the magic, which, in turn, broke the spell.

On top of that, this particular spell should only last about thirty minutes.

All that information should have made me feel better, but it didn't. I wouldn't feel better until the spell my potion put on Dorian was broken. Guilt and fear swirled in my gut. Guilt for accidentally giving him a potion, fear my potion was defective and Nora's antidote wouldn't work. I felt nauseous.

"Lizzy," Dorian said on a sigh. "Short for Elizabeth?" he asked.

"Aliza actually."

"A more beautiful name I have never heard!" Dorian exclaimed. "A beautiful name for a beautiful lady. A lady who would make any man want to become a poet. Lizzy, oh Lizzy, oh you make me dizzy. You make my heart all... fizzy. When I am with you, I am never chilly..."

"Got it!" Nora exclaimed, peeking her head out of the van. "Get him in here."

Relief coursed through me. "Want to come in the van?" I asked Dorian, cringing immediately after the words left my mouth. I might have known this wasn't a pedo van, and that I was inviting him in to help him, but he certainly didn't.

Dorian, however, didn't give it a second thought, and he jumped into the van. I quickly followed and Nora shut the door behind us.

I took a second to ground myself. As I took a big breath in, I noted the familiar surroundings. Pink fluffy carpet, mini kitchen with mini fridge, fold out couch bed in the corner, and a mix of herbs, cast iron pots and other random potion items hung from the ceiling and walls. To top it all off, a small TV was suspended from the roof of the van and a small gaming console lay on the armrest of the couch.

Nora was sitting on said couch with a vial in her hand.

"Easy fix," Nora said, pulling me back into the issue at hand. "You certainly aren't the first person this happened to. And on the bright side this must also mean you got it right... So, congrats!"

"Ya, maybe," I said unsure. Nora had tasted my potion and she said it was almost right, but something had felt off. She had good instincts, instincts that I hadn't seen be wrong yet. She also didn't sound fully sure when she said that last part. The one about me getting it right.

"Come sit," Nora said to Dorian.

He spared her a glance but then went back to staring at me in wonder.

I groaned. "Come on Dorian. Let's have a seat." I took his things from his hands and placed them on the counter before gesturing to the couch.

"Alright," Nora said, turning to me. "The plan is we give him the antidote potion, when we see it's working, we send him on his merry way, and then we get out of here fast, before he fully gets out of the post-potion haze."

"You know he's sitting right beside me and just heard our plan, right?" Witches weren't a secret anymore, but we also weren't generally liked by humans. That and giving a human a potion without their consent meant we were both in huge trouble if someone found out.

"New lesson, Lizzy. When a person is under a spell like this one, it will feel like they are in a dream of sorts. If we are gone before the spell fully clears, he will probably think he imagined it all. If he reports it, but no longer has the spell on him, it will be hard to prosecute us. Witch lawyers cut down things like this all the time. The courts usually let them go too, as they have much bigger fish to fry." She uncorked the small bottle and handed it to me. "Let's do this."

I guessed the faster I got this over with, the faster I could process this whole experience and move on. I let out a sigh and turned to Dorian who was sitting patiently beside me.

"Here," I said, handing him the vial, which he took with all the care in the world. "Drink that."

"Of course, goddess!" He lifted the vial to his lips and chugged the contents.

Nora and I watched him closely.

At first nothing happened. Nora frowned in confusion; my heart started to thump. It seemed something was wrong with my potion.

Then, ever so slowly Dorian's expression shifted, he frowned, his eyebrows bunching.

"Where am I?" he asked.

"And that's our queue." Nora said. She grabbed Dorian's things and shoved them at him. He took them mechanically, his movement stilted.

Nora didn't waste a moment and immediately moved to wrench the van door open. She gestured to me to help nudge Dorian out of the van. Dorian was still confused so he followed our gentle shoves without much protest. Once fully out of the van, he stood there, looking at us with slightly unfocused eyes.

Nora went to pull the door closed when Dorian's hand suddenly flew out, stopping the sliding door from moving.

Shit.

"Where am I?" he asked again, more lucid this time.

"How are we supposed to know?" Nora retorted, feigning ignorance. "You just walked up to our van and tried to get in. Well, not today, buddy!"

He faltered for a moment, his right leg took a step backward and Nora took the opportunity to try to close the door again. She didn't move it more than a few inches when Dorian straightened and stopped the door from closing once again.

His eyes were steely and clear as he looked us over. "You're witches."

My blood ran cold. Double shit.

"And you're a pink rainbow unicorn. Get out of here, creep." Nora said, trying and failing to pull the door shut. Being a witch didn't come with superhuman strength, unfortunately.

Dorian wasn't falling for it. "I study human witch relations and magical theory for a living. I think I know what I'm talking about. You both are witches, and you used a spell on me. No, a potion."

And... triple shit with a watery bowel movement on top. Nora and I shared a concerned look.

"Tell me what's going on or I'm calling the cops. I remember bumping into you, then taking a sip from my drink... everything is a bit fuzzy after that." His face scrunched in concentration as if he was trying to make out the details.

As far as I was concerned, we were screwed either way. We couldn't make him forget, we couldn't ditch him and run, because then he would call the cops and it would make us look really bad if this came to a legal matter. He was also a scholar studying magic and witches. He wouldn't fall for any old lie. In my mind that left me one option, the truth, and maybe we could reason with him.

So that's what I did. I let the story come out, told him everything, and prayed he let it go.

When everything was out there, he stood in thought for a moment. The silence stretched over us, oppressive in its weight.

"I'll let it go." Blessed relief flowed through me. "On one condition." My mind plummeted back to the earth, leaving a crater from the strength of its fall.

Nora opened her mouth, but I cut her off. Out of the two of us, she was usually the more impulsive and vocal one. This was my mess. I would handle it.

"What's your condition?"

"I told you, I study magic for a living. My condition is that you both provide me with, let's say, three hours of time where I can ask any question I want about magic and witch life. It's been impossible to get a witch to answer my questions seriously."

Ok, that was doable I thought. We would have to be careful on how we answered his questions, but three hours of questions was better than cops.

"And," he continued, pausing for a moment as if he was thinking on his words, before blurting out in one breath, "I get to kiss you."

"Say what now?" Nora said.

"On the cheek of course," Dorian continued, sheepishly "Just to make sure there are no lingering effects of the potion."

Nora laughed and I gave her a death glare.

"Sounds reasonable to me," she said cheekily.

I looked between my friend and Dorian, both waiting expectantly for my reply and I gave in. This situation was technically my fault, and a kiss wouldn't kill me.

"Deal."

Dorian grinned. For someone who had just got unexpectedly drugged with a potion, he sure was chipper. Though I guessed that if he really was someone studying witches, this was almost like winning the lottery for him. Witches were notoriously tight lipped to outsiders.

Dorian moved all his things, minus his travel mug which was still in the van, to one arm and then took out his wallet from his back pocket. He slid out a business card from it and handed it to me.

Dorian Longley was written in plain black text on the top, I briefly noted the phone number and other basic information on the card, then went back to the matter at hand.

No one moved. Dorian cleared his throat awkwardly and I took that as my cue.

I moved so that I was standing outside the van beside him, and I turned my head to the side to give him access.

He moved in, giving me a quick peck to my cheek, then lingered for a moment. I felt warmth radiating from him and his lips, the scent of aftershave and manly musk. Then he slowly pulled away. Our gazes connected, lingered once again. There was something there. Some kind of energy passing between us. I couldn't quite put my finger on it, and then he pulled away, breaking the moment.

Silence stretched for a moment before Nora broke the silence.

"So?" she asked.

Dorian cleared his throat. "No unadulterated admiration," he said, though his gaze held a touch of heat.

"Then we're good here. Here's my number." She handed him a small piece of scrap paper with her number on it. I didn't know when she had had time to scrawl that out but that wasn't my biggest concern right now.

"We'll talk later and iron out when we will meet," Nora added.

Dorian nodded at her, his gaze going back to me for a moment before he took a step backward. "I'll see you then. If there is one thing I'm good at, it's finding information, so I hope you two keep your end of the bargain. It wouldn't be too hard with my skill set to find out where you both are and get the cops involved."

"Ya, ya. See you at hour one of the interrogation," Nora quipped, retreating farther into the van.

Dorian's stare was back on me, almost expectantly.

"Bye." I said lamely, all thoughts of possible replies had fled my brain.

He simply nodded, a slight frown on his face as he turned and walked away.

As soon as I was back in the van, Nora closed the door and locked it. Then she made her way to the couch and sat on its edge. Now that we were alone, her easy going and carefree attitude was gone. Lines of worry creased her forehead.

"What's wrong?" I asked her.

"Well, the antidote seems to have worked, but it wasn't instantaneous. It took a second to kick in which isn't normal, and I have this nagging feeling... I don't know. I think we may need to follow up with him. Just to be safe. It's probably a good thing that we made this deal with him. I'll be able to double-check everything is OK next time we see him and do some tests on your potion in the meantime too."

"Ya, I guess so," I replied, my gaze on the closed van door, and my thoughts on the man who had been on the other side of them.

"You totally like him," Nora teased, flopping back onto the couch pillows.

I opened my mouth to deny it, but then shut it. I had only gotten to know him when he wasn't under the influence of a potion for mere moments. Yet there were some odd elements to what happened. My gut had told me the last batch of my potions was right. Something had drawn me to keep talking to him so he wouldn't leave while we were in the coffee shop, and something had definitely passed between us when he had kissed my cheek.

It could all be coincidence; it was probably nothing. Or maybe, just maybe, there was such a thing as fate and this man was meant to be in my life. A picture of his smirking lips and deep green eyes flashed in my mind's eye as an unbidden smile graced my lips. A warm gooey feeling was starting to simmer inside me, and I couldn't help but think that fate had played a role today. Call it witchy intuition, or womanly instinct, but whatever this thing we had between us was, I felt it had a great possibility of turning into something truly, and spectacularly magical.

I HOPE YOU ENJOYED THIS STORY! BE SURE TO LEAVE A REVIEW online! It is always very appreciated and helps us authors in so many ways! More stories are always in the work so don't forget to sign up to my newsletter by going to my website www.aureliafoxx.com to not miss out on any details on upcoming releases or pre-order goodies!

About the Author

Aurelia Foxx is a Canadian Author of romance books. She likes to showcase the power of love and the magic of a story. Her romance books range from clean romance, young adult, to new adult, adult, and spicy romance. You can expect a good amount of banter, quirky humor and swoon-worthy scenes thrown into that mix.

When she is not writing, you can find her spending time in nature, crafting, or letting her creative mind dream up a million and one new ideas.

Join Aurelia Foxx Online

Join Aurelia Online by visiting her website and signing up to her newsletter. You can also find her on the social platforms below.

Facebook

Instagram

Follow Aurelia on Amazon and don't miss out on any new releases!

https://www.amazon.ca/Aurelia-Foxx/e/B0CH56Y3P5/ref=dp_byline_cont_book_1

Office Hex

BY REBECCA CONRAD

Ever since freshman year, Basil has been suffering from a crush on his classmate, Sage. As clever and pretty as she is, they're all wrong for each other. That's what he's been telling himself for the past six years anyway, especially since they started sharing an office space.

One rainy morning, his hopes for solitude are dashed when Sage comes into the office to catch up on work. Then everything goes wrong. Thunderstorm. Power outage. Sage finding an unlabeled magic pink powder.

*

Grateful for the waterproofing spell he had carefully mastered, Basil–and his ever present book–arrived at the TA's office dry as a crow's bone. The early hour and threatening storm left the short trek from his dorm to the office silent as the other witches and warlocks remained in their cozy beds. He knew the office would be just as deserted, save the one TA who could not leave her post.

The young witch, Alexis, somehow magicked herself into a bluetooth device, and no one had been able to find a reversal. As the door silently clicked shut, a rainbow of LED lights came to life on the windowsill. "Good morning, Basil."

"Morning, Alexis." He sat down at his desk with a sigh, rubbing his eyes. He'd been up for the better part of the night at the library working on his dissertation. Now he needed a few quiet hours to answer emails and input grades before returning to the library. He flicked his fingers behind him, the water kettle in the corner starting to bubble and he reached for his mug and box of lapsang souchong tea.

"You're here early."

He pushed his glasses up his nose. "I wanted to get these grades in."

"Sage had the same idea. She should be here soon."

His hand froze over the mouse.

There went his quiet morning alone.

Sage had been disrupting his peace since freshman year, but the tension ramped up when they began sharing the office. He didn't like that she was always looking over his shoulder and offering unsolicited suggestions, and he hated it even more that she was always right. And he definitely hated the crush he'd been nursing almost since they met.

At first, he tried to rationalize his attraction and ignore it. But now that they were working in the same office, it was all he could think about. Too many moments he couldn't quite forget. Like May Day.

As he answered emails, he drank another mug of the smoky-smelling tea. He was almost finished with one response when his phone buzzed. He knew who it was before he even looked at the screen.

Sage.

Basil let out a sigh, reading the message.

Stopping at the cafe. Want something?

He shook his head, typing a reply. *No, thanks. I have tea in the office.* He debated for a moment, then typed a second message. *See you soon.*

She asked him that every workday, and he'd never taken her up on it. He'd always wondered what it would be like if he said yes. If her offer meant anything to her.

He went back to his emails, trying to ignore the anticipation brewing in his gut as he counted down the minutes until Sage appeared.

The door opened and there she was.

A cloud of dark hair, a tight strappy top, and those pouty berry-red lips she was always biting. She wore a flouncy little skirt that ended above her knees. He couldn't quite take his eyes off the patch of skin between the hem of her skirt and the tops of her stockings. *How was she not cold?*

Sage's face was flushed, breath a little ragged, and her cardigan and hair sparkled with raindrops. She sat at her desk across from him and gave him a smile. "Morning, Basil."

"Morning. Do you have a lot of work today?"

She nodded. "Put off grades last week 'cause I was behind in my own stuff."

"Mm."

"You look tired. Hot date last night?"

"What?" he choked. "No, I was in the library." *Smooth. Why don't I just say "I have no life?"*

"Didn't see you."

He cocked his head. "You looked for me?" *It doesn't mean anything.*

She shrugged. "Not specifically. I usually look for people I know."

He started to say something, but then Alexis interrupted.

"Why didn't you greet me?"

Sage rolled her eyes, grinning at Basil. "I greeted you when I texted to let you know I was coming in. Now, I have work to do." They sat in silence for a while, both working on their own tasks.

Basil was deeply aware of her presence in the office. The cramped, narrow room had them brushing by each other, casual, light touches that left her dark vanilla scent on him at the end of the day.

Sage finished her coffee, slurping the last bit in a way that made him wince. The light drizzle he'd walked through earlier had turned into a full-on storm. Sage sighed, looking out the window as lightning flashed.

"Shit, even the best waterproofing spell won't hold up against *that* on the walk home."

He glanced outside. This was stay-at-home weather. Tea, books, and his cat. He would have stayed home, but he worked better in the office. And now he was going to have to spend who knew how long with Sage in this tiny, cramped room.

"Alexis, how long will the storm last?" he asked.

Alexis's light flashed. "Break in the storm projected for noon, however–" She broke off, light blinking rapidly. "Power's going out all over campus, I–"

The lights flickered before the room plunged into darkness. Muffled shouts of surprise came from the hall. Alexis would be fine. She'd be back when the power came on, no worse for wear.

"Guess that's all the work we'll be getting done today," Sage announced.

Basil grunted in agreement and moved to the altar, lighting some of the candles with a snap of his fingers. He heard the click of a lighter and turned.

Sage lifted her chin in challenge. "What? I like the clicky noise." She set a lit candle on the windowsill and retrieved another. "Y'know, I always found it weird you're the one out of the two of us to use magic to light candles. I thought you would understand the attraction to non-magical items, especially with your love for physical books and that huge-ass printer you insist on having." She pointed the lighter at his printer perched on a file cabinet.

Basil rolled his eyes. "I don't need *toys* to get a job done."

Sage's eyebrows lifted, and she snorted. She set the lighter down deliberately, then, holding his gaze, lifted her arms, snapping her fingers on both hands.

All the unlit candles ignited, illuminating the entire room.

She cocked her head and grinned. "I'm good with my hands."

It was then Basil realized certain *implications* of his earlier statement. He huffed and looked away before sitting back down and opening his book. If he couldn't work, and he couldn't leave, at least he could do something he liked. Especially if it meant he could ignore Sage. And her hands.

"I'm going to organize Alexis's mail. It's taking over her desk."

This was why his crush was a bad idea; Sage wasn't happy unless she was getting involved in things she didn't need to be into.

"Whatever makes you happy." As he continued reading, Sage rustled envelopes and catalogs, muttering to herself.

"Hey, Basil?" she asked, turning around, holding a small and battered brightly colored cardboard box. "This is for Alexis, but it says 'fragile' and looks pretty destroyed."

He wrinkled his brow. "Does it say who it's from?"

She shook her head. "Label's water damaged beyond what any spell can do for it." She turned the package over in her hands, frowning before looking at him again. "Maybe there's a packing slip inside? We can at least let her know what she ordered was damaged. Maybe she can get her money back?"

"I think getting her money back isn't currently in her top fifty concerns."

Sage rolled her eyes, sliding behind him to get to the altar, her fingertips brushing against his shoulders.

"Just because our dear friend and co-worker is trapped in a home assistant doesn't mean we can't support her. Besides, she can't open it herself to find out." Sage narrowed her eyes and Basil's face heated in shame. She was right.

He got to his feet, looking over her shoulder as she opened the box. She sifted through layers of blue tissue paper before holding up a small vial with a glittery pink powder in it.

"It's cracked," she said. "Not enough for it to have spilled, but... here." She handed it to him. "Let's empty it into a new thing for her." She opened the wooden chest with supplies on the altar, looking for another vial.

He sighed as he turned the vial over. The dust inside sparkled, catching the candlelight, shifting from pink to purple to gold. His mouth felt dry. He should probably drink some water before he made another cup of tea. The magic coming off the vial felt strong, thrumming in time with his pounding heart. It smelled like Sage—or maybe Sage was standing way too close.

She held up an empty jar, shaking it at him impatiently.

He gave her a nod and wiggled the cork, trying to be mindful of the damaged glass. The seal was tight, and just as the cork gave, his hand slipped. The sparkling substance burst out of the bottle, covering both of them in glittering dust.

Their eyes met.

"Apologies. Allow me–" He raised his hand, preparing to sweep the glitter off her face with a cleansing spell. At least magic made spilling glitter less annoying.

But his fingers got caught in her dark hair.

Her eyes went wide as she inhaled sharply and Basil jerked his hand away, surprised at the way his stomach flipped. He felt as if he'd been struck by lightning. His skin felt tight, his earlier sleepy rainy day mood gone, replaced with a sudden sharp awareness of Sage.

"I hope this isn't dangerous," he said.

"Depends how you define dangerous." She gave him a sheepish grimace, waving the packing slip weakly. "It's Lust Dust."

Fucking hell.

He let out a frustrated breath and pushed his glasses up his nose, closing his eyes. Aimed at intimate partners, Lust Dust was one of a handful of magical 'relationship enhancers' that heightened sensation and loosened inhibitions. But it wouldn't work on strangers; even magic couldn't create feelings from nothing.

Basil inhaled. "It smells like vanilla." He let out another sigh and felt his cock twitch. That was odd.

She wrinkled her nose. "Vanilla? No, it smells like that smoked tea you're always–shit!" she exclaimed, clapping a hand over her mouth.

His eyes narrowed, thoughts going a million miles an hour, but he couldn't latch onto any of them long enough to think. "Why would you think it smells like my tea?"

"Why do you think it smells like vanilla?" she shot back. Her cardigan slipped from her shoulder, revealing the strap of her top. A simple thing he'd seen a thousand times before; three times that morning even. (Not that he was counting.) But now, under the muted glow of candlelight, with her skin sparkling in that shimmering dust, he wanted to lick her until the glitter disappeared and all that was left was her skin.

He shook his head. "That doesn't mean anything. You always wear vanilla perfume. The office reeks of it."

She lifted her chin triumphantly. "So you admit the Lust Dust smells like something you associate with *me*."

Basil's face heated, the way it always did around her when she was giving him that look. He frowned. "I gave a logical answer. I don't have a crush on you."

She cocked her head, looking at him intently as if she could read his mind. Her tongue ran across her teeth and he had the distinct feeling she would eat him.

Sexually.

Not that he'd mind. He shook his head.

"Who said anything about a crush?" Her voice was deceptively sweet.

His eyes widened as he pushed his glasses up his nose. She had him trapped. "I do not have a crush on you," he repeated. He blinked, his tone unconvincing, even to his ears. "You're ridiculous to even think such a thing."

"Ridiculous? You're the one who can't stop looking at my tits."

His gaze snapped to hers, face burning. He'd never been that obvious before.

She grinned that feral cat grin, the one which foretold imminent doom upon those at whom she directed it. It was dazzling.

Dangerous.

"I think we should kiss," she said.

He shook his head. "That's the Lust Dust talking."

"So you've never wanted to kiss me before now?"

Their eyes locked and Basil knew what she was alluding to.

May Day, two years ago. A party before finals. Far too much mead. The ribbon dance.

In a flash of reckless impulsivity, he'd grabbed the other end of Sage's ribbon. He'd told himself it was because she looked so sad, waiting for a partner, and he couldn't leave her alone like that, but the truth was he wanted to dance with her. She gave him a warm, bright smile, keeping her eyes on him as they spun, clutching the ribbon until it broke. He pulled her to him with magic, and they held each other as other couples spun around them.

It could've been *the* moment, *their* moment, but then someone jostled them and the spell was broken.

She'd slipped through his fingers as easily as sand, and Basil decided then it wasn't meant to be. They would never share more than that moment.

"Prove it," she said.

"What?"

"Prove you don't have a crush on me."

"How?"

She shrugged, smiling up at him with that sweet, dangerous grin. "Kiss me."

He huffed, shaking his head. Preposterous. Just like almost everything else she said or did.

"Alright, well if you don't, I'll have to assume you *do* have a crush on me and are scared."

The Lust Dust was definitely taking full effect now. He could feel it in the rush of his blood, the racing of his pulse, the throb of his cock. He could kiss her, but it would confirm all the things he'd been ignoring and then she'd *know*.

He shoved a hand through his hair, glaring at her.

Her eyes traveled down and up his body before she did that head-tilt-smile combo. "Looks like your temper isn't the only thing I can make rise."

"Don't for one second think you have any effect on–"

"Your boner?" she suggested with that sharp little smile. She shook her head. "Of *course* it's not me. It's the Lust Dust doing that." Her voice was a purr. "You know it only works if you're attracted to the other person, right?" She stepped closer to him, breasts brushing against his chest, and he swore her nipples tightened through her shirt. She was playing with the zipper on his hoodie, glancing up at him. "You have a crush on me."

"It's not a crush," he ground out. *It was so much more than that.*

"Then what is it?"

He shook his head. "We don't have to do this. We can go home and shower."

She raised a brow.

"Separately," he hastily clarified.

White teeth sunk into shiny, full, berry-red lips. "Is that what you want?"

He clenched his jaw. No. But any feelings he wanted to explore, he would. Later. Alone. In a cold shower.

"It shouldn't be an issue, right?" he asked quietly. "It's not as if we have romantic feelings for one another."

Lust Dust amplified feelings that already existed. His only feelings for Sage were annoyance. Usually.

She dropped her gaze, pulling her cardigan up over her shoulder.

"Might be an issue for me," she said so softly he wasn't sure he'd heard her correctly.

"What do you mean?"

His heart was hammering, his mouth was dry, and he could not stop staring at Sage. The flush creeping up her face from her chest, the way she kept licking her lips as she stared back.

She shook her head, those smoky brown waves brushing against her shoulders. She was acting... shy? Was it possible she felt the same way?

His fingers itched to touch her hair again, to bury his hand at the back of her neck and cradle her head. She twirled a lock of her hair between her fingers, watching him with a heated look that warmed his blood. His cock twitched again, and he shifted his weight, trying to alleviate the building pressure.

"You're right," he agreed. "We need to kiss."

"Why?"

"Because otherwise, I'm going home to masturbate until my hand falls off." That settled it. The Dust *definitely* lowered inhibitions. That was something he would have never admitted out loud alone, never mind to the person that fueled those fantasies.

"Oh." Her eyes widened. He couldn't stop looking at her. The quick rise and fall of her chest, the glitter on her cleavage, face, even her lashes, catching the light. And the naked want in her eyes.

He was definitely semi-hard now. Clenching his fists at his sides, he tried to keep from pulling her into his arms and burying his face in the front of her shirt. The Lust Dust was certainly living up to its name.

"I..." he started to say, with no clue where he was going.

"Shut up, Basil."

He snapped his mouth closed.

Sage's hands balanced on his chest, and he put his own hands on her hips. Their lips met. He wasn't expecting a peck, but he was surprised at how she lingered, a soft, slow kiss of curiosity. Her hands wandered, exploring, slipping between his hoodie and henley as she moved closer.

Her mouth on his felt like relief. No longer trying to fight the Lust Dust, he surrendered to sensation.

Basil put an arm around her waist, one hand on her face as he pulled her against him and kissed her hard. Her squeal of surprise turned to a hum of pleasure.

Her arms twined around his neck, plastering her body against his, deepening the kiss. Her fingers ran through his hair, tracing the nape of his neck, sending shivers up his back.

Sage broke the kiss with a moan, hands still on his chest, and pulled away, just barely. Her nose brushed against his. She was staring at him wide-eyed. His hands twitched on her hips before he cupped her face between his palms, crushing his mouth to hers, and pressed her back against the wall.

Her mouth was warm and soft, his nose filling with the scent of her, earthy and sweet.

Basil's fingers caught in her hair, tongue slipped between her lips and she moaned, her hands tightening their hold on him.

All he could think about was Sage, the taste of her mouth, the soft sounds she made, the feel of her under his hands. Basil could feel his control slipping. She was pliant under his hands, moaning against his mouth.

It wasn't the first time he'd tasted magic on another person's lips, but with Sage there were honest-to-god *sparks*. Like static electricity, every touch of her lips ignited something he had buried so deep within him he was only just discovering it.

It could've been the Lust Dust, but Basil knew it was *her*. He didn't know how he knew, but he *knew* he wanted to keep kissing her.

His cock was harder than he'd ever been and every touch, every kiss, every sound was both too much and not enough. Her hands yanked at his hoodie, trying to pull it off. Basil pressed a slow, deep kiss to her mouth before removing it himself, dropping it to the floor.

Her fingers tangled in his hair, her touch against his scalp shooting sparks down his spine, straight to his cock. He wanted more of her touch. How had he gone this long without it?

They broke apart, breathing heavily, arms still wrapped around each other.

"That was technically two," he said, mouth pressed against her neck, his hard length pressed between her thighs.

"Fuck's sake, you're counting?" she said, whimpering as she moved against his erection. She slid one arm out of her cardigan, and he hooked his fingers in the other sleeve, feeling the goosebumps on her skin as he dragged it down her arm.

"I like being precise."

She waved her arm wildly behind her, trying to encourage the objects on the altar to slide to the other end. Wax spilled across the wood when she only managed to knock a candle over.

Basil chuckled, lacing his fingers with hers and helping her with the spell, roughly shoving everything out of the way.

"Thank you," she muttered. She sat on the edge of the altar, pulling him between her legs.

Basil could feel the heat in the desperate way she moved against him.

He dragged a hand from her face, locking their office door with a twist of his wrist, then added a silencing charm for good measure. He'd be damned if he let anyone interrupt this.

He put a hand on her hip, but she took his hand and pressed it between her legs. He stroked her, pressing harder at her breathy moan, wanting that sound again.

"You want me to touch you?" she asked.

He nodded.

Her hand slipped between them, palming the front of his pants. The brush of her fingers on the head of his cock, even through the layers of his clothes, had him shuddering. He couldn't seem to touch her *enough*, wanted to touch her everywhere, to see what other noises she could make under his hands. He ran his hand down her spine, under her shirt.

She opened his pants, hands slipping into his underwear, drawing him out. The first touch of her cool hands on his hot cock almost had his knees buckling. The knowing little giggle she let out when he groaned in her ear was almost enough to make him come right there. He knew Lust Dust increased sensitivity beyond belief, but there was a difference between reading the warning label and actually experiencing it.

He squeezed her thigh. She bucked her hips, her hot center rubbing against his hard length.

"Can I take these off for you?" he asked, hooking his finger in the waistband of her underwear.

She nodded, pressing her forehead against his neck.

He drew two fingers down her underwear, whispering against her skin, the fabric tearing under his spell, allowing him to sink his fingers into that wet heat.

Sage gasped. "You ripped my underwear." Her accusation turned to a whine as he continued stroking.

"Never attempted it before."

"Lucky me."

He slid a finger into her, then two, thumb circling her clit. She moaned in his ear, wrapping her leg around his hips, riding his hand.

He knew Sage well, but this side of her was brand new. She was looking at him like he was the only thing in the world.

He liked watching her as she came apart for him. There were so many words he wanted to say, but he couldn't voice them. So he decided to do something that didn't need words. Lowering himself to his knees, he pressed a kiss to the inside of her knee, trailing his fingers across her skin.

She gasped, fingers digging deeper into his hair. "Please, Basil. Don't tease."

"Teasing's fun, Sage. Haven't you ever been teased before?"

"I'm usually the one teasing you."

He slid his glasses off, tucking them in his pocket, chuckling. "Yeah, consider this payback." He put his mouth to her and licked. She moaned, sliding one of her legs over his shoulder. His cock twitched, and he wrapped his hand around it, stroking himself as he tasted her.

"Oh fuck, you're good at this." Her thighs tightened around his head.

He grinned, sliding two fingers into her as he sucked her clit.

She almost came off the edge of the altar as she clenched around his fingers. He wanted more. The clench of her body around his fingers was good, but he wanted to feel her on his cock.

She exhaled shakily, her hands dropping from his hair, her thighs still twitching.

He got to his feet, and she looked at him. He felt woozy, the cloud of lust still on him, his cock still hard.

Her eyes were glazed over, but he could see a bit of clarity returning as she came down from her orgasm. "I always wanted this to be different," she said.

It took him a moment to realize what she meant. That she had thought about this, had wanted it, with him.

That knowledge allowed him to finally admit his feelings for her to himself. To admit that she always slipped, unbidden, into his thoughts. That he watched her, just to be able to admire her. Everything made sense.

Unfortunate that it'd taken him this long to realize it. He wasn't rash enough to call this love. Not yet, at least.

He stroked her cheek with his thumb. "This isn't ideal for me either. I'd rather not feel like if I wait any longer to get my cock inside you, I'll die. I mean, I imagine I might feel like this any other time around you, but the Lust Dust is making it unbearable."

She giggled, wrapping her arms around his neck as she kissed him.

"Hey, uh, before we... d'you have protection?"

She nodded. "Magical and mundane, you?"

"I can do magic," he said. "Is that okay with you?"

She cupped his face, smiling. "Yeah."

He closed his eyes, whispering hoarsely, hands shaking as he did a protection spell. He couldn't resist running his thumb across her cheek again. "Ready?"

"More than you know."

The slow slide into her stole his breath. He locked eyes with her and she looked as surprised as he felt. Before he could say anything, she took his face in her hands, covering her mouth with hers and rolled her hips against him.

Basil groaned, arms tightening around her as he thrusted into her, every stroke deep and hard. He ran his fingers up and down the back of her neck, threading them through her hair. Her legs wrapped around his hips again, urging him closer. He gave her hair a gentle tug, her head falling back and he buried his mouth in the valley of her cleavage.

Basil could feel his climax building fast thanks to the Lust Dust. It worked quickly on Sage too, as she let out a cry, not even bothering to muffle it against his shoulder as he felt her come around him. He thrust against her one last time, finding his own release.

He pulled away, grabbing the box of tissues on the shelf behind him to clean up. He offered one to Sage before putting his glasses back on. "How long?" he asked.

She looked up at him before dropping her gaze. "Most of undergrad, but right before... the May Day *thing* was when I realized it wasn't going away anytime soon."

"Sorry for chickening out then."

She shook her head. "I chickened out too." She shot him a grin, pushing off from the table, but stumbled, holding tight to him.

"You okay?" he asked, putting an arm around her waist.

She nodded. "Sorry, if I'd known today was going to be the day for this," she said, motioning between them, "I'd've had something more substantial than an almond croissant for breakfast."

He laughed. "I can pick up lunch for us."

"It's a date," she said.

He chewed on his lower lip, cocking his head to the side as he ran his fingers through his hair. "Bit of a shitty first date, isn't it? Come over tonight for dinner and..."

"And round two?" she interrupted with a grin. "I'd like that a lot."

Basil sucked in a breath, pushing his glasses up his nose. "Maybe—maybe you could bring me a tea tomorrow? Y'know, if the offer still stands."

She smiled. "It always stands."

Alexis's speaker trilled and they both jumped. "She's been carrying a box of that tea in her bag for over a year just in case you ever said yes."

Basil looked at Sage, her face beet-red. He raised a brow and she nodded in confirmation.

"How long's the power been back, Lex?" Sage asked.

"About five minutes. Heard the end of... Anyway, two things: First, fucking finally. Second, if going at it in the office is going to be a thing, please unplug me next time."

"Got it," he said as he reached for Sage's hand, any embarrassment vanishing from her face as their fingers laced. Fucking finally was a great way to put it, Basil thought.

About the Author

Rebecca Conrad has an education day job and reads and writes romance novels whenever and wherever she can (there are at least a dozen legal pads full of writing in her desk drawer). She likes good food, walking around Target with no purpose, and documentaries about scandals.

She lives in the greater Houston area and spends most of her time indoors because she's a delicate flower and wilts dramatically if the temperature is above 75 F. She has an FB page she rarely does anything with, so look for her on Instagram (mostly food) and the app formerly known as Twitter at @ByRebeccaConrad.

His Little Devil (Sneak Peek)

BY AMBER NICOLE

This book is dedicated to my step-mom, Jessica, who fought a hard battle with breast cancer. I love and miss you every day.

NB: Please know this is book two of Alistar Academy. Please read The Forest Witch Lies first.

Prologue

Donovan

"We don't have much time. That spell will only keep Luke down for so long," I grumble as Jade places the crystals all around Silver's sleeping body. Clara lights the candles as the storm rages behind the cave walls.

"Arrow, grab the dagger and start carving," I order and he grunts in answer before picking up the thin silver blade and dragging it across his arm, letting his blood drip onto Silver.

Blood magic. Our last resort to get our girl back. He hands me the dagger and I do the same, holding back my flinch as the cut stings.

"I pray this works," Clara mutters before tossing the herbs onto Silver. A glow emanates from her body as the blood mixes in with the leaves. Jade gasps as Silver's body starts to levitate in the air, and her hair starts to change back to a blood-red color.

"It's working," Jade cries in joy, and Clara starts to chant. My heart races as I watch the transformation, but something isn't right. The blood-red strands turn a piercing white and Silver's eyes open, a horrifying scream leaving her lips.

"No, no!" Arrow shouts, getting angry. A portal opens beside us and I'm frozen as a figure steps through. Silver lands back onto the ground with a whimper and I watch as the person shuffles closer to us.

A wave of their hand has us being pushed away from Silver and restrained against the cave walls with a powerful force.

Clara starts to yell and shout as they reach for the blade and thrust it into Silver's chest. I watch in horror as our last chance to save the woman we love is fading from existence.

This wasn't supposed to happen. Not like this. I just wanted to get her back. Bring Silver into the light like before. Now everything has gone to shit.

How is she even here right now?

One

Donovan

"What the fuck just happened?" I growl at Arrow as we catch Wells before he hits the cold stone floor. "Did Silver seriously just disappear into some portal after giving up her fucking soul?" I roar and Arrow glances back to where we just watched our girl pop out of thin air.

Wellson gasps and I bring my attention back to my brother who is dying before me. Arrow is muttering spells under his breath, trying to heal him, but nothing is working.

"He needs water," I grumble, then do a small incantation, bringing water to my palms. I cup my hands and pour it into his mouth. It trickles out, and I grip his throat.

"Wells, you have to drink," I plead and his eyes roll back into his head as his body goes limp.

"No! We need to get him to Clara now," Arrow shouts doing a transportation incantation. I grip his arm and wait for the spell to work, but something is blocking it.

"We don't have time for this," I say, picking up my brother and tossing him over my shoulder, then rushing out of the dungeon and up the stairs until we reach outside.

The cold air is like a slap to the face, allowing me to take my first deep breath.

"Call Clara," I tell Arrow as he runs beside me. If anyone can heal Wells, she can.

She's more than just a clairvoyant music teacher. She was once the best healer our coven had. Before my father and Alara decided to get involved and take over.

Arrow freezes in place and I don't have time to see what's wrong. I have to save Wells.

❧

Arrow

A VISION HITS ME SO HARD I FALL TO MY KNEES WITH A GASP. Donnie runs ahead with Wellson and I fight the full body shivers as images flash through my mind: Silver on a throne covered in bloody skulls; Wellson in a bed surrounded by his family; Donovan missing; a young child.

They keep flashing like a movie trailer and I can't slow them down. Nothing is making any sense.

I knew our powers were amplifying since Silver's ascension, but this is far more than I expected. I feel powerful, but weak at the same time.

I don't know what any of these premonitions mean, but the way I'm lying on the ground in the fetal position when they start to fade away proves that it's not a good omen.

Two

Luke

I watch silently as Silver looks around. My bedchambers are one of my favorite places. The black stone walls and the large four poster bed, with the blood-red satin sheets, give me a taste of luxury that I never had before I got this job.

I have a bookshelf full of my favorite reads over the decades, and a nice comfy couch to relax on too. She shuffles over the stone floor and runs her black nails over the back of my leather chair, before sitting on the edge of my wooden desk and giving me a look.

"So... you're not really a professor, are you?" A laugh bubbles out from my chest and I move closer to her. She gasps with surprise as I grasp the back of her neck and pull her lips to mine. I have been dying for another taste of her, and now that she's all mine, I plan to indulge.

She moans softly as the flames between us rise. I have never felt a connection to someone like I do her. I move my lips from hers and kiss down her neck, leaving small nips and sucks.

She tastes like the sweetest dessert... and mine. Her porcelain skin pinks from my marks and I can't wait to really claim her. To show her the true devil that lies beneath this façade.

"Luke... please," she whimpers and it's music to my ears and cock. She reaches down for my belt, but I grip her wrists tight and shove them away.

"Did I give you permission to touch me?" I growl. She squirms below me and I fight like my hellhounds are nipping at my ankles to not give in to her allure. I know she is only acting this way due to the darkness enveloping her.

I may not have a cause for doing what's right, but I will wait until her body, soul, and mind are all mine and only mine. Her heart is still conflicted, but not for much longer.

I may not give her what she wants in this moment, but that doesn't mean I can't torture her a little. It is a favorite pastime of mine, after all.

"Luke, what are you... oh God," she whimpers, as I slam her back down onto the hard wood and reach up between her thighs. I laugh as I lean over and growl into her ear.

"God won't help you here, little devil." Her legs shake as I bite down on her collarbone, my fingers slipping beneath the flimsy scrap of cloth she wears under her dress.

I place her fingers into my hair and let her pull as hard as she wants, the pain making me unbearably hard. I move along her body, lifting the material so I may bite her inner thigh leaving another mark, but not deep enough to break the skin. Even though my body shakes with the thought of claiming her, it's not time yet.

But soon.

"Hold on, I haven't had a meal this delicious in years and I'm famished." I growl before ripping her flimsy panties off, and eating her like I know those boys never did.

Her moans turn to screams as I flip her legs up to my shoulders and bend her in half, licking up all the cream she gives me.

Fuck, my dick is rock hard and I thrust a few times against the edge of the desk to relieve the pressure. I'm close to making a mess in my pants like some worked up schoolboy when we are interrupted.

Someone knocks on the door and I growl. Silver whimpers when I lick her one last time and press a kiss to her abused slit.

"Sir, you're needed in the office. Time is of the essence," one of my worms shouts through my door. They know better than to enter my private chambers.

Sighing, I release Silver's shaking legs. I take in the view of her glazed, sated eyes and move away from her.

"Wait, where are you going? Luke!"

I don't bother with a response and slam the heavy door in my wake. Thimon is standing guard in the hall and jolts to attention when I face him.

"Don't let her leave," I tell him sternly and he bows his service. I lock the door then stride to the office. I slam the door open not caring that the measly worm jumps out of his skin.

"This better be good, Blackwell, or I may just have Merida cook you for dinner." He audibly gulps and drops his eyes to the floor.

"Donovan Blake has decided to leave Alistar Academy, Master, Wellson Birch is hanging on by a thread, and Jaxon Arrow's powers have amplified at an alarming rate. Half the coven are still unconscious and the rest are lost and confused. This wasn't part of the plan, Master."

I roll my eyes and take a seat behind my desk, licking my lips, still tasting my queen. I wait for him to look me in the eyes and raise my hand to get him to stop his sniveling.

He doesn't take my warning.

Dropping to his knees and bowing his head he starts to beg and plead. I find it funny though that he never asks for mercy for his daughter. Only his life.

"Your Lordship, please, I beg of you."

Yeah, I've had enough of this. I slam my fist on my desk and the whole room shakes from the force, stopping this incompetent worm of his sniveling. I take a deep breath and reign in my powers.

"I have heard enough, Blackwell. Silver is mine now, as she was always meant to be. I could give a fuck about your measly little coven. Give it to Blake and Alara. As we all know they have been gunning for it from the beginning. Silver has ascended, as was prophesied. Now she will rule by my side as my queen. That is my final word on this discussion."

I stand and walk out of the room, leaving him behind as he cries my name, thanking me for allowing him to breathe.

I don't acknowledge him and continue on my way. I have more important matters to take care of. First up a cold shower, with only my fist, memories, and the taste of Silver on my tongue.

Silver

Luke leaves me breathless, and sweaty on his desk, walking from the room and slamming the door. I take a minute to get my legs working, then jump off, chasing after him, not caring that I'm now naked.

I grip the door and pull with all my might, but it doesn't budge. Did he seriously lock me in here? I yell and pound on the wooden door with my fists, but after a few minutes I give up.

Today has been horrific. This whole week has been. I can feel the darkness pulling me down into the depths away from what I used to be.

I know I should fight, but after everything, would it be so bad to just give in and give up? My family is gone, my friends will be fine without me and I hope the guys understand everything I did was for them.

Even though they lied and kept secrets, I forgive them. I see red when I think of all they could have warned me from, but I know that they love me.

I wipe my eyes, and walk over to the large bed. The satin sheets feel cool to the touch and I collapse on top of them, exhausted.

❧

My eyes feel gritty when I pry them open some hours later. Luke is in bed with me, clutching my back to his chest. His deep slow breaths prove him to be asleep. The red from the firescape gives an eerie glow along the stone walls.

My heart aches and I'm not sure why.

Darkness is taking over me and I'm scared. I know I did this. There was no other choice but watching Wellson fall as I left him...

I hope he's okay. I know I'm losing my sanity and my soul to Luke's madness.

I don't know how I didn't figure out that he was a liar and a fraud. The journals basically told me exactly who he was, but I was blinded. Or maybe he spelled me.

I still can't believe magic is real. Or that I'm in actual Hell. Not just an expression anymore.

How am I going to get back to the academy? Will Luke ever let me return? What about the stipulations I still need to uphold? Will any of these things even matter to me anymore in a few hours?

I can feel the change coming over me. I know it won't be much longer. I guess my one good thing about all of this is Luna and my family aren't here to see it.

Tears fill my eyes as I think about my parents and siblings one last time. I hope I never forget them and my memories. Even without a soul, I should still have those right?

Luke groans behind me and cuddles me closer and I try to relax. My mind won't stop racing, I'm filled with guilt and sorrow. I let the tears fall as I feel myself finally slip into the darkness.

❧

I storm into Luke's chambers with an attitude that would rival Winnie. Huh, I wonder what happened to that little bitch.

Maybe I should ask Luke to bring her to me, so I can play with her a little bit. He owes me now.

I can't believe he took my toy away. I was having fun tormenting that mean, nasty man. Who cares if I went a little too far, he was a murdering rapist and deserved to have a lifetime of torture in Hell.

"I was wondering how long it would take you to come track me down, Little Devil." Luke growls in my direction but doesn't bother lifting his eyes from the tablet in his hands.

I sway my hips as I stride his way. When I reach his chair, I wrap my arms around his neck, before sliding my fingers down his chest. He grabs my hand and presses a kiss to my knuckles, but that's not what I want.

I'm so bored and for some reason he still won't fuck me. I slip around the side and smack the tablet from his hands ignoring his snarl when it lands on the stone floor.

"Whoops." I shrug and climb onto his lap, straddling him and grabbing his throat forcing him to meet my eyes.

"I shouldn't have had to track you down. You should have been by my side instead of reading that boring journal again. If it wasn't for your full devotion to me, I would be jealous."

He rips my hand from his throat and grasps mine tight.

"Just because I may be devoted to you, Silver, does not mean that you will be the one in control in this relationship. I am and will always be your lord and savior, so you better start treating me with respect and stop acting like a little brat, or you will not like the consequences."

His palm pulses against my neck and I roll my eyes. At this point I would take anything he gave me. His nostrils flare and he stands up abruptly, slamming my back against the hardwood of his desk.

A small breath of air leaves my lips from the jolt and he wastes no time restraining my wrists in his other hand.

My body heats and my panties flood. I love making him snap and show his true colors. He may call me a brat and at times that's true, but I'm mostly bored and just wanting his attention.

He was the one to drag me away from the people who cared about me. He wanted me all to himself, so now he will have to deal with his consequences.

"I don't have time for this, Little Devil," he growls before kissing me hard and I melt. I kiss him back and squirm, but before things can get too heated he pulls away like always and then snaps his fingers.

"Take her away and give her a new toy," he orders one of his servants as they appear and I pout.

"You're no fun. I just want to play with you," I whine and he sighs, shaking his head.

"Silver, I have to work. Maybe in a few days we can go tour the other realms, okay?" He gives me a kiss on the forehead, then waves me away.

I stomp out and behave for now, but only because I have a plan for later.

Three

Arrow

I SIT BESIDE HIS BED AND READ TO HIM. HE DOESN'T RESPOND OR even twitch but I know he can hear me. I try to get in here once a day and give him some company. Donovan took off the night Silver chose the devil over us and hasn't been home since.

I'd be worried about him if I didn't have eyes on him at all times. Since Silver ascended, my powers have been amplified and I have been taking full advantage.

A knock on the door pulls me from this riveting story I found in Silver's room about a woman named Queenie. She may have no magical nature but she reminds me of Silver a little. I know I may not trust her and she broke everything I fought to keep, but I can admit to missing her.

I miss her homemade muffins. The random songs she would sing while in the shower. I even miss her damn annoying need to touch me and push my boundaries. Since she betrayed all of us, this house has felt empty. It's too quiet.

I place the book on the bed, and lean down to press a kiss on Wellson's temple. "I miss you, brother." I stand back up and head toward the incessant knocking. I close my eyes and take a deep breath to see who is at the door and groan, rubbing a hand along my face. I place a bright, fake smile upon my lips and open the door.

"Jade, what can I do for you today?" I ask Silver's persistent friend. She stops over three times a week to check on Wells and ask for news. She doesn't wait to be invited in and pushes me aside, stomping towards Silver's room with a purpose.

I follow, wishing she would just give up. It's been almost two months now since the night she left us for him. I guess Wells was right about her cheating on them with the professor.

"It's so creepy how much hasn't changed, though everything has." Jade mutters, taking in the messy bed and clothes strewn around the place. I haven't had the foresight, or energy, to clean out her room.

I may not trust her, or be her favorite person right now, but I do have hope she may return to us one day.

"Jade, you need to stop doing this to yourself. Silver is gone. I watched her step through that portal with my own eyes. She accepted darkness. Even if she were to return...she wouldn't be the same." I place a hand on her trembling shoulder, and turn her back to the hall. Her eyes meet Wells, lying on his bed.

"Will he ever wake up?" I sigh, and shake my head.

"I don't know. The doctors say physically, he's fine—but still, he sleeps. What worries me is I can't see his future. Even with the advancement to my powers. I'm blocked from him, same with Silver."

Her bottom lip trembles and she gives me a nod before rushing from the house. I wave my hand and shut the door behind her. I take a seat on the couch and stare at the fireplace. I haven't been down to the chambers since the last time with Don.

I tug my phone from my pocket and try his number, not surprised when it goes straight to voicemail. I hang up and toss it to the table, then lean back and concentrate on his face.

"THANKS, BABE. KEEP THEM COMING." SLUMPING ON A BAR stool on the beach, Don tosses some cash a waitress's way. She gives him a beaming smile, but he ignores her advances. He looks like absolute shit and I wish he would just come home. A presence comes beside him, but it's fuzzy. I can't tell who it is, but I know it's not good.

MY EYES SNAP OPEN AND I JUMP TO MY FEET. DON'S IN TROUBLE. I have to get to him before I lose another piece of my soul.

THE END... FOR NOW...

Want to know what happens next? His Little Devil will be released in February 2024.

Click the link now to pre-order.

HIS LITTLE DEVIL

About the Author

Before accompanying her military husband across the United States, Amber Nicole was born and raised in upstate NY. An avid reader and baker, she always has something cooking, whether in the kitchen or in her mind. She is well known for her international best selling duet *Forever Changed,* and she has a wide range of tropes to choose from. Whether it be why choose, MF, MM, FF, paranormal, or contemporary.

She also has two incredible children who help inspire her every day and a husband that pushes her to follow her dreams. She's an animal lover and has many of her own.

Stay tuned for more from this incredible author.

If you want to come hang out with me and talk about books, come—join my author's group!

AMBER NICOLE'S TRAUMA QUEENS

Also by By Amber Nicole

Reverse Harem:

THE FOREST WITCH LIES

Forever Changed Duet: Completed!

FOREVER CHANGED

FOREVER YOURS

Solidarity Academy: Cheerleading Bully Academy RH Co-write with Alisha Williams

KNOCK 'EM DOWN

TAKE 'EM OUT

RAISE 'EM UP

Forbidden Truths Duet:

FORBIDDEN LIES

FORBIDDEN SECRETS

Quiet Confessions Duet:

QUIET CONFESSIONS PART 1

QUIET CONFESSIONS PART 2

Locked Hearts, Locked Souls Society Book One (Co-write with Jenn Bullard)

LOCKED HEARTS

LOCKED PROMISES

FF, Dark, Bully, Stepsister Romance: (Co-write with Jenn Bullard)

THE MIDNIGHT CONFESSIONS 1

Shared World:

KARMA

She Put A Spell On Me

BY JENNA D. MORRISON

Robbie, the typical boy next door, has had a crush on McKenzie for ten years but she has never noticed him. He is determined to catch her attention before their senior year is over, but he has been unsuccessful. Charli is one of Robbie's closest friends and a witch. Can he convince her to help him win McKenzie's love, or will she convince him that love freely given is better?

One

For as long as I can remember, I've had a thing for McKenzie Meyer. The first time I saw her, she had begrudgingly come into my classroom on our first day of second grade, eyes wide and just about to cry. She was the new kid in a new school, and even my seven-year-old self recognized her vulnerability, even if I didn't quite grasp the word for it, yet. She walked in like a bat out of hell with cast down eyes and slumped shoulders, and whispered to our teacher, Miss Wren, who directed her to the seat right in front of mine. I was smitten. Mesmerized by the waves in her hair, In my brief life, I had yet to see the back of someone's head that was as captivating.

Ten years later, I'm still sitting in the seat behind her, staring at the back of her hair and daydreaming. However, I have still not developed the courage to even talk to her. These days, her vulnerability has grown into full-blown confidence. McKenzie is the most beautiful girl in school. Head cheerleader, most popular, nominated for Homecoming Queen. Every guy here wants to date her, and I suspect I'm not on her short list of prospects. Mind you, I'm not on the bottom of the food chain here, at school. But, I'm also not at the top, either. I'm somewhere in the middle of the pack. But I'm more into art than sports, unlike the guys she goes out with. Others might consider me attractive, but I don't presume that anyone would consider me "hot," by any means.

Now we are in our senior year, and this is my last shot to make her to take notice of me. I have loved her for years and I don't reckon she even knows who I am. But I had a plan that would change all of that! I live in a small town called Welty, and it is an interesting place, unlike most small towns. It is dollars to donuts, one of the most interesting places in the entire country. My town comprises many people whose very existence is the stuff of myths. Shifters, vampires, witches, you name it. In fact, I am acquainted with a few witches from my high school, and I am friends with most of them.

Charli was one of my best friends, so I approached her first. But, while sympathetic to my plight, she turned me down flat, after she explained to me that, as a Wiccan, she won't cast a love spell because it would take McKenzie's free will away. I understand why Charli said no, and felt guilty, but I wanted McKenzie to like me, so I stuck with my plan.

So I asked another friend, Katrina, who told me the same thing, but she said she could put a spell on me to make me more attractive and maybe it would catch McKenzie's attention. She called it a glamour, which should only be temporary, but would allow her to get acquainted with me before I returned to my normal appearance. Unfortunately, she said she would do it for a price; I explained to her that my parents won't let me work because of school, but she only said that she's sorry, but she doesn't work for free, and if she does me this favor, others will demand the same. I grasped the situation, yet I was crestfallen.

I sulked most of the walk home, but as I approached my house, I had an idea. Thanks to Katrina, I was now aware of what type of spell I was after, and with ease I could research online how to do it myself! As I looked it up, the task seemed daunting. Thousands of entries flooded my screen. But I took my time, and I found three in particular that seemed promising, but I didn't grasp which to choose. I thought to myself, If one works, I bet three will work even better. The first one I chose used crystals for the spell. The second, a bag of herbs, one with some random found items like a black rooster's feathers and limestone, and at last, the last one, which required a blessed candle. I set off for one of our town's local magic shops that I believed would have what I needed, and bought everything on my list, except the rooster's feather, but that was easy enough to get on one of my walks home from school. The salesperson talked me into getting a bundle of something that smells weird as well. But she told me it was a good idea to burn some before I start any rituals. I figured it was best to cover all of my bases. Happy with my purchases, I headed back home.

Once back at the house, I first burned the bundle until its rich scent filled my bedroom. I took my time trying to decide how best to combine my magical items for maximum potency, opting to just combine it all together. "Go big or go home", I thought to myself, as I placed the rose quartz and pyrite onto my chakras according to the texts, and the herbs, feathers and limestone are supposed to go in a bag that is to be worn around my neck. Since they all would touch my body, anyway, I decided it was best to just put it all in the bag. I lit the candle, chanted the words that I had found online, put everything in the bag and figured that was it, but in a flash, something went wrong. The spell backfired and instead of glorious hair and a god-like physique, I ended up ugly and awkward. My body was a gangly mess, my hair and skin were extra oily, and my two eyebrows became one, and on top of everything else, my feet grew, causing me to become more clumsy as I tried to figure out how to walk with my massive feet. I began tripping over nothing and everything all at once. It was awful, and I did not know what I had done wrong.

Two

Embarrassed, I threw on a hoodie and covered my face as much as I could, before crawling to Charli for help, like a dog with its tail between its legs. As we both stood in the doorway, she stared at me with wide eyes and her mouth agape. "What on earth did you do, Robbie?" she whispered in an exasperated tone. I recounted my conversation with Katrina, and the basic steps I had taken, and my brilliant idea about mixing the spells, thinking a more potent effect would make me substantially more difficult to resist, which earned me a well-deserved eye roll from my friend.

"Can you explain what ingredients you used and what words you used for the incantation? I can undo this, but it's going to be difficult, and it will only happen if I know just what you have said and done. Not everything works in harmony together, Robbie. Be careful, untrained, non-magic wielders should not mess with this stuff. You just do not have the experience."

I felt admonished, but seeing the concern on her face let me know that at least she wasn't angry with me, despite reading me the riot act. Which was important, because I already felt foolish enough, and I needed her more than ever right now. Knowing my friend was there for me when I needed her put me at ease. Coming to Charli was definitely the right call.

"Everything is still in my room, including all the words that I had found online to use. I didn't know if I should even touch it, so I just left everything out. You okay with heading to my place?" I asked.

"Yes. We should get over there right away! We will head over and get started," Charli sighed with a smile. Although I knew I exasperated her,

Charli smiled and showed amusement at my situation. I didn't blame her. I would be, too, if it were happening to somebody else.

❧

"First, I need to know all the ingredients you used. Leave nothing out. Just one thing out of place or forgotten can cause the whole thing to backfire." She paused as she looked around at the mess that was left in my room before adding, "Oh! I also need the words for the spell you used. I can't believe you tried this on your own, Robbie. It could've gone even worse. Only hereditary witches should attempt magic. They did not design these spells for human consumption."

"What do you mean?" I asked her. "How is it different from what you do?"

"Well, Wiccans and other modern witches' covens are primarily made up of humans learning to harness the power of nature. Hereditary witches are genetically predisposed to our own powers. We also use nature, but our powers are part of who we are, not something that we learn to be. And no disrespect to anyone who wants to learn, but we will always be more powerful and better at controlling that power. So don't try anything like this again. Okay?" Charli admonished, before softening up and giving me a small smile. "I'm sorry, Robbie. I don't want to fuss at you, but this is dangerous and worries me. We will fix it though, okay?"

"Okay. I know we will, or rather, you will. There was no reason for me to even give it a go. It was a dumb move, I suppose, but I'm desperate for McKenzie to look my way this year. I want her to like me. I just feel like it's my last chance, you know, before we all grow up and head off to college."

Charli lifted an eyebrow at me and smirked. "No one ever leaves Welty for good. You know that. Whether or not we go to college, this town has a way of dragging everyone back. Even people who have left and been somewhere else at least keep vacation homes here. You have plenty of time to charm the pants off of her. But why do you want to so much that you would alter yourself for her? You've been obsessed with this chick for as long as I can remember, but for the life of me, I can't understand what's so special about McKenzie Meyer."

Charli seemed curious, but I didn't have an answer. I hadn't given it much thought about it, but she's stunniing. I remained quiet as I handed her the bag. She began pulling the magical items out and laying them on my nightstand. "How many spells did you combine? You've got a lot of things going on here."

"Three, plus I took a few words from another, so three and a half?" I answered sheepishly. Now that I had done it, I understood why humans shouldn't play with it. She's right. Humans shouldn't experiment with this stuff.

"Oh boy. You're not making this easy, are you? No worries, though. I can fix it."

And she was right. It took several excruciating hours, but she got me back to my normal self.

"Thank you so much, Charli! You're incredible and I can't put it into words! I'm still attempting to get McKenzie to pay attention to me. Are there any other methods you can think of that would help me get her attention besides using that type of spells?" I felt foolish asking right after she's done so much for me already, but desperate times come with desperate measures. I was desperate to get McKenzie to like me.

Charli sat there, studying me quietly. She didn't speak for several minutes. As she answered me, a sadness appeared on her face, perhaps because she knew of my foolishness. "I asked before what you like so much about McKenzie and you couldn't even answer. How much do you know about her? The more you can tell me, the better I can help. For instance, what is her favorite class? Who is her best friend?"

I gave her all the information I could. McKenzie is popular, the stereotypical cheerleader and student council member. I don't know her favorite class, but she is decent at all of her subjects. Her best friend is Sabrina White. And the only activity I know she takes part in outside of school is hanging out at the coffee shop near the college campus.

"Robbie, I don't mean to be insensitive, but hanging out where the college kids hang out? It sounds like she's trying to snag a college boyfriend. Are you sure you are up to the potential heartbreak?" Charli asked with concern in her eyes.

"Yeah. If it won't happen, then it won't happen, but I need to make one last ditch effort, then let it go if she rejects me. Obviously it would hurt, but I've been obsessed for ten years. I need to get the girl or get over it."

"Do you realize that some changes we make won't have anything to do with witchcraft?"

"Right. I'm ready for whatever," I exclaimed.

Three

We met back up a few days later. Charli came prepared with bags upon bags of items, both of the magic and non-magical sort, along with her coven members. It was overwhelming, but I trusted her. I had to. She was my only hope.

"Robbie, I think you know most of us here, but just in case, let me introduce you to everyone. This is Annabelle, Stacy, Amanda, and Kathy. I could tell right away that Annabelle didn't want to be here. She wasn't rude about it or anything, but the situation put her off. She even rolled her eyes more than a few times as Charli went over the situation. Maybe I can't blame her. I did something stupid, after all. I imagine she must think I'm a complete idiot.

"Wow! You guys sure brought a lot of stuff! I must be quite a project!" I tittered.

"Not every idea we've had is based in witchcraft," Charli dismissed, ignoring the joke I was making at my own expense, as she started pulling clothes out of one bag. She was single-minded with her mission, and I nodded, grateful that she was taking my situation seriously.

"My brother left for college and left behind a lot of his clothes that still have the tags on them. Mom bought them, but they aren't his style. He's more of a t-shirts and jeans kind of guy and prefers comfort over style." Kathy said, "Try them on and see if they fit!" She smiled as she gave the order.

I went to the bathroom and tried everything on. They fit just right, and although they weren't my style, I knew it was time for a change. Who am I kidding? I didn't even have a style. I kept the last outfit on and went back to my room.

Kathy clapped. "I thought they would fit! You look fantastic!" she laughed gleefully.

Next, Stacy told me that when we finish, I have an appointment for a haircut with her stylist. Considering she has the coolest hair I have ever seen, I was pretty stoked.

"Oh! Wow, that is generous, and your hair is absolutely amazing, so I can't wait to see what mine will look like. Thanks so much!" I was pretty stoked. Stacy's hair was the coolest I think I've ever seen..

Next up was Amanda. She circled me as she spoke, studying my imperfections. "I will add a light glamour. Nothing drastic. We will straighten up those teeth and give them a nice whitening. Smooth your skin, and brighten up your eyes. While I like the gray, it doesn't really pop. You need to get her attention. How about a beautiful shade of blue? Wait!" she exclaimed. "No, a stunning Caribbean aqua green! That will definitely get her attention. Hell! It might get mine!" she winked and laughed.

"That sounds great!" I returned with a small laugh, feeling pleased at all the progress.

I looked at Annabelle, assuming she had something to add, but she just stared at me with her arms crossed. Alrighty then. Clearly, she still doesn't want to be a part of this. That's alright. But I can't help but wonder why she even came.

❧

After my glamour was in place, my hair cut and properly styled, I was looking pretty damn good. Charli and I said our goodbyes to her friends and then went somewhere quiet where we could sit down to think about other ideas that would grab McKenzie's attention.

"Do you know if she's a reader?" Charli asked.

"Not that I know of. I've never seen her with anything but school books and fashion magazines," I admitted sheepishly.

"From everything you've said about her, you guys don't seem to have much in common. If she were a reader, I would have book recommendations you could share with her, but that won't work. Me personally? I love books and that would be a great conversation starter for someone like me."

"Oh yeah? What books? While I don't know if she enjoys it, but I love to read!" She had genuinely piqued my interest.

"Well, there is this author that I have really enjoyed, Mark Silas. He writes fantasy, really magical realism, and he just released the last book of his latest series about a secret door to a magical city, and it's fantastic!" Charli was really excited about this author. Her hazel eyes sparkled and her entire face lit up. I don't think I had ever seen her so happy before. It was a good look on her. I don't think I ever noticed that about her. She nearly glowed with joy. I have never seen her this happy before. It looked good. Beautiful even. I felt a strange stir in my gut and a slight dizziness in my head. "I need to focus on the mission", I thought to myself, but for the first time I felt a little confused.

"That sounds like something I would read. McKenzie probably wouldn't be interested, but I will check him out."

"Do you know what her favorite song is? Or at least her favorite band?"

"No," I said, feeling fairly defeated. Beyond her physical features, I had hardly any knowledge of McKenzie. Until now, I did not know how shallow I was. I wasn't happy about this new discovery about myself.

"Okay. Do you know anything about her hobbies? Things she is interested in? Anything?" Charli was being so supportive and kind about it, but I've known her long enough to know when she's a bit frustrated. I wasn't exactly being helpful here, after all.

"No, I'm sorry Charli. It's unbelievable how little I understand about her as a person. I should have been more prepared. I should know something about the girl that I love, right?"

"That's alright, Robbie. We will just have to do some recon. Pay attention, I'm about to give you some homework!" She grinned. "We've given you a new look, and that's half the battle." She paused, looking like she thought she had said something wrong, quickly added, "Not that this has been a battle. I'm always happy to help my friend." She softly smiled. I couldn't help noticing how much I really liked her sweet smile. How pretty she actually is. How caring and attentive. I shook my head, annoyed with myself. "Focus dumbass!" I thought to myself. "What is wrong with you?" I felt like I was losing sight of what was supposed to be important here: McKenzie.

"Now you have to pay attention and focus on finding out what she likes, what she cares about and, just as importantly, what she doesn't. So, more than just her being a popular cheerleader." She giggled.

She had put me in my place, but I accepted her point. "I will start learning as much as I can. I know her friends, so maybe I can find out from them," I replied. "Subtly, of course."

Four

It was funny how many people noticed my new look, even people I didn't know outside of classes we shared. "Looking good, Robbie," a kid in my English class exclaimed.

"Wow! Look at you," Andie said, batting her eyelashes at me. I was really enjoying all this attention. Attention from everyone but McKenzie.

I was noticing how unfriendly she was with everyone outside her circle. Maybe not unfriendly, per se, but at least oblivious. Like none of us were even in her universe. I thought back to how friendly Charli and her crowd were, and honestly, the two groups didn't even compare. Charli's friends were definitely the people I would rather hang out with. Had I been chasing the wrong girl all along?

But I wasn't willing to give up on McKenzie just yet, so I followed Charli's instructions to the letter. I watched McKenzie closely over the next week. As I had noticed before, she was middle of the road academically, but wasn't particularly attentive in any class we shared. The only books I saw her with were textbooks. I paid attention to her in the computer lab, and other than assignments, all she did was check her social media. Her favorite hobby seemed to taking selfies with duck lips. Not attractive. She always hung out at the coffee shop with her clique, and their conversations were typically about stuff like makeup and making fun of other kids at school. That was something else I hadn't noticed. The more I observed about her, the more my attraction to her faded. Ten years wasted on this girl when I could have found someone more compatible years ago.

My mind kept going back to Charli. She and I had been friends since kindergarten, and I knew a lot more about her than McKenzie. We were both readers, liked the same books. We're interested in the same subjects in school, both wrote for the school newspaper. I didn't have magic of my own, but I had learned about hers and recognized now how difficult it is. My respect for her had grown, if that was even possible. How had I never noticed her before? We were friends, but could we be more? Could she ever be interested in a guy like me? I would only find out by testing the waters.

❧

Charli and I met at the diner the next day after school. We got some homework out of the way, then started talking about our project to get McKenzie to notice me. "Okay, what have you learned in the past week?" Charli asked.

"Not much good, to be honest. She doesn't like school. She does like socializing with her friends, but no one else is even in her orbit. Her favorite hobby seems to be social media and looking good for the camera. And she doesn't like dogs. I saw her walking one the other day and got brave enough to talk to her. I told her she had a cute dog, but she just rolled her eyes, told me he wasn't hers, and walked off."

"How rude," Charli exclaimed. "I'm sorry, Robbie, but the more you tell me about McKenzie, the more unappealing she sounds. Do you have anything in common with her at all?"

I had to think hard about everything I had learned. "Well, we go to the same school?" I said, knowing in my heart that wasn't enough.

"You know that won't sustain a relationship, right?" Charli asked, with sadness in her eyes. "At least not the relationship I think you are looking for. It might work for a short-term casual booty-call type thing, but not for something serious. As long as you have been focused on McKenzie, I'm pretty sure that's not the guy you are. You are one of the rare good ones looking for something long-term. Am I right?"

"Yeah, that's me," I said glumly. But I noticed what she said and how she said it. Charli had a way of paying attention to the people around her. She obviously cared for her friends, I mused. I wondered if she and I could work as a couple. So I changed the subject away from our experiment.

"Have you decided where you want to go to college yet? Applications are due soon," I asked.

"Probably State, here in Welty. My coven has decided to stick together. It's not exactly easy to bring up magical things outside of here, and the thought of trying to find new covens for our rituals is pretty daunting. How about you?" she asked with a seemingly genuine interest.

"I'm not really sure, but probably State, as well. I may have an opportunity in California, but I'm not sure I'm ready for Los Angeles. It's pretty intimidating, and I'm pretty happy here for the time being. Maybe after graduation, but I think being comfortable in my environment will make it easier to settle into my studies." I was glad our plans seemed to align. Even if we were just friends, it would be nice to have friends already.

"Do you know what you want to major in?" Charli asked.

"Engineering, or something else involving math, I think."

"I figured as much," she laughed. "Math has always been your best subject." I was stunned she had noticed that. And I couldn't help but break out in a smile. "How about you?"

"I'm struggling to figure that out," she admitted. "I would love an English degree, followed by a Master's in Creative Writing. But other than teach, what would I do with it? I know I want to write, but I can't expect to finish school and jump right into being a full-time author."

"How about a Master's in Library Science?" I suggested. Your love of reading would enable you to write in your spare time until you become experienced enough to quit your day job.

"That's a good idea. I could just kiss you!" she said before realizing how it sounded. She turned bright red, so I pretended I didn't notice.

"Well then, I'm glad I thought of it," I breathed, and gave her what I hoped was a flirtatious smile. She just looked at me, and I just looked back at her. Then, before I realized what I was doing, I was kissing her. Just a whisper of a kiss, but I panicked and drew back. Her breath caught, and she searched my face, then leaned back in and kissed me softly and slowly, but decisively.

I pushed hair away from her face and spoke with a crack in my voice, "What does this mean?"

"I should ask you that question, Robbie. What about McKenzie?" Charli asked.

I had learned a lot since the day I went to Charli for help. The McKenzie I had created in my mind wasn't real. The real McKenzie was shallow and didn't care about any of the same things I did. Suddenly, I recognized something that shocked me. The McKenzie I believed in all these years was just Charli in disguise. She is the one who shares my interests, who I can be myself with no matter what. How had I not seen it? It was probably glaringly obvious to anyone who paid attention.

I looked Charli in her enormous hazel eyes. I was terrified to say what I needed to say. In fact, I was so nervous, I just blurted out "Charli, I think I've been in love with you all along. The more attention I have paid to McKenzie, her habits and interests, the more I compared her to you and she came up lacking every time."

Charli just stared at me with no emotion showing on her face for what seemed like an eternity. Then, slowly, she began to smile. "It's about damned time, Robbie. I've been waiting for you to notice me since sophomore year. If you're asking me to be your girlfriend, I'm all in."

I laughed, "What if I'm not?"

"Oh, you definitely are," she teased.

"Are you flirting with me, Charli? I think I like this side of you, girlfriend."

"Same, Robbie. Same," her voice broke.

"Hey! What's wrong? If you want me to back off, it's okay. It's a lot to process. Just know I'm here for you, as a friend or whatever you want. Don't feel you have to do anything right away. I wasn't able to get a read on her.

"No, no. Just the opposite, silly. But you are right. It is a little overwhelming, but I meant it when I said I was all in, boyfriend."

And just like that, Charli's smile was back. I took her in. I wanted to remember this moment and her smile forever. Hopefully, I will be the reason for that smile for many, many years to come.

About the Author

Jenna D. Morrison is an up-and-coming author of young adult and new adult fantasy, paranormal, and science fiction, with a side of romance (under the pen name Kenna Campbell). She has been an avid reader since she was four and started writing for her own enjoyment in middle school.

She lives in Tulsa, Oklahoma with her family and their very spoiled fur babies. When she is not reading or writing, Jenna is a Zen Buddhist priest, an amateur genealogist, a daughter, sister, mother, grandmother, and aunt.

Potion Control

BY KAT WEBB

In the middle of decorating the house for your daughter's eighteenth birthday party, you (a divorced witch mom) discover that the birthday girl spilled your latest concoction on herself–a love potion that only works on adults (aka anyone eighteen or older). What will happen when the (also eighteen and up!) party guests start arriving? A parent frantically calling poison control–or its witch-world equivalent–isn't typically romantic, but in this quiz-format choose-your-own-adventure bewitched tale, there's more than one high-flying happily ever after.

*

As you're draping sparkly black streamer over a chandelier, your daughter, Bianca, shouts. You run to follow the sound, and find her holding an empty bottle and looking guilty, and smelling like cinnamon ... no no no no NO. She screwed the top off of your homemade potion for adult romance to sniff it, thinking it was perfume (it was on your dresser with other perfume–you were thinking about testing it on yourself, but also how many times have we talked about asking first before just using my stuff?! Anyway, need to focus). But Bianca spilled some of it on herself, on her eighteenth birthday. Lots of other 18-year-olds are headed to the house for the party, including her very handsome BFF, Briar. What do you do?

A. Call regular human poison control hotline.

B. Call 911.

C. Just keep Bianca away from anyone over the age of 18—including 30 party guests, no biggie—and anything that breathes (at what age is a bee considered an adult? A tree?).

D. Call the witches' potion control hotline.

Answer: C, then D

❧

Bianca asks: Why do I have to stay in my room?

A. Because I just ... you'll be fine, but ...

What?! What was in that bottle, Mom?!

A. Nothing! It's fine. Like, water, basically. Lemon juice. It's ... you shouldn't mess with my stuff! ... I'm sorry, OK? You know what? I forgot to give you your birthday present. Here's a hundred dollar bill.

Ew, it's all crumpled. And wet ...

A. Yep! It's soaked in ... birthday-happiness potion. Happy birthday! Now. Don't call anyone, don't text anyone, don't even say anyone's name out loud or wave to a neighbor walking a dog, don't even look at the dog, especially that really cute old Westie that lives at the corner, got it?

Should you also:

A. Spray yourself with enough LovBlok Potion to launch a thousand divorces–or, based on your romantic history, maybe your body manufactures it naturally.

B. Turn off the wifi–people can fall in love via FaceTime, right? Can't be too careful.

Answer: Shit! Yes.

Mom! I was FaceTiming with Briar!

A. He's her best friend since third grade. It's fine.

B. The hell it is.

C. He'll be here in 30 minutes! You'll live.

Answer: B, and C, and ... she will live, right? Yeah. Yep. Hmm.

Agent asks: Hello, Poison Control Hotline, how can I help you?

A. Um, hello, did you say poison control or potion control, I wasn't sure?

B. How do you pronounce ibuprofen?

Answer: B

Agent: I pronounce it eye-BOO-pro-fin.

A. Uh, what the? That is unhinged, who pronounces it that way?!

B. As do we all.

ANSWER: B

Agent: Thank you for your patience. As you know, we are required to verify your status as a magical being through that security check.

A. Yeah, of course.

So. My daughter just sprayed herself in the face with my homemade romance potion for anyone 18 or older, and I have a list of the ingredients but I've already locked her in her room, sprayed myself with LovBlok, gave her a hundred-dollar bill soaked in LovBlok, blocked the windows, unplugged our router and there's no other adults in the house.

Answer: None required at this point, but quietly sob to yourself anyway.

Agent: Thank you, ma'am, so if I've got this correct, you are seeking guidance for an accidental dosing of your daughter with a romance spray formulated for adults, and your daughter just turned 18 today and therefore is an adult. Is this correct?

A. Yes.

B. Yesssssssugggggghhhh. (Oh my GOD, get on with it already.)

Answer: B

Agent: Thank you, ma'am. Is it OK if I ask you some questions to make sure I have the information I need?

A. Yes, thank you.

B. Ugh, just ask instead of asking to ask, go go go.

Answer: A (out loud), B (internal thoughts)

Agent: I'm sorry, ma'am, I should've disclosed at the start of the call that one of my skill sets is that I am clairvoyant, so I unfortunately can't guarantee the privacy of your thoughts during this call. Do you still wish to proceed?

A. Oh. Shit. I'm sorry. I'm just nervous.

B. It's my daughter's 18th birthday today and I'm freaking out.

C. We're having a party, and there will be a bunch of her friends here, but also adults, and friends who are already 18, and I don't know whether the person who gets sprayed just has to be an adult, or who they fall in love with .. I haven't tested it yet. That was why I had it on my dresser–I figured, hey, she's an adult today, time to get a life of my own again, maybe with the dad of one of her friends, I mean, only if they're single ...

Answer: All of the above

Agent: Ma'am, do not worry, I am here to help you. I understand this can be a stressful time. So I was going to ask you how old your daughter is, but you said 18.

A. Yes.

Agent: And please, ma'am, is this spray:

A. Commercially manufactured

B. Homemade, but ingredients and ratios are listed in the Book, or

C. Homemade, but with an original formula and you do have a list of ingredients and ratios, or

D. Homemade, but improvised, with no list of ingredients and ratios

Answer: So it's kind of a hybrid B and D, like it's an adaptation of an original—not every blend is the same, so not every spell can work on everyone, which is what my business is about, I adapt existing recipes based on my reading of the person's body chemistry and other factors.

Agent: Thank you, ma'am. At this time, I'd like to place you on a brief hold while I access official Potion Control resources. Is that OK?

A. Ugh, the party starts in 5 minutes!! Never mind, I'm hanging up.

B. Yes, thank you.

Answer: B, but with resigned, biting insincerity

Agent: Hello, ma'am, are you with me?

A. Ugh. Unfortunately.

B. I mean, yes! Hello. So grateful. Thank you! What do you have for me?

Agent: It's OK, ma'am, you wouldn't believe the things callers think about me on here. So I searched for resources, but I did not find any that adequately address your question. So I have on the line one of our resident potion experts, is that OK?

A. Well, yes, great, just as long as it's not—

new voice Your ex-husband? Yeah, sorry, Wera, but there's only one of us on duty at a time, and you're stuck with me. Now what can I help you/my custody attorney with?

A. You hateful piece of frog scrotum, I swear to all that is dark, I will not rest until—

B. Hang up.

C. Ask the potion control agent to not relay those thoughts to your ex-husband, Davos.

Answer: C

DAVOS, I'D THINK A LITIGIOUS, CLAIRVOYANT WIZARD LIKE YOU would realize that on our daughter's 18th birthday, the custody broom has flown?

DAVOS: I WOULD REALIZE THAT. EXCEPT THAT BIANCA'S birthday is tomorrow.

A. Oh shit, is it?

B. No, it isn't, but nice try, you little shit. Was she cut out of your body, or no? Yeah. I remember.

C. Maybe I should check on our daughter.

ANSWER: B, THEN C.

DAUGHTER IS NOT IN HER ROOM

A. Tell Davos—he's her dad, after all, and he can help

B. Are you crazy?

C. He heard you shriek "she's gone!"

Answer: C

DAVOS: SO THERE'S ONLY ONE POSSIBLE EXPLANATION FOR HER being gone:

A. The love potion spray already worked and she's eloping with a werewolf. Or that Westie down the street.

B. She left because she's never respected your authority.

C. She was already in love—love potion and love-blocking potion can't work if you're already in love. Check the front yard.

Answer: C (B came from your own head)

DAVOS: HE ASKED FOR MY BLESSING.

A. Who did?

B. Blessing to do what?! Torment me?

C. Nothing? Fine. Going to front yard. You're the worst. God.

Answer: A,B,C

YOUR DAUGHTER'S CHILDHOOD BEST FRIEND, BRIAR, IS ON ONE knee in the front yard, as your daughter floats on her broom above. She pulls Briar up to the broom, nods, kisses him, and he puts a ring on her finger.

A. You ... knew about this?!

B. She's only eighteen!

C. Why wouldn't he ask me?!

D. Ah, yes, you can see the future, great. Well, I've always wondered, Ye Gifted One, why marry me if you knew it would end in divorce?

DAVOS: BECAUSE. IT DIDN'T END IN DIVORCE.

A. Ha. What? Why do I even bother? I'm hanging up.

DAVOS: I DIDN'T SAY THERE WASN'T A DIVORCE. I'M SAYING IT didn't end in divorce.

A. What?! It's about to be the end of you if you don't shut the ...

DAVOS: I HAD TO LEAVE.

A.What?

DAVOS: FOR THIS TO HAPPEN.

A. For what to happen?

DAVOS: OUR DAUGHTER WOULDN'T FIND HER TRUE LOVE IF I HAD been around. It's complicated.

A. Fuck you.

DAVOS: CHECK THE INSCRIPTION ON YOUR RING.

A. There was no inscription. And I pawned that like five years ag—

DAVOS: NO, YOU DIDN'T.

A. No, I didn't.

B. Open your jewelry box.

Answer: "I had to leave my love so our daughter could find hers. Forgive me. Happy our daughter's 18th birthday. I'm almost there."

And there he is. Jet-black hair, but with swooshes of white in it now. Walking through the overgrown lawn, wet from the recent rain. Walking to Bianca and Briar, giving them a hug, Bianca playfully swatting her dad when she sees he knew before she did. And now walking toward you.

"I never knew," you say. "It never made any sense. I figured you'd cheated on me, and just couldn't bring yourself to admit it to me. The only reason I could think for you to leave when things were so good between us. Weren't they good?"

"One night, I saw it—the end of my life," Davos says. "Wrapped around a tree, driving after dark. Swerving away from a car that looked a lot like Bianca's best friend's parents' car, with a face a lot like Briar's but seven years older. But the worst part is it also wrecked you. And Bianca. And she didn't even have her best friend to help her through it. And I couldn't have that. We sacrificed—you and me. To give her a best friend. To give her a husband. To give her a dad that didn't die while she was still just a kid. But I'm so sorry it was a blind sacrifice, on your part. I'm so sorry I couldn't tell you. I couldn't risk it."

"Can you say something?" Davos says.

A. No.

B. Yes.

C. I don't know.

D. You ... still love me?

E. I hate you for this.

F. You'd do that for her? It's been nine years! You did this to me too. There was a custody battle, for God's sake.

G. Oh, for believability? I don't care that it only went on for a month and I won, it sucked! And you owe me five thousand dollars!

H. Come inside. Now.

He steps inside, to ... home. To what was his home, at least. Is it again? No time. That can wait. What do they do when they get home?

A. Scream (her)
B. Cry (both)
C. Blame (her)
D. Sob (both)
E. Hug (everyone)
F. Cake and champagne (everyone)
G. Presents (Bianca)
H. Flushing a potion down the toilet.
I. Good night, sweet girl. Happy birthday (both)
J. Go to the garage to talk.
K. Hop on a broom to ... not talk.
L. Discussing can wait. Flying on a full moon with your lost love cannot.
M. The pleasure of this kind of riding a broom cannot be overstated.

Answer: All of the above, while flying above everyone below.

About the Author

Kat Webb is a government writer and editor in the streets, steamy contemporary romcom writer in the sheets (of paper). She lives in Georgia with her husband, son, puppy, and two underused kayaks.

Made in the USA
Middletown, DE
07 November 2023